THE SORCERER'S OA

Bronze Magic

Jenny Ealey

To Becca
Love
from
Jenny.

Eskuzor Publishing

Eskuzor Publishing
1 Monash St,
Melton South,
Victoria, Australia 3338

www.jennyealey.com

Published by Eskuzor Publishing 2013

ISBN 978-0-9876017-0-4

Printed and bound by CreateSpace, USA

Acknowledgements

I would like to thank Paddy Mary Stentiford who, from the other side of the world, painstakingly edited my novel with me through all its myriad drafts. I would also like to thank my sister Wendy Ealey who produced the cover design and interior typesetting, and Burnham Arlidge who painted the marvellous tree filled with bronze magic that appears on the front cover and throughout the book.

Dedication

I would like to dedicate this book to single parents everywhere.

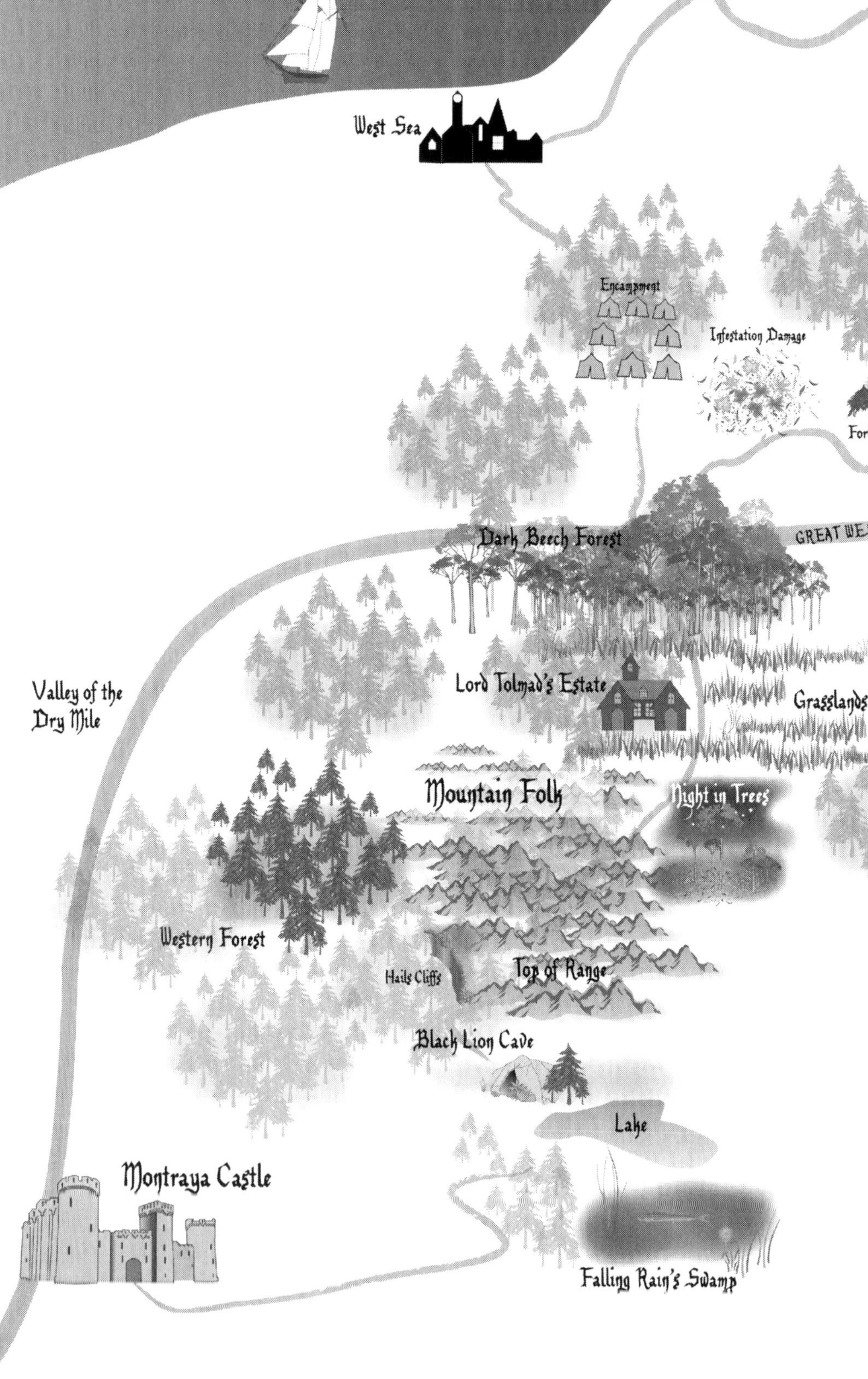
West Sea
Encampment
Infestation Damage
Forest
GREAT WEST
Dark Beech Forest
Valley of the
Dry Mile
Lord Tolmad's Estate
Grasslands
Mountain Folk
Night in Trees
Western Forest
Hails Cliffs
Top of Range
Black Lion Cave
Lake
Montraya Castle
Falling Rain's Swamp

Wood Nearing
Wooding Deep

TORMADELL
CASTLE

Borovan's Ride
Eagle Cliffs
Wolves Burial
Ancient Elm's Firesite
First Firesite
GREAT WEST ROAD
Second Firesite

N
Not to scale

Characters

Sorcerers

Tamadil Royal Family:
King Markazon (deceased)
Queen, Markazon's wife
King Kosar, eldest son of King Markazon
Prince Jarand, second son of King Markazon
Prince Tarkyn, third son of King Markazon

Courtiers:
Danton Patronell, Lord of Sachmore, Tarkyn's friend from childhood
Andoran and Sargon, friends of Tarkyn at court.
Stormaway Treemaster, wizard for Prince Tarkyn and King Markazon
Journeyman Cloudmaker, Prince Jarand's wizard
Sergeant Torrigan

Thieving Family:
Old Ma
Gillis, Old Ma's son
Tomas, Old Ma's son
Morayne, daughter of Tomas
Charkon, son of Tomas

Woodfolk

Wanderers:
Waterstone
Sparrow, Waterstone's daughter
Autumn Leaves
Thunder Storm
Creaking Bough, Thunder Storm's wife
Rain on Water, Thunder Storm's son
Rustling Leaves
Grass Wind
Lapping Water
Summer Rain, healer
Falling Rain, Summer Rain's exiled brother

Forestals:
Raging water
Falling Branch, his son
Sun Shower, Falling Branch's wife
Rainstorm, Falling Branch's son

Gatherers:
Ancient Oak
Tree Wind
North Wind
Running feet

Mountainfolk:
Dry Berry
Woodfolk near Tormadell
Ancient Elm

Captured Woodfolk:
Golden Toad
Rushwind
Ibis Wings

Part 1: Into the woods

CHAPTER 1

Tarkyn threw himself to the ground and rolled beneath the red streak of light, coming up fast, close to his attacker. Before the other sorcerer could change the direction of his shaft, Tarkyn had surrounded himself in a translucent bronze shield. Gasping for breath, he stood within a foot of his opponent, hands on hips, giving what he hoped was an unnerving smile.

As soon as he had recovered, he spun himself behind Andoran, his long black hair fanning out behind him, then dropped his shield and threw a shaft of bronze power at his opponent's back. Andoran ducked. Tarkyn's bronze beam shot over his opponent's head and slammed into a rickety spectator stand. A wooden upright gave way with a resounding crack.

Tarkyn watched in horror as, with ponderous grace, the makeshift stand sagged to one side. Dozens of panic-stricken spectators scrambled over each other, swarming onto the arena of the Harvest Tournament, desperate to get clear before the stand collapsed. Immediately, Royal Guards surrounded the prince and his opponent to protect them from the rabble.

From within the ring of guards, Tarkyn glanced up at the strong, well-built grandstand where the nobility and the rest of the Royal Family sat, well out of reach of any stray tournament-strength shafts of power.

"I warned them that we should have stronger boundary shields," he muttered. "It is not right to place people needlessly at risk."

Gradually, the exclamations and shouts died down as the stand stayed stoically, if drunkenly, upright.

With a show of bravura, a scruffy young lad with more courage than wisdom, vaulted back onto the stand and seated himself in the front row.

On hearing no creaking, a prim lady poked her beau in the ribs to push him up the steps before her. Then she gathered her skirts and calmly followed him to sit beside the scruffy youth in the best seats the stand had to offer.

Seeing that the stand still held firm, the rest of the crowd, first in dribs and drabs, then in a steady flow, remounted the structure to resume their seats. Once the last of them was re-seated, the guards returned to their positions around the stadium and the competitors squared off once more.

"Resume!" bellowed the referee.

The two sorcerers circled each other, each protected within his shield. Suddenly Tarkyn's shield winked out and he stood exposed but safe, as long as Andoran was putting his energy into maintaining his own shield. Andoran was now a step behind in the attack. After feinting right, then left, the red-headed sorcerer threw himself to the left, winked out his shield and thrust a shaft of power at the prince. But Tarkyn anticipated him and as he sidestepped the red attack, drove a shaft of power at Andoran that caught him cleanly in the chest.

Andoran yelped with pain, the referee blew his whistle and Tarkyn was declared the winner.

As the prince reached out to haul his opponent up and shake his hand, tumultuous applause erupted from thousands of watching sorcerers. They rushed onto the arena, young and old, rich and poor, eagerly clustering around their victorious prince, but kept at bay by a ring of protective guards. Tarkyn grinned and waved in response, then placed his arm across his worthy opponent's shoulder to draw him into the congratulations. Andoran mastered his disappointment enough to produce a rueful smile and wave his acknowledgement to the crowd.

Only the reaction of Tarkyn's twin brothers marred the occasion. Even while responding to well-wishers, Tarkyn noticed the look of consternation that passed between Prince Jarand and the king. *Concerned for my safety in the midst of this large milling crowd, he thought glumly. I hope Kosar is not so worried that he refuses me permission to compete again next year.*

The trumpets sounded, summoning Tarkyn to stand before King Kosar to receive the Harvest Tournament trophy. Still grinning at his achievement, Tarkyn strode across the arena but as he approached the king, he sobered up and with due decorum, produced a respectful bow. When he straightened before his brother, he expected Kosar to be smiling with pride. Instead, he received only a curt nod and a smile that did not reach Kosar's hard grey eyes.

"Congratulations, Tarkyn. Your power rivals our late father's. Impressive." The king's voice was formal. As he handed his youngest brother the trophy, the crowd broke into renewed shouts of approbation. Kosar frowned. "You appear to have developed quite a following amongst the rabble."

"Yes Sire. I believe all your subjects are enjoying the Harvest Festival. Thank you for granting me the opportunity to compete."

Throughout the presentation, Tarkyn mulled over the significance of Kosar's lack of enthusiasm. Kosar seemed distracted. Someone or something had upset him. *Probably Jarand,* thought Tarkyn. *It usually is.* At nineteen, Tarkyn was seven years his brothers' junior and, whenever possible, avoided the constant tensions that surrounded the throne. Nevertheless, he passed his own actions under quick review, to assure himself that nothing he had done could be the cause of Kosar's ill humour.

With the formalities over, Tarkyn withdrew to change into more formal attire; a deep blue surcoat embroidered with gold thread over a white shirt tucked into black leggings. As soon as he returned to the Royal Box to view the afternoon's events, a blonde, purple-eyed sorcerer bounced up to him and gave a small bow.

"Ah, I am pleased to see that you managed to get away from your guard's duties for a while, Lord Danton," said Tarkyn, formal in a public forum.

"Yes, Your Highness. So am I. I didn't want to miss your match. Well done, Sire. That was a great effort to beat Andoran. He has been practising for weeks, you know."

Tarkyn smiled, "I wondered about that. I was sure he had improved."

As the afternoon wore into evening, the Royal party retired to the great dining hall in the castle to preside over the Harvest Feast. The great dining hall was rarely used; only on Festival days and for visiting heads of state. Its stone vaulted ceiling soared above three rows of long, heavy oregon tables, lit by huge candelabra and three enormous chandeliers. Today, representatives of every guild, town and shire had been invited but only the highest nobility sat at the king's table.

All evening, Kosar was unusually genial to his twin brother.

Tarkyn leaned over and murmured in Danton's ear, "The king seems more at ease now. It is good to see my brothers getting on so well. They seem to be at loggerheads more often than not, these days."

"Yes Sire, it is certainly more congenial when they are in harmony with each other," said Danton carefully.

Tarkyn raised an eyebrow. "But…?"

Danton grimaced, "But someone else always suffers when they unite."

"With justification, I presume?" A note of hauteur warned Danton to go no further.

Danton met the unwavering gaze of Tarkyn's amber eyes and heaved a small sigh. "Just so, Sire." A few minutes later, he stood and bowed, "If you will excuse me, Sire, I am on guard duty on the east gate of the city in two hours' time. I will attend you tomorrow."

Tarkyn nodded farewell and returned his attention to the steady but discreet stream of well-wishers who, throughout the evening, had been vying for a chance to offer their congratulations.

By midnight, the last guests had been finally ushered out. The rigours of the tournament followed by an afternoon in the glare of the public eye, had taken its toll. Tarkyn took his leave of his family and fell into bed exhausted, his mind spinning with the events of the day. Gradually, the castle fell silent and Tarkyn fell asleep.

In the early hours of the morning, his quiet was shattered by someone thumping on his bedchamber door. When he dragged himself out of bed to answer the door, tousled and half asleep, Tarkyn found himself surrounded by embarrassed guardsmen who requested politely but firmly that he accompany them to the Great Hall.

The prince frowned, then nodded curtly, "Send for my man."

When the guards hesitated, Tarkyn met the eyes of one man he had known since childhood and raised an eyebrow, "Is it so urgent? Surely you do not expect me to present myself in my night garments?"

Despite his orders, the guard bowed, "Your Highness, the king is even now awaiting your presence. But I will assist you to dress, if you will allow me."

As the prince inclined his head graciously, no one could have known the disquiet he felt at being isolated from his servants. The guards waited awkwardly while the prince dressed, unhurriedly but not gratuitously wasting time until, with a final nod at his reflection, Tarkyn indicated that he was ready.

Under normal circumstances, no guard would dare to lay hands on him, and Tarkyn was not sufficiently concerned at this point to put it to the test, instead allowing himself to be escorted to the Great Hall. For their part, the guards made no move to restrain him.

Their footsteps echoed in the quiet of the night as they strode down the polished stone corridor of the palace, past closed bedchamber doors behind which palace advisors, courtiers and their families lay sleeping. For the guardsmen, the statues and portraits that they passed represented the history of Eskuzor and the bedrock of its society, while the quiet prince they escorted was a living embodiment of that heritage. But for Tarkyn, it was more than that; he walked between ranks of his own family, stretching back over forty-eight generations of monarchs:

some frowning down at him, some regarding him benignly, many of them great rulers, and others whose lives were mentioned only in hushed whispers. Their heritage demanded high expectations of him but also provided a foundation of strength and dominion stretching back over a thousand years.

They reached the top of the sweeping stone staircase. Except for the guards standing on either side of the great, carved wooden doors at the front of the palace, the entrance hall was deserted. Without a word, the soldiers marched with their charge down the stairs and out into the night.

The shuttered shops of Tormadell's main street presented blind eyes to the procession that passed before them. If anyone watched, they did so without betraying their presence. As they passed an alley, an orange cat streaked out into the road and seeing the soldiers, stopped dead, arching its back and hissing its displeasure at them. In an upstairs room, a baby started crying and a dim light was kindled but no one came to the window to witness the passage of the prince.

When they entered the Great Hall, Tarkyn saw that it had been set up as a court. At the far end, the king sat behind a huge raised wooden table with Prince Jarand by his side. Tarkyn's stomach turned over as he wondered wildly what he had done. He realised his knees had begun to tremble and he hoped desperately that they would hold him as he walked down the length of the hall. When finally he stood before his brother, Tarkyn gave a low bow. His heart thumped slowly within his chest, beating time with a vein in his temple, as he straightened and stared up at his brother, "You sent for me, Your Majesty?"

Suddenly Tarkyn found himself plunged from lauded victor to accused felon, standing trial on a charge of damaging public property and endangering life. In a daze, he listened as his own brother passed sentence on him; that he must foreswear his magic for four years or face imprisonment. With rising panic, he knew he could not allow them to take his magic. Nor could he face imprisonment. Once he was away from public sight, he knew he would never see the light of day again. Faced with the horror of such a future, Tarkyn threw up his shield.

Kosar leaned forward and glared down at him. "Tarkyn, how dare you defy me? You will accept the judgement of this court."

"My liege, please, I cannot." Tarkyn went down on one knee. "Sire, I have always been your loyal subject. The public stand should have had shields to protect it from off-target shafts of power. I raised this with the organisers before the tournament, but they dismissed my concerns. Other shafts went wide. The only difference is that mine hit a stand. Please reconsider."

But justice played no part in Tarkyn's trial and so his plea was irrelevant.

"Even if I may have reconsidered before, the fact that you raise your shield against me shows us all too clearly the limits of your loyalty and the reason that your magic must be forfeited." Kosar glared at him, "My judgement stands. Release your shield!"

Tarkyn's heart hardened within him. Never again would he bend his knee in submission. He stood slowly and straightened to his full height. He glanced around the room at the closed faces of the guards. No one met his eyes. He brought his gaze back to bear on his brother and said with quiet dignity, "I am truly sorry, Your Majesty...but I will not."

A charged silence followed. At the king's nod, the guards closed in.

"Bring him to me when he succumbs," ordered Kosar. With that, Jarand and he rose and passed through a private exit, leaving their younger brother to his fate.

Tarkyn stood motionless within his bronze dome, head held high, masking his desperation. For a moment, no one moved.

Then one guard, more jittery than the rest, threw a bolt of blue power at him. Tarkyn flinched. But instead of blocking the power, Tarkyn's shield reflected it, dropping the guard like a stone.

Pandemonium broke out. Tarkyn held his focus, knowing nothing could touch him, if he held firm. But now, every guard in the room attacked. Swords, arrows and beams of magic drove at the beleaguered prince from all sides. Every arrow or shaft of power that struck the bronze dome around him reflected back at a different angle, ricocheting around the Great Hall, injuring and killing guards randomly.

The air fizzed with a maze of dazzling colours as shafts of magic zig-zagged crazily around the Great Hall. All around him guards died, either killed by reflected power or arrows. The constant assault of ricocheting power pockmarked the vast cream walls of the Hall, sending chunks of plaster spraying down on the unshielded guardsmen. But still the guards kept up their attack. In the midst of it all, Tarkyn simply stood there, stunned into immobility but rigidly holding his focus, as arrows, beams of magic and masonry assailed him from every side before careening off his shield to add to the bedlam.

Then cracks began to appear in the ceiling and pillars. Within moments, aggression turned to fear. Anyone left standing turned tail and ran. With the imminent collapse of the Great Hall, the guards' desperate efforts to save themselves thrust all other considerations aside.

Dimly, Tarkyn realised that while the guards were preoccupied, he had to find a way out. Unnoticed, he crawled beneath the huge wooden table and finally released his shield. He strained his mind to remember the words of the re-summoning spell he had read, desperately hoping that he could make it work. He drew a deep breath and, focusing his will on his surcoat, muttered, "*Maya Mureva Araya....*" Between one breath and the next, he felt himself disintegrate into oblivion before landing nauseated but safe, at the origin of his clothing in a tailor's shop near the edge of town.

CHAPTER 2

For some little while he lay there, wrestling with the shock of the disintegration that he had endured in the course of his translocation. He nearly vomited at the thought of it. But as he recovered, he felt a certain satisfaction that his spell had worked. The events in the Great Hall crowded at the edges of his mind, but he could not yet allow himself to think about the scene of devastation he had left behind.

Once the feeling of sickness had passed, Tarkyn realised he was lying on a long wooden workbench. He rolled off the bench to land cat-like on his feet, then stood up slowly, grasping the edge of the bench for support while he regained his sense of balance. A strange combination of dull orange light from a street lamp a little way down the road and moonlight, picked out vague shapes in the darkened workroom. As his eyes became accustomed to the dim light, he realised that the mounds in the corner were in fact neatly stacked piles of cloth. Completed shirts, surcoats, cloaks and leggings hung in racks along the rear wall. It was the middle of the night and the workmen were all at home in their beds. It seemed no apprentices slept on the premises. He let out a sigh, thinking that luck was with him.

"Oh, very lucky!" he said sourly to himself.For a moment, the enormity of his situation threatened to overwhelm him, but he resolutely kept his mind in the present, knowing he could not afford the luxury of reflection until he was well away from Tormadell.

Although his own surcoat had been made here, he had never been to this workshop himself. All fittings were done at the palace. So he had no idea where he was. As he sat on a pile of cut cloth wondering what to do next, he gradually became aware of distant shouting. Several times, he heard running footsteps on the cobbles outside the factory. When the shouting drew nearer, for horrified moments he thought that the guards had worked out his location. But no. It was merely townsfolk regaling each other with the drama of the Great Hall's collapse and urging each other to venture forth to see the spectacle.

Tarkyn considered his situation. He knew how to fight, but other than that, he had had no training in looking after himself. He had been pandered to from the moment he was born. Now, the obstacles facing him even to procure breakfast in a few hours' time, seemed insurmountable. He had never had to deal with money and did not have any on him now. And even if he did have money, he could not risk being seen to buy anything. Not only was he a well-known public figure, but any circulated description of his long black hair, his height and his unusual amber eye colour would make him eminently recognisable.

After some careful thought he decided that with an uncertain future ahead of him, he would need resources. He would not turn to his friends and jeopardise their safety but somehow he had to get back into the palace and retrieve at least some of his personal jewellery. Now seemed as good a time as any; in fact better than most. All eyes would be on the demise of the Great Hall.

With a wry smile, he focused carefully on himself, better prepared this time for the feeling of disintegration and murmured, "*Maya Mureva Araya...*"

He expected to land in his mother's bed where he had been born but in fact, he landed in the king's huge four-poster bed. As he fought against the nausea, he shook his head. *This spell is dangerously unpredictable. Returning to the place of one's creation is open to more than one interpretation.* He shuddered as a thought struck him, *Oh lord. At least it didn't try to put me back inside my mother.*

A sound in the corridor brought his attention back to his surroundings. Even if the present king were elsewhere, he realised, there would always be a guard at his door. A fire glowed in the stone hearth, keeping the room warm, ready for the king's return. Bright moonlight streamed in through the window, bathing the padded armchairs and the fine, ornate writing desk in soft, silvery light. In the distance, Tarkyn could still hear the sounds of turmoil but within the palace, everything seemed quiet.

Tarkyn considered his options. He could take some of the king's jewellery in exchange for his own, leaving a note to that effect, but he suspected that Kosar would publicise the loss of his jewellery and suppress the explanation. Tarkyn did not want grand larceny added to the other accusations against his name.

He could not hope to beguile the guard by passing himself off as his brother. The king and Jarand were noticeably shorter than he, had grey eyes and wore their auburn hair shoulder length. Only the set of their features showed their relationship.

Tarkyn crossed to the window and opened it. Two hundred yards away, crowds of people clustered around the remains of the Great Hall. Only one corner of the monumental old building was left standing. The rest lay in piles of tumbled stone. Even as he watched, the last section gave way and crashed to the ground, sending up a billow of white dust. The sounds of shouting redoubled as spectators and workmen scrabbled away from the falling masonry. A knot of activity centred around one particular group and when the crowds parted, he could see his mother the dowager queen, talking intently with guards, workmen and townspeople. Tarkyn felt sick at the thought of the guardsmen who must have been trapped inside the building as it fell.

He shook his head to clear it. There was nothing he could do to help them. He had to find a way out of the king's room, retrieve what he had come for and leave. He took a moment to peer down two storeys to the lawns below. Too exposed. No way of escape there. After a bit of thought, he moved quickly to the king's writing desk and rummaged around until he found some parchment. He tore it quietly into strips and placed it along the inside of the door. Then he lit a taper from the coals of the fire, set the parchment alight and waited.

As the smoke seeped out into the corridor, he heard a muttered exclamation, followed by the precipitous entry of the guard. Tarkyn stepped behind him and closed the door. At the sound, the guard swung round, his eyes widening at the sight of the prince.

As the guard's hand went to his sword, Tarkyn sent a thin blast of power into the man's forearm. The guardsman reeled back, clutching his arm in pain. Tarkyn said quietly, "I do not want to hurt you further. But if you make any move to attack me, I will retaliate."

The guard lurched towards Tarkyn, "I cannot allow you to threaten our king. I must protect him, even if it means my life."

Tarkyn waved his hand languidly and muttered, "Shturrum", freezing the man in his tracks. The prince raised his eyebrows. "I would expect no less. That is, after all, your duty. However, you have my assurance that I intend the king no harm. I am merely passing through." He considered the guard dispassionately, "I am afraid I will have to tie you up so that I can make good my escape. I will not gag you if you hold your peace." He shrugged, "Besides, I doubt that there is anyone near enough to hear you at the moment." Saying that, he dragged the tasselled rope from the king's dressing gown and used it to tie the guard's hands behind him, before waving his hand to release the spell. Then he frogmarched the guard over to the huge four-poster bed, sat him down unceremoniously on the eiderdown and tied him to an upright.

The guard watched warily as Tarkyn stepped back to survey his handiwork. After a moment, Tarkyn met his eyes, "And now, guardsman, if I leave you like this, you will avoid excessive punishment, I think."

"I do not wish to avoid punishment. I have failed in my duty," replied the guard stiffly.

"Don't be such a martyr. I have already told you; the king is safe. And I do not wish my actions to be the cause of your suffering, any more than they already are."

"Huh! From what I hear, your actions tonight have caused a great deal more suffering than this. I can't imagine why you would concern yourself with me."

The prince's mouth set in a thin line. "You forget yourself."

Under Tarkyn's unbending stare, the guardsman lowered his head. "I beg your pardon, Your Highness. Tonight's events have confused us all."

"That may be so," Tarkyn conceded, "But whatever else I may be held to be, I am still a prince of Eskuzor…and you and anyone else who crosses my path would do well to remember it."

At that, the guardsman raised his head and subjected Tarkyn to a long considering stare. But before he could voice his thoughts, Tarkyn crossed quickly to the door, listening intently. With a brief nod at the guardsman, he opened the door and slipped out into the dimly lit corridor. It was deserted. He headed to his right, his nerves jangling, expecting at any moment that one of the doors he passed would open. The sound of his footsteps, despite his best efforts at stealth, echoed around the stone walls. With a grimace at the delay, he risked a few moments to take off his boots. Holding them in one hand, he crept on stockinged feet to the top of the staircase.

Suddenly he heard the voices of his brothers coming towards him, somewhere below him in the central hallway. He stepped back and pressed himself into an alcove, finding shelter behind a large statue of his great grandmother. As he listened, a messenger ran to catch up with the king and reported, "Your Majesty, there is still no news. The entire building has collapsed in on itself. Workmen are even now trying to reach those trapped beneath the rubble. The streets are filled with anxious relatives and onlookers. There have been no sightings of your brother the prince, Sire, and until what is left of the interior is breached, it is too early to say whether he still lives."

"Thank you," said Kosar gravely. As Tarkyn heard the messenger's footsteps gradually fade into the distance, the king spoke again. "Jarand, I think we must go out into the street and show our concern for our people." He sighed heavily. "Blast Tarkyn! How did he have the power to destroy the Great Hall? It will cost a literal fortune to rebuild."

Relieved, Tarkyn realised that Kosar had no immediate plans to climb the stairs and return to his bedchamber.

"Unfortunate, I agree," Jarand's voice echoed up the stairs, "But at least we have achieved what we set out to do. We have removed the risk of Tarkyn's pretensions to your throne."

Above them, Tarkyn listened in stunned disbelief.

"Just as well. Clearly his power is – was excessive...and far too many people applauded his victory. But look at that mess out there! I was hoping to remove him with a minimum of fuss." Kosar came into sight, heading towards the front door, his twin brother beside him. "I don't know what happened after we left, but somehow he held off my entire Royal Guard and then destroyed the building around him."

"Pointless. Juvenile theatrics; petty revenge at the cost of self sacrifice. He must have known he could not win. And now he has been crushed with all the others." Jarand sounded spine-chillingly unconcerned. "Even if Tarkyn has somehow survived, his popularity won't have. He will be the most reviled man in Eskuzor."

"I will make sure of that," said the king grimly.

Tarkyn gave a little frown, knowing these words should upset him. And yet his brothers' betrayal, followed by the horror of his trial and its wake of destruction had so numbed his mind that his popularity seemed of little significance. In fact, when he thought about it, his unpopularity would be merely one more obstacle in his already impossible future.

As their voices faded away, Tarkyn found he had no energy left to care that the cost of the Great Hall mattered more to them than he did. He waited for a few minutes before easing himself out from behind his great grandmother's statue to resume his journey across the top of the staircase. He followed the corridor for another fifty yards until he came to the door of his room.

He listened briefly before slipping into the haven of his own bedchamber. He glanced at his mahogany four-poster bed, noting that someone had already pulled the embroidered eiderdowns straight and plumped up the pillows. All around him were the objects of his life that he would have to leave behind: his trophy, books that he treasured, a small painting of his father, and various gifts and mementoes that he had kept despite carefully worded protests from his servants about the clutter. Almost he wished that he had not returned. Seeing what he must leave behind, highlighted the extent of his loss.

Thrusting his regrets aside, Tarkyn walked to his dressing table where his jewellery box stood in full view. He searched through his drawers until he found a drawstring leather bag and, with no regard for the beauty or delicacy of the finely wrought, gem-encrusted pieces, shovelled his jewellery wholesale into it. He glanced at the door of his dressing room, considering the wisdom of taking some clothes with him but he had limited time and no idea what clothing he should pack for himself. He had to return to the tailor's, well before the start of the working day.

In the end, he stuffed a couple of shirts into a bag and grabbed only his travelling cloak and hunting knife. Then he spent precious minutes penning a note to say that he had taken his own jewellery, to protect his servants from accusations of theft.

As he blotted his note, he took one last look around. He attached the sheath of his knife to his belt, and slipped the leather purse into a deep pocket in his leggings. Then he placed the cloak around his shoulders and took a firm hold on his bag, before focusing on his surcoat one more time.

CHAPTER 3

As soon as he had re-oriented himself in the quiet of the tailor's shop, Tarkyn crossed to the door and turned the handle. The handle turned, but the door did not give when he pulled or pushed it.

"Blast. It's locked, of course. And no doubt the tailor has the key on his person." Tarkyn threw his hands up, "Now what?"

After a few moments of frustration, it occurred to him that there might be another exit. Sure enough, a sturdy wooden door, bolted on the inside, led into a back alley. Tarkyn cautiously drew back the bolt, opened the door and peered out into the darkness. This established little more than the fact that no one was standing beside the door waiting to pounce on him. Taking his chances, he slipped out into the alleyway, pulled the door to behind him and waited for his eyes to adjust. The alley was in deep shadow; the buildings too high to admit the moonlight and no streetlamp nearby to cast away the darkness. He stood with his back to the door, listening. Off to his left, he could faintly hear the noise of the crowd gathered at the remains of the Great Hall. With his hand trailing against the alley wall for guidance, he headed to his right.

He crept along until the alley intersected a small road. Here he took a left and then a right hand turn into another alley that led him all the time further from the sounds of the crowds and hence away from the centre of the city. This was, in fact, the sum total of his plan at this stage; to reach the edge of the city and from there, to get well away from houses and people. Without having thought it through, Tarkyn had a vague idea that the further from Tormadell he went, the less likely people would be to recognise him or to have heard what had happened tonight.

He moved quickly and quietly through the dark streets, pulling back into the shadows to wait, each time he heard a noise or saw any signs of movement. But very few people were out and about in the depth of the night so he was able to make good time. Twice a small band of soldiers marched past down a cobbled street but the alleys provided plenty of cover at night and Tarkyn was able to draw back into doorways and remain unobserved until they passed.

At times, his nose screwed up at the smells of urine and refuse that wafted at him through the darkness. Once, he tripped over a pile of rubbish and his foot clanged loudly against a metal drum. An upstairs window opened abruptly and the tousled head of a middled aged woman popped out, "Who's down there making all that noise?"

Another window opened and a raucous voice demanded, "What's going on? Who's sneaking around my back gate?"

Tarkyn stood still in the shadows, scarcely breathing. Suddenly a cat broke cover and, with a bloodcurdling yowl, tore off down the alleyway.

"Oh! Bloody cats! I might have known," The owner of the first voice slammed the window down in disgust and retreated. The second window banged shut in answer.

Tarkyn waited, hunkered down beside the metal drum, until he was sure that all was quiet again. *A lot of cats in Tormadell,* he thought, before feeling his way carefully past the offending metal drum and resuming his journey.

By the time he had neared the edge of town, he found he was moving more surely and realised that the first faint touch of dawn was showing him the details of the buildings around him and the cobbles beneath his feet. He noticed with distaste the grime ground into the walls of three storey dwellings, gates hanging askew and rotting food scraps strewn carelessly into the alley. Everywhere around him were signs of poverty and decay. Anyone who lived there, would have seen that, in fact, some of the buildings were well kept; clean, and recently painted. But Tarkyn, overwhelmed by his first sight of the poorer quarters of town, was horrified.

His next disquicting discovery was that many people rose a lot earlier than he did. Even on mornings when he made an extraordinary effort to rise early to go hunting, he still left his bed well after sunrise. He was aware that his servants had to be up before him but he had somehow assumed that their early rising was peculiar to their profession. Yet out here in the town, many people were appearing on the streets well before the sun had risen.

And with the brightening light, Tarkyn was in real danger. The safety of his dark back alleys was being stripped from him minute by minute. At any time, someone could give him a second look and recognise him. And his travelling cloak, beautifully tailored from fine russet-dyed wool and embroidered with silver thread, although workaday by his standards, stood out like a beacon of excellence among the clothes of tradesmen.

For the time being, he could think of nothing to do but keep his hood up, his head down and walk on, looking for somewhere to lie low as he went. As a strategy, this was destined for failure.

He had not gone two blocks before he became aware that someone was quietly following him. As he passed a side alley, he caught a glimpse of a slight, ragged figure running parallel with his course in the next alley along and another creeping up through the shadows towards him. When a larger figure appeared in the mouth of the alley ahead of him, Tarkyn gave up all hope of passing undetected, backed himself up against the side wall and waited.

In all, there were five of them; two tough-looking men, an even tougher-looking old woman and two scrawny teenagers; a boy of about fourteen and a girl of thirteen. They closed in on him slowly until they stood just beyond arm's length in a semi-circle around him.

The silence lengthened but none of them made a move towards him. Eventually Tarkyn, never good at waiting, cleared his throat and asked, "May I help you?"

The taller man guffawed, "Oh, that's good one. Can he help us?" He turned to his companions, "What do you think? Can he help us?" Suddenly he turned back to the prince and snarled, revealing yellowed, jagged teeth, "Of course you can bloody help us. You're rich. We're poor. We want your money."

It dawned on Tarkyn that they would not believe him if he told them that he had none. So instead he said, "I can imagine you might. You certainly look to be in need of a good meal and decent clothes. Perhaps we could come to some arrangement."

"Perhaps we could." The old woman's mouth stretched into a sneer as she drew a long knife from within her skirts. "We can agree to let you live, if you agree to give us your money."

His would-be attackers saw a slight smile appear within the hood's shadow. "That was not quite the arrangement I had in mind."

The smile unnerved them. Suddenly the boy asked, "Where's your sword? Someone like you usually has a sword."

The smile broadened. "I only use my sword for show. I find it a clumsy weapon and have no need of it to defend myself."

"Hmp. Dad uses magic to fight too, you know. So don't think you're safe."

Although the thieves were unaware of it, Tarkyn did not want to use his shield or his attacking power. His magic's colour was unique and would give away his identity as surely as his physical appearance would. He inclined his head, "Thank you for warning me, young man. And what about the rest of you?"

"Shut yer face, you stupid lad!" The shorter man cuffed the boy across the back of the head before snarling at Tarkyn, "Don't think we're going to tell you what magic we each have. We're not. You don't need to know about us. All you need to know is that we all carry knives and know how to use them."

"I'm pleased to hear it. This looks to be a rough area. I can imagine you might need to defend yourselves."

The two men looked baffled as their attempts to intimidate Tarkyn met with frustration. The old woman sighed in irritation, and snapped, "Idiots! Don't stand there talking. Get his purse."

As the thieves surged forward, Tarkyn waved his hand and incanted, "*Shturrum.*"

They froze where they stood. Tarkyn then bodily lifted the girl to hold her against him, facing outwards. With a flourish, he produced his hunting knife and, with the eyes of his victims following his every move, placed the knife carefully against her throat. He could feel the coarse material of her dress, stiffened with dirt, beneath his hand as he waved his fingers to release his spell. He had not mistaken the thieves' closeness. With the girl in his power, the rest of the family backed off.

"Now, about that arrangement we were discussing..."

Half an hour later found them in a disused, partly demolished warehouse, down near the river. Tarkyn noted the pitiful rags and scrounged implements of their belongings piled against a wall. Threadbare blankets were strewn in cleared patches in the rubble. They were not very clever thieves, he decided.

Tarkyn still held the girl in front of him. With his face in the shadow of his hood and the knife at the girl's throat, his tall cloaked figure exuded menace. The other four thieves stood around him, taut and wary, waiting for the slightest opportunity to recover their kin.

"And now that we are safely out of view, we can talk." Tarkyn studied their thin, sullen faces. "You seem to have a lean hungry look about you. Perhaps you need to eat first."

"We was just off to pinch something from the baker's when we spotted you, prime for the picking...at least that's what we thought." The boy scuffed his foot in the dust. His shoe was coming apart at the seams and the sole was hanging off at the front.

"I see. Perhaps I can do something about that." Tarkyn glanced at the old woman. "Now, I wish to make you a proposition. Although at the moment, I hold the balance of power, I do not hold all the knowledge and so I will listen if you raise objections. Do you understand?"

"Some of us are not as stupid as others," said the old woman acerbically. "State your terms."

"I need something sold for me. In return, I will give you one half of its value. Unless I am much mistaken, even that will set you up for life."

The old woman folded her arms, "And why would you pay us when you don't need to?"

He looked around at their squalid living conditions. "Because I am not a thief and will pay you for your services. Besides, you are right. You are poor and need the money."

"And if we agree to do this, will you let my granddaughter go unharmed?"

Tarkyn shook his head regretfully. "Not until you have delivered all of the money to me with a receipt from the buyer. And in addition, I will need to be safely out of town before I let her go. I don't want you sneaking up on me again as soon as my back is turned."

The old woman glanced a query at the two men and received brief nods in return. "Yeah, we agree." She spat on the ground, "Don't have much choice, do we? What do you want sold?"

"Just a minute," Tarkyn stood up, transferred his knife to his right hand, and held the tip of it against the girl's ribs so that he could free up his left hand to feel in his pocket and rummage through the leather purse. After considerable fumbling through larger pieces, his hand finally closed on a small diamond pin that he used to hold his necktie in place.

As he withdrew his hand from his pocket, the girl took her chance on his divided attention. She yanked herself to her left and around, driving her right arm back towards him. A small knife flashed in her hand. All Tarkyn could do in time to avoid the knife, was let her go and jump backwards out of range. At the same time, the two men came at him from either side, the grandmother closed in beside the girl and the boy circled around to come at him from the back. With the thieves so spread around him, Tarkyn could not use his freezing spell on all of them. The girl swivelled into a crouch, her eyes filled with hatred, ready to slash up at him. *No use now,* thought Tarkyn, *to tell her that I would not have harmed her.*

Then, as Tarkyn stood balanced on the balls of his feet, preparing for the inevitable attack, the fire died in her eyes and she sank to kneel on one knee. Slowly, she turned her knife and presented the hilt.

"Your Highness, forgive me," she whispered. "I would never have attacked, if I'd known it was you."

The grandmother put her hands to her mouth and gasped before she too sank to her knees. The two men, a little slower on the uptake sent puzzled glances at the two women before turning to stare at him. Then they too knelt before him.

Belatedly, Tarkyn realised that his hood had fallen down as he had jumped backwards. "Oh blast," he murmured to himself, unmoved by their obeisance, "This was not my intention at all."

Neither the prince nor the thieves found it at all strange that they who defied the law on one hand, could still revere the royal family on the other. But now Tarkyn was in a real dilemma. Obviously, the family knew nothing about the events at the Great Hall, but as soon as they ventured forth into the market place, they would hear. While he pondered what to do, a slight sound from behind made him spin around just as the boy's arm whipped forward. Tarkyn ducked, even as the men shouted, "No. Stop!" and a knife whistled over his head to lodge in a wooden upright, only inches to one side of the women.

"No. You stupid boy!" yelled his father, desperation in his voice. "Don't you know your own prince? Get down on your knees and beg his forgiveness."

Dawning understanding of what he had just done brought horror to the son's eyes as his gaze swang wildly from father to prince. Knowing he had just committed a hanging offence, he turned on his heel and bolted.

Tarkyn was not sure that a clear command would penetrate the boy's panic so he murmured "*Shturrum*," and dropped the boy in his tracks. "Bring him to me," he said quietly.

"Please, Your Highness," pleaded the father, "He was behind you. He didn't realise who you were."

"I said, 'Bring him to me,'" repeated Tarkyn evenly.

It occurred to none of them that, at five to one, the odds were still stacked well in the thieves' favour. Centuries of rule by the Tamadil family had elevated its members to almost omnipotent status in the minds of the common people. Tarkyn removed his spell and waited until the man and his son were knelt before him. Tears rolled down the boy's face, leaving pale streaks on his dirty face while beside him, the father's face was a mask of misery. For the longest minute of their lives, the prince looked down on them silently.

Then he said, "You did well to do as I asked." The father looked, if anything, more stricken, until Tarkyn added gently, "I would not be so cruel as to force a man to bring his son to his own execution."

Relief washed over the father. "Thank you, Your Highness. Thank you."

Tarkyn considered them, kneeling before him, "It is not just your son who has transgressed against me. You know, don't you, that all your lives should be forfeit. But because you did not know who I was, I will not exact that punishment. Equally, for reasons I will explain later, I will not turn you over to the city watch."

"See? He's a fine young prince, he is," cackled the grandmother, an hysterical edge of relief in her laughter. "He's kind, this one. That's why he's the best loved of the royal brothers."

Tarkyn was startled, but after a moment's reflection, smiled wryly to himself. Even if that were true yesterday, it won't be today.

"Here grandmother. Let me help you up." As he put out his hand and drew the old woman to her feet, he could see that, much as she tried to hide it, it was a struggle for her to get herself up off her stiff knees.

"Thank you, Sire." She cocked a sharp eye at her sons, "You two could learn some manners from His Highness here."

The taller man grunted, still on his knees, "You don't have to kneel for us in the first place."

Tarkyn raised his eyebrows and the man muttered an apology and subsided into silence. "The rest of you may also rise." He turned to the girl and offered her his hand, "And I am sorry that I treated you so poorly. It is not my usual practice to intimidate young ladies. I hope you were not too afraid. I would never have hurt you."

The teenager blushed at being called a young lady then nodded casually, "Yeah, I didn't think you would, Your Highness." In response to Tarkyn's evident surprise, she explained, "You were not very rough, you know. And half the time you forgot to hold the knife against my throat. Your hand kept dropping. And even when you did, you did it gently."

"Hmm. Well, I must say it is not a skill I wish to develop." Tarkyn shuddered inwardly at the experience of violence that lay behind her casually uttered words. He sat down on the large block of stone and crossed his ankles, "So now that you know who I am, we may need to renegotiate our terms."

The grandmother bowed, "Of course, Your Highness. You have only to request it, and it shall be done."

"Blast!" muttered the shorter man to his brother, "I thought we was onto a bit of a winner here."

Tarkyn raised his eyebrows, "I beg your pardon?"

The shorter man pulled his forelock, "Beg pardon, Your Highness." He glanced sideways and murmured, "Sharp ears."

"Very sharp," said Tarkyn, "And I would appreciate it if you would refrain from making little asides in my presence." He waited for them to absorb this. Several glances passed between them but when they refrained from speaking, he nodded, "Good. And now, to return to our negotiation. I will not renege on our previous agreement. You will still receive one half of the value of this," here he held up the diamond pin, "on delivery to me of the money and receipt." He gave a faint smile, "So you may still make your profit."

"You are a true man of honour, Your Highness," said the taller man, still grateful for his son's life.

"Of course I am. And despite your profession, I expect you to be men and women of honour also, in your dealings with me."

The taller man's chest swelled with pride, but the grandmother glanced contemptuously at her son. She had heard token words like these before.

Tarkyn crossed his arms. "And now there is something I need to tell you before you venture forth on my behalf. You may be seated while you listen." He waited until they settled themselves on various tumbled chunks of masonry. Now that the time had come to tell them, Tarkyn was almost unable to continue. After a moment, he drew a deep breath and began, "Yesterday, during the Harvest Tournament, a shaft of my power went wide and hit a spectator stand. The stand was knocked awry but no one was hurt. In fact, after the initial panic, everyone climbed back onto it to watch the rest of our match. But…" He took another deep breath, "But the king brought me up on charges, because of it."

Tarkyn stood up and began to pace back and forth, ignoring the little intakes of breath that he had heard. After a few moments he turned to his small audience and said, "And I did not accept his judgement. I threw up my shield and after that…well… after that, everything went a bit haywire and most of the Royal Guardsmen were killed and the Great Hall opposite the Palace was completely destroyed," he finished in a rush, grimacing.

Five pairs of round eyes stared at him from slack faces.

"You defied the king?" the taller man breathed. "In public?"

"I'm afraid so."

"So that was why you were alone and kept your hood up," said the boy, pleased that a puzzle had been explained for him.

Tarkyn nodded.

"And the Great Hall has been destroyed?" asked the shorter man, eyes wide with astonishment. "What? You mean, gone? Completely gone?"

Unconsciously, Tarkyn wrapped his cloak around himself against the onslaught of their reactions. "Pretty much. There is only a big pile of rubble left."

"You must have put up one almighty struggle," said the shorter man, in some awe. "And killing all the king's guards too. Wow! That is some feat."

Tarkyn frowned. "No. It wasn't like that." He hunched deeper into his cloak "All I did was raise my shield. But something went wrong with it, and instead of blocking, it reflected back their own weapons at them... and at the walls. I didn't intentionally kill anyone."

"I'd hate to see you try, then," quipped the shorter man, who did not count sensitivity among his virtues.

"Yes, you would," said Tarkyn coldly.

"Now, stop it, Gillis. I beg your pardon for my son's behaviour, Your Highness. He never has known when to stop." The old woman sent a scalding glance at her errant son before beginning to talk to the prince in a soothing voice, almost as though she were calming a wild animal. "Hmm. I expect those guards' deaths must have been quite shocking for you. You probably knew some of them personally. And you know, I had you down as a pretty harmless sort of a character."

Tarkyn's eyes gleamed in appreciation of her tactics as he replied, "You can never know what a man might do when he is desperate. But you are right. I am a pretty harmless sort of a character. It saddens me that those guardsmen lost their lives." He gave a rueful smile, "And I could not have hurt your granddaughter."

With a conscious effort, Tarkyn pushed his cloak back and sat down, spreading his hands wide. "So there you have it." It went against all his instincts and upbringing to present himself for comment to anyone but the king. But he had never been in such an invidious position before and could think of nothing else to do, if he wanted their help.

The taller man gave a small chuckle, "You're in one bloody great pickle then, aren't you, my lord?"

The shorter one whistled, "And you thought we were bad. We're just petty thieves. But you, Your Highness! You've committed high treason, and destroyed a whole public building... Well, they'll say you did, whether you did or not. You're in a league of your own."

"And you're no master criminal, that's for sure," cackled the old grandmother. "You've cut the ground from under your feet, good and proper. Now we know you won't hurt Morayne and probably not any of the rest of us either. You're too much of a gentleman, Your Highness. Not wise to have told us that."

The prince considered her, unsure whether she spoke a warning or a threat. After a moment he shrugged and gave her a faint smile, "I have placed my fate in your hands and my faith in your honour. Was that so unwise?"

She stared at him, stunned. And as she thought about it, she realised that what he said was true. He was no longer using force. And hard upon that, came the realization that no one outside the family, let alone a prince, had ever even conceived that she might be honourable, let alone staked his or her life on it.

"You really have, haven't you?" A slow smile appeared on her sharp, wrinkled face. The grandmother put hand on her heart and bowed. "No, Your Highness, that was not unwise. You do us great honour and we will live up to your faith in us."

A short time later, Tarkyn heard her berating her tribe as they left, "Now, not a word to anyone. Do you understand? I know this is the biggest news we've ever had but we can't tell people. Not anyone. Got it?"

Then followed a long tedious wait. Tarkyn prowled the inside perimeter of the warehouse, then paced back and forth across the floor until he felt he knew every stone and scrap of rubbish intimately. He tested the rear doors and found that they were all locked. The only way out was through the gaping front door at the front of the building. If his thieving family brought back the city guard, he was trapped.

He considered using a blast of magic to destroy a lock in a back door but he hesitated to betray his uncertainty in their honour. Sooner or later they, and in particular the old grandmother, would notice what he had done.

After two hours, his nerves were worn thin with apprehension. He crossed to the front door for the umpteenth time and peered out from within the shadows. Always there were people within his line of sight, carrying goods down to the river docks or hurrying about their business. And everywhere he could see animated knots of people standing and talking in the morning sunshine, arms waving in graphic description. Even from a distance, it was clear that last night's events were dominating the town.

Tarkyn sighed and retired into the gloom of the derelict warehouse to sit dispiritedly against a wall. He pulled his hood up and tried to doze, knowing he had slept little last night and would have to travel again tonight. But he was too much on edge and every slight sound from outside jerked him back to wakefulness. After a while, he gave up and renewed his prowling.

Finally, when the sun was near its zenith, the taller man slipped quietly into the warehouse. He gestured for Tarkyn to be quiet and to follow him to a dark recess at the rear of the building. He shrugged a heavy bag off his shoulder before bowing briefly to the prince.

"Where have you been?" hissed Tarkyn. "And where are the others?"

"Your Highness, soldiers are everywhere. We had to travel far across town in case someone wondered where we got your pin. Then we split up and are all coming back by different routes making sure we're not followed. Your life wouldn't be worth a small tasty sausage out there at the moment." He glanced sympathetically at the prince. "You're worth just as much dead as alive to the king, and most people want you dead."

Although he had known this would happen, still Tarkyn's stomach knotted. "And how much is the reward?" he managed to ask casually.

The taller man's mouth quirked in a half smile, "I don't rightly know, Sire. Town criers came through earlier this morning and they'll be posting up notices this afternoon. But rumours are flying so hard and fast that it's difficult to tell what the town criers actually said."

"What is your name?" Tarkyn, suddenly aware of this man as more than just one member of a thieving family.

"Tomas, Sire."

"And so, Tomas, were you tempted?"

"Tempted? No Sire. Honour amongst thieves, so to speak. Not that you're a thief, Your Highness – I didn't mean that. But you are firmly on the wrong side of the law now, just as we are, and under our protection. Besides," Tomas gave an embarrassed shrug, "the chance even to meet you, let alone talk to you and do you a service is beyond my wildest dreams. In my whole lifetime, I have never come within a hundred yards of anyone in your family and even then it was only a glimpse at a parade."

Tarkyn was saved from responding to this by the advent of Morayne followed at discrete intervals by the rest of the family. The grandmother was last to arrive. Like the others, she dropped a heavy bag on the floor before bowing to Tarkyn. "Your Highness, there are soldiers at the top of the road conducting a door to door search. We must hide you." In a complete change of voice, she said sharply, "Come on you lot! We'll have to go down in the cellar. Move that stone."

Then, to Tarkyn's intense interest, the five of them trained their variously coloured beams of magic on a large stone block, slowly pushing it sideways. When he realised what they were doing, he joined his bronze beam to theirs. Immediately, the stone moved noticeably more easily.

"It's true, innit?" observed the shorter man, "His magic is strong."

Tomas snorted, "Of course it is. He won the tournament, didn't he?"

"Nothing to do with it," snapped the grandmother. "The whole Royal Family's magic has been strong for generations. Well known."

"I am right here," said Tarkyn, with a clear note of annoyance, "should you wish to speak to me rather than about me."

Tomas flashed him a smile, as he continued to train his orange beam on the slowly moving stone. "We're used to talking about you, not to you, Your Highness. It's hard to change the habits of a lifetime."

A reluctant, answering smile broke through the prince's reserves as he remembered their previous conversation. "Make the most of it, Tomas. Talk to me while you can." A shout and the sound of running feet further up the road made Tarkyn start in alarm. "Where do you want this blasted stone?" he demanded.

"Another foot should do it."

Tarkyn focused and sent a pulse of power at the heavy stone, thrusting it away from him the required distance along the floor. A trap door now came into sight that had been hidden beneath it. There was a rope attached to the middle of the underside of the stone that fed along a narrow channel cut into the wood of the trapdoor and from there down a hole into the cavity below.

The shorter man drew up the trapdoor and as they all clattered down the ladder, Tomas explained, "There's a slight slope to the floor. That's why it's so hard to push the stone away. But we can pull the stone back over the trap door from within the cellar. All that is left are a few rub marks. And we make sure there are rub marks beside many of the fallen rocks so that this one doesn't stand out. It's worked so far."

"Hmph. Very ingenious. I saw those marks while I was pacing around waiting for you. I vaguely wondered what they were but to be honest with you, my powers of concentration aren't up to much at the moment."

As soon as all people and bags were at the bottom of the ladder, the trapdoor was closed behind them and the two men pulled hard on the rope until it was hanging straight down and they knew that the stone was back in place. It was pitch dark in the cellar.

A thought suddenly occurred to the prince. "And how do we get back out of the trapdoor? How do you move that stone away from down here?"

The shorter man chuckled in the dark. "We don't, Your Highness. We can't move the stone from down here."

Something in the quality of the silence that followed, let them know that Tarkyn did not like being toyed with. After waiting in vain for him to ask the obvious question, the voice continued, this time more carefully courteous, "There is a series of small rooms beyond this one, Your Highness, and from the last of them, a small grating leads down onto the mudflats of the river. Only Morayne and Charkon are small enough to climb through the gap. So, later, when all is clear, they will go back up and release us."

"But surely that stone is too heavy for them to move on their own?"

"It just takes longer to move, Sire," came Morayne's voice, "with only two lots of magic to move it. But we can do it."

"And do we intend to sit in pitch darkness all afternoon?"

"No, Sire. But it is not safe to strike a light in here in case any glimmer of it shines up through the cracks. If you will allow us, we will guide you through into the next room and there we can be less cautious."

"Thank you. I do not think I could endure hours of this." But when a hand landed gently on his back to guide him, he still flinched at the unaccustomed touch.

Ignoring his reaction, Tomas said from beside him, "This way, Your Highness. Just be warned. There is step upwards in a minute," as he used his hand to guide the prince through a doorway into the next room.

Suddenly, they heard shouting and the sounds of heavy boots on the wooden flooring above them. Tarkyn and the thieves froze where they were. As the footsteps milled around straight above them, Tarkyn felt the thief's hand on his back give him a reassuring pat. Once he had quelled his initial affront at Tomas' over-familiarity, Tarkyn found the gesture surprisingly comforting.

After a few fraught minutes, as the footsteps gradually diminished and the thieves and Tarkyn resumed their manoeuvres in the dark into the adjoining room. Once the door had closed behind them, Tarkyn waited for a light to appear but instead he heard the sound of scrabbling and quiet cursing. With a slight smile, he intoned, *Lumaya,* and a soft ball of light appeared in his hand. "Will this help?"

"Oh, thanks very much, Sire," said the shorter man. "You're pretty handy with your magic, aren't you? Ah, here we are. I couldn't find the flint in the dark. It must have been knocked off the shelf as we came through."

Once the lamp was lit, there was a moment of awkwardness while the family realised that the only place to sit was on the floor. And none of them could sit down while the prince stood. In a flash of inspiration, Charkon emptied the contents of his bag and lay it out on the floor, "Perhaps you would like to sit here, Your Highness. Then your clothes will not get too dirty."

"Thank you," said Tarkyn gravely, not actually as concerned as they feared. "Perhaps you would all like to be seated too, if we have a long wait ahead of us."

Not being totally clear on court etiquette, each of them gave a short bow before sitting down on the ground around him.

"And now, Your Highness," the old grandmother's eyes were shining with excitement as she began to unpack her bag, "we have brought food and drink such as you have never seen before."

"Actually, old Ma," said Tomas dryly, "he probably has. It's us who haven't."

The grandmother waved away his objection as she produced a large square of bleached linen. "And look! I even bought a cloth to put it all on."

From every bag came pies, meats, fruit, breads and cakes, yellow butter and soft white cheeses. Bottles of wine, ale, milk and fruit juice were distributed around the little room and then, when all was set before them, the family heaved a collective sigh of contentment and sat back, looking expectantly at the prince.

Tarkyn smiled, "It is indeed a magnificent spread. Shall we?"

With permission granted, the feasting began. There were no plates or cutlery. Everyone used their knives to cut portions or spread butter on hunks of bread and held their food in their fingers.

When the first frenzy had passed, and they were sitting around drinking and picking occasionally at the remnants, the family turned their attention to other items in their bags. Under the grandmother's strict directions, they had all been allowed to buy one personal item each on their way back, partly for the joy of it and partly to give themselves time to check that they weren't being followed. These items were now paraded before Tarkyn and each other. The boy had a fine new pair of boots and the girl had bought a warm, hand-woven shawl. Tomas and Gillis had bought shirts and the old grandmother held up a smart black jacket that contrasted noticeably with the worn material of her present garb.

There was a lull after this and Tarkyn spotted members of the family exchanging surreptitious glances as they reached for a bottle or more food. He had a fair idea that they were waiting for him to ask for his money but he refused to accommodate them. He was determined that he would not show the slightest doubt in their honour.

Eventually, the grandmother gave a deep sigh and shook her head, smiling, "Oh, Your Highness, your patience and courtesy are beyond belief."

"I am not renowned for my patience actually," said Tarkyn dryly, "only in some situations."

From one of the bags that was still fuller than the others, she produced a well-filled rucksack. She handed it to Tarkyn saying, "This is from all of us. It is a sturdier, more practical bag than the one you carry and we have filled it with supplies for your journey. Your money is in an inside pocket."

A rush of feeling threatened his equanimity as he realised that once he left them, he would encounter no one well disposed towards him. He swallowed before replying, "Thank you. I did not expect such kindness."

"You have a hard road ahead of you, my lord," said Tomas. "We have just done what we could to ease your passage."

Chapter 4

An eerie silver glow on the eastern horizon signalled the imminent rise of the moon as Tarkyn and the family of thieves parted company on the edge of town. In the gloom of the pre-moon night, Tarkyn could just make out the track ahead skirting the cornfields close to the bank of the river.

Tomas's last words to him were, "And Sire, at your first opportunity you should find somewhere safe to hide the rest of your valuables." The thief smiled at Tarkyn's look of surprise. "You are not good at dissembling, my lord. It was obvious you had more in your pocket than your diamond pin. Don't keep it all on you. If you get rolled, you don't want to lose everything." He bowed, "It was a privilege to spend this time with you, my lord. We will never forget it. Fare well."

"Fare you well also. I, too, will not forget you," Tarkyn replied as, with a final wave, he hitched his rucksack and strode resolutely into his future.

The thieves had offered to procure a horse for him but after some discussion, he and they had felt that he would be more obvious mounted and would be forced to keep more to the roads. By foot, he would be slower but better able to hide. Since he had no particular destination, his speed of travel was less important than remaining hidden.

Tarkyn walked steadily through the night, keeping the river on his left as Gillis had suggested. But the trouble with following the river was that its waters attracted home dwellers and provided transport for barges and sailboats. Several times, he had to detour though the fields to avoid homesteads and twice he came around a bend in the river to be confronted by a small river port, complete with garrisoned soldiers.

The second time, he walked within ten feet of two sentries. The first he knew of them was a tense voice to his right, asking, "Did you hear that? Hoy! Is anybody there? Stand and show yourself."

Tarkyn froze and edged slowly back into the shadow of the thicket from which he had just emerged. Just as he heard the sentry start towards him to investigate, a small deer brushed past and crashed its way through the undergrowth, out into the open in the direction of the sentry. As the sentry started in surprise, the deer zig-zagged past him, back into the cover of the trees and out of sight.

Another voice laughed, "Huh. So much for your prowler."

Soon after this, the moon deserted him, hiding behind a heavy bank of clouds that came in from the south. He couldn't use his lumaya spell to light his way for fear of drawing attention to himself. So he walked slowly, straining his eyes to see where the path led him and occasionally tripping over unseen tree roots or rises in the path. After a couple of hours of excruciating concentration, he gave up and found a log to sit against near the riverbank.

As soon as he sat down, the clouds whimsically disappeared, revealing a moonlit stretch of water spread before him. He glanced around, seeing the path ahead winding off to his right, clearly visible at last. With a wry smile, he decided to take a chance on the clouds staying away and settled down to investigate the contents of the rucksack. With a piece of game pie in one hand and a bottle of ale in the other, he looked out over the dark waters of the river and finally let his mind drift unfettered over the events of the last two days.

He still felt breathless with shock every time he thought of his brothers' betrayal. Being straightforward himself, Tarkyn had never come to terms with duplicity in others. And if his brothers could discard him like that, what about his friends? Were any of them true to him or had they just been using him for their own ends? He shook his head as he thought about it. He had no idea.

Then his mind turned to the guardsmen. How quickly their lifelong respect for him had turned to enmity, as the king willed it. He remembered the hatred and dawning fear in their eyes as their attempts to hurt, kill or capture him had been frustrated by his shield.

Tarkyn looked down at the moonlight glinting on his signet ring, carved amber embedded in bronze. It had been his father's ring, fashioned for him to blend his eye colour and the colour of his magic. When he was younger, Tarkyn had been a reflection of the late king's colouring but in the eleven years since he had died, Tarkyn had carried the black hair, the amber eyes and bronze magic alone. Staring down at the ring his father had left him, his resolve hardened. Whatever happened to him, he would not forsake his heritage. He hoped his father would have understood that Tarkyn had not betrayed the Tamadil line by refusing to bow to Kosar's decree, but that a Tamadil monarch had betrayed him.

He gave his head a slight shake and took another bite of pie, stamping firmly down on the feelings that threatened to well up. There was no point in dwelling on them. He had survived and escaped. That was the best he could ask for. These people were in his past. Now he must look to his future.

Tarkyn studied the dull gold of lamplight in a cottage window on the other side of the river and wondered what life was like for the poor farmers in that cottage, as they ate their evening meal and prepared for bed. As he watched, a man came out of the side door of the cottage and the leashed dogs sent up a chorus of welcome as he crossed to a shed and disappeared from sight.

Tarkyn took another bite of pie and tried to envisage his own future. But try as he might, nothing came to him. Everything he was and everything he knew lay in ruins behind him. He spent another few minutes while he finished his food, trying to come to terms with the black void ahead of him. He was not cast down by it. It was his past, not his future that upset him. In fact, there was a spark of excitement in him at the prospect of the complete unknown that lay before him.

Tarkyn stood up, brushed his hands and stowed the rest of the ale in his pack.

"Well, I know I am going away from Tormadell and I think I must also leave this river. It is too populated," he said to himself. "Other than that, I will let my future come to me. Each time I reach a fork in the road, I will follow the road I like the look of, the road with heart. And I will let my heart lead me into my future." This idea was so absurdly whimsical that it brought a smile to his lips, but at least it gave him a basis for deciding on his route.

Before he left the river's course, mindful of Tomas' advice, he wanted to find somewhere to hide the bulk of his valuables. Just after dawn, the path narrowed and became difficult to negotiate, as it wound its way over and around tumbled rocks at the side of a narrow pass. Ahead, Tarkyn could see the path disappearing up into the damp undergrowth beside a series of waterfalls. Spray filled the air and obscured his views of immense cliffs that towered on either side of the waterfalls as the valley narrowed to a deep ravine. In those cliffs, he decided, he would find his hiding place.

It took him over an hour of solid climbing to reach the top of the cataract. The path he had been following ended there. Before him, the river filled the ravine from cliff to cliff. Tarkyn's only choices were to turn back or to climb. He studied the cliff face on his right, looking for some likely cranny in which to hide his leather bag. Then, a little distance along the right hand cliff, a hundred feet up but nowhere near the top, he spotted an eagle's nest perched on a small ledge. Sorcerers respected eagles, both for their strength and beauty; no one would dream of attempting to invade their nests. If Tarkyn could secrete his valuables there, no one would find them

Perfect, he thought, Impossible, but perfect. Tarkyn shrugged and grinned to himself. He had nothing to lose. He was a man without a future. He would attempt the impossible.

It was not reaching the nest that was the problem. He and many other of the stronger sorcerers could levitate, not necessarily a hundred feet, but enough to rise from one foothold to the next. It was running the gamut of the eagles that made it so tricky. And if he was busy levitating, Tarkyn could not raise his shield or fire a beam of power at the eagle to defend himself. Besides, killing the eagle would defeat the whole purpose of hiding his valuables behind its nest.

Tarkyn settled down on a wet rock to eat while he watched the eagle's nest. It was hard to see exactly what was happening but from time to time, he saw the head of a large golden eagle jutting over the top of the nest. Judging by the way it kept shifting its position, he was fairly sure that there must be an insistent chick beneath it. He wondered why the eagle didn't take off straight away to hunt until he remembered that it would be waiting for the air to heat up.

It was still early morning and the air was cool and fresh. Tarkyn decided that he might as well find himself somewhere in the undergrowth to doze until the warming air created the thermal currents the eagle was waiting for.

The sound of voices woke him a little before noon, dragging him up out of the depths of a sound sleep. For a few moments, he lay groggy and disoriented, trying to remember where he was and why. He gave his head a shake and rubbed his eyes, glad that he was safely out of view behind a curtain of overhanging branches. He listened carefully for a few minutes and caught enough snatches of conversation to decide that the voices belonged to a group of sightseers, out on a walk to view the spectacle of the falls. Not as dangerous as soldiers, but still able to report a sighting of the renegade prince on their return, even if they chose not to tackle him themselves.

Tarkyn was just about to let himself doze off again until they left, when it occurred to him that he might snore and alert them to his presence. So, instead, he spent the next half an hour, jerking himself awake every time he felt himself nodding off.

Luckily, the dampness underfoot and the spray in the air were a little too uncomfortable for the day trippers to stay long. But just as he was about to emerge, he heard more voices coming up the track from the bottom of the falls.

Oh Blast, thought Tarkyn, *I've trapped myself, right in the middle of the local attraction.* He thought back to the last large village he had passed. It would have been about two hours from the bottom of the falls. So it was reasonable to assume that the last day trippers would leave the top of the falls at least three hours before dark. Tarkyn heaved a sigh and resigned himself to a long wait.

Inactivity was not natural to him and by the time the last voices had died away down the side of the valley, most of his supplies had been drunk and eaten, out of pure boredom. By the time Tarkyn could crawl out of his hiding place, he felt damp through to his bones. The sun was heading towards the horizon but once he was away from the overhang of the trees, there was still a sting of heat in the air. Without further ado, Tarkyn hitched his pack firmly on his back and walked to the bottom of the cliff to plan out his route. The cliff was not completely sheer. In fact, an experienced climber could probably have scaled it without ropes. However, Tarkyn planned to climb where he could, and levitate to the next ledge whenever he got stuck.

This plan worked well, but he had underestimated the height of the cliff and the difficulty of the climb. When he was only half way up, the eagle had swooped back onto its nest. Tarkyn pressed himself in against the rock face and waited motionlessly while it fed a large rat to its insistent fledgling before taking off again. After a few minutes, Tarkyn cautiously resumed his ascent but by the time he was sitting on a ledge just below and some thirty feet short of the eagle's nest, he was running out of both time and energy.

Here, he could hear the incessant squawking of the eagle chick. He could see the eagle far above him, circling in a thermal that brought it out over the ravine and then sent it out of sight over the top of the cliff. Each time it disappeared from sight, he scrambled a few feet closer to its nest, and froze each time the eagle's path brought it back into the open sky above him. At last, he was within ten feet of the nest. Now that he was close to it, Tarkyn could see that the ledge on which it rested was wider and deeper than it had appeared from below and there would be room for him to stand on it while he found a secure place for his leather pouch. The eagles had chosen well. The cliff face was completely smooth in every direction around the ledge, so Tarkyn would have to levitate himself across the last stretch.

He waited until the eagle circled out of sight then made his move. He glided the short distance across the gap, to land in a crouch next to the eagle chick. The chick immediately addressed its complaints to him, at double the volume. Before he could even straighten, the sun was blotted out by huge wings as a second eagle came at him from behind, its fearsome talons spread before it. Tarkyn threw up his shield, instinctively cowering back against the cliff face as the enormous bird swooped in to land straddling its chick defensively, its hooked beak only inches from Tarkyn's face.

Oh no! Of course there are two of them. I should have known that. Tarkyn lowered his arms and slowly uncurled himself. He leant, still crouching, against the back of the ledge, and raised his own amber his eyes to look directly through the bronze haze of his shield into the hard amber eyes of the eagle. Tarkyn was by no means safe, even within his shield. If the eagle forced him off the edge of the ledge, he doubted whether he could wave away his shield and then incant his levitation spell as he plummeted downwards, in time to avoid smashing onto the rocks below. And when the time came to leave the eagle's ledge, he would have to drop his shield before he could levitate. No, not safe at all.

Slowly, Tarkyn removed the pack from his back and set it down in front of him. Without taking his eyes off the eagle, he felt around inside until his hand closed on the last of his game pie. He brought it out slowly and raised the edge of his shield so that he could push the offering towards the eagle. The eagle tilted her head so that she could see what Tarkyn had laid before it. Then she shrieked her derision at him.

With no conscious effort at all, Tarkyn found himself slammed hard against the cliff face as the sound assaulted him. But despite this, he kept his eyes firmly locked on the eagle's. At the smell of food, the chick's cries became even more plaintive as it struggled beneath its parent to reposition itself and stretch out far enough to reach the pie. The eagle gave it an impatient nudge back with her beak but the chick was not to be denied. After several frustrated attempts to quell her chick, the eagle flapped into the small space between Tarkyn and her nest so that she could reach the piece of pie.

Pastry was not the easiest substance for an eagle's hooked beak to grapple with and it took several attempts before most of the pie had disappeared down the chick's throat. During the whole procedure, she alternated her baleful stare between the food and Tarkyn. Overall, Tarkyn felt that his gift had probably antagonised the eagle more than pacified her.

Minutes later, the male eagle landed on the nest and, ignoring Tarkyn, used beak and talons to rip apart a large crow and feed it, piece by piece to the squawking chick. At last the chick's cries subsided and Tarkyn felt his nerves settle slightly as silence descended. But now he had two huge birds glaring at him from inches away and the ledge had become extremely crowded. Slowly he stood up so that he was taking up less space. As he rose to his feet, he saw a deep recess at waist height. With a very slow wave, he changed his shield from a dome to a curved wall in front of him. Then he reached into his pocket, drew out the leather pouch and, keeping his eyes all the time locked with the eagles', pushed the leather pouch deep into the crevice with his right hand. All was going well until his hand flinched back from a sharp piece of rock.

At the sudden movement, pandemonium broke out. Both eagles spread their wings and battered at the outside of his shield, shrieking and snaking their heads towards him, their beaks and talons hooking onto the bronze hazy barrier. In the background, the chick squawked in alarm. Breathing hard, Tarkyn resisted the urge to back away. Bringing to bear the natural arrogance of his heritage, Tarkyn outfaced everything the eagles threw at him. He would not let them drive him from the ledge. He brought his hand slowly down to his side and forced himself to stand motionless before them, keeping his eyes on theirs.

Gradually, as their aggression had no effect on the intruder, the eagles quietened and after ruffling their feathers into place, reverted to glaring at him. Slowly, more slowly than he had ever done it before, Tarkyn faded his shield away. After a minute, the female jabbed her head forward and used the rounded part of her hooked beak to push Tarkyn in the chest.

Tarkyn kept rigidly still. Then slowly, keeping his eyes trained on theirs, he placed his hand over his heart and gave these lords of the air a small bow, as the acknowledgement of one equal to another. He doubted that they had any idea what he meant by it, but it felt the right thing to do, to pay them homage and to thank them for protecting his valuables. They cocked their heads at him, as though studying the gesture. Suddenly with a parting shriek, the female took off and with a few strong wingbeats, rose swiftly on the air to become a silhouette against the sky. The male stepped into the nest and settled himself on top of the chick, muffling its cries.

Tarkyn could hardly believe his eyes. Returning stare for stare with the remaining eagle, he muttered under his breath, "*Ma liefka*" and rose gently into the air. The eagle stayed where he was and let Tarkyn go.

When at last Tarkyn had levitated and clambered his way to the top of the cliff, he stretched himself out on the grass and found that he was trembling, whether from exertion or reaction he wasn't sure. He was still dazed by his escape. He reflected ruefully that even for a man with no future, his venture into the eagle's domain had been foolhardy.

CHAPTER 5

Over the next few days, Tarkyn skirted villages and farmsteads, losing all idea of where he was heading. Twice he waylaid a small child to ask him to buy something for him from the village shop in exchange for a small fee, but these villages were so small that everyone knew everyone's business, and both times he had had to run for his life as suspicious villagers had come looking for the stranger. By the fourth day, he was living mainly on berries and some apples he had found in an old gnarled tree by the side of the road. His big frame demanded more than this and his stomach growled constantly as he walked along mile after mile of dirt roads.

It was nearing sunset on the fifth day away from Tormadell when he sat down by the side of the road to rest before finding somewhere safe to spend the night. Up ahead of him, Tarkyn could see the beginnings of a forest and he hoped that it might provide him with some respite from the constant tension he had endured since leaving Tormadell.

He was tired and dispirited after days of living on his nerves. He had travelled fast, avoiding villages and farmhouses, shying away from contact with people. He was becoming very weary of detouring around the slightest signs of humanity and starting at every sudden sound. After days of unaccustomesd solitude, he was sick to death of his own company and was beginning to think that his unknown future would be slow starvation if he could find nothing better than berries and apples to eat. Heaving a disconsolate sigh, Tarkyn put his hood up and dozed for a while in the shadows of an old oak.

When he awoke, an old man was sitting beside him. Tarkyn retreated further into his hood and glanced around to check whether the old man was alone. He seemed to be.

"Good evening," said Tarkyn warily.

The scruffy, old man seemed to be completely relaxed, "Good evening, young man. I was wondering, if you are going my way, whether you might like some company for a while, going into yonder forest? I have been travelling alone for some time and would appreciate a bit of company. Besides, the forest always feels safer when there is more than one person travelling through it, if you know what I mean."

Tarkyn studied him for a minute, trying to discern any guile in his voice. Then he realised that the old man could have captured him while he slept, had he known who he was.

"I don't suppose," ventured Tarkyn hopefully, "that you're any good at hunting or trapping, are you?"

The old man snorted, "Of course I am. Lived in these parts for years." He peered at Tarkyn, "Hmph. Can't see your face but your voice sounds a bit strained. After a feed, are you? Well, I think I can help with that. Got a good plump rabbit in my bag, all ready for dinner. Glad to share it, in exchange for the protection of your company."

"Agreed," Tarkyn stood and held his hand out to help up the old man. Together, they walked along the dusty road towards the forest.

Long before they reached the treeline, the heat from the waning sun made life inside Tarkyn's hood uncomfortably warm. He was not particularly practised at withstanding discomfort and so, readying himself in case the old man attacked, Tarkyn threw caution to the winds and dropped his hood. At first the old man didn't even look at him but when he did happen to glance around, he showed no sign of recognition. For several minutes longer, Tarkyn stayed on tenterhooks, waiting for a surprise attack from the old man, but gradually, as nothing happened, he relaxed his guard.

Once they were well inside the forest, the old man made a fire for them and set about skinning the rabbit. Tarkyn watched this operation carefully, realising that he might have to learn how to do this himself in the coming days.

"I think I could stalk and kill an animal," said Tarkyn. "I have hunted before. But I have never prepared an animal for eating." He grimaced, "I can't say it appeals to me all that much."

The old man glanced up at him, his green eyes strangely piercing. "And where have you been, my young buck, that you have hunted, but not had to do the dirty work?"

Tarkyn cursed his unruly mouth. "I come from the city and have only been on organised hunts."

The old man grunted, and returned his attention to the rabbit. "You may find stalking animals more difficult without beaters to flush them out and gamesmen to track them down in the first place."

"Yes, I think I may." The prince was beginning to realise that life was lot harder than he had expected.

As the evening progressed, his spirits seemed to sink even further, despite his first good meal for a couple of days. The prince and the old man were seated on the ground, leaning against forest trees, the remains of cooked rabbit lying on a piece of bark near the fire.

After days of solitude, Tarkyn began to talk, "I don't know where I'm going, you know. I have lost myself, my way of life and everything that has mattered to me until now. All the roads ahead of me lead nowhere."

He smiled with a touch of embarrassment, "I decided that, at each intersection, I would follow the road that felt best, the one with heart." He shrugged, "But I'm finding that is easier said, than done. Sometimes, none of them feels good."

The man across the fire from him maintained a companionable silence, prodding idly at the coals with a long stick.

Somehow encouraged by this, Tarkyn continued, "It has not been in my nature to be so feckless. In fact, it has come upon me quite suddenly. Last week, my life was laid out ahead of me by the expectations of the c... those around me. But this week...this week, I am cut loose by circumstance and running hard from those very people who held me so closely before." He gave a mirthless grunt of laughter. "Strange, isn't it?"

His companion directed one quick calculating glance at him before letting his gaze drop back to the fire. "Woman trouble?" he asked sympathetically.

Tarkyn gave a slight smile, "No."

"If it's not woman trouble and you're on the run, I'd say you might have a price on your head." The man's eyes glinted in the firelight. "Do you?" he asked slowly.

The prince's eyes narrowed. Incurably honest, he replied, "Yes, I do. I don't know how much, but I do. Why? Thinking of turning a quick profit?"

The old man looked up at him and shrugged, "To be honest with you, it would depend on what you'd done."

"And on what grounds would you base your decision? If the crime were sufficiently dire, would you feel honour-bound to bring me in, but for a lesser crime you would show mercy?" His voice hardened, "Or perhaps, it's the other way around? If I seemed relatively harmless then it would be safe to take me in for a quick profit, but you would not risk it if my crimes suggested that I might be dangerous?"

The older man shifted uncomfortably. "Stars above, young man! No need to get so touchy! I am not planning to turn in someone I am sharing my fire with. I was talking generally, not specifically."

"I beg your pardon. It did not come across that way," said Tarkyn stiffly.

"You're a courtly sort of a character, aren't you, my young buck?" The old man leaned forward and pushed a stick further into the fire. "So," he asked casually, "Are you going to trust me with your name?"

There was a long pause. The old man kept his eyes trained on the fire as the minutes ticked by.

"My name is Tarkyn Tamadil, Prince of Eskuzor."

Without a word, the old man rose to his feet and bowed deeply. "It is an honour, Your Highness."

Tarkyn looked up at him and inclined his head in acknowledgement, "And may I ask who you are?"

"Certainly, Sire. I am Stormaway Treemaster, Wizard of the Forest."

The prince raised his eyebrows. "Are you indeed? I have heard of you, Stormaway Treemaster." His eyebrows came together in a slight frown. "You were at court, were you not, in the service of my father?"

The wizard inclined his head but made no further comment.

"Please be seated." Tarkyn smiled. "I have always thought Stormaway Treemaster to be such an excellent name. I wish I had one so colourful."

"Do you?"

Tarkyn drew his cloak around himself against the cooling night air. "Any name but my own would be better right now."

For the first time, the forest wizard returned his gaze levelly and said with unexpected sympathy, "I imagine it would be." He leaned forward and poked the fire again, "Even if you weren't sharing my fire, I wouldn't attempt to turn you in. You are far too dangerous."

Tarkyn gave a short mirthless laugh. "I see my reputation precedes me."

"It certainly does. But I suspect the tales of your misdeeds may have been vastly exaggerated."

"Maybe. Maybe not. I don't know what they are, but I can't imagine that they are much worse than the reality."

"But regardless of the rumours," continued the wizard, "the strength and skill required to win the Harvest Tournament is indisputable."

A genuine smile lit the prince's face. "Thank you. I had almost forgotten that achievement in the turmoil that followed."

Stormaway stirred the fire then asked in a completely different tone of voice, gentle and firm, "Would you like to tell me about it?"

After a minute's silence, he looked up to see Tarkyn staring at him, considering his decision. The wizard, who seemed to have grown in assurance, said, "Take your time deciding. We have all night if we need it." His eyes fell to the fire once more as he continued, "If you trust me not, so be it. Perhaps the truth is worse than the rumours, but I doubt it. But knowing who you are, places you in as much danger as anything you could say."

Tarkyn eyes narrowed. "I thought you said you would not betray me?"

The wizard frowned impatiently, "I won't. I'm saying that I need no further information to betray you, should I choose to do so. Therefore, you can tell me your story without fear of further consequence."

Tarkyn re-evaluated his impression of the wizard. The man before him, who had seemed shifty and shiftless, now exuded natural authority. "I've been watching you, Stormaway. You're like a chameleon. The person I sat down with, is not who I see before me now."

"We must all wear disguises in the face of potential danger, Sire."

"And you would consider a lone stranger to be a potential danger?"

The wizard spread his hands disarmingly. "Often, Your Highness. But in your case, absolutely."

"I hope you realise that I intend you no harm," said Tarkyn quietly. Suddenly, he hit his hand on his thigh in irritation. "Blast it! I am not used to being treated as such a pariah."

Stormaway smiled condescendingly. "Might I suggest that you are not used to being without a bevy of toadeaters and sycophants?"

The prince glared at him, "You would not say that of me, if we were at court."

"My point exactly."

"That is not what I meant," retorted Tarkyn hotly. The air around him shimmered with anger. Then suddenly, he gave a short laugh. "You're deliberately goading me, aren't you?" He looked at the unremarkable, tatty figure before him with dawning respect. "Despite what you say, you must be pretty sure of yourself to take that risk."

"Oh, I get by," replied the wizard airily. "So, will you deign to tell me your story?"

The prince stood up and towered over him for a moment, clearly annoyed. But then he merely turned and walked over to the woodpile. Between gathering dry branches into his arms, he looked over his shoulder and said, "I don't know you well enough yet to know what I think of you, but you seem to have formed a very poor opinion of me." He brought the branches across and fed them into the fire before he sat down again.

The wizard watched and waited.

"Not only that," continued Tarkyn as he brushed the wood dust off his hands, "Having said that I could take my time deciding whether to tell you what happened, you are now trying to goad me into it...Why?"

The question hung on the night air for what seemed a long time. Then Stormaway leaned forward to adjust a burning branch and replied gravely, "Because I would trust you, my lord."

Tarkyn was taken aback. After giving it some thought, he said slowly, "And I would value your trust, should I earn it. You say the rumours are bad but you may think the reality is little better. Still, I will tell you what happened and you must judge for yourself."

He settled himself against the tree, drew his long legs up and rested his arms on his knees. Then he began.

"As you no doubt know, I have twin older brothers. One of them is king; the other would like to be. Kosar and Jarand have grown up in fierce competition with each other and their common ambition to assume the monarchy has overshadowed all other loyalties."

The wizard frowned, "You have not been brought up in a moral household since your father died, then."

Tarkyn threw an impatient glance at the wizard, "Stormaway, don't judge my worth too hastily – and when you do, judge me on my own merits, not on my family's."

As Stormaway gave a short nod, Tarkyn continued, "The Harvest Festival was when it all went wrong." He shifted his weight a little as he grimaced at the memories, "I think it might be about here that my tale will part company with the rumours...During the final bout, my shaft of power went slightly off target and damaged one of the wooden spectator stands. People jumped off in a panic as the stand sagged to one side but as soon as they could see it wasn't going to collapse, they came back and sat down to watch the rest of the tournament."

"That's it?" demanded Stormaway.

Tarkyn gave a lop-sided smile. "The damage to the spectator stand is the only incident of any note that occurred during the tournament. More happened later of course, but I will come to that.

"Unfortunately, as you know, I won the whole tournament. I say unfortunately, because I gather it made my brothers realise how strong my magic had become and that I now have… or had, a following among the people. From what they said afterwards, they seem to have thought I might mount a challenge for the throne." The prince shook his head in bewilderment, "But just because I possibly could, doesn't mean that I would. The thought never entered my mind. I want nothing to do with the throne. All my life, I have watched the misery and anxiety caused by the manoeuvrings around the monarchy. I find even the peripheral intrigue of being the king's brother enough to manage. I have never had any wish to become the focal point."

Tarkyn ran his hand distractedly through his hair. "They didn't even ask me my intentions." He lapsed into silence, staring moodily into the fire. After a few minutes he stirred himself enough to glance up at Stormaway with a wry grimace, "Still, I suppose they wouldn't have believed me anyway, once the idea was planted in their heads."

Not wishing to stand up this time Tarkyn, with a flick of his wrist and a muttered "*Liefka,*" floated another branch onto the fire and when the branch was settled, he continued his story.

"For the first time in who knows how long, they acted in concert instead of vying with each other. They had me arrested late at night when no one was there to raise objections. I don't know if you can understand how embarrassing it is to be arrested by Palace Guards whom you have known all your life?" He shrugged, "Hard for them, hard for me." He waved a dismissive hand, "Anyway, because of the incident at the tournament, Kosar sentenced me to foreswear my power for four years, on pain of imprisonment."

"What?" demanded Stormaway, incensed. "For misdirecting one blast in a tournament? If they were worried about it, they should have organised boundary shields."

Tarkyn shrugged. "That's what I said, but I realise now it was never about that. The twins just wanted me disarmed and that was their excuse."

"So what did you do?"

"I couldn't let them take my magic. It would have been like...I don't know... losing my arm, being blinded, having my heart ripped out of me."

Stormaway nodded sympathetically. "Totally barbaric, even to consider it."

"So I defied the king and threw up my shield..." He trailed off and glanced uncertainly at Stormaway before clearing his throat, "Hmm. This may be the point where the rumours have a greater basis in truth..."

"Go on, Sire," said the wizard gently, "I don't have to agree with everything you've done, to be able to trust you."

The prince grimaced, "I'm not sure how far that holds.... However... Basically, things spun out of control. I think perhaps the intensity of my emotions altered my shield's composition. Instead of blocking, it reflected.

"If no one had attacked me, nothing would have happened. But one guard threw a bolt of magic at me and my shield reflected it straight back at him. Next thing I knew, every guard in the room was sending beams of power and arrows at me and coming at me with swords. They were all reflected back, knocking out guards and ricocheting around the walls."

Tarkyn rubbed his hands up and over his face and down his hair, to hold his head with linked hands at the nape of his neck. He sighed, "I don't know how many died that night. My brothers didn't die. They left me to my fate. I saw them later in the palace. But many guards were killed or wounded."

"So how did you escape?"

"As the building collapsed and the guards were running for their lives, I finally recovered my senses enough to use a re-summoning spell on my surcoat that took me to the tailor's out in the town. And then, while everyone's attention was still on the Great Hall, I went back to the palace and collected enough valuables to sustain me, at least for the foreseeable future."

Seeing the speculative gleam in the wizard's eyes, Tarkyn added hastily, "No. I'm not carrying them all with me, if that's what you're wondering.

The wizard smiled disarmingly. "Just trying to gauge your level of competence, Sire."

Tarkyn grunted in self-deprecation, "It was not my competence. In fact, I heeded the advice of a thief, and went to some lengths to hide them."

Stormaway blinked. "Not where he could find them, I hope?"

Tarkyn sent him a look of pure derision. Stormaway assumed he had received the look for stating the obvious, but in fact it was because he had cast aspersions on a thief whose honour Tarkyn trusted.

Stormaway hastily changed the subject, "And what about your friends? Did they help you?"

"I didn't ask them," replied the prince shortly. "I didn't want to compromise anyone else's safety. One life in tatters seemed plenty for one day without dragging my friends down with me."

"Not to mention the guards," added the wizard dryly.

"I did have some particular friends among the guards but none of them was there that day. So I wasn't talking about them"

"Obviously."

Tarkyn stopped short and stared at the wizard.

"You really don't think much of me, do you?"

"On the contrary, Your Highness. I think more of you than I expected to."

"Stars Above! The rumours must be bad then"

"They are." Stormaway looked at him sympathetically, "But it's obvious to me now that none of this was your fault. You were just the fall guy."

The prince stared at him. "What? Weren't you listening? I caused the death of all those guards and the destruction of the Great Hall. Something went wrong with my shield."

"I wondered if you would see that," said the wizard mildly.

"Oh, you condescending, old hedge-dweller!" exclaimed Tarkyn, outraged. He stood up abruptly and shook out his cloak. "I find," he said icily, staring down at the wizard, "that I am no longer interested in gaining your trust. You hold me in such low regard that it would be pointless. Believe what you choose. There is no good version. But don't bother telling me what you decide, because I am no longer interested."

So saying, Tarkyn pulled his cloak around him and turned to stalk off into the night.

He found his way blocked by a slight, green-eyed man with light brown hair, dressed in a brown jerkin, loose-fitting leggings and soft leather boots. Tarkyn turned and realised that he was surrounded by similar figures. They looked harmless enough, but he wasn't silly enough to believe appearances. A trap, after all, he thought bitterly. Why did I trust a complete stranger when I can't even trust my own brothers?

Fighting panic, he took a breath to slow his heart rate then flicked up his shield, hoping that calming himself first would make his shield absorbent, not reflective.

A deep voice rang out from behind him. "Woodfolk of the forest, you are right to appear before him. He has passed my final test."

Tarkyn took a moment to recognise the wizard's voice. He spun on his heel and beheld Stormaway exuding power, resplendent in emerald robes, brown hair smoothly spilling over his shoulders. As the prince watched, Stormaway raised his staff. But before he could bring it down, the sounds of the forest seemed to swell into a frenzied cacophony.

Tarkyn looked up into the trees in confusion. He could hear the sounds of wind blowing through the trees, water gushing over rocks, leaves and rain falling, thunder rumbling and a myriad of other sounds that should have accompanied the sight of a storm surging through the forest. But none of the trees moved.

Slowly, Stormaway lowered his staff and nodded his head. He did not look pleased as he addressed the people standing around them, "If I am right, the spell's binding will begin to take effect over the next twenty four hours. At moonrise tomorrow night, I will seal it beyond return unless you give me good reason not to. You have until then. But remember; only I can make the final decision."

"What is going on? What test, what spell are you talking about? And who are these people?" Tarkyn asked wildly.

With an effort, Stormaway brought his attention back to the prince's confusion. "I thank you for taking care with your shield, Sire." He waved his arm in invitation. "Why don't you come back and sit by the fire so that we can discuss this further?"

"I would know your intentions first. There is some sorcery here that I do not understand. And are you planning to turn me in, despite your assurances? You have me surrounded," said Tarkyn stiffly, "so is your request an invitation or an order?"

Hand on heart, Stormaway bowed low, "I would not presume to issue an order to you, Your Highness. You are free to leave if you choose. I am hoping your curiosity will get the better of you."

"Hmph." After careful consideration, the prince returned to resume his seat at the fire, while the people surrounding him remained watching him, faces impassive.

"This is very unnerving," Tarkyn muttered to himself.

"These people are the woodfolk, Sire. Although unknown to the sorcerers of Eskuzor, they inhabit these forests. And they have been here all evening. It's just that you can see them now."

"That's even more unnerving. They could have attacked me at any time. I've been completely unshielded."

The wizard gave a low chuckle. "Now you know how high the stakes were, when you told your story."

Tarkyn mouth tightened. He took in a deep breath and composed himself, as he thought back over what he had said.

"Don't worry, Sire. You have acquitted yourself well." The wizard. At his request, a couple of the woodfolk brought them goblets containing an oaky silver birch wine.

Tarkyn gazed in bemusement at the goblet in his hand. After a moment, he sniffed it surreptitiously before trying it. His brow cleared as he said, "This is an excellent wine. I'm sure I've tasted similar before."

"The woodfolk supply wine to many great houses in the country, including your own."

Tarkyn looked up from the wine and asked, "And what was this final test of yours? That I accepted responsibility for the deaths?"

"No, although that was one of them. The final test was that you held to the truth of your tale, when you no longer cared for my good opinion."

The prince frowned as he considered this.

Stormaway leaned forward, "You do understand, don't you? I had to be sure you weren't lying to gain my trust."

Tarkyn scowled, "Oh I understand, all right. I've been played like a fish on a line from the start. You couldn't lie straight in bed."

"I do apologise, Your Highness. However, I have found that being devious provides a much more accurate estimate of character than straightforward questions and answers." The wizard sipped his wine and looked at Tarkyn over the rim of the goblet. "And now, at least to my satisfaction, I have established your integrity."

Tarkyn looked at him long and hard. Then in a sudden movement, he clicked his fingers and the shield winked out of existence. "It seems I am in your debt. I thank you for giving me the chance to explain myself to you. I hope I will not disappoint you in the future."

He waved his hand to indicate that he was also talking to the woodfolk, only to find he was waving at empty space. They had disappeared. Tarkyn scanned the woods around him then turned back to the wizard.

"Where have they gone?" he demanded in hushed tones. "Or are they still here and I just can't see them?"

The wizard was chuckling quietly. "I think waving your arm around on such a short acquaintance and with such a dire reputation as yours may have pushed the friendship a bit far at this stage."

"Oh lord! I'd better not drink any more wine then, if people are going to run for cover every time I gesture."

Stormaway did not try to reassure him, "I think it would be wise to be careful. They have no reason to love you... And anyone branded a rogue sorcerer is bound to be feared."

"What!" Tarkyn was stunned. "Is that what they are saying? A rogue sorcerer?"

"I'm afraid so, young man."

Panic flared in the young prince's eyes. "But I'm not a madman. I defied the king but the rest... the rest just happened."

"So it would seem – but the evidence against you is quite damning. You fled, leaving a pile of corpses behind you. The popular belief is that you went berserk in the Great Hall and lashed out at everyone in sight."

The colour drained from Tarkyn's face. "No! No. I thought the truth was bad enough... It's bad enough being branded a traitor. But a rogue sorcerer!" He dropped his eyes to the fire and said in quiet despair, "They will proclaim it across the kingdom, you know. I will be hunted down like a rabid dog." After a few moments, he frowned, "Why didn't you kill me as soon as you knew who I was?"

Stormaway picked up a branch and stirred the fire. "Ah. I thought you might ask that."

"And the answer?"

"Well, to be perfectly honest with you...." began the wizard.

"No, Stormaway. Please," said Tarkyn wearily. "Don't lie."

The wizard scowled at the prince and said sharply, "I don't think, young man, that you are in a position to take your welcome for granted. A little civility would be appreciated."

Oh ho. So now the claws are out. "In case you hadn't notice, Stormaway, I said, 'Please.' Frankly, I am too confused and too overloaded to cope with any more of your games tonight. "

"You are too smart by half, my young buck," snapped the wizard. "I think you should consider your position very carefully. If I send you away from here, what chance will you have of survival?"

The prince lifted his head from his contemplation of the fire and raised supercilious eyebrows. "I would say that depends very much on whether you choose to kill me, once my back is turned. Other than that, I am prepared to take my chances. At least I now know what I'm up against.

And I can assure you that I have no intention of becoming a slave to your every whim to buy myself safety."

The wizard grunted. "Stinking Tamadils! So stinking arrogant! You're no better than the rest of them, that's obvious."

"You're no shrinking violet yourself," retorted the prince and then added for good measure, "except when you're prevaricating!"

They locked gazes for so long that it became a battle of the wills.

Finally Tarkyn said quietly, "Stormaway, I find your behaviour towards me offensive. You may have the right to be master of your hearth and forest. But you do not have, nor ever will have, the right to be my master." The young prince drew his cloak around him and rose to tower over the wizard, sending bizarre shadows dancing up into the trees. "You will treat me with respect, or not at all."

Then he strode off into the dark, leaving Stormaway to contemplate his words.

The wizard's eyes narrowed in appreciation, "He's his father's son, that one." As the minutes ticked by and Tarkyn did not return, Stormaway started muttering to himself. "Oh well done! You wait for years to see him and then you antagonise him. Brilliant! Your age is really serving you well. Now you've got him up on his high horse –and let's face it – it's all because you didn't like him rumbling your tactics. He's pretty sharp. You're going to have to do better than this, if you don't want to lose him."

A resounding crash made the wizard jump as a branch landed on the fire, thrown from behind him. Stormaway swung around to find Tarkyn standing behind him, casually leaning against a tree, arms and legs crossed and looking as though he had been there all evening. Even more disconcertingly, he was grinning.

"Come on then. Out with it! Why don't you want to lose me?"

Mindful of the prince's stricture, the old wizard began to scramble to his feet but was waved to stay where he was. Reassured, Stormaway said grumpily, "Blast you, Your Highness! You shouldn't eavesdrop on a man's conversation."

The grin broadened. "I agree. I apologise. Still, the question remains... given that I did overhear you...Why don't you want to lose me?"

The wizard looked distinctly flustered. "To be perfectly honest with you...." he began. In response to the prince's delicately raised eyebrow, he re iterated firmly, "To be perfectly honest with you, Sire, it's complicated and will take a bit of telling...and to be perfectly honest," Stormaway continued with a challenge in his eye, "I would rather tell you when you have a better gauge of my calibre."

"I see," said Tarkyn slowly, "At least, I don't see but I will accept that you don't want to tell me yet. Frustrating, but at least honest." He grinned, "And at least someone doesn't want to lose me. That has to be an improvement."

CHAPTER 6

Tarkyn woke to a cold grey dawn. The fire had long since died and the cold was seeping up through his cloak. He could feel a sharp stone digging into his thigh. He reached out and felt under his cloak to remove it. Feeling stiff and poorly rested, he hunched his shoulders against the cold and tried in vain to go back to sleep.

After a few minutes, it dawned on Tarkyn that he was alone. He sat up abruptly and looked around. There was no sign that anyone else had even been here. He scanned the woods carefully trying to spot the elusive woodfolk but, as far as he could see, no one was there.

"Hmph," he grunted, in disappointment. He wandered down to the stream to splash his face and freshen himself up. Then he sat down on a rock and watched the water running by. The sun had risen and golden shafts of light spread between the branches and leaves of the trees. For a time, Tarkyn amused himself by sending flat stones skimming across the water.Then he just sat in the sun and drowsed, all the while mulling over the events of the previous night. Maybe he'd dreamed it but he didn't think so. That conversation had been too convoluted for him to dream up.

A short time later he noticed a grey heron working its way methodically along the edge of the stream. He sat very still and watched it prodding its beak in amongst the reeds. Slowly it made its way along the bank to where he was sitting then, to his amazement, came to stand on the rock next to him, now and again jabbing its beak into the water and occasionally coming up with small fish.

Tarkyn moved position very gingerly and started to talk softly to the heron."Well, I'm still alive and still have nowhere to go. So not too much has changed since yesterday. I'm back to being by myself which might be safer, all things considered, but also, to be honest, a bit lonely. I quite liked that wizard even if he was as slippery as an eel...and grumpy. Still, I think he must be some sort of bigwig around here. Those clothes he was wearing at the end of the night wouldn't have been out of place at court... What?Yes, I agree with you, perhaps a little overdressed for sitting around a campfire but no accounting for taste...and I suspect he was making a point...What do you think?"

Tarkyn fell silent for a few minutes as he watched the heron surveying the stream. After a while he gently continued his one-sided conversation. "You know they're saying I'm a rogue sorcerer? Do you know how bad that is? My nursery maid used to make me fear the woods by telling me that I might meet a rogue sorcerer. Now I'd be frightened to meet myself." He shook his head, carefully so as not to startle the big bird, "That doesn't make any sense, does it?"

The heron eyed him, spread his wings and rose slowly into the air.

"Hmph. So much for that."

Tarkyn could feel a pall of melancholy settling on him. He bent over the stream to splash his face and shake himself out of it. Suddenly there was another face beside his, staring up at him.

He yelped and sprang back, throwing his arms up in shock

Next thing he knew, he was sprawled on his back with an arrow tip pressed firmly against his neck. He stared wild-eyed at the person behind the drawn bow. Tarkyn lowered his hands very, very slowly and tried to calm his racing heart.

As he gazed up into the implacable, hate-filled green eyes above him, the sorcerer considered his options. He could summon a ball of air and blast the woodwoman backwards but he did not want to provoke an attack from other nearby woodfolk. He couldn't raise a shield unless there was a gap between the arrow tip and his throat, which, at the moment, there wasn't. He could feel his hand touching a leaf that he could possibly use to translocate but that would take him to the source of the leaf. That might be in the bough of a great oak, at the top of a spindly sapling, or at a point only feet from where he was presently. Worse still, he would arrive there disoriented and unable to protect himself for several seconds.

As he lay pinned down, Tarkyn began to relax. A scattering of dead leaves fell around him. Gradually, he began to feel that the woodfolk would know what to do and he could simply follow their directions. The best course was simply to do as they wished. Suddenly he realised that his will was slowly drowning in the green eyes above him. Outrage at such a violation came to his rescue and as the anger surged up, he regained enough control to close his eyes and break the contact.

Immediately, he felt the arrow tip press harder and a sharp pain as it pierced his skin. A sudden eddy of wind picked up dust and leaves and sent them with unexpected force across the clearing. Tarkyn could feel the skin on his face stinging under the onslaught of sand and swirling leaves.

"You may kill me," he whispered, "but you will not control me." He waited. Nothing changed so he continued to speak softly even though he could feel the arrow cutting into him as his throat moved. "I would sooner die than subvert my will to you or anyone else. So, go ahead. I have little left to lose." Another silence. Still the arrow pushed into his throat but no deeper than before. "But I could offer you my friendship, or at least a truce, until we become better acquainted."

Tarkyn opened his eyes to see a ring of faces above him, their owners gesturing to each other in silent communication. They seemed to be having some sort of altercation. As soon as they saw him watching, they stopped. He let his gaze travel around the six pairs of green eyes, taking care not to stay focussed on any particular one. No one moved.

Lying on his back under the weight of a woodwoman with an arrow sticking into his throat, Tarkyn was becoming impatient. He thought of another option, waved his hand and muttered, "*Shturrum!*"

He saw the eyes widen in shock as the woodfolk realised they couldn't move anything else. In a split second, the sorcerer had reached up and pushed the woodwoman off his chest. He scrambled to his feet and, in quick succession, released the woodfolk from their paralysis then raised his shield.

He now found himself surrounded by a sea of angry faces. At least forty woodfolk had appeared, each with an arrow aimed straight at his heart. None of them made a sound, and the silence seemed to intensify the hostility they exuded.

The sorcerer stepped back slowly to seat himself on a rock by the stream. The angle of forty arrows followed his movements to stay aimed directly at his heart. His skin crawled, even though he knew he was safe behind his shield, as long as he had the energy to maintain it. He could hear the wind brushing through the trees and dry leaves dancing through the air to settle on the ground around him.

"We seem to have reached an impasse," observed the prince. "Do you have a spokesman or is Wizard Treemaster the only person who communicates with outsiders on your behalf?"

A sound like the susurration of wind through pine trees reached his ears. After a few moments, he realised that the woodwoman who had held the arrow to his throat was speaking, "We may speak for ourselves if we choose, but we are not used to speaking with strangers. My name is Tree Wind."

A voice like rustling leaves cut in. "No one who has seen us leaves the forest alive. My name is Autumn Leaves."

"If you prove false, we will kill you before you reach the forest's edge," sighed Tree Wind eerily, her arrow aimed steadily at his heart.

"But if you prove true, and stay amongst us, our lives as we know them will be at an end," rumbled another woodman despondently, "I am Thunder Storm."

"Then, to preserve both you and myself, I will have to prove myself true and leave."

A young woodman, whose arm was in a sling, gave a slight, sympathetic smile. When he spoke, his creaky heavy voice issued incongruously from his lithe body."No. If you prove true, you cannot leave the forest. My name is Ancient Oak."

"So, either you kill me or force me to stay within the forest?" Tarkyn felt a rising panic threatening to overwhelm him. He had come all this way, simply to exchange one prison for another. Without conscious effort, his shield strengthened against the threat. Dimly realising what was happening, Tarkyn said urgently, "Don't shoot at me! The shield is changing! I can't control it. I think your arrows will rebound and kill you if you shoot."

A babble of voices followed this pronouncement, then suddenly no one was there. Even as Tarkyn blinked in surprise, a lone arrow streaked towards him. He flinched automatically but the shield held and, as he had suspected it might, sent the arrow flying back out into the woods. In the distance, Tarkyn heard a large branch crack and crash to the ground. Around him, whirls of leaves spiralled to the ground.

Tarkyn could hear the sounds of the forest increasing in volume. Then suddenly the woodfolk were again surrounding him. His heart thumped in fear until he realised that this time their bows were slung on their shoulders and their arrows were back in their quivers.

The sound of water running over pebbles resolved itself into a fifth voice, "We thank you for your warning. My name is Waterstone. Why did you try to ensorcel Tree Wind?"

"I didn't," replied the sorcerer flatly. "I am not casting a spell every time I move my arms. Look!" He waved his arms around and took perverse pleasure in watching the woodfolk cower. "I simply threw my hands up in fright, just as you would if you were startled. Nothing more or less."

A symphony of forest sounds broke out around him and continued for several long minutes. Tarkyn sat listening with little understanding. Each different voice took so long to tune into that by the time he did, another was speaking. They seemed less hostile, so he flicked out his shield while he was waiting. As his attention wandered, the young prince put his hand to his throat to feel out the damage caused by the arrow. His fingers came away sticky with blood but the cut beneath was disappointingly small. After all, this was his first real combat wound. He gradually became aware that the woodfolk had fallen silent and were watching him expectantly.

He looked around them, "I beg your pardon. I lost track of the conversation. Did you ask me a question?"

The wind had dropped. The forest was still, filled with an air of expectancy.

Tree Wind glanced at the set faces around her and her gentle, sighing voice continued, distant and formal, "We accept your explanation. But we are not used to sorcerers and you have a frightening reputation. So, until the issue is decided, will you agree not to use your magic?"

The sorcerer did not hesitate. "No. You know I will not." He overrode the ripple of consternation that spread through the woodfolk."Besides, if I am false, my word would be without value."

"Perhaps instead, you will guarantee not to harm us?" responded Waterstone.

The prince looked around the ring of earnest faces. "Again, I do not see what use my guarantee is to you, until you decide my worth. However," he shrugged, "I am prepared to make that undertaking, but on three conditions; firstly, that you do not try to use your mind control on me, secondly, that I may leave the forest at any time, and thirdly, that you in turn will guarantee not to attack me."

"We agree to the first and third but not the second," murmured Tree Wind.

"Then I will make no guarantee – and I will not allow you to keep me prisoner in your domain." Before any of the woodfolk could reply, the sorcerer pulled from his pocket a rather squashed berry he had picked a couple of days before and focusing on it, incanted, "*Maya Mureva Araya....*"

The scene before him faded. Closing his eyes, he felt the sick dizziness of disintegration but then, instead of a gradual return to a new location, he felt as though he had hit a wall and was wrenched backwards. He opened his eyes to find himself lying defenceless and nauseated on the ground with concerned woodfolk bending over him. He felt too sick and battered by the aborted translocation to resurrect his shield.

"Keep away from me," he snarled.

The woodfolk jumped back, but the voice of Waterstone said gently, "We know nothing of sorcery. We did not interfere with your spell." He waved his arm around him, "I am not sure why, but the forest appears to be keeping you here to protect you."

Tarkyn was fighting too hard against nausea and anger to hear a word that Waterstone said. He heaved himself upright, using the rock to haul himself to his feet. He stood there, furious, gasping for breath, his long black hair framing a deathly white face, his amber eyes burning.

As soon as he could control the waves of nausea, he roared at them, "I will not be held prisoner. So now, let us see how the forest protects you against a caged, angry sorcerer." He swept his arm around in an arc and yelled, "*Shturrum!*"

The prince glared around at his captive audience. "So what should I do now? Consume you all with a fireball?" In quick succession, he released the paralysis spell and threw a small fireball over their heads to ignite a nearby bush. "Perhaps I should summon a mighty wind and send you smashing into the trees?" Tarkyn flicked his hand and a tree behind them thrashed suddenly in a brief gale. He strode up and down between the stunned woodfolk. "I know... I could lift you all up to the height of the trees and then let you drop so that you smashed on the rocks beside the stream." With that, he incanted, "*Ka Liefka!*" and lifted one of the woodfolk and suspended him ten feet above the ground.

The sorcerer allowed his gaze to sweep slowly across his audience. "Should I drop him, do you think?" He paused then his voice came again, bitter and taunting. "Will I drop him, do you think? I am, after all, a rogue sorcerer... And if you value your friend's life, you will not disappear into the woods." He shrugged. "Besides, I could set the whole woods alight if I wanted to flush you out."

Even as he spoke those last words, Tarkyn knew they did not ring with the same conviction as his earlier tirade. His rage had burnt itself out. The woodfolk stood silently, rooted to the ground with fear as Tarkyn gently lowered the woodman to the ground.

With his anger spent, the prince was mortified by what he had done. He placed his hand gently on the shoulder of the terror-stricken woodman and said quietly, "I am so sorry. I had no right to use you thus. I may be outraged at being held in the forest against my will, but that does not justify my treatment of you."

A voice that sounded like scrabbling claws in the undergrowth replied, "Perhaps not, my lord, but unless I'm much mistaken, your actions now have sealed our fates." The woodman looked around at his companions who all nodded silently."You may do with me as you will." There was no mistaking the undercurrent of bitterness. "You are my liege lord and these forests are yours – my name is Running Feet"

The prince rocked back on his heels, stunned. "This is my domain? And if so, has it not been forfeited?"

"No one can overturn your father's will in this, my lord," answered Ancient Oak, "And we could not accept it, even if they tried."

The prince slowly surveyed the woodfolk. "I am truly sorry that I subjected you to such unkindness. If, as you say, I am your liege lord, there is even less excuse for my behaviour, not more. – And Running Feet, I may not use you as I will, neither by right of might nor by birth right."

A soft sighing heralded Tree Wind's voice. "My lord, the issue is decided. The wizard accepted your integrity and now, so do we." She sounded resigned. "Each word you speak proves it more. You are true."

Tarkyn frowned in confusion. "Why? How have I suddenly achieved that? By ranting and raving, and throwing dire threats at you?"

"Exactly that," rumbled Thunder Storm. "Even at the height of your rage and even under attack, you did not harm anyone. If you didn't hurt us then, we believe that you won't hurt us at any other time."

"Oh." Tarkyn sat down quite suddenly, so surprised was he, by this response.

Thunder Storm heaved a sigh, "And now we must accept that Stormaway will irrevocably bind us into your service at moonrise tonight."

Tarkyn, who was used to people clamouring to serve him, did not consider this an issue, "And if I insist on leaving the forest?"

"Sire, you cannot stop the process. The spell has already begun to work. Only if you had proved to be really evil, could it have been reversed."

Tarkyn waved his hand, "I am not concerned about reversing the process. I am concerned about my free will. I wish to be able to leave the forest when I choose."

The woodfolk exchanged glances.

"Your Highness," said Waterstone, "We did not stop you. The forest did. The forest wards, which are part of the trees themselves, are not letting you leave while the danger to you is so great beyond their borders."

"We could not harm you, if you insisted on leaving." Autumn Leaves' voice was sullen, "But we are sworn to protect you. So, if you place yourself in jeopardy, you risk all of us."

Tarkyn did not see that this was a logical progression but decided it was pointless to pursue the argument while the forest held him anyway.

CHAPTER 7

Dusk was gathering as four woodfolk strode into the clearing, carrying a long twisty branch, from which hung a slain deer.

Ancient Oak nodded at them, "There'll be some fine spit roasted venison tonight." The woodman had spoken very little, and seemed at a loss to know what to talk about, most of the time. Tarkyn suspected that the task of entertaining him had fallen to this particular woodman because of his injured arm. Ancient Oak turned to the prince, and spoke formally, "Tonight we will honour your arrival among us, Your Highness. We have long awaited the day when you would come to claim your own."

The four hunters handed the deer over to a waiting group of woodfolk who immediately set to skinning and cleaning the carcass. Meanwhile, others were tidying the clearing, gathering firewood and setting the fire.

If the prince was disturbed by the woodman's cold tone, he gave no indication. "I am honoured by your kindness, Ancient Oak," he replied with equal formality. He was seated on the ground next to the woodman, his back leaning against a tree. "Tell me, are your homes nearby? I cannot see them."

"They are all around us, my lord, scattered through the nearby woodland, although the untutored eye cannot distinguish them." Did the prince discern a note of derision in the woodman's voice? "Each dwelling is constructed within a thicket of shrubbery. Branches from the growing plants are woven into a small dome that is lined with grasses and mud to make it waterproof."

"I see, or rather I don't see because, as you so rightly point out, I am untutored in your ways."

"That is how I injured my arm," said Ancient Oak, in a sudden burst of confidence.

"I beg your pardon?"

"One of the saplings we were using to build a shelter was not secured properly and flicked back into my arm." He gave the prince a shy smile, "It's not broken, you know. Only bruised. But if I don't have it in a sling, I might forget and climb into a tree and then find my arm unable to support me when I need it."

"You climb trees a bit, do you?"

Ancient Oak smiled at the prince's lack of knowledge, "All our lookouts are stationed up in trees. We spend nearly as much time in trees as on the ground, especially if there is a potential danger."

"Interesting." Tarkyn was watching another group of woodfolk prepare vegetables to be roasted in the fire. "And I suppose you can quickly obliterate all of this, should the need arise?"

Ancient Oak nodded, "Yes. The lookouts will warn us of any outsiders' approach. We can pack away the food and put out the fire, then scatter leaves and forest debris to disguise our presence within minutes. By the time outsiders arrived here, they could walk across this clearing and never know we had been here."

Tarkyn studied his companion. Ancient Oak was not old, as might have been expected. He was named purely for the qualities of his voice. Tarkyn was beginning to be able to differentiate the woodfolk from each other. At first, the similarity in their stature, dress, hair and eye colour had made them all appear alike to him. However, as they became more familiar, he could discern differences in hair length, shade and style and in facial shape and expression. Ancient Oak was young but more fully grown into manhood than Tarkyn. He wore his hair straight and shoulder length and sported a small goatee. Now that Tarkyn knew him better, he couldn't imagine how he had ever been unable to tell him from the others.

"So when will your leader present himself... or herself to me?" asked the prince. "I would have expected to be introduced by now."

Ancient Oak raised his eyebrows, "But Your Highness, did we not make it clear? We have had no leader until now."

"Don't play games with me, Ancient Oak. You know what I mean. Who organizes the lookouts and the arms practice? Who adjudicates arguments? I haven't been here. There must be someone who leads you.... and why have they not presented themselves to me?"

Ancient Oak looked distinctly uncomfortable at Tarkyn's sharp tone. "We don't have leaders. Different people tend to direct different activities depending on the knowledge and skills needed...." He trailed off.

The prince merely waited, keeping his eyes fixed on the woodman's face. Ancient Oak was watching, with slightly unfocused eyes, the woodfolk hanging garlands of flowers in the trees around the clearing. Finally, he glanced at Tarkyn. "Your Highness, there is no-one to dispute your claim, if that's what's concerning you. We have known for years that you would one day come to claim our fealty."

"Yet, despite this," said Tarkyn dryly, "my arrival has been greeted with hostility, not welcome."

"I do not see why knowing about something for years should make it any more welcome," retorted the woodman.

Tarkyn raised his eyebrows. "You have a bit to learn about being a liegeman, Ancient Oak. That is not how you speak to your lord."

The woodman's cheeks tinged with colour, not with embarrassment as Tarkyn first assumed, but with anger. "I beg your pardon, Your Highness. I had not realised that dishonesty would be a requirement of serving you."

Tarkyn was completely taken aback. No one spoke to him like that. And yet, he found himself in a quandary. He did not want dishonesty from his liegemen and women. He had never enjoyed the guiles of court, so why recreate them here? On the other hand, he would not countenance impertinence.

"Ancient Oak, I expect the highest standards of courtesy and honesty both from my liegemen and women, and from myself. This does not necessarily mean that I will rub unpleasant truths into people's faces. Perhaps you could also learn to avoid that practice."

Ancient Oak's mouth tightened but he gave no response. Again, his eyes lost focus.

The prince frowned and looked away quickly. Watching the preparations for the feast, he mulled over its significance. The woodfolk had agreed not to use mindpower on him. So if it wasn't that, what was it? The woodfolk may have declared their intention of trusting Tarkyn, but he was a long way from trusting them in return.

Suddenly, Autumn Leaves and Tree Wind appeared on either side of them.

"Go on, Ancient Oak," said Autumn Leaves, waving his hand. "You're needed to help mind the children. Creaking Bough needs a break."

Tarkyn frowned as the woodman left without his dismissal, but decided that he could not spend the entire afternoon berating him. And although he had not seen Ancient Oak gesture, he was fairly sure that the arrival of the two woodfolk was not coincidental.

"Had enough of enduring my company, has he?"

A glint in Autumn Leaves' eye acknowledged the prince's acuity. He smiled, "We try to be fair in apportioning onerous tasks, my lord."

"And exactly how did you two turn up so fortuitously?"

"Sire, since you value honesty, I will tell you." Tarkyn frowned in a suspicion that was confirmed by Autumn Leaves' next words. "Ancient Oak relayed your conversation to us and asked us to come."

"How dare he share with others his private conversation with me?"

Autumn Leaves shrugged disarmingly, "Sire, we all do it. We speak with our minds, as much as with our mouths."

"Perhaps you do, but I do not appreciate having an unseen audience to my conversations."

A tense glance passed between the two woodfolk. At a slight nod from Autumn Leaves, Tree Wind cleared her throat and said in her sighing voice, "Your Highness, would you be kind enough to walk with me awhile? We have some time before the food is ready and the moon is not due to rise for another hour."

Tarkyn stood up and inclined his head, "It would be my pleasure, Tree Wind."

The prince and the woodwoman walked away from the bustle of the clearing into the quiet gloom of the forest.

Tarkyn murmured, "*Lumaya,* " under his breath. Slowly a gentle radiance spread around them allowing them to find their way beneath the huge overhanging trees. "You must let me know, Tree Wind, if the light may endanger us and I will extinguish it."

The woodwoman nodded but said nothing. Tarkyn glanced at her set face and wondered why she had offered to walk with him if she felt so ill at ease in his company. Finally, he said, "It seemed to me that there was a point in time this morning when my fate held by a thread. I would like to thank you for resisting the impulse to kill me."

Tree Wind pushed a strand of hair back from her face and forced herself to look him in the eye. "I apologize for reacting so hastily. I understand from Stormaway that it is a heinous crime to attack a member of the Royal Family." There was no vestige of warmth in her soft voice. "Besides, in hindsight, it was not warranted by your actions."

Tarkyn looked at her quizzically. "No, but at the time, you thought it was. You thought I was placing a spell on you. Why did you not kill me? I could feel it. Every fibre in you wanted to plunge that arrow further into me and yet you held."

"If I had been able to kill you with impunity and save us all from the future that lies ahead of us, I would have done so. But if you remember, Stormaway reminded us that only he could make the final decision. And only if you were totally corrupt, would the binding spell not take hold. If we had killed you and you were true, we would all have perished." The woodwoman drew herself up. "In the end, the forest saved you."

Tarkyn stopped walking to look at her. "It did?"

"Don't you remember the wind that sprang up? The swirling leaves?"

Tarkyn thought back and nodded slowly.

"Our oath to you is bound in sorcery to the welfare of the forest and therefore to our own welfare. The effects of the binding spell had already begun to work. Because I was threatening you and your claim was just, the binding spell was threatening the forest." She continued impatiently,

"It is not yet autumn. No leaves should have been falling. Fey whirlwinds do not spring up in the middle of the forest."

The young man raised his eyebrows. "No, I suppose they don't." Tarkyn frowned in an effort of memory, "So when did you swear this spellbound oath to me?"

"Twelve years ago, my lord. My people and I made a solemn vow to your father that we would protect you and recognize you as our liege, should you return to the forest."

Tarkyn brow cleared. He looked around the overhanging trees of the surrounding woodlands. "I've been here before, haven't I?" he said slowly. "I vaguely remember coming into the woods for a long ceremony of some sort. A long time ago, when I was very young. It is one of the last vague memories of my father."

Tree Wind considered Tarkyn for a moment then offered, as though the idea had only just occurred to her, "If you wish, I can show you. You will need to look deeply into my eyes so that I can share my memory with you."

She must have known that Tarkyn would be wary of her mindpower but she did not offer any reassurance. He thought it unlikely that she would try to control his mind again and he felt reasonably sure that, if necessary, he could resist as he had before. So, after a slight hesitation, the prince agreed.Nevertheless, it took a leap of faith to look into her eyes.

"So, stand relaxed and focus deep into my eyes," instructed Tree Wind calmly, "Now let your mind drift and allow the images to form. You will not lose your own self awareness. You will simply gain the awareness of my images and feelings."

The night is bitterly cold. I can feel my legs stiffening up. We have been warned of their arrival at the forest edge half an hour ago and we have been waiting in readiness. I can hear the jangle of harnesses as they draw near: now the quiet thudding of horses' hooves on the forest floor. Three riders emerge from the gloom. A large burly man with black hair and beard mounted on a strong black horse. He is wearing deep burnt orange robes and cloak, richly embroidered in silver thread. Behind him on a grey pony sits a much smaller, slighter, beardless replica of the first, white-faced and swaying with fatigue. There is a shimmering light around them, possibly a shield of some sort. The third rider is Falling Rain, one of our number who has been missing for over a week. He is slumped over the neck of his pony with his wrists tied to the pommel of the saddle. Outrage ripples through those of us waiting. Many people notch arrows ready to attack as a fourth rider appears.

With a start, Tarkyn recognised Stormaway Treemaster, resplendent in his green court dress, stronger and more confident in the vision than the wizard he had met recently.

King Markazon's hawk-like gaze sweeps across us. He dismounts and indicates that we should assist the little boy and our stricken companion down from their mounts. Although he sanctions releasing Falling Rain's bonds, no one is clear whether the woodman has been bound in captivity or merely kept tied for his safety. Falling Rain collapses when he is set upon the ground and has to be supported to a comfortable spot against an old oak. No one has yet spoken and the air is filled with mistrust and foreboding. No one has ever before come into our woodland home. The wizard watches warily from horseback then, when all are settled, dismounts and joins the king and the rest of us seated around the firesite. Food and drink are brought forth for our guests.By previous agreement, it falls to me to greet our visitors.

"Welcome to our forest, Your Majesty. We are honoured by your presence among us. My name is Tree Wind."

The king's frown is forbidding. "I thank you for your welcome. However, you labour under a misapprehension. These are my forests and you live here at my discretion." He glares around the circle at our ashen faces. "I have not been pleased to discover a whole community of people who have never sworn allegiance to the Crown."

A stricken silence greets this pronouncement. Then one of our number breaks the silence.

"But Your Majesty, you cannot rule a people you cannot find. My name is Autumn Leaves."

All eyes turn to glare at the speaker of such provocative words. We glance nervously at each other around the firesite, acutely aware that Autumn Leaves' words are ill-chosen. Surprisingly, no explosion of wrath follows. Perhaps noting our reaction, the king merely waves an impatient hand and declares calmly, "All that is at an end. Now that the illness of Falling Rain has betrayed your presence, your unnatural, treasonous independence is at an end."

We are filled with dread at what that may mean but before we can respond, Stormaway cuts in smoothly but respectfully, "However, we understand that many of your people are near death from this sickness and we have come bearing medicines that will heal them. Beyond the forest edge, this malady is common enough and easily cured but because you woodfolk have never been exposed to it, you have no resistance to it or knowledge of the cure."

"I am concerned for Falling Rain. Should he not be put to bed?" I ask.

The wizard produces a small packet of herbs from an inner pocket and hands it to the nearest woodman.

"Here. Make a tisane from these. Hopefully, now he is back amongst you, that will revive him. The journey has tired him excessively as I feared it might. But for some reason, he did not respond to my treatment while he was within the palace. I believe he may need to be within the forest to recover."

"So, you will help us, but the cost of this help is the loss of our independence? A high price indeed," observed a scratchy voice. "I am Running Feet."

"Without our intercession," interjects the king, "You would all be dead within the month. Being independently dead seems quite pointless to me."

"However, being independently alive does not," I retort, but my sighing voice robs my words of rudeness. "You could choose to save us but leave us as we have always been, elusive and not answerable to anyone."

The king glowers at me but speaks mildly, "My Lady, I cannot countenance having people within my realm who have not acknowledged me as their rightful ruler. And you cannot expect my support unless I, as your liege lord, accept responsibility for you."

Tarkyn experienced a strange sensation of thoughts and impressions travelling back and forth between the woodfolk around the circle. Because the sensation was alien to him, he couldn't grasp the content clearly but could only be aware, through Tree Wind's vision, that it was happening.

After an appreciable pause in the proceedings, a burbling voice takes up the negotiations. "Sire, our need is dire and so we may be forced to accede to your conditions. However, two things concern us. Firstly, what would you demand from us as your subjects? I am Waterstone."

The king glances impatiently at his wizard, but then draws a breath and answers with a stern calm. "My demands are not excessive. I require your loyalty and your obedience, should I need it. I wish you to continue to care for these vast forests. In time of conflict, which I hope will never arise; I will require your service either at arms or in gathering intelligence."

Again Tarkyn experienced the sensation of thoughts racing between the minds around the fire.

"These conditions do not seem unreasonable," states Waterstone on our behalf.

"I should think not. I have not even demanded a tithe from you." The king's amber eyes sweep around the circle. "And your other concern?"Before we can answer, Markazon notices his son seated next to him and smooths his tousled hair. He leans over and whispers sotto voce, "Not long now. Bear up." In a quick change of role, the father becomes the king as he straightens up and raises his eyebrows. "Go on. I'm waiting."

Waterstone clears his throat nervously. "Your Majesty, we have heard you are a just monarch, firm but fair." The king inclines his head in acknowledgement. "If we swear an oath of fealty to you, does that bind us to all future kings?"

Our uncertainty and unhappiness with this is apparent without words. Before any of us can raise an objection, the king lifts his hand.

"Obviously, I will not be here at the crowning of the next king to make sure you transfer your oath. However..." The king breaks off and looks at the wizard who looks pointedly at the little boy who is now leaning against his father.

"Sire, you must."

The king takes a deep breath and begins again. "However, much as it pains me, I can understand your reservations. There are some uncertain portents regarding the future King Kosar and his brother Jarand, particularly in relation to young Tarkyn here. Since I will not be here, I would protect Tarkyn's future as best I can, from beyond the grave, so to speak." After his momentary show of vulnerability, King Markazon draws himself up and sends his harsh glare across us all. "So, to ensure that two generations of my family have your fealty, I will require you to swear the oath of fealty to both my son Tarkyn and me. In return for this, I will apprise no-one else of your existence and I will save your people from this sickness."

After another period of mental communion, Waterstone presents our view, "We have one more reservation. Prince Tarkyn is still very young and has not yet passed through the trials of childhood and adolescence. Although unlikely, Your Majesty, it is possible that by the time he reaches manhood, he may have become embittered or cruel or even unbalanced. Swearing a lifetime of service to an unformed child is too uncertain."

The king stands up abruptly, sending the little boy falling sideways as the shoulder he has been leaning against disappears.

"Enough!" roars the king. "I have been patient and I have negotiated when I could simply have enforced my will. You will give me your oath and you will give Tarkyn your oath. I have placed my shield around this clearing so you cannot melt away into the forest and choose to die unaided. I have had enough of this charade. This is my kingdom and I will be obeyed."

A horrified silence ensues. No one moves. Then Stormaway Treemaster speaks in a matter-of-fact voice as though the conversation were proceeding as before. "Perhaps a slight modification can satisfy all parties."

"What?" snapped the king.

"When Prince Tarkyn first enters in these forests as a grown man, I will undertake to evaluate his worthiness to be their liege lord."

Markazon barks, "He is worthy because he is my son."

Stormaway holds the king's gaze for a notable pause. "Just so, Your Majesty." The wizard looks down at his hands, "And yet should the unthinkable happen, I know you would not wish any people of your realm to be bound to evil."

The king looks at his tired son and gently strokes his hair. Tarkyn turns his head to look up at his father and smiles at him sleepily. The king raises his eyes and says, "Because I have faith in Tarkyn, I will concede this point. But be warned! The oaths you swear to me and my son will be bound in sorcery to the welfare of the forest."

Despite his concession, the air sizzles with resentment. Running Feet's scratchy voice speaks for us. "Since you have already removed our freedom and our right to choose our own fate, we must inform you that we will be making these oaths under duress."

"Of course you will be. But that won't make your oaths any less binding." The king tosses off the contents of his goblet. "You are out of touch with the ways of the outside world. Although it does not generally arise in times of peace, the basic premise safeguarding the monarchy is "Submit or die." Treason has always been punishable by death. In your case, I would not have to order your executions. You will simply die from sickness if you do not swear fealty. And in the future, if you betray your oath to my son, it will not be you but your forest that will die. Perhaps you may think that is too lenient," he says dryly, "but unless I am much mistaken, the death of your forest would destroy your souls."

Tarkyn closed his eyes and pulled himself out of Tree Wind's memory. "Enough. I have seen enough," he said thickly. "More than enough."

He opened his eyes to find Tree Wind regarding him with long-nurtured loathing etched in every line of her face. In an instant, the expression was gone but Tarkyn knew he had not been mistaken. The prince thought of trying to explain his father to Tree Wind but, watching her closed face, he realised there was no chink in her resentment. He would be wasting his time.

He managed to find his voice again and to speak with a quiet assurance he did not feel. "Thank you for sharing your memory. I believe you have made your point quite clearly. I can see now why you are so unhappy about being bound into my service. I think I will take a walk before dinner. You may leave and return to your people."

Once he was rid of her, Tarkyn blundered into the comforting darkness of the forest. He crawled into the heart of a huge overhanging pine tree and threw himself down on the soft bed of pine needles. He extinguished his light and felt the velvety blackness pressing on him. A seething roil of images and emotions swirled round and round inside his head.

In turns, Tarkyn wept for the loss of his father all over again then railed against him for the impetuous nature that had turned the woodfolk against them both. In the end, when his emotion was spent, he was left with the implacable hatred in Tree Winds' eyes. He sat up shivering and drew his cloak around him.

"What am I going to do?" he whispered into the darkness. "I'm locked in a forest with a horde of people who detest me."

He thought about all he had lost and of what lay ahead of him and felt desolation wash over him. Eventually, a rustling in the branches above him caught his attention. Curiosity and the need for self-preservation dragged him up out of his pit of despair.

"*Lumaya!*" he murmured and by the gentle corona of conjured light, he spotted a tawny owl staring unblinkingly down at him. They regarded each other for several seconds. Then the owl scratched under his wing with his beak, and ruffled his feathers. Tarkyn felt a gentle surge of reassurance. He heaved a huge sigh and said with quiet resolve, "You're right. Life must go on and I must face these people." So saying, he pushed his way between the pine's branches and back onto the forest path.

As he neared the clearing, Tarkyn could hear the sounds of revelry. "I can see they are celebrating already," he said dryly to himself. "Perhaps Tree Wind has convinced them that I will stay away from them... Maybe I will, but not until we all know where we stand."

He took a deep breath, squared his shoulders and walked into the clearing, his heart hammering in his chest. It was every bit as bad as he had anticipated. A sudden hush fell. Only the crackling of the fire broke the silence. Hundreds of pairs of expressionless eyes turned to look at him.

"Good evening," he said quietly to everyone and no one in particular. "Don't let me interrupt your festivities."

A small child holding a goblet of wine responded to a gentle shove in the back and came forward to offer it to the prince. Tarkyn inclined his head and accepted the drink.

"Thank you, young one," he said gravely.

He sipped the wine and commented on its quality. Still no one else spoke. Tarkyn resisted the temptation to feel foolish, clenched his teeth and walked slowly through the circle to the other end of the clearing. Woodfolk parted silently to let him through. When he reached his chosen vantage point, he turned and swept his gaze around the waiting throng.

"Since I have your attention," he began with a touch of irony, "I will take this opportunity to thank you for providing this welcoming feast. I am honoured by your hospitality..." Still no one spoke. Tarkyn could almost feel their antipathy pulsing against him. "As some of you may know, Tree Wind was kind enough to share her memory of my father's visit to you over a decade ago." He took a sip from his goblet.

"And I believe, as a consequence of that meeting, that you were all required to swear an oath of fealty to both my father and myself? Is that correct?"

Several heads nodded slowly, either uncertain or unwilling.

"It is a long time since my father was here. Memories fade and new children have been born. I also have changed. The child to whom you gave your oath is, in many ways, not the person you see before you today. As Tree Wind has already inadvertently demonstrated, the consequences of breaking the oath would be dire." He saw several heads turn to look at Tree Wind. "So, now that I have returned, I believe that the oath must be renewed."

The moon had still not appeared, but a silver glow lit the eastern horizon. He saw a few people at the rear moving. "I do this to protect you. Because of the danger to your forests, it is important that all of you are made to remember your oath before the moon rises and the spell takes full effect."

Angry mutterings greeted this pronouncement until Tarkyn raised his hand.

"I am aware that you resent the oath and resent me. But believe me; I equally resent being forced to abide in this forest against my will. This covenant between us was none of my making and it is not within my gift to remove it. However..."

Whatever else Tarkyn had been going to say was lost, as the voice of Stormaway Treemaster rang forth at its most theatrical, as he moved forward to stand beside the prince, "However, I have judged Prince Tarkyn fit to rule and events today have confirmed my decision. Prince Tarkyn's integrity has galvanised the binding spell of the oath. The forest itself, just as bound as you are by the oath, has already acted to protect your prince and your actions have already endangered it." He swept his arm in an arc. "So kneel before your prince and give him your oath."

As one, the woodfolk sank reluctantly to their knees. To Tarkyn's surprise, Stormaway also turned and knelt before him as he led the oath-taking.

"On behalf of the forests of Eskuzor, the creatures of the woods, the birds of the air and the fish in the streams, I give my solemn vow to honour, serve and protect you, Tarkyn Tamadil, Prince of Eskuzor, until the end of my days. I give this oath in the knowledge that the woodlands and all who live in them depend on my good faith."

"Thank you," said Tarkyn quietly. "And in return, I make my pledge to you."

Guided by some force within him, the prince produced a bronze pillar of flame in the palm of his hand and focused on its brilliance. For a moment, he wondered whether he would know what to say but then he felt the words he had spoken as a child emerge from deep within him. As soon as he began to speak, the oath took over and the words poured forth without conscious volition.

"I, Tarkyn Tamadil, Prince of the Forests of Eskuzor, give my solemn vow that I will fulfil my obligations and responsibilities as your liege lord and will protect the woodfolk and the forests of Eskuzor. Your just cause will be my cause and your fate will be my fate. This is the covenant bequeathed to me by my father, Markazon Tamadil, 48th King of Eskuzor."

As the last words faded away, the bronze flame shot skyward and disappeared. Sparks spiralled upward from the fire as Stormaway brought down his staff with a sound like thunder. A shock wave of air blew outward from the centre of the clearing and the ground beneath them shuddered. In the quiet that followed, the first silver rays from the rising moon washed over the clearing.

Tarkyn stood there, stunned. Nothing had prepared him to expect the level of commitment he had just given to a people he hardly knew. He collected himself enough to say, "People of the Woodlands, you may rise. The venison smells as though it is nearly cooked. Please, resume your festivities."

The woodfolk rose to their feet and began to disperse. A few of them looked uncertainly at the prince as though they would have spoken with him but he gave them no encouragement so they too melted into the night's festivities.

Tarkyn turned glazed eyes slowly to look at Stormaway. "How could I ever have forgotten that?" he said shakily.

Stormaway put a fatherly hand on the young man's shoulder. "Tarkyn, my friend's son, you were so young you would not have understood what you were saying, let alone remembered it. No one has been there to remind you. Your father died within the year and I was banished from court by your brothers."

"So now what?" asked Tarkyn. "Am I now condemned to live within the confines of this forest, my fate entwined with people who hate me? I might have been better off in prison."

Stormaway took care not to roll his eyes. "My lord, I am aware that you, no less than the woodfolk, were given no choice about entering into this pact. However, you overstate the case. I think you will find that not everyone resents you with the same ferocity as Tree Wind."

Tarkyn ran a hand through his hair. "I have seen no sign of any friendship. Ancient Oak is the only person I have conversed with and he was doing it out of obligation."

"You have only been here for one day," the wizard pointed out gently. "Give them and yourself a chance to get to know each other."

"I feel as if I've been drafted into the role of an unwelcome conqueror who has magic at his back instead of an army."

"I am afraid, Sire, that you have summed up the situation quite succinctly." said Stormaway in the same matter-of-fact voice that Tarkyn had seen in Tree Wind's memory, "And now, you are going to have to rise to the occasion and learn to live with it." The wizard turned to leave but stopped when he saw Tarkyn's mutinous face. "Now listen to me, my lord. Did you like what you saw of your father in Tree Wind's memory?"

Tarkyn glowered at him. "Yes, I did. I loved him and I have always missed him." His throat ached with the effort of not shedding tears.

"And did you like everything he did?" pressed Stormaway.

The young prince's eyes flashed in instant defence of his father but then his shoulders sagged and he conceded, "No. Not everything. If he had been more patient and tactful, the woodfolk could have given their allegiance with much less ill-feeling and I wouldn't be in this mess."

"Your Highness, I too loved your father. I served him to the end of his days just as I will serve you to the end of mine. But he had a tempestuous nature which sometimes marred his actions." Stormaway shook his head slowly from side to side. "From what I have seen, you are very much your father's son. Learn from him. Take from him wholeheartedly what you admire and learn to manage the rest."

Tarkyn gave a short derisive laugh. "Pull myself together, in other words."

The wizard smiled. "Basically, yes. These people have just unwillingly sworn their lives to you. They have every right to feel resentful. The least you can do is deign to speak to them and treat them with courtesy."

"Stars above, Stormaway! I don't know how my father put up with you."

The wizard actually grinned. "I can assure you, Your Highness, it was a struggle for both of us." He clapped his new charge on the shoulder. "Come on. Let's get some of that fine wine and a plate of venison."

For better or for worse, Tarkyn's future had found him.

Chapter 8

Tarkyn took a deep breath, squared his shoulders and walked over to the nearest group of woodfolk who were standing with drinks in their hands, waiting for the venison to be carved. As he approached, he saw two of them exchange glances.

At a nudge from Waterstone, Autumn Leaves held up a large flagon. "Would you like a refill, Your Highness?"

Tarkyn blinked. None of them bowed or even inclined their heads in respect, as he walked up to them. "Thank you. I would. Your wines are very good." He glanced sideways to share his surprise with Stormaway only to find that the wily old wizard had melted from his side. He gave a rueful grimace. "Hmm. I seem to have misplaced my wizard."

A woodwoman smiled at him, "He's as slippery as a snake, that Stormaway. Disappears for weeks at a time. Then suddenly, one day, he will just stroll in and help himself to a cup of tea as though he'd never been away. I am Creaking Bough."

Tarkyn inclined his head in acknowledgement, "Pleased to meet you. I hope you will forgive me if I take a few days to remember all your names. I am meeting so many of you all at once. But I promise you, I will do my best."

The venison and roasted vegetables filled the clearing with glorious aromas as the food was served onto large pieces of bark lined with plaited vines.

"At last. Food's ready," said Autumn Leaves. "You wait here and I'll bring you over a plateful."

Tarkyn watched in bemusement as the woodfolk moved in to help themselves without serving him first, or waiting for him to be ready to eat, before they started themselves. A few minutes later, Autumn Leaves returned with two filled plates. He handed one to Tarkyn and kept one for himself.

"Come on then, Your Highness. You may sit with us if you like."

Waterstone had already sat down with his meal on his lap. "Look," he said, patting a mossy patch next to him on a log. "I've saved you a spot."

"Thank you." Tarkyn sat down, looking a little dazed. He had never been treated so casually in his life. And yet he could tell that they were not being deliberately disrespectful. In fact, he thought they were making an effort to include him and make him feel at ease.

After a wry glance at his friend, Waterstone smiled at the prince, "Autumn Leaves is trying to make up for his previous misdeed."

Privately reeling that Autumn Leaves wasn't simply serving him out of duty, Tarkyn asked as lightly as he could manage, "And what misdeed was that?"

"Sending you off with Tree Wind on your own."

"I see." Tarkyn's gaze slid along to watch Autumn Leaves eating his meal. "It was indeed unpleasant, but I did need to see her memories. So that I knew what you all knew."

Waterstone waved his hand, "I agree. You did. Still, any one of us could have shown you, perhaps more kindly, or supported you when you saw hers."

Tarkyn frowned, unconvinced, "Surely you all relished the opportunity to wreak a small revenge. I cannot imagine that any of you feel well disposed towards me after what I saw."

Just as Waterstone was about to reply, Autumn Leaves cut in, "I believe you said that you did not want unpleasant truths rubbed in people's faces, so I will not comment on that. But I do offer you my apology. However we may feel about you and the situation, you are alone, one among many." The woodman stopped to consider for a minute, "Even if I were as strong as you, I cannot imagine that I would feel comfortable if I found myself surrounded by sorcerers." He gave a slight smile, "So it was not kind of me, and I apologise."

"Thank you. Although it is not perhaps as strange for me to be one among many, as it would be for you. "

"But, Your Highness, you have been with your own kind until now," protested Creaking Bough.

"It is clear, both from your words and your actions, that you do not understand the enormous gulf that lies between sorcerers and the Royal Family. I do not consider commoners or even lords to be my peers. My family has ruled Eskuzor for over a thousand years. Our heritage sets us apart. When I enter a room, no one continues to behave as they did before I arrived. So it happens frequently that I am one among many."

"That sounds very lonely, my lord," said Creaking Bough.

Tarkyn raised an eyebrow and gave a faintly derisive smile, "It is merely the expected order of things, Creaking Bough. It is neither good nor bad. It just is."

Despite his words, he did feel more isolated than he ever had before. These people were alien to him. He knew nothing of their customs, way of life, or attitudes, and they were not behaving as he was used to. His gaze travelled around the clearing. He could see that despite their disregard for protocol, they were still keeping a weather eye on him while they ate.

As he suppressed a sigh, an owl swooped in a low arc over their heads and up into an oak tree to land high above Tarkyn. Although not unheard of, an owl flying through the firelight was enough to cause a ripple of comment through the woodfolk. Tarkyn smiled slightly, pleased to share a moment of common interest with them.

"Do you know much of birds, my lord?" asked Waterstone.

"Enough to know that owls generally keep away from light. He's a beauty, isn't he?" Tarkyn pointed upward, "Look. He's still there. Right above me."

Autumn Leaves squinted upwards. "As far as I know, you can't tell the sex of a tawny owl by its appearance."

"He's a male," said Tarkyn with quiet confidence. At their looks of surprise, he added, "I saw him earlier, before I returned to the clearing." He shrugged, "Besides, I just know he is."

"You must have studied birds a good deal to know the difference between the genders, particularly if we can't tell," said Waterstone with a note of scepticism. "Unusual in a town dweller."

"No, I hate to disillusion you, but I haven't." Tarkyn's eyes twinkled, "But despite that, you will find that our owl is male." For the first time, they saw a chink in his courteous formality. His smile broadened, "And there is no way you can disprove it, short of following him for weeks and waiting for him not to lay an egg."

This drew reluctant smiles from the woodfolk who were not quite sure how to take him. Above him, the owl ruffled his feathers and settled down.

"Your Highness, what is it about our actions that makes you say we don't understand the gulf between you and other sorcerers?" asked Waterstone suddenly. "After all, we have never met any sorcerers, other than you and your father... and I suppose, Stormaway. He, I believe, is a type of sorcerer."

"In that case, it is not surprising that you don't understand." Tarkyn knew the woodman was waiting for further explanation. He also knew that he did not want to get into a wrangle about expected behaviour after the trauma of the oath-giving they had just been through. "Waterstone, we have time ahead of us. Tonight, the oath is raw in everyone's minds. My expectations of your behaviour are clearly not aligned with your own, at the moment. But now is not the time to remedy that." When he saw Waterstone about to protest, he raised his hand and said firmly, "No. I will not discuss this tonight. I am well aware that no one is intending me any disrespect. If I had thought otherwise, presumably the forest would have let you know."

The three woodfolk retreated into tense silence. When he had finished eating, Autumn Leaves quietly gathered up everyone's plates and took them over to woodfolk who were waiting to clear away. While he was exchanging a few words with them, Waterstone explained in a subdued voice, "Normally, each woodman would attend to his own utensils."

Tarkyn's eyes narrowed, "But tonight they are doing yours in exchange for you keeping me entertained. Is that right?"

Waterstone shifted uncomfortably, "It is not quite so blatant as that. It is more that that is their contribution towards serving you." The woodman glanced anxiously at the nearby trees.

"I see. I can accept that."

Waterstone let out a small sigh of relief. Around the fire, more woodfolk were watching the prince and exchanging anxious glances. There was a building undercurrent of tension.

As Autumn Leaves returned, Tarkyn snapped, "Will you please keep private conversations with me private?" He waved his arm around the clearing, "Now look! Everyone is waiting to see what I will say next."

For a moment, the heavy woodman glared at him, resentment smouldering in his eyes. "What do you expect?" he snapped back. "Of course they want to know what you're going to demand of us."

The prince's face stiffened with shock.

Autumn Leaves took a deep breath."I beg your pardon, Your Highness, but everyone is clamouring to hear what you have been saying to us. I said as little as I could." He sat down, unknowingly offending Tarkyn even further by not waiting for permission. He added firmly, "I do not think you appreciate how frightened we are for our forests. How can we keep them secure if we don't even know how to act to meet your expectations?"

Tarkyn eyed him, deciding whether to reprimand him for his presumptuous attitude. Finally, he reminded himself of his decision to make allowances tonight. "Very well. I will speak once more on this subject. I will not stand up and make an announcement but this time, I give you permission to convey my words to all other interested parties. That will then be the end of it for tonight. Is that clear?"

Autumn Leaves glanced at Waterstone as he nodded, "Yes, Your Highness. Quite clear."

Tarkyn then spoke quietly so only those close to him could hear, but he paused every few sentences to give Autumn Leaves time to transmit his message to everyone watching. "Perhaps you were not listening, but

I have just sworn an oath to protect your forests. As you will come to realise, I am a man of my word. I will not try to ambush you, nor punish you or your forests, for expectations of which you are unaware. When I have decided what I expect of you, I will make sure you know. Only then, will I insist on compliance."

He took a sip of wine. "I am aware that you feel jarred by my arrival and by the commitment you have had to give me. That is why I will not impose any expectations tonight." He looked around the assembled woodfolk but continued to speak softly, "While I have your attention, thank you for your fine food and wine. Please feel free to come up and speak to me, but do not feel obliged to."

Little did the woodfolk know, but even this last offer was an enormous concession from a prince who would normally have had everyone presented formally to him in the course of the evening.

Tarkyn watched with interest as several people melted into the forest and the same number swung down out of the trees to take their place. The newcomers helped themselves to food and drink, and two of them wandered over to join the prince.

"Good evening, Your Highness," said a middle-aged woodwoman whose soft brown hair hung well down her back. "I noticed last night that your face was showing signs of strain. No doubt being on the run is bad for the nerves." She put her plate down on the log, in order to produce a small phial of dark green liquid. "This should reduce some of your tension, my lord. I am Summer Rain."

"Thank you." Tarkyn took the phial from her and held it up to study it in the firelight. Out of the corner of his eye, he saw woodfolk exchanging knowing looks. He turned his gaze to confront Autumn Leaves. "Am I being made fun of?" he demanded.

"No Sire," said Autumn Leaves hastily. "Summer Rain's tonics are renowned for their efficacy."

They waited until he had taken out the cork and tossed off the contents before Thunder Storm, who had just joined them, added, "But they taste horrific."

With his face screwed up from the bitterness of the brew, Tarkyn eyed their grinning faces balefully. Waterstone could see that he was not pleased. "Sire, we are not laughing at you. We are laughing out of fellow feeling. All of us have endured Summer Rain's tonics."

Creaking Bough refilled Tarkyn's goblet and smiled at him, "And thank you for putting our minds at rest, Your Highness. The fact that you even considered our concern gives me the first glimmering of hope."

When Tarkyn had regained control of his facial muscles, he said kindly, "I believe that no one in my acquaintance or service would tell you that I am a harsh master. I try to be fair. I will always listen, though I will not always agree. Of course, once the issue is decided, I would expect my orders to be obeyed without question. And needless to say, my word is final. But I will listen." He sipped his wine, blithely unaware that the smile had slowly died on the woodwoman's face.

Creaking Bough swallowed, and tears started to her eyes. "Oh, Ypur Highness. No matter what your expectations, this is going to be so hard."

Tarkyn, who had thought he was being reassuring, looked at her in some surprise.

"Your Highness, Ancient Oak told you, but you did not take it in," rumbled Thunder Storm quietly. "Other than the two days when your father was here, no one here has ever taken orders from anyone. Certainly not as a way of life. We are used to deciding for ourselves. Until today, we were all equally in charge of our own lives."

"No matter how fair you are, or think you are," said Autumn Leaves, "while you have the final say, you hold our freedom in your hands."

Tarkyn resisted the urge to retort that that was exactly how it had always been. In Tormadell, he had held the freedom of all his friends, acquaintances and staff in his hands. He could have ordered their imprisonment at any time, on the slimmest of excuses, if he chose. He could see, however, that these woodfolk were genuinely upset and he remembered how it felt when his own freedom had been held in the king's hands, and Kosar had chosen to crush it. But even though he had hated it, he had accepted Kosar's right to do it.

No, that was wrong, he realised. He hadn't accepted it at all. He had rebelled and thrown away his whole life to save his freedom.

Suddenly the prince smiled. "Perhaps you and I are not so very different. I refused to let my brother take my freedom from me. Saying that, until then I would have followed his orders without question." He shrugged. "However, I can see it is different for you. Strange as it seems to me, you are not used to following orders. But unfortunately for you, your oath has given you all into my service. So, whether you like it or not, and whether I like it or not, you do owe me your obedience, and as your liege, I do have the final say. But I will bear in mind how much it grates with you." He spread his hands, "That is the best I can do. Even if I decide to relieve you of my presence, it is still my decision, not yours."

Autumn Leaves looked startled, "Are you considering that possibility? Sire, you can't. We are sworn to protect you. If you leave the forest and anything happens to you, the forest will be destroyed."

"So that's what you meant when you said that if I place myself in jeopardy, I risk all of you. It makes sense, now that I know about the sorcery in the oath." Tarkyn took a deep draught of wine. "I will not place you at risk, but I may perhaps choose to live alone somewhere in the forest until the risks outside subside." He glanced uncertainly at Waterstone. "All my life, people have fallen all over themselves to be of service to me. I am not sure that I will enjoy, or even be able to endure, being surrounded by people who are serving me under duress and who resent my very existence."

The woodfolk were stunned. They knew the prince was not happy about being trapped in the forest but it had never occurred to them that he, too, might not relish the consequences of the oath. After a moment, Waterstone sent Autumn Leaves a sharp glance. "You see? I told you Tree Wind might have been too unkind."

Tarkyn waved his hand, "No. All she did was show me her memories...." He thought back to the hatred in her eyes and added, "...and perhaps a little of how she felt about them." He took a breath, "And if you all feel the same way about it, I may end up preferring my own company. We'll see." Primed by now with several glasses of wine and Summer Rain's tonic, he stood up. "And now, I think I must circulate amongst my reluctant liegefolk. Even if they are unwilling, I owe them the courtesy of my attention."

Part 2: Waterstone

CHAPTER 9

Tarkyn rolled over, then wished he hadn't. His head hammered with the aftermath of last night's wine. Small twigs and leaves kept landing on him and annoying him. He pulled his cloak up around his head and went back to sleep. Not long afterwards, he felt something scrabbling under him. He jerked in alarm and, without opening his eyes, managed to feel around and drag out a cockroach that had made its way beneath his cloak. The red inside his eyelids told him it was daylight so a short time later, he gingerly opened his eyes a crack to see what effect this had on his head.

The first thing he saw was a pair of boots on the other side of the fire. When he looked again, he realised they were attached to the legs of a sorcerer who was sitting watching him from across the clearing. His groggy brain struggled to work out what was going on. The clearing seemed much smaller than it had last night and the fire was only the size of the remains of a small campfire. There was no sign anywhere of the woodfolk.

Looking at the sorcerer's clothes, Tarkyn judged him to be an emissary from one of the rich merchant sorcerer's houses. The next thing he noticed was that he was within the sorcerer's pale blue protective shield. This was not a good sign, he decided.

Tarkyn was just coming to the conclusion that he might be in danger when rough hands grabbed him from the back and dragged his arms together behind him. Before he could react in any way, his hands were bound roughly and he was yanked to his feet. His head pounded in protest but adrenaline was acting swiftly to dispel his hangover. He shook his head to clear it but was thumped hard from behind.

"None of your tricks!" growled an unpleasant, gravelly voice from behind him. For a moment, Tarkyn thought something about the voice sounded familiar but no-one he knew spoke in such harsh deep tones. "Keep still, you stinking rogue. One false move and we'll take you in dead instead of alive. The reward's less if you're dead but there's no risk then, is there?"

Tarkyn decided the question was rhetorical and didn't answer. He was busy thinking furiously. What had happened to the woodfolk? So much for protecting him. He peered around at the surrounding trees. They all looked healthy enough. The woodfolk could not have abandoned him, then. This made him feel a little more hopeful, although what arrows could do against sorcerers' shields he didn't know. He wondered what would happen when they reached the edge of the forest. What could the forest or the woodfolk do to prevent him from being dragged away?

He was returned to the present by a hefty shove in the back that nearly sent him sprawling.

"Get moving. We don't want to stay in this dreary forest any longer than we have to."

Suddenly, the last thing in the world Tarkyn wanted to do was to leave the forest. Yesterday he had hated the forest's protectiveness. Today, faced with the brutality of these men, it was borne home on him that a countryside full of vengeful sorcerers was not a tempting prospect at all.

For four hours, Tarkyn was force marched along forest paths, moving awkwardly because his arms were pinioned behind him. He was belted hard on the head from behind each time he stumbled. In the end, his vision began to blur and the cycle of stumbling and being hit became more frequent as he began to lose his balance. He dimly realised that his captors were taking pleasure in inflicting pain and that no matter how hard he tried, he would still be punished. He wondered if there was anything he had done to them that could justify their treatment of him. He hadn't recognised the sorcerer he had seen, and the other two were careful to stay out of his field of vision.

Finally, when Tarkyn thought he would have to collapse and endure a beating, they turned off the path into a small clearing. Before he could look around and get his bearings, someone lifted one side of the shield, kicked him in the back and sent him flying to land at the foot of a large pine tree. He twisted in mid air so that his shoulder, not his head, hit the tree with a sickening crunch. Even so, the pain was severe and he lay there gasping for breath. No one came near him and he was given nothing to eat or drink. Tarkyn could hear them setting about lighting a fire and making themselves a midday meal. They were paying him scant attention but they probably knew he was too spent to move.

Suddenly he felt a small object hit his hand. He felt around on the ground behind him and closed his fingers around an acorn. Tarkyn frowned in perplexity. Was that the object? He gazed blearily around and realised that he was lying deep within a stand of pine trees. The acorn was definitely out of place. How could an acorn help him? Did it have some mystical properties that the woodfolk thought he would know about? Then Tarkyn knew. He checked the sound of his captors then tried to twist his hands to the side so that he could focus on the acorn. To his frustration, his hands wouldn't reach around far enough for him to be able to see them. He thought hard then dropped the acorn and twisted himself around so that he could see it lying on the ground. He knew he needed to hold it and to focus on it for a re-summoning spell to work. He turned onto his stomach and picked it up in his teeth. By manoeuvring it to the side of his mouth, he could, with one eye, just see it sticking out of his mouth. The next challenge was incanting clearly enough without dropping the acorn. Before Tarkyn could begin the incantation, he heard the sound of a sorcerer coming over to check on him.He pushed the acorn inside his cheek and tried to act semi-conscious. Considering how he felt, it wasn't difficult.

The sorcerer yanked the prince's head up by the hair and brought his face up close. "Not so fearsome now, are you?" Tarkyn wisely decided not to reply. "We're leaving soon. You can look forward to another four hours of forced marching. I hope you can keep your feet better this time....That should just about get us back to civilisation and a good night's sleep in a comfortable inn. Not for you, of course. Floor's good enough for you." He threw Tarkyn's head back down, gashing his cheek on a rock and stomped away to join the others. Tarkyn could hear him saying, "The weak bastard is almost gone already. You might have to lay off a bit if we want to make it to the inn in time for dinner."

A voice in the distance that seemed almost familiar replied gruffly, "Don't go soft on us, Fallorick. You're supposed to be the professional. We're not going to let that pampered, arrogant Tamadil slow us down. If he's fit enough to win that tournament, he's fit enough to make the distance. Don't let him fool you. He'll be able to cope with a little more punishment. Just watch and learn."

Ignoring his bleeding cheek, Tarkyn manoeuvred the acorn back into position, focused his will, and hoping devoutly that someone would be there to catch him, incanted, "Maya Mureva Araya!"

The familiar swirling nausea of translocation swamped him. Next thing he knew, Tarkyn was lying sprawled along a large branch of an oak tree. Twenty feet below him, he could see a crowd of shocked upturned faces. Even as he watched them galvanise into panicked activity, Tarkyn felt his weight sliding off to one side. He tried to grapple with his legs but with his hands tied, he was unable to fight the inexorable pull of gravity. Helpless, Tarkyn thumped down through the great oak, crashing from one branch to the next. He was unconscious long before he hit the ground and so, was unaware that the last part of his fall was cushioned by several woodfolk who were borne to the ground under his plummeting weight.

Chapter 10

"Blast him! He's gone!"

Fallorick stood staring at the empty space under the tree with his hands on his hips and growled disgustedly, "Oh you stupid bastard! How far do you think you can get with your hands tied behind you? You'll fall over the first log you come to." He yelled across at the other two, "My lords, he's bloody run off. Come on. We'll have to find him. He can't have got very far."

Just as the other two arrived, the sound of something crashing through the undergrowth directed their attention to a figure moving awkwardly away from them through the trees.

"There he goes!" exclaimed Fallorick. "Follow him!"

The three of them plunged through the sharp, dense brush towards the retreating figure. As they came closer, they realised their prisoner had now managed to undo his bonds and was picking up speed. They redoubled their efforts to gain on him but always the figure with the black flowing hair remained the same distance ahead of them.

"You see?" panted one of the lords, as they struggled to keep up "He's as fit as a fiddle. You should have hit him harder. Now look what's happened!"

As the figure neared the edge of the woods, he glanced around quickly and then raced off across the fields towards a village with the bounty hunters in hot pursuit.

Stormaway stayed in disguise until he had run loudly past the village pub of Wooding Deep, making sure people had time to catch sight of him. The wizard kept looking over his far shoulder and puffing loudly so that he generally made it obvious that he was being chased. In actual fact, he really was beginning to tire at this stage so the puffing was quite genuine. Once people emerged from the pub to see what was happening, he ran on to the other end of the village until a curve in the road took him out of sight. Then he reverted to his own colouring and clothes and doubled back to join the crowds. By the time the bounty hunters had arrived, Stormaway had the villagers convinced that they had seen the prince cutting across the fields towards the next village of Woodland Nearing.

His actions at Wooding Deep were just the first of the wizard's deceptions. While the sorcerers followed the villagers' reported sightings of Tarkyn on foot, the wizard procured a horse and reached Woodland Nearing by a circuitous route, left the horse tethered outside the village and played a repeat performance. Over the next six days, he lead them through a series of villages way up to the far north west of the country to the seaport of Westsea.

Stormaway left the horse tethered outside the town in a disused barn. Once more, he assumed his disguise of long black hair, creating an increased sense of height and hauteur. He kept his eyes averted or shadowed by a hat wherever possible because although they were more yellow than his own, his eyes were by no means the electric amber of Tarkyn's. He judged he had about three hours' lead on his pursuers so he took his time finding the docks and seeking out departure times of the vessels moored there. Stormaway entered a seedy dockside pub that rejoiced in the name of the Leaky Barrel. He pulled up a stool to the bar and asked for a beer. The barman, a short stocky man with thinning red hair and a grand moustache, stared suspiciously at him while he complied with his request.

"Not from around these parts, are you?" he asked slowly.

Stormaway kept his eyes on his beer mug as he answered carefully, "I would have thought most people passing through here weren't from these parts."

The barman shrugged, "No offence meant, I'm sure. Just making conversation. You planning on hanging around or are you waiting for a ship?"

"Don't know yet. Haven't decided."

The barman leaned in towards him and said quietly, "There are some very nasty rumours circulating at the moment. Now, I'm not saying whether I believe them or not but I'll tell you for nothing that a young man looking like you would be wise to get on a boat and get out of here as quick as may be." He hesitated for a minute then added, "And I'd be tucking that long hair of yours inside your collar."

Stormaway stared fixedly into his beer. "Why would you not give that young man away?"

The barman gave a short grunt of laughter, "Because I always liked the youngest prince and it's my guess that his brothers are out to discredit him."

Stormaway risked a quick glance up then returned his gaze to his beer. "And what would you say if I told you that some of those rumours may be true."

"Oh, there's no smoke without fire, young sir. I'd say there'd have to be some truth at the bottom of those rumours but I'm not ready to condemn a man out of hand until I hear his own story."

The barman moved off to serve some other customers but returned as soon as he was free. He leaned in again and said quietly, "There's a small ship called the Roving Seadog that's due to sail on the tide. That's in about two hour's time. It's not the flashest vessel at the docks but if you tell them that Beer Barrel Benson sent you, they'll take you on." He leaned even closer and whispered, "But I'd lose that hair, if I were you."

"Thanks," said Stormaway gruffly, drank down the rest of his beer and left.

Once outside, the wizard wandered along the street towards the docks, loudly asking directions to the Roving Seadog from several people he passed. He wandered into another pub, the Sailboat on the Sea, and asked loudly for directions in there too. Stormaway saw a few frowns and at least two people slipped quietly out behind him.

The wizard judged it was time to leave. He ducked into an alley and returned to his own shape and size, turning his cloak inside out so that the green lining became the outer surface and then sauntered back out into the street. A group of four soldiers was just entering the Sailboat on the Sea.

Stormaway wandered down to the docks and, when he had located the Roving Seadog, assumed his Tarkyn disguise once more and headed purposefully towards the shabby old trading vessel. He glanced around the dockside. The last of the stores and cargo were being loaded onto the Roving Seadog.

He reached the bottom of the gangway and remarked to one of the dockers, "Good to see she'll be well stocked. I wouldn't want to go hungry halfway through the journey, now would I?"

The dockers glanced impatiently at him, clearly thinking his comments inane. Stormaway wandered off, waving over his shoulder, "See you in a while."

He rounded the corner of a loading shed then let the long black hair shorten and fade back to brown and his eyes resume their natural green. He switched the cloak inside out and his return to Stormaway Treemaster was complete. He sauntered back along the docks and found a sheltered spot from which he could watch the Roving Seadog completing its loading. He waited until the gangway was drawn up then turned away.

At the edge of town, the bounty hunters had arrived. It was immediately apparent that their enthusiasm for each other's company had worn very thin.

As they trudged heavily along the roadway, one of the lords said to Fallorick, "You're a hopeless bloody tracker. We've been travelling after this elusive character for a week now. We had him in the palm of our hand and you let him get away." He waved a hand around him, "Now look where we are. A seaport. No prizes for guessing what he's planning here. And how far ahead of us is he?"

Fallorick cleared his throat nervously, "I'm not sure, my lord. But we must hurry. Let's see if we can get word of him. I suggest we head straight to the docks."

A speaking glance passed between the two lords as they grudgingly followed their guide. A few enquiries lead them to the Sailboat on the Sea where there had been a reported sighting of the prince. The three bounty hunters strode into the bar.

Without any preamble, Fallorick demanded, "Has anyone seen the fugitive prince?"

A seedy looking character sitting in the window alcove answered roughly, "Yeah. We seen him. Someone even called the soldiers but they were too late. He was looking for some ship.... I've forgotten what it was called." He looked around. "Anyone remember?"

A tatty individual with wispy light brown hair stammered, "It w-was the R-roving S-seadog, milords."

"So, anyone know where this ship is?"

"Try the docks!" yelled a would-be comedian.

Everyone sniggered. The barmaid raised her eyebrows, "If you're quick, you might just make it." As the door shut behind them, she turned to the crowd in the bar and said innocently, "Oops. I forgot. Isn't that the ship that's sailing at full tide?"

Among the guffaws that greeted this, the tatty individual frowned at her, "Are you a s-supporter of the p-prince then?"

"I wouldn't go that far," she replied with a significant glance around the bar. "But I don't like seeing anyone used as currency."

The tatty man finished his beer thoughtfully and followed the path of the bounty hunters down to the docks. From within the shadow of a huge stack of cargo waiting to be loaded, Stormaway watched the two lords vent their frustration on their hapless guide as the scruffy little ship disappeared into the middle distance. Finally, they turned on their heels, leaving the guide in a huddle on the dockside. As they passed within feet of the wizard, he could hear them still muttering angrily. Once he was sure that they had given up the chase, Stormaway heaved a sigh of relief and turned his footsteps to his waiting horse and the long trip back to his liege.

Chapter 11

The world seemed to rush at him and then recede through a sea of pain. Sometimes he tried to move but something was restraining him and he couldn't summon enough strength to resist it. Each breath sent a searing pain up his back. From time to time, gentle arms lifted his head and some sort of thin broth was poured between his lips. Tarkyn dreaded these times because he could not control his swallowing and would end up coughing. Then as the pain became excruciating, he would collapse back gasping for breath and drift back into oblivion.

As the days and nights passed, his awareness of the world gradually expanded beyond the pain. He realised his movement was restricted by a strap that held his right arm close to his chest. He became aware of people coming and going, talking quietly. There was one woodman in particular who spent many hours sitting quietly beside him, but Tarkyn had no desire even to acknowledge him. He could not summon enough energy to engage in a game of courtesy with an unwilling liegeman.

Tarkyn's body slowly recovered but his spirit sank deeper into isolation. He had spent all his life surrounded by friends and liegemen, ostensibly well-liked. He questioned every past image. Would he have been so popular, had he not been the king's son? Obviously not. But how far did that go? And now none of those friends, even if they had remained true to him, was available to him now. He relived over and over again his mistreatment at the hands of the bounty hunters. It wasn't the physical pain that had disturbed him. It was the experience of being regarded as nothing more than a commodity. Nothing in his life, not even his arraignment, had prepared him for being treated with such malice and contempt.

Sometimes in the night, Tarkyn would hear the sound of running water and realise that a woodman was talking quietly to him. The sound was soothing and gradually, as his strength returned, he began to take in the stories the woodman was telling him – old stories of the history of the woodfolk, mythical legends and newer stories of the day-to-day events that were taking place outside the shelter. The woodman did not seem to require any response from the ailing young man.

Finally, Tarkyn asked, "Are you the healer?"

"No, my lord. I'm not. With food, water and rest, your body is healing itself now."

"Are you guarding over me?"

"No, my lord. Others outside are keeping watch."

There was a long pause. Then the prince said, "Nothing in that wretched oath compels you to sit here hour after hour."

"No, Sire. But not all actions are governed by oaths and people don't act only under compulsion."

Tarkyn turned dark, haunted eyes to regard the woodman. The man was older than he, strongly built with a square jaw and firm mouth but kind eyes "Then why are you here?" Tarkyn croaked, his voice dry from lack of use.

"I am here because I choose to be."

"Oh." Tarkyn closed his eyes while he thought about this. A few minutes later, he asked snakily, without reopening his eyes, "I suppose you feel sorry for me? Are you one of those do-gooders looking for a pet project?"

A rippling laugh greeted this sally. "I think you must be feeling better. You're getting tetchy."

Tarkyn opened his eyes and glared at the woodman.

"And in answer to your question," continued the woodman mildly, "yes. I do feel sorry for you. I would feel sorry for anyone who had been bashed around as much as you have been – severe concussion, at least three broken ribs, a dislocated shoulder, multiple bruising…."

Tarkyn waved a feeble hand to tell him to desist.

The woodman smiled and kept burbling, "And I like to think that I am reasonably kind, although do-gooder might be an exaggeration."

Tarkyn waved his hand again and mumbled, "All right, all right. You've made your point."

He closed his eyes again and took a few slow deep breaths. When he had recovered, he looked once more at the woodman.

"However," burbled the woodman before the prince could speak, "I think it is fair to say that you are my pet project." Then, with a grin over his shoulder, the woodman was gone.

For the first time since his accident, Tarkyn thought about something other than his isolation and misery. The woodman had intrigued him and he didn't know whether to be amused or annoyed to find that he had become someone's pet project.

When the woodman returned the following day bearing his breakfast, Tarkyn was ready for him. Between mouthfuls of porridge, the prince said, "Now I'm beginning to feel better, I have a lot of questions that need answering."

"I thought you might have," said the woodman warily. "Go on."

"Can you begin by telling me your name? I think I have met you before but I'm not sure. My memory is a little hazy."

"I am Waterstone, my lord."

The prince smiled faintly. "Yes, I should have known from the sound of your voice." After a pause, he asked, "And where is Stormaway? I thought he would have been in to see me." Tarkyn tried not to sound plaintive, but a glance from the woodman told him he had not completely succeeded.

"He should be back soon. He's been gone more than a fortnight," said Waterstone reassuringly.

Tarkyn stared at him. "A fortnight?"

The woodman smiled. "You were badly injured, you know. You didn't regain consciousness at all for the first week." While the prince mulled this over, Waterstone continued, "The wizard left the forest with the three sorcerers who captured you on his tail. He had some plan of leading the bounty hunters off on a false trail." Waterstone leant down and picked up the spoon that Tarkyn had just dropped onto the earthen floor and handed it back without giving a thought to washing it. The prince accepted it without comment and wiped it on his sleeve.

"Does he know what he's doing? I wouldn't want him or any of you to be hurt by those bounty hunters." Tarkyn glanced at Waterstone. "They were an unpleasant lot," he added a little too casually.

"Yes, I know. I was shadowing you for a large part of that morning," Waterstone took away the breakfast plates and stood looking down at the prince, "You didn't once look for us or give any indication to those bastards that we might be nearby. That wasn't a bad effort, considering that you had only just met us."

The sorcerer smiled self-deprecatingly. "I didn't need to look to see if you were around. I knew you must be trying to protect me somehow, because the forest was calm. Besides which, I am honour bound to protect you, even as you are to protect me."

"Anyway, you needn't fear for the wizard or the woodfolk. Those sorcerers wouldn't even have known the woodfolk were there and Stormaway is a master of disguise. From what I hear, he led them through the woods and out into a nearby village, looking very much like you from the back." The woodman frowned. "They sound as if they were very easily fooled. Why wouldn't they have thought of you translocating?"

"People believe what they see." Tarkyn shrugged awkwardly, using only one shoulder. "I suppose it didn't occur to them, if there was a figure like me running off through the woods. Besides, very few sorcerers can translocate and I don't think anyone, other than Stormaway and you woodfolk, knows that I can do it. Everyone else will have assumed that I just run away from the Great Hall in the general confusion." He raised his eyebrows. "I must say, after my last two inauspicious attempts, I won't be rushing to try it again." He looked quizzically at Waterstone. "On which topic, who do I have to thank for giving me an acorn from halfway up a great oak tree?"

Waterstone grimaced, "To be honest, it could have been any one of us. Someone thought of the idea of giving you something to use to translocate. So we hunted around under the oak tree, came up with a selection of good, healthy acorns and chose the best looking one. We thought you would come back to where we picked the acorn up."

"And instead, I came back to exact place where the acorn had been created, halfway up the tree."

"Yes. As soon as you appeared up there in the tree, it was blindingly obvious what had happened, but hindsight didn't stop you from falling. Actually, several woodfolk are also sporting injuries from that incident, you know."

Tarkyn frowned, "No. I didn't know. So, what happened to them?"

"You fell on them, Your Highness!" replied the woodman shortly. "But they'll be all right. One has a wrenched knee; another has a couple of bruised ribs. I think the rest have pretty much recovered by now."

"Oh, I see. Oh dear. I'm quite heavy when I'm close to the ground, let alone when I'm thrown from a great height." The prince closed his eyes for a few minutes. This much talking required more energy than anything he had done in the last fortnight. Then his curiosity overcame his exhaustion and he asked, "And how did I come to be lying unprotected in the middle of that clearing when the sorcerers found me? I noticed that you had all found time to cover the signs of your own presence but had left me to my own devices."

Waterstone stood up and poured a cup full of water from a stone jar in the corner and brought it over to Tarkyn while he considered what to say. "It was a series of wrong assumptions and errors on our part and, I suppose, a lack of preparation. You had slept out in the open the night before and all had been well. So we didn't fully appreciate how much danger you might be in." He glanced at the prince, "To be honest, we were all struggling to come to terms with our new status that night and a lot of wine was consumed in the process. And I'm afraid, because of that, we did not get around to building a shelter large enough to house you. So we just hoped for the best. When the lookouts sent warnings that strangers were approaching, we tried to wake you to get you into hiding but all our attempts were unsuccessful."

The prince frowned, "What attempts? I didn't hear anyone."

The woodman considered him for a moment. "You may not remember… Firstly, someone dropped leaves and twigs on you. Then, when that didn't work…'"

Light dawned on the prince's face. "You sent in a cockroach, didn't you?"

Waterstone gave a little smile. "So you remember the cockroach then."

"Now you mention it, I even remember the annoying twigs and leaves. I just didn't realise what they signified." Tarkyn gave a wry grin, "I'm afraid your wine was stronger than I bargained for, especially combined with that tonic. I began the day with a terrible headache which events conspired to make worse by every conceivable means until I was finally knocked out." He leaned back and closed his eyes. "I'm afraid my head is beginning to pound again at the moment."

"Perhaps that's enough questions for now."

The prince nodded slightly but didn't speak. After a while, the woodman stood up quietly and left him to rest.

The next morning, the little girl who had given him the wine before the oath-taking, brought him his bowl of porridge. "My dad says you're getting up today. I am Sparrow."

The prince stopped eating to smile at her. "Hello Sparrow. My name is Tarkyn." He took another mouthful of porridge. "Who is your father? The healer?"

The little girl shook her head vigorously. "No. My dad's Waterstone." She frowned reprovingly at him. "You should know him by now. You've spent enough time with him."

The prince smiled, "Oh, is that your dad? You're right. I should know him by now, but I have been sick and haven't been listening very well."

"I get into trouble if I don't listen." Sparrow confided.

Tarkyn gave a short laugh then gasped as a pain shot through his chest. The little girl put down the porridge and frowned with worry. "Are you all right?"

The prince nodded mutely as he breathed in gently, trying not to move his damaged ribs.

"I think I'd better get my dad," said Sparrow nervously and disappeared outside.

By the time Waterstone arrived, Tarkyn was lying down again. He opened his eyes when he heard the woodman enter and said, "I'm sorry if I frightened your daughter. I'm afraid something she said made me laugh."

"Oh, I see. That must have hurt. I'll tell her to stop cracking jokes."

Tarkyn put up a hand. "Please. Don't. It hurts too much."

Waterstone was unrepentant. "It's going to hurt more when I get you up."

"Oh stars above, do I have to? I don't think I'm ready."

"Your Highness, your body has been well enough for several days now. It is your spirit that has been ailing."

"I see," said the prince. "Now I know why you're here. You are a spiritual healer."

The woodman rolled his eyes. "No Sire! Can no-one speak to you unless they have a role to fulfil?"

Tarkyn glanced at Waterstone and then looked away. "Anyone can speak to me. I just assumed that after having that oath forced on them, no-one would want to unless they had to."

"I have already told you that I didn't have to sit with you all that time and I didn't have to talk to you either. Did you think I was lying?" Waterstone sounded distinctly annoyed.

"I beg your pardon," the prince said stiffly. "I did not mean to offend you." He smiled faintly. "Your daughter told me she gets into trouble if she doesn't listen to you. Looks like the same holds true for me too."

The nuggety woodman smiled perfunctorily in return, then gave Tarkyn's good shoulder a pat and sat down next to him. "I can see you won't let this rest, Your Highness, so I will save you the trouble of continuing your guessing game and tell you why I've spent all this time with you."

Tarkyn could feel his stomach tensing as he waited to hear what would be asked of him. In his brother's court, no one did anything for anyone without a reason.

The woodman looked him straight in the eye and said, "It's simply this. I watched you talking to Stormaway and I saw how you handled Tree Wind and the rest of us - and I liked what I saw. Most of it, anyway. Since then you've become confused by the whole oath business and for a while there, you were downright maudlin after your run-in with the bounty hunters but basically, you seem to be an interesting sort of character with a dry sense of humour and more integrity than many people I've met. And right now, despite your title and your exalted status, you could do with a friend. So here I am." Waterstone cleared his throat self-consciously. "I know that sounds a bit wet. That's why I didn't want to tell you, really. It's better if friendship can just develop over time. But that bloody oath has made you so mistrustful…." Waterstone gave a grunt of laughter. "It's paradoxical really. The oath was designed to bind us together but instead it has pushed us apart."

Tarkyn desperately needed a friend but a lifetime of disingenuity had taught him to trust no one. He could not easily accept this man or any other as a friend. The offer of friendship just raised his suspicions and highlighted his aloneness. He could make no reply. Waterstone heard the prince swallow and saw a solitary tear escape from the side of his eye to trace its way down his cheek. Tarkyn turned his head away and put his hand over his eyes.

For a long while, the woodman sat there quietly. Then when he judged the time was right, he stood up and clapped Tarkyn on his good shoulder and said briskly, "And now Your Highness, I am going to submit you to the torture of standing up."

Tarkyn sniffed, uncovered his eyes and said flatly, "I can't."

"Oh yes, you can. Bring your knees up, and then roll onto your left side. From there, get onto your left hand and knees… That's it! Now I'll help you get up from there."

Tarkyn gritted his teeth and complied. It was a trying process. Every muscle in his body was stiff and protested at being moved. On top of this, his ribs sent stabs of pain through his chest and back. As he prepared to straighten up, the woodman resisted him.

"Whoa. The roof's too low. You'll have to stay bent over until we get outside."

"Bent over is good." Tarkyn managed to say. "I think straightening up will be a whole new challenge."

"I think you could be right," agreed Waterstone. He called out to his daughter. "Sparrow, can you move the screening aside please?"

A rustle of leaves and branches followed this request and the prince looked through the doorway to discover that they were in the middle of a huge bramble patch. Waterstone supported the prince outside and through a short series of winding paths until they found themselves at a point halfway between the clearing and the river.

"All right?" asked Waterstone.

When Tarkyn nodded, Waterstone said, "Now try straightening up. Take it slowly."

Tarkyn grunted as he straightened but gave no other sign of the effort it cost him.

"Come on," encouraged the woodman, as he placed Tarkyn's good arm across his shoulders. "Let's walk down to the river and rest on those rocks."

Tarkyn sent him a sideways glance. The river looked a million miles away. However, he said nothing, clenched his teeth and set himself the task of making it the forty yards to the river.

Halfway there, Tarkyn's legs were trembling and his weight bore down ever harder on Waterstone's shoulders. The woodman was contrite. "My lord, I believe I have set you too hard a task for your first time out of bed."

"Maybe, but I would like to get down to the river, if I can." The prince took a slow deep breath then asked, "I know I'm pretty heavy. Do you think you can make the distance?"

"Of course I can ma…" Waterstone stopped mid-word and looked around to see the prince's eyes twinkling at him. "Very funny," grunted the woodman but he was not deceived. He knew it was costing the young man an enormous effort to keep going. For a couple of seconds, Waterstone's eyes went out of focus but Tarkyn's reaction was immediate. He pulled away and scowled down at the woodman.

"Not you too," he growled. "I should have known I couldn't trust you,"

Waterstone was honestly bewildered. "What are you talking about? What have I done wrong?"

"Don't give me that! I can tell when you're doing your mind talking and I really object to sharing my conversations with other people without my knowledge or permission." Tarkyn was swaying slightly but held Waterstone at arm's length.

Now it was Waterstone's turn to be offended. "And I object to you doubting my integrity like that."

"It's nothing to do with your integrity. It's to do with loyalty, and obviously your loyalty is going to lie with your people above me."

"Oh good! I'm glad you sorted that out for me. I wouldn't want to make my own decisions about it," responded the woodman sarcastically. He stood with his hands on his hips, green eyes blazing. "I don't know what your problem is. All I did was check with the lookouts before I allowed us to get too far away from the shelter. I can't see you being able to run for cover if the need arises and you're too heavy for us to carry back quickly."

They stood glaring at each other for a long moment before Tarkyn conceded, "If that's what you were doing, Waterstone, I apologise. When Ancient Oak did that, he was passing on everything I said to Tree Wind and Autumn Leaves.

The woodman raised his eyebrows. "I see. No wonder you don't like it then... Come on. Let's just get you down to the river. Put your arm across my shoulder again before you fall over."

Once they had reached the riverside, Waterstone lowered the prince carefully onto the ground so that he could lean against the rocks. They sat in silence for several minutes while they both recovered their breath. Tarkyn was looking grey and pinched around the mouth. His head throbbed in time with his heart but despite that, he felt a sense of satisfaction at having reached the goal he had set himself. While he was recovering, Waterstone pulled out bread, meat and fruit from a bag he had slung on his back. He walked down to the river and filled two small cups with cold water and brought them back. He handed a cup to Tarkyn and sat down next to him.

"Well done. That was a good effort," said Waterstone, "You're determined, aren't you?"

Tarkyn smiled faintly in acknowledgement.

The woodman cleared his throat. "I think we have a few things we need to clear up, Your Highness."

Tarkyn considered the man sitting next to him. Waterstone was very different from anyone the prince had met before. He was tough and kind, and although ostensibly respectful, treated Tarkyn as his equal.

"I'm listening," said the prince quietly, wondering where this was going.

"Firstly, I suppose we had better sort out the mind talking. I don't want you jumping down my throat every time I mind talk to someone. It's a natural part of the way we work with each other." Waterstone's voice blended with the sound of the running water and Tarkyn had to concentrate hard to discern what he was saying. "We rarely shout because that might inadvertently give our presence away. So it's the only way we can talk over longer distances and it is essential when we wish to remain hidden from strangers. It's also very useful for co-ordinating hunting parties without alarming the quarry."

"And for eavesdropping," added Tarkyn but without rancour.

Waterstone gave a little smile. "Only on outsiders, I'm afraid. Any one of us would hear the thought if the person we were talking to transmitted our conversation." He picked up a couple of pebbles and started bouncing them up and down in his hand. "But you seem to have tuned in pretty quickly to what was going on, even if you can't intercept the thoughts."

"When Tree Wind showed me her memory, I could almost hear the thoughts. I could feel they were happening but not what was being said."

Waterstone considered him thoughtfully, "I wonder if we could teach it to you?"

"It is not a sorcerer ability as far as I know, but I would like to try. I haven't had much formal training in magic, you know."

The woodman frowned. "What? You must have. Don't all sorcerers get training as part of their education? Especially you. How can you win a tournament with no training?"

Tarkyn grimaced as he shifted his position against the hard rock, "Tournaments are quite restrictive of the skills you can use. You don't use much beyond shields and shafts of power. You mainly need good reflexes and some agility."

"So why haven't you had much formal training?"

"You have no idea what it's like at court," began the prince and promptly looked stricken. "I didn't mean that to sound rude…." Waterstone waved his hand dismissively and Tarkyn continued, "What I meant was, you can't imagine how complicated and devious the relationships and the manoeuvrings are around gaining favour with my brothers."

"And with you, I presume."

"To a lesser extent. I was merely seen as way to my brothers. Anyway, so much time was spent on all the intrigue and scandal that no one ever seemed to have time to get around to organising my education. My father would have made sure I was trained properly, but he died when I was eight and my mother's time has mostly been spent adjudicating my brothers' arguments and indulging in court intrigue."

Waterstone stopped bouncing his stones up and down and threw them, one at a time, into the river. "That sounds hideous."

Tarkyn grinned suddenly. "Oh, I don't know. A lot of people would give their eye teeth to be able to have and do virtually anything they wanted."

"And you…?" asked Waterstone as he picked up two more pebbles and started to bounce them.

The prince flicked him a glance. "I suspect you would like me to say that I don't care about all those things but the truth is that I do. I've been brought up in a life of luxury, had everything I wanted at the lift of a finger, been surrounded by people wanting to please me…either for their own ends or from a loyalty that has been bred into them over generations. It will take some getting used to, not having all of that." Tarkyn took a sip of water and gave a lop-sided smile. "On the other hand, I won't have to dress for dinner every evening and endure hours of sycophantic conversation…."

When Waterstone remained silent, Tarkyn looked at him. The woodman kept his eyes on the pebbles he was bouncing and waited. Finally Tarkyn sighed and said, "All right. You're right. In many ways, it has been... difficult. Life in court since my father died has been tense, and even dangerous, most of the time. It hasn't been easy sharing a life with two pathologically jealous brothers. I lost my father. My mother loves me, I think, but can't cope with my brothers, and certainly has never had time for me. But don't treat me like a poor little rich boy. I'm not…. At least, I wasn't until a couple of weeks ago," he added with a flash of dry humour. Tarkyn picked up a stone and threw it hard into the river. "Anyway, all families have their problems. It's just that ours is played out in the public arena."

The woodman walked down to the water's edge and re-filled their cups. As he handed Tarkyn his water, he said, "Public arena or not, most families can't order the imprisonment of a family member on a whim… and wouldn't, even if they could."

Tarkyn put down his cup, "You're determined to feel sorry for me, aren't you?" He picked up a stone and threw it hard against a nearby tree. "Look. In another family, the precocious younger brother might be relegated to the rotten jobs around the farm, get beaten up behind the barn, forced to work longer hours, sent away on long tedious errands... I don't know…but in my family, everything is on larger scale. There is influence riding on everything. So, all the actions are more extreme. I don't know that the ill-intent is any greater, just the power is."

Waterstone snorted. "That's the whole point though, isn't it? That power has corrupted all the relationships within your family and within the court. No wonder you struggle to believe in friendship."

The prince stared hard at Waterstone then looked away to contemplate the sun sparkling off the rippling water of the river. After a while, he returned his gaze to the woodman. He nearly spoke, but hesitated and instead returned to watching the river. The woodman began to pack away the remains of the lunch while he was waiting. Then he just sat there quietly. Finally, the prince dragged his eyes back around to meet and hold Waterstone's.

"You're right," Tarkyn said slowly. "If anyone ever professes their friendship, my mind automatically asks, 'What does this person want from me? What do they hope to gain? Why are they doing this?' I've thought about all my friends back at court and I think I can answer those questions for every one of them. I don't know whether any of them will remain true to me now that I no longer have influence. Some might, but I honestly don't know and even then I would be wondering what they would be hoping to gain." He shook his head and looked down at the ground as he selected some pebbles to fiddle with. He shifted position a little, then looked back up at Waterstone. "And then we come to you. I can think of a lot of things you would gain from having my friendship."

The woodman's face suffused with anger and he would have interrupted but Tarkyn held up his hand and said peremptorily. "No. Let me finish. You may be angry with me at the end, if you wish to."

Waterstone subsided but was clearly simmering.

The prince gazed down at the pebbles in his hand as he continued, an unpleasantly cynical edge to his voice "As I was about to say, there are a lot of things you might gain from having my friendship. I am a powerful sorcerer, certainly more magically powerful in most ways than your people. Because of the oath, I could insist on absolute power over your people, if I so choose, and who knows, you could possibly share that power. In fact, I have much more influence here than I ever had in my brother's court. Then, notoriety is always a great draw card." Tarkyn brought bitter eyes up to face the angry woodman, "And yet, Waterstone, despite all the advantages you might gain from my friendship, I think I believe that your offer of friendship does not depend on them and may be truly genuine."

"Oh for heaven's sake!" growled Waterstone, not at all gratified, "That's the weakest, most conditional avowal of good faith I've ever heard… 'I think I believe' and 'friendship may be genuine'. That's pathetic! Make your bloody mind up!"

Tarkyn smiled ruefully, "I'm sorry. That's the best I can do at the moment."

"You poor bloody bastard!" the woodman spat out, unappeased. "It must be a lonely world for you."

"It is," said the prince shortly. Then, much to Waterstone's further irritation, Tarkyn shook his head, guffawed with laughter and immediately wished he hadn't. He gasped at a sharp stab of pain but managed to get out, "I love it when you get angry! No one else has ever dared to."

The woodman stared at him belligerently then suddenly broke into a smile. "Well, that's taken the wind out of my sails then, hasn't it?"

"And if you want to know," said Tarkyn, still struggling not to laugh, "It's the one thing above all else that persuades me that your friendship may be genuine. No one else would risk losing my goodwill by being so openly angry."

"Oh good!" retorted Waterstone, "So all I have to do to prove my friendship is just get angry all the time and endure you laughing at me. Well, that is something to look forward to."

They both found this exquisitely funny, much to Tarkyn's extreme discomfort. When they had recovered themselves, Tarkyn had his good arm wrapped protectively around his ribs. "Oh my aching ribs! I think I'm dying," he groaned, still with a smile on his face. "I can't stand much more of this."

Waterstone eyed him and, deciding he could stand a bit more, said flippantly "Well, you had better not make me angry again then."

Tarkyn spluttered with laughter then groaned again in pain. "Stop! Don't make me laugh."

The woodman relented and did his best to become serious again. "All right. I'll stop. Otherwise you won't have enough energy to walk back up to your shelter. I'll get you another drink of water and then we'll head back."

The trip up the hill was much slower and more tiring than the journey down had been. Tarkyn had been out of bed too long for his first day and Waterstone was bearing most of his weight by the time they made it into the shelter. The prince was near exhaustion as the woodman helped him carefully down onto the bed. Tarkyn went almost instantly to sleep, but from that point onward, made a more rapid recovery.

CHAPTER 12

Next morning, the darkness lingered and Tarkyn could hear heavy rain pounding on the roof of the shelter. When the rain finally ceased, he could see chinks of sunlight through tiny gaps in the shelter's structure. But still no one came to see him. By mid-morning he was very hungry and becoming concerned at the unexplained change in routine. Eventually a gentle rustling heralded the arrival of Sparrow. However, she did not pull back the screening as usual but slithered in through the lower branches of it, clutching a small bag. Even before she stood up, she put her finger to her lips to signal silence. Quietly, she opened the bag and set out meat, bread and jam on a plate that she gave to Tarkyn with a flask of water. Then she sat down and watched him eat.

After a few minutes, the intensity of her gaze gave the prince pause. He looked at her, pointed to the food and then to her. Sparrow hesitated then shook her head. Tarkyn thought for a moment then pointed separately to the meat, bread and jam and put his hand on his heart and his head on an angle after each one. She smiled and nodded in response to the bread and jam but pulled her mouth down at the meat. So then Tarkyn awkwardly spread some jam on a piece of bread, using his one available hand, and held it out to her. Sparrow put her head on one side and screwed her face up in uncertainty but the prince nodded emphatically. So she accepted the bread and jam with a beaming smile.

Then, clear as a bell in Tarkyn's mind, appeared the image of the water flask. He picked it up and offered it to Sparrow who accepted it with a casual smile of thanks. Tarkyn was just congratulating himself on having picked up a mind picture when suddenly they heard the sounds of shouting and crashing through the undergrowth in the woods outside. The prince's eyes widened in alarm, as he imagined woodfolk being hunted down and injured. Pictures of an intense sorcerer on horseback searching through the woods flowed into his mind. Tarkyn brought two fingers from his eyes to indicate looking, and then pointed to himself with his head on one side. The girl shrugged and pointed to him then put her head on one side and mimicked an animal running with her hand and shrugged again.

In answer to an unspoken query, Tarkyn received a picture from Waterstone high up in an oak tree, well hidden and looking down on an unshielded sorcerer passing below. The prince recognised the sorcerer and even as he concluded that it must be the king's Hunting Party, he sensed Waterstone's eyes widen and lose focus, as he received the image.

Tarkyn was so distracted that he didn't realise Sparrow was trying to get his attention. She came over and tapped him on the arm. Once he was looking, she put out her hand raising different numbers of fingers with a look of query on her face. The prince thought about a full hunting party and using her fingers, Sparrow checked with him that twenty was about right. He nodded and immediately sensed Waterstone passing the message on to other woodfolk in nearby trees.

Then, way below Waterstone, on the forest path, the king and his twin brother came into view. A jolt of fear, loss and rage blasted through Tarkyn and his mind went blank. In consternation, he saw Sparrow give a little whimper and crumple onto the floor. He threw himself out of bed, sending the food flying. In a panic, he placed his hand on her neck and felt for a pulse. Beneath his fingers he could feel her heart beating strongly but very slowly. He breathed a sigh of relief and hoisted himself down onto the floor to sit with his back against the bed. Then he gently lifted Sparrow's head, put it on his lap and began to stroke her hair. He tried to project calm soothing images but he could feel his mind blocking him. Gradually, by calming himself first and then focusing his will, he relaxed his mind barrier and was able to send waves of reassurance into the little girl's mind.

After what seemed an eternity, Sparrow stirred. She stared up at the prince looking down at her in concern, and tears began to roll down her cheeks. She picked herself up and climbed onto his lap, snuggling her head against his good shoulder so that he could wrap his arm around her. Then she quietly sobbed her heart out. Tarkyn held her, stroking her arm and whispering softly in her ear until her sobs subsided and she gradually fell asleep.

Not too much later, sounds of shouting drew closer. Tarkyn hugged Sparrow closer to him and with an awkward flick of his hand, threw a shield up around them. He could hear the wind picking up outside, throwing leaves and small branches spattering against the outside of the shelter. The shouting resolved itself into the voice of Waterstone yelling, "Her mind link stopped. Where is he? I'll kill the bastard if he's hurt a hair on her head," followed by a crackling voice saying, "Calm down. Let's just see if she's safe first," and another voice rumbling, "You can't. You have to think of the forest."

The screening was thrown aside and Waterstone, blood running from a gash in the side of his face, stormed in flanked by the two woodfolk who were trying to calm him down and restrain him. He threw them off and seeing his daughter, pale and still, in Tarkyn's arms, rushed at the prince.

"I'll kill you, you bastard," he shouted. Outside, the wind roared through the trees and they could hear branches cracking and crashing down. Not far away, a ponderous series of crashes signalled the death of some large tree as it fell victim to the howling gale.

The sorcerer expanded the shield to keep Waterstone at bay. The woodman hit the barrier and became, if possible, more angry.

"How dare you keep me from my daughter?" he raged.

Tarkyn sent a look of appeal to the other two woodfolk but Waterstone threw off all attempts to contain him.

"Waterstone. Waterstone," said Tarkyn urgently, "She's all right. She's not dead. She's sleeping," but the woodman was ranting so much, he didn't even register that the prince was speaking.

With a mute apology, the sorcerer, in quick progression, dropped the shield then incanted, "*Shturrum.*" The three woodfolk froze.

"I'm sorry, Waterstone and you others. I don't want to use strong-arm tactics but Waterstone, you must listen; Sparrow is all right. She's sleeping – Do you understand? It's taken a long time to get her to sleep and I was hoping not to disturb her. It is your choice, of course. But if you're going to beat me up, do it somewhere away from Sparrow." The prince smiled wryly at the other two. "And don't worry about your forests. As long as he doesn't actually kill me, he has my permission to do to me what he needs to."

As soon as he said this, the wind outside dropped and an uneasy silence settled on the forest. The sorcerer waved his hand again, removing the paralysis spell but not re-instating the shield. He braced himself for Waterstone's next move but the woodman now had himself in check.

"Give me my daughter," he demanded flatly.

"Here." Tarkyn gently shrugged his shoulder to push Sparrow forward towards her father but the movement woke her.

The little girl opened her eyes sleepily and smiled at her father, "Hello dad. Tarkyn's been minding me." She started to nod off but murmured, just before she went back to sleep, "Actually, we've been minding each other."

Tarkyn and Waterstone were left staring at each other across the sleeping form of the woodman's daughter.

"I'll speak to you later," said Waterstone shortly and walked out bearing Sparrow.

The prince looked at the other two woodfolk.

"Have the huntsmen gone?" he asked urbanely to cover the awkward moment.

"They've been gone for an hour or more," rumbled one of them.

"Just as well, with Waterstone shouting like that." The prince frowned. "I thought woodfolk weren't supposed to shout."

The woodmen exchanged glances. "We don't, in the normal course of events."

The prince smiled disarmingly at them. "Would you mind telling me your names again? I have become confused." He hazarded a guess. "Are you Thunder Storm?" He received a nod. "And you?"

"Autumn Leaves."

"I thought you were, but I wasn't sure."

Tarkyn flexed his shoulder and asked, "Could you two help me back into bed. I've been sitting in the same position for a couple of hours. It is not that I minded holding Sparrow, but my arm and shoulder were screaming by the end of it.

Once he was settled back in bed, Tarkyn asked, "What happened to Waterstone's face?"

The two woodfolk looked at each other again, then Autumn Leaves shrugged, "We're not sure. Just as the king and his brother were riding underneath, Waterstone's eyes went wide and he lost his balance and nearly fell out of the tree. Luckily Thunder Storm was near enough to grab him but he swung in against the trunk of the tree and gashed his cheek. After that, all he wanted to do was get back here but we couldn't move until the hunting party had left the area."

The prince ran his hand through his hair. "Poor Waterstone. No wonder he'd worked himself into such a frenzy."

"My lord," rumbled Thunder Storm, "It is important that Waterstone is made to realise that he must control himself. He endangered the forest with his behaviour towards you."

The prince raised his eyes brows superciliously. "He has indeed, but that will be the last time you pass judgement on my actions. Perhaps you have forgotten that I, too, have sworn to protect the forests. I will deal with Waterstone as I see fit. The mindblast that hit Waterstone was a fraction of what hit his daughter, and I was its source. He was frightened for his daughter. He had every right to be angry with me, even though he must have known it was unintentional."

"But my lord...,"

"But what?" asked the prince icily. "Do you expect a man to stand by and accept his daughter being hurt?"

"Perhaps not." rumbled Thunder Storm stiffly.

"Do you have a daughter, Thunder Storm?"

"I have two sons, my lord, five and seven years old."

"And how would you feel if I or someone else injured one of your sons?"

"I would be upset, of course, but I would like to think that I would maintain a sense of proportion and put the welfare of all woodfolk before my own concerns."

"It has obviously not happened to you yet," observed the prince tartly. "We would all like to think that we could act rationally in times of stress, Thunder Storm, but we often don't."

"But, my lord," insisted Thunder Storm, "how could you give him permission to assault you?"

The prince looked at him steadily for a few moments, deciding whether to answer. Finally, he said, "Once Waterstone knew his daughter was safe, he was never going to attack me. I gave him permission, both to appease the sorcery of the oath and to give Waterstone an even playing field." The prince shrugged and smiled wryly. "If he does come back seeking vengeance, I will just have to accept it."

"I think that's very generous of you, Your Highness. I would almost say courageous, given you have your arm in a sling. But I gather, since you won that Harvester tournament, that you must be a skilled fighter."

Tarkyn narrowed his eyes, finding Thunder Storm's remarks sychophantic."Thank you. And now I think I need to rest." *Mostly from you,* Tarkyn added to himself.

It was several hours before Waterstone reappeared. He eyed the prince and sat down next to him. His face was pale and there were signs of strain around his eyes.

"How is Sparrow?" asked Tarkyn with some restraint.

"She is well," replied Waterstone shortly.

Silence ensued. Waterstone cleared his throat a couple of times but said nothing. Then they spoke simultaneously.

"Waterstone..."

"Your Highness..."

Tarkyn nodded to the woodman. "You first."

Waterstone cleared his throat again. "Autumn Leaves told me that you defended me against Thunder Storm."

"Thunder Storm is a sanctimonious, old bore. He questioned my judgement and I was not pleased."

Waterstone glanced at the prince, taking in this disdainful side of him. After a moment, he asked, "How would you react if I questioned your judgement?"

The prince raised his eyebrows. "You are not a prosy old bore. So I would listen." He shrugged, coming down off his high horse. "I mightn't agree with you, but I would listen. And in fairness, I did listen to Thunder Storm. I just didn't like the way he spoke. He did have a point though. You did endanger the forests and your people."

Suddenly, Waterstone's eyes glistened with tears. "I know I did. You should see the damage out there. At least one grand old oak tree has fallen and many trees have been damaged. Birds' nests on the ground…." Waterstone cleared his throat again. "And although you stood up for me, I actually think my behaviour was reprehensible, regardless of the oath."

"Do you?" The prince's amber eyes considered him, giving him time to squirm. "I suppose it depends on how you look at it. From the point of view of court etiquette, it was almost a hanging offence. In fact, in my brother's court, I doubt that I could have saved you." He paused to let this sink in. "From the point of view of a father protecting his daughter, it was perhaps a little aggressive but understandable – and at least you haven't hit me yet." Suddenly, Tarkyn twinkled at the woodman. "But the offer still stands." Before the woodman could respond, he became serious again, "To be honest, I feel I almost deserve it. I'm afraid my reaction to seeing my brothers sent a huge jolt of emotion through the mind link and Sparrow caught the worst of it." The prince ran his hand through his long black hair. "Waterstone, you have no idea! I was so frightened that I might have killed her. She just collapsed. Then when she opened her eyes and looked up at me, she started crying. I held her and did the best I could, one-handed, but it was ages before she went to sleep. I am so sorry, Waterstone. I would never do anything to hurt her intentionally."

The woodman waved his hand dismissively. "I know. Of course you wouldn't. I knew at the time."

"But you were crazy with fear for Sparrow."

Waterstone nodded shortly.

The sorcerer gave the woodman a little smile. "I'm sorry about the spells. I do not generally resort to magic to impose my will, but I couldn't make you listen and the forest was suffering."

Waterstone glanced at him then looked away. "Hmph. I didn't leave you much choice. Anyway, it's a great leveller to be reminded from time to time how powerful you are."

The sorcerer grimaced. "Actually, I think we both need to know more about each other's magic. For a start, had you people understood my magic better, I wouldn't be carrying so many injuries and had I had time to learn about your mind linking properly, I may not have endangered Sparrow as I did."

Tarkyn saw Waterstone hesitate and added quickly, "Not today but soon. Tonight you need to go home to Sparrow."

CHAPTER 13

The next morning, Sparrow and Waterstone came in together with the prince's breakfast.

"Good morning, you two. Are you better now, Sparrow?"

"Morning, Tarkyn. Yes, I'm better. Are you?"

Before he could answer, Waterstone's voice cut in sharply. "I beg your pardon, young lady. What did you just say?"

Sparrow thought back and repeated faithfully, "Morning Tarkyn. Yes, I'm better. Are you?"

"Sparrow, you do not call a prince just by his first name," scolded her father

"But I did yesterday and you didn't say anything."

"Hmph. I may not have noticed at the time, but I'm noticing now."

The prince in question coughed apologetically, "My fault, I'm afraid. I introduced myself to Sparrow as Tarkyn"

"I see," said Waterstone, although he was clearly at a loss about what to do next.

The prince smiled, seeing his dilemma. "You may also call me Tarkyn, if you would like to. Maybe not on formal occasions, but the rest of the time. It seems a bit pointless to keep using titles so far from court."

Waterstone frowned. "I'll think about it. I might forget who you are, if I stop using your title."

"I doubt it, especially after yesterday. Besides, I stand out like a sore thumb amongst you woodfolk. I can't see you ever forgetting who I am."

Sparrow, who was waiting impatiently for this conversation to end, asked her question again. "So, are you better?"

"Sorry, young one. I guess I'm getting better but I still have my arm strapped up..."

Sparrow waved a dismissive hand. "Not that better. You know - feel better."

Tarkyn flicked a discomforted glance at Waterstone then looked back at Sparrow in some confusion. Sparrow frowned at him reprovingly. "You should feel better. I cried all your tears for you."

Light dawned. "Oh no, Sparrow. Oh, Stars above! You should never have had to deal with that." Tarkyn shot an apprehensive look at Waterstone to find the woodman watching silently, his mouth set in a grim line.

Sparrow shrugged and smiled, "Maybe it was easier for me. I'm still young."

Tarkyn thought about the enormity of his reaction to seeing his brothers. "No, Sparrow. It is not the job of a child to bear an adult's burden for them." Despite that, he realised that the big knot in his stomach had nearly disappeared. "But you know, I think you're right. I do feel better, as in feel better."

"And I feel better because when I was crying for you, I started crying for me."

"You did? Why?"

"Because I lost my mum."

Tarkyn glanced up over Sparrow's head and briefly met Waterstone's eyes before returning his attention to Sparrow. "That is sad. I bet you miss her." When Sparrow nodded, the prince added, "I lost my dad too, you know, when I was your age."

"And now you've lost your brothers and your mum and everyone else and that's why you were sad."

"Hmm. Yes." Tarkyn sent a wry grimace in the woodman's direction. "Neatly put, Sparrow."

The little girl hopped up and sat on the bed with her feet dangling over the edge. Once she was settled, Tarkyn put his arm around her. Sparrow smiled sunnily, "See Dad. Tarkyn and I are friends."

Waterstone ruffled her hair. "You don't know what an achievement that is, young Sparrow."

After a while, it became apparent that Tarkyn had no hands left with which to eat his breakfast. So Sparrow was shooed off to play and Waterstone waited with him until he had finished.

There was an air of constraint around the woodman and his previous confident style in his dealings with the prince was conspicuously absent. He did not use the prince's title but neither did he call him by name. "I think your strapping is coming off today," he said neutrally. "Once you have both arms free, we can get you into a new set of clothes. Your own clothes were badly torn by your fall through the oak tree."

Even as he finished speaking, an older woodwoman entered the shelter. She nodded her head and said in a soft shushing voice, "Good morning, Your Highness. It is pleasing to see that you are looking better. It was uncertain for a while whether you would recover at all and whether you would have your wits, if you did. I don't know if you remember me, I am Summer Rain."

Tarkyn smiled and inclined his head, "I believe you gave me a tonic on the first night. Am I right in assuming that you are the healer?"

"I do have some knowledge in that area," came the cool response.

"I thank you for your care. I believe I do have my wits, at least as much as I ever did, although Waterstone may be a better person to attest to that." When Waterstone merely smiled perfunctorily, Tarkyn gave a mental shrug.

"How are your ribs, my lord?"

"Very sore, especially if I laugh."

The healer delicately raised her eyebrows. "I would not advise laughing for the time being, if you wish to avoid pain."

Tarkyn glanced at Waterstone who did not show any reaction. Tarkyn felt his good humour evaporating. The healer seemed to have no sense of humour and Waterstone had become distant. For some reason, the woodfolk seemed to be closing ranks against him. Inevitably, Tarkyn became more aloof in response. He did not reply but waited for the next question.

"And how does your shoulder feel?" asked the soft emotionless voice.

"It is painful if jolted but quite comfortable if it is still," he replied briefly.

"Your shoulder has had over two weeks tightly strapped in place. I believe it will be safe to take the strapping off now." The woodwoman, with Waterstone's assistance, removed the prince's shirt and then the strapping. The woodman's eyes widened, when he saw the extent of the bruising that was revealed. Even after two weeks of healing, Tarkyn's back and shoulders were almost totally covered with dark blue almost black bruising, a greenish tinge around the edges where the bruise was beginning to fade.

"Wolves' teeth!" exclaimed Waterstone, his voice, for the first time betraying some feeling. "You're a mess. That walk to the river must have been agonising."

"Agonising might be too strong a word but it was difficult," replied Tarkyn coolly.

"However," interrupted the healer, "a little exercise will be helpful in reducing stiffness." She lifted his arm and moved it gently through its range of movement. "How is that?"

Tarkyn flexed it carefully and grimaced, but said, "It is a great relief to be able to move it."

"As long as you are careful, it should be all right now." Summer Rain picked up the bandaging and prepared to leave.

"Thank you for all you have done to help me," said Tarkyn with a smile.

In return, he received a curt nod and no eye contact. His smile faded and his face became stony. Tarkyn struggled to contain a wave of anger that washed through him at her discourtesy. "Summer Rain, although I will make some allowances for your natural resentment of me, I will not brook deliberate rudeness. Do I make myself clear?"

The healer nodded and looked up reluctantly at him, her face set. "Yes, my lord. Your pardon, my lord."

He took a steadying breath and asked, "Is something amiss, that you did not reply?"

"Yes, my lord. There has been something amiss for more than a decade."

"Has this oath affected you so badly?" asked Tarkyn.

"No, my lord. Not until your recent arrival. But because the king found us and forced us to foreswear our independence, my brother was exiled."

"And your brother is…?"

"Falling Rain."

"Oh, I see," said Tarkyn slowly as he thought back over Tree Wind's memories. "But surely his self-betrayal was inadvertent? Didn't he become so ill that he was found after falling from a tree?"

"That is so, but he should have refused to answer questions. Instead he chose to betray our existence to the king and then show him how to find us."

"And the most fundamental tenet of woodfolk is that we remain hidden from the outside world," put in Waterstone. "Our way of life and our safety depends on it."

Tarkyn began to feel he was fighting a rear guard action for this woodman he had never met. "But as I understand it, had he not brought help, many woodfolk would have died." He looked at Summer Rain. "You're a healer. In your opinion, how many would have died if help had not arrived?"

"My lord, the sickness was virulent. More than half of the woodfolk were ill by the time the king and the wizard arrived. As it was, many people died. Without aid, our numbers would have been decimated. We may even have been wiped out completely."

Tarkyn frowned, "So how could such actions be condemned?"

The healer shrugged, "The woodfolk decided that Falling Rain had betrayed the sacred trust of his people and that, regardless of his reasons, should be banished."

Tarkyn whistled under his breath. "For pity's sake! That is a harsh judgement, when one could equally argue that he should be regarded as the saviour of his people"

"Yes, my lord. It was very harsh. Yet a people's saviour does not lead them into subjugation."

"Death or submission. That was the choice presented by my father." The prince ran his fingers through his hair. "Stars above! Your poor brother. What a choice!"

"In the end, it was all of us who made that choice," Waterstone pointed out. "Falling Rain's crime was making our existence known to the king."

"I see."The prince thought for a moment. "And am I right in saying that this choice has not affected your lifestyle in the intervening years?"

"Yes, that is true." answered Summer Rain. "Except in the abstract, of course – in our view of ourselves and in knowing that one day, our debt would be called in."

"In the shape of myself." Tarkyn considered the healer as she packed away her herbs and bandages. Finally he asked, "And do you think Falling Rain should have been banished?"

"Excuse me," interrupted Waterstone quietly, "I have to go and check on Sparrow." Since the woodman could easily have mind linked with his daughter, Tarkyn raised his eyebrows slightly in query. "And I'll fashion a walking stick for you while I'm there," added Waterstone quickly. "I'll be back shortly."

When he had gone, the prince turned to Summer Rain. "What was that all about?"

The woodwoman gave a gentle smile. "Waterstone does not want to become involved in influencing your decisions."

"I presume that means he has a strong view on this subject." observed the prince.

"Yes, he does but I would not betray his intentions by telling you what it is," said the healer firmly.

"Nor would I expect you to," the prince retaliated stiffly. "But you have not yet told me your own views on your brother's banishment."

The healer met his gaze steadily. "Until recently, I have always advocated that Falling Rain should not have been exiled, certainly not for such a long period of time. Many woodfolk agreed with me, especially those who had been saved or whose relatives had been saved by your father and the wizard."

"But then," continued the prince for her, "I came into the forest and now the debt has been called in."

Summer Rain nodded. "And the forest has already been damaged twice in the short time you have been here."

Tarkyn thought of saying that the incidence of damage to the forest was likely to decrease as the woodfolk came to terms with the power of the oath, but on balance he decided that the comment might be more harmful than helpful. So he merely asked, "So, what is your view now?"

"As both a healer and his sister, I still believe that his betrayal of us did more good than harm. But now memories of the sickness have faded and the reality of your presence has swung away most of the support I might have had."

Politics is alive and well and living in the woodlands, thought the prince. He closed his eyes imagining the pull of opposing forces dragging at him. He took a careful, deep breath and gazed steadfastly at the floor as he thought through what he was saying, "So, on the one hand, you resent me and all I represent but on the other hand, you know I could choose to end your brother's exile." He raised his eyes to look at her. "And because Falling Rain was exiled for complying with my father's wishes, it seems likely that I would champion his cause."

She returned his stare in silence. When he said nothing further, Summer Rain swallowed and said tightly, "And yet you will not."

The prince shook his head slowly. "I have not said that. I will think on it. However, I am facing enough resentment at the moment without overturning such a pivotal decision. I can't do that on such short acquaintance. It would look as though I had no respect for woodfolk lore."

The healer's gentle green eyes flashed. "I doubt there is much you could do to persuade us that you respect us. Meanwhile, my brother will suffer in exile to ease your passage into our society."

"Charmingly put, ma'am," said the prince with heavy irony. "And on that note, might I suggest we close the discussion?"

Summer Rain looked as though she would say more but the forbidding expression on the prince's face stopped her. As she left the shelter, bearing her bag of herbs and bandages, Tarkyn relented enough to say stiffly to her retreating back, "Do not despair. I will not forget your brother's plight. Thank you for your care."

By the time Waterstone returned, Tarkyn had managed to wash himself using the basin of water that had been left for him in the corner of the room and had dressed himself in his new woodfolk garb. The effort of this activity had depleted his reserve of energy and he was lying down recovering when Waterstone walked in, bearing a long sturdy staff of wood.

Again the woodman's face showed signs of strain and although he smiled as he presented Tarkyn with the staff and commented on his new clothes, there was a haunted look at the back of his eyes.

Tarkyn frowned in concern. "What is wrong, Waterstone? I feel you have withdrawn from me. Are you still angry with me because of Sparrow? What is it?"

Waterstone looked at him without speaking for several seconds, and then made up his mind. "Come. I will show you."

When they had emerged from the winding path through the brambles, the prince found himself facing a scene of devastation. Twigs and branches littered the ground. Broken branches hung, half ripped off standing trees. And some smaller trees had been virtually stripped bare of leaves. From where he stood, Tarkyn could see at least three fallen trees other than the great oak. The prince stood and surveyed the scene for long minutes before asking, "How far does the damage go?" he asked quietly. "Is it like this throughout the forest?"

"No." Waterstone shook his head, his eyes bright with tears. "Probably thanks to your intervention, the damage is all within a two hundred yard radius. But look what I've done," The woodman waved an encompassing hand. "How can I live with this?"

Tarkyn remembered his father saying that breaking the oath would destroy the woodfolk's souls. The sorcerer glanced at the distressed woodman and without thinking about it, sent waves of understanding and strength to him, as he said, "Waterstone, you do not bear all the blame for this. We both did something wrong but more than either of us, my father let loose a great evil when he created this sorcerous oath in the first place. If he had to impose an oath, it should have been an oath of honour. He showed no respect for the integrity of woodfolk when he bound your compliance to the welfare of the forest." He looked at the woodman. "Can we walk down to the river? I can't stand up for long."

Waterstone nodded and they set off slowly, Tarkyn using the staff for support as his back and legs muscles complained. He still found the walk difficult but was able to make the distance without a break or assistance. He lowered himself down against the rocks with a sigh of satisfaction. Waterstone did not sit down but paced around tidying up debris or gazing up into damaged trees. Finally, he sat on a rock opposite Tarkyn and ran his hands through his light brown hair. He gazed at the river for a few minutes then took a deep breath and swung his eyes around to face the patiently waiting young sorcerer.

"Tarkyn, I don't know whether I can do this."

Tarkyn could feel his heart beating slow and hard. He knew what was coming and thought it ironic that Waterstone had finally used his name. "Go on," he said.

"When you were unconscious, when you were ill and isolated, I didn't understand the complications of ...I don't know... spending time around you." The woodman picked up a couple of pebbles and started tossing them up and down, just as he had when they had been beside the river two days earlier. He took his eyes off the prince to focus on the pebbles."There are so many things that are difficult...I don't know where to start. There's your enormous magical power that seems to become erratic when your emotions get the better of you. You have absolute dominion over the future of the woodfolk if you want it and I can already see the vultures gathering already, waiting to use your influence. I don't know how to act to keep neutral. I don't know how to be a friend and not have opinions. And if I have opinions, you'll start thinking I'm trying to use you.... and I'll be drafted into one camp or the other and people will try to make me influence you. But if I don't have opinions, who am I? And on top of all that, there's the stinking oath. I don't blame you for it, but now I know how destructive it is, how can I risk being unrestrained around you. When does anger start a windstorm?" He dropped the pebbles and shook his head. He looked back up at the prince. "It's all so hard," he finished disconsolately.

Tarkyn gave Waterstone a rueful smile. "I know it's hard being around me. I have to do it all the time, but at least I'm used to it. I do understand and I'm sorry you have had to go through all this when you have done so much to help me. If you cannot cope with me and all that goes with me, I will miss your company but I will understand."

Waterstone stood up and started to pace up and down in some agitation. Finally, he came to stand in front of the prince and glowered down at him. "The trouble with you is that you're too bloody noble. If you were less understanding, I might be able to walk away and leave you to your fate but I can't. Anyway, I don't want to. I just don't know how to deal with it all."

Such a wave of relief came flooding into Waterstone's mind that he blinked. "And that's another thing," said the woodman, half crossly and half laughing, "You work out how to use mind links and then develop your own weird style. We use images and words. You use images and feelings. Do you realise you're flooding me with your relief at the moment?"

Tarkyn managed to look guilty and embarrassed all at once. "You're right, aren't you? My emotions do run riot at times, don't they?"

"Yes, they do. And when they do, things tend to go haywire. You're an absolute disaster area, all things considered."

Tarkyn shrugged, "That's how I got into this mess in the first place." He realised what he had just said and added quickly, "Not that I mean to imply that...."

Waterstone interrupted him with a half smile, "Don't even try to get out of that one. You'll just tie yourself in knots and won't convince me you didn't mean it anyway." He sat down on the ground next to Tarkyn and became serious again. "You will have to help me, Tarkyn. I'm not used to people pulling at me and judging my every move and questioning my motives." He looked around at the prince. "I know you can't completely trust me and, having seen just a little of what goes on around you, I can understand why, much better than I did two days ago. But maybe you could tell me when I do or say something that arouses your suspicion, so we can sort it out."

Tarkyn grimaced, "I am hard work, aren't I? Thank you for sticking with me. If I have any doubts, I will talk to you about them. I have been honest with you so far, haven't I?"

"Blindingly."

"But you are also badly upset about the forest, aren't you?" When Waterstone nodded, Tarkyn continued, "I know the forest has a different, deeper meaning to you and that it is hurting you to see what has happened to it. But if my welfare is tied to that of the woodlands, then your support of me is supporting the woodland. So please don't let this one mistake eat away at you. Just help me to make sure it doesn't keep happening as woodfolk test me out." The sorcerer looked around the nearby trees and pointed at some of the half torn off branches. "Perhaps we can repair some of these trees. In the palace nursery, they used to graft branches onto other trees by tying them until the tree grew strongly enough around the joint to hold the branch without support. Can't we do that for some of these trees?"

The woodman looked perplexed. "I can't hold a branch and tie it at the same time while dangling out of the tree. And there wouldn't be room for two of us to reach one branch at the same time, even if you were strong enough to climb up."

Tarkyn gave a self-satisfied smile. "You forget. I'm a sorcerer. Watch." He pointed one of his fingers at a branch and incanted, "*Liefka.*" The branch lifted up into its original position on the tree. "Now, all you have to do is get up there with something to bind it."

Waterstone's eyes lit up. "Well, isn't that amazing?! I never thought of sorcery being used to do something good!"

Tarkyn let the branch back down and stared at him. "What do you think? That all sorcerers go around using their power to hurt people?" He frowned. "And if you think sorcerers are so evil, what on earth are you doing spending any time with me at all?"

The woodman was nonplussed. "Well, I don't know. I suppose I thought sorcerers only used their powers for attack or defence. I've only ever been near five sorcerers, you, your father and those three bounty hunters - and I've heard about your brothers of course."

"And it didn't occur to you that we might not be typical sorcerers - two kings, two princes and three vicious bounty hunters?"

Waterstone raised his eyebrow. "No. Not really. Though, when you put it like that...."

"So, I suppose you thought I was the best of a bad lot."

Waterstone gave an embarrassed smile. "Something like that. To be honest, I thought you were quite remarkable when you didn't hurt anyone even though you were under attack and then only used your powers for defence - well - except for that flashy display when you thought we were keeping you in the forest, but even that was pretty harmless." He flashed Tarkyn a cheeky grin. "Just another example of your emotions running riot."

Tarkyn raised his eyebrows, "That was you, wasn't it? I've just remembered. You were the person trying to tell me that it was the forest not the woodfolk that was stopping me from translocating."

The woodman smiled and nodded. "For all the good it did us."

"Oh dear," grimaced the prince. "You and I are not very good at listening to each other when we're angry, are we?" He thought through what Waterstone had said, "So all any of you knows of sorcerers is my family and those bounty hunters throwing our weight around. I have a lot of bad impressions to overcome, haven't I?" He looked at Waterstone thoughtfully, "Just to set the record straight, sorcerers are just ordinary people with varying degrees of magic. Some are good. Some are bad. Most are a mixture of both. Just like woodfolk, I would imagine. Most sorcerers use their powers to ply their trade, whatever that is; gardener, groom, craftsman, cook..."

"And what useful, helpful things does a prince do with his magic, as a general rule?"

The prince started to reply, but hesitated. Then he came up with another idea but again stopped himself before he spoke. Finally, he said with a wry grin, "Actually, not a lot, but it doesn't mean I can't start now. So let's get on with fixing these trees."

"Yes, if we are to have any successes, we must start soon. Many will already be too far gone to repair." Waterstone's eyes went out of focus for a couple of seconds. Tarkyn did not say anything but Waterstone could see he was waiting for an explanation. "I'm recruiting help. You probably didn't pick it up because it was mainly words."

Shortly afterwards, Autumn Leaves, Thunder Storm and three other woodfolk arrived. Right behind them, Sparrow came running up, carrying twine and bandages.

A woodwoman with a soft sighing voice said, "Good morning, Your Highness. I am Grass Wind."

"I am Cracking Branch," said another woodwoman with a sharp staccato voice.

"And I am Rustling Leaves," said a woodman in a voice similar to Autumn Leaves but harsher.

The prince did not rise, but inclined his head in acknowledgement. "I am pleased to meet you all."

Instead of instructions being issued, there was an intense silence followed by the woodfolk glancing sceptically at the prince. Nevertheless they then fanned out to inspect nearby trees and to climb into the branches of those that had broken boughs that could be saved.

"Ready, Your Highness," instructed Waterstone cheerfully. "Let's see this magic of yours. Start with mine. As soon as I have it partly secured, you can move onto the next one."

The sorcerer nodded, waited until the woodman was ready in the tree, held out a finger and incanted, "L*iefka!*" A shaft of bronze power raised the bough into position.

"It won't burn if I touch that beam, will it?" queried Waterstone suddenly.

"Don't you think I would have told you if there was any danger?"

"You might have assumed I'd know."

"No. After the acorn episode, I wouldn't assume anything about your knowledge of my magic. Don't worry; I will remember to tell you if there is anything that might harm you....Now, can we get on with it?"

Waterstone grinned and immediately set to work with the twine. After a while, Tarkyn worked out that once he had one branch held in place with a steady shaft of power, he could transfer his focus and use his other hand to create a second shaft of magic to raise another branch. He was not used to performing two spells at once and he found that it required intense concentration. Once a broken branch was bound in place, Sparrow would tap him on whichever hand was supporting that branch and he would know to transfer his power and attention to a new location. When all the trees in a thirty yard radius of Tarkyn had been repaired as well as possible, everyone took a break while the sorcerer hauled himself up and moved to a new position. Once he had seated himself in a new location, the process started again.

When they broke for lunch, there was notably less restraint in the attitude of the other woodfolk. The work continued deep into the afternoon until Waterstone noticed that the branch he was trying to secure kept wavering out of place. He sent a mental image of the problem to Tarkyn and received back such a weak response that he immediately sent an urgent query to Sparrow. Sparrow transmitted an image of Tarkyn's face, which was deathly white with dark smudges under his drooping eyes. As one, the woodfolk descended from the trees to return to Tarkyn's side where he was seated, leaning against a tree.

Waterstone passed the exhausted sorcerer a drink. "Why didn't you tell us you were tiring? I didn't realise you would be tired, just sitting there sending up shafts of light."

Tarkyn blinked owlishly up at him, almost drunk with tiredness. "In case you hadn't noticed, I've been lifting tree branches and holding them up in the air all day."

"Doesn't the magic do that for you?"

"Yes and no. But where do you think the power comes from?"

"Oh dear," said Waterstone, "We've made another wrong assumption about your magic, haven't we?"

"I believe we have tired you excessively, Your Highness," rumbled Thunder Storm.

"You look like a corpse," observed Autumn Leaves, with his characteristic lack of tact. "Do you have enough strength to walk?"

Tarkyn leant his head back against the tree and closed his eyes. "I don't know. Maybe in a while." He opened his eyes and gave a tired smile. "At least we've repaired a lot of trees, haven't we? I'm sorry I can't keep going but I'm afraid that's the end of the road for me today."

A gentle chorus of forest sounds let him know that they were all pleased with what had been done and reassured him that they were all tired too and ready to stop for the day anyway. With a satisfied sigh, the overtaxed young sorcerer drifted off to sleep.

Tarkyn woke to find himself in the dark, still leaning against the tree. In that moment of disorientation between sleep and wakefulness, his mind jolted with alarm as the memory of the last time he had awakened out in the open in the forest flooded through him.

"Whoa," said Waterstone as he received a wave of Tarkyn's reaction, "It's all right. We're all here. We haven't left you on your own this time."

As Tarkyn became wider awake, he realised that a fire was crackling cheerfully a short distance away and there was a lovely aroma of roasting meat wafting through the air. He hauled himself up and wandered over to join the woodfolk sitting at the fire.

He turned a perplexed face to Waterstone."Where are all the others? There were many more people here when I first arrived in the forest."

"We don't usually congregate in such large numbers," explained the woodman. "We were all gathered for your welcoming feast. But aside from that, most of the gatherer woodfolk have gone up to the east of the forest to harvest the blackberries. The harvesters are collecting the last of the summer flowers and will soon move further north for the sweet chestnuts and hazelnuts. And the rest of the wanderers could be anywhere by now, gathering information and taking wares from one group to the next as they go."

Tarkyn took a few moments to absorb this then asked, "But aren't there blackberries here? My shelter is in the middle of a big patch of them. Why aren't the harvesters still here?"

Waterstone nodded. "The best crops are in particular areas. So the harvesters and gatherers tend to move around with the seasons to gather the best harvests."

Autumn Leaves brought him a cup of wine. The prince thanked him and asked, "So how many of you have stayed here?"

"There are twenty of us still here, my lord," replied Autumn Leaves. "Ten men, six women and four children."

"And on what basis did you people choose to stay rather than go with the others?"

The woodfolk all looked at each other, then eyes went out of focus as they conferred mentally with each other. Tarkyn picked up a feeling of embarrassment but no explanation.

"Well?"

"Well… " said Waterstone, clearing his throat, "It was done on a voluntary basis. Basically, those of us who were least frightened or least resentful of you stayed to look after you and protect you."

Tarkyn picked up a wave of consternation rolling around the campsite in the wake of Waterstone's words. The sorcerer raised his eyebrows and swung his eyes slowly around the group. "Don't worry. I know where I stand with you people, particularly after talking with Waterstone earlier about your experience of sorcerers. I can appreciate what a courageous decision it was to stay anywhere near me. I don't think my behaviour on the first day in the woods did anything to improve matters. I can only say that I am not usually in the habit of throwing my weight around as I did that day."

Unexpectedly, Thunder Storm came to his support. "Prince Tarkyn was very careful with his use of power yesterday when there was a need to calm Waterstone."

"No one was fearful today when you were using your power, at least not once we became used to it," added Grass Wind.

There was a lull in the conversation as the roasted meat was taken off the fire and thick slices were handed around with small, soft loaves of warm bread.

After a period of silent concentration on eating, the prince looked around the group thoughtfully then asked, "So what would you do next time if another group of sorcerer bounty hunters threatened me? What can you do against sorcerers' shields?"

"You'd probably know the answer to that better than us." Waterstone pointed out. "What can we do?"

The sorcerer shrugged. "Not much with bows and arrows, and you can't break through their shields and grab them." He paused while he thought about it. "A shield takes power and focus. Most sorcerers can't maintain them for long, if at all. Those who can, would eventually run out of power but possibly not for a long time. It's not as hard to maintain a shield, as it is to lift tree branches, for instance. If you could hold the sorcerers somehow until they went to sleep, they would be vulnerable. We can't maintain our shields while we're asleep."

"What about using nets or misleading them so they can't find their way out of the forest until they tire?" asked Rustling Leaves.

"Yes. That would work." Tarkyn frowned. "But what would you do with them once they were asleep? If you kill them, mightn't someone come looking for them?"

"For that very reason, killing them would be the last resort," said Waterstone. "Keeping you hidden is the simplest solution. It works for us. We may need to teach you some of our camouflaging techniques. How are you at climbing trees?"

The sorcerer smiled, and incanting "*Mayareeza Mureva,*" rose gently into the air and drifted into the nearest tree. "Not bad," he said, grinning down at them.

"Good. That's sorted then," continued Waterstone with a completely straight face. "So now we have to deal with your hair..." He broke off and stood looking up at the sorcerer with his hands on his hips, laughing. "Get down from there before you fall down. You're too tired to go mucking about in trees tonight."

Tarkyn floated gracefully back down, staggering slightly as he landed. "Whoops! You may be right, at that."

Waterstone grabbed his arm to steady him. "I think you've had about enough for your third day out of bed. Why don't we help you back to your shelter now, to save us having to carry you later?"

Tarkyn's smiled tiredly down at him and nodded.

Chapter 14

The prince suffered no ill effects from his over-exertion and for the next three days, the sorcerer and the woodfolk worked hard on repairing the damage caused by Waterstone's rage. By the afternoon of the fourth day, most of the repair work that could be done had been completed. Tarkyn was sitting under a tree directing two shafts of power up into the last group of trees that they had decided was worth working on.

Suddenly, a booming voice rang out from behind him, "What on earth do you think you're doing?"

Tarkyn jumped and both branches juddered out of place, unbalancing Waterstone and Autumn Leaves in two separate trees.

"Tarkyn!" yelped Waterstone, "Help!"

Ignoring the intrusive presence behind him, the sorcerer refocused his will and steadied both woodmen in their respective trees. Then he maintained steady shafts of power to hold the boughs in place until they were secured, despite the reproachful voice behind him that grew in intensity as it insisted on knowing what had happened to his sense of consequence. Once the branches and the woodmen were safe, the sorcerer released his power and without looking around, said politely, "Good Afternoon, Stormaway. I am sorry. I was concentrating. Could you repeat that, please?"

The wizard stomped around, to stand glaring down at the young prince. "Where is your sense of propriety?" he demanded. "A prince of the realm is not a gardener. A person of your consequence does not lower himself to working on manual tasks in the company of common woodfolk."

The prince hauled himself up from the ground until he stood looking down at the wizard from his superior height, his amber eyes blazing. There was a long silence. When Tarkyn finally spoke, his voice was pitched low and was shaking with anger. But the anger in his voice was nothing compared to the blast of rage that silently hit Stormaway's mind. "I believe you forget yourself. It is not I but you who have forgotten my consequence. I will spend my time as I choose, with whom I choose. You may offer me advice but you may not dictate to me and above all, you may not insult these people."

The wizard stared back up at him for a moment. Then his stance relaxed and he bowed low, hand on heart. "I beg your pardon, Your Highness. I am pleased to see that you have not forgotten your status completely."

The prince merely raised his eyebrows as he sent an image of his staff to Sparrow. When it arrived, Tarkyn broke eye contact with Stormaway to look down at Sparrow. He smiled and thanked her as he took hold of his staff and leant heavily on it. "Come," he invited the wizard, "Let us get settled at tonight's firesite. You must need some food and drink after your journey." Tarkyn noticed that the woodfolk had melted away into the surrounding woods. He sent out an image of a firesite coupled with a feeling of uncertainty to Waterstone and received back an image of a nearby clearing. "This way," he said as he altered the direction of his steps. As they walked, the prince commented, "I believe I have to thank you for your efforts on my behalf."

"A pleasure, Your Highness, a pleasure. Come on. I'll tell you all about it.

Once they were comfortably seated at the firesite, wine in hand and food on its way, Stormaway began his story.

"By the time the sorcerers returned to collect you, I was waiting nearby in the forest, making a lot of noise to entice them to chase me."

"How did they think I had managed to free my hands?"

Stormaway shrugged, "I don't think they did, at that stage." He took a sip of wine and gave a satisfied sigh before continuing

Tarkyn frowned, "Weren't you worried they would capture you instead?"

The wizard raised his eyebrows. "Have you so little faith in me?"

"I hardly know you," retorted the prince tartly.

"Hmph. Well, be that as it may, I was never in any danger. I didn't let them get anywhere near close enough to attack me. I just let them catch tantalizing glimpses of me running off through the trees, long black hair streaming out behind me!"

Tarkyn put his head on one side. "Go on, then. Show me how you do the hair!"

It wasn't just the hair. Right before his eyes, Stormaway's body slimmed down; his face grew longer, his cheekbones higher and hair long and black. His eyebrows blackened and swept upwards in pronounced arch. His eyes became yellower but were still greenish and nothing like Tarkyn's extraordinary amber ones. Overall, however, there was a clear resemblance that would certainly have passed muster from a distance, even more so from the back view.

The prince laughed, "That's pretty good!"

"I can do better if I spend longer on it. I can even improve the eye colour but no one I have ever met other than you and your father have those amazing amber eyes and I just don't seem to be able to replicate them." The glamour faded and the wizard's real form re-emerged. He took another sip of wine. "Ah, that's better. Can't really relax when I'm maintaining a disguise."

The sorcerer nodded slowly as he absorbed this information then asked, "So what happened after you left the forest?"

Stormaway settled down to telling the story of his escapades with the bounty hunters.

The prince's smiles of appreciation did not reach his eyes. He was too busy trying to gauge the calibre of this disingenuous wizard. When there was finally a gap in the wizard's flow, Tarkyn asked, "But didn't all this take place over two weeks ago? Where have you been since then?"

"I kept leading them further away until we reached the northwest coast. A false trail to the docks led them to believe you had left the country. So they gave up the chase."

The younger man frowned "That won't bring them back through the forest, will it?"

The wizard raised his eyebrows. "No, of course not. I wouldn't put in all that effort otherwise. No. They will travel back home well to the north of the forest edge." He regarded Tarkyn thoughtfully. "Outsiders don't usually venture into these woods unless they are in large groups or have a particular reason for doing so. Those who live near the woods know that many who have ventured in, have failed to come out."

Tarkyn looked at him sceptically. "But I thought it was very rare for woodfolk to need to kill outsiders. They're so good at staying hidden that the need rarely arises."

Stormaway swept his arm around in a semicircle. "These woods are not as benign as you may think. Many people lose their way and die from cold or lack of food in the depths of the forest. In some parts of the forest, there are savage wolves and dark creatures of the night that attack without warning. Besides these, there are refugees from justice."

"Not unlike myself," quipped the prince.

"Very unlike yourself," returned the wizard repressively, "Renegades who, as I was going to say, skulk in the woods and prey on unwary travellers."

"Oh dear," said Tarkyn, rolling his eyes. "Yet another bunch of reprehensible sorcerers that have helped to form the woodfolk's less than favourable impression of us."

Stormaway frowned. "What about the travellers? Most of them would be perfectly well-behaved sorcerers."

The prince shrugged. "True enough. Maybe the woodfolk have only seen them using magic to defend themselves against the renegades you spoke of."

"That doesn't make them bad," protested the wizard.

The sorcerer shook his head smiling. "I know it doesn't. It's just that Waterstone was shocked that magic could be used for something productive. So it made me think about how sorcerers appeared from the woodfolk's point of view." In answer to the wizard's raised, interrogative eyebrow, he answered, "Generally, not very well at all. Waterstone thought that magic was just used as a weapon. No one realised that sorcerers' magic could be used for anything else." Tarkyn grimaced, "It's been quite salutary, becoming aware of the woodfolk's impressions of us."

The wizard frowned. "I can't help deploring a lack of respect for your person that seems to have developed in my absence."

The prince raised his eyebrows with a hint of disdain. "Are you implying that respect and honesty are mutually exclusive?"

"You will not intimidate me that easily, young man," chuckled the old wizard. "It depends very much on how the honesty is delivered, wouldn't you agree?"

Tarkyn nodded shortly, thinking back to what he had said to Ancient Oak. "It was said courteously, Stormaway. We just became aware that we had different impressions of sorcerers."

Stormaway shook his head dolefully. "I should not have left you so long alone and vulnerable with these woodfolk."

"Why not?" demanded the prince, "There is the oath to protect me and they have looked after me well."

"Ah, Your Highness," The old wizard shook his head sagely, "You don't realise how people can take advantage of you. When you are alone and injured, as you have been, your emotions are rawer and your need for support is so much higher." He smiled condescendingly. "You know so little of the intricacies of personal influence within circles of power."

The prince stared at him. "What utter rot! I have spent the whole nineteen years of my life living and breathing those intricacies. You haven't even been at court for the last eleven years!" But despite his protests, Tarkyn could feel the seed of doubt implanted by Stormaway's words beginning to fester as he remembered that he was, in fact, not particularly good at discerning duplicity.

As dusk fell, the woodfolk reappeared to set the fire and gather together food for the evening's meal. The camaraderie that had developed over the last three days had been replaced by formal courtesy. Although he noted it, Tarkyn did not try to rekindle the earlier congeniality. He could see that the woodfolk had backed off as his father's faithful retainer assumed his place at the prince's side. Tarkyn suspected that the wary woodfolk would watch his interchanges with the wizard and take their time to gauge where they fitted into the new regime that Stormaway had brought back with him.

Waterstone was uncharacteristically quiet all evening and excused himself early, on the pretext of putting Sparrow to bed. However, unlike other evenings, he did not return.

While the woodfolk listened or talked amongst themselves, Stormaway spent the evening enquiring after various people he had known and encouraging the prince to tell him about his recent life at court. Now, as the prince talked about his companions and their exploits, he found himself re-evaluating every chance remark and gesture his friends and acquaintances had made. "Why am I being so hard on my old friends?" he wondered. "I wasn't betrayed by them. None of them even had the chance to choose whether or not to support me."

Then Stormaway's voice broke in on his ruminations. "I am not just asking these questions for my own entertainment, Your Highness. It helps all of us," Here he swept his arm around the gathering, "to know something of your associates if we are to serve and protect you."He paused and prodded at the fire with a stick, clearly uncertain how to continue. As he stared into the flames, he said awkwardly, "So. There is something I think you should know".

A stillness settled on the clearing.

"Yes?" Tarkyn's voice seemed unnaturally loud.

Stormaway flicked a glance at him before seeking the refuge of staring into the flames. "The two bounty hunters who kept out of sight were your friends, Andoran and Sargon." The wizard cleared his throat. "I noticed you mentioned them a few times. They seem to have been regular companions of yours from what you were saying."

The young prince felt as though he had been punched in the stomach. All his doubts clicked into place as he realised that some part of him must have recognised his unseen captors. There was an awkward silence while Tarkyn mustered his thoughts and resources to say, "They were not among my closest friends but you're right. I did spend quite a bit of time with them, one way and another. I defeated both of them in the tournament. They always did like any excuse for an adventure. I knew there were times when they were thoughtless pranksters but I never knew they were cruel." He could not keep the bitterness out of his voice, "No doubt they thought it might be a good bit of sport. At the same time they could gain favour with one or both of my brothers since they have now lost their route of influence through me. In fact they were probably very angry that my exile had ruined the value of their carefully nurtured friendship with me." Tarkyn turned bleak eyes towards the wizard who was still gazing studiously into the fire. "You see, Stormaway, this is not the first time that apparent friendships have winked out of existence when these so-called friends have realised that they would not get the influence they craved, through me." Tarkyn managed to raise a half smile as he hauled himself to his feet. "Anyway, the good thing about it is that it keeps me from having too high an opinion of myself. With all that power I wield, it would never do to be blindly arrogant as well, would it?... And now, if you'll excuse me, I will take a short walk to ease my stiffness before retiring."

Tarkyn walked away from the gentle light of the fire into the gloom of the forest, heading down to the river. He did not choose to use his sorcery to give himself light and so had to pause every few yards to allow his eyes to adjust. He heard a spate of talking break out soon after he left. From what he could tell, the woodfolk were reproaching the wizard and Stormaway was having to defend himself. In the darkness, despite himself, Tarkyn smiled.

When he reached the river, the moon had just cleared the top of the trees and had turned the river into a ribbon of silver. His whole being felt jarred by the betrayal of his erstwhile friends and their brutal treatment of him. More than this, Tarkyn's faith in his own perceptions had once more been undermined.

He sat on a rock at the river's edge and let the peace of the forest wash over him. After a while, he became aware of an otter working its way busily upstream, ducking into side pockets and sliding up and over small rocks. When it noticed Tarkyn, it did a double take then flicked out of sight under the far bank. A few minutes later its head gingerly re-emerged and it watched Tarkyn for several seconds before disappearing again. After several repeats of this performance, it glided slowly across the river and emerged right beside Tarkyn to shake itself off at his feet. Tarkyn smiled but other than that, did not dare move a muscle.

He remembered the mind linking and worked on sending out waves of friendship. The otter stared up at him and Tarkyn realised he was receiving curiosity, wariness and a dawning hint of trust.

Am I just reading this from its body language or is this animal actually sending me messages? wondered the prince.

This uncertainty was rewarded by a clear wave of irritation and a view of the river from where the otter was standing. Tarkyn raised his eyebrows in amusement, and sent ruefulness and an invitation, which the otter accepted by scuttling up the rock to sit next to him. The sorcerer visualised a tentative image of patting, and received consent. So he reached out slowly and started to stroke the otter in slow gentle movements. The otter was cold and wet under his hand and not particularly enjoyable to stroke but the wonder of being able to pat a wild otter more than made up for it.

Suddenly the otter flicked back into the water. Almost simultaneously, Tarkyn heard the thrum of a bowstring and saw an arrow streak past his face. Even as he threw up a shield and dived for cover, he heard a dull thwack and a strangled snarl as the arrow found its mark. Gasping in pain from his abused ribs, he emerged to find himself face to face with a huge black wolf, its teeth bared and its dulling, yellow eyes staring into his. Waterstone was calmly removing the arrow that stuck out of its neck.

Fear made the prince angry. "Why didn't you warn me?" he demanded.

Waterstone shrugged. "Didn't want to warn the wolf."

"Couldn't have that, could we?" returned Tarkyn sarcastically. "And you didn't feel the need to kill it before it sprang at me?"

Waterstone grinned, "Not really. Anyway, I'm not even sure it was springing at you. I got a clearer shot at it, once it came out from the trees. If I'd told you it was coming, the wolf would have known it was being watched"

"Hmph."Tarkyn digested this, not sure how keen he was on being used as bait. He flicked out his shield and ran a hand over his head. "I'm sorry. I'm just a bit shaken. Thank you for saving me."

A certain dryness in the look the woodsman sent him reminded the prince that Waterstone had no choice but to protect him. Tarkyn smiled ruefully and said, "Nothing's easy, is it?"

"No, it's not," replied Waterstone shortly, "And I hope you know that I did not kill that wolf because of the oath."

Tarkyn smiled, "Well, obviously not. You were just protecting the otter, weren't you?"

Waterstone shook his head and smothered a smile as he walked down the few steps to the river. As the woodman crouched at the water's edge, rinsing his arrow tip, Tarkyn suddenly became aware of an unnatural stillness around them and received an image from a viewpoint within the overhanging branches. A dark shape, slinking low and dangerous, was closing in on Waterstone from the other side.

"Stay down," ordered Tarkyn sharply. As the wolf emerged from the trees, the sorcerer yelled, "*Fierspa!*" and threw a blast of power at it. The wolf recoiled howling in shock and pain, but regrouped and sprang at the crouching woodman, who had whirled to face it, knife in hand. Another wild streak of fire slammed it to the ground and this time it didn't move.

Waterstone sprang to his feet, knife at the ready and stood staring down at the smoking wolf."Stars above!That was careless. The lookouts spotted the first wolf coming this way but I assumed it was alone." He shook his head, "It is unusual to see this type of timber wolf so far east. Usually they are either sole travellers or in packs. Not this time, apparently. The lookouts must have missed this one while they were watching the other."

The sorcerer frowned. "I thought I was warned by a lookout. Isn't there one up in the overhanging trees over there?" he asked, pointing to the patch of forest the wolf had come from. Just then, a large tawny owl took off from the trees in that area and swooped down over him before heading off across the river to hunt. The sorcerer picked up a wave of approval as it flew past.

Waterstone turned puzzled eyes on the prince. "There are no lookouts this close to us. What warned you?"

"Maybe the silence. Maybe I caught a flash of its eye." Tarkyn wondered about the owl but didn't feel sure enough to mention it. He shrugged. "Maybe I saw a shadow moving. I don't know."

The woodman considered him silently for several moments. "I guess it's my turn to thank you," he said quietly. "I might have to revise my opinion of sorcerers. You're definitely becoming an asset. Thank you."

"A pleasure." Tarkyn smiled as he walked over to join Waterstone in looking down at the singed carcass. "That wolf took a lot of stopping, though. That power blast would have knocked most men or beasts unconscious with a direct hit like that. Are there likely to be any more?"

"I would hope not, but I think we'll put on extra lookouts until morning." Waterstone's eyes lost focus as he relayed this message. When the woodman's eyes cleared, he returned to the river's edge and crouched down again, arrow in hand.

"So what brings you down here?" the prince asked. "I thought you were going to bed."

Waterstone looked at Tarkyn over his shoulder before calmly returning his attention to cleaning his arrow. "I did go back to be with Sparrow for a while and I decided to stay there. I didn't want the wizard focusing on me as a potential rival for your attention. He needs a bit of time to piss on his tree."

"Me being the tree, I presume?"

Waterstone smiled, "I'm afraid so" He turned back to the river to give his arrow a final shake to clear it of excess water and walked up to sit near Tarkyn. "Autumn Leaves mind told me about the identity of the bounty hunters. When you left to walk down here, we thought I should come down and see how you were. I hadn't decided whether or not to intrude on your solitude to talk to you, but events made the decision for me." Waterstone saw the prince thinking this through and added, "To forestall any suspicions you might have about Autumn Leaves' motives, I might point out that he has no expectation that I would tell you of his concern." The woodman grimaced, "In fact, I don't think he would be very pleased to find out that I had told you."

"I had already figured that out, actually." The prince grinned sheepishly

The woodman shook his head ruefully. "I knew it. You can't take anything at face value. You have to analyse everyone's actions to the last detail."

Tarkyn snorted derisively. "Do you blame me? Especially tonight, after what Stormaway told me. Andoran and Sargon have been amongst my circle of friends for years. They may not have been my closest friends and I may not have liked everything they did, but I would never have expected this of them." He ran his hand through his hair. "And yet no matter how hard I try to second-guess people's motives and protect myself, look what happens."

Waterstone shook his head slowly. "No, I don't blame you. The longer I know you, the more I understand why you do it." He shrugged, "I just think it's a shame that those stinking sorcerers have jaundiced your view of people so much."

The princes raised his eyebrows, "And are woodfolk so far above reproach, then?"

"Of course they're not, though I think they're better. All right. I'll retract that. It's not sorcerers or woodfolk. It's the power that corrupts the people around you."

"That's a refreshing point of view, Waterstone," remarked Tarkyn caustically. "It is generally held to be the power wielder who is corrupted by the power."

Waterstone eyed him thoughtfully. "Considering your family, I would have to say there's a lot of truth in that. However, power does not corrupt everyone within its sphere and therein lies your hope. Except for your deep-seated and let's face it, justifiable paranoia, I think your integrity remains remarkably unscathed by the power you wield and there will be people around you whose integrity overrides the lure of power." Waterstone picked up a stone and threw it forcefully into the river. "Your problem is finding out who they are."

The prince stared out silently across the river. He was quiet for so long that Waterstone nudged him to see if he had gone to sleep. Tarkyn came out of his reverie with a start. "Ow! Don't forget the ribs!" He rubbed his side. "I was thinking back over all the times I spent with Andoran and Sargon, trying to find the clues that should have alerted me. People are so good at prevaricating. Either that, or I'm easily fooled." He swung haunted eyes around to regard the woodman. "I feel as though

I'm walking in quicksand. Each step is sucking me in deeper and deeper until finally I'll have nothing solid left to hang onto."

Waterstone knew it would be pointless to reassure Tarkyn of his friendship. He cursed the invidious people who had so often betrayed the young man's trust. Overwhelmed with frustration, the woodman leapt to his feet and started pacing back and forth. Finally, he stopped and stood staring down at the prince, his hands on his hips. "There must be some way to test people, to decipher their motives." He paced up and down a few more times, then came back to stand over the prince, completely oblivious to the breach of etiquette he was committing. "What about the mind linking? You've never had that at your disposal before. What do you pick up? Images and feelings? Could you use that to check someone's motives?"

Tarkyn focused on Waterstone for a minute, then shook his head. "I don't know. All I can pick up from you is exasperation and frustration. The thinking component is missing. So I can't know from mind linking whether you're frustrated out of care for me or because you can't get me to trust you so that you can use me." Seeing Waterstone's quick frown, Tarkyn hastened to add, "I'm not saying that's what I think. I'm just showing you the limitations."

The woodman stared at him for a minute before resuming his pacing. The next time he stopped, he asked, "But it could be useful in some situations, couldn't it? You might discern nervousness or feelings of guilt, for instance?"

Tarkyn nodded. "Yes. I can imagine times when it could be quite revealing."

"Hmph" Waterstone set off on his pacing again. Then he stopped abruptly, looking out over the river. He stood there for several seconds before turning slowly to face the prince.

"What if you could search through a person's memories? Through all their impressions and feelings?"

"Tree Wind showed me some of her memory," said Tarkyn slowly. "It certainly revealed her antipathy, although it was only a short segment." He frowned. "She could equally have shown me a bland unrevealing memory if she had chosen to be duplicitous. I can see two difficulties with that idea. I don't have whole lifetime to spend viewing someone else's lifetime of memories and it is very intrusive. I could not demand it of anyone."

The woodman came back and sat down opposite the prince. "Memories don't use up real time and many similar memories tend to compress into one impression with the changes in attitudes overlaying them. Even so, you're right. A whole lifetime of memories would take too long." He paused while he thought it through, "So, what if the person gave his permission freely and you chose which segments to view?"

Tarkyn did not pretend to misunderstand the woodman. He eyed Waterstone. "I couldn't ask it of you."

"But would it convince you?"

The young prince studied the woodman for a long time, as he searched for possible loopholes. He turned his head look out across the silvery river. Finally, he returned his gaze to Waterstone. "Yes. It would."

Waterstone took a deep breath, let it out, then said formally, "Then I freely give you access to whatever of my memories that you wish to view."

"But if I do this, it will be difficult for you, won't it?"

"Yes. It will. I am placing great faith in you to allow you to do it. But it will be even more difficult to keep living with your continual mistrust. You have no notion how hard it is not to feel hurt, each time there's an indication that you don't trust me."

"Oh Waterstone, I am so sorry!" Tarkyn ran his hands through his hair. "And I wish I could say that your offer alone were enough."

Waterstone gave a sad smile. "But I know it is not and I knew, when I offered, that it would not be. Sooner or later, the suspicion would cross your mind that I might have banked on you not taking up my offer."

Tarkyn grimaced. "Stars above! I am hard work, aren't I? I don't think my company is very good for you. You're starting to learn my warped thinking patterns." He took a deep breath and looked the woodman. "Very well. I accept your offer. When?"

Waterstone's eyes went slightly out of focus for a few seconds as he checked with the lookouts. He re-focused and said, "Now. If I have to wait, I'll get too nervous."

Tarkyn frowned, "Are you sure about this?"

The woodman nodded shortly. "Come on. Just get on with it. When and what do you want to see first?"

The prince didn't hesitate. "My father's visit to the forest."

"All of it?"

"From just after the oath is given."

"Right. Relax and look into my eyes."

The king's and the little prince's final words die away. The king stands glowering over us as we kneel before him. My stomach feels tight and sick. We all stare at this tyrant who has come among us. No one can think of anything to say.

Suddenly, the king's whole demeanour changes. He smiles benignly around him and rubs his hands together.

"Good!" he exclaims, "Now that is settled, we had better get started on helping you people to recover." He stands up from the table. "Stormaway! Get your herbs, medicines, whatever. Quickly, man! We have work to do."

The king raises his eyebrows until I realise that he is waiting to be shown where to go. I lead him to the nearest shelter. He has to duck to enter, and then the restricted height forces him to kneel down at the bedside of a sick woodwoman. He looks at me. "Her name?"

"Cracking Branch, Your Majesty."

"Hmph. How long have you been ill, Cracking Branch?"

"About four days, Your Majesty."

"And how are you feeling?"

"I don't have any strength left and my head and limbs are all aching."

In a surprisingly gentle voice, the king says, "Let me assure you that help is on its way." He looks over his shoulder towards the entrance and frowns ferociously. "Where is that dratted wizard? Ah, Stormaway. Took your time, man. Now, what are we doing for these folk?"

Stormaway produces a quantity of various herbs and hands them to me. "Can you boil some water and make a strong tea with these, please? We also need flannels or rags and bowls of cold water to bathe people's foreheads to reduce the fever."

I emerge from the shelter to be surrounded by wide-eyed woodfolk. I ignore their questions and organise the wizard's requirements.

After this, Tarkyn experienced a blur of memories, all similar, with the king visiting every sick person, reassuring them in his bluff manner, and ensuring that they received treatment. Tarkyn could feel Waterstone's attitude to the king gradually shifting from horror and distress to reluctant respect and admiration as the king persevered through the night and deep into the next day without a break. Then the memory became clear again.

The king enters a shelter to kneel at the bedside of a young woodwoman with gentle green eyes and a musical voice, my wife.

"Good morning, Your Majesty. I am Skylark."

"Good morning Skylark. How long have you been ill?"

"Not as long as many others. Only three days but it is very wearying."

The king takes her hand. "Well, I hope you will recover soon with this fine tea that young Waterstone has summoned up for you."

I smile at her and give her the tea. The king looks from one to the other of us and raises his eyebrows. "You know each other, I gather."

We both grin and chorus, "Yes, Your Majesty."

"Hmph, well, Skylark. You should be proud of this young man. He has worked with me through the night to bring aid to those of you who are sick."

Skylark smiles and says, "I am."

I leave the shelter with her voice ringing in my ears.

Tarkyn pulled out of the memory and gave Waterstone time to recover. The woodman had tears in his eyes as the prince smiled mistily at him. "I'm sorry. That must have been hard for you to remember Skylark."

"It is, but no worse than all the other times I remember her."

Tarkyn sniffed, "It is also hard for me, seeing my father like that. It's clearer than any memories I have of him."

Waterstone cocked his head to one side. "I suppose it would be. I hadn't thought of that."

Tarkyn gave a small smile. "It's one of the reasons I drank so much at the feast that first night. I'd just seen my father in Tree Wind's memory and even though he must seem ruthless and bombastic to you, I still miss him."

"He was ruthless and bombastic, as you put it, but he was also dedicated and passionate and true to his word that he would care for our people," replied the woodman. He walked down to the water's edge and splashed water on his face and hair. Then he returned and unloaded an earthen bottle and two cups from his knapsack. "I've just remembered. I brought provisions with me in case I decided to sit and talk with you." He poured golden liquid into a cup and offered it to the prince. "Wine?"

Tarkyn accepted it and took a long draught. "Thanks. This is quite a torrid process, isn't it?"

Waterstone looked at him for a moment, then dropped his eyes to his cup. "Yes, it is." He took a deep breath and looked up. "Where next?"

"When you first saw me a couple of weeks ago."

The prince caught a flicker of hesitation but Waterstone closed his eyes, composed himself then looked unwaveringly into Tarkyn's eyes, "All right. But I warn you, you may not like some of this. Look deeply and relax."

It is a soft sunny afternoon. We are posted in the trees near the eastern edge of the forest awaiting the arrival of this renegade prince whom we may have to serve. We have heard dire tales of his misdeeds and we are hopeful that he will not survive Stormaway's testing. He appears around a bend in the road, walking in the company of Stormaway and talking. This prince is very tall; his hair is black like a raven and very long. He glances up into the trees and I see his father's face and electrifying eyes. Yet despite his bulk, his demeanour is not intimidating as he bends slightly so that he can hear what the wizard has to say.

An impression of mental discussion reached Tarkyn but no words. He pulled out of the memory and instructed, "Now, that same evening from where I try to leave and you woodfolk stop me."

This time, the memory was images with a running thought commentary.

We have taken an irrevocable step in revealing ourselves. Either he will die or he will rule us. His shield will not save him against Stormaway's and our combined forces. Even though I know which way Stormaway's judgement will go, my heart sinks as I hear the words, "He has passed my final test." We make a desperate plea to Stormaway to postpone the final sealing of the binding spell. We have to be sure, before we are forced to accept this young inexperienced sorcerer as our liege lord: we who do not even have leaders among ourselves. I am almost old enough to be his father. Suddenly, he waves his arm. My heart leaps in fear and I flick into the cover of the trees. Silly young man looks surprised that we have vanished. What does he expect? The wizard is not getting things all his own way, for a change. This prince is nobody's fool. Stormaway's attempt to force his hand by threatening to make him leave the forest fails signally. The young man calls his bluff immediately. Stormaway is right. He is arrogant and easily angered but so far, only when he's challenged. He has a better sense of humour than Stormaway and he is smarter and better at manipulating people than his father. Therefore, possibly more dangerous.

Tarkyn broke contact. "On my oath, Waterstone! You're more calculating than I am."

The woodsman rubbed his eyes with the back of his hand. "I would say analytical, not calculating. I was, after all, trying to work out what the future held for us all." His voice sounded tired and despondent.

The prince frowned in concern. "Are you all right? Do you want to continue at another time?"

Again Waterstone stared at him then dropped his eyes. He sighed. "No. I couldn't do this again. Not like this, being judged. It's now or never. I just hope you don't end up trusting me but disliking me." He took a long pull on his wine with a hand that trembled, then closed his eyes to gather his resources. When he was ready, he opened them and looked once more at Tarkyn.

Tarkyn thought hard. He realised that more than one extra memory might push the woodman too far. He would like to know Waterstone's reaction to his display of temper when he had frozen the woodfolk and threatened them all but he decided on balance that he would gain more from seeing the woodman's memory of the time when Tarkyn was injured.

"Very well, one more only. Your memories of being with me from when I translocated up into the oak tree."

There is a sound like rushing air above us. We look up and see Prince Tarkyn suddenly appear way up in the boughs of the tree. My stomach lurches with horror knowing that he will fall and there is nothing we can do to prevent it. He hits branches on the way down with a series of sickening thuds. I cannot imagine that he will survive. I fear for his survival but even more for what his death will mean to the forest. When he lands, he is deathly pale and barely breathing. I cut his bonds and organise a litter. Summer Rain attends him. She gently feels around his chest and places some strapping around his side. She manipulates his shoulder back into place and straps it.It is probably just as well that he is not conscious for this part. Summer Rain leaves instructions for his care and moves on to attend to the others who have been wounded by his fall. There is a delay in moving the prince while a larger shelter is constructed to house him. We are all anxious and realise that we have been forced to taken on a bigger responsibility than we had expected.

Many memories of coming to check on the prince and talking to people around him blur into one general theme. The predominant feeling moves from fear for the forest and the life of the prince, to compassion for his suffering.

I watch him grimace with pain after he gags trying to eat and I sit with him as he thrashes around in the night, reliving horrors of bounty hunters and his arraignment before his brothers. I start talking to him to calm his distress. As he hovers in some twilight world between waking and sleeping, I gradually tell him everything about me and about the woodfolk. I feel I have let him into my world and trusted him with things I have needed to say but have never said to another. Then he awakens fully and the reality of who he is opens a yawning gap between us. I am jolted by his mistrust and realise that my imagined friendship with him is all in my mind and not in his.

Suddenly, Tarkyn found himself back at the river at night. Waterstone had closed his eyes to break contact. Before Tarkyn could re-orient himself, Waterstone scrambled to his feet with an uncharacteristic lack of grace and disappeared into the trees. The prince was left sitting alone, shaken by the depth of feeling in Waterstone's memory and wondering what to do next. He did not have long to wait.

Twenty minutes later, Autumn Leaves came trundling down the track and plonked himself down near the prince. "Evening, Your Highness."

"Good evening," replied Tarkyn uncertainly.

Autumn Leaves stared earnestly at the sorcerer. "Now I know you're a high and mighty sorcerer and you can burn me to a crisp or throw me about or whatever takes your fancy, but I'll risk all that to protect my friends."

The sorcerer in question looked blankly at him and said faintly, "I applaud your courage." When there was no further response, he asked, "Which of your friends needs protecting?" although he felt sure he knew the answer.

The solid woodman eyed him belligerently. "You know perfectly well I mean Waterstone. I don't know what spells you've magicked on him but he's a total wreck. He looks, I don't know, wounded, like a whipped cur…even though there's not a mark on him that I can see. His hands are shaking so badly I had to pour the wine down his throat myself. So what do you have to say for yourself?"

The sorcerer's face had stiffened with shock. "Autumn Leaves, I promise you, I have not used my magic on him. It is his magic, not mine, that has led to this."

The woodman glared at the sorcerer scornfully. "I am surprised that you would try to dodge your responsibility for this. You must know we do not have any magic."

"Oh yes, you do," Tarkyn gave a slight smile. "It's just so natural to you that you don't think of it as magic. You mind talk and use mindpower to control people and you can let people see your memories. I suspect you have other magic that helps you disappear into the woods but I'm not sure about that yet."

Autumn Leaves continued to stare at the sorcerer as he absorbed this information. "Hmph," he said at last, "but none of this tells me what has happened to my friend."

Tarkyn hesitated. Somehow he felt he might be betraying Waterstone's confidence if he told Autumn Leaves what had happened. He was beginning to think that Autumn Leaves would not approve of Waterstone's actions. The prince was prepared to deal with Autumn Leave's disapproval but he didn't want to put Waterstone in that position, especially now.

Tarkyn drew a deep breath, "If I tell you, I don't want you to remonstrate with Waterstone for what he has chosen to do. You can say what you like to me but not to Waterstone unless we agree it together." He paused, "Do I have your agreement?"

Autumn Leaves narrowed his eyes as he considered his options, then nodded. "I can't imagine that I would want to get angry with Waterstone anyway."

The prince kept his eyes on the woodman. "Waterstone allowed me to see some of his memories."

The woodman shrugged. "So? I've often done that to pass on information. I can't see a problem with that."

"Waterstone allowed me to choose which memories. He gave me free rein to see whatever I asked for."

Autumn Leaves froze. The sorcerer could see him imagining what it would be like to have his memories unprotected by his own choice. He gave a low whistle. "For pity's sake, I hope you at least negotiated it with him, gave him some kind of veto."

The prince shook his head, "No negotiation. Purely my decision."

Autumn Leaves blinked. "You're not going to tell me you've been trawling his memory ever since those wolves were killed, are you?"

Watching the anger gathering in the woodman's eyes, Tarkyn winced inwardly as he nodded. "He wanted to prove to me that I could trust him."

The storm broke. Autumn Leaves did not rage as Waterstone would have done. Instead he slated the prince carefully with biting scorn. "So you have violated a man's innermost privacy, cast aside the layers of protection that keep him strong, and safe against the world. And how long did you subject him to this flaying of his soul? Three hours? I can understand that you might need a gesture of good faith to earn your trust – but three hours? You either have no imagination or you're an utter bastard or both."

The prince sat white-faced as the woodman slammed home to him what he had done. "Oh no! Oh, for pity's sake," he breathed as he bowed his head beneath his hands, "I think I'm both." He lifted his head to look the woodman resolutely in the eye, "I knew he was finding it difficult. I suggested postponing but I never offered to finish it even when he started to worry that I wouldn't like him."

Autumn Leaves snorted derisively. "I'm not surprised he was worried. Now you've seen parts of him that should never have been seen by anyone else." He scowled at the prince. "I don't much care whether he has earned your trust. Personally, I think the cost was way too high. But you had better make sure you earn his trust."

Tarkyn looked away towards the river but its silver beauty brought him no comfort. "I fear I have already betrayed his trust by abusing the gift he offered me." He put his forehead in his hands. "Oh Waterstone, I'm so sorry." After a moment, he raised his head with an air of decision. "Can you send a message to him for me? I can only send feelings and images and I need to send him some words."

"I believe you said that we would agree together what is said to Waterstone?" Autumn Leaves raised his eyebrows. "I presume that still stands?"

"Of course it does. I need you to help me repair this mess, Autumn Leaves. I didn't mean to hurt him. I just took a lot of convincing. But in my need to have someone to trust, I forgot to look after him." He thought carefully how to phrase what he wanted to say. Although he hadn't told Autumn Leaves, he felt sure that the very last part of the memories he had seen were the main cause of Waterstone's distress. "Will you tell him that he has earned my trust beyond any doubt and that there is no aspect I saw that I disliked? He is welcome to the poor opinions he has had of me and they come as no surprise. – And tell him that, in my mind, he is one of the best, truest people I have ever known and I am proud to be his friend." He cocked his head to one side. "And that I am sorry….Will you agree to send that? Will it help or should I just go and talk to him?"

Autumn Leaves shook his head decisively. "He wouldn't let you anywhere near him at the moment. He's too raw. I will send your message as long as you really mean it and are not just saying it to make him feel better."

The prince stared at him. "Of course I mean it. I wouldn't dream of saying something like that if I didn't mean it. I could easily find something tactful but less emphatic to say if I needed to."

The woodman's eyes lost focus for several seconds.

"That took a while," commented Tarkyn.

"I replayed the whole conversation from where you said you needed my help right up to where you said you could think of something less emphatic to say." The woodman smiled for the first time since he arrived. "Pictures and sound."

The sorcerer raised his eyebrows. "That's impressive. I didn't know you could replay whole scenes. I thought you could only send events as they happened."

"No. You can send old memories too, if you want to. Helpful if someone needs directions to somewhere you have been before."

"I suppose so." A silence fell. Then Tarkyn asked, "Do you think Waterstone will respond to the message?"

The woodman shook his head. "I doubt it. Not tonight anyway. Give him time. He almost has to re-assemble himself, I'd say." For a solid man, Autumn Leaves rose nimbly to his feet. "Anyway, I'd better go back and see how he is." He gave a little smile. "Thank you for not burning me to a crisp."

The sorcerer waved a dismissive hand and returned a rueful smile. "A pleasure. Thank you for coming to sort it out with me. I'll see you tomorrow."

For a long while, Tarkyn sat there thinking through all that had happened that day; repairing the trees with the woodfolk, Stormaway's arrival and disapproval, learning of his friends' treachery, Waterstone's sacrifice and now, Autumn Leaves intervention. He was glad Stormaway hadn't seen the interaction with Autumn Leaves.

These woodfolk weren't used to being ruled. They had no ruling class of their own and no experience of royalty. Even with the threat of the oath and his power hanging over them, they still confronted him and let him know when they weren't pleased. It wasn't just Waterstone who showed his anger, as it turned out. He thought back and realised he had probably been too harsh with Thunder Storm. Passing judgement on the prince's actions seemed to be as natural as breathing for all of them.

They were courteous to him – when they weren't angry with him, he added wryly – but when he thought about it, they were just as courteous to each other. The only real difference was the use of his title. They had given him a bigger shelter because of his size but it was not grander and he suspected that he had been waited on only because he was ill.

Now Stormaway had blustered back in, throwing around expectations of both his and the woodfolk's behaviour. Despite the justification that Stormaway had given for enquiring into activities at court, Tarkyn was fairly sure that the wizard's main motivation had been to impress the woodfolk and set him, the prince, apart from them. That being the case, it had probably been a tactical error to speak about Andoran and Sargon since their treachery had tarnished the mystique of court life Stormaway was trying to build up.

Tarkyn thought about the servants, the grand banquets and balls, the exquisite furnishings and clothes he had left behind. He thought about the ordinary everyday artisans and workers he had barely brushed up against and the nobles and courtiers who had been his constant companions. With a smile, he thought about his thieving family and wondered how they had spent the money.

He remembered that he had told the woodfolk on the first night that he would make clear his expectations. In theory, the prince could demand that he should be treated with greater respect, be waited on hand and foot as he was used to. In theory, he could insist that the woodfolk lowered their eyes, bowed in his presence and performed all the obsequities that he had taken for granted in his past life. In reality, he knew he could not.

On the other hand, although he did not dislike the unaccustomed familiarity of the woodfolk, the prince did not think he could ever accept simply being on equal terms with them, as they were with each other. And there were many tasks he had no intention of ever doing himself.

In the dark, Tarkyn smiled wryly as he pulled himself stiffly to his feet. It was a little levelling to discover that, after all his discussion with Waterstone, in actual fact he liked and needed his power and would feel too vulnerable without it. Of course, it was his refusal to lose his magical powers that landed him here in the first place but now he had the added, greater power of the oath. Tarkyn was dismayed to realise that, even though the oath was so extreme in its consequences, he was not ready to lose the power it gave him. Without the oath, he knew the woodfolk, with a few possible exceptions, would almost certainly kill him now that he knew of their existence, particularly if he tried to leave. But it wasn't that. With a mixed sense of shame and excitement, he knew that he liked the power for its own sake. After a lifetime of living in the shadow of his brothers or his father, for the first time he was the indisputable seat of ultimate power. *Stars above!* he thought, *I hope Waterstone hasn't overestimated me.* As he walked stiffly back up the path to his shelter, it crossed his mind that there would be interesting days ahead as he strove to find a balance.

Part 3: Guardian of the Forest

CHAPTER 15

Driving rain pounded on the roof of Tarkyn's shelter all morning. At some point, a plate of bread and soft cheese accompanied by a jug of berry juice was thrust into his tent with a brief "Good Morning," but no one came in. After four days of repairing trees, followed by the discovery of Andoran and Sargon's duplicity and his run-in with Autumn Leaves, Tarkyn was quite happy to spend the morning in bed.

When the rain passed, he lay listening to the birdsong around him until the gruff voice of the wizard sounded at the entrance to his shelter.

"Come on, young Sire. You can't lie abed all day. Rain's stopped. Sun's out...well, most of the time anyway."

Tarkyn grumbled to himself, but he was used to being ordered around by familiar retainers, whose lives revolved around his. As soon as he emerged from the bramble patch, Stormaway pounced on him. "I thought you might like to see some little concoctions I am experimenting with."

Rubbing his face, Tarkyn looked around at the glistening leaves, damp logs and mud underfoot. The air was lively with the chirruping of small birds, cheerful after the rain. The woodfolk were nowhere in sight.

As he began to walk towards Stormaway, the wizard said, "Sire, if you wouldn't mind, stand on stones as much as possible, especially after rain. It reduces the amount of work required to hide your presence, if strangers should happen by."

The prince was grumpy at being woken up, so he snapped, "Stormway, I have a whole nation of people to look after my needs. I am sure they can find the time to disguise my footsteps. After all, I have made few demands on them so far and their service is casual, to say the least." Nevertheless, from then on, he did try to minimise the trail he left behind him.

Stormaway led him to an array of small bottles that he had laid out on a tree stump. "Now Sire, stand back a few feet and watch while I have a little dabble with these new potions I picked up on my last trip."

He spooned out a small quantity of bright yellow powder from a little packet onto a tiny dish. Then he unstoppered one of the bottles and poured a few drops of magenta liquid onto the powder. At first nothing happened. Then the powder began to fizz and a pungent smell wafted out from the dish.

Tarkyn coughed and his eyes watered, "Ugh Stormaway. That's vile. What's it for?"

Stormaway grinned, "I don't know. I'm just playing. But I would say a larger quantity of that could be quite debilitating, wouldn't you?" He produced a small tattered book and wrote furiously in it. When he had finished, he looked up, "Ready for another one?"

This time, he mixed silver and white powders together before pouring a thick, light blue liquid over them. Nothing happened. This did not seem to perturb the wizard. He hummed to himself as he worked the powders and liquid into a thick paste. Then he rolled it into a small damp ball and placed it in the palm of his hand.

"Ready, Your Highness?" With that, he threw it hard onto the ground.

There was a blinding flash of light and a loud report.

When the smoke cleared, Tarkyn found himself surrounded by woodfolk, facing the wizard with arrows drawn.

Stormaway was chuckling to himself, quite unconcerned, "Whoops! A bit more potent than I anticipated. I think I've singed my eyebrows." He smiled approvingly at the woodfolk. "Very quick. I felicitate you."

Thunder Storm scowled at him, "Stormaway, you play fast and loose with our prince and our forest. Desist."

"Hmm. You do have a point. I had better be a little more careful." The wizard bowed slightly to the prince, "Your Highness, I think it might be better if you watch from further away next time. I really didn't mean to put you at risk."

The woodfolk put away their arrows and turned to the prince.

"I hope that wasn't too casual for you, Your Highness," said Thunder Storm with awful sarcasm.

Before Tarkyn could reply, they had disappeared. The prince was left feeling torn between chagrin and anger.

Woodfolk turned up briefly for lunch but remained reticent. Tarkyn could think of nothing to say to bridge the widening gap, since their disappearance without his leave had effectively proved his remark.

Eventually, he said, "I am sorry that I spoke about you instead of to you."

Summer Rain gave a small sniff, "I doubt it. I expect you are just embarrassed that you were caught out."

"Summer Rain," cut in Stormaway. "You clearly have no idea of the honour it is to have a prince apologize to you."

"Thank you Stormaway. I will manage my own affairs, if you don't mind." The wizard's interference had done nothing to improve matters. Tarkyn tried again. "You people are very quick at responding to perceived threat."

"Yes, we are," rumbled Thunder Storm. "We have to be."

Tarkyn wasn't sure if this was a reference to the oath or their secretive way of life. Both, he suspected. "Better now than when Andoran and Sargon came into the forest."

"That won't happen again." Creaking Bough glanced at him but didn't meet his eyes. "We don't make the same mistakes twice, especially when the stakes are so high."

"So I see."

When no one spoke, Tarkyn gave up and ate the rest of his lunch in silence. Either the presence of the wizard or his chance remark had soured the camaraderie he had begun to establish. As one who was used to constant formality, he was surprised at how quickly he had come to look forward to their friendliness. He glanced around at the woodfolk's closed faces and repressed a sigh. And to his growing concern, there was no sign of Waterstone, Sparrow or Autumn Leaves. However, he respected Autumn Leaves' evaluation that Waterstone would need time to regroup, so he made no attempt to contact them.

With lunch over, the woodfolk melted away, leaving Tarkyn with his wizard. Although Stormaway intrigued him, Tarkyn did not want his time monopolised by him but for the time being, he let it ride.

Stormaway settled back and said, "Since your father imposed the oath, Your Highness, I have kept up constant contact with the woodfolk. I act as their agent to sell their wines, preserves, nuts and berries. They now have access to many goods that they didn't have before your father came here."

"What did they do in those days?"

"They were totally self sufficient before I came along. I am still the only link they have with the outside world," said Stormaway with a self-satisfied air.

Tarkyn looked askance at him. Something in his tone of voice disturbed him. Only one route for goods out meant that Stormaway had a monopoly. This arrangement would bear further scrutiny, he decided. "So do you exchange for goods or money?"

"I sell the woodfolk's goods, then use the money to buy whatever they request, mainly cloths, metal arrow tips, knives, that sort of thing. Sometimes stockpiles of foods, if the winter looks like being very hard or the harvests have been particularly poor. Sometimes I bring back money to use on the next trip."

"And I presume you receive a commission?"

"Of course I do. Nothing unreasonable, though. Ten percent." Stormaway added stiffly, "You can check with them if you doubt me."

"That is very fair of you." The prince smiled disarmingly and said, "But if I did check with them, how would they know what price you received for their goods in the first place?"

The wizard's eyes narrowed dangerously. Just as Tarkyn braced himself to deal with a tirade, Stormaway suddenly smiled, "Oh Your Highness, you will be a fine liege lord for these people. Already you are working to protect their interests. It comes as naturally to you as breathing."

Tarkyn thought about Sparrow and Waterstone, and grimaced, "I doubt that they would agree with you. Not only that, but even if they did, I doubt that they would thank me for it. They have managed without my protection for centuries and I am sure they would prefer to continue to manage without it."

"Give it time, Your Highness."

"I will, Stormaway, but not too long. There are some among them who are almost heroic in their efforts to overcome our differences and yet it is these very people whom I have inadvertently hurt the most. I will not persist in a situation that is too difficult either for them or me."

The wizard was clearly not happy with this response but decided to hold his peace.

Almost as a defence against Stormaway's silent rebuke, Tarkyn picked up a stick and concentrated on methodically breaking bits off the end of it. After a while, he looked up and asked, "And who among the woodfolk keeps the money for you between trips? Who keeps the accounts?"

Stormaway scratched his head. "That depends, really. Different woodfolk look after different enterprises, so to speak. So I receive hazelnuts from Ancient Oak, blackberries and preserves from Tree Wind, and so on. If there is a stockpile of money, Waterstone takes it and hides it somewhere in the forest until it's needed. I think all the woodfolk know where it is. They only hide it to keep it safe from intruders, not from each other. They are amazingly trusting, these woodfolk."

The more Tarkyn heard, the more he realised how hard it must have been for Waterstone to be doubted. Aloud he said, "Perhaps it is harder to be deceitful when they share their thoughts with each other constantly."

"You know about that, do you?"

"Yes. I can even do a version of it myself, you know."

"Can you, Sire?" The wizard was impressed. "I didn't know any sorcerers had that facility."

"Neither did I." Tarkyn stood up and walked around the clearing as he spoke to stretch his limbs. "I can't do it in the same way as the woodfolk. I can only use images and feelings. No words. It has caused a few small problems because it is so new to me. I haven't really mastered it yet." He didn't think he would go into the details of the disaster with Sparrow and its consequences. "What about wizards? Can you use any form of mental communication?"

Stormaway frowned. "Well, I didn't think so, but thinking back to yesterday…Did you send me a wave of anger when you were objecting to my interference. Somehow I felt that I was on the receiving end of a right royal rage, far beyond the degree of anger in your voice."

The prince grinned. "Yes. My latest technique, designed to give a private dressing down in a public place."

"Very good, Your Highness," replied the wizard dryly.

"Thank you," responded Tarkyn, not about to be daunted, "Just be glad I have more tact than you do." He considered the wizard. "Something's been puzzling me. Why were you so sure of yourself when you were goading me when we first met? You professed to know how dangerous I could be but then deliberately set about drawing my fire. Are you so powerful?"

Stormaway smirked. "I was while you had no shield up and there were forty arrows aimed at you from within the trees, by woodfolk who were looking for any excuse to kill you."

Tarkyn gave an involuntary shudder. "Stars above! I'm lucky to be alive!"

"Not lucky. You proved yourself. It was you, not luck that pulled you through that situation."

The young man thought about this for a moment then gave himself a mental shake and asked, "So, what are a wizard's specialities? I know you serve an apprenticeship and have much more detailed training than your average sorcerer, but what do you gain?"

"A true Master Wizard spends years studying his or her craft, well beyond the four year apprenticeship. Our powers develop, although none would have greater power than you. However, I expect I have a greater knowledge of how to use those powers effectively and for a wider range of uses. Sorcerers generally just take their powers for granted and, except for a few, learn as they go. Wizards also tend to have more skill in healing, partly because of the knowledge they accrue. No mental communication that I know of, though some of us can use mind control, of course."

Tarkyn frowned. "Can you? How strongly? Could you use it on me? Not that I am going to let you try."

Stormaway glanced sideways at the prince. "I have used it on sorcerers sometimes when I was in the king's service."

"Did you know that Tree Wind tried to use it on me the day after I met you?"

"Outrageous!" The wizard was scandalized. "Didn't they realise how dangerous that was? I told them the binding spell would already be working. Did the forest suffer? What happened?"

"I realised what she was doing and resisted just in time. There was little damage to the forest."

Stormaway huffed, "Lucky for them that you are so strong... If you don't mind me asking, how did you manage to resist?"

Tarkyn gave a lop-sided grin. "I was outraged when I realised what she was trying to do. The anger gave me the energy to resist her and close my eyes."

"Hmm. You are an unusual sorcerer. Most untrained sorcerers are a walkover, to be honest."

"Are they? And what about woodfolk? They too use mind control. What happens when two people try to use it simultaneously on each other, I wonder." At last he had an expert in magic to tap. "And is it easier to resist, if you are a user of mind control yourself?"

Smiling, the wizard put up his hand to stop the deluge of questions. "One step at a time, my boy... In answer to your first question, I haven't had much need to try mind control on woodfolk but I have had one signal success. It was a little unfair, I suppose, since the woodman was very weak at the time...."

Tarkyn went very still. "You're talking about Falling Rain, aren't you?"

The wizard's head whipped back. "Sire! What was that? I've just been hit by a wave of what? – Outrage, anger, disgust?

"Looks as if you can pick up emotions after all," said Tarkyn tightly.

"Well, I don't know what gives you the right to be sanctimonious, Your Highness. If it weren't for our discovering the woodfolk, you'd be isolated, out in the open and on the run."

"Stormaway! Don't you realise that Falling Rain was exiled all those years ago for betraying the woodfolk?"

The wizard shrugged. "Better him than you. My loyalty lies with you, not the woodfolk. If I knew it would ensure your safety, I would do it again without a second thought."

Tarkyn stared at his determinedly faithful retainer, aware that they had reached an impasse. After a moment, he asked, "Did you think to tell the woodfolk that you had forced the information out of Falling Rain?"

"I didn't even know until now that he had been exiled. They don't tell me their business any more than they need to."

"And would you have told them, if you knew?"

Stormaway thought carefully. "On balance, I think, yes. I can't see that it would have damaged your cause if they had known that."

"In actual fact, it would have meant one less pocket of resistance for me to overcome."

"They're a funny lot. It was entirely up to them what they did about it. Why do they direct their resentment towards you?"

"Not all of them agreed with exiling him and those that disagreed were making some headway with overturning the decision until I turned up."

Stormaway smiled cheerfully. "So it's good we had this little chat isn't it? Because now you have a good reason for overriding the exile, haven't you? I presume you want to, judging by that flood of emotion I received."

"I do, but I don't want to enforce my will on them."

"Your Highness!"Stormaway scowled at him. "I thought I detected some flaws in your attitude. You are their liege lord. They do as you say. No questions asked. That's the end of it. What's the point of the oath if you don't use it?"

Tarkyn looked at him out of the corner of his eye and let out a long sigh. *Well, that's one side of the argument,* he thought. His reaction to Stormaway's stance gave him some hope, though. He was relieved to realise that, although he liked to have the power, he didn't necessarily like to use it. *Maybe I deserve Waterstone's faith in me after all.* He let his faithful retainer know none of this, but simply asked, "I wonder how one overturns a decision when there is no court to inform that you are doing it."

"Obvious. You simply inform the exile that he may come back."

"What? And let him walk back into a disapproving society? That would be no life for him. I have to sort it out with the rest of the woodfolk first." Tarkyn thought for a few moments. "I'll start by discussing it with Summer Rain"

The prince sent out an image of Summer Rain, with a feeling of uncertainty attached, into the trees generally and hoped that someone would pick it up and pass it on. In a surprisingly short amount of time, Summer Rain came running.

"What's wrong?" she asked, panting as she caught her breath.

"Oh dear," said Tarkyn, "I'm sorry. I didn't mean to alarm you. I'm fine. I just wanted to talk to you about something."

The healer scowled at him.

"Please sit down," he invited urbanely, "Have you met Stormaway Treemaster? Of course you have. You would have worked together to heal the sick when my father came here, wouldn't you?" Tarkyn realised he has babbling and promptly stopped himself.

"You wanted to speak to me about something?"

"Yes," replied Tarkyn more slowly. "And if I could just ask you ahead of time not to relay any of this conversation? That might save any unpleasantness later on. I will be able to tell if you do and I really do not like people sharing my conversations without my permission."

Summer Rain's eyes narrowed. "I see. Not that I had planned to do so."

"No, perhaps not but I know it is natural for you to share information while for me, it is not."

"I'll remember that, Your Highness."

"Thank you. Now, if you remember, I said I would consider Falling Rain's plight." The prince considered her gravely. "I don't think you set much store by that at the time, but I don't usually make hollow undertakings." He glanced sideways at the wizard. "It has now come to my attention that mind power was used on Falling Rain to discover the location of the woodfolk. Were you aware of this?"

Summer Rain shook her head emphatically. "No... So it was not his choice to betray us. This information changes everything."

"I thought it might. Given that I now have new grounds for overturning an old decision, I am quite prepared to do so. Consequently, I need to know how to go about it. I can't just order Falling Rain back if everyone is still shunning him."

"I can send out a message explaining the new information. I think...."

Tarkyn interrupted gently, "I don't mean to cast aspersions on you but would this information be better coming from a more disinterested party - perhaps someone who had been opposed to your brother's return?"

The healer's eyes flashed but she took a moment to think about it before nodding reluctantly. "Why don't you just send it?"

The sorcerer shook his head regretfully. "Can't send words, I'm afraid. I'm happy to have the message sent in my name, but I need an intermediary."

"What about Waterstone?"

Tarkyn boggled. "Waterstone! I thought he would have been on your side. No wonder he left the discussion. We'd have had a war in my shelter."

"No, Your Highness," Summer Rain replied without a vestige of humour, "I would have considered your need for quiet and drawn him outside. He has always believed that betrayal for whatever reason deserved exile, at the very least. He has always been very firm about the old rules."

Tarkyn absorbed this new information into his view of the woodman. Then he remembered Waterstone's present situation and said, "I think you'll find Waterstone is unavailable for the time being. Who else can you think of?"

"Thunder Storm?"

"Agreed. Could you ask him to come here please?" While they were waiting for Thunder Storm's arrival, Tarkyn asked, "How will we inform Falling Rain? How far away is he? Could a mind message reach him from here?"

Summer Rain shook her head, "And even if it could, I'm not sure that he'd agree to come back. He may need some persuasion. No one has seen him for years. Last sighting of him was way down in the south west."

"I see. And who would go to tell him?"

"I don't know yet. We will work it out amongst ourselves."

Restless after his recuperation, Tarkyn came to a sudden decision. "I shall go."

Immediately, the wizard cut in. "You cannot go without a retinue. It would be improper."

"I came to the forest without a retinue, Stormaway." The prince reminded him gently.

Summer Rain's joined forces with the wizard. "You can't go on your own. Without us, the wolf would have killed you yesterday. The bounty hunters would have carried you off."

"And I wouldn't have three broken ribs," quipped Tarkyn. *I don't learn, do I?* he thought, as she stared at him stonily. After a moment, he said more seriously, "I had no intention of going alone. I have very limited experience of woodcraft, hunting, cooking, navigating or possible dangers. Even if I wanted to, I know I couldn't go alone. But it would give me a chance to see some of the woodlands and to help to redress the wrong done to Falling Rain." He grimaced. "The biggest problem I can see is that you might find it harder to recruit woodfolk who would be willing to fetch Falling Rain, if they know they will have me with them."

Summer Rain looked at him for a long time. "Have we been so hard on you?"

"Not everyone, and not all the time. But I know most woodfolk resent me," remembering Waterstone's memory, he added, "and consider me a liability."

For the first time, Summer Rain smiled. "Not completely. I think a travelling party might appreciate the talents of a sorcerer on their side. I don't know that you're ready to travel yet, though."

"How long?"

Summer Rain shrugged, "You are pretty tired again today. Aren't you?"

"But I just spent four days lifting branches." He saw her about to protest and cut in, "And in answer to your next question. No, I wasn't just sitting around and yes, it does tire me even if it's only magic. You don't do physical magic, so you don't understand."

"If that's the case, you shouldn't have done so much then."

Tarkyn smiled, "No pleasing you, is there? No, I probably shouldn't have. But we only had a short time to repair the trees before they would have been too dried out. So, better to work too hard for four days and recover on the fifth, don't you think?"

The healer nodded reluctantly. "I think you will need another few days or you will just hold everyone up. Then you would be a liability. We don't want you overstraining yourself trying to keep up. But we will need time to assemble supplies and equipment, so you may be well enough by then, anyway. If not, we will wait. After twelve years, another week will not matter." He remembered this was not what she had said to him a few days ago but saw no point in mentioning it. She smiled at him. "And thank you."

By the time Thunder Storm arrived, it was almost dinnertime. A huge pot of stew hung over the fire, its tantalisingly smell wafting over the clearing. Thunder Storm filled two bowls and handed one to the Tarkyn as he sat down next to him.

The prince blew on the hot food and ate a few mouthfuls. "This is good stew, a bit gamey perhaps but plenty of herbs...Hmm, very tasty indeed."

"Thank you, Sire," Thunder Storm took a mouthful himself, "Ah yes. You need the herbs. It takes a fine chef to cook a good wolf stew. Taste's too strong for roasting."

Tarkyn choked. "Did you say wolf? Not the wolves we killed yesterday?"

"Of course." Thunder Storm rumbled happily. "You have to cook it quickly so that it doesn't go off.

This answer was so eminently sensible that Tarkyn was left with nothing to say. He peered into his bowl, steeled himself and kept eating.

"Mind you, there's a lot of meat on two wolves. We should have plenty of stew for the next few days, at least. And not only that," continued the woodman, blithely unaware of the prince's heroism, "I think the pelt of the wolf Waterstone shot down will be large enough to make you a good thick cloak for winter."

"Marvellous," said the prince with as much enthusiasm as he could muster, as he thought of the finely tailored cloaks he had left hanging in his wardrobe at the palace.

"However," rumbled Thunder Storm with a disapproving frown, "Your fireworks didn't do much for the quality of the other pelt. Probably worth bearing in mind next time, Your Highness." he added kindly, giving the prince's knee an avuncular pat.

The prince nearly choked again and cast a weather eye in Stormaway's direction to see whether he had noticed Thunder Cloud's over-familiarity. Luckily, the wizard was intent on listening in on someone's conversation, a common activity for him, Tarkyn suspected. "I'll try to do better next time," he managed, smothering a laugh.

Thunder Storm beamed at him and asked why the prince had wanted to see him. When Tarkyn explained, he was relieved to find that once Thunder Storm had expressed his shock and dismay, he was quite happy to send out a message on the prince's behalf even though he had previously been an advocate for Falling Rain's continued exile. Almost at once, Tarkyn was rocked backwards by a wave of outrage followed by a deluge of relief and rejoicing.

The prince grinned. "Did you feel that? I think my first decree, or whatever you call it, has met with approval."

Thunder Storm smiled. "No. I didn't feel anything but my mind is jammed up with excited messages coming from everywhere. People are so pleased to hear that Falling Rain did not willingly betray us after all. Glad for him that he can come home, and glad for all woodfolk that the pact we have amongst ourselves is still intact."

Chapter 16

Early the next morning, Tarkyn slipped down to the river before anyone, and in particular Stormaway, could accost him. He loved the river's tranquillity and the way its moods changed at different times of the day and night. But more than this, he wanted to try to develop his mind links with the otter again, if it reappeared.

He sat quietly in the sun for a while and tried to send out waves of invitation into the river. As he gazed down into the water, he suddenly realised he was staring at a huge golden fish that was looking expectantly up at him. *This is getting a bit silly,* he thought. *What do I say to a fish?* He produced a picture of the otter and a feeling of uncertainty. He received a frisson of fear followed by an image of the otter far downstream heading the other way. Then he received a view of the river directly below him, with an understanding of all the safe holes, feeding areas and smaller fish accompanied by a sense of pride. Somehow, the prince realised from the vision coupled with the fish's size that he was communing with the old man of the river, so to speak. In return, the prince sent a picture of himself in the surrounding trees with woodfolk in the background, also with a sense of pride. The huge fish rose slowly to the surface and watched him for a few minutes before turning and swimming slowly down into the shadows. *I must say, conversation tends to be laboured without words, no matter whom you're talking to,* he thought.

Tarkyn lay on his back and focused his will on trying to tune in to any feelings or images around him. Slowly he became aware that he was being watched and opened his eyes to find himself being scrutinised by the heron he had seen on his first morning in the forest. The sorcerer radiated calm and sat up slowly while the heron watched patiently. Tarkyn received a clear impression that he was wasting time moving slowly and that the heron was quite disdainful of any danger he might represent. Slightly riled, the sorcerer sent the bird an image of a fireball blasting towards him, but the heron merely tilted his head disbelievingly. Having had his bluff called, Tarkyn shrugged and grinned. The heron looked him sternly in the eyes then flapped his wings slowly and took off. At first, Tarkyn was disappointed but suddenly realised he was seeing trees gliding past and below as the heron gained height. Soon, the sorcerer was viewing the forest from above the treetops as the bird glided in ever-increasing circles higher in the sky. With a sense of wonder, Tarkyn realised that the domain of his forest spread as far as the eye could see in every direction but one, which he presumed was the north eastern approach from which he had entered. In the distance to the southwest, he could see wooded mountains soaring above jagged cliffs that rose from the forests below. He could see the changes in foliage from one area to another and thought he could pick out the route he had been forced to take by the bounty hunters, which had ended in a large stand of pines to the north northwest. Then the river came back into view as a shining, snaking line partly covered by trees. As he watched, the river drew closer and closer until he was streaking headfirst towards it. At the last minute he saw a fish just below the surface before the image was lost in a blur of white water.

A splash slightly downriver signalled the return of the heron. A minute later, it stalked into view carrying the hapless fish firmly in its beak and settled down on the rock next to the sorcerer to eat it. Just a small fish, not the old man of the river, Tarkyn was relieved to see. Tarkyn sent a message of thanks to the bird who ruffled his feathers nonchalantly and concentrated on devouring his catch. When the heron had finished his meal, he flapped his wings slowly and rose into the air without any further communication.

After a while, Tarkyn's mind turned to Watertstone. He still hadn't seen him or Autumn Leaves. He didn't want to intrude on him so he decided to send a message to Autumn Leaves instead. He couldn't use words but he could use gestures, he realised. Targeting the right person was another issue. He shrugged. *I can only try.* He thought hard about Autumn Leaves; how he looked and sounded, what he knew of his personality then sent an image of himself signalling for Autumn Leaves to come to him.

When Autumn Leaves arrived, his face was tight and closed and he spoke formally with no trace of his former familiarity.

"Yes, Your Royal Highness. I believe you required my presence."

"Please sit down. I need to talk to you." The prince eyed the woodman who showed no sign of thawing. "Autumn Leaves, unless I am mistaken, you appear to be annoyed with me. I can think of a few reasons why that might be, but to save me guessing, why don't you just tell me?"

Autumn Leaves glanced at him coldly then looked away. "I am not used to obeying commands, Your Highness. Hopefully, it will become easier over time but at the moment, I resent it."

"Autumn Leaves, when you are up in the trees and on lookout duty or whatever, are there not times when one of the other woodfolk instruct you to do something?"

"Of course, but that is on equal terms. I can just as easily instruct them, if the need arises."

"I see. And yet you seemed to be instructing me quite forthrightly the other night," observed the prince dryly. He thought for a moment. "I think we may be at cross purposes here. I did not really intend to command you to come down here. Admittedly, there might be times when I would, but this wasn't one of them. I wanted you to come but if it had not suited you, I would have accepted that. Perhaps the problem lies in my mind message. Was it too peremptory? Without the words, you can't build in phrases like 'could you' and 'please' that turn a command into a request."

Autumn Leaves finally met the prince's eyes properly for the first time since he'd arrived. "Your gesturing was pretty emphatic," he said shortly.

Tarkyn gave a self-conscious smile. "I have only just started using mind messages. Maybe I need to add a feeling of uncertainty to make it a request."

"Go on then. Try it and I'll tell you what I think." After a moment, the woodman shook his head. "No. That comes across as a question; 'Are you coming here?'"

"Maybe just less emphatic gesturing?"

"All right. Try that." Autumn Leaves frowned. "That's better, but I think you're going to have to talk to people about it, so they understand. Especially with the oath, they're going to assume, as I did, that they have no choice."

The prince eyed him speculatively, "I would like my requests to be acceded to unless there is a good reason not to be, but I don't want to create unnecessary antagonism and I don't want a request to be confused with a command. Will I show you what I'd send if I really were sending out a command? I warn you it would probably only be in a situation where I was angry or in some kind of danger so there would be a strong emotion attached."

"Go on then. To make sure we can tell the difference."

Tarkyn thought for moment, imagining such a situation. Then he sent Autumn Leaves the gesture to come to him accompanied by an intense wave of anger, hauteur and compulsion.

Autumn Leaves went white. "Stars above! Well, that's certainly clears one thing up. You didn't send me a command."

Tarkyn smiled disarmingly. "No. Something to be used fairly sparingly, I would have thought."

The woodman studied the smiling prince for a few moments. "I'm beginning to see why Waterstone likes you so much."

The young man coloured slightly, more nonplussed by this one grudging remark than by any of the beautifully phrased compliments he had had thrown at him throughout his life at court. Noting the prince's discomfort with some amusement, Autumn Leaves kindly moved the conversation on. "So why do you want to see me? About Waterstone, I presume."

"Yes. I haven't heard from any of you and I want to know how he is and what, if anything, I can do to help."

"Well, do you know," said the woodman thoughtfully, "I think he's all right now. He's just feeling embarrassed about seeing you for some reason.He won't tell me why, but no doubt it has to do with whatever his private thoughts or feelings he exposed to you, so I'm not going to press him." He looked at Tarkyn. "Maybe we just need some way to break the ice again before it becomes too thick."

They sat and pondered in silence for a few minutes.

"If I were in any sort of danger, he would come," said Tarkyn, considering possibilities.

"True. So would everybody else. But you're not in danger and hopefully unlikely to be for a while."

They fell silent again.

"What if I have something of interest to show him?"

Autumn Leaves looked at him speculatively. "Depends what it is. He mightn't find it interesting at all."

Tarkyn subsided. "You're right. It may be commonplacc to woodfolk." He thought it through, before continuing with more conviction. "But it is not at all commonplace to me and I would like the chance to discuss it. That in itself should be enough, surely?"

"I suppose so, if it's important to you."

The sorcerer hesitated. "The only thing is, I'm not sure that I can show him."

"Why not? Don't you trust him?"

"Very funny. Of course I bloody trust him. That's what this was all about in the first place." Tarkyn scratched his head. "I'm just not sure how to do it."

"Well, you can either figure that out with Waterstone or you can work it out with me as a dress rehearsal, so to speak." Autumn Leaves shrugged. "Personally, I think a practice run will just make you self-conscious."

"It is quite unnecessary to make elaborate preparations. All I need is a pretext for visiting Waterstone the first time, which I now have, however flimsy. Let's just find him and get on with it. At the very least, I can tell him about it even if I can't show him." Tarkyn pulled himself to his feet, accepting the offer of Autumn Leaves hand. "Where is he?"

The solid woodman guided Tarkyn through a stand of small silver birches then deep into a thicket of hazel trees where they came upon

Waterstone sitting outside his shelter, whittling a new arrow into shape. There was a certain tension in his movements and he sent a singeing glance at Autumn Leaves as the two of them approached.

Obviously he knew we were coming, thought the sorcerer. *He's a woodman. Well, at least he hasn't avoided us.*

"Please don't blame Autumn Leaves," said the prince, his voice sounding formal because of his tension. "I have something I wanted to show you." Tarkyn heard the cold tone of his own voice and took a moment to thaw. Then he swung from one extreme to the other and began to blither. "Well actually, I wasn't going to show you yet, because it's a bit of a work in progress but I decided I would, anyway. Autumn Leaves thought it mightn't be as interesting to you as it is to me even though he doesn't actually know what it is…." He rolled his eyes beseechingly at Autumn Leaves. "I'm not doing too well here, am I?"

He broke off as he realised that both woodmen were grinning broadly at him.

"No wonder you're so blindingly honest. You couldn't lie to save yourself," chortled Waterstone. "Come on. Come and sit down. I'll get us something to drink and you can tell me what's so interesting, if you can think it up before I've brought you some juice."

Once the three of them were seated with cups of apple juice, Tarkyn said, "Actually, I do have something interesting to tell you and hopefully show you. But first I need to clarify something. If someone has sent you an image at some time in the past, can you send that image on to someone else?"

The woodfolk nodded. "It's just like sending a memory," said Autumn Leaves, "An image is an image, wherever it comes from. It can be a real view of something, it can be imaginary or it can be from your memory."

Tarkyn smiled in satisfaction. "Good. In that case, I think I should be able to do it. I'll send you the image first and tell you how I got it second. Are you ready?" He closed his eyes and brought back the views he has seen from the heron's eyes - lifting up over the river, soaring high above the woodlands, then swooping back down into the river. When he had finished, he opened his eyes and looked at them expectantly. "So, what do you think? Can you all do that?

Waterstone and Autumn Leaves both looked stunned.

Waterstone was the first to speak. "That was…unexpected. I have never seen the forest from above, except from the mountain peaks. But can we all do what? Are you imagining how the forest would look? Where did you get the images from?"

Tarkyn beamed at them. "From a heron. That's what I've been learning to do, mind link with animals."

The woodmen exchanged glances before Waterstone spoke, "None of us can share images with animals." He shrugged, "Maybe it's because we use words so much. Your mind linking does work differently from ours. Have you tried it with any other animals?"

Tarkyn grimaced. "I haven't yet instigated an exchange. The animals seem to come to me, really. Like the otter, the other night. It just happened to be there, working its way up the river so I sent out waves of reassurance and it came over to me. I could show you the whole exchange but I'd have to explain the feelings afterwards.

"Go on," said Autumn Leaves quietly.

Once he had sent the image, he said, "The otter sent me the river from her point of view to make sure I knew she was mind linking with me." Tarkyn smiled, "She was irritated with me because I was a bit slow on the uptake." He shrugged, "Hardly surprising I was slow, since it was the first time." The sorcerer frowned suddenly, "Actually, now I think about it, it wasn't the first time. On the night of the feast, I was upset," here he glanced self-consciously at Autumn Leaves, "after seeing Tree Wind's memory of my father and the way he enforced the oath taking. Anyway, there was a tawny owl up in the pine tree above me... the same one that came swooping over the firesite later that night... and now I think about it, he sent down some sort of comforting waves so that I could pull myself together and come out to face you all." Before the woodfolk had time to absorb the prince's admission of vulnerability, an idea suddenly struck him, "... The owl that warned me about the wolf the other night was female." He grinned suddenly, remembering the woodfolk's disbelief on the first night. "Maybe it was the other one's mate?"

Waterstone directed a frown at him. "An owl warned you? You didn't tell me that at the time. You gave me all sorts of other explanations...."

Tarkyn shrugged and smiled ruefully at him, "I was just trying to come up with explanations I could believe myself. I hadn't had time to put all the information together then and I couldn't really credit that I'd just looked down on the woods through the owl's eyes."

"Understandable," put in Autumn Leaves, the peacemaker. "Not the first thing you'd naturally think of really, is it? Mind-reading an owl." The other two looked at him without saying a word. "I'll get some more juice then, shall I?" he said, getting to his feet.

As soon as Tarkyn and Waterstone were left alone, an air of constraint descended. After too long a pause, Tarkyn said, "You have a good friend in Autumn Leaves. He risked being burnt to a crisp for you."

"Oh really?" responded Waterstone, not at all impressed, "He didn't think you'd do anything of the sort. Not for a second."

The sorcerer pulled the corners of his mouth down in mock dismay. "That's quite lowering, isn't it? To realise I'm already losing my fearsome edge."

Waterstone watched him with his head on one side, a sardonic glint of amusement in his eyes. "And yet, if you think it needful, I'm sure you will easily create a twinge of apprehension to keep us all in line."

Tarkyn's stomach tightened. There could be no mistaking the bitter edge to Waterstone's words...and he had said 'us all', not 'me'. Until now, their conversations had been person to person, not prince to woodfolk. Tarkyn stood up and walked to the edge of the small clearing. He looked out, hands on hips, into the tangle of branches as he tried to work out what he could say. Before he spoke, the prince sent Autumn Leaves an image of himself gesturing for the woodman to wait. He vaguely hoped that it wasn't too emphatic. He turned on his heel and stood looking down at the Waterstone.

"Waterstone," he began, but faltered as he saw the woodman's set face. He sat down again on the log next to Waterstone and leant forward, resting his elbows on his long legs. He drew a breath and tried again. "Waterstone, I couldn't help not hearing all those things you told me when I was unconscious. I couldn't help not knowing what a true friend you had been to me. How it was when I awoke is not how it is now. I had hoped the message I sent through Autumn Leaves would have reassured you of that." He glanced at Waterstone but still the woodman did not reply. Tarkyn leant down and picked up a long twig and methodically began to break bits of the end of it, as he talked. "Now it is I who feels a yawning gap opening between us. I don't really know what else to say... Yes, I do. Autumn Leaves explained – quite forcefully in fact – what it meant to expose your memories without choice, as you did. Although I knew that beforehand at one level, I didn't fully appreciate the courage it required of you to keep going. I can only say that I am sorry I pushed you so far. I can't undo it. Autumn Leaves was horrified at what I had done and so am I. My only defence is that, as you so rightly judged, I am an inexperienced young man and on top of that, I have had no training in mind linking of any sort."

There was a long silence. Tarkyn picked up another long twig and started breaking bits of it while he waited. When that twig was in little pieces on the ground, he debated whether to pick up yet another twig or whether just to get up and leave. He decided for one last try. He picked up a third twig and said inconsequentially, "Of course Autumn Leaves may be right. I might just be an utter bastard... in which case you're better off keeping well away from me, like most woodfolk do."

Waterstone finally spoke. "Autumn Leaves said that?" He smiled reluctantly. "Maybe he really did think he risked being burnt to a cinder, after all."

The sorcerer shook his head, smiling. "I doubt it. Not by then, anyway. But I do know he would have risked it, if he felt he had to."

At last, Waterstone turned his head to look at the prince. "Do you know what upset me most?" Tarkyn decided this was rhetorical and didn't answer. "I wasn't able to do what I had contracted to do. I pulled out of the memory instead of allowing you to choose. After all that effort, I wasn't able to prove that there was nothing I couldn't show you because I stopped the memory, not you."

"Waterstone, you're too hard on yourself. I understand completely why you were unable to continue at that point."

"You may understand but that will not stop the doubts."

The prince smiled wryly. "I may be an utter bastard but I am neither an utter fool nor a liar. I said I trusted you beyond any doubt and I do. That last memory and your strong reaction to it showed me the motivation for your friendship. That's what I needed to know. The earlier memories didn't, which was why I asked you to keep going." Tarkyn threw down the remains of his twig and sat up. "I hope the cost wasn't too high - Autumn Leaves tells me it was – especially when the trust you won from me is something you take for granted from everyone else. I hope it was worth it to you. It is beyond value to me."

The woodman's face broke into a slow warm smile. "Now I understand all that, it was worth it ...and I'm glad you pushed the point until you were satisfied. So, if you still wish to maintain this friendship, even knowing the unkind thoughts I had about you when you first arrived, I suppose I can deal with your occasional flashes of ruthlessness." Waterstone rocked backwards as a wave of relief poured over him. He shook his head, laughing. "You are hopeless. Your emotions get the better of me, let alone you."

A few minutes later, Autumn Leaves finally ran out of patience and turned up with a stone carafe of apple juice.

"Whoops. Sorry," said Tarkyn. "I forgot to send you another message. How was the last message?"

Autumn Leaves blinked as he thought about it. "Hard to say. Since I now know more about your attitudes, I wasn't offended by it. I think people will have to get to know you better to interpret your messages properly, though. So", he said, as he poured the juice into the three goblets, "Have you two sorted yourselves out?"

"Yes, thanks," replied Tarkyn with laughter in his eyes.

The other two looked at him. "What's so funny?" demanded Autumn Leaves.

"I've never had so many people treating me in such an avuncular manner before."

"Who else is?" asked Waterstone. He frowned. "Not me?"

"No. Not you, but Stormaway and Thunder Storm both seem to have taken me under their wings." He chortled. "And of course Autumn Leaves is busy looking after both of us.... now that he's stopped lecturing me. Even Summer Rain had an unexpected moment of kindness last night." He shook his head. "I am struggling to maintain a dignified distance, I can tell you."

The two woodfolk stared at him. Then, their eyes glazed slightly as they thought amongst themselves. As the seconds drew out, Tarkyn cocked his head to one side and asked, "Would you mind sharing whatever thoughts you are having? It's becoming a little lonely out here."

Waterstone came back into focus "Sorry. We were discussing whether there is a need for a dignified distance, as you call it. From your point of view, from our point of view, practically and traditionally, especially when we have such different societies. We got carried away." He nodded thoughtfully. "It's complicated, isn't it?"

Tarkyn nodded, suddenly nothing more than a young man trying to make sense of the world from a very strange standpoint.

"And really, it is your sole decision, isn't it?" Waterstone shook his head slowly. "It's a big decision to make, for a young prince who has suddenly become the liege lord of such a different society."

"And because of all that has happened, I still haven't stated my expectations as I promised I would on the night of the feast," said Tarkyn.

Autumn Leaves was regarding Tarkyn with some concern. "I hope I haven't offended you, Your Highness," he said, "I am not used to dealing with princes. None of us is."

"No. You haven't offended me...At least no more than anyone else has, given the differences in our customs." The prince smiled and shook his head."You will know if you really offend me, I can assure you. You have not behaved around me as I have been used to, but it becomes increasingly obvious that the woodlands are nothing like court and, without wishing to be rude, woodfolk are not very good at being courtiers."

Seeing Autumn Leaves frown, Tarkyn continued, "It does take years of training, you know. You have to grow up believing in the monarchy and its importance to the whole structure of the nation. Everything in our society - all the feast days, all the customs, all the routes to wealth and power - originate from my family."

Tarkyn picked up another twig and set about destroying it slowly, like those before it. "You people have only known a king for two days and me for how long - three weeks? Nothing in your society depends on the monarchy except, of course," he put in dryly, "the safety of the forest." The prince shrugged, "But your society and customs and etiquette are not built around the monarchy. You don't even seem to have a hierarchy. So you don't know how you should behave towards a nobleman, let alone towards a member of the royal family."

He stood up and walked a little away from the two woodmen. Standing with his back to them, hands on hips, the prince stared unseeingly into the tangle of hawthorn and said quietly to himself, "And therein lies the dilemma."

He swung around and walked back to stand towering over them, his long black hair framing his face, his drawn brows shading his strange tawny eyes. "And the other side of that dilemma is that I am not used to such familiarity. Even within my family, there have always been protocols, particularly but not only, when members of the public are present. Even close friends are expected to show deference and follow rules of etiquette."

The two woodmen sat watching him intently, waiting to see where this monologue was heading. The prince glared down at them. They waited. Finally the prince threw up his hands. "You see! With the best will in the world, you have no idea what I'm talking about."

"Well, why don't you stop standing over us like some looming bird of prey and sit down, have another drink and explain it better so we do understand?" suggested Waterstone mildly.

At that, Tarkyn broke into laughter tinged with more than a little hysteria. He threw himself down on the log next to them and gulped down the best part of a cupful in one draught. He looked at Waterstone and Autumn Leaves incredulously. "Don't you know you shouldn't sit in my presence if I'm standing?"

"No," they chorused. "How would we?" added Autumn Leaves.

"Or that you shouldn't lean over me, as both of you have done in the past?"

"Obviously not or we wouldn't have." replied Waterstone tartly.

"Or that you should bow every time you approach me?"

The woodman goggled at each other.

"Or that you shouldn't raise your voice to me?"

"Well," said Waterstone promptly, "I've failed signally on that one but I bet Autumn Leaves kept his voice down. He's good at saying what he wants to without raising his voice."

"Or that you shouldn't speak to me until I address you first?"

"Oh, I certainly failed on that one," chortled Waterstone, rolling his eyes at Autumn Leaves. "I talked to him for days when he was unconscious, before he addressed me."

A wave of frustration tinged with anger rolled into the minds of the two woodmen.

"Now settle down, Waterstone." said Autumn Leaves gently. "You're starting to upset him."

Waterstone calmed himself and smiled ruefully at the prince. "I'm sorry, Tarkyn. I shouldn't tease you when you're trying to be serious." He gave the prince a friendly pat on the knee not realising that, once more, he was transgressing. "Look, if you want us to learn these things and behave in certain ways, we'll just have to learn. I'm sure Stormaway would be happy to teach us." Waterstone smothered a smile as he added, "It could take us a while to get the hang of it and there are quite a large number of us to teach. Still, it will keep Stormaway out of mischief."

The prince frowned suspiciously, "What are you laughing at?"

Waterstone whooped with released laughter, "I'll show you," he gasped. He sent the other two a mental image of groups of woodfolk trying to remember to stand and speak at the right times using Stormaway as their guide. *Woodfolk are bobbing up and down in confusion as Tarkyn stands or sits. Since they are mainly sitting on the ground or low logs, by the time they scramble to their feet, Tarkyn is sitting down again. The woodfolk then all look uncertainly at each other and subside slowly to sit again apprehensively, ready to bounce back up at any moment. Then they sit in deathly silence around the fire, waiting expectantly for Tarkyn to say something. Needless to say, it is not long before the woodfolk revert to mind talking and simply leave the prince out of the equation.* "You'd certainly create distance between yourself and us but I'm not sure how dignified it will be."

Although he was smiling, Autumn Leaves shook his head. "I don't think that's kind, Waterstone. Tarkyn is trying to...."

The prince waved Autumn Leaves to silence. He, too, was smiling, if a little reluctantly. "Thank you for your support, Autumn Leaves, but Waterstone is not just teasing. He's showing me the reality of trying to impose my culture on yours." He took a sip of wine and looked at the woodmen over the rim of the goblet. "You will be pleased to know, Waterstone, that I had actually figured that out already."

"So why are we talking about it then?" asked Waterstone impatiently.

"I suppose, because I need to work out what is reasonable to expect," answered the prince. "From my framework of understanding, ever since I arrived here, I have been constantly overlooking transgressions, some of them severe enough to merit banishment or even imprisonment."

Waterstone smiled. "I know you have. I've seen you do a double take when someone is unexpectedly familiar with you. Anyway, you don't need any of these niceties from your society to keep your distance, if that's what you want. All you need is a few of those withering words of yours and a few of your supercilious looks and people will never take you for granted."

"And there's always the oath to fall back on." added Autumn Leaves encouragingly.

Tarkyn was visited with a queer sensation of wading through treacle. *At least it's friendly treacle,* he thought.

Waterstone stood up and walked a few steps away before turning to look at the prince. Tarkyn realised that, despite the teasing, the woodman had carefully made sure he wasn't standing over him. "Tarkyn, in your society we wouldn't stand a chance because we don't know your rules. But from our point of view, everyone has tried to treat you with respect and to overcome whatever resentment they might be feeling. You feel you have been generous with us. We feel we have been generous with you."

"You have. You have been much kinder to me than I expected. Not everyone, but certainly most of the woodfolk who stayed here with me have been."

"And another thing you haven't considered," said Waterstone, crossing his arms, "You're assuming we're all commoners. But we see ourselves as all of equal rank. Why do you assume that it is the lowest possible rank?"

Tarkyn stared at him for a moment. "I suppose because in a hierarchy, the vast majority of people are commoners."

"But we're not a hierarchy. The lowest possible rank here is also the highest possible rank" As he saw the prince frown, Waterstone added, "Don't worry. I'm not mounting an argument to usurp your authority. No matter what rank you may consider us, you still outstrip us all, because of the oath."

A wave of uncertainty rolled around the clearing. The young exiled prince put down his wine and stood up. He picked a small green shoot off his staff before setting it firmly on the ground. "I'm sorry," he said, "I'm going to have to think this through on my own. Thank you Autumn Leaves, for all your help and Waterstone, I'm glad we're back on an even keel. Don't worry. I'm not offended by anything you've said. I just need time to think. I'll see you this evening."

Chapter 17

Tarkyn wandered out of the hawthorn patch, not sure where to go next. He didn't want to run into Stormaway at the moment, whose strong views would only add to his confusion.

Suddenly, he was seeing the forest far below him. Tarkyn staggered as the image overwhelmed him and he lost his balance. He clung to his staff for support as his mind soared in a great arc across the top of the trees. As his vision swung around across the river, Tarkyn's body lost its battle to stay upright and crumpled in a heap on the ground. His staff crashed away from him and skittered down a slope.

His mind raced low over the trees heading towards the west. Ahead of him he could see grey shapes moving beneath the trees. Wolves. He felt a fugue of anger and hatred emanating from them as they ran single-mindedly, the lead wolf clearly sniffing its way along a specific trail through the woods. His mind swung up higher to show him the scope of the danger. There were wolves spread through the trees, all headed towards where his body lay. His mind soared away from the wolves and back over the river. He watched as two woodfolk rushed up to his prostrate form lying in the middle of a path. With a sickening lurch, he was back in his body; lying on his back and watching a huge golden brown eagle glare down at him through the trees, before it slowly flapped its enormous wings and glided out of sight.

Within moments, his view was filled with the faces of Waterstone and Autumn Leaves bending over him in concern. Tarkyn put up a restraining hand. "Don't." he said peremptorily. "Just let me get up in my own time. I'm all right."

The two woodfolk backed off and waited. Tarkyn sat up and moved a few yards so that his back rested against a tree. As soon as he was able to focus his mind, Tarkyn said, in a voice that brooked no argument, "Sit down. I have an image to show you and you need to be seated to see it."

He transmitted the eagle's vision to them. Then it was his turn to wait. Waterstone and Autumn Leaves stayed out of focus for quite some time. Finally, the prince lost patience. "I presume you are informing the others and making plans?" He waited until this brought Waterstone's eyes back into focus. "It may not have occurred to you but I would like to be included in those plans." It was not a request.

Unmistakably, he saw Waterstone's expression move from impatience through resigned acceptance to calculation.

"Yes," responded Tarkyn, with a wry smile. "I do not have to be a millstone around your neck. I can assist you. I will show you your choices. You tell me what you want to use and how." He closed his eyes and sent images of a power ray, fireball, magical net, levitation and shield.

"I will have to relay this," said Waterstone apologetically. "Try to focus on my thoughts and you may be able to see some of our discussion. I will get back to you as soon as I can."

The sorcerer saw woodfolk posted in trees all along the river. There was a particular concentration of them in trees around a ford about half a mile south of where they were seated. Even the children were up in the trees. Two of them were under the close supervision of Summer Rain, behind the line of fire. Sparrow and another child were standing in the branches, bows at the ready. Tarkyn could not pick up any of the discussion but he could pick up Sparrow's and the other child's carefully controlled fear. He sent them a feeling of reassurance and an image of himself and the other woodfolk stationed all around the children looking calm and ready. He was rewarded with the sight of them squaring their shoulders and smiling, albeit a little tightly.

Waterstone re-focussed. "We need to get down to the river near the ford. As soon as we can, we must get up into the trees for safety. If by any chance we are caught out before we reach the river, you must get yourself up into a tree before you do anything else. Once you are safely out of their reach, you can attack. Not before. Your safety is paramount. I'll explain the rest as we go."

Once Autumn Leaves had retrieved Tarkyn's staff, the prince and the two woodfolk walked down towards the river as quickly as Tarkyn was able.

"How high can you levitate yourself?" asked Waterstone.

"I don't know. I usually lift myself no more than ten feet or so, but I can't see why there would be limit."

"If you could rise high enough to see where the wolves were coming from, we would know where to concentrate our attack. There aren't very many of us and we have to maximise what we have."

If Tarkyn was disappointed with the passive role they had given him, he didn't let it show. He merely nodded and focussed on moving as quickly as he could, given his stiffness.

"Why don't you just levitate yourself along sideways?" asked Autumn Leaves suddenly. As the other two stopped and looked at him, the woodman shrugged and said with his usual candour, "Well, you are holding us up. Your magical strength won't have to fight against strained muscles like your physical strength has to."

The sorcerer smiled, "Good idea. I should have thought of it myself but I'm not used to using magic for everyday activities." He muttered, "*Maya Reeza Mureva*" and rose gently into the air. From that point on, the sorcerer floated himself along above the ground while the woodfolk jogged to keep up with him. When they neared the river, Waterstone checked in with the woodfolk in the trees.

"No sign of them yet," reported the woodman. "Do you want to lift yourself up and see if you can find them? Autumn Leaves and I will climb up into the trees while we're waiting. We don't want to get caught on the ground either"

With a quiet, "*Maya Reeza*", the sorcerer rose up through the trees until he could see across the canopy of the forest. He had never before levitated so high and he could feel the strain on his untrained powers. He centred himself and then looked down into the trees on the far side of the river. He saw a small pack of wolves headed for the ford but not the large number he had noted previously. He scanned the trees and finally caught sight of another larger group heading north along the river. As he watched them, the front guard jumped straight into the fast running water and swam strongly across. The lead wolf shook himself and set off immediately into woods, heading in a direction that would cut in behind the woodfolk's position.

The sorcerer brought himself back down onto the firm branch of a large horse chestnut tree, and then relayed the image of what he had seen to Waterstone. Tarkyn picked up a quickly suppressed flash of panic and an image of woodfolk in trees, no arrows left and wolves surrounding them on every side. Tarkyn sent back a wave of reassurance, with an image of himself alternately blasting wolves and retrieving arrows and sending them back up to the woodfolk. A faint ripple of amusement reached him before he was left alone with his own thoughts while the woodfolk planned their strategy.

Not long after this, Tarkyn heard the first howls as woodfolk arrows struck home. He felt restless not knowing where everyone was in relation to him and not being part of the attack. With nothing better to do, he rose above the trees again to track the wolves' progress. Eight more wolves had crossed the river and were circling around through the trees towards the woodfolk. The sorcerer could feel their snarling hatred as they closed in. Tarkyn descended quickly into the cover of his own tree and found himself a secure position where he could sit straddled across a bough and lean against the trunk of the great horse chestnut before transmitting the image. Twenty long minutes passed. Nothing further happened. It felt like hours of waiting

They're waiting for us to drop our guard and come down out of the trees, thought Tarkyn, *I hope the woodfolk realise that and are patient.* He thought about sending a message to wait, as he had to Autumn Leaves, but decided that it was his own need to be doing something rather than any real need to warn the skilled woodfolk that would be driving him to send the message.

Finally, he saw the wolves emerge from the cover of the trees. Two of them passed directly beneath him but even though he was clearly visible and they must have smelt his scent, none of the wolves stopped to try to attack him. All their attention was focussed on reaching the woodfolk. As he watched, they seem to cluster around particular trees. Arrows sped through the air, dropping one wolf after another. But then the last group of three ran at a nearby oak in sequence, each using the one in front as a ladder to get further up its trunk. Once the leading wolf gained the lower branch, it bounded up from one branch to the next at the beleaguered Waterstone.

Tarkyn could feel the savagery directed against the woodman and received a strong image of Waterstone, hard-pressed and climbing further up into the tree. The sorcerer aimed carefully, spoke "*Fierspa!*" firmly and sent forth a blast of power at the leading wolf before it could climb up out of sight. The huge wolf howled and, losing its footing, crashed to the ground. Tarkyn blasted it once more before it had time to recover. He sent one more streak of power at the second wolf but by then, Waterstone had had time to regroup higher in the tree and his arrows struck the remaining wolves with fast, deadly accuracy.

Suddenly it was over. Tarkyn rose once more above the trees to check for any strays but there was no sign of the running grey shapes. He relayed this information to Waterstone and slowly the woodfolk descended from the trees and congregated next to the river.

As the sorcerer landed gently on the ground to join them, a ball of energy threw itself around his waist. He staggered slightly under the impact and looked down to find Sparrow's upturned face, beaming up at him.

"Tarkyn," She beamed at him. "You saved my dad with that fantastic beam of light and you told us the wolves were coming and then told us about the sneaky ones. Thank you. Thank you. Thank you."

The young prince grinned back down at her and, ignoring the protest of his ribs, swung her up into his arms and gave her a big hug. "You're welcome, young Sparrow. I think everyone did a great job of looking after one another, don't you? And do you know, I think if I hadn't been here, your dad would have just climbed up out of the way faster." He swung her onto one hip so he could see the other woodfolk and asked, "Is everyone here and all right?"

"Thanks to your warning, we were never in any danger," rumbled Thunder Storm. "Things would have been a lot different if we'd been caught out of the trees. We needed more preparation time than the lookouts would have given us to meet such a large number of wolves."

Tarkyn spotted the other child who had been in the tree with Sparrow. The young boy was peeking out from behind his father, Rustling Leaves, watching the prince. Tarkyn swung Sparrow back down and crouched next to her.

"Are you going to introduce me to your friend?" he asked her, nodding at the boy.

"This is Breaking Twigs. We are both ten years old and this was our first hunt," said Sparrow proudly. "Come on. Come and say hello," she urged the boy.

Breaking Twigs disengaged himself from his father and walked forward uncertainly. "Good afternoon, Your Highness," whispered the little boy, clearly over-awed by meeting the prince.

"I am pleased to meet you, Breaking Twigs. You and Sparrow have been very brave fighting those fierce wolves. I was too far away from you to see. Did you hit any of them?"

Sparrow and Breaking Twigs looked at each other then back at the prince before the little boy answered with resolute honesty, "I think one of us might have hit one in the rump but they didn't come to our tree. So we didn't get a close shot."

Tarkyn smiled. "That was a very good effort for your first hunt. I am glad the wolves didn't come any closer to you. They were fearsome, weren't they?"

Both children nodded solemnly. The prince stood up and ruffled their hair. "Well done, you two. Now, would you happen to know where there might be some wine and food? I think lunchtime came and went while we were up in those trees."

A short time later, the woodfolk were seated around a firesite in a nearby clearing, eating a selection of fruits, nuts, cheeses and berries. The conversation was revolving around the disposal of the wolves' bodies.

"Fourteen wolves. That is going to take a lot of cleaning," said Creaking Bough, as she reached for another handful of nuts. "We won't be able to use that much fresh meat. We'll have to dry most of it. There'll be plenty of warm furs for cloaks and blankets."

"I suppose there are only thirteen good furs?" asked the sorcerer apologetically.

Thunder Storm smiled understandingly. "You did better this time, my lord. There is only a small singed area where you struck the wolf. The rest of the hide is quite retrievable this time."

Waterstone looked from one to the other and smiled to himself as he correctly surmised the previous conversation. Tarkyn caught his eye and looked away quickly with a slight smile before Thunder Storm noticed.

"And how are you after your exertions?" enquired Summer Rain. "Not resting as instructed, I notice."

The prince wondered if she was attempting a joke but one look at her serious face assured him that she wasn't. "There are times," he said carefully, "when rest and recovery must take second place."

The healer frowned at him. "First the trees drying out. Now the wolves, my lord. I wonder what your next excuse will be?"

Much to Tarkyn's relief, Thunder Storm butted in and said firmly, "Summer Rain. If it means a few extra days before we depart to seek your brother, then you must be patient. Prince Tarkyn's actions today saved many of us from injury or even death. Do not demean his contribution by calling it an excuse."

Summer Rain coloured slightly. "I beg your pardon, Your Highness. I am merely concerned for your welfare."

Tarkyn smiled at her placatingly. "In answer to your original question, I am feeling stronger today than yesterday despite today's exertions which, after all, were not so great." He threw a glance at Waterstone, "Nothing like so hard as holding up tree branches for hours on end." The prince looked around the group of woodfolk. "Since the topic has arisen, have you decided who will be travelling with me to find Falling Rain?"

There was a short unfocused pause that Tarkyn endured with patience. Finally, Waterstone spoke for them, "All of us who are with you now will travel with you. The others will continue with the harvesting."

A wave of pleasure and gratitude spread out from the prince over the group.

"Tarkyn," said Waterstone with a slight shake of his head. "You are doing it again."

After a slight hesitation, Tarkyn realised what he meant and smiled. "It's just as well I reacted well to the news then, isn't it?" After a moment's thought, he frowned, "What about the children? Will they be all right to travel so far?"

Rustling Leaves answered him "Most woodfolk are itinerant, your Highness. We never stay long in one place anyway. The children are used to travelling although perhaps not so far at any one time. They will learn much on the way. They will be just as safe travelling as they would be staying in one place within the forest."

Tarkyn looked around them. "So when do we leave?"

A lovely young woodwoman with soft eyes and shoulder length shining hair answered him in a soft rhythmic voice. "My Lord, the arrival of the wolves has set us back a little. We must attend to the wolf carcasses before we leave. It will take us several days to prepare and cure the meat and hides. By then we will be ready to leave and you may be recovered, if nothing else happens to distract you. I am Lapping Water."

With some amusement, Waterstone noted an arrested expression in Tarkyn's eyes as he registered Lapping Water for the first time. However, the prince's court training clicked in and he didn't miss a beat as he answered, "Thank you, Lapping Water. I do not believe I have met you before and am pleased to do so now." To cover his confusion, Tarkyn glanced around the group and said, "We have fought together and will be travelling together and yet I still have not been introduced to everyone here. This seems most remiss. Could those of you who have not yet introduced themselves, please do so now?"

Once the seven remaining adult woodfolk had introduced themselves, the prince asked, "And your children, Thunder Storm?"

"I beg your pardon, Your Highness," answered Creaking Bough for him. "These are our sons Trickling Stream and Rain on Water." Trickling Stream was a scruffy, bouncy five year old, with a couple of front teeth missing who bounded forward to meet Tarkyn without a second thought, while Rain on Water was much neater, more reserved and clearly intimidated by talking to the prince. Tarkyn made a mental note to get to know him better away from an audience.

Once introductions had been completed, the prince addressed the whole group. "I would like to thank all of you who are here for having chosen to stand by me. I did not ask to be introduced only for form's sake. I need to know your names if we are in situations such as we were today so that I can call out to you if I need to. All of you need to learn to understand my way of mind talking. I cannot use words, only images, gestures and feeling. As Autumn Leaves can attest, this can lead to some misunderstandings. I will leave him to explain that to you at some other time."

Tarkyn took a sip from his goblet before continuing. "I don't know how you do things here, but where I come from, we discuss a battle of any sort afterwards to ensure we learn from it to improve the next time. Do you do this?"

A few embarrassed glances between woodfolk answered his question.

"You have done it already and not included me?" Tarkyn blinked in disbelief. A wave of outrage burst forth from him and rocked the entire group backwards. As leaves began to dance on the trees, the woodfolk glanced at each other with stricken faces. "So. You use my power and knowledge and then close ranks against me as soon as the danger has passed."

Their new liege lord grasped his staff and struggled to his feet. Gusts of wind picked up leaves and threw them across the clearing as he spoke, his voice intense with anger. "Perhaps you are unaware of the honour I bestowed on you by letting you choose which of my powers to use. By rights, I should have led that attack on the wolves. Instead, I allowed you to make the decisions. But at the very least, I expected to be treated as a valued contributor. You mistake the case completely if you think I am some tool to use, as and when it suits you."

Giving a significant glance at the gathering storm, Autumn Leaves said bravely, "Sire, on the feast night, you said that only when you had made your expectations known, would you demand our compliance – and yet now you are angry even though you have not stated your expectations."

The prince glared down at him. "No, I have not yet stated them. And I am not angry that you remain seated while I stand even though you, Autumn Leaves, know that is not what I am used to. But I am angry that the common courtesy you extend to each other does not also extend to me. Even without court training, I cannot imagine that any of you thought that you were honouring me by excluding me."

Small trees were bending in the rising wind. Dust and leaves gusted around the firesite and someone's cup skittered away into the bushes. But no one moved. They watched transfixed, as the sorcerer stood glowering at them, his long hair whipping around his face.

Thunder Storm found his voice enough to say, "We thanked you for what you did."

"As a general would thank a foot soldier," snapped the prince.

A particularly strong gust of wind sent sparks spiralling into the air. A glowing branch rolled off the fire. With a distracted flick of his wrist, Tarkyn murmured "*Liefka,*" and glided the burning branch back onto the coals.

Then Waterstone stood up. He looked steadily at the prince and gave a self-conscious bow. The gesture was so uncharacteristic of him that it brought Tarkyn up short. When Waterstone straightened, he said quietly, "Tarkyn. Your Highness. Please listen to me now, as I did not listen to you when I was angry."

He waited while Tarkyn absorbed his words and actions. When the prince had focused his unnerving gaze solely on Waterstone, the woodman continued, "You are right, Tarkyn. We have taken what you offered and continued to treat you as an outsider. On behalf of everyone here, I apologise for our behaviour and I particularly apologise for mine. Knowing you better, I believe I have less excuse than they do."

The wind dropped a little although the air was still not calm. Encouraged, Waterstone continued, "As you are aware, until recently, we regarded you as dangerous and a liability." A wave of apprehension rippled around the group in response to this, but the wind did not pick up again. "Over the last few days though, some of us have come to realise that you could actually be an asset to us."

Tarkyn crossed his arms. "I am no more gratified to be considered an asset than I was concerned at being considered a liability. Every one of us is an asset or a liability at different times in our lives. I don't see how this justifies your behaviour."

Waterstone frowned. "It doesn't. I was trying to explain that it is only recently that there has been a shift in our attitude towards you. But we are still nowhere near thinking of you as one of us."

"I am not one of you. You have made that patently obvious," said Tarkyn coldly. "I am your liege lord. Clearly, despite your words this morning, you prefer to keep me at a distance. So be it. But it will be reciprocal. I will insist on being accorded the signs of respect that are my due. You will not take me for granted again."

Autumn Leaves lumbered back into the conversation, "Sire, we made a mistake, an oversight. Please don't force us to follow all that protocol of yours because of one mistake. The problem is your mind talking disability. We have to make a conscious effort to include you. Your inability to pick up words makes it very difficult... even if you do have other strengths."

"Don't patronise me." Tarkyn said sharply. He waved his hand dismissively, and began to pace. He realised he was hurt, as much as angry. He had let down his guard and risked a closeness that did not come easily to him, only to have it thrown back at him. As he paced, he struggled to overcome his desire to avenge himself.

Finally he turned and faced them all. His voice was low and controlled, his anger tightly in check. A swirl of leaves behind him was the only remaining evidence of his displeasure. "I will give you two choices: either you will include me in all discussions relevant to me that you have amongst yourselves, no matter how hard that is or I will simply assume total control and expect you to behave towards me in accordance with court protocols. If you continue to close me out, then I shall act strictly as a prince of the realm and will treat all of you as no more than my subjects. Then we shall all be clear about where we stand, won't we?"

The prince watched them exchanging glances, staying strictly in focus, not daring to mind talk.

"Waterstone, Autumn Leaves, you may share with the others the protocols I mentioned this morning, but no other part of the conversation. Be aware that there are other expectations that I have not yet mentioned. I will give you an hour to discuss it among yourselves and give me your decision." So saying, the prince turned on his heel and walked off down to the river.

CHAPTER 18

It seemed like years since Tarkyn had last been here, but it was only this morning. The river bank was not a pleasant place at the moment. It was littered with wolf carcasses and blowflies were beginning to gather. However Tarkyn was not about to make a fool of himself by walking back up the hill to go off in another direction. As the minutes ticked by, the prince's heart sank. He had thought the woodfolk would find the choice easy. He could not imagine that they would want to be ordered around by him all the time. Tarkyn did not want to be isolated from all of them either, but equally he would not put up with being marginalised. As time passed and he calmed down, the young man wondered if he had just let his feelings force him into a confrontation that could have been avoided, just as his father had done before him. He wandered down to the water's edge and squatted down, looking into the depths of the river.

"Oh stars above! I'm a bloody idiot. Now what have I done?" Tarkyn said quietly to himself. "All I had to do was point out what was wrong and work it out with them. Now I've upset everyone again and they will, quite rightly, feel more resentful of me than ever." The prince moodily threw pebbles into the water. "Maybe my first instinct was right. Maybe I should just go away from these people and leave them in peace. There is plenty of forest to live in. And maybe I can find a way for the forest to release me, once the hunt has died down, and I can take my chances on the open road again."

"I don't think we could let you do that, you know," came a familiar voice.

Tarkyn spun around to see Waterstone sitting on the stone behind him. Being stiff and not as agile as usual, the spinning sent him off balance and only Waterstone's outstretched hand saved him from falling backwards into the water. The prince thanked him gruffly and stood up. He walked over to a nearby tree and sat down with his back to it. He sighed, "How long were you listening and what can't you let me do?"

"Long enough." replied Waterstone with a slight smile. "Even if you're a bloody idiot, we can't let you go off and be miserable on your own. After all, we have vowed to protect you and that's a bit hard to do if we're nowhere near you."

Tarkyn glanced up at him but looked away. "You will have to find a way if that's what I choose to do." His ultimatum had still not been answered. "What have you all decided?"

Waterstone gave a short laugh. "There was never any decision to make. Nobody wants you ruling us like some sort of tyrant, least of all you, I suspect."

The prince nodded reluctantly. "So what took you so long?"

"Trying to figure out how to make sure we keep you in the loop. Someone has to be posted with you all the time to act as mediator. I should have thought of that and had you in the same tree as I was. Then I could have told you what was being said and let everyone know your ideas."

"I don't need someone with me all the time," protested the prince, "only when something important is happening or being discussed. I do need time on my own sometimes, you know."

Waterstone leaned down and picked up a couple of pebbles and started to toss them. "That's a problem, you see. How do we judge what is important and what is not?"

Tarkyn brushed his hand over his eyes. "For heaven's sake, Waterstone. I really do think we might all be better off if I just go away somewhere. You can keep watch from a distance if you're worried about me being safe. I just don't know how to do this."

Waterstone dropped the pebbles and came over to squat in front of Tarkyn with his hand on the prince's knee. "Tarkyn, don't give up now. You're nearly there. Your ultimatum has presented a few problems but we just have to find ways around them."

The prince brought his eyes up to look into his friend's face. "Waterstone, despite your best efforts back there, I still behaved just like my father. Threatening when I should have been talking it through."

The woodman gave the prince's knee a pat and stood up."You know, I don't think it will hurt everyone to think they haven't any room to move. It will make it easier for them and me to break the habit of mind talking automatically and leaving you out." Waterstone held out his hand then pulled the prince to his feet. "Anyway, I don't think you did behave like your father. You are much more controlled than he was. Mostly, you were just clear about the choices."

As they walked back up the hill, Tarkyn said resignedly, "Still, I presume resentment is running high again?"

Waterstone thought for a moment before answering, mostly to ensure that Tarkyn didn't think he was producing an empty reassurance. "Actually, I think your ultimatum made most people realise for the first time that you did not intend to exercise absolute control. Since they had not been party to the discussions we have had, they didn't know that before. Not only that, we all understood why you were angry. It made us realise that you require more than the respect based on protocol or fear. You are demanding the type of respect we give each other." The woodman shrugged, "To be honest, that is much harder to give."

Tarkyn stopped walking, a frown gathering on his brow. Before he could say anything, Waterstone pointed to a side path. "Come on. Let's take a longer way back. We need to sort this out before you face everyone, and I think they need to get on with cleaning those wolf carcasses." At a nod from the prince, Waterstone went briefly out of focus.

After a moment, Tarkyn followed the woodman's suggestion and turned down the side path. He was still frowning as he asked, "Are you saying, that after all you and I have been through, you don't respect me as you do, say, Autumn Leaves?"

Waterstone flicked a glance at the prince, then cleared his throat nervously, as he returned his gaze to the path. "In some ways, yes," he replied resolutely. He held his breath and waited for the explosion. When it didn't come, he turned his head to find the prince staring at him incredulously.

"Waterstone, your courage never ceases to amaze me. I wish I had known you for longer." For one hideous moment, it flashed across the woodman's mind that the prince was going to kill him, but Tarkyn merely clapped him on the shoulder and continued in amazement, "I don't think there is another person I have ever met who would dare to say that to me."

The woodman let out a quiet sigh of relief and shrugged. "Autumn Leaves would. Maybe others. Saying that, I have to admit I thought I was taking a risk."

"Oh, you were. Believe me, you were." The prince's eyes glinted. "The things I accept here that I would never have countenanced at court continue to astonish me." He studied the woodman unnervingly for several seconds. "So tell me, in what ways do your friends merit more respect than I do?"

Waterstone took a deep breath to steady himself. He knew he was pushing the limits of this strange friendship. "This is very difficult. I risk offending you with everything I can think of to say. But basically it simply comes down to this. They are woodfolk. You are not." The woodman glanced at the sorcerer for a reaction but as far as he could see, there was none. He continued, "I share a thousand, two thousand years of ancestry with them. I know how they think, how they react in every situation. I know their skills. I know how they behave in danger. I know how we work together. I know them as I know myself."

"And you do not know me." It was partly question, partly statement.

Waterstone shook his head. "Not like that, I don't. How could I? I have known you for three weeks. I have known them all my life."

"So in the short time you have known me, where have I fallen short?"

The woodman did not like the detached tone he was hearing in the prince's voice. He could feel Tarkyn withdrawing but he was now committed to this uncomfortable expose.

"Tarkyn, it is like playing with fire, being around you. You are unpredictable. In a dangerous situation, you are an unknown quantity. How could you expect me to respect your judgement in a situation that you have never been in before and that we have been in a hundred times over?" He paused and looked at the prince who was still gazing expressionlessly straight ahead as they walked. "Tarkyn, imagine if I came to court with you where I know little or nothing of the expectations and dangers....You would probably have to explain and excuse my behaviour and endure my ignorance embarrassing you in front of your peers. Would you have as much respect for me there as for your fellow sorcerers?"

The prince smiled sadly. "Knowing you as I do, if I took you to court, I would respect you far and away more than anyone else there. That doesn't mean you would be the best at everything or that you would shine in all situations." He considered carefully, "I must admit that in some circumstances, my greater knowledge could mean that I did not respect your judgement there as I do here. But I would hope that I would give your opinions due consideration because you also would know your limitations." He shrugged, "I might point out that I did not even attempt to air any of my opinions during the fight with the wolves."

Waterstone stopped dead. "I have done you a disservice, haven't I? Both now and after the wolf fight when I didn't ensure that you were included in the post mortem." He frowned as he turned to keep walking. "Now it is I who needs time to think all of this through."

The sound of hurrying footsteps made them turn in their tracks. Up the path behind them came the wizard, green robe flapping around him as he rushed to catch up with them.

"My lord, I don't know what you said to them but the woodfolk seem to be very pleased about it."

The prince raised his eyebrows. "Do they?" He frowned as he thought through what he had said, "I was concerned that I had been overly harsh with them."

"I told you that they were relieved," said Waterstone.

Stormaway looked suspiciously from one to the other. "What have you made the prince do?" He demanded of the woodman. "I'm not a fool, you know. I know you've been working on him, taking advantage of his illness to work your way into his good opinion. Now you've used your influence to manipulate him, haven't you? Even with the oath, one man against a nation is poor odds."

Thank heavens I trawled Waterstone's memory. I'm not sure I could withstand this barrage otherwise, thought the prince. As it was, he let loose a warning wave of anger which he allowed Waterstone to feel as well to make sure the woodman realised that he had the prince's support. *Interesting. I wonder if Stormaway can tell that I also let Waterstone know that I'm angry? Probably not.* "Stormaway, there is no point in you blustering in here after the fact and throwing your weight around. While I have been trying to work out my role among the woodfolk, you have been conspicuous by your absence." Tarkyn conveniently forgot that he had been at some pains to avoid Stormaway at various times. "And where were you when the woodfolk were fighting the wolves?"

Stormaway waved a hand vaguely. "Oh, here and there. Nowhere near the river though. I leave that sort of thing to the woodfolk. Not my place to get involved in it." He regained some of his bluster and put his hands on hips. "So what have you done?"

"Stormaway," the prince's voice held a warning tone, "you are not my keeper. You are my advisor. Be calm." Tarkyn picked small green shoots from his wooden staff while he waited for Stormaway's stance to become more respectful. When the wizard had dropped his arms and nodded a brief apology, Tarkyn answered, "I told them that they must not mind talk about anything that concerns me without keeping me informed."

"Very sensible, Sire, but I can't see them being relieved about that."

Tarkyn grimaced, knowing that the wizard would not like what he was about to say. "I told them that the alternative was that I would assume control of everything."

He wasn't wrong about the reaction. Stormaway almost danced up and down with frustration. "Your Highness! You are their ruler. You are supposed to take control."

Tarkyn took a deep breath and brought his eyes up to hold the wizard's gaze. "Stormaway, I am not my father. I may be passionate, but I am not my father. I am not a king and never will be. I may be a prince, but I am far from court and the rules are different here."

"But my lord, it is up to you to impose the rules."

"Stormaway, it is up to me. And I choose not to." The calm authority in his voice forestalled any argument.

Tarkyn looked down at the particular shoot he was trying to remove. When he had managed to twist it off, he looked back up to find the wizard staring at him. The prince met his gaze squarely, waiting for the next sortie. To his surprise, Stormaway turned instead to Waterstone and demanded, "You made this staff for the prince, didn't you? I would have expected you to do a better job of it. When did you make it?"

It struck Tarkyn that Stormaway never asked questions of Waterstone. He always demanded. Meanwhile the woodman was frowning down at the staff in some perplexity.

"I made it five, no six days ago. How can it still have green shoots on it? I trimmed it right back."

Even as they watched, a tiny pale green shoot pushed its tip through a small fissure in the side of the staff. Tarkyn raised his eyebrows and looked from one to the other of them, a slight smile dawning on his face.

Suddenly, Stormaway was all business. "Waterstone, take us to the trees you repaired the other day. I want to look at them."

The woodman glanced askance at him but complied without comment. However, as they moved off, the wizard was taken aback by a firm but gentle wave of disapproval.

A few minutes later they were standing amongst a group of trees that Tarkyn and the woodfolk had worked on three days before. The prince looked up but could not see any sign of the bandaging the woodfolk had done. "What has happened to the bindings you placed around the breaks?" he asked.

Waterstone came to stand beside him and gazed up into the trees. "They're still there." He said, pointing at an apparently undamaged branch. He looked at Tarkyn then back up into the trees. "Look. Just there. We cover the joints with sap and bark so that they blend in; otherwise a stranger passing might see our repairs." As he turned to look at the wizard, his gaze hardened. "So, what did you want to see?"

"If it is at all possible, I would like to see how well one of your mended joints is recovering…If you wouldn't mind, could you please take the wrappings off one and have a look?"

Waterstone blinked in surprise at the change in Stormaway's tone. A flicker of surmise crossed his face but he answered with equal courtesy, "I would be pleased to assist you. No doubt you will tell us why, in your own good time." The woodman climbed nimbly into the nearest tree and began to unwrap the layer of sap and bark. "Tarkyn, can you hold up the branch to support it when I take away the bindings? Otherwise we may damage it beyond repair."

In answer Tarkyn muttered, "*Liefka!*" and a beam of bronze light shot up to hold the weight of the bough. If the wizard deplored such familiarity, he refrained from saying so. He was gazing intently at the branch that was being revealed beneath Waterstone's hands. As the binding was removed, both wizard and woodman stared in wonder at the smooth, unscarred branch that appeared before them. Tarkyn was too busy concentrating to realise what was happening, as Waterstone asked, "Can you reduce your support gradually?"

Tarkyn thought about it and grimaced, "I don't think so. It's all or nothing. Perhaps you can hold it for a moment and let go gradually yourself. Then I'll take the weight again when you're ready."

The woodman nodded and placed his arms around the place where the join had been. "Right. Let go." Waterstone gingerly reduced his support of the bough. Nothing happened. The branch stayed in place and was able to take its own weight. "Can you two come up here?"

"I'm getting too old for this," grumbled Stormaway. Nevertheless, wizard and sorcerer rose from the ground and hung in midair to inspect the branch.

Tarkyn stared at the unbroken bark of the healed bough. "These trees have healed quickly, haven't they, Waterstone? I would have thought they would take a lot longer than this to heal."

The woodman nodded slowly. "They should take much longer than this. Several weeks at least....and even then, they would always bear a scar of some sort."

"Hmm," said the wizard thoughtfully, "Interesting. - Waterstone, would you mind if we looked at another mended branch?" he asked politely. The woodman flicked a suspicious glance at Tarkyn who blinked but otherwise remained deadpan.

It was the same with every branch they inspected. Beneath the wrappings, there was no sign of damage at all. When they were all back standing on the ground, Stormaway asked, "Have any other strange things been happening?"

Waterstone scratched his head. "Obviously, the wolves are strange. It is unusual to have even one coming this far to the east of the forest, but first two arrived more or less together then today, two days later, another fourteen attacked us. If it hadn't been for Tarkyn's warning...." The woodman looked decidedly embarrassed, the prince was pleased to note.

Stormaway shook his head, clearly perturbed. "I don't like the sound of all this. Something is wrong." A thought struck him. "I am shocked that the woodfolk allowed you into a position, Your Highness, where you were the first to see the wolves. They cannot be protecting you properly. It is not funny." He added in response to a ripple of dry amusement that pushed against him.

Tarkyn smiled at him. “Stormaway, I am pleased you are looking after my interests but I was not in the first line of fire. In fact, I had more than the woodfolk looking after me. In the latest incident, I was assisted by an eagle. The time before, I believe it was an owl,” said Tarkyn casually, grinning hugely by this time at the stunned look of amazement on the wizard’s face. He exchanged grins with Waterstone while the poor wizard struggled to get his head around it all.

“Explain to me,” demanded Stormaway. “What do you mean; you were assisted by an owl?”

As Tarkyn explained, Stormaway’s eyes widened, then a deeply satisfied smile spread across his face. “Marvellous!” he exclaimed. “That I should live to see this in my own lifetime. I saw the portents all those years ago but until now, I didn’t really believe they could be true.”

Tarkyn stared at the wizard as though he had gone mad, but Waterstone reacted quite differently. The woodman became very still and then, as the wizard watched, pieces fell into place and realisation dawned. Waterstone turned to regard Tarkyn with a strange mixture of suspicion and wonder on his face that the prince found very unnerving.

“What? What are you looking at?” demanded Tarkyn.

Ignoring him completely, the wizard kept his eyes on Waterstone. “You know it’s true, don’t you?”

The woodman gave his head a little shake. “But Stormaway, can’t all sorcerers do this type of mind linking?”

“No. None that I am aware of…and I did train many sorcerers, the king among them. That’s why they’re such a pushover for mind control” He raised his eyebrows at the woodman. “You are aware, I presume, that our young sorcerer here was able to withstand Tree Wind’s attempt at mind control?”

“Yes. She wasn’t pleased, was she?” Waterstone smiled reminiscently. “I don’t think any of us was too pleased about it at the time, to be honest,” he added with a wry smile at Tarkyn.

“Oh good. So you’ve remembered I exist then,” responded Tarkyn sarcastically. “You still haven’t answered my question. Why were you looking at me in that strange way? You know something I don’t and I would appreciate being included.”

Waterstone gave him a cheeky grin that went a long way towards making the prince’s blood boil. “At least you know we’re not mind talking. Stormaway’s mind is a closed book.”

As a sharp wave of annoyance hit him, Waterstone added quickly, “Sorry. It’s a bit like that owl you didn’t tell me about. I’m struggling to believe what Stormaway is proposing and I don’t want to say anything until I’m sure.”

The prince's eyes flashed. "I am quite happy to hear theories. Stormaway, I insist you tell me what this is about." A jab of anger hit the wizard's mind.

"For heavens' sake, Tarkyn," he said, rubbing his forehead, "I will tell you. Exercise some control."

"I am." answered the prince flatly.

"Sire," The wizard wandered over to a nearby log. "I suggest we sit down. This could take some time." He waited until Tarkyn was seated before sitting down himself. Then he began. "For you to understand, I will have to tell you one of the old tales of woodfolk lore." He paused as he gathered his thoughts. "There is a legend that has passed down through generations of woodfolk of a mystical being who appears among the woodfolk in times of great need. This being, sometimes male, sometimes female, possesses powers far beyond those of any woodfolk and is given the name of…"

"Guardian of the forest" said the prince slowly, glancing at the woodman. "You see? I remember some of what you told me."

"So you know this story?" asked the wizard.

Tarkyn shrugged apologetically, "Actually I only have a vague recollection of it. Waterstone did tell me but I only remember that there was a wondrous being with mystical powers that emerges, what? every four or five hundred years."

"Yes," replied the wizard, "There is no set time but that seems to be roughly how often one will appear. Not every generation of woodfolk has seen a guardian but the legend is passed down for safekeeping in the lore of the woodfolk so that when he or she appears among them, they will recognise and remember. The appearance of a guardian of the forest is greeted with both fear and rejoicing; fear because his or her coming is a portent of great strife; rejoicing, because the forest guardian has come to stand beside them in their time of need."

"I do remember most of this." The prince absent-mindedly picked off another green shoot that had started to grow on his staff. "So are you seeing signs that this marvellous being may be coming among the woodfolk again?" He thought about it for a moment. "The wolves? The trees growing back more quickly….What else?"

"Tarkyn, look at me." The wizard's voice grew tense with suppressed excitement. "Among the powers possessed by a guardian of the forest are the ability to commune with the creatures of the woodlands and the ability to heal and foster growth."

Tarkyn stared at him as the significance of his words hit him, and then turned to stare at Waterstone. "Oh, Stars Above! You two have completely lost the plot," he said, revolted by the whole concept. "I am not some marvellous, mystical being. I am simply a sorcerer – perhaps more powerful than most, but still just a sorcerer."

Tarkyn stood up and started pacing up and down in agitation. "And I have not just appeared miraculously among you. I have been forced upon you by the oath. Not only that, I walked for five days to get here from Tormadell then walked into the forest in plain view of everyone, in the company of this devious, delusional hedge-dweller here." He smiled faintly. "Although I did appear above you when I translocated with the acorn."

He stopped to look down on them, hands on hips, his eyebrows raised in derision. "And I may have been met with fear, but certainly not with any rejoicing that I've noticed." He scowled at them, "Is that enough for you? Can you stop looking at me as though I'm some kind of freak now?"

The woodman and the wizard exchanged glances and shook their heads. Waterstone smiled fondly up at him. "Tarkyn," he said quietly. "I think you have to give a legend a bit of poetic licence. Over the years, the logistics of how the guardians appeared would have become irrelevant. The tale has blurred each arrival into one description. And anyway, it doesn't say 'miraculously'. It just says 'appeared.'

Tarkyn looked askance at him then bent down to pick up his staff. He started to pick a green shoot off it then, realising what he was doing, threw it down in disgust.

"Oh for heaven's sake. Can't you see? I'm not mystical," Tarkyn raised his hands and twinkled his fingers to demonstrate what he was not. "And I don't have mystical powers. I've just been trying to mind talk like the woodfolk and it has gone a bit awry."

The wizard shook his head. "No, it hasn't gone awry. You have unearthed unique powers within yourself. No other sorcerer has them. No one else on Eskuzor, wizard, sorcerer or woodfolk, has them."

A hint of panic flickered at the back of the sorcerer's eyes. He looked wildly around, like a cornered animal. "I can't handle all this," he said imploringly. "I'm only just coming to terms with being exiled, trapped in a forest, hated by an entire nation of people.... actually two nations of people, if you count the sorcerers as well." He ran his hand through his hair in distress. "Finally, I start to find a basis for living with the woodfolk with some degree of acceptance and now you're trying to tell me I'm some kind of mystical being from one of their legends." He sank down onto a log, closed his eyes and hid his face in his hands.

No one spoke. After a while, a feeling of warm reassurance pushed at the edges of Tarkyn's mind. He felt something nudging against his knee.

Being used to having dogs, he put his hand down unthinkingly to pat it. Then, as he remembered where he was, his hand stopped in mid-pat and he looked down to see the broad, striped face of a badger looking calmly up at him. As his eyebrows snapped together, the badger shied away from him. Tarkyn sighed and sent a wave of contrition to the badger who eyed him uncertainly for a moment before returning within the sorcerer's reach. He stroked the badger gently for a few minutes, focusing on the feel of her coarse hair under his fingers as he grappled with his confusion.

He had an idea. "Maybe it's the oath. You woodfolk did swear it on behalf of the woodland creatures, didn't you? Maybe they're protecting me because of that."

Surprisingly, it was the wizard who replied. He shook his head firmly and said, "No, Your Highness. Woodfolk have no authority to speak for the forest creatures. Those words simply meant that by obeying the oath, the woodfolk would be acting to protect the forests and the creatures within them. Besides, it doesn't explain the regeneration of the trees and the staff."

The sorcerer ran his hands through his long hair. "This is crazy. Anyway, call me what you will, it won't change who I am."

"Now there is a fraught statement, if ever I heard one," commented Waterstone. "Would you still be the same if you were no longer called Prince of Eskuzor?"

Tarkyn stared at him for several seconds. "To be honest," he said at last, "I am struggling to imagine what that would be like. I don't know. It is not just a title. It is a role that comes with huge expectations of myself and everyone around me; expectations which, I might add, are shifting like quicksand beneath my feet at the moment." The prince felt the badger nudge him again. "Sorry," he said distractedly and began to pat her again.

Waterstone watched him quizzically.

Tarkyn sighed. "Don't tell me. I can see where this is going already." He saw them both watching him expectantly and tried a last ditch stand. "I can't be a guardian of the forest.I am sure a guardian would have to be old and wise with grey hair and long flowing beard. I am just an untried, callow youth. You said so yourself," he added with a tinge of resentment, glancing at Waterstone.

Stormaway looked profoundly shocked, but the woodman laughed. "I didn't quite say that, but you are certainly inexperienced in the ways of the woodlands." Waterstone gave another chortle as he echoed the prince's own words, "You may not be the best at everything and you may not shine in all situations…. and you are certainly not old and grey," suddenly he became serious, "but against all the odds, you are wise."

The wizard and the sorcerer both stared at the woodman. Tarkyn's cheeks burned with embarrassment. Despite all the flattery he had received over the years, he did not know how to respond to such a profound compliment.

"And," continued Waterstone quietly, sliding in under his guard, "amazingly, you are a guardian of the forest."

After a few moments, Tarkyn picked up his staff and watched as small green shoots pushed their way out of the wood. As an experiment, he focused his will on the staff and found that he could accelerate the speed of growth. He gave a small private smile and looked up to find the other two watching him. He shrugged self-consciously, "Just seeing what I can do."

Wizard and woodman were staring at him appraisingly. Neither spoke. Lacking a response from them, Tarkyn ignored them and, hunting around for a sharp dry stick, used it to dig a narrow hole in the ground. When he was satisfied, he jabbed one end of his staff down into it and pushed the soil back into place around it. He grasped the rod with both hands, closed his eyes and focused his being into it. The tiny green shoots expanded and grew into the beginnings of small branches even as they watched. Within minutes, a healthy young sapling was growing in the ground. Tarkyn opened his eyes and stood back to admire his handiwork.

After a moment, he smiled apologetically at Waterstone, "I still need a staff. Do you think you could make me one from a dead branch this time? Then I won't have the embarrassment of green shoots bursting forth all the time."

Waterstone, who was staring in bemusement at the new sapling, nodded distractedly.

Tarkyn tried again. "Waterstone?" His voice became sharper, "Waterstone!" Once the woodman had dragged his eyes away from the resurrected sapling to look at him, Tarkyn said, "Hello? It's still me. You're the ones who told me I could do it. So don't act so surprised when I do what you're expecting me to do."

Waterstone gave his head a shake and blinked, "Sorry Tarkyn. It's going to take a bit of getting used to – living with a legend."

The sorcerer rolled his eyes. "Oh for heavens sake, Waterstone! Pull yourself together. I'm still the same person I was an hour ago."

Waterstone smiled ruefully. "You haven't grown up listening to the legends as I have. It's truly amazing."

Tarkyn looked to the wizard for support but found him, too, gazing at the resurrected sapling. "Not you too," said Tarkyn in disgust.

Stormaway shook his head in wonder, "Marvellous. Just marvellous."

"Well, that settles it," exploded the prince, "I'll be experimenting in private next time. If you two, who know me, behave like besotted fools, what will everyone else do?"

Consternation showed in the woodman's face. "The others. We must tell the others. There must be danger coming."

"No," said the prince flatly. "I forbid it."

"But Your Highness…" began the wizard.

Tarkyn put up a hand. "No. Not yet. The woodfolk and I must work out our terms of engagement as we are. That's hard enough to sort out as it is. I have to consolidate where I am before everything starts to shift again."

Stormaway came in firmly. "You can't have long. The threat to the woodfolk, whatever it is, must be discovered and prepared for."

"I have sworn to protect the woodfolk and I will not forget." Tarkyn frowned at him. "You seem remarkably concerned for the woodfolk all of a sudden. And yet you were party to creating the oath."

Stormaway considered carefully before answering, aware of the prince's reservations. "Yes and no. Yes, I constructed and delivered it but I did so under orders from the king."

"I thought you were his advisor. Could you not have dissuaded him from it?"

The wizard shrugged. "You saw in Tree Wind's memory what type of man he was. Sometimes I had very little influence. Other times, I had more. Sometimes I had to be, hmm, what shall we say?… creative… to protect people's interests."

Tarkyn glanced at Waterstone but the woodman was watching quietly, keeping well out of the conversation. The prince turned back to the wizard. "So, if you created it, can you also destroy the sorcery in the oath?"

Stormaway looked squarely at him."I could but I would not. I know how to destroy it but I promised your father that I would not." Seeing Tarkyn about to protest, he too glanced at Waterstone. "I would suggest that we continue this discussion at another time."

Waterstone stood up. "I can leave if you would like."

"Yes. That would be helpful, I think," said the wizard at the same time as the prince said, "No, stay. This concerns you and the woodfolk every bit as much as it concerns me."

The woodman waited irresolute while the balance of power wavered. After a fraught moment, Tarkyn said quietly to the wizard, "Despite your misgivings and for reasons I am not prepared to go into, I have complete faith in Waterstone. I would appreciate it if you felt able to continue the discussion now. However, if it involves something about you personally that you don't want to reveal, then of course we will wait for another time."

A slight smile of satisfaction appeared on the wizard's face. "My boy," he said, "Your father would have been proud of you. I am even prouder of you because I understand, better than he would have, the subtlety of your style." Stormaway addressed the woodman. "Waterstone, I hope Tarkyn's faith in you is justified. I suspect it will be because I am beginning to develop a healthy respect for his judgement." The wizard shrugged, "So be it. Shall we take up the discussion where we left off?"

Tarkyn looked down at the badger and kept stroking it gently. "What would happen, Stormaway, if I ordered you to remove the sorcery in the oath? After all, you too have sworn the oath."

Stormaway breathed a sigh of relief. "I am so glad you phrased it like that. What would happen is that I would refuse."

"Hm, I see. No surprises there. And is this because your loyalty to my father is greater than your loyalty to me?"

"No, Your Highness, it's not. It's because the oath was designed to keep you safe and without it, you might find it difficult to leave the forest alive, should you ever choose to." The wizard glanced at the woodman as he said this but Waterstone offered no reaction.

The prince frowned, "And what about the safety of the forest if I insisted on ordering you? Would you see it destroyed?"

The wizard smiled with a hint of smugness, "My concern for your wellbeing far outweighs any consideration I may have for the forest. Now that you know I would refuse, you could not order it because you have vowed to protect the forest."

Tarkyn rocked back to sit upright as he considered this. His hand came away from the badger who, having had her fill of being stroked, took the opportunity to head off into the undergrowth. "I can see why you didn't want Waterstone to hear this. Not," he added hastily, looking at the woodman, "that I regret my decision to allow you to stay," He returned his gaze to the wizard, "but I understand your reservations."

He asked Waterstone. "What are the exact words of the oath?"

The woodman did not make the mistake of parroting the whole thing and merely repeated the relevant section. "To serve, honour and protect."

"According to your understanding of honour and service, Your Highness, not Markazon's. I achieved that much for you."

"I suppose I should at least thank you for that, Stormaway" said Tarkyn gruffly. He rolled his eyes at Waterstone. "You really wouldn't want to live under my father's regime."

Waterstone stood up and looked up into another repaired tree, his face closed. After a moment's scrutiny, he lifted himself up into the branches and began to unwrap the injured bough. He looked down at the prince and said tightly. "This is actually a difficult conversation for me to listen to. I feel like my future, my whole life is being bandied around like some sort of commodity."

Tarkyn was instantly contrite. "Oh Waterstone, I'm sorry. We are both affected by the terms of this oath, but of course, for you, it is even more critical. I need to know how much leeway I can safely give without destructive forces coming into play. I didn't even think to ask you if you wanted to stay to hear all this. I just assumed you would. I think your perspective may help us all in coming to terms with managing this oath but I can come and talk to you about it afterwards if you prefer."

Wizard and woodman both smiled at this little speech. "Tarkyn," said Waterstone, "You make it just as impossible for me to leave as you did for Stormaway not to speak in front of me. I don't think you have any need of an oath to get what you want."

Tarkyn, embarrassed by this vote of confidence, bent down to pick up a dry stick which he then began methodically to demolish. "I did mean it, though," he said, without looking up. "You don't have to stay if you would rather go."

"I know you did. That's what makes it so convincing." Waterstone shook his head, smiling, and turned his attention to the wizard. "You need have no fear that your young prince will compromise his authority. He just goes about it differently from his father."

Tarkyn looked up at this and his eyes narrowed as he considered the wizard. "Out of those who swore the oath, you alone can oppose my will if you decide it serves my best interests to do so. Is that right?"

"How do you work that out?" asked Waterstone, as he climbed back down out of the tree.

Tarkyn smiled ruefully. "Because no one else, not even I, would place my welfare above the welfare of the forest."

Waterstone considered him for a long time. "I'm not sure that's true," he said slowly, "although it may be true of most people." He shrugged, "I would hope that you will never put me in the position where I have to oppose you to protect you – but I will remember this if it ever happens."

Tarkyn frowned as he tried to work out the complexities of the oath. "It seems to me that anyone who calls my bluff will have the upper hand, whatever the issue. I can't afford to order someone to do something that they don't want to do. If they tell me they are going to refuse, I will have no choice but to back down. I'm honour bound to protect the forest so I can't allow anyone the option of opposing me and invoking the destructive force of the oath."

The wizard nodded. "Now you see why I didn't want any woodfolk here for this conversation."

"Waterstone is not just any woodman, even as I am not just any sorcerer." The prince replied stiffly. "But I do see what you mean," he conceded. He looked at Waterstone. "So where does this leave us then?"

Waterstone's green eyes travelled slowly from the prince to the wizard and back again. His eyes were glittering with anger. "Both of you have forgotten that the woodfolk are also people of honour. We agreed to swear that oath in good faith as a debt of gratitude for the assistance rendered to us by King Markazon and you, his wizard.He did not respect us enough to trust our word. Obviously you do not either."

"Oh no, Waterstone, don't think that." The prince was mortified. "I do trust you - you the woodfolk, I mean, to keep your word. I had just forgotten that angle on things because I was focusing on the danger to the forest. I have to be sure we know how to manage the destructive magic in the oath." The prince turned impulsively to the wizard. "Couldn't you find your way clear to neutralise your spell?"

"No, Your Highness. Do not demand it of me." Stormaway shook his head regretfully. "I am sorry if I offend you, Waterstone, but I do not know or trust the woodfolk well enough to risk the prince's safety. I will not break faith with his father."

Waterstone shrugged. "You have certainly offended me but there is not much I can do against blind prejudice." There was a pause while he visualised Sparrow going to live among a large group of stern, unfriendly wizards and sorcerers. He shared the image with Tarkyn and sighed. "I suppose I can understand how you might feel, at least to some extent."

Tarkyn smiled wryly and sent an image back to Waterstone of Sparrow ordering the sorcerers around, with the sorcerers glancing sideways at her with their eyes filled with resentment and malice.

Waterstone raised his eyebrows in response. "True. To an even greater extent, I understand, but I am still offended." He shrugged, "However, I suppose I can still work with you, Stormaway. I cannot purport to be honourable and, at the same time, expect you to break your own oath to Markazon."

"Good." said, the wizard, suddenly all business, "because if this young man is truly a guardian of the forest, there are bad times coming and you are going to need all the help you can get."

CHAPTER 19

Night had fallen. Everyone was sitting around a new firesite. After some discussion earlier in the day, it had been agreed that mind talking was permissible if it was for private conversations or routine communications. There was some initial constraint, but gradually the atmosphere around the firesite had become more congenial than it had been previously. The woodfolk were not as relaxed with the prince in the way that they were with each other but they were making a clear effort to include him and to fill him in on any mind talking that occasionally wandered into the middle of conversations in which he was involved. As for Tarkyn, he was used to being set apart and felt that he had achieved as much familiarity as he could manage.

"Tarkyn," said a little voice at his side. The prince looked around to see Sparrow's upturned face. "Could you hold these for me while I finish making this village?"She held out an assortment of rocks, twigs and leaves. Tarkyn held out his hands and she tipped her treasures into them. "I've just collected them all and I don't want them to get dusty sitting on the ground while I finish this bit off." She pointed at several little assemblies from bark and small branches that Tarkyn rightly surmised to be houses.

"They're not woodfolk houses," he pointed out. "Have you ever been to a village like that?"

Sparrow shook her head. "No, but I've seen one from the forest edge." She gave an anxious frown. "Have you been to one? Do you think I've got it right?"

Tarkyn smiled. "Near enough. There's usually one bigger house called an inn which is where everyone goes for a chat and a drink in the evenings."

Sparrow scowled at her creation. "I don't think I have time tonight to build a bigger one as well. This will have to be a village without an inn." She set to, smoothing out the dirt between the houses to make roads and straightening up her houses. Then she began to place her collected items around the village as decoration. By the time she reached into Tarkyn's hand for the last stick, tiny green shoots were clearly developing on it. Sparrow shot a sharp glance up into Tarkyn's face. An image of him asking her to be quiet accompanied by a feeling of complicity appeared in her mind. She barely missed a beat. "This will look good as a tree in the front of this little house," she said placidly as she dug the sprouting twig into a small hole.

Unfortunately, woodfolk are very attuned to anything related to plants and the forest. Added to that, the novelty of the prince's presence meant that at any one time, several people were likely to be idly watching him while they chatted among themselves. Sparrow and Tarkyn gradually became aware that everyone had fallen silent. Many eyes were out of focus as the embargo on mind talking was forgotten.

Nearby, Waterstone was staying determinedly in focus, clearly resisting a battering of silent questions. On the pretext of bringing Tarkyn another drink, he leaned over and whispered in the prince's ear, "The game is up, my friend. How do you want to play it?"

Tarkyn's mouth quirked. "Since it is now inevitable, I think I'll just go for the grandiose," he whispered back. "Anything else will seem apologetic." He sent Sparrow a request for a bigger, green stick. In less than a minute, she returned with a stick about the length of his arm. Tarkyn thanked her and held it upright between his hands.

He drew a deep breath and focused his will briefly on the stick before addressing the woodfolk. He allowed his voice a degree of severity. "It does not seem that agreements made with you endure for long. Already you are excluding me from your present conversation which, unless I am much mistaken, closely concerns me."

Around the firesite, woodfolk eyes snapped back into focus and they looked uneasily at each other, aware that they had transgressed. Then, as one, their green eyes became fixed on the new shoots that were curling forth out of the stick that Tarkyn held. The silence lengthened.

"I didn't say you had to stop talking all together," observed the prince dryly, firmly suppressing a smile. "Who among you would like to tell me what you were saying? Perhaps you would like to ask me a question?"

Waterstone's mouth twitched in appreciation but he held his peace and turned away to help Sparrow pack up ready for bed.

Finally Thunder Storm's voice rumbled into life. "My lord, would you mind explaining how you became aware of the impending wolf attack?"

"Did Autumn Leaves or Waterstone not tell you?"

Thunder Storm shook his head. "No, my lord. We assumed that you had been levitating yourself for some reason and just happened to see them." He paused, "But now, that explanation has been called into question."

The prince glanced in turn at Autumn Leaves and Waterstone. "I appreciate their discretion. However, it would now be my pleasure share the source of my knowledge with you. If you all make sure you are seated, I will show you." The sorcerer waited until they were ready, then asked them to close their eyes. Tarkyn centred himself then sent them the image from the eagle's eyes of the wolves running through the forest as it wheeled below them. He took them right through to where he was looking up from the ground at the eagle flapping slowly away through the trees above his prostrate form.

There was a mass expulsion of breath. Tarkyn steeled himself. All around him, eyes opened and woodfolk gazed at him in wonder. In his hands, the stick had become a flourishing young sapling.

Ignoring the woodfolk's reaction, Tarkyn spoke to Thunder Storm, "Where are your children? Are they still up? And Breaking Twigs?"

"Yes my lord. They are all playing over near the trees."

"Could you send for them please?" He turned to Waterstone, "And Sparrow."

Once the children were arrayed before him, the sorcerer said, "Before you go to bed, I have a very special job for you. Can you four take this sapling and choose somewhere to plant it to commemorate the coming of a guardian of the forest?" He ignored the mass intake of breath that this elicited and kept his eyes firmly on the children who nodded solemnly. "Each of you has to have an equal share in the task. Is that clear?" He handed the sapling to the quiet Rain on Water and nodded dismissal to them.

Inevitably the moment came when Tarkyn had to raise his eyes to meet the awed gazes of the woodfolk gathered before him. "Could I just ask," he said diffidently, "that you don't treat me as more of stranger than you already do?" His voice gained assurance. "You all knew I had strong magical powers before this. Can we just keep it in perspective and think of the mind linking and the tree healing as another couple of powers to add to the rest that you already know about?"

Suddenly everyone was smiling and shaking their heads. They swarmed forward and surrounded Tarkyn, patting him on the back, angling to get close to him and pressing wine and food into his hands. Flowers that seemed to have appeared out of nowhere were festooned over him and he was surrounded by a symphony of excited forest voices. The reticent prince blinked and, after a brief flicker of panic, succumbed to the kindness and enthusiasm of the woodfolk, a surprised smile dawning slowly on his face.

Among the general hubbub, the prince was finally able to make out Autumn Leaves' voice. "Don't you realise, Tarkyn? The guardian of the forest is no stranger to us. You have been here a hundred times before. You just don't remember. But we do."

Long into the night the festivities raged. Everyone sang, danced and retold all the old tales of the guardian of the forest. The people on lookout were rotated so that everyone could join in. No one remembered to put the children to bed and they gradually fell asleep in little heaps at various points around the fire. Everyone congratulated themselves that they were the ones who had stood by Tarkyn and were now the chosen few to have first met the new guardian of the forest. Stormaway looked on benevolently and drank solidly.

All evening, the prince was plied with wine and carried along on the wave of the woodfolk's excitement. As the dawn crept slowly across the sky, Tarkyn weaved his way ponderously up to his shelter and collapsed inside, watched from afar by Waterstone.

Part 4: Life Force

CHAPTER 20

The following day dawned grey and chilly. A sharp wind blew through the trees and twitched at leaves that were beginning to change to shades of autumn.

When Tarkyn finally emerged nursing a sore head, the air of celebration had completely evaporated, but the acceptance of him had not. He was greeted by friendly, relaxed nods from those woodfolk who were still clustered around the breakfast fire. Someone thrust a bowl of porridge and a cup of warm tea into his hands as he sat down with his back against a tree.

Summer Rain looked over at him, "Would you like something for your head?" she asked sympathetically.

Tarkyn squinted at her and nodded. "Ow. That hurt. Yes please. Probably a double dose of whatever you were going to give me."

Thunder Storm and Waterstone walked into the clearing, deep in discussion. They helped themselves to cups of tea and sat down near Tarkyn.

Waterstone studied the prince's grey face. "How's the head?" he asked.

Tarkyn rolled his eyes at him. "Not good, but at least this time I'm not being beaten around the head by bounty hunters on top of the hangover." When the woodman smiled, he demanded, "And why are you looking so disgustingly healthy?"

Waterstone shrugged, "I had things to look after; lookout duty, Sparrow, you. I couldn't afford to get too drunk. I'm glad you did, though. It was about time you let yourself go."The woodman laughed as he saw the classic doubts of the morning after the night before chase across Tarkyn's face. "No. Don't worry. You didn't make a fool of yourself."

Summer Rain handed him a cup of some murky green herbal concoction. Tarkyn sniffed it suspiciously and screwed up his nose at it. "Can I gulp it down or do I have to endure it slowly?"

"It's not as bad as it smells, but you can take it how you like. Fast or slow. The quicker it's in your blood stream the quicker it will work. As long as you don't drink it so fast that you can't keep it down."

"Thanks." He took a deep breath and slugged it down in one draught. For a few seconds, he turned greenish and it was touch and go whether it would stay down, but then he let out a long breath and the colour returned to his cheeks. "We're a tough lot, we guardians, you know," he chortled.

"I think you're still drunk," said Waterstone dryly.

"No, I'm not," said Tarkyn indignantly. He waved his cup of tea. "Well, actually I might be, but I don't think so. I'm just relieved everyone's not goggling at me as you and Stormaway did yesterday." He gave a post-concoction shudder. "Strange, isn't it? You two struggled more than anyone else did, coming to terms with me being a forest guardian."

"Not so strange." Waterstone gave a little smile. "It is harder for those who know you well to accept that you are something as amazing as a forest guardian... But now, if you're feeling up to it, we need to address the second aspect of the advent of the guardian of the forest."

Tarkyn looked at the three serious faces surrounding him and immediately sobered up. "We have to figure out what is threatening us, don't we?" he said, unaware that he had used 'us' instead of 'you'. It was not lost on the woodfolk, however. "Where do the wolves fit in? Anywhere?"

Thunder Storm shook his head. "We don't know. It seems likely that they are part of it in some way since their attack is so unusual, but we don't know."

"What about the other woodfolk? Have they noticed anything unusual?" Waterstone and Thunder Storm glanced at each other uneasily, but Tarkyn forestalled them, "Don't look so guilty. I'm assuming you're gathering information. As long as you share it with me when it matters, that is what we agreed."

Thunder Storm rumbled, "They report an increased number of attacks on people travelling through the forest but other than that, nothing."

"Attacks on travellers do not affect us, do they?" asked the prince.

"Not directly," replied Summer Rain. "Although groups of stranded and injured people are inconvenient when we have to skirt around them."

No overdose of the milk of human kindness running through those veins, thought the prince.

"And we have to be very wary of the marauders," added Waterstone, "especially as they are sorcerers with powers we don't possess."

"Hmm. So where do these wolves come from?" asked Tarkyn.

"From the western pine forests near the foothills of the Ridgeback Mountains," rumbled Thunder Storm. "Interestingly, not far from the greatest concentration of attacks on travellers."

Tarkyn looked around the group. "So what happens now? Does anyone else have any other ideas about the source of this danger?"

A protracted mind conference, punctuated by conscientious liaison with the prince, yielded no new suggestions.

Between updates, Tarkyn used the time to ponder the cause of the wolves' attack. He thought back over his eagle's view of the wolves. Eventually he offered the observation, "The second lot of wolves were following someone or something's trail, you know."

When the woodfolk looked sceptical, he showed them the image again.

Waterstone frowned. "He's right. They are definitely following the trail of something. What? What else has been through near here that they might be interested in?"

"The first two wolves," answered Tarkyn slowly.

The three woodfolk stared at him.

"Can anyone control wolves?" he asked. "Can they send them out searching? Or even just in a particular direction?"

"I don't know," answered Thunder Storm, "but if you could control the lead wolf, you could control a pack."

The prince frowned in thought. "Stormaway may know about this. Where is that lazy wizard?" He pictured Stormaway then sent out a wave of impatient summoning, making it strong so that the wizard would pick it up.

A few minutes later, the grumbling wizard wandered into the clearing and sketched a half hearted bow. "Stars Above, Your Highness. Can't a man get a little sleep?" He shook his head then looked up in surprise. "My headache's gone." His face broke into a smile. "Well done, young guardian. Your peremptory message has cleared my hangover."

Tarkyn flicked a smile at the healer. "Watch out, Summer Rain. I might be taking over your job, if you're not careful."

"I think you are meant for more important tasks, my lord," replied the woodwoman dispassionately.

Oh stars! When will I remember that she doesn't have a sense of humour? Tarkyn met Waterstone's eyes and grimaced. The woodman's eyes lit with amusement but he turned quickly to address the wizard before Summer Rain noticed, "Stormaway. Are there people who can control wolves?"

The wizard huffed. "Don't worry about me. I can snap straight from a deep sleep to full alert. I'll get my own breakfast when I've finished answering your questions."

The prince laughed, "Stormaway, I'm sorry we are being so brutal with you. Could someone get a cup of tea and some food for him while we interrogate him, please?"

The wizard glowered at him. "Don't think you can charm me, young man. I will answer your questions when I'm good and ready"

A sudden heavy gust of wind blew dust and leaves across the clearing. The smile faded on the prince's face. "I think not. We are not prepared to wait on your convenience." The blow of anger that hit the wizard's mind sent him staggering, as the prince's voice continued calmly, "We must act with all speed to find out what threat is facing us."

Thunder Storm caught the wizard as he toppled sideways. "Are you all right?" he rumbled in some concern.

Stormaway gave a short nod and allowed Thunder Storm to help him to a seat on a nearby log. He sent a fulminating stare in Tarkyn's direction as he struggled to deal with the incongruence between the prince's transmitted ire and his dispassionate voice. Realising that no one else was aware of the extent of Tarkyn's displeasure, he said hurriedly, "Probably just the after-effects of the wine." He took a deep breath to steady himself, accepted a cup of tea and addressed himself to answering Waterstone. "In answer to your question, yes. Of course people can control wolves. Not many do. They generally prefer domestic breeds of dog but wolves, if taken young enough, can be trained up. I suppose older wolves could be trained but I doubt that they would stay willingly. They would have to be forcibly confined when not under direct command."

"If someone has trained these wolves, what are they hoping to achieve? What command would send them deep into the forest away from their own territory?" pondered Thunder Storm as he sat down next to the wizard.

"They would have to be searching for something," said Tarkyn. "There are two possibilities that would concern us; if they are looking for woodfolk or for me. The second is much more likely since we know a lot of people are hunting me and no-one even knows woodfolk exist, do they?"

Waterstone leaned forward, suddenly intense. "When the first wolves did not return, the second wave of wolves must have been sent to find the first pair of wolves….And now the second lot of wolves will not return."

The five of them exchange glances. "And if someone is sending wolves, that person will know that something or someone in the woods is killing their wolves and will follow the wolves' trail to us," said Summer Rain, voicing the thought in everyone's minds.

An urgent image of packing up and fleeing swept through the woodfolk's minds.

"Sorry," said Tarkyn shortly, concentrating on a little ladybird running across his hand to hide his embarrassment. He raised his head and smiled ruefully. "I'm not trying to issue orders. That was my reaction, not my decree. It is up to all of us together to decide what we should do."

Stormaway glanced at him, correctly surmising the cause of his apology. "How long do we have?" he asked.

Thunder Storm calculated, "The first wolves arrived here three nights ago. The second wave arrived late yesterday morning... That means it takes 36 hours for whoever it is to realise the wolves aren't returning, to dispatch more and for them to travel the distance. He scratched his head thoughtfully, "I'd say we have 12 hours at the outside before the next lot arrives."

"We need to mind conference," said Waterstone shortly. "I'll get back to you two soon."

The three woodfolk went out of focus, leaving Tarkyn sitting with a resentful wizard.

"You were pretty harsh with me back there, Sire," Stormaway protested.

The prince raised his eyebrows. "I will not have you gainsaying me, particularly in front of other people. Unlike the woodfolk, you have little respect for your oath to me or for the welfare of the forest. I am not going to risk the forest's welfare to indulge your whims. So the lines need to be drawn. You may think that I do not demand enough respect from the woodfolk, but none of them has ever refused a request nor spoken to me as you just did. Therefore I have not needed to impose my will." With the slight exception of Waterstone when he was upset, he added wryly to himself.

The wizard didn't say anything further but was obviously still disgruntled. Tarkyn picked up a green stick and focused on it for a minute. When the green shoots began to curl out from it, he handed it to the wizard.

"There," he said, with a gentle smile "Peace offering."

Stormaway accepted it reluctantly. "You'd do the same again though, wouldn't you, Sire?"

The prince looked quizzically at the wizard, "Yes, but I hope it won't come up again... Stormaway, I value your counsel and your stiff, old-fashioned ideas. In some ways it gives me an anchor to hold me as I am swept along by new circumstances. But I told you when we first met that I would not be dictated to by anyone and that holds for you as much as for anyone." He watched the wizard appraisingly and after a moment, added, "Don't go away."

Stormaway looked at Tarkyn in some surprise. "How did you know I was thinking of it?"

"Because you have operated alone for years now. You seem to come and go at will, with no ties to anyone. So, I would imagine that if things became uncomfortable for you, the simplest thing would be for you to leave."

The wizard scowled, "And will you forbid me to leave, or force me to stay?"

"No, but I will ask you to stay. And I will ask you to come to me if you are thinking of leaving, to see if we can sort things out so you can stay." The prince stood up awkwardly, still not fully recovered from his fall through the branches of the oak, and took his cup over to the fire to refill it from the large kettle that was hanging there. He looked over his shoulder and asked, "Would you like a refill?"

This drew a grudging smile from the wizard. He accepted the offer as the conciliatory gesture it was.

Tarkyn filled both cups, handed one to the wizard and sat back down. "Stormaway, do you realise I have had almost no formal training in using my powers?"

The wizard, in the middle of taking a sip of hot tea, choked. After several slaps on the back, his coughing subsided enough for him to exclaim, "What? You, a prince of the realm, uneducated in the ways of magic? That is scandalous!"

"For years, everyone talked about organising a tutor for me but no-one actually took the time from scandal-mongering to do it." The prince watched the horror reflected on Stormaway's face with some amusement. "I learnt everything I know by playing with my brothers and friends or by watching other people. Sometimes I went to the library myself and browsed through books on magic, but that's about it."

"Your Highness! I had no idea." The wizard looked at Tarkyn in some awe. "Then that was an amazing feat, winning that tournament."

Tarkyn shrugged deprecatingly, "Thank you again, but tournament magic is reasonably straight forward. Actually, attempting the resummoning spell was much harder." He leaned forward. "But Stormaway, do you see why I want you to stay? I would love to learn from you. I need to learn from you to protect myself and to protect the woodfolk. You have so much knowledge that none of us has."

"Hmm. I don't suppose I could make it a condition of my staying that you don't hit me with another of those waves of anger, could I?"

The prince shook his head regretfully. "I'm sure we can agree not to ride roughshod over each other. If you treat me with respect, I will do the same for you. But I'm afraid there are times, unlike this morning when it was controlled, that my anger bursts forth unexpectedly and I could not guarantee you any immunity from that."

"I think I can live with that. I put up with a lot worse from your father, after all." The wizard transferred his attention to the woodfolk. "What is keeping them? They should have reached some decision by now." He leant over and gave Waterstone a firm jab in the ribs.

"Ow." The woodman flicked back into focus."You could have just asked. I'm not oblivious to my surroundings, you know."

"Sorry," said Stormaway, but Tarkyn suspected he was passing on a bit of the pain he had suffered himself. "Don't know much about mind talking, you know."

"Let me demonstrate," offered Waterstone dryly. In a normal conversational voice, he addressed the two woodfolk, "Thunder Storm, Summer Rain. Leave them for now. Let's discuss it with Tarkyn and Stormaway." As soon as the woodfolk's attention was back with them, he began, "Getting away is not the problem. We can be ready to leave within an hour, although we will have to travel through the treetops so that our scent can't be followed."

"The problem is making sure that we keep our existence secret," rumbled Thunder Storm. "We need to cover up the fact that we have killed the wolves. So we have to create another explanation for the wolves' deaths."

"And we can't leave the corpses and simulate any sort of a fight," said Summer Rain, as she added more water to the kettle from a hessian bag, "because we have cleaned, skinned and dismembered the wolves. So we'll have to conceal the skeletons and innards that we haven't used. And we can't just bury them at the site, because any wolves following will sniff them out."

"Throw them in the river?" suggested Tarkyn.

Waterstone grimaced. "That would prevent them from being sniffed out but if I lost a trail, first place I'd look would be in the river. Can't hide them in the trees either, because the scent would be carried downwind."

"We'll have to take them with us then," said Stormaway decisively. Seeing the sceptical looks on the woodfolk's faces, he added, "At least some of the way. So there's a break in the trail."

"He's got a point," Summer Rain conceded. "But the carcasses are so heavy and there are so many of them. We would have to carry several loads each, over a considerable distance, to break the trail."

"But the scent of their deaths will still be all around the riverbanks, won't they?" asked Tarkyn. "Perhaps we could set it up to look as though travellers or bandits had killed them?" He tried to remember the details of the heron's flight but failed. "Is there a road anywhere nearby that travellers could have come from?"

Thunder Storm frowned. "Yes. That's a possibility. There is a road about four miles to the south. But travellers wouldn't neatly dissect a wolf's carcass for future use. So we would still have to conceal their remains and account for their disappearance." He smiled at the prince, "Travellers don't seem to eat wolf unless they're starving."

"Oh really?" said Tarkyn, trying to sound surprised.

Stormaway huffed thoughtfully, "A small switch from each carcass would need to be dragged to lay a false trail to the road. The switches could then be levitated straight upwards from a position close to cart tracks and carried through the treetops to be buried them somewhere else. Then if the trail to the road is followed, the trackers will think that the wolves' bodies were carried away in a cart out of the forest."

"We will also have to create evidence of sorcerers being at the river and travelling between the road and the river," Waterstone added, as he pulled a branch from the woodpile and fed it into the fire, "No one will believe that the wolves all died, then dragged themselves off to the road to load themselves onto the back of a cart."

"Very droll," said Stormaway dryly. Suddenly, his eyes gleamed as he began to scheme. "What oddments does anyone have that come from villagers or travellers? We need some scraps of cloth or buttons. Anything really... except the remnants of the prince's clothing, obviously. Then we can salt the ground near the river with evidence of a fight between travellers and the wolves. Combine that with our trail to the road and we should create a convincing story."

Waterstone considered it from all angles before replying, "Yes. I think that might work. And we can hide the bulk of the carcasses nearer to hand." He finished placing another piece of wood on the fire and settling the kettle more firmly in the coals. Then he brushed his hands and stood up, before going into a short mind conference. Once he had re-focussed, he nodded briskly, "Agreed. It's not perfect. It will require a lot of work to cart the carcasses through the trees and to bury them. And it's going to be hard to cover up such a large excavation, but it will have to do."

"I think I can help with disguising the burial site," said Tarkyn diffidently. "I could plant a stand of saplings over it."

"And we can both add our fire power to the excavation," put in Stormaway. "And of course, levitate the wolf switches at the road." He rolled his eyes at Tarkyn. "You realise what this means, Sire? You and I will have to walk to the road laying the false trail. We are the only ones who have the right type of scent, big enough feet and the right sort of boots to make the tracks. Blast it! I don't want to have to walk all the way to the road but I can't see any alternative."

Thunder Storm raised an objection. "But mightn't they recognise Tarkyn's scent?"

"If they do, they will already know he is here somewhere from the scent around the river." said the wizard. "It will be better, in that case, to lay his trail to the road and out of the forest anyway."

The prince leant forward and adjusted a branch that was threatening to roll out of the fire, "Besides, it is much more important to conceal woodfolk's presence."

"Not if the cost is your safety. Then we wouldn't have a forest to hide in anyway." Waterstone felt a flicker of hurt wander past his mind. He reached across and patted the prince on the knee. "Don't get confused. I can care about you and the forest all at once, you know."

A ripple of embarrassment hit the woodman as Tarkyn muttered, "My blasted feelings! I wish they would keep to themselves."

The woodman smiled and looked from the wizard to the sorcerer. "So. Are you two prepared to walk to the road, dragging the wolves' scent? Tarkyn, are you recovered enough to walk that far at the moment?"

Tarkyn glanced sideways at Summer Rain who was still in discussion with other woodfolk and gave a crooked smile. "I'll have to be. To be honest, I will find it hard, I think. But the hardest part will be enduring Summer Rain's disapproval."

"Don't worry about that." Waterstone shrugged. "Unless someone comes up with an alternative, she will support you to succeed."

Summer Rain came back into focus and nodded. "But you and Stormaway must save your strength for the things that only you can do. Don't push yourself too hard. You would be too heavy for us to carry."

Tarkyn stared at her for moment, thinking that finally she had cracked a joke. But no. She was, as usual, completely serious. The sorcerer flicked a glance at Waterstone and blinked.

Waterstone smothered a smile but he did not allow himself to become distracted. "We have decided on a suitable patch for burying the remains about half a mile to the north. If you both follow me, I'll show you where to start excavating."

With that, the woodman swung himself lightly into the nearest tree and headed off up into the higher boughs of the tree.

Chapter 21

Waterstone ran lithely up one long branch until it began to bend under his weight, then jumped down and across into the next tree. From there, he climbed up higher again to repeat the manoeuvre to land in the tree after that. Sorcerer and wizard incanted, "*Maya Reeza Mureva!*" and rose gracefully to drift along beside the woodman. Stormaway sighed and rolled his eyes. "I'm getting too old for this, you know," he said in an aside to the prince.

Tarkyn raised his eyebrows. "That's what you said yesterday but you don't seem to have suffered any ill effects."

"That's what I always say, but no-one listens to me," responded the wizard mournfully.

"Maybe that's because you never stay anywhere long enough for people to care," suggested the prince kindly.

"What rubbish! We all care about him, as much as one can care for a slippery, devious, bigoted chameleon." Waterstone broke off for a moment as he launched himself into the next tree. Once he had landed and recovered his balance, he added, between breaths, "Maybe it's because he loves melodrama. He's not that old, you know. Unfit perhaps. It's not his age that's the problem."

Stormaway glared at the woodman. "As you can see," he said to the prince, "respect is a sadly rare commodity among these folk."

Tarkyn thought about all the conversations about respect he had had with Waterstone, Autumn Leaves and Stormaway and found himself so overwhelmed with possible responses to the wizard's throwaway remark that he couldn't respond at all. He resorted to diversionary tactics. "How much further is it?" he asked.

Waterstone pointed ahead. "It's over that next rise. There's a rocky clearing on a gentle slope not far from the river. It needs to be somewhere that won't be washed away if there is heavy rain."

"Hmm." Tarkyn digested this then asked, "Not too rocky, I hope, or the trees won't grow. Are we going to have to keep off the ground while we do this excavation?"

The woodman landed neatly on the bough of a large horse chestnut, then shook his head. "I don't think so. The site is a good half mile from where the wolves were killed and in the opposite direction from the trail we will lay to the road." He considered as he stepped around the trunk of the tree and pulled himself lightly up onto a higher branch. "Maybe we'll throw some water over the area when we've finished, to wash away your scent and footprints, just to make sure."

"Good idea," said Tarkyn. "That will also help the saplings to establish themselves."

"Hmm. For someone who has never been a farmer or a gardener, you seem to know a lot about plants all of a sudden."

The prince looked a little startled. "I suppose I could have learnt it from the gardeners," he said slowly, then shook his head. "No. I didn't really talk to the gardeners much. I was more interested in chatting to groomsmen and men at arms." He grinned, "Perhaps being the guardian of the forest comes with knowledge as well as power."

"Perhaps the knowledge is part of the power," suggested the wizard, as they topped the rise and looked down a gently sloping, heavily wooded gully.

Slightly ahead of them, Waterstone had now swung down out of the trees and was inspecting the ground in front of them. He stood in a small clearing, next to a low pile of tumbled rocks. The grass was sparse in this particular spot and the ground was strewn with small pebbles.

"That's not a cairn, is it?" asked Stormaway, frowning at the rocks.

The woodman stood with his hands on his hips, studying the rocks. He bent over and pulled a couple of the rocks aside. "Not that I know of. I might just check."

After a couple of minutes out of focus, he reported that no one knew of any reason that a cairn should be there. "It must just be a natural grouping of rocks, I suppose." He sounded doubtful. "Well, why don't we keep away from it just in case it is marking something for someone?" He pointed to a space on the other side of the clearing. "We can dig our hole over there."

"And where is your shovel?" demanded Stormaway. "You don't expect us to do it all, I hope."

"Of course. I thought I'd just sit back and watch." Stormaway's face darkened but before he could explode, Watertone said calmly, "Shovels are coming with the first load of carcases."

"So I assumed," said Tarkyn dryly.

The wizard glowered at them but Waterstone returned his gaze, completely unmoved, a cheeky grin hovering around his mouth.

"Bloody cocky woodmen." grumbled Stormaway, as he turned away.

"Stormaway," said Tarkyn, "do you have any suggestions as to how we might tackle this – other than just blasting the ground with power?"

Waterstone intervened hastily. "You don't want to send the soil too far away. We'll need most of it to refill the hole."

Stormaway raised his eyebrows, "Obviously. We are not complete idiots, you know."

Since Tarkyn wouldn't have thought twice about where the soil ended up, he nodded then shook his head in agreement, a smile lurking in his eyes as they met Waterstone's across the back of the wizard.

If Stormaway was aware of his antics, he gave no sign. "If we aim our power beams across each other's and then moved them both in clockwise direction, the power rays should wrap themselves around each other. Since our individual power rays will have a different frequency of vibration, this should set up a dissonance and gradually destabilise the soil in that area, turning it from a sol to a gel; a similar effect to an earthquake. Then the loosened soil can be removed with very little effort."

"You see," said Tarkyn to Waterstone, "how much I need to learn. I didn't even realise our power rays vibrated, let alone at different frequencies."

The wizard shook his head solemnly, "Shocking. Truly shocking, that your magical education has been so limited."

"For once I agree with you," said the woodman, "I think Tarkyn has been sorely neglected over the years since his father died."

Not wishing to add more fuel to their fire, Tarkyn kept a close guard over his feelings and said brusquely, "If you two have finished commiserating over me, do you think we could get on with it? How big do you want this hole?"

Waterstone shot him a glance but said nothing and turned his attention to the question. "If we don't want foxes or other animals digging the carcases straight up again, it will have to be at least six feet deep, and I'd say about seven feet in diameter." He looked at Stormaway. "What do you think? Does that sound about right?"

"Quite large, but I think we can manage it." Stormaway's tone was noticeably more cordial towards the woodman.

Oh save me! thought the prince, *My neglected education has provided them with a common cause. Oh well, at least some good has come out of it, I suppose.*

"Come on then, Sire," said the wizard as he positioned himself in front of the area to be excavated. "Stand next to me, about four feet to my right and let us begin. You will need to sweep slowly around the whole perimeter and then gradually speed up. Once my beam has travelled halfway around the circumference, focus your beam on the place I start from, then follow my lead."

Stormaway closed his eyes to draw on his power. After a moment, a strong green ray of light sprang forth from the wizard's hand. It travelled slowly in a large arc. Tarkyn followed with a bronze beam that moved slowly along the same path as the green one. As bronze ray travelled the last quarter of the circle, it crossed over and touched the green beam of power. There was a sharp thwack as they connected followed by a persistent thrumming that grew in intensity each time the rays crossed each other again. Soon, the intensity of the light and vibration drove Waterstone back into the shelter of the trees. As he watched, the bronze and green rays twisted themselves around each other, over and over again. As the green and bronze rays swept more and more quickly around the circumference, the thrumming became louder and higher in pitch until Waterstone imagined he could almost hear the earth screaming. The earth within the circle was trembling and small stones bounced up and down as each ray swept past. Suddenly, the green ray snapped out, quickly followed by the bronze. An eerie silence filled the clearing.

Waterstone and Tarkyn were both shaken by the intensity of the display of power, but Stormaway was quite matter-of-fact. "There. That should do it." He stooped over the circle and effortlessly scooped up a handful of soil. "You see? We have shaken apart the connections between the particles of soil. It will take no time at all to clear this out. We could do it with our bare hands if we had to." He looked from one to the other and added jauntily, "but I think we'll leave it to those with shovels." He frowned at the prince, who was looking a little wan, "Are you all right? "

Tarkyn waved a hand, "I will be. I just need a rest after levitating myself here, then doing that." He frowned irritably, "I'm getting bloody tired of being below strength." He looked at Waterstone, "I seem to spend my entire life becoming tired and overtaxed. You people must think I'm a complete weakling."

"We do," the woodman assured him, enjoying the shocked look from Stormaway that he spotted out of the corner of his eye. "'Why can't he hold up tree branches all night as well as all day', we said to ourselves? 'Why is he only holding up two at a time?' we wondered. 'Surely he could manage at least four?''Why didn't he fight off all the wolves single-handedly and keep us from having to use up our arrows?' We've talked of nothing else, ever since you got here."

"Very funny," responded Tarkyn trenchantly.

Waterstone smiled unrepentantly. "It's probably just as well you've been sick. Otherwise we'd all have been frightened off by the extent of your power.Well," he qualified, "we wouldn't be allowed to be frightened off. At least some of us would have to stay and be terrified. But if you had carried on like you did the first day, we would all be quivering wrecks by now."

"And if you lot had carried on the way you did that first day, I'd be dead by now," retorted Tarkyn.

"Ah, but of course, that was before we realised that only you can have any sort of power in any confrontation between us. In our dealings with you, even our physical prowess has been effectively stripped from us by the oath." Waterstone spoke lightly but there was no mistaking the bitterness in his voice.

Suddenly the bantering had turned sour. Chagrin swept across the clearing and the woodman received a clear image of the prince pulling away from him.

"I am sorry, Waterstone, if I have made you feel powerless," Tarkyn said stiffly. "That has not been my intention. Since that first day, I have tried not to flaunt my power. If you remember, I even gave you permission to hit me at one point."He ignored the strangled gurgle that emitted from the wizard, "I cannot undo the oath. If it chafes you so badly, I give you permission to leave so that it doesn't continue to confront you. Others of the woodfolk can protect me."

Waterstone stared at him, white faced. "Are you ordering me to leave?"

Much to the two antagonists' surprise, Stormaway intervened, "Now hold it right there. This is getting out of hand. I don't want either of you to do irreparable damage to what is clearly a strong friendship." Woodman and prince turned to stare at him. "Tarkyn, beware of your feelings riding your actions. Waterstone, the prince has given you the choice because he cares about you and doesn't want to force you to stay in a difficult situation. Don't force him to make your choice for you. If you do, he may send you away for your sake so that you don't have to make the decision to leave him." He frowned ferociously at them "And one more thing, Tarkyn. I've told you this before but listen again. For heaven's sake, give people the right to feel resentful sometimes, without taking it too personally, especially if you are looking for honesty from them."

The prince let out a deep breath and relaxed. He ran his hand through his hair. "Thank you, Stormaway," he said quietly. He turned back to his friend. "In answer to your question... no. I wasn't ordering you to leave....and I don't think I was going to, before Stormaway spoke. I have not been in the habit of ordering you around and I am not about to start now. I did note what you said though, that you wouldn't be allowed to be frightened off. That's why I gave you the permission to go. At least then, you can have choice about that."

Waterstone eyed him uncertainly, battling against a wellspring of previously concealed resentment. He put his hands on his hips and stood there looking at the prince silently for a few moments. Then in a sudden rush, he swung his arm up and around and punched Tarkyn hard on the jaw. Unprepared, the prince staggered backwards. A shimmering green wall flashed up between them. Any relief the woodman may have gained by lashing out at the prince was replaced by irritation at finding himself cut off.

"Remove your shield," Tarkyn snapped at the wizard. Rubbing his jaw, the prince glanced around at the trees. Not a leaf had moved. He returned his attention to the tense woodman who stood confronting him. "Come on then," he invited, with a sparkle in his eyes. "Clearly my permission still stands. Finish what you've started." He did not demean himself by offering assurances that he wouldn't use magic and Waterstone did not need them.

The woodman rushed at him low and hard. As he fell onto his back, Tarkyn brought his arms up before him, grabbed Waterstone by his shirt and hurled the woodman over his head. Waterstone rolled easily and turned in a couch to rush at him again. Tarkyn twisted himself around and threw himself upward from prone into a crouching position and put his arm across his chest as a barrier against the impending force of Waterstone's next attack. Just before the woodman reached him in his headlong rush, the sorcerer twisted sideways, then swung his arm around to thump Waterstone's back as he passed. The woodman went flying, driven by his own impetus with the added force of Tarkyn's thrust. Waterstone lay still where he had landed.

After a long moment, Tarkyn stood up and walked over to where the woodman lay unmoving. As he bent over him, a fist shot up and caught him between the eyes. Tarkyn went down like a stone and shook his head to find Waterstone laughing and sitting on top of him.

Seeing a spark of anger in the prince's eye, Waterstone shook his head. "Enough! Don't go hurling me off into space again. I concede." He laughed as he felt the prince's muscles reluctantly relax under him. "I know it was a dirty trick but you're bigger than me."

Tarkyn frowned up at the woodman, "I don't see why you're conceding, when you have me pinned down."

Waterstone smiled, "I'm not fool enough to think that I have you helpless, but I don't want to fight any more. You fight pretty hard and so do I. One of us might get badly hurt and I don't want that." He climbed off and stood up before offering his hand to help Tarkyn up.

The prince's face was sporting two bruises and a cut on his eyebrow dripped blood down his front. Waterstone had come off relatively unscathed with a graze down one side of his face and a slight limp. They stood there looking at each other, breathing hard. Then a grin split Tarkyn's face and they descended into relieved laughter.

"Well," gasped Tarkyn between breaths, "That made a change. I haven't had a good wrestle for ages, even if it was short-lived."

Waterstone chuckled, "You're a skilful fighter, aren't you? No wonder you won this tournament of yours. I was being flung all over the place and you didn't seem to be putting in much effort at all."

"You pack a pretty hefty punch and you're devious, but I'll remember that next time." He pressed his arm around his ribcage. "Oh, my aching ribs," gasped Tarkyn. "Remember the ribs? I don't know how much good it did them, having you sit on me."

"Of course I remembered the ribs," chortled Waterstone. "I'd never have tackled you otherwise... Laughing is probably still quite difficult with your sore ribs, is it?" he asked with spurious sympathy.

"Yes, it is," said Tarkyn grinning hard and trying not to laugh any more. "At least I gave them a good workout."

"Yes. Thanks for that," replied the prince dryly. Tarkyn looked at Stormaway and smiled warmly. "Thank you for not intervening. I suspect that may have cost you quite an effort."

Stormaway gave a reluctant smile. "Except for the fact that we are in the middle of a complex operation and you will need your strength for other things, I would say it probably did you both a power of good. Unorthodox behaviour for a prince to spar with a commoner but I suppose there is no one else."

"Not so unorthodox. I have often trained with men at arms." The prince glanced at the woodman, "Besides which, Waterstone assures me that all woodfolk are noblemen and women." The prince entertained himself watching Waterstone do a double take while the wizard frowned in disapproval. Before Stormaway had time to remonstrate with him or the woodman, Tarkyn added fuel to the fire by adding silkily, "And I don't think I would describe it as sparring really, would you, Waterstone?"

"Uh, no. I'm afraid not. If we had been sparring, we could have kept going for longer." There was a tiny pause. Then Waterstone cleared his throat self-consciously. "And Tarkyn, thanks."

At this juncture Thunder Storm, Autumn Leaves and six other woodfolk wearing backpacks swung down out of the trees. Thunder Storm took one look at the prince and asked around for some bandaging. While Stormaway directed the woodfolk to the excavation site, Waterstone and Thunder Storm sat the prince down and set about tidying up his face.

"So, my lord, you finally had to wear it, did you?" said Thunder Storm noncommittally as he dabbed at Tarkyn's split eyebrow. "I'm surprised at you, Waterstone. You're not usually one to hold a grudge like that. Not once you've calmed down."

"Old permission. New argument." said Waterstone shortly.

Thunder Storm nodded slowly. "That's interesting. I wonder if your permission stays in place until you revoke it or until it's used?"

The prince shrugged. "I don't know. I can't think of a safe way of finding out either. For the meantime, I'll just re-iterate it so then we at least know where we stand." He winced as Thunderstorm gave his cut a final wipe. "So Waterstone, you still have my permission to hit me if you have to. Actually, that goes for Thunder Storm and Autumn Leaves too. Just don't do it too often."

Waterstone looked at him strangely. "We would also know where we stand if you revoked it."

The prince gave his head a little shake. "Would we? Yes. I suppose we would. I'm not thinking too straight at the moment. Let's leave it how it is for now. Thanks Thunder Storm," he said as he stood up. As he straightened, his face went white and he grunted with pain. He doubled back over and stood clutching his side. "I think I'll sit back down for a minute," he gasped between gritted teeth.

"Stay there!" rumbled Thunder Storm as he went out of focus, "I'll get Stormaway and Summer Rain."

A few minutes later, Stormaway arrived with Autumn Leaves and Summer Rain in tow, all of them looking anxious. Tarkyn waved a dismissive hand at them. "Don't worry. It's not hurting while I'm sitting down. At least not as much. I'm having a bit of trouble catching my breath though. It's probably because I haven't done much strenuous exercise until now." He coughed suddenly and everyone was horrified to see a fleck of blood appear at the side of his mouth. Now he was beginning to wheeze. He coughed again bringing up more blood.

"I think we had better lie you down, even of it hurts you to straighten." said Stormaway.

"Wait. I have to plant the trees over the hole first," protested Tarkyn feebly as he was manhandled down onto the ground.

"You have to be alive to do it. Let's get that bit sorted first." Stormaway knelt beside him and felt gently around the prince's chest. "Where did it hurt when you stood up?"

Tarkyn indicated a point halfway down on his left side. He was struggling for breath and each exhalation brought up further flecks of blood.

Stormaway looked into his eyes. "Tarkyn. Focus on me. You have a punctured lung. One of your broken ribs has pierced the wall of your lung and your lung is filling with blood. That is why you can't get enough air. Do you understand so far?"

Tarkyn nodded.

"It is beyond the normal practice of medicine to repair it and you are in danger of drowning in your own blood. But Tarkyn, you are a forest guardian and you possess the power of healing. I will guide you to heal yourself."

Tarkyn was fighting for breath and fear flickered in his eyes but he nodded and kept his focus on the wizard.

"Now, you will have to close your eyes but you must not let yourself lose consciousness…Think down inside yourself. Go to the source of the pain. Look at what is happening. You will have to straighten the rib back into position so that it is no longer piercing your lung."

Tarkyn's eyebrows twitched then drew together. His face grimaced with pain but he kept his eyes closed. His breath was gurgling now but he maintained his focus. He coughed again and a small gush of blood burst forth between his lips. He dragged in a slow wheezing breath.

Stormaway kept his voice steady and low. "Don't concern yourself with repairing the rib for now. Just make sure it is clear of the lung." He waited until he saw a minute nod from the prince. "Now, move your attention to the wound in your lung. Can you see it?" Another tiny nod. "Focus your will on the wound. Use the same power you used to grow the sapling from the staff. Draw on your life source, your *esse*, and knit together the damaged blood vessels. If you can, use the blood that is in your lungs as material for the repairs."

Tarkyn's chest rose and fell in great heaving motions. He was struggling to get any breath at all. Each breath brought fresh blood. Still he kept his focus but he was already living on borrowed time. Stormaway looked around at Waterstone, Thunder Storm, Autumn Leaves and the newly arrived Summer Rain who were gathered ashen faced around the prince who was slowly but surely losing his battle to live.

"He's going to need our help. Put you hands on my shoulders. Now focus inside yourselves. Find your life force and let it flow through your hands into me. Do not fear that you will lose it all but you may lose some. However, like blood, it replenishes itself." They nodded and did as he had asked. "Tarkyn, keep going. Keep focussing on repairing the damage. The woodfolk and I are going to join our *esse* to yours to give you the strength you need."

Tarkyn felt a soft infusion of strength but by now he was struggling to focus on anything but drawing his next breath. A soft green glow swirled around the small group huddled over the prince. Drawn by the spectacle, the other woodfolk left their digging and came over to watch. Summer Rain sent a brief mind message, explaining what was happening, then re-focussed her attention. The other woodfolk, as one, placed their hands on the shoulders of those already in place. The green mist spiralled lazily, growing in density, the centre of it swirling down the vortex of the whirlpool into the prostrate figure on the ground.

An uncanny silence descended. With a start, the woodfolk realised that they could no longer hear the gurgling and wheezing of the prince's laboured breath. His chest was still. A sense of dread crept over them. They redoubled their efforts to channel their combined life force into the prince.

Inside a private hell, Tarkyn had given up the fight to breath. He was using what energy he had left to focus on drawing together the tear in his lung. He knew he was failing but he kept fighting. A ponderous, rolling wave of strength washed into him and he drew on it desperately to create new fibres to weave closed the puncture in his lung. Suddenly, in the far distance he heard a voice that he thought he knew calling out to him. The voice became so strident and insistent that Tarkyn finally decided he should leave his task and listen to it.

"Breathe, Tarkyn. Breathe. Come on. Listen to me. Change your focus. For pity's sake, breathe!"

Shocked, Tarkyn realised he had forgotten all about breathing. It had been such a relief to stop trying. He steeled himself and forced himself to drag in a breath. Immediately, he started coughing and his chest seared with pain. Tarkyn opened his eyes and hands propped him up while he coughed over and over again as blood and sputum forced their way up out of his lungs. Finally, the coughing stopped and he lay back exhausted, but with his airways clear. He heard cheering in the background and wondered vaguely what it was for. Then Tarkyn finally gave in to the terrible tiredness he had been fighting against and slipped into unconsciousness.

Stormaway looked up, grey faced, from the prince to all those gathered around him. "I thank you all. Without the strength from all of you, he would surely have died." He stood up wearily. "I am afraid we are going to have to change our plans. The prince's rib is still hanging broken and sharp right next to his lung. Until he has the energy to repair it, he can only be moved with extreme care. I don't know when he will be well enough to grow plants on your excavation. I think you'll have to disguise it as best you can without him for now." He looked at Thunder Storm."How long do you estimate we have left before the next attack?"

"Still a while. About nine or ten hours. Assuming the gap is the same as last time, of course."

Stormaway shook his head. “There is no way Tarkyn will be able to walk to the road. I’ll have to do it on my own. I need a rest first. Things have been rather busy here one way and another since we arrived. Any chance of a cup of tea and something to eat?”

“Don’t worry. We’ll find something for you.” Summer Rain frowned at him in concern. “You look close to exhaustion yourself”

Stormaway sat down on the log next to Tarkyn’s unconscious form and nodded. “I am, but I’ll recover in a while.” He looked at the woodwoman, “I think it was fear that drained me the most. I’ve never done anything like that before. I have never worked on anyone who has the gift of healing to draw on. I think it was desperation more than anything that guided me through it.”

“Thank you for saving our forest guardian. I was very impressed. I should have asked you to attend to the prince earlier.”

“I didn’t realise he was a forest guardian before and it wasn’t desperate enough to try something so different.” Stormaway considered her thoughtfully for a moment, “Did the welfare of the forest not cross your mind?”

Summer Rain looked startled then angry. Before she could speak, Stormaway put up a hand. “No, sorry. Don’t answer that. It was an unworthy of me to say that, after all you have done. I apologize.”

She considered him silently for a moment, obviously debating whether to take issue or to let it drop. Finally, she said merely, “I’ll get you some tea and some food,” and left.

Stormaway looked around, “Waterstone? Where are you?”

“I’m here,” came the woodman’s tight voice from just behind him.

“Come around and sit next to me.”

Waterstone sat down and put his head in his hands. “Go on,” he said in a muffled voice. “You won’t say anything I haven’t thought of myself.”

Surprisingly, Stormaway wasn’t full of recriminations. “Waterstone, I have seen enough of your dealings with Tarkyn to know that you would not want to hurt him like that. I was there when you stopped the fight for that very reason. None of us knew the damage had already been done. He is as much to blame as you are for fighting like that before he was properly healed.”

The woodman lifted a tear stained face. “That’s not strictly true. He’s only young and he would never have refused because he knew it mattered to me. I was the only one who could have prevented it and I didn’t.” He shook his head. “I didn’t realised he was still so injured. He covers it up a lot, you know.”

The wizard put his hand on the distressed woodman’s knee. “Waterstone, I too allowed the fight to continue. Let us not dwell on what could have been and instead focus on repairing what now is. Tarkyn needs your help. You are closest to him and he trusts you. I want you to sit beside him, keep your hand on his shoulder and join your life force, your *esse* to his. Don't give it to him and don't drain yourself. He will need you strong when he wakes. Just join your *esse* with his. Can you do that?"

Waterstone frowned, "I'll try. I'm new at this. Do I just do the same as we all did before?"

Stormaway nodded, "Yes, more or less. I want you to do something else as well."

"Anything. Whatever it takes."

The wizard considered the woodman. "No, Waterstone. You can't make extravagant promises like that. You have a daughter. But I am not asking you to do anything excessive. You can send images to Tarkyn, can't you?"

"Yes, but not words."

The wizard nodded, "Images will do. Can you send him an image of everyone linked, helping him with their strength and waiting for him to come back? Once he has understood that, send him an image of you waiting for him and calling him back. Something like that. Can you do that? I know he's exhausted but I don't want him to stay unconscious for too long. I want to make sure he's all right."

Waterstone sat down cross-legged next to the prince and placed his hand on Tarkyn's shoulder "I will do what I can. Could you ask someone to send Sparrow to me please? She will want to look after Tarkyn as well… and I want her beside me."

"Of course I will." Stormaway stood up to leave then turned back, "One more thing. Whatever you do, don't let him get up when he wakes. That rib could re-puncture his lung."

CHAPTER 22

Stormaway wandered off to track down Summer Rain and the food. The area that sorcerer and the wizard had loosened had now been emptied of dirt and was already half full of parcels of wolf remains. A cooking fire had been lit off to one side.

Summer Rain saw him coming and had a meat roll and a cup of tea ready for him.

"Hmm, wolf sandwich," he murmured to himself.

Summer Rain's eyes brows twitched, "What? Don't you like it?"

Stormaway smiled. "Actually, I enjoy it tremendously. I'm not so sure how keen our young friend is about it, though. It is a bit of an acquired taste, don't you think?"

The woodwoman shrugged, "Maybe. I've eaten it all my life from time to time. So it's hard to say." She nodded at the hole. "The last loads are coming in now. Then we'll all have lunch before we move on to the next phase."

"Once we had laid the trail to the road," said Autumn Leaves who had come over to join them, "our plan was to travel through the trees so that we would leave no scent or tracks." He glanced over at Waterstone sitting beside the forest guardian's still body. As they watched, Sparrow arrived and took up position opposite her father, placing her hand on Tarkyn's other shoulder. Waterstone smiled gently at her and ruffled her hair. "I don't know what we are going to do about Tarkyn. We can't leave him lying here. We have to get him up into the trees if wolves are coming."

Creaking Bough who had just emptied her load into the hole, brushed her hands off as she suggested, "What about a stretcher arrangement that we could haul up into the trees. Two poles and a large piece of sheeting tied between them."

"We couldn't take him very far through the trees like that, but at least it would get him up off the ground." Autumn Leaves turned to the wizard. "Can you lift things in the same way as Tarkyn?" Seeing the hesitation on Stormaway's face, he added hastily, "We would be hauling up at the same time. It just might make the lifting smoother."

The wizard gave a tired smile. "I will do what I can. I am hoping he will recover enough to make that unnecessary. How long would you need to rig up a stretcher?"

Creaking Bough shrugged, "Not long. Half an hour maybe. Another half hour to get him up into the trees. Probably a lot less but we wouldn't want to cut it too fine."

Autumn Leaves frowned suddenly and went out of focus. After a few seconds, his eyes cleared but he looked puzzled. "I received some confusing images but basically Waterstone needs us over there."

Waterstone looked up as they approached. "Tarkyn wants us to position him next to a large tree so that either he is touching it or someone is linking him to it."

Summer Rain smiled in comprehension, "He is a guardian of the forest. If we can give him life force, so can the trees. And they will, because he is the guardian,"

"Is he awake?" asked Stormaway.

Waterstone frowned uncertainly. "No. Not exactly. I know he has been receiving my images and now he has sent this one to me about the trees but he's not stirring yet. I don't think he has enough energy to come back yet."

Autumn Leaves looked around. "You're very close to that young elm. There's a huge old oak over there but that's twenty yards away."

Waterstone shook his head. "Tarkyn won't use a young tree. He doesn't want to risk draining it too much."

Autumn Leaves raised his eyebrows. "Is he listening to us, then?"

Waterstone put his head on one side. "I don't think so. I'm sending him the images of what you're saying and he's sending back reactions." He looked at the wizard, "Can we move him to that oak?"

Stormaway considered. "If you all place your hands under him to support him and keep him straight, I will lift him and transport him over there. Agreed?"

Once the woodfolk had positioned themselves along either side of their guardian, Stormaway said, "On count of three, I will lift. One.. two..three."

Tarkyn rose into the air, hands holding him unbending as he sailed gently towards the great oak.

"Now, I am going to lower him slowly. Is everybody ready?"

The woodfolk maintained their pressure under him until he was lowered onto the ground next to the gnarled trunk of the great oak. During the whole operation, Tarkyn did not so much as flutter an eyelid. Except for his chest rising and falling slowly, he seemed uncannily like a corpse. Several worried glances passed between the woodfolk.

"Are you sure he's all right?" asked Creaking Bough.

Waterstone grimaced, "I don't know. I hope so. He is still in mental contact with me." The woodman took Tarkyn's limp hand and placed its palm against the trunk of the tree. He looked at Stormaway. "You know about these things. Should we be doing anything else?"

The wizard shook his head. "This is well beyond the range of my experience." He frowned down at the still figure while he thought for a moment. "Still, I suppose the same rules would still apply. Tarkyn, can you hear me?"

Waterstone nodded.

"Relax your barriers. Open yourself up to allow the flow of energy in from outside. Join your own with that of the oak. Don't let your own life force become too diffuse. The oak is much larger than you." He paused. "Are you connected with the oak?"

Waterstone nodded but his communication was almost unnecessary. Beneath the woodfolk's stunned gaze, their forest guardian was slowly taking on an unmistakable, greenish tinge.

Stormaway frowned but continued as though unperturbed, "Now, do you have enough strength to repair your broken rib?"

Waterstone nodded.

"Good. Then focus in on it and draw the two ends together - Now use your tree growing abilities to grow new tissue and weld the bone back together, just as you did for the tear in your lungs." The wizard waited for some time before asking, "Are you able to do that? Is it working?"

Waterstone's face lit up. "He's done it."

Sighs of relief ran through the surrounding woodfolk.

Stormaway watched the prince for signs of recovering consciousness but none came. He gestured to Waterstone to leave Tarkyn's side and to join him a short distance away. Sparrow stayed steadfastly beside Tarkyn, keeping her hand firmly on his shoulder and stroking him gently from time to time.

"What is happening now?" the wizard asked in a hushed voice. "Why is he not waking? I am fearful that he may become inextricably entwined with the oak's life force. Do you get any sense that that may be happening?"

"He is joined with it at the moment, but he is still himself," answered the woodman slowly.

"Are you concerned or do you feel he is just not yet ready to awaken?"

Waterstone put his hands on his hips as he considered the matter, "I don't feel at all qualified to answer that, but Tarkyn doesn't seem to feel intimidated by the oak. I don't think he is fading into it, at least not at the moment. My best guess is that he still needs the oak's strength." He looked anxiously over at the prone figure lying so still under the tree. "I'd better go back so I can keep an eye on him." The woodman's eyes suddenly went out of focus. "Whoa. He's panicking."

"Dad!" yelled Sparrow in the same moment.

Waterstone ran the few steps back to Tarkyn's side. He threw himself down and put his hand on Tarkyn's shoulder. The woodman sent an image of himself and Sparrow seated on either side of him, gesturing for the prince to return. A wave of relief rolled into Waterstone's mind, followed by a wave of reassurance. Waterstone received a clear image of Tarkyn with his hand up asking them to be quiet. The woodman relayed all of this to the surrounding woodfolk.

Stormaway stared down at the Tarkyn's prostrate form. "Tell him we must leave soon. He can have another half an hour, hour at the most. I need time to check if he's all right before I lay the trail to the road."

Waterstone frowned. "How do I do an image for time?"

"Sun going down a certain distance over the trees," suggested Autumn Leaves.

Waterstone pictured the sun going down, as suggested. Much to everyone's relief, they saw the side of Tarkyn's mouth twitch in a minute smile. "He would really like everyone to go away and get on with preparations. He needs to concentrate. That includes you, little one." The woodman smiled, "He wants me to stay but to be quiet!"

Sparrow gave Tarkyn's shoulder a final pat and headed off with the others to have some lunch. Another twenty minutes passed, during which the woodman sat patiently and resisted the temptation to talk or to reassure Tarkyn. Finally, Waterstone's anxiety became too much for him and he transmitted a look of enquiry.

An amused smile appeared on Tarkyn's face, followed by an image again asking Waterstone to be quiet. Then the prince opened his eyes. The amber eyes in a greenish face were quite shocking to behold.

"Shh," he whispered, "Just give me a minute to pull myself together without having everyone crowding around me,"

Tarkyn let his eyes travel over Waterstone then up into the boughs of the tree. He brought his gaze across and down through the branches then down the trunk until he was looking at his hand with the palm still firmly touching the oak. He took a long, clear breath and took his hand away. In the centre of his palm was a deep green circle.

He smiled, "Interesting. Let me look at the palm of your hand."

Waterstone put out his hand for inspection and saw that his palm had a dark pink, perfect circle in the middle of it.

"What about my shoulder, I wonder?" mused the sorcerer. He went to pull away his shirt to look at his shoulder and recoiled in disgust. "Oh yuk! My shirt is covered in blood and mess. What are we going to do about that? No one else has a big enough shirt to fit me. We'll have to wash it."

Waterstone gave a shout of laughter. "Frankly, your shirt was the least of our worries. We couldn't have moved you to get you out of it, even if we'd thought of it."

Tarkyn grinned, "Fair enough. Just commenting, not complaining." He took another deep pain-free breath and sighed with relief, "Right. Well, your guffawing will have given the game away. So I might as well get up and get on with it. I have to take this shirt off though."

So saying, the prince jumped nimbly to his feet and strode over to the group gathered around the fire, removing his shirt as he went. He didn't even notice the biting wind against his bare chest. "So, any food around? I'm starving. And is there any chance of someone washing this shirt? It's absolutely putrid." He looked at his shoulder. "Oh my stars! I'm green all over. That is a little unexpected. I hope it's not a permanent state of affairs." He looked back at Waterstone. "Hah, you see? There is a round mark here on my shoulder where you put your hand, matching the circle on your palm. I thought there might be."

The entire group stood transfixed as their pale green guardian of the forest stood amongst them, prattling on as though nothing had been amiss. He looked around at them all and beamed, "How are the plans going? Is the hole filled in and ready for me to do some planting?" He glanced at Autumn Leaves and grinned, "I'd say the sun is in just about the right place in the sky, according to Waterstone's marvellous image. So I must be about on time."

Tarkyn put his hands on his hips as the silence stretched out and demanded, "What is the matter with you lot? Have you never seen a green man before?" He then proceeded to chortle at his own joke. Realising he had unnerved them; he took a deep breath and slowed himself down. "Sorry. I'll try to be sensible. But at the moment, just the fact that I'm still alive is pretty exciting." He let his gaze travel around them all and carefully slowed down his speech, "And I have everyone of you to thank for it. I could not have made it without you. Thank you to you all for sharing your life force with me. It feels as thoughI have been gone a long time and travelled far and now I am just glad to be back among you again."

At last the tension broke. The woodfolk and the wizard crowded in around him smiling and asking questions and telling him what was happening all at once. When the hubbub died down, Tarkyn found that his shirt had been whisked away and he had a plateful of food in his hand. "While I'm eating this, could someone get some green sticks or small shrubs organised so that I can get on with disguising this hole as soon as I've finished. I believe a stand of poplars once grew here," he said, unwittingly betraying his unconscious knowledge of the forest. "Are there any around we could get cuttings from?"

Stormaway managed to make himself heard above the general chatter. "Shouldn't you be resting? You nearly died back there. You can't recover that quickly."

Tarkyn raised his eyebrows. "I wasn't quick. I kept you waiting, as I recall." He looked over at the oak tree. "That fine old oak has completely replenished my strength and has aided me in repairing all my injuries, not just the most recent ones. You can check if you like. No bruising anywhere, I bet….and I can't see, but how's the eyebrow where you hit me, Waterstone? I'll bet it's completely healed."

Waterstone and Stormaway both nodded slowly, amazed.

"That's why I took so long. I realised I could heal myself completely, not just make running repairs." The prince smiled gently at the wizard. "I'm sorry if I frightened you. I was a long way down – down, is that the right word? – It's the best I can do to describe it. So, anyway, I was a long way down and I needed to focus hard on each part of my body in turn to inspect it and repair it as needed."

"Why did you panic when Waterstone was over talking to me?"

Tarkyn shot Waterstone a glance and smiled crookedly. "Because he was my hold on the outside world. I needed him linked to me to stop me from going too far down and getting lost…Like a lifeline, I suppose. Sparrow wasn't solid enough on her own." He looked around, "Where is Sparrow?" Then he spotted her a little way off, hanging back from the crowd and looking less sure of herself than usual. He smiled at her and beckoned, "Come here, little one."

Sparrow walked slowly towards him. When she reached him, he swung her up onto his left hip and gave her a big smile, "Thank you for helping me."

Sparrow stuck out her bottom lip. "Why didn't you let me stay?"

"Because, young Sparrow, it was too long for you to sit still and I needed to concentrate." He ruffled her hair. "I'm sorry I didn't have time to explain. Even your dad only lasted twenty minutes after you left, you know."

She smiled reluctantly, "Did he?"

"Yes, I'm afraid so."

"Oh," Sparrow gave this some careful thought. "So you weren't cross with me?"

"No, of course I wasn't. Don't worry. You didn't do anything wrong." He smiled at her. "Still friends?"

Sparrow nodded and smiled, although tears sprang to her eyes. "I was very worried about you, you know. It was very scary."

"I'm sorry, little one. Look! I have a smudgy round mark on my shoulder where you put your hand. Let me see your hand."

Sparrow turned her palm up for inspection.

"See?" said Tarkyn. "You've got a matching smudgy mark on your palm. He looked at her, "So. What do you think of me being green?"

Sparrow screwed up her face. "Terrible. You look like you've gone mouldy."

The prince grinned. "Well, thanks very much! I knew it was bad, but not that bad." He swung her back down onto the ground. "We'll just have to hope it goes away then, won't we? Go on. Off you go and have some lunch."

"I've had lunch."

"Sparrow!" cut in her father. "Go and play! We have to do grown-up things now."

Sparrow threw a cheeky smile over her shoulder and looked much happier, as she skipped off to join the other children.

Tarkyn watched her for a moment then turned back to Waterstone and Stormaway. "Come on then. Let's get this grove of poplars planted then I need to speak to you, Stormaway."

The woodman and the wizard exchanged glances and followed the boisterous forest guardian to a pile of poplar cuttings that had been prepared.

Tarkyn caught their glance and raised his eyebrows. "Waterstone, be afraid! Be very afraid! Because now I am completely well, and in full possession of my powers." He grinned rather evilly. "As I recall, you thought my full powers might be enough to frighten you off and in a moment of weakness, I gave you permission to go. Well you've had it now, because I retract my permission for you to leave. In fact, I absolutely forbid it. However you may feel, you're going to have to stay and cope with me." Tarkyn beamed at the woodman, totally confident that his words would not be taken amiss.

Tarkyn knelt down, pushed the first poplar cutting into the ground and focused his attention on it for a couple of quiet minutes. As soon as green shoots began to sprout from it, he relaxed his focus but still held the cutting until it had become more established. Within an hour, there were twenty young poplars four to six feet in height, sprouting forth green leaves and reaching for the sky.

Waterstone looked Tarkyn up and down. "It's a bit hard to tell but I think you're a paler shade of green now."

The guardian of the forest smiled, still full of energy. "That's hopeful. Sparrow may be able to stand the sight of me soon."He turned to the wizard, "And now for you, Stormaway. Thank you, my friend, for your courage and your skill. You orchestrated my whole recovery and now I would like to return some energy to you. You are looking very drained and, after all, if you are to be believed, you are getting too old for all this excitement."

The wizard shook his head wearily. "No, Tarkyn. You must preserve your strength. There is still a lot to do and a long way to go."

Tarkyn considered him for a moment. Finally he said, "Stormaway, your skill and care saved my life. I assure you I have energy to spare. Please let me repay you just a little by giving you a bit of my life force." He gave a wry smile, "It might help to get rid of some of this green!" He shrugged, "Besides which, now that I know about it, I can replenish my strength from any large tree if I need to. The advantage of being a forest guardian... Come on," he urged, "let me do this for you."

"Oh my word, young man. It is tiring just being near you at the moment. Maybe you do need to get rid of some of that excess energy," he conceded grudgingly.

Before the wizard could change his mind, Tarkyn placed his left hand on Stormaway's shoulder and closed his eyes. The wizard felt strength pouring into him so fast that it made him gasp. As quickly as it started, the sensation stopped. Tarkyn opened his eyes and said casually, "There. That should help."

Stormaway stared at him. "The combined efforts of twenty woodfolk and me didn't produce anything like that life force."

Tarkyn smiled strangely, "You're dealing with the strength of the forest now. You can't compare the life force of twenty woodfolk and a wizard to the strength of an ancient oak and the forest guardian."

Waterstone felt his stomach turn over. This Tarkyn was not the person he had spent the last week with. This Tarkyn was stronger, more sure of himself, less compromising and infinitely more powerful. Maybe the prince was just revelling in being well again, but Waterstone didn't think that was all there was to it. In his connection with the ancient oak tree, Tarkyn had actually taken on the persona of the guardian of the forest.

The woodman gradually became aware of a gentle wave of amused reassurance wafting around his mind. He glanced at his green friend to discover that he was being watched with raised eyebrows and an understanding smile.

Waterstone scowled at him, "Don't tell me you have added mind-reading to your ever increasing list of skills."

Tarkyn shook his head. "Who needs mind-reading when dealing with a face as expressive as yours?" He stood up. "Come on my friend. We have work to do. When all is done we will talk, but meanwhile be assured that although I may have changed, I have not forgotten our friendship." He walked over to the cooking fire and requested in a clear, carrying voice. "Would everyone gather together here, please,"

If the woodfolk were surprised at the unexpected assurance in his voice, they did not show it, but simply did as he asked. When they had gathered around him, their forest guardian said, "I hope I have not disrupted your plans too much. However, there are a few things I need to clear up. Firstly, who will be tracking the wolves' spoor back to their source? We need to know where they originate from, don't we?" Following nods of agreement, he continued, "Secondly, are we still setting off to find Falling Rain? My opinion is that we should not leave him to face this threat alone. And thirdly, I think that if there is a significant, unidentified threat to us, all woodfolk need to be together to protect each other."

Tarkyn looked around the group of woodfolk before him. "So. Any comments? Opinions? I'm assuming you will need to discuss it with the main body of woodfolk. However, fear or dislike of me will not be sufficient reason for them not to join us."

Autumn Leaves cut in at this point. "We can't gather together for too long. A large group is too conspicuous and too hard to keep hidden."

"We can make sure we stay within easy reach of each other," suggested Thunder Storm.

The prince nodded decisively. "That will have to do then. At least until we know what is threatening us. Agreed?" When he had their consent, he continued, "Meanwhile I will head back up to the site of the wolf fight. Now that I do not have to struggle against cracked ribs, I am quite capable of walking to the road with the full load of wolf remains." He paused, "I presume you have used minimal pieces of each wolf to provide the scents for the trail?"

The woodfolk nodded, mesmerised. The aloofness and formality that attached to Tarkyn in his role as imposed liege lord had disappeared. His linking with the oak had transformed his view of himself. Now he accepted the authority that came from being their guardian of the forest. From Tarkyn's point of view, the oath was no longer the driving force behind his relationship with the woodfolk. Although he still abhorred the fact that the woodfolk were effectively held in thrall by it, he now felt that he had a different, legitimate, untainted basis for his authority. It restored in him his natural assurance as a leader of men that he had been bred for.

Then a soft rhythmic voice asked "My lord, are you able to find out, as you did before, when the next attack may arrive?" Tarkyn looked around.

Lapping Water's soft green eyes met his gaze nervously but with quiet determination.

Tarkyn suddenly became very aware of the fact that he wasn't wearing his shirt and that he was an unwholesome green. His newly found confidence threatened to desert him. He blinked and smiled wryly. "I can try. I have not yet been able to instigate a mind link with a bird or animal. Up until now, it has always been the creature who has contacted me. When I get to the river, I will spend a few minutes trying to link with the eagle or may be the heron. I will do what I can."

"Thank you," said Lapping Water with a gentle, uncertain smile.

Tarkyn felt that perhaps his new strength wasn't going to last as long as he thought. His knees seemed to have gone a bit wobbly. With an effort, he tore his gaze away from Lapping Water. "Stormaway, I would still like you to walk to the road with me, even if I carry all the wolf scents. Two sets of tracks will be more believable than one."

"Your wish is my command, Sire," replied the wizard with a heavy touch of irony.

Tarkyn raised his eyebrows. "Not that I've noticed," he said dryly. "However, I will give you the choice because I know you are tired." The prince returned his attention to the woodfolk. "So, if there are no further comments, I'm off. Someone needs to come with me, but only if Stormaway doesn't. I'll need some directions from the river to the road."

There was a general clamour of offers. Their forest guardian smiled to himself and said, "You sort it out among yourselves. And don't forget to water in my poplars. I'm heading off. Give me an hour. I'll meet you down at the river." He rose gently into the air and then glided off through the trees in the general direction of his favourite spot by the river.

CHAPTER 23

When Tarkyn reached the site of the battle against the wolves, there was little sign of the carnage that had been there earlier. Under a shady tree, there was a neat pile of black and grey switches, tied together at one end, presumably trimmed from the skins of the wolves. Tarkyn looked around carefully and spotted a small torn piece of brightly coloured fabric caught in the low branches of a spiky bush - definitely not from woodfolk clothing. Further scrutiny discovered a small spray of blonde human hair tangled in the branches of a hawthorn. Tarkyn wondered, with a frisson of dismay, where the woodfolk had procured it.

Very subtle, he decided, *not the scattering of belongings I was anticipating. You have to be looking carefully to find them but if someone is tracing the wolves, they will be looking everywhere for clues. Clever people, these woodfolk. Still, I suppose they are masters of tracking.*

Tarkyn sat down against a rock near the river and watched the water rolling over stones and spreading out to flow peacefully downstream. He could feel the roughness of the rock slightly scratchy against his bare back. Tarkyn shivered as the biting autumn wind played over his bare skin but he drank in the sensations, still so pleased to have survived. He took a deep pain-free breath and relaxed back, relieved to have some time away from everyone's attention. The novice guardian of the forest slowly opened up his mind to his surroundings to see if some creature would make contact with him. As he relaxed his boundaries, a kaleidoscope of images flooded into his mind. He could see the woodlands from above, from within, from ground level, from the treetops all at once, and all superimposed over each other. He dragged his mind back from the edge of chaos and closed its boundaries with a snap.

Tarkyn let out a long breath. "Whoa. That was excessive. Now everything's trying to talk to me at once." He shook his head to clear it and looked around him. "I need something specific to focus on."

As he watched, a swallow skimmed over the water near him twisting and swooping to catch the midges that were hanging there. Tarkyn focused narrowly on the swallow and sent a query about wolves. The swallow flicked past him and then suddenly the sorcerer was seeing the world through the swallow's eyes. The little bird soared up into the treetops and swooped and swung its way through the air until she was above the woodlands. Tarkyn could feel his stomach struggling to keep up with the rapid changes of direction. He tightened his stomach muscles against the sudden lifts and dives that seemed to be a natural part of the little bird's flying pattern. The sorcerer sent an image of the direction from which the wolves had come and the swallow banked sickeningly and flew swiftly westward, bobbing and swooping as she went to catch any insect she spotted on the way past. The woodland spread out below as the swallow climbed higher. Every now and then she swooped down and back up in an arc that made Tarkyn's stomach lurch. Tarkyn gradually became aware that the swallow knew what effect these acrobatics were having on him and was playing with him.

"Very funny," he murmured through gritted teeth as, once more, the swallow took a joyous dive.

After several more minutes of swooping dives and climbs, Tarkyn was feeling decidedly queasy. Just as well I'm already green, he thought grimly... saves me the trouble of going green around the gills now.

Just when he was thinking that he would have to pull out and leave the swallow to her teasing, Tarkyn spotted a faint cloud of dust rising above the height of the trees in the distance. The sorcerer directed the swallow towards it. With cheerful good grace, the little bird swooped and flitted her way towards the dust cloud. As the swallow drew closer, Tarkyn could see, not the wolves he expected, but flashes of sunlight reflecting off the harnesses of a large group of horsemen riding hard. A lone wolf flitted ahead of them leading them towards the river. The next attack was not six hours away as the woodfolk had expected. These horsemen were less than two hours away.

The sorcerer sent a quick sense of appreciation and pulled out of the swallow's mind. He nearly vomited as he returned suddenly into his nauseated body, but a couple of deep breaths restored his equilibrium. As soon as he was re-oriented, Tarkyn searched out Waterstone's mind and sent a clear image of the last part of the swallow's journey above the trees.

Half a mile away next to a new stand of poplars, Waterstone suddenly reeled, lost his balance and fell over as the swallow's images sent his mind swooping and diving across the top of the forest.

"Blast it, Tarkyn," he exclaimed, even though the prince couldn't hear him. "A bit of warning would have been nice."

Despite the urgency of the situation, Tarkyn chuckled quietly to himself, knowing exactly what havoc the image would be causing the woodman. When he had given Waterstone time to pick himself up, he sent a spurious wave of sympathy then a query about Stormaway. Once he knew that the wizard was coming to join him, Tarkyn sent a directive that the woodfolk should skirt around the area of the wolf fight and meet him nearer the road.

A few minutes later, Stormaway appeared drifting through the air between the trees. He alighted neatly and presented Tarkyn with his freshly washed shirt. "One shirt, washed in a forest stream and dried over a wood fire," he said with a small, courtly bow. "You may need this too," he added, handing Tarkyn a long, light brown cloak."

The prince stood up and smiled his thanks. "What? No wolf cloak?"

"No. It takes longer than a couple of days to cure the skins."

"Well, I would rather wait and not stink of wolf," said Tarkyn, as he put on his shirt. "I'm glad you're here. We have to move fast." He flung the cloak around his shoulders. "There is a large group of horsemen heading this way. I'd say we have only an hour and a half safely, perhaps a bit longer but not much."

Stormaway raised his eyebrows. "And you know this how?"

"Swallow," replied the forest guardian briefly. "Let's grab those switches and be on our way."

Forty minutes later, the wizard and the sorcerer stood beside the road through the forest. They had scuffled around the clearing and had left many heavy footprints at every point along the way. The wolf remains had been artistically dragged along the ground and against bushes and tree trunks on the way past to emulate carrying a large load. Now they were inspecting the road surface for signs of cartwheel tracks.

Stormaway squatted down and studied the gravel surface. "There are a few sets of tracks going through," he reported. "These ones here are the most recent, earlier today sometime, I think. We just need to deepen them a little at the point where we would supposedly be loading the wolves into the cart. Cartwheels leave slightly deeper impressions when they have been left standing in any one place for a while and the wind tends to build up sand and dirt into a small ridge against the side of the wheel." He looked up into the gently waving branches of the trees. "There has been a sharp wind all day today so there would be quite a build up on the windward side of the tracks. Right!" said the wizard as he began some delicate sand sculpture along the edge of the wheel track, "I'll sort the wheel tracks while you make some boot prints back and forth behind where the cart would have stopped and then down one side as though you are walking around to get into it. Then levitate yourself and the wolf remains straight up and out of here. I'll do the same and be right behind you."

The sun, low in the sky, cast strange long shadows down the road. The wizard and the sorcerer hung in the air, trailing pieces of fur, giving their handiwork a final inspection.

"I'm impressed, Stormaway, came a voice out of the trees on the southern side of the road. "Unless I was expecting to be tricked, I would be convinced by your creation... and I am considered to be one of our best trackers." Creaking Bough smiled at them. "Let's go. We have to get those remains buried and set up camp before nightfall. We estimate from your images, Tarkyn, that the riders will be arriving at the riverside in less than an hour, around dusk."

Part 5: Betrayal

CHAPTER 24

When dusk came, Tarkyn was sitting with his back against an old elm, a little distance away from the others. He had reached out carefully and after searching specifically for the male tawny owl, had made contact. Now he was looking down on the riverside clearing through the owl's eyes.

Ten riders stream into the clearing behind the wolf. They are roughly dressed, each carrying knives, axes or staffs. Most have a bow and a quiver of arrows strapped to their saddles. They mill around, fighting to control their excited horses as the wolf sniffs back and forth around the clearing then sits down on his haunches, throws back his head and howls.

One rider snarls something, obviously disliking the wolf's howling.

A weedy young man snaps out orders and the riders dismount and begin to search the area. The piece of bright material and the blonde hair are quickly found but each is discarded out of hand. The wolf, when he has finished his tribute to his kin, responds to the young man's call and trots over to him. He sniffs at a piece of brown cloth that the man has tucked into his waist. Then the wolf snuffles back and forth around the clearing again. He finds the trail left by Tarkyn and Stormaway but after zigzagging along it for several yards, returns to the clearing. Suddenly, the big wolf starts to bark at the base of one of the tree, lunging at the trunk in an attempt to jump up into the branches.

The young man exclaims in triumph then slaps his thigh in frustration as he looks up into the empty tree. By his facial expressions and his gestures, it is clear that he knows his quarry has escaped him but it is equally clear that he is not looking for sorcerers or wizards.

Tarkyn walked back to join the weary woodfolk around the fire. They seemed to be lower on energy than usual. Tarkyn sat on the ground near the fire leaning back against a large log. He feared the image would dispirit them even further. He was right.

A horrified silence hung over the firesite once Tarkyn had relayed the owl's images. Finally, Stormaway could stand it no more. "Could someone fill me in on what is happening? I don't pick up images, remember."

Tarkyn dragged himself out of a reverie to answer, "Ten riders and a wolf are in the riverside clearing, as we speak. They were not interested in our carefully laid trail or in the evidence of travellers that was so neatly planted. There is a young man who seems to be in charge. The wolf was directed to seek out a particular scent, which led him to the base of the tree that the woodfolk must have climbed to leave the clearing. These people, whoever they are, are specifically hunting for the woodfolk."

"How did the young man direct the wolf to look for woodfolk?" asked the wizard.

"He has a piece of our clothing," said Waterstone tightly.

Stormaway frowned, "I see. And is there any way you can be tracked from there to here?"

Thunder Storm shook his head slowly. "No. Our scent will be all around that area and where we buried the wolves but we have only just come back down from the trees now." He looked wearily at the wizard. "It has been a long hard day travelling everywhere through the tree tops but it looks like it was worth it."

Tarkyn realised with a jolt that he hadn't considered the effort it would have cost them to climb up into the heights of each tree and jump down into the next one over several miles of woodland. He thought over the events of the day and worked out that they would all have had to travel at least five miles, some further if they had done more than one trip with wolf remains. No wonder they seemed dispirited. They were bone tired.

The forest guardian stood up, still pleased with how little effort it cost him. He let his gaze travel around them all. "I know you are all very tired but will you please stand up and come to stand on either side of me? We can discuss these developments afterwards. You don't need to do this, Stormaway."

For the first time, disgruntled glances were exchanged and some people were clearly reluctant to comply. Tarkyn made no comment but simply waited until they had all done as he asked.

"Now, put your hand on your neighbour's shoulder." Their forest guardian placed his hands on the shoulders of the two woodfolk nearest to him on either side. "I am now going to replenish your energy."

A mutter of dissent and uncertainty ran through the woodfolk.

Tarkyn spoke gently but with an underlying edge to his voice. "I am not offering this or requesting that you take it. I am requiring you to take it." He paused. "Now. Close your eyes. Do not resist. Allow the energy to flow." Tarkyn closed his own eyes and focused deep inside himself. He drew forth his *esse* and sent out a warm wave of strength into the exhausted wood folk. There was a communal intake of breath as the wave of gentle power washed into them. "You may open your eyes when you are ready."

When the woodfolk opened their eyes, they found themselves encased inside a warm bronze haze. Even as they gazed at it, it faded away. They looked at each other, saw renewed vitality in the faces before them and broke into smiles. Their forest guardian took his hands down and gestured that they could take their seats again.

Tarkyn smiled and sent out a wave of gratitude and bonhomie as he sat down himself. "Thank you for your cooperation. I realise it took a big effort to stand up after your long day. I can't thank you enough for what you all did for me today and I wished to give you something in return. Not only that, but as your forest guardian, I need to make sure you have enough strength to face whatever the next few days brings us." He looked around at them all. There was still some residual tension among them so he sent out a ripple of reassurance and added, "And that's it. I may have been a little too exuberant this afternoon but true to my word, I am not going to keep ordering you around – at least, only occasionally. As agreed, we will work together."

"Tarkyn," said Sparrow, coming up to stand in front of him to peer at him closely, "You're not green any more."

"Thank heavens for that!" exclaimed Tarkyn. He smiled at Sparrow and said in a loud voice. "Are you hungry?" She nodded. "So am I." He looked around the side of the little girl and addressed no one in particular. "Without wishing to be too demanding... does anyone have enough energy now to make some dinner? I'm starving – and I don't know how to cook." He looked back at Sparrow and grinned, "And I don't particularly want to learn how, either."

"That's very lazy of you, Tarkyn," said Sparrow severely.

The prince didn't look one bit abashed. "I know, but equality can only go so far, in my opinion."

Sparrow seemed a little confused by this answer but was rescued by her father who interceded to say dryly, "What His Highness means, is that he has other jobs to do that other people can't do. So it's fair if he doesn't do any cooking."

"Is that what I meant? Thank goodness you're here to keep me informed," chortled Tarkyn.

Sparrow frowned repressively at him, "I think you're just trying to get out of it."

The prince smiled sweetly at her, "Oh no, I'm not trying. I'm determined. There are limits, you know. Now, haven't you got something better to do than stand here telling me off?"

Suddenly she smiled sunnily, and flung her arms around his neck before plonking herself on his knee. "I think you're being very naughty but I'm not sure. Anyway, I'm glad you're not mouldy any more and I'm glad I'm not feeling as tired as I was. I was aching everywhere. We did a lot of climbing today, you know. It stops being fun after a while."

"Well, I hope it becomes fun again tomorrow when you've had a good sleep." He said, wrapping his arm around her.

She nodded and settled herself against his shoulder. "I expect it will be." She answered drowsily. In the next breath, she was asleep.

Tarkyn gazed down at her, "Oh dear. Maybe I should have given the children a double dose. Poor little things must be exhausted. The adults were close to exhaustion, let alone the littlies." He looked at Waterstone, "What is she going to do about dinner?"

Waterstone smiled down at his daughter, lying peacefully in Tarkyn's arms. "If she is very hungry, she will wake up. If not, she can make up for it with a big breakfast in the morning."

Tarkyn stroked Sparrow's hair. After a while, he asked quietly, "What did you decide about finding Falling Rain?"

"That you're right. We need to find him and bring him back into the fold. He is in the southwest beyond the mountains." As he spoke, Waterstone drew a map in the dirt to demonstrate what he was saying. "We can travel parallel to the road until we reach the area where the attacks on travellers are increasing and see what we can find out on the way past. Then we'll turn due south and travel over the mountains."

"And who is back-tracking the wolves?"

The woodman glanced at Tarkyn. "We decided that those of us with you are a bare minimum for your safety really, and ours. So, another group, the harvesters, will track the horsemen and follow the wolves' trail back to its source. We'll send in more if we need to."

Tarkyn smiled wryly, "They're still avoiding me, aren't they?"

Waterstone grimaced, "Well, they're not exactly rushing to meet up with you, I would have to admit."

"Autumn Leaves said woodfolk don't all meet together very often - or was it, don't meet for very long?" The prince shrugged. "Anyway, how many groups are there? In fact, how many woodfolk are there?"

Waterstone stared off into the fire. "There were about two hundred of us at your welcoming feast. Usually we work together in groups of somewhere between forty and eighty, depending on what we are doing."

Tarkyn did a quick calculation. "So there must be three or four other groups."

The woodman kept his eyes firmly on the fire, "Mm. Yes. Something like that."

For the first time since Tarkyn had known him, Waterstone was being evasive. The prince didn't challenge him but frowned in thought trying to work out what the woodman was avoiding telling him. *What is most important to Waterstone?... Sparrow?* Tarkyn looked down at her and stroked her hair again. Yes, but not relevant to this conversation.He glanced sideways at the woodman's profile. Usually, Waterstone caught his eye but this time he kept his gaze steadfastly forward. Tarkyn thought back over the conversation, word for word. *Two hundred on the first night but somehow my calculations aren't right and Waterstone doesn't want to tell me what's wrong with them. What does he care about so much that he won't be straight with me?* Suddenly he knew.

"How many woodfolk were present when my father made them swear the oath?" asked the prince slowly.

Finally, Waterstone dragged his eyes away from the fire to face him. "About one hundred and sixty."

"Oh no!" breathed the prince. "That means I forced forty more woodfolk to swear the oath who had avoided it before. Blast it! I wish I had known." He looked at Waterstone. "Not you though. You were there the first time, weren't you?"

Waterstone nodded and looked morosely back into the fire.

"Where's Stormaway?" asked Tarkyn suddenly.

The woodman glanced around the firesite and spotted the wizard on the other side of the clearing. "Over there," he replied shortly.

"Good." He returned his attention to the woodman and regarded him through narrowed eyes. "You're struggling, aren't you?" asked Tarkyn. Then he shrugged, "Well, maybe you're not. Maybe your loyalties are totally clear to you. Maybe I'm just hoping you're struggling."

"Of course I'm bloody struggling," snapped Waterstone. "I'm always bloody struggling around you. If it's not for one reason, it's for another."

"I know. I think we both agree I'm hard work." Tarkyn seemed completely unmoved by the woodman's outburst. He gave a crooked smile. "Let me put you out of your misery and save you having to betray, or consider betraying, your fellow woodfolk. There are many more woodfolk, aren't there, than I have ever met?"

Waterstone let out a long breath and, after a moment, nodded.

"Does Stormaway know this?" asked the prince.

The woodman's eyes flickered in alarm. "No."

Now Tarkyn did become annoyed, "Oh Stars above, Waterstone, don't look like that! Have you learnt nothing about me in the time you've known me?"

Waterstone had the grace to look embarrassed. "Sorry. Knee jerk reaction."

"Let us agree to keep Stormaway out of this. If I ever meet with these other woodfolk, I'll do it on my own terms, not his." Tarkyn was struggling to keep his unruly feelings in check. He glanced sideways at Waterstone and said, "I'm sorry. Can you take Sparrow? I can't sit here any longer. I need some time on my own to think."

When Sparrow had been safely transferred over into Waterstone's arms, Tarkyn stood up and stretched, forcing himself not to rush. "When's this food coming?" he asked irascibly.

"Here you are," said Thunder Storm, appearing at just the right moment and handing him a bowl full of rich stew.

"Wolf?"

Thunder Storm beamed, "Nothing but the best."

Tarkyn managed to return his smile and thank him. Then he took his stew and headed off into the quiet of the trees. Once he was beyond the circle of firelight, the reaction set in. His mind was overwhelmed with trying to re-think every incident and conversation and agreement in view of this new information. He blundered through the woods, barely aware of where he was going until he found a comfortable tree to prop himself against that was shielded from view and surrounded by soft moss. He sat down and concentrated on eating his meal to still his raging thoughts. When he had finished, he leaned his head back against the trunk of the tree, closed his eyes and began to re-assess everything.

All those times I thought they were mind talking with the group of woodfolk I had met, they had actually been talking to many more. Every one of the woodfolk around me, probably even Sparrow, knew that there were other woodfolk that I hadn't been told about. I am in the middle of a huge tacit conspiracy against me. And what would happen if I met one of the woodfolk not bound by the oath? These people would have all the resentment but none of the restrictions provided by the oath. Would they kill me as an outsider to protect the secret of their existence? Would they kill me to rescue their kindred from the oath? Not if oathbound woodfolk were present because the threat to the forest's wellbeing would guarantee my protection, but probably they would otherwise. And what difference does it make to these unknown woodfolk that

I am this forest guardian of theirs? Would that stop them from attacking me?

And what does this all mean for my relationship with the woodfolk I thought I knew and was beginning to trust? And where does it leave my friendship with Waterstone? Nowhere, was his immediate reaction. After a few minutes of further thought, he decided his immediate reaction was correct. *How could Waterstone have been so confident about concealing this information when I scanned his memory? Obvious, really. He knew I wouldn't know woodfolk well enough to notice if I saw different woodfolk in the memories from the ones I had met. As it turned out, the issue didn't even arise.*

And the agreement I thought I had with the woodfolk here tonight - so much for sharing vital information. It slipped their minds, did it, that they were discussing everything I said with a whole host of other people I knew nothing about.

A tidal wave of anger and desolation burst forth from the sorcerer and rolled off through the woods. Its passage was marked by ruffled feathers, grunts of discomfort from a passing badger, and starts of fright from various, completely innocent night creatures in the woods. As it reached the campsite, every waking person rocked back in their seats, their eyes widening in apprehension. But even though he was also swamped by the wave, Stormaway alone did not understand its cause.

Twenty minutes later, unaware that his untamed feelings had once more betrayed him, Tarkyn walked out of the woods and sat down with an appearance of equanimity at the firesite.

"So," he said urbanely, "As I remember it, I interrupted the discussion we were having about the owl's image of the hunters. I think the main issue, as far as I can understand it, seems to centre around the fact that somehow they seem to know that woodfolk exist and that they are looking specifically for you. I am sure that will be concerning you. Any ideas how that may have happened?"

A prolonged, strained silence greeted the prince's words. Stormaway frowned at the lack of reaction, "Perhaps everyone is too tired to discuss it tonight. Maybe we'll do better after a good night's rest."

The prince produced a courtly smile. "I'm sure you're right. I should have realised everyone would be too tired this evening. Have shelters been constructed or are we sleeping outside tonight?"

"Of course shelters are ready," growled Stormaway, now becoming seriously unnerved by the silence of the woodfolk. "Yours is over there."

The prince raised his eyebrows. "Is it? Thank you to whoever prepared my shelter when you are clearly still so exhausted. Well, I will bid you goodnight. To be frank, the conversation at the moment is less than stimulating. I will see you all in the morning." So saying, Tarkyn rose to his feet and left the stunned woodfolk to the rest of their evening.

There was no way that Tarkyn was going to be able to sleep. He was wound up like a taut bow, rage simmering just below the surface. He had tried, successfully he thought, to maintain a front of friendly courtesy but the effort had been extreme. He couldn't possibly keep it up for long, certainly not day after day for the rest of his life. He tossed and turned, trying to find a way out.

I can't just leave them, much as I want to. I have sworn that blasted oath to them. Their fate is my fate. Their cause is mine. What a bloody one way street that is, he thought bitterly. *But I can't stay. I just cannot do it.*

Inspiration struck him in the early hours of the morning. He rose quietly and crept away from the campsite. Spotting the lookout just before the lookout spotted him, he muttered "Shturrum!" without any compunction. Tarkyn caught Grass Wind as she fell paralysed from the tree. "When I release this spell, I forbid you to let anyone know I'm gone, at least until you are directly asked. Is that clear?" The prince did not waste time on courtesy. "Do not try to follow me and do not try to dissuade me. Do you understand?" He released the spell.

"My lord," whispered Grass Wind, "Take care. My thoughts will be with you."

Tarkyn recoiled as if bitten. He shook his head to clear it, unable to reconcile her intended kindness with his knowledge of her duplicity. Without another word, he turned and disappeared into the woods. Once he was beyond the scope of the other lookouts, he levitated himself and travelled above the forest so that he couldn't be tracked by anyone wishing to follow him. The moon shone intermittently between scudding grey clouds. The sharp autumn wind was stronger and colder without the trees to provide shelter from it.

When he was an hour away from the campsite, he returned to the forest floor and sat with his back against a tree while he sent out his mind to find the tawny owl he knew. He pictured the occasion under the pine when he had first met the owl, then sent a request for it to make contact. After a short wait, he found his mind scanning the forest floor looking for rodents. The sorcerer sent an image of the woodfolk he knew with him shaking his head then a vaguer image of woodfolk with a query. It wasn't very clear as communication went but it was the best he could think of. Tarkyn's mind took off and flew low through the forest until it came to a firesite he had never seen before. Tarkyn sent a message indicating himself, then the place. A sense of ruffling feathers came to him and he realised that the owl was not keen to come and fetch him. The sorcerer persevered with his request and eventually the owl conceded. Tarkyn sent a wave of gratitude.

A good half hour passed before the owl arrived. He alighted in the branch above Tarkyn and sat glaring down at him, ruffling his feathers, clearly in a huff. Tarkyn wished he had some titbits of wolf to give him. The owl sank his head down into his shoulders and closed his eyes. Tarkyn waited patiently. After a short nap, the owl blinked, shook himself and took off without further warning. The sorcerer scrambled to his feet and levitated himself to follow. Half an hour later, as they drew near their destination, Tarkyn sent the owl a query about lookouts. In response, the owl took them both above the height of the trees, curved around and dipped slightly above and behind a still figure positioned high in a horse chestnut tree. Tarkyn sent out his thanks to the owl and began his descent behind the lookout into the middle of the firesite.

CHAPTER 25

No one was yet stirring. The sorcerer debated with himself about whether to erect his shield. It would be safer but it would also be regarded as a sign of hostility. On balance, he decided to take his chances unprotected, and settled himself to wait beside the cold remains of their last night's fire, wrapping his cloak tightly around himself to fend off the dank chill of pre-dawn.

As the first pale rays of the sun filtered through the glowing golden autumn leaves, the first woodman emerged. The man was middle aged and scruffy after a night's sleep. He wandered about collecting sticks and branches to get the fire started. As he brought them over to the firesite, he finally noticed Tarkyn sitting there, waiting. The woodman dropped the sticks with a loud clatter. His eyes went briefly out of focus and within seconds the clearing had filled with belligerent, wary woodfolk; many with raised bows in their hands, arrows notched. Through all of this, Tarkyn didn't move a muscle. When everyone had gathered around him, he stood up very slowly and took his hands slowly out from within his cloak.

"Who are you?" demanded a young woodman rudely.

Tarkyn raised his eyebrows. "But surely you know." He let his amber eyes travel around them all and sketched a shallow bow. "I am Tarkyn Tamadil, Prince of Eskuzor and of these forests, also known as guardian of the forest."

"And also known as rogue sorcerer," added the belligerent youth.

The prince grimaced, "Yes. I had forgotten that one."

"We are under no obligation to you," growled the first man he had seen. There was a tiny pause, "I am Falling Branch and we people are known as the forestals."

"I am aware that you are under no obligation to me, Falling Branch."

"Who betrayed us?"

"No one has betrayed you. Waterstone made a slightly evasive reply to one of my questions that alerted me to your existence." The prince drew himself up. "They betrayed my trust but they have not betrayed yours. I found my own way here," he added.

"So you have come to force us into taking your oath, have you?"

Tarkyn looked around at them all with a slight smile. "And how would I do that?"

The woodfolk looked at each other then a woodwoman replied, "With your sorcery. I am Sun Shower"

The sorcerer frowned, "I did not create the sorcery of the oath."

"We have heard what you did to the other woodfolk," she persisted.

Tarkyn crossed his arms. "And have you heard that I hurt anyone?"

There were reluctant shakes of heads.

"I don't think I could force you into taking that oath" said the sorcerer thoughtfully, "but I wouldn't want to, even if I could."

Murmurs of surprise and disbelief emerged from the crowd.

"What do you want with us then, that you come sneaking into our firesite like a thief in the night?" demanded Falling Branch.

The prince wrinkled his nose in distaste, "Hardly like a thief. A thief would not wait quietly for you all to get up and speak with him." He wrapped his cloak back around himself and shivered. "No. I have come here to allow you the opportunity to kill me if you must, or to come to some sort of working arrangement with me, otherwise." He looked around calmly at the boggling faces. "One of the first things Autumn Leaves said to me was that anyone who saw the woodfolk did not leave the forest alive. That group of woodfolk has not been able to kill me because of the oath. But you people have no such impediment. I have come here alone so no oathbound woodfolk is forced to protect me." He swung his arms wide, flinging his cloak open. "So here I am. Do with me as you will."

He saw them go out of focus. "Might I suggest that you make your own decisions? If you confer with the oathbound woodfolk, they will have to try to persuade you to spare me. So, for more honest opinions, ask the rest of you."

Sun Shower looked at him strangely, "Do you want to die?"

The prince shrugged. "Frankly, at this stage in my life, that's a rather moot point. I don't think I care very much one way or the other."

"Why shouldn't we kill you?"

Tarkyn smiled faintly. "Two reasons. Firstly, if I am truly a guardian of the forest, you will need me to protect you from whatever danger threatens you. Secondly, there may be repercussions to the forest for the oathbound woodfolk failing to protect me – I hope not. I tried to make it virtually impossible for them to protect me in order to minimise that risk."

"And why do you think we would kill you?"

"Again two reasons." The prince's voice was completely dispassionate. "Firstly because I'm an outsider who has seen you woodfolk and secondly, and I would have thought more importantly, to release your fellow woodfolk from the oath."

Falling Branch raised his eyebrows. "You're a pretty cool customer. You're being remarkably forthright for someone in your position."

Tarkyn shook his head. "Not really. You have to remember I put myself in this position. There's no point in entering the lion's den and then trying to wriggle back out of it. If I live long enough for you to get to know me, you will learn that I am, as Waterstone puts it, blindingly honest." Just mentioning Waterstone made Tarkyn's stomach turn over.

"Can you prove that you're a guardian of the forest?" demanded the belligerent young man.

"I beg your pardon," said the prince urbanely, "I don't believe I know your name."

"I didn't give it."

The prince looked around enquiringly. "Is this young man special in some way? Am I mistaken in thinking it is common courtesy for woodfolk to give their name the first time they speak to someone new?"

Falling Branch cleared his throat. "No. That is correct."

"I see," said the prince and waited.

As the silence threatened to become awkward, the young man finally rolled his eyes and said grudgingly, "I am Rainstorm."

As though nothing untoward had passed between them, Tarkyn said mildly, "You would probably know better than I, Rainstorm, what characteristics you would expect in a forest guardian. I presume you have been sent images by the other woodfolk. What further proof do you require?"

The young woodman seemed startled at being taken seriously. He frowned as he thought. "I don't know. I just want to see it for myself. Hmm, I suppose the legends talk of a mystical being that comes among us" He looked Tarkyn up and down. "Well, your eyes are a bit strange and your hair's very long and dark, but other than that you don't look very mystical to me."

The sorcerer smiled approvingly, "I couldn't agree more."

The young man tilted his head to one side as he considered, "You're supposed to have great magical powers…"

"Yes. Well, I am a sorcerer and a powerful one at that, so I more or less qualify on that front."

"Well, go on then. Show us," demanded Rainstorm.

"What would you like to see?"

"I dunno. You're the sorcerer, not me."

Tarkyn considered for a moment. "Very well. I will blast a small branch off that elm over there and then transport it over here. Then it will be ready for my next little demonstration." He looked around, particularly at those with strung bows and asked, "Are we agreed?"

When he had received a general consensus, the sorcerer sent a harsh bronze beam of power against the base of one of the elm's branches. The branch broke off with a loud crack and fell to the ground. Tarkyn could hear the soft menacing sounds of bows being pulled tighter. "Is everybody all right so far? I don't want an arrow in the neck because someone is getting too edgy. If I'm going to die, I would rather it were for a better reason than that." Murmuring, "*Liefka*," he gently lifted the branch on a softer beam of bronze and floated it through the air to land just in front of him. He looked at the young woodman. "Anything else?"

Rainstorm had had time to think this time. "Well, go on then. Make it grow."

The guardian of the forest squatted down and forced a hole in the ground with a sharp stick. Then he placed the damaged end of the elm branch into the hole and closed his eyes. He drew gently on his *esse* and channelled it into the branch. Beneath his hands, he could feel the sap swell and small leaves twisting up out of the stem and opening up. He opened his eyes and held the branch for a few more moments until it was firmly established. Once he was sure it was secure, he smiled contentedly at his creation and stood up. His smile faded as he remembered where he was.

He sighed and looked once more at the young man. Rainstorm had forgotten him and was staring in amazement at the new little elm.

Sun Shower spoke instead, "Can you show us how you communicate with animals?"

Tarkyn shook his head decisively. "Not directly. I will not ask forest creatures to perform for you. I can share the image of my journey here if you like, but we will all need to sit down." He paused. "I don't suppose we could have a short break while you get the fire lit. You're all looking very cold and I would love a cup of tea if you happen to be making one. I've been up all night." He ran a tired hand through his hair and suddenly found himself up close and personal with six arrows virtually touching him. "Oh for heaven's sake," he snapped irritably, "If I were going to hurt you, I could have killed you all when I first arrived. You were all fast asleep and I sat out here for well over an hour before anyone stirred."

Falling Branch frowned, "Why did you come here? Why didn't you just stay with the oathbound woodfolk where you were safe?"

"Before I answer that, can we sit down? And do you think you could put away your arrows, just for a little while? Otherwise, I'm going to have to raise my shield. I can't stand the tension much longer."

"I thought you didn't care whether you lived or died," said Sun Shower.

Tarkyn glanced sideways at her, "It's one thing to die and quite another to endure the constant expectation of it."

"What will the shield do to us?" asked Rainstorm with narrowed eyes.

"Nothing. It will simply protect me. But I have been going to some lengths not to frighten you. So I don't want to start now."

None of the bowmen relaxed their stance so Tarkyn breathed in resignation and threw up a bronze shield around himself. Immediately, four arrows pinged against the outside of the shield.

"Oh, what a bloody silly lot you are!" exclaimed the prince in extreme annoyance. "I'm beginning to lose patience with you! I come here in good faith, completely unprotected, try to have a sensible discussion and you act like a bunch of hooligans."

Sun Shower stepped up to the outside of the shield. "We do not want to be tricked into your oath."

"I don't blame you, but I give you my word that I don't want your oath."

Sun Shower shook her head regretfully, "Unfortunately we do not trust you, so your word is valueless."

A strong wave of anger hit the surrounding woodfolk, rocking them backwards with its intensity. Several bowmen notched arrows and prepared to fire. Tarkyn was almost certain that his anger would have altered the composition of his shield to make it reflective. He removed his focus from the shield but managed to hold it in place as he muttered, "Shturrum!"

He glared around at the stationary woodfolk. "Why does it always come to this? I have done nothing to you. I intend to do nothing to you. I have had to stop the bowmen because my shield will reflect the arrows back at them now that I am angry. I do not want them to die from their own arrows." He waited to give his message time to sink in. "Do you understand? Stop shooting at me! … At least until we have finished talking. Then if you still want to kill me, so be it." He swept his gaze around the angry woodfolk before him. "I will now release you but whatever you do, don't shoot at my shield. When you lower your weapons, I will lower my shield. Everyone clear?"

The sorcerer released the woodfolk and watched as their eyes went out of focus.

"Fine," said Tarkyn quietly to himself. "Chat among yourselves. See if you can sort this bloody mess out."

At last Falling Branch spoke. "Will you agree to have your hands tied while we talk?"

Tarkyn felt sick at the memory of the last time he had had his hands tied. "I will. I won't like it but I will"

Falling Branch raised his eyebrows. "You are in no position to dictate terms."

The sorcerer rolled his eyes. "Oh for heaven's sake. I'm in every position to dictate terms at the moment. I'm just choosing not to."

The bowmen released the tension in their bows and Tarkyn lowered his shield and turned around to have his hands tied.

"There is no need for your hands to be tied behind you. That will be uncomfortable. We will simply bind your hands in front of you."

Tarkyn turned his head to look over his shoulder at the woodman. "Unless you want this to be a complete farce, you will have to tie my hands behind me. I can perform nearly all of my sorcery with my hands in front of me, bound or not."

Without further discussion, someone tied his hands together firmly using rough hemp. When he was facing Falling Branch again, he asked irritably, "Can we sit down now?"

The woodfolk sat Tarkyn on a low log and sat themselves around him. The prince stretched out his legs and crossed his ankles. "So, what do you want? To see how I came here or to find out why?"

"Tell us why," said Sun Shower. "If you wanted to leave the other woodfolk, why didn't you just walk away from all of us?"

The prince took a deep breath. "You have no idea how much I want to do just that. But I too am bound by the oath to protect you woodfolk whether you have taken the oath or not. And if I am indeed the guardian of the forest and the legends are true, you are going to need me. So I can't just walk away from you."

There was a surprised silence at these words. Mind messages passed back and forth. Then Falling Branch asked, "But why did you come to us when you knew it was so dangerous?"

"Because I can't allow woodfolk to be opposing woodfolk for my protection. You will need to be united to face whatever threat lies ahead and I will not allow this cursed oath to destroy your unity. If it means I have to die, then at least I have kept my word to protect you as well as I could." Tarkyn flexed his shoulders. "If you allow me to live and work by your side as your forest guardian, I may be able to provide even greater protection, but I can't guarantee it. I don't know what dangers lie ahead. Anyway, the choice is yours."

With the unblunted perception of youth, the angry young man asked, not unkindly, "There's more to it than that, though, isn't there?"

The prince nodded reluctantly. "Yes." He moved his wrists trying to ease the pressure of the ropes. "How can I explain it to you? - The woodfolk I know have chosen to protect you from me. They didn't trust me enough to take the risk that I wouldn't try to force the oath on you. In the time I have known them, they have never let on that woodfolk existed who had not sworn the oath. So the fact that they are protecting you from me has undermined any relationship I had with them." Tarkyn looked around at the unsympathetic faces surrounding him. "You probably think that's a good thing but it's not from where I'm sitting. And if I can get rid of any need for subterfuge in woodfolk's dealings with me, then I will."

Rainstorm considered the prince who was sitting surrounded by enemies, looking remarkably relaxed, if a little awkward, with his hands tied behind him.

"How old are you, prince?" he asked suddenly.

The young woodman found himself being scrutinised in return. Tarkyn's eyes narrowed as he tried to judge the woodman's age. "I am nineteen. Maybe slightly older than you?"

Rainstorm reddened at the implied compliment. "I am sixteen, but I will be seventeen soon." He paused and added self-consciously, "I hope that by the time I am nineteen I have as much courage as you – and less need to use it."

Tarkyn smiled. "Thank you." A wave of fellow feeling rolled out from the prince to the youth before he could stop it.

Rainstorm's eyes widened in surprise then smiled in return.

A rough voice cut across this interchange, "And how did you find us and avoid our lookout?- I am Raging Water."

Tarkyn transferred his gaze to a tough old woodman with gnarled hands and a weathered face. His smile faded and he gave a small sigh, "It would be easier for me to show you. It's like mind talking but no words. It may affect your balance but it is not a trick. You can block it out at any time, just like mind talking. Agreed? So, is everyone seated? I can't see who's behind me."

"Sun Shower is just bringing you a cup of tea. Wait for a minute," replied Rainstorm.

"No thanks. Forget the tea. Too hard in my present situation." There was a slight but definite bitterness in Tarkyn's voice. He looked at Rainstorm. "Is she ready?"

At a nod from Rainstorm, the sorcerer closed his eyes and took the woodfolk on his journey following the owl across the moonlit treetops, down behind the lookout and into their clearing. He opened his eyes and waited.

"You lucky bastard!" breathed Rainstorm.

Tarkyn raised his eyebrows and gave a short laugh. "I suppose I am. I hadn't thought of it like that."

Raging Water stood up and stomped around to stand over the prince. He glowered down at him. "You really are a bloody guardian of the forest, aren't you?"

Tarkyn shrugged, "So I have been led to believe." He stared the old woodman straight in the eye. "It's not my legend and I hadn't even heard of a forest guardian until a week or two ago. So you must be the judge of it, not I." He flicked a glance at Rainstorm, "To be perfectly frank, I find it all a bit embarrassing."

Rainstorm roared with laughter but was quickly quelled by disapproving looks from the older woodfolk.

Raging Water had not moved from his aggressive stance over the prince. "So even if you are a guardian of the forest, there are still a few things we need to sort out before we let you go. Now we have you here bound and helpless, it seems to me that we should be forcing you to release our kin from the oath."

"I couldn't agree with you more," said the prince, "but would you mind moving back just a little while we discuss it because I'm beginning to get a stiff neck looking up at you."

"Sorry, young man," said the old woodman moving back a couple of paces. Then he frowned in confusion at his own compliance and shook his head a little to clear it. He looked severely at the prince and began again, "So, as you are now our prisoner, we demand that you release our kin from their oath."

Tarkyn put his head on one side as he thought about what to say. "I do not know how to release the sorcery in the oath. If I did, I would have done it as soon as I knew about it. The one person who does know how to release the spell has refused to do so because he fears that I will be killed by the woodfolk if they are released from the oath. If I survive today, I will be in a better position to persuade him." The prince flexed his shoulders again as they stiffened from being in one position. "However, there is a slight hitch to this."

"Go on," growled Raging Water.

"Waterstone assured me that woodfolk are people of honour and that since they swore the oath in good faith as a debt of gratitude, disarming the oath will not remove their commitment to honouring it." Tarkyn looked around at his captors. "The only sure way I can think of releasing them is to kill me. – Of course you do run the slight risk that the allegiance may automatically revert to my brother King Kosar, but I think that is unlikely."

"Blast you!" roared Raging Water in the prince's face.

Tarkyn jumped in fright. "Why? What have I done? I have offered myself up as the sacrificial lamb. I can't do much more than that."

"You have reminded us that we are indeed people of honour," explained Falling Branch. "We are all one people. If we kill you, we will have betrayed the honour of our kindred."

If Tarkyn was relieved, he didn't show it. "Perhaps then, the best solution will be for me to stay away from the oathbound woodfolk. Then they won't have to 'serve, honour and protect me.' I can easily override their vow to protect me by ordering them to stay away."

"Then, prince, you will have the situation you were trying to resolve in reverse," pointed out Rainstorm. "You'll still have some woodfolk having to stay away from other woodfolk if you are with them." The young man eyed the prince uncertainly for a moment while he decided whether to say what he was thinking. Finally, he drew in a breath and said quietly, "You are going to have to face them sometime, you know."

Flinging a look of defiance at his elders, Rainstorm walked around behind the prince and untied his bonds.

"Thanks," said Tarkyn quietly and brought his hands around to the front. He focused briefly on his wrists and the pink weals from the rope disappeared as the woodfolk watched. He looked up and let his gaze travel around the woodfolk. "So, is it safe for me to get up and move around? I would swear that I mean you no harm or tell you what I have sworn as my part of the oath but there's not really much point if you don't trust me anyway." He waited until he saw a couple of grudging nods, then stood up. "I will try to move slowly for a while until you get used to me. There's something I need to do."

Tarkyn walked across the clearing and bent down to inspect the damaged elm. He placed his hands on the scar made by his blast of magic and waited until he felt the trunk's bark become smooth under his hand. "There," he said to himself. "That's the best I can do." He gave the tree a final pat and walked back to join the woodfolk who were silently watching him from around the firesite. Sun Shower gave him a cup of tea that, this time, he accepted.

"At least," said the prince between sips, "I know where I stand with you. You can behave as you like around me. I know you won't trust me so I won't be disappointed when you don't. And this time, this time, I will have learnt my lesson and will know not to trust you either." He gave a wry smile, "It's not much as working relationships go, but at least it's clear…and so far I'm still alive." He paused and added, not very convincingly, "And that has to be a good thing."

Falling Branch scowled at him. "I do not like your implication that we are not trustworthy."

"I beg you pardon. I did not mean to offend you. I am sure you are all as trustworthy as any other folk amongst yourselves." Tarkyn took another sip and looked at the woodman over the rim of the cup."From what I have seen, more so than most. But as Sun Shower has already pointed out, you don't trust me. So, in that case, I can hardly expect that you will be forthright with me, can I?"

"No, I suppose not," conceded Falling Branch grudgingly.

"And unfortunately, over time, the mistrust does not seem to abate. So I think I will be safe in always assuming that, at least on the issues most closely concerning you, woodfolk will never be open with an outsider." The prince looked around them and was saddened but not surprised when no one challenged his statement.

CHAPTER 26

The sun had reached its zenith and was beginning its journey down to the horizon when Autumn Leaves finally trudged into the firesite. Tarkyn was kneeling beside a small stream being shown how to tickle trout by Rainstorm. The other woodfolk had become more or less inured to the sorcerer's presence and were going about their own tasks with only the occasional glance in his direction. In actual fact, they were quite pleased that Rainstorm had found a way to keep himself gainfully occupied.

Autumn Leaves sat down quietly under a tree on the opposite side of the stream and waited. Tarkyn held his arm in the water up past his elbow. Amidst an enormous splash and a great deal of shouting, he flicked a good-sized trout up out of the water onto the grass. Before he could grab it, the slippery trout catapulted itself back into the water and swam off downstream.

Tarkyn grinned at the other youth, "Nearly. I'm getting better." His smile faded when he caught sight of Autumn Leaves.

Rainstorm took one look at the prince's face and said, "Right, I'm off." Then he thought better of it and offered, "On second thoughts, prince, I'll stay if you want."

Tarkyn smiled his thanks. "That is heroic of you, Rainstorm, but I think I'll let you off the hook."

As soon as Rainstorm had left, the smile dropped from his face. The prince regarded Autumn Leaves stonily. "I presume you have been sent to pour oil on troubled waters?"

The big woodman nodded, "Something like that."

Tarkyn produced a court-bred smile but his eyes glittered. "There is absolutely no need to concern yourselves. As you can see, no one is trying to kill me and you'll be even more pleased to know that I haven't yet found a way to make them take the oath. That must be a great relief to you." The sorcerer stood up and stared down on the woodman, "I must warn you that I am a lot closer to burning you to a crisp now, than I ever was when you were defending your friend." He shook his arm free of excess water and rolled down his sleeve. "I hope you have not had to travel too far. Enjoy your trip back." Tarkyn turned on his heel and walked way.

As the prince walked past the firesite, Rainstorm fell in beside him. "You can't just leave him there when he's walked all this way to talk to you."

Tarkyn stopped and looked at him. "Did he ask you to say that?"

Rainstorm shifted uncomfortably and dropped his eyes.

"You're very compliant, all of a sudden," observed Tarkyn dryly, "I haven't noticed you cooperating with other people like that."

Rainstorm brought his eyes back up and squared his shoulders. "That's because I don't necessarily agree with other people."

"But you do agree with Autumn Leaves."

The young woodman nodded.

"What is the point of talking to people who don't trust me?" exclaimed Tarkyn bitterly.

Rainstorm gave a little smile, "You spent all morning talking to people who don't trust you."

Tarkyn frowned at him, "No wonder you drive people crazy."

"How do you know I do?"

"It's obvious." The prince considered his words carefully. "You're the most perceptive person among them but you don't know when to say what you think and when to keep your peace. So you tell people things they don't want to hear… and then they get angry with you. Now you've sidelined yourself by being difficult and they've stopped listening to you." Tarkyn bent down and picked up a dead stick. "Pity really. You're worth listening to."

Rainstorm, unsure of how to respond, changed the subject, "Are you going to make that grow?"

Tarkyn looked down at the stick in his hands. "This? No, it's dead. I was planning on destroying it further, actually." He grinned and said, "Watch."

With Rainstorm's eyes on his every move, Tarkyn methodically broke piece after piece off the end of the stick until there was nothing left in his hands. There was a silence.

"That's it?" asked Rainstorm eventually.

Tarkyn laughed, "Yep. That's just a little something I do to fiddle while I'm chatting."

Rainstorm scowled. "Very funny."

"Come on," cajoled the sorcerer. "You have to admit it was pretty funny – you waiting to see a fireworks display and me just breaking twigs like everyone else."

"Hmph. I suppose it was," conceded Rainstorm grudgingly. Then he grinned as he overcame his wounded pride, "All right, yes. It was very funny. I'll have to remember not to take you too seriously."

"And in return, I'll take your advice and go back to talk to Autumn Leaves."

Rainstorm's eyes met Tarkyn's. "Good luck."

Tarkyn returned to the side of the stream and sat down opposite Autumn Leaves.

Silence reigned for an appreciable length of time.

Finally the woodman began. "Tarkyn…."

Tarkyn's eyes shot up from his contemplation of the river.

Unnerved by their severity, Autumn Leaves faltered. "Your Highness," he began again, "we have been desperately worried about you."

Tarkyn raised his eyebrows and said coolly, "You had no need for concern. I made it impossible for you to protect me when I left. So your precious forest was safe."

Autumn Leaves frowned, "We were concerned for you, not the forest."

"You don't even know me," replied the prince sharply. "So how could you care for me?"

"Of course we know you," said Autumn Leaves in some bewilderment.

The prince's temper snapped. "If you knew me, you would know better than to double cross me. If you knew me, you would have trusted me with the knowledge of your fellow woodfolk. And if you knew me, you would have known that your duplicity would destroy the last vestiges of my trust." Tarkyn got up and squatted beside the stream so that he could splash water over his face. When he looked up, he was calmer but his voice was hard. "But you do not know me and so we shall proceed from there. I now realise that none of you trusts me, and you know that I no longer trust you."

"Oh come on, Tarkyn."

"Oh come on, Tarkyn what? Come back so we can string you along again? I don't think so." Tarkyn rooted around among the rocks until he found a nice long dry stick.

He sat down again and concentrated on demolishing it. After a while he looked up and said, "You haven't got much to say, have you? Not like the time you were defending your friend Waterstone. You had plenty to say then. It's not the same this time, is it? No righteous indignation this time. You haven't got much to be righteous about, have you?"

At last Autumn Leaves found his voice. "No, Tarkyn, we haven't. We are all feeling very unhappy about what has happened."

"Am I supposed to feel gratified? No doubt it feels uncomfortable for you to have been caught out." The prince flicked the last of the stick into the water. "My commiserations. I'm sure you'll get over it."

"I don't know that Waterstone will get over it."

"Waterstone," said Tarkyn with venom, "will be weak with laughter at having duped me so completely, ably assisted by you, one must hasten to add."

"Neither of us has ever lied to you," protested Autumn Leaves.

"No need, when ambiguity and omission will serve you just as well."

"Stars above, you're hard work, Tarkyn," said the woodman, beginning to lose his temper.

"So I have been told," replied the prince maddeningly

"I have come all this way to tell you we are sorry.... and we are. We were all caught between loyalties." Autumn Leaves raised eyes to meet the prince's. "If you think about it, you weren't planning to tell Stormaway about these woodfolk, were you? So you too can be torn in more than one direction."

The prince raised his eyebrows. "The cases are not at all the same. Stormaway may feel loyalty to me. That is his prerogative, but I feel none towards him. He has foisted himself upon me and won't destroy the oath at my request." Nevertheless, Autumn Leaves' words had at last opened a slight chink in Tarkyn's armour.

The heavy woodman stood up and stretched. He paced up and down a few times then turned and looked down at the prince. He took a deep breath and said, "Your Highness. Imagine if a foreigner came into your kingdom and took it over. Imagine that the person was actually quite reasonable and you grew to like him. At what point would you be prepared to tell this foreigner about all your friends and family hiding in the woods behind the palace? After a week? A month? A year? What if you knew that no matter what you thought of this foreigner, your friends and family would not want to meet him and would definitely not want to be ruled by him?"

"If I knew and liked this foreigner so well," replied the prince coldly "could I not have told him about these friends and family, knowing he would not interfere unless I agreed?"

"What if you had sworn an oath from the first day you could talk, never to reveal the presence of your kin?"

Tarkyn stared at him. Finally, he heaved a deep, deep sigh. "Then," said the prince slowly, "I would have no choice but to remain silent."

A strange mixture of sadness, loneliness and resigned acceptance welled up out of Tarkyn and rolled out across the clearing and into the forest. All the woodfolk stopped what they were doing and looked across at him. Tarkyn, unaware of his public reaction, stood up and put his hand out to Autumn Leaves, "Here. I'll help you across the stream. It will save you walking around."

"Thanks," said the woodman, about to grasp it. Instead he found himself floating in the air and being drawn across the stream to land neatly beside Tarkyn. He staggered slightly and looked at the sorcerer with big round eyes, "Wow. I wasn't ready for that!"

Tarkyn smiled slightly but not with his usual exuberance. "Come on. Let's see if we can get you a cup of tea or something." He turned and waved his arm around. "I presume you know all these people?" It was then that he realised that everyone was staring at him. He stopped and frowned. "Is anything wrong? I didn't promise not to use magic, did I? And I'm not threatening anyone…"

As Raging Water came stomping forward, Tarkyn braced himself for another tirade. The gnarly old woodman surprised him by giving him a couple of friendly thumps on the back and saying, "Come on, young man. It can't be all that bad. Maybe we've all been a bit hard on you." He steered the bewildered young sorcerer over to the firesite and sat him down, with his hand still on his shoulder.

All the woodfolk gathered around him. Tarkyn was not fearful because they all seemed relaxed and even friendly, but he was confused. Even Autumn Leaves did not look sure that he knew what was happening. Someone produced cups of tea for everyone and they all sat themselves down around him.

Raging Water addressed himself to Autumn Leaves, "I think you should know that this young prince of yours was willing to sacrifice himself to preserve unity among the woodfolk." He drew his brows together in a fearsome frown. "And he nearly talked us into killing him so that you could all be released from the oath. The only thing that saved him was that we couldn't assist you to betray an oath of honour." The old man huffed, "It was a close run race, though."

Autumn Leaves was looking a bit sick. "Stars above, Tarkyn! What were you thinking? We don't want to lose you."

Tarkyn who had been gazing steadfastly at the ground, looked up at this and said with a wry smile, "I'm glad there was a reason I could accept, for you not telling me about these other woodfolk. At least now I know that you would not have willingly misled me."

"But things are still not well between us, are they?"

Tarkyn took a sip of tea, "They are as good as they can be," he said carefully.

Autumn Leaves frowned at him, "What's that supposed to mean?"

"It means," put in Rainstorm, rolling his eyes at Autumn Leaves' need for clarification, "that since he is not woodfolk, there will always be secrets he can't know. So in some ways, he will always be isolated."

Tarkyn glanced at his feisty ally but his attention was then diverted by hearing sympathetic mutterings around him and receiving several more kindly hands patting him on the back. He shook his head slightly, thinking this was a very strange day.

"Tarkyn, my boy," said Raging Water, "I'm afraid things may get a little worse for you before they get better but I'm thinking there are some things we need to discuss amongst ourselves.And with a forest guardian arrived among us, we must bring together representatives from all regions of the forest and all groups of woodfolk to convene a gathering."

Tarkyn glanced at Autumn Leaves, "Remember when you said that we couldn't gather all woodfolk together because it was unsafe to have large numbers together for too long? Was that reason genuine or was it really because of the existence of woodfolk who hadn't sworn the oath?"

The heavy woodman shook his head. "No Tarkyn. My objection still stands. We can't have too many people congregated together for long. Raging Water's intention of convening a gathering will help us to pool our knowledge without having a dangerously large group."

"I see." A certain reserve in Tarkyn's tone betrayed his belief that this suggestion would have been put forward earlier if they had been able to be straightforward with him.

Before Autumn Leaves could fashion a reply, Raging Water cut in, "Even in doing this now, we are honouring you with our trust by introducing you to woodfolk you should, by rights, never meet."

"I would not wish you to betray your woodfolk oath," said Tarkyn stiffly. "I suggest you confer amongst yourselves and keep me informed, as you see fit."

Autumn Leaves privately mourned the change in Tarkyn. His newly found, effusive assurance as guardian of the forest had evaporated. "What about your demand that we always keep you informed?" he asked.

"I cannot make demands on people who are not under oath to me. And I can no longer expect you to keep me fully informed either, since you are restricted by your obligations as woodfolk. I would not use the threat of the forest's destruction to override your woodfolk oath," said Tarkyn, tacitly pointing out that he could if he chose to. "I will leave you to your planning. Rainstorm, do you think that if we persevere, we may be able to contribute a trout or two towards dinner?"

For once, Rainstorm glanced a request for approval at Raging Water, before agreeing to accompany Tarkyn. This was not lost on Tarkyn who asked, as soon as they were clear of the others, "What was that all about? I thought you kept you own counsel."

Rainstorm gave a wry smile. "It was out of care for you, if you must know. I wanted to make sure they had said all they wanted to say to you, before we left. I know they were trying to make you feel better, even if they weren't succeeding."

Tarkyn stopped and put his hands on his hips as he thought back over the conversation. "Hmm. I made it pretty hard for them, didn't I?"

Rainstorm grinned. "Very. But don't think they've given up. They're just regrouping."

The prince gave a short bitter laugh as he dropped his arms and resumed the walk to the stream. "It might be better if they didn't try. Seeing the kindness that exists within woodfolk just makes the distance between all of you and me all the more difficult, now that I have lived… or thought I had lived, without that distance."

As they reached the stream, Tarkyn knelt down on the bank and rolled up his sleeves. "Never mind," he said bracingly. "I am back in the role I was bred to. A prince exists above and apart from his people." He smiled at the young woodman as he dipped his arm into the water, preparing to make a fool of himself again, as he tried once more to tickle trout. "And despite it all, I am still not as aloof as I was when I entered the forests."

Having no experience of princes, Rainstorm forbore to mention that he could not imagine anything more aloof than Tarkyn's behaviour had just been towards Autumn Leaves. Instead, he addressed himself to diverting Tarkyn by tickling trout with him.

Chapter 27

Waterstone and the rest of Tarkyn's woodfolk arrived, footsore and weary, just as the evening meal was being prepared. Rainstorm warned Tarkyn of their impending arrival several minutes before they came into view.

Tarkyn walked to edge of the clearing so that he could greet them away from the forestals. He had no real wish to see them but his sense of duty upheld him. As Rainstorm had pointed out, if woodfolk were to be united, he could not avoid them. Using all of his court training, Tarkyn produced a welcoming smile and let his eyes rove so that everyone mistakenly assumed that he was spending more time looking at someone else, when in fact he was avoiding everyone's gaze. His determination to remain aloof was nearly undermined by Sparrow who ran at him beaming, and forced him into catching her by launching herself up into his arms.

"Tarkyn. Tarkyn. We were so worried about you. I'm so glad you're all right."

Tarkyn smiled down into her earnest little face. "I'm sorry, Sparrow. I didn't mean to worry you. I had urgent business with these woodfolk."

Sparrow nodded wisely and said with a resigned sigh, "I know. Adult's business." Then she gave him a cheeky grin and kissed him on the cheek. "Well, I'm glad we found you." She leaned in and whispered in his ear, "Dad has been so grumpy, you wouldn't believe it."

Tarkyn gave a short laugh. "Has he? Well, let's hope his mood improves with some food in his stomach." He dragged his eyes away from Sparrow's to address his group of woodfolk. "I apologise for alarming you. As you no doubt know from Autumn Leaves, the issues have been explained to me and I am now clearer about the expectations that are placed on you as woodfolk. In future, should I unwittingly trespass on sensitive areas, simply tell me that you are unable to answer. Now that I understand that you cannot be open with me, I revoke my requirement for you to keep me informed in circumstances where it conflicts with your woodfolk covenenant. I do not want to make your situation more uncomfortable than it already is."

The woodfolk before him glanced uncertainly at one another, wanting to talk to him and reassure him, but kept at bay by the formality of his words and demeanour. Waterstone made no attempt to approach him in such a public forum, knowing from Tarkyn's courteous tone of voice, devoid of any true warmth, that the damage ran deep.

Tarkyn waved an arm invitingly. "Do come and settle yourselves down. Dinner will be ready shortly and you will be astonished to know that Rainstorm and I have actually contributed three fine trout to the evening's meal."

His attempt at lightness drew smiles from his audience and Lapping Water managed to say teasingly, "But I doubt that you cooked them, Sire."

Tarkyn looked at her, felt that he was a hundred miles from her and produced a smile. "No. I would not want to ruin our afternoon's work."

Raging Water stomped over and gruffly reiterated Tarkyn's invitation, adding suggestions on where to erect additional shelters. He glanced at Tarkyn's set face and thumped him bracingly on the back. "Come on, young fellow me lad. Come and try some of that fine trout you caught." As they turned to walk back to the firesite and Sparrow skipped off to play with some forestal children, the gnarly old woodman leaned in and said quietly, "And just remember, they did the best they could with the restrictions they had at the time. Do not condemn them for holding true to their heritage."

Tarkyn looked down at the old woodman. "I do not condemn them, Raging Water…and I am trying to be conciliatory. But I no longer know where I stand with them, except that it is not where I thought I stood. And I would rather err on the side of caution than be caught again thinking that there was openness where in fact, none exists."

Raging Water wagged his finger at him. "Now, don't overstate the case. As I understand it, they have been open with you except for keeping a few private woodfolk matters to themselves. Now, get down off your high horse and give them some respect for the support they have given you when the rest of us shirked the responsibility."

"Yes sir," said Tarkyn meekly, his eyes shining with laughter.

Raging Water scowled. "And don't you laugh at me, young man. I won't have it. Just you remember that it is by our grace that you are still alive."

If Raging Water expected this to wipe the smile off Tarkyn's face, he was sadly mistaken.

Tarkyn gave a crack of laughter. "No it's not. Your sense of honour saved me. Nothing else. You didn't confer a favour on me. You were forced into a corner by your own principles."

"Don't you dare speak to me like that!" exclaimed Raging Water, incensed.

There was a fraught silence. Tarkyn became aware that everyone was watching their interchange. Tarkyn took a deep breath to control his immediate outrage and then spoke in a low calming voice, "I beg your pardon for offending you, Raging Water. However, whether you have sworn the oath or not, I am still a prince of the realm and a forest guardian. And I have the right to speak to whomever I like, however I like!" Seeing Raging Water's face suffuse with anger, Tarkyn waved a placatory hand, "But I do not choose knowingly to offend or upset you… and so I offer you my apology."

Raging Water's eyes narrowed as he considered the prince's words. "You're pretty precious about your status, aren't you?" Gradually a little smile began to play around his mouth. "I accept your apology, young man. If you think you are that important, I suspect that in your eyes, you are making quite a concession."

"Cutting, Raging Water, very cutting." Tarkyn shook his head, a smile on his face."If I were merely vainglorious, I might take offence at your provocation…But as it is, I will simply assure you that although I am, as you so accurately point out, cognisant of my status, I have no wish to abuse my position." He gave a shallow courtly bow. "And let me assure you that I respect your words and have taken them to heart."

Raging Water waved his hand irritably, "Oh for goodness sakes! Now he's bowing. Someone take him away and feed him before he drives me to distraction."

Rainstorm appeared out of nowhere with a big grin on his face and dragged Tarkyn off to partake of their marvellous trout. When they were settled with a portion of their trout that had been baked slowly in the coals, Tarkyn asked, "And what are you looking so pleased about?"

Rainstorm chortled, "You winding up Grandpa like that. Even I rarely make him as angry as all that." He speared a piece of trout and waved it about as he talked. "It's a very good sign, you know. He only gets mad at people he likes. He mutters behind the backs of people he has no respect for."

"He's kind, isn't he? Gruff but kind. My father was like that, from what I remember of him."

"Who? King Markazon?"

Tarkyn nodded and said dryly, "Yes. The dreaded King Markazon,"

"Hmm." Rainstorm lapsed into silence as he picked his way carefully through the bones of the trout.

Eventually Tarkyn could no longer contain himself and asked, "Hmm?"

Rainstorm shrugged, "I was just thinking that your father and my grandfather are very alike, according to you, and yet their reputations and their places in history are so different."

"Not just according to Tarkyn." Waterstone casually sat down next to Rainstorm with his own plate. "I worked with Markazon when he helped our people through the illness. Tarkyn's right. He was tough but he was also kind in some circumstances." He smiled disarmingly. "Very good trout, boys."

Tarkyn's eyebrows flickered at the form of address but he gave Waterstone a genuine smile. "I'm very proud of it. It's the first trout I have ever caught."

"We will make a woo… forester of you yet." Waterstone grimaced at his faux pas.

"Yes," said Tarkyn heartily. "That's what I'll become. Not a forestal or a woodman, of course, but a forester. Good term, Waterstone. Perfect description for an outsider living in the woods."

"Ah sorry, Tarkyn." Waterstone ran his hand across his eyes. "This is hard for all of us. You don't have to pretend you're all right, if you're not. In fact, please don't."

Tarkyn realised that Rainstorm had mysteriously disappeared. "He's developing tact, that boy," he muttered to himself. As he returned his attention to Waterstone, the need for revenge warred inside him against his understanding of the woodman's predicament. As he remembered everything Waterstone had done for him, rationality won by a slim margin. "Autumn Leaves is a very good advocate. He champions your cause against me over and over again. He produced all sorts of hypothetical arguments but in the end, all he ever needed to say was that you were under oath. I know you are people of honour and that you could not break your avowed commitment to your people." He gave a little shrug, "So. There it is. The beginning and the end of it. Nothing else needs to be said."

Waterstone looked sideways at the prince, trying to gauge the innuendo beneath the words. "Yes, it does."

"No," said Tarkyn firmly. "I accept that your friendship is genuine but also that it has limitations. And you and I will have to live with that, just as we live with so much about the oath that is distasteful." He glanced briefly at Waterstone before looking away. "Obviously, from now on, we will both be aware of the distance in our relationship whereas before, only you were."

Waterstone threw his plate down with a clatter. "No Tarkyn. It was not like that."

Tarkyn looked at his friend with some sympathy. "Yes it was, Waterstone. You just assumed that woodfolk business was exclusively between you people. And you were right. It was and still is. I will not insist on intruding. When you want my assistance as forest guardian, no doubt you will decide among yourselves what I need to know. Hopefully, you will not inadvertently exclude me from any vital information."

"That sounds very lonely, Tarkyn."

Tarkyn bit his lip. After a few moments he said, "For a woodman, used to sharing every thought, that may be lonely. But I was brought up to stand apart. For a while, I nearly escaped my heritage. But it was an illusion, and now my heritage has come back to haunt me." He gave a wistful smile, "We are what we are, Waterstone. You are a woodman and I am an exiled sorcerer prince, an outsider among you, made more welcome than I could have dared to hope."

Waterstone grimaced, "Stop being so bloody noble about it. I think I would prefer anger from you, rather than this stoic acceptance."

Tarkyn gave a grunt of laughter. "I'll admit I did consider raging at you but Raging Water saved you. He said you did your best under the circumstances and I believe you did. So," he shrugged, "what else can I do but accept the situation?" He slapped Waterstone on the knee. "Come on. Cheer up. From your point of view, you are in a less invidious position than before, because now you don't have to conceal the fact that you woodfolk harbour secrets between you. Just tell me and I won't ask any further." And because Tarkyn had years of court training behind him, he almost convinced Waterstone that all was well.

But as the week wore on, and various woodfolk new to Tarkyn arrived, the change in the prince became apparent. As soon as he knew of an impending arrival, he would absent himself, going off for long solitary walks, albeit overseen by a discreet lookout, or retiring to his shelter. He made no attempt to meet these new woodfolk and would not allow anyone to speak to him about them, reasoning that the woodfolk were under oath not to reveal the presence of their kin.

"But you already know of their presence," protested Waterstone on the third day, catching up with him as he headed off once more into the woods. "Stop being such a martyr. You are making everyone feel uncomfortable. Don't make the situation worse than it is. There will be times when we confer on our own but we have agreed that you, as forest guardian, should be able to meet these people. Besides, the fact that you have vowed to protect us, and that you already know of woodfolk presence, means that the rules apply differently to you."

"As and when the mood takes you," retorted Tarkyn, making no attempt to slow his pace.

"No. As and when we get full agreement from all woodfolk." Waterstone grabbed the prince's arm. "Tarkyn. Stop."

Tarkyn stopped and swung around to confront Waterstone. "What?"

"Despite your best intentions of accepting the situation, your actions are reeking of anger… Has it occurred to you that if I had broken my woodfolk covenant and told you about the existence of other woodfolk, I could have been exiled?"

Tarkyn stared at him. Several times, the prince went to say something but didn't. Finally, he simply turned on his heel and headed back to the firesite. As they emerged from the shadow of the trees, he said, "You just make bloody sure, Waterstone, that you don't ever take that risk. I need you. Sparrow needs you. We all need you. And I can tell you from experience that exile is … " Tarkyn hesitated, realising that his exile coincided with his life among woodfolk, "… exile is not easy," he finished lamely.

"No. So I gather." Waterstone patted Tarkyn on the back. "Come on. Come and meet those who have arrived so far."

From then on, Tarkyn allowed himself to be included in the discussions but his participation was characterised by formal courtesy, and the dry humour and exuberance that he had brought to his life among the woodfolk had disappeared. Even so, without conscious intention, the prince became the focal point of ensuing discussions, bringing to them his perspective as a prince and sorcerer, and his potential as a forest guardian.

With growing concern, Tarkyn listened as wolf attacks were reported from two other groups, and tales of sorcerer unrest, and increasing attacks on travellers and isolated homesteaders were brought in from all parts of the forest with each new arrival.

Chapter 28

On the fifth day after Tarkyn's confrontation with the forestals, the last of the woodfolk arrived. Tarkyn had been cajoled by Rainstorm into helping him gather firewood after lunch. As they walked between towering chestnut trees, the prince said firmly, "Just don't come to expect this. I do it because I enjoy your company and it gives me an excuse to get away for a while."

Rainstorm grinned, not at all abashed. "Understood, Your Highness." Just as he reached to break off a dry branch, the young woodman went still for a moment. Then, in response to a distant request, he continued as though nothing had happened.

Minutes later, a woodman came into view, walking towards them from the direction of the clearing. As he drew nearer, Tarkyn recognised him as Ancient Oak, the woodman who had sat with him on his first day among the woodfolk. Remembering how they had sniped at each other, he understood why Ancient Oak had chosen to leave his vicinity but equally, was surprised to see him now.

The two woodmen nodded to each other in greeting before Ancient Oak presented himself to Tarkyn. "Good afternoon, Your Highness. I thought I would lend you a hand since the numbers at the firesite have swelled in your absence."

"Good afternoon, Ancient Oak. I am pleased to see your arm is no longer in a sling. So the harvesters have arrived, have they?"

"Yes my lord, and so too have some of our kin from the mountains and others from the forest near Tormadell. Our gathering is now complete."

"But are you not tired after your journey? I understand that you people have had to travel some distance."

The woodman inclined his head. "That is true, my lord, but some things cannot wait."

When Tarkyn looked puzzled, Rainstorm said, "Woodfolk business, I'm afraid, prince."

"I see," Tarkyn replied non-committally. He cracked a long branch over his knee, and placed both pieces neatly on the ground before straightening and looking Ancient Oak in the eye, "I believe I owe you an apology, Ancient Oak." At the woodman's look of enquiry, he replied, "As I recall, the last time I saw you, you had just enlisted Tree Wind and Autumn Leaves' help to escape from my presence after I had berated you about the expected behaviour of a liegeman." He gave a wry smile. "In view of all I have learnt since, I can imagine that didn't go down too well with you."

Ancient Oak returned his gaze steadily. "No Sire. It was indeed hard to stomach. But I am led to believe that your expectations have mellowed somewhat since you discovered how the oath was imposed."

Tarkyn snorted, "Between Tree Wind and you, I was left in no doubt as to how unwelcome I was. But I think you people owe more to Waterstone for any changes in my attitude… and possibly Autumn Leaves." He smiled wryly, "And Thunder Storm, for that matter, and Sparrow… and all of those who stayed with me." He cleared his throat and concentrated on breaking another long branch. He glanced up and said gruffly, "Are you going to gather any wood, or do you just plan to stand there staring at me?"

"Whoops. Sorry." Ancient Oak hastily addressed himself to the task of collecting smaller pieces into a pile. "It is just that I am stunned by the vision of Rainstorm actually doing something useful." He promptly ducked as a wad of bark sailed past his left ear.

Rainstorm scowled at him, "I'll have you know that it was I who suggested it… And just so you're clear, Tarkyn is gathering wood purely for the pleasure of my company." He threw a wicked grin at Tarkyn. "Aren't you, prince?"

"Stop bragging. Yes." He smiled at Ancient Oak. "My attitude has not changed so much that you could expect me to do anything I chose not to. But collecting wood can be quite recreational, when I am in the mood."

Ancient Oak paused in what he was doing to scrutinise the prince.

"What?" demanded Tarkyn.

Ancient Oak gave his head a little shake and smiled, "Nothing, Your Highness. It is just that since you are both so feisty, it is amazing that you get on at all, let alone choose each other's company."

Tarkyn was not sure that this had actually been the subject of the woodman's thoughts but let it slide. "I have found that many woodfolk, you included, speak to me with a forthrightness that I find…hmm… shall we say, unexpected?"

Ancient Oak returned his attention to collecting small branches. After a few minutes, he said over his shoulder, "I heard about your confrontation with the forestals, Sire. Everyone is talking about it."

"Are they?" Tarkyn raised his eyebrows. "I thought we were all discussing wolves, and woodfolk being hunted, and sorcerer attacks."

Ancient Oak straightened up and continued as though Tarkyn hadn't spoken, "It was very kind of you, Sire, to try to release us from the oath."

"No, Ancient Oak, it wasn't an act of kindness. It was an act of desperation. I couldn't bear the duplicity I had suddenly discovered around me so I took the risk of meeting the oathfree woodfolk to blow apart the conspiracy."

"Prince, that is only part of the story," broke in Rainstorm. "I was there, remember," He turned to the other woodman. "Tarkyn offered his life to release you all and to make sure that we could stand united against the coming threat."

"And do you still feel let down by Waterstone and Autumn Leaves and the rest of them?" asked Ancient Oak.

Tarkyn frowned, "How do you know so much about this, if you have just arrived?"

The woodman looked a little puzzled, "I thought Waterstone would have told you by now. I have a particular interest in some of the people you travel with, and keep in closer contact with them than most."

"Do you now? Then when you are next mind talking with them, you may report to them that I would never have wished them to risk exile or retribution by compromising your woodfolk code. I should have known an outsider couldn't just walk into the middle of an established society and be accepted without reservation." Tarkyn gave a rueful shrug. "They have given me far more than the oath required… And for my part, well, I would not have reacted so strongly if I had cared about them less."

"I think they also care about you, Sire," said Ancient Oak gently.

Tarkyn glanced at him but did not reply. Instead he wrenched a large branch off a sagging dead tree. "Don't you two have woodfolk business to attend to?"

Rainstorm raised his eyebrows at Ancient Oak, who smiled and said, "I think it is almost concluded, Sire."

Tarkyn frowned irritably. "I have no idea what you're talking about, but I suppose that is a state of affairs I will have to become inured to. If possible, I would appreciate it if you could deal with your private affairs away from me."

Ancient Oak's smile broadened, "I understand. You do not want unpleasant truths rubbed in your face, if I remember correctly."

For a moment, Tarkyn glared at him. Then he broke reluctantly into a smile. "We did get off to bad start, didn't we? I can't imagine why you're not still avoiding me."

Ancient Oak hesitated, "I'm afraid I can't answer that at the moment, Sire." He looked uncomfortable, "And I should perhaps warn you that now the gathering is complete, we… er…"

"Come on. Spit it out," said Rainstorm. "He's trying to tell you, prince, that we have a few things to discuss amongst ourselves this afternoon."

CHAPTER 29

When they returned to the firesite, a silent conference was in full swing. Several newcomers glanced nervously at the sorcerer prince, but so intent were they on their discussions, that no one broke off to speak to him. Even Tree Wind and the harvesters merely nodded in acknowledgement.

Tarkyn parted company with Rainstorm and Ancient Oak as soon as they had offloaded their wood; they to join their kin while Tarkyn wandered off down to the stream. No one even seemed to register him leaving.

Tarkyn meandered a little way along the stream, watching moorhens strutting among the reeds and a couple of wood ducks alternately floating downstream on the current then paddling back upstream. The forest guardian was not feeling very communicative so kept his mind closed against any attempts to contact him. When he found a soft grassy patch, he lay down on his stomach with his head propped on his hands, and stared morosely down into the water, watching tiny fish darting in amongst the weeds. Slowly the weak afternoon sun relaxed him and he fell asleep.

When he awoke, it was dark and cold. Someone had thrown a warm blanket over him but left him to sleep. Tarkyn rolled over and looked up into the sky. Thousands of stars winked down at him and a golden glow near the horizon heralded the rising of the moon.

He peered over the top of his blanket at the woodfolk sitting around the fire. He studied them as they talked and laughed quietly among themselves. In many ways they looked just like a group of sorcerer troops gathered after a day's patrol. A wave of homesickness washed over the prince. Then he remembered the wary courtesy that sorcerer troops would have accorded him and laughed softly to himself when he contrasted it with the memory of Waterstone yelling at him, Ancient Oak snapping back at him and Autumn Leaves berating him. Despite their oath to him and their secrets, woodfolk were still less guarded than most sorcerers in their dealings with him.

Tarkyn sat up and ran his hands through his hair. His mouth twitched in a half smile as he remembered he had nearly been killed for doing that in his confrontation with the forestals. He leaned over and scooped up some water to splash his face. Then he took a deep breath, stood up and walked into the light of the fire.

A hush fell over the woodfolk. Tarkyn blinked as his eyes became accustomed to the light. "Good evening," he said, as he gathered his thoughts. His amber eyes swept slowly around, studying the assembled woodfolk. "I believe there are many new arrivals I have not yet met. I look forward to making your acquaintance. I am Tarkyn Tamadil to those of you who have not yet met me." He waved a hand and immediately wished he hadn't, as several people blanched in fear and more than a few ducked for cover. "Don't let me interrupt you. Does anyone happen to have a spare glass of wine?"

Tarkyn didn't really know where to sit. Wherever he chose to sit would be making a statement. In the end, he walked over to a group of complete unknowns and sat with them. They eyed him uncertainly and unconsciously pulled their cloaks in tighter around themselves.

He smiled ruefully at them, "I beg your pardon. I forgot you'd be frightened of me if you hadn't met me." He went to stand up again. "Would you rather I sat somewhere else?"

A dried up old woman waved a thin, long-fingered hand at him from inside her cloak. "No. Stay. We did not mean to be unwelcoming. You're just a bit unnerving on first sight, you know. I am Ancient Elm."

"I am pleased to meet you. Where have you come from? Or is that classified information?"

Ancient Elm frowned at him, "I suspect your navigational skills in the forest wouldn't get you to us even if I told you."

Tarkyn eyes glinted in the firelight, "You may keep your secrets. Now that I have seen you, I could find an owl or an eagle to guide me to you, wherever you are."

The old woodwoman glared at him. "You are not helping your cause threatening me like that, you know."

"I was not aware that I had a cause. Besides, I am not threatening you. I am merely stating a fact." The sorcerer took a slow sip of wine. "All right. I apologise. I admit I was feeling a little snaky. I am just becoming tired of being surrounded by secrets. I have no wish to intimidate you." Tarkyn smiled at her disarmingly. "Actually, I seem to spend most of my life carefully not frightening people."

Another scrawny old woman piped up, "What's this oath you made to the woodfolk then? I am Dried Berry."

Very apt. Tarkyn looked at her in some surprise. "If you know about the oath, why don't you know the contents?"

"Not my business, until now."

"Why is it your business now?" asked the prince.

"Now that is none of your business," she said severely. When he blinked at her in confusion, she snapped at him impatiently. "Well, go on. Tell us your vow, all of it."

"If you insist." He took a deep breath, remembering the words. As soon as he began, the words reverberated around the clearing and all the woodfolk fell silent to listen. *"I, Tarkyn Tamadil, Prince of the Forests of Eskuzor, give my solemn vow that I will fulfil my obligations and responsibilities as your liege lord and will protect the woodfolk and the forests of Eskuzor. Your just cause will be my cause and your fate will be my fate. This is the covenant bequeathed to me by my father, Markazon Tamadil, 48th King of Eskuzor."*

A babble of discussion broke out after this, followed by the silence of intense mind talking.

Eventually, Autumn Leaves came over and sat down next to the prince, "You know, none of us really listened to what you vowed at the oath-taking. We were too concerned about ourselves at that stage. But you made an even bigger commitment than we did."

Tarkyn went to run his hand through his hair but stopped himself. He let his hand drop to his side. "I know I did and I had no more choice than you about doing it."

"Yes, but you're not our liege lord," objected Dry Berry. "So it doesn't apply to us."

The prince narrowed his eyes, "I have vowed to protect the woodfolk. I didn't say the woodfolk who swore the vow or who are my liegemen. I simply said the woodfolk. As far as I'm concerned, I have made a commitment to all of you."

"Well, don't think we're going to make one in return because we're not," snapped the scrawny old woodwoman.

Tarkyn raised his eyebrows haughtily, "I didn't ask you to and I had no intention of doing so."

The first old woman he had spoken to, Ancient Elm, looked at him sharply, "But you must feel pretty hard done by, now you know there are others of us who haven't taken the oath."

The sorcerer waved a dismissive hand and saw fewer heads duck instinctively for cover than previously. He ignored them and continued with their public conversation. "I certainly feel hard done by, but it's not because of that." Tarkyn broke into a rueful grin. "In fact, when I first heard the words I had vowed, I was absolutely horrified. Having my whole fate entwined with the fate of a people I didn't even know..." He glanced at Autumn Leaves. "That was another reason I drank too much that night."

Tarkyn looked around. Everyone was hanging on his every word. Some were frowning at what he had just said so he moved on quickly. "Anyway, once I came to know the people I was with and we had worked out a way of living together, I became truly committed to the words I had vowed. Then came the day I realised that other woodfolk existed… The best and worst day of my life."

Tarkyn took another sip of wine and finally looked over at Waterstone and his group of woodfolk. "I don't know if you are all aware of this but, six days ago, each of these woodfolk gave me a part of their life force to keep me alive. Then, only hours later, I worked out the existence of the other woodfolk they had told me nothing about and felt totally betrayed." He took a breath to steady himself and looked around the rest of the audience, "I now realise that, as a people, you are vowed to secrecy. So they and you have no choice but to hold me at arm's length." The prince returned his gaze to Ancient Elm and shrugged, "As a prince among my own people, I have been used to living like that. So I suppose I can continue as I always have."

"And can you prove that you're a forest guardian?" she demanded in a total non-sequitor.

Tarkyn regarded her stonily for a moment. "Yes, I can, but I have no intention of doing so. I proved it for the forestals. But I am not a walking, talking freak show, here for your entertainment. Believe your fellow woodfolk or not as you choose. I am not going to prove myself to you."

Ancient Elm waved a skinny hand, "Fair enough, young man. No need to get hoity-toity."

Another intense silence descended on the clearing as woodfolk conferred. After several minutes, they stood up and gathered in a large semicircle with Tarkyn at its centre. Feeling it was required of him, Tarkyn also stood up. He towered over the two little old ladies on either side of him.

Raging Water hobbled over to stand before him. "Tarkyn Tamadil, Guardian of the Forest, we have considered your words and your deeds. The vow you made to us might have been only words: but by giving your fate into the hands of the forestals, you proved to us that you do indeed place the welfare of the woodfolk above your own life. This being the case, we have decided, in an unprecedented move, to ask you to become a member of the woodfolk nation."

Tarkyn's heart missed a beat as he bowed his head in acknowledgement. "I would be truly honoured."

Thunder Storm came forward to join Raging Water. "In all the history of the woodfolk, no outsider has ever been granted membership of the woodfolk. So we have no ceremony for accepting you into our nation. However, all woodfolk must be a member of a family. If all of a person's blood relations die, then that person, no matter what their age, is officially adopted into a new family. All woodfolk must have kin - and we do have a ceremony for that."

And now Waterstone, Ancient Oak and Sparrow stepped forward and stood beside the other two in front of Tarkyn.

Waterstone looked Tarkyn squarely in the eye and spoke formally, "Tarkyn Tamadil, I offer you membership of my family that you may share with us the joys and trials of kinship and that we may call upon each other's strength in times of need. Do you accept?"

For a heartbeat, there was silence. Then Tarkyn gave a courtly bow of his head and spoke equally formally. "I am honoured by your offer and I accept."

Did he mistake it, or did Tarkyn see a slight release of tension in Waterstone's shoulders? Before he could be sure, his attention was drawn to Raging Water who now addressed the whole assembly. "To establish a new blood tie, blood must be shared." So saying he produced a wickedly sharp knife and advanced towards Tarkyn. For a wild moment the thought flicked across Tarkyn's mind that it had all been a ruse to kill him but he decided almost simultaneously that any one of them could have stuck a knife into him while they were talking.

"Roll up the sleeve of your right arm," instructed Raging Water. "Now hold out your arm, palm upwards." He waited until both Waterstone and Tarkyn were standing with their bared right arms held out. Then in two swift movements, he sliced each arm from wrist to elbow.

As the blood welled up, Waterstone grasped Tarkyn's arm near the elbow so the two long cuts lay over each other. Tarkyn grasped the woodman's in return. As their blood intermingled, a deep hush fell upon the forest. Not a leave stirred. Then a faint shudder ran through the ground beneath them. A cascade of red and golden leaves swirled down from the trees around them and all was still again.

Keeping his eyes firmly on the prince, Waterstone intoned, "We are now of one blood. My kin are your kin. My ancestors are your ancestors. Ancient Oak and I welcome you as a brother. Sparrow welcomes you as her uncle."

Tarkyn's eyes narrowed slightly at the confirmation of his dawning realisation that Ancient Oak was Waterstone's brother. He realised he didn't know what he should say next. He had winged it so far but now he was stuck. He took a breath and kept improvising. "I thank you for your welcome. I will do all I can to bring harmony and honour to my new family and to fight with you all against the dangers that lie ahead."

Thunder Storm leant over and whispered in the prince's ear. Tarkyn's mouth quirked a little as he added, "Waterstone, we are now of one blood. My kin are your kin. My ancestors are your ancestors. I welcome you and Ancient Oak as brothers and Sparrow as my niece."

Raging Water addressed the woodfolk, "Tarkyn Tamadil, Guardian of the Forest, is now a member of a woodfolk family and no longer an outsider." He turned back to Tarkyn, "Welcome to our nation."

Tarkyn's face relaxed into a huge smile and an enormous wave of gratitude emanated from him, rolling over the crowd and bowling many woodfolk over onto the ground. Tarkyn and Waterstone wrapped their left arms around each other in an awkward bear hug as everyone crowded around offering congratulations. Someone came forward with cloth to bandage their right arms while Sparrow burrowed her way through the crowd to give Tarkyn a hug.

Ancient Oak embraced him stiffly and Tarkyn grasped him warmly in return. As they broke apart, Ancient Oak said quietly, "Welcome to our family. I am truly proud to have you as a brother." And Tarkyn understood that he was proud despite, not because, Tarkyn was a prince.

"I passed your vetting process then, Ancient Oak?"

The woodman's eyes gleamed briefly in acknowledgement, before he replied gravely. "It is no small step to adopt a brother. So I knew Waterstone would not make such a request lightly. It clearly mattered a great deal to him."

"It matters a great deal to me also."

Ancient Oak gave a slight smile. "But although I have implicit faith in his judgement, I preferred my welcome to be based on my own opinion."

Tarkyn looked into the depths of the woodman's eyes, a softer green than his brother's. "You have a quiet strength that rivals Waterstone's, don't you? I am proud to be your brother. Thank you for your welcome."

Part 6: Unrest

CHAPTER 30

When the fuss following the ceremony had subsided, Tarkyn found himself seated with his back against a log between Autumn Leaves and Waterstone. Despite a lifetime of adulation, he was still dazed by the honour the woodfolk had accorded him. Sparrow was asleep on his knee, leaning into the crook of his left arm and he was already the worse for wear to the tune of several glasses of wine. He leaned his head back and said dreamily, "What a long week… Firstly, I was bashed up and nearly died from my injuries." He rolled his head towards Waterstone to watch his outraged expression. "And I was nearly killed by the forestals for sweeping my hair out of my eyes. Then I let them tie me up. I hated that bit, but what else could I do? You can't talk sense with frightened people. Then I endured a week of being sidelined… Actually, I mostly expected to be dead by now but instead, amazingly, I am now officially a woodman." Tarkyn grinned. He fiddled with the bandage on his right arm, his eyes idly roving over the similar bandage onWaterstone's arm. After a moment he said, "You never told me Ancient Oak was your brother. More classified information, was it?"

Waterstone shook his head and smiled, "No, I did tell you about him… in that time when you were semi-conscious. I suppose you just don't remember."

"Oh. And have we been waiting all week for Ancient Oak to arrive so that he could be at the ceremony?"

The woodman laughed. "Partly. I could not have done it without his agreement or without his presence at the ceremony. But for such a momentous occasion as this, we needed a full gathering of woodfolk to reach an accord and to witness it. So we were also waiting for people from the more distant groups to arrive."

"I see. So was the true purpose of this gathering to consider making me a woodman?"

"Partly." Autumn Leaves raised his eyebrows. "Although, in case you've forgotten, there is still someone out there trying to hunt us down."

"Oooh dear," Tarkyn gave a gusty rather wine-soaked sigh. "I'm being a very bad forest guardian. I had forgotten all about that." His eyes twinkled, "Well, almost."

Autumn Leaves gave a grunt of laughter. "I'm not surprised. You have other things on your mind at the moment."

The prince looked rather owlishly at him, "And what do you think Kosar and Jarand are going to think of their new brothers, when I tell them about Waterstone and Ancient Oak?"

Autumn Leaves' eyebrows snapped together before his eyes narrowed as he realised Tarkyn was winding him up.

"Ha! Nearly had you." Tarkyn smiled. He wagged his finger at the woodman. "You see, old habits die hard, don't they?" He snorted derisively, "As if I could go anywhere near either of them, even if I wanted to - and as if I would tell them anything, even if I did. You're lucky I've had a drink or two to mellow me, or I might have taken offence at that." He looked up as Rainstorm came over to join them. "Enjoyed scheming with Ancient Oak this afternoon, did you?"

"Hi, prince," said Rainstorm cheerily as he plonked himself down on the grass in front of Tarkyn. "Or should I say princes?" He grinned cheekily at Waterstone who turned a dull red. "I'm not sure about this adoptive family thing. Do you gain Prince Tarkyn's ancestors and kin, or does he just get yours?"

"Rainstorm," said Tarkyn repressively, acutely embarrassed for his friend, "I don't know how you managed to live to be sixteen but if you don't shut up, you may not make seventeen."

Autumn Leaves, the peacemaker, waded in, "Among woodfolk, the ancestors are combined, as I'm sure you know perfectly well. However, since this is an exceptional situation..."

The prince looked reproachfully at Waterstone, although his eyes were still twinkling. "Is he trying to tell me that you don't want to share my family?" Tarkyn shrugged, "Well, I suppose I can understand it. I know my father was not a great hit with everyone and frankly, Kosar and Jarand are significantly worse.You might like my mother, if you could get her on her own. She's really quite a kind person, intelligent in her own way, but just too much of a pushover. Can't stand up to my brothers. Still, you can now lay claim to forty-eight generations of kings and queens of Eskuzor and that has to be worth dropping into conversations, if nothing else."

"Yes," persisted Rainstorm, "but does it make him a prince too?"

Tarkyn wrinkled his brow in thought. "Now that is a very tricky question. Since you don't have ranks among woodfolk, then I would say no. But if Waterstone ever came among the sorcerers, then I would say yes."

"So what about you? Are you a prince among the woodfolk if we don't have ranks?"

Tarkyn rolled his head from one side to the other to look at each of the woodmen in turn, "You can see, can't you, what a thorn in the side this young man is?" When they had both nodded, he continued, "But a very astute thorn in the side." The prince turned his head back to regard Rainstorm, "Sometimes in life, a person has to make an executive decision… and I'm afraid, for better or worse, I can't get my head around being totally equal," He gave a crooked smile and tightened his arm around the sleeping Sparrow, "...especially if it might involve me having to cook."

Rainstorm frowned, "That doesn't answer my question."

Tarkyn sighed, "No, it doesn't really. I was hoping you wouldn't notice that. As you can see," he added in an aside to the other two woodmen, "persistence is another of his endearing traits." Tarkyn sat himself up a little straighter against the log and shifted Sparrow more comfortably against his left shoulder. "Very well, Rainstorm. It comes down to this. I was born and bred to be a prince and in my mind, I probably always will be. In your mind, I don't know, I'm probably some delusional fish out of water." He grinned rather sheepishly, "I keep setting out to say that I'm not your prince but… truth is, I am. You mightn't acknowledge it, but my father decreed that I would be liege lord of the woodfolk… although he was unaware that not all woodfolk had sworn that oath to me."

Tarkyn saw Rainstorm's eyes dilate in shock and added hastily, "No. Don't panic. I have no intention of ruling over you. Ask these two. Even with the oath, we negotiate nearly everything…and you aren't even subject to the oath."

A few minutes of intense mind talking ensued while Autumn Leaves and Waterstone tried to use images of past conversations to reassure the young woodman.

Tarkyn frowned, "Why is this taking so long?"

Waterstone laughed. "Because, for all your good intentions, you are quite clearly exerting authority in most situations we can think of."

The prince looked quizzically at Rainstorm. "Well, I did say I couldn't come to terms with being totally equal, didn't I?"

Rainstorm scowled at him, "You had better not try to order me around."

Tarkyn could feel that the other two were also waiting to hear what he was going to say. "My friend, from what I have seen of you, you make your own judgements on the value of people's requests to you and act accordingly. If you do the same for me, I could ask no more."

The young woodman raised his eyebrows and nodded. He looked at the other two woodmen. "He's not bad, this prince of yours. Friendly, but with just a hint of menace!"

The sorcerer looked crushed, "What do you mean, a hint of menace? I bend over backwards not to be intimidating."

"Exactly," exclaimed Rainstorm. "None of us needs to do that." He laughed. "You should have seen him when he first got here. We're trying to kill him and he's getting crabby because people are firing arrows at him. Not frightened, mind you, crabby. He called us a bunch of hooligans!"

Autumn Leaves and Waterstone both turned their heads to stare at Tarkyn. Then they looked back at Rainstorm. "And exactly how close did he come to getting himself killed?"

"Oh, he was safe enough then," replied Rainstorm airily. "He had his shield up at that point." Just as the other two began to relax, he added, "But it was on a knife edge for the best part of an hour at least - only because he chose it to be, by relinquishing all his defences. He even made sure his hands were tied behind him not in front, when none of us would have known the difference."

Tarkyn was looking steadfastly at the ground, "Ah, but in time you would have discovered that I had made fools of you if I pretended to be helpless with my hands tied in front." He looked up, "Besides, I am not in the business of giving false impressions."

This statement, which began as a simple explanation of Tarkyn's actions, ended hanging in the air as an indictment of the fact that the woodfolk sitting on either side of him had concealed the presence of their kin from him. "So, on that topic… " said Tarkyn slowly. The two woodmen braced themselves as the prince picked restlessly at the bandage on his arm. Rainstorm was intrigued to notice a wicked little smile playing around his lips. Then, seemingly unaware of their tension, Tarkyn continued, "So on that topic, what are we going to do about Stormaway?"

Two relieved woodmen punched him simultaneously on the nearest shoulder to them.

"Ow. That is a serious question," said Tarkyn, laughing.

"You're a bastard. Do you know that?" said Waterstone, half smiling, half frowning. "Exactly how long are you going to make us pay?"

Tarkyn put his head on one side, a smile lurking in his eyes, while he considered it. "Well, let me see. I had to endure total misery for nearly twenty-four hours, deal with isolation for a week, not to mention the previous weeks of deception. So I think you might still have a bit more coming to you." He put up his right hand to forestall a sudden movement of Waterstone's. "Now stop. You can't punch me any more. You might wake Sparrow!"

As Waterstone subsided, Rainstorm asked, "So who is this Stormaway?"

"There you are," said Tarkyn, smiling at the young woodman."At least someone is taking me seriously. For your information, Stormaway is the wizard who devised the spell-bound oath for my father and is my faithful but determinedly disobedient retainer."

Rainstorm nodded, catching on. "I know. He's the one who thought that woodfolk would kill you if you didn't have the oath to protect you."

"Yep. That's the one."

"He wasn't far off, was he?" observed the young woodman dryly.

"No," said Tarkyn, "but just far enough." The prince rolled his head from one woodman to the other, "So, the question remains. What are we going to do about him?"

Rainstorm frowned. "Am I to understand he's an outsider who knows about woodfolk?"

Waterstone nodded.

"Well. It's easy then. We will just have to kill him before he tells anyone," said the young man with an air of finality.

Tarkyn shook his head, smiling. "Much as I admire your straightforward, bloodthirsty style, I should point out that Stormaway has already known about woodfolk for some twelve years and if he dies, I will never be able to find out how to release the welfare of the forest from the oath."

Rainstorm gave this some thought, then said, "Right, then. Let's find out how to disarm the oath. Then we can kill him."

Tarkyn raised his eyebrows. "If I had realised I had such simplistic minds as this around me, I might have taken a few less chances with the forestals."

"Very funny," growled the young woodman.

"Stormaway has visited us, off and on, ever since the oath was first sworn to Tarkyn's father," explained Waterstone. "He was appointed as judge of Tarkyn's fitness to assume the role of liege lord. So he had to stay in contact with us. Over the years, we began to use him as an agent to sell produce to outsiders so we could buy things we don't want to make or can't obtain ourselves." He smiled at Rainstorm. "I think you'll find that all woodfolk products that go to outsiders are channelled through him."

Tarkyn looked puzzled. "If everyone is using Stormaway as an agent, why doesn't Rainstorm know about him?"

"I can answer that myself," put in Rainstorm. He cleared his throat self-consciously. "I have only just reached an age where I have any interest at all in adult affairs. So there are still a lot of things I know little about."

Tarkyn smiled warmly at him, "Now there you are, you see. That is the advantage of not being a prince. I've been forced into adult affairs ever since I can remember. Do you know how old I was, when I first swore that oath?' Seven."

Rainstorm whistled. "Wolves' teeth! You didn't have any choice, did you?"

The prince laughed. "No. None at all. But I wouldn't change it now, even if I did have." He fiddled with his bandage again, lost in his own thoughts for a while. Then he looked up again, "So, we still haven't sorted this out. What are we going to do about Stormaway?" He gave a wry smile. "I have to warn you; he is only an hour away. So you'd better get it sorted somehow."

Autumn Leaves showed no surprise but heaved himself to his feet. "I'll go and talk to the others about it. Come on, young man. You can help me as long as you don't advocate killing off the prince's loyal retainer."

"Autumn Leaves, please let us know if there is likely to be any danger to Stormaway," said Tarkyn gently but firmly. "Despite my differences with him, I really couldn't countenance any harm coming to him, after all his years of holding true to my father and me."

Autumn Leaves smiled reassuringly, "Tarkyn, if we don't want him to find us, he won't. We don't need to kill him. If he is nearly here, he is following the path we have laid out for him."

When they had gone, Tarkyn turned his head to look at Waterstone.

"I haven't had a chance to thank you yet," began Tarkyn.

Waterstone shook his head, "And I haven't had a chance to apologise for my presumption."

"No." said the prince softly. "Don't say that. I meant what I said. I am truly honoured to be part of your family." He looked down at his bandage and pulled at a loose thread.

"What's wrong? You keep fiddling with it. Is your arm hurting?"

"Hmm? No. My arm is fine." Tarkyn threw the woodman an embarrassed glance and looked back down. "I just like having the bandage on there. It keeps reminding me that you..." he shrugged, "I don't know....that you were willing to risk me rejecting you in front of all those people, that you are willing to have me in your family."

Waterstone shook his head in wonder. "You're a strange character, young Tarkyn. One minute, you're the most arrogant thing on two legs. The next minute, you are so humble, it's scary. I can't work you out at all."

Tarkyn stroked Sparrow's head and kept his eyes down. "It is one thing to know your worth as a prince or leader among men. It's quite another to be accepted by someone when they don't have to accept you and when you know most people are either scared stiff of you or resent you."

The woodman patted him on the shoulder. "You know, Tarkyn, I think you're a little out of date with your perceptions. Thunder Storm and Autumn Leaves would have gladly taken you into their family too, you know. I nearly had to fight them for the privilege."

Tarkyn looked up in surprise. "Really?"

"Yes, really. None of us who knows you is frightened of you any more. We might be frightened for you after your shenanigans with the forestals, but not of you."

The prince gave a slight smile. "You know, I was beginning to think things were settling down," the smile faded, "but when I found out about the other woodfolk, everything I thought I knew, fell apart."

Waterstone heaved a sigh, "I can imagine it did. I am so sorry, Tarkyn, that you had to go through feeling betrayed again. I was as open as I possibly could be, given the demands of secerecy placed on us by woodfolk lore." He looked at the prince. "I really don't have any ulterior motives for my friendship with you.... And I've done the best I could to repair the damage."

Tarkyn gave a relaxed smile as he went back to fiddling with his bandage, his arm still around Sparrow. "Don't worry. Your best is well and truly good enough."

After a minute or two, the forest guardian shifted his weight under the little girl and said, "I keep receiving images from various animals and birds warning me of Stormaway's impending arrival. I don't know why - maybe because he is very angry and they can sense his antipathy towards us. I think we had better go and meet him before he storms in here and wreaks havoc. What do you think?"

Waterstone nodded, "Good idea. Then we can stall him, if we need to, to give those woodfolk who wish to, time to leave. I'll ask Creaking Bough or Thunder Storm to mind Sparrow. They can keep her with their two kids."

"So, do I need to ask a creature to guide us to him?"

"Much as that would be entertaining for me, no," replied the woodman. "I know where to find him. He will be following our trail."

Twenty minutes later, on a thin deer track through the depths of the forest, Stormaway rounded a corner and came into view. When he spotted Tarkyn and Waterstone, he stopped dead and put his hands on his hips.

"So, you found him, did you?" said the wizard sternly. Stormaway then ignored Waterstone and turned the full strength of his wrath on Tarkyn, "Heavens above, Sire, what on earth did you think you were doing, disappearing like that?" He waved his hand in the woodman's general direction. "I'm used to this lot disappearing but not you. The forest's a dangerous place. There are all sorts of people lurking in the forest who might wish you harm."

Tarkyn raised his eyebrows. "What? Me, in particular?"

"Yes. You, in particular. In case you've forgotten, you've been branded a rogue sorcerer."

The sorcerer grimaced. "Hmm. I do keep forgetting that, I must admit."

"So what were you doing with yourself?" demanded Stormaway angrily. "And why didn't you let anyone know where you were going? You left everyone in a total panic."

Waterstone waited with interest to hear how Tarkyn was going to respond to this.

The prince looked his retainer in the eye and drew a breath. "Stormaway, I apologise if I distressed you in any way. However, I was upset and needed time away from you all to sort things out." He let a faint note of hauteur enter his voice. "Beyond that, there is nothing else I am prepared to tell you. My business is my own, after all."

"Bloody arrogant Tamadils!" exclaimed the wizard. "I don't know how I've put up with you all. You're as bad as your father. Use you one minute. Freeze you out the next."

Tarkyn relented, "Stormaway, I don't mean to freeze you out. However, equally, there will always be times when what I am doing is not necessarily your business, or anyone else's, for that matter." He paused. "I don't know everything about you. You don't need to know everything about me."

Stormaway eyed him, only half placated. "But you can't just run off when it suits you. You need the protection of the woodfolk."

"If it makes you feel any better, I can tell you that I do not intend to make a habit of running off, as you put it." The prince raised his eyebrows derisively, "And I think I have made it clear in the past that I value the woodfolk rather more than you do."

As they neared the clearing, Tarkyn could see that there were notably fewer woodfolk. However, he was shocked to realise that many who had attended the ceremony had remained. He spoke quietly to Waterstone, "We can't just walk in without preparing him. He might attack them to protect me."

Once the woodman had nodded his agreement, Tarkyn turned to the wizard and placed a restraining hand on his shoulder. "Stormaway, before we go on, I must ask you to trust me. Whatever happens, do not attack anyone. At the very worst, raise your shield if you must."

Just as he finished speaking, Raging Water stomped up to Stormaway. "Good evening, old man. You'll be wanting something to eat and drink after your long walk, I'm thinking. I am Raging Water."

Stormaway, with years of court intrigue behind him, barely missed a beat as he replied, "Good evening. I would indeed be glad of some refreshments after my long solitary journey here." He sketched a slight bow, but tension showed in every line of his body. "I am Stormaway Treemaster, wizard." As he fell in beside the old woodman, he asked tightly, "Would I be right in assuming that you are not bound by the oath to His Royal Highness?"

"That would be correct, wizard."

Stormaway sent a sharp glance to Tarkyn. "And this would be your private business you would say nothing about, I presume?"

The prince nodded.

They reached the firesite and Stormaway was introduced to the wide array of woodfolk from different parts of the forest. He sat himself down on a log and was given wine and a plate of spit roast deer, bread and fruit.

Everyone seated themselves comfortably around him and indulged for a short time in a desultory chat about the weather, the harvests and the potential for marketing.

"I did have my suspicions that there might be more woodfolk than I had met," said Stormaway eventually. "There was so much produce from such a small number. However, I thought the prince would be safe enough as long as he was with woodfolk who were sworn to protect him." The wizard took a sip of his wine and turned to frown at Waterstone. "I am surprised you brought him here, nevertheless. I don't know how you could be sure that you could protect him against so many, if it were needed - no offence intended." he added, glancing around the group. "Besides, don't you have a code of secrecy?"

Amused glances passed between the assembled woodfolk.

Raging Water answered. "Wizard, your young prince appeared among us many hours before Waterstone and his lot arrived." The woodman bent a rather evil smile on the wizard. "He'd have been long dead by then if we had decided to kill him."

Stormaway turned a stony face towards the prince.

Tarkyn smiled cheerily at him. "But as you can see, I am still alive and kicking. Better still, woodfolk don't have to worry about protecting me against each other and we can all get on with facing the coming threat together."

If Tarkyn thought this would mollify his faithful retainer, he was sadly mistaken. Stormaway glared furiously at him and demanded angrily, "Your Highness, how could you place yourself at such risk? Have you no understanding of your importance both as prince and as guardian of the forest?"

For the first time, the new woodfolk saw Tarkyn's arrogance emerge. In a cool voice that sent a chill up the spine of his listeners, the prince replied, "I know exactly how much or how little I am worth. I will place myself at risk when and where I see fit and, unlike you, I will place my trust in the good sense and honour of the woodfolk. Not only that, but I will thank you to remember to whom you are speaking and to treat me with some vestige of respect."

The woodfolk watched him in shock. Gone was the placating, self-deprecating sorcerer with whom they had spent the week. In his place, was the proud, sure prince of the realm asserting his authority. Then Tarkyn's anger was gone as quickly as it had come. He took a short breath and continued more calmly, but still in a manner that would brook no opposition. "Stormaway, I am not answerable to you. I know you have my best interests at heart and I will always listen to your advice, but I will not be called to account by you."

The wizard looked steadily at him. "I beg your pardon, Si````re," he said stiffly after a moment. "Perhaps I did not express myself very well. I would appreciate it if someone could take the time to tell me what happened that has led us to where we are now."

Stormaway frowned as he learned the reason for the prince's flight. As several woodfolk filled the wizard in on Tarkyn's deliberate surrender to the woodfolk's will, his mouth became set in a thin tight line. Then his eyes grew round as he heard about Tarkyn's inauguration into the woodfolk as a member of Waterstone's family.

When he was clear on the details, Stormaway turned once more to Tarkyn who was quietly concentrating on demolishing a long dry stick while everyone around him talked about him. "My lord, I wonder if you realise how great your achievements have been? The honour you have been accorded is breathtaking."

Tarkyn dropped the last of the stick and straightened his bandage a little. He smiled around at everyone and said, "Oh yes, Stormaway, I do. I told you before; I know exactly how much and how little I am worth."

Stormaway cleared his throat. "And might I enquire where I am left amidst all these changes?"

"Stormaway, I cannot decide for the woodfolk. I don't think you are in any danger, though, or Autumn Leaves would not have let us bring you to this firesite. Is that correct?" Several heads nodded. The prince placed a hand on the wizard's shoulder and addressed the woodfolk. "As forest guardian, I need Stormaway by my side. He is a skilful powerful wizard who can teach me to use my own powers more fully. I know we don't agree on the oath but I cannot force him to change. However, I'm sure he and I will continue to discuss it." His amber eyes swept around the woodfolk. "Have you worked out what you are going to do?"

Ancient Elm's creaky old voice made itself heard. "We have decided to put up with you, Stormaway Treemaster, even though you created that disgraceful oath. Not only that, we have decided that, as our forest guardian's companion, you should be included in woodfolk affairs as they concern our guardian. From what we understand, you have already assisted woodfolk against the evil that hunts us." Her bony shoulders twitched in a shrug. "And if you've known about woodfolk for twelve years and haven't let on, there's no reason to suppose you would start now." She gave a little cackle. "Besides, it is very handy to have a link with the outside world. We have all used you to trade our goods for us and it would be churlish to turn on you now."

The wizard raised his eyebrows. "I must admit I am pleasantly surprised that woodfolk not involved in the oath are willing to work with me. I can see I may have to re-evaluate my preconceptions of all of you woodfolk, but particularly of you, Your Highness."

CHAPTER 31

Lapping Water carried the empty skin bag down to the stream and walked along a little way looking for a place where she could easily draw clear water. The morning sky was heavy with dark rolling clouds and the stream had swollen with overnight rain. She pushed past a bush growing close to the stream water's edge and found herself standing only feet away from the prince, who was seated on the bank.

When Tarkyn started and looked around, clearly discomforted, Lapping Water stepped back and prepared to withdraw.

"I beg your pardon, my lord," said the woodwoman nervously, "I did not mean to intrude."

Tarkyn reddened and held out his left hand, which was trailing his bandage, in a restraining gesture. "No. Please don't go. I was just fiddling with this bandage and trying to get it back on." He looked around him and nodded slightly downstream. "There is a good spot just there for drawing water."

"Thank you, my lord." Lapping Water walked around him and knelt to fill her waterbag. She watched Tarkyn out of the corner of her eye as he made one attempt after another to wind the bandage neatly around his right arm. When her waterbag was full, she hung it from a nearby branch and came over to him.

"Here. Let me do it," she said quietly. "It will be much easier with two hands."

Tarkyn glanced up at her. "Thanks, but I think I just about have it in place now." Even as he said it, the other end of the bandage came loose and started to unwind. "Blast! No, I haven't. Drat the thing." He grimaced at her and gave a little sigh. "Very well, thank you. I accept your offer."

He held out his right arm and the bandage in his left hand. As she took the bandage and began to straighten it out, she asked, "Why didn't someone do this for you in the first place?"

"Someone did. I just took it off and now I can't get it back on again."

A slight frown appeared on Lapping Water's face but she didn't ask anything further. As she began to wind on the bandage, her frown deepened and she looked more closely at the cut on his arm. "You can't re-bandage your arm like this. There's dirt in the cut."

"I know there is," said the prince in a tight voice.

Lapping Water brought her soft green eyes up to meet Tarkyn's. "So why are you leaving it there? You must know it will hinder the healing?"

A dull red had seeped into the prince's cheeks. He dropped his eyes. "If you must know..."

Lapping Water put a gentle hand on his shoulder. "No. I don't have to know if you don't want to tell me. I did not mean to make you feel uncomfortable."

Tarkyn raised his eyes and gave a half smile. "No. Having come this far, I will tell you…although I admit it is a bit embarrassing." He took a breath. "I want to make sure the cut leaves a scar so I can carry it as a reminder…of being accepted by Waterstone and by all of you woodfolk."

Lapping Water smiled as she resumed the bandaging of his arm. "I think that is a fine thing to do. I suppose you could heal yourself anyway if it became infected, couldn't you?"

He nodded, rather surprised that she had taken it so prosaically. After a minute, he said, "Did you know I could actually feel Waterstone's blood going around inside me? It's beginning to fade now. I suppose it's been absorbed into my own blood now, but to start with, I could have told you where every drop of it was inside me."

"Ooh, that sounds quite horrible." She wrinkled her nose. "Did it make you feel queasy?"

Tarkyn laughed. "No. It was just interesting." He shrugged. "I don't suppose Waterstone felt anything at all. I think it's part of the forest guardian thing." He glanced at the woodwoman to gauge her reaction.

She finished tying the bandage then looked at him. "You still don't feel comfortable about being a forest guardian, do you?"

The prince shook his head. "It's getting better but it's all moving so fast: all of these new abilities emerging and developing. Growing plants. Talking to birds and animals, not in words, but you know what I mean. And weird things like turning green and healing myself and feeling Waterstone's blood. Even being able to send images and feelings. I couldn't do that before, either." He shook his head again and smiled ruefully, as he rose to his feet. "It's a lot to get used to."

"I suppose so."Lapping Water walked over to the tree and retrieved her waterbag. "Still, it must be exciting, having all these new experiences. I'd give my right arm to be able to do what you can do."

Tarkyn smiled. "Would you? That's pretty much what Rainstorm said. Well, words to that effect" He reached for the waterbag. "Here, let me take that."

"Why?" she asked unexpectedly.

The prince frowned in confusion. "Why what?"

"Why should you take the waterbag?"

Tarkyn was taken aback. He suddenly realised any argument about gentlemanly courtesy wasn't going to cut the mustard. "Well," he said, "because I am repaying the kindness you showed me in re-bandaging my arm."

She glanced at him uncertainly. "I'm not sure that it's proper."

"What sort of proper?" Tarkyn asked in some alarm.

"Well, you're the prince and we're supposed to be serving you."

The prince breathed a sigh of relief. "Oh, is that all? I can get around that easily enough. I insist that you let me carry your water."

"I can't argue with that then, can I?" Lapping Water grinned. "You realise that if we hadn't spent all this time talking about it, we could have been back at the firesite with the water by now."

"I can see gratitude is not one of your strong traits then," said Tarkyn dryly as he walked back up the stream beside her, carrying her waterbag.

Lapping Water flashed him a smile and answered, "Not for anything as trivial as that."

Just as he began to frown, Tarkyn realised he was being deliberately provoked. Hard on the heels of this realisation, came the uncomfortable knowledge that he didn't know how to respond. He was rescued from his predicament by the spectacle of a large group of woodfolk congregated in the clearing, clustered around Tree Wind and the harvesters.

"Oh look, the harvesters are about to report on what they found at the end of the wolves' tracks." Lapping Water's eyes twinkled at him, "They would have done it yesterday but other issues took precedence." She took off and called over her shoulder, "Come on. The harvesters should be able to tell us where the riders and wolves came from."

Tarkyn followed more slowly, surveying the clustered woodfolk. He skirted the edge of the firesite and found somewhere to hang the waterbag. Then he stood under the shadow of the tree and watched while everyone milled around, smiling, chatting and mind talking to each other. The prince felt a deep sense of contentment that these were his people. But at the same time, he knew that when they became aware of him standing there, he would become the centre of attention. Standing apart was a quiet pleasure, he reflected, when one could choose to be a part of things.

Inevitably, someone noticed him standing there and almost immediately there was a lull in the conversation.

"Ah, Your Highness," said Tree Wind, "Now that you have graced us with your presence, we can begin."

Tarkyn inclined his head, thinking that his new status as a woodman showed no signs of shielding him from Tree Wind's antipathy. "I beg your pardon. I did not realise that you were waiting for me."

Tree Wind continued as though he hadn't spoken. "There is an encampment of many men about forty miles due west of here," she explained out aloud, mostly for the benefit of Stormaway and Tarkyn. "The horsemen and the wolf returned there. The young man who led them has other trained wolves chained up in the encampment."

"How many sorcerers? Any wizards?" asked Stormaway.

Tree Wind shrugged, "I don't know the difference between sorcerers and wizards but I can tell you there were at least three, maybe four hundred of them."

"Three or four hundred?" The wizard whistled. "That's the beginning of a small army. Were they all men? Or were there women and children as well?"

The woodwoman thought carefully. "I would say about three quarters were men. The rest were women and children. Many of them looked like the travellers you see along the woodland roads."

"So, were they bandits?" asked Tarkyn.

Tree Wind avoided his eye but answered his question, "No, my lord. I don't think so. I don't know what they are doing in the forest but they don't look like they are planning to clear trees for farming and they don't look as rough as the usual bandits. I think we will have to watch them and try to work out what they are up to."

"Other than trying to hunt down woodfolk, you mean," said Thunder Storm dryly.

"Yes." After a slight hesitation, Tree Wind added, with the faintest undertone of derision, "Although perhaps His Highness was mistaken in his vision of that."

"Perhaps I was," answered the prince silkily. "For those of you who did not see it the first time, would you like me to repeat the image of the wolves' attack and the arrival of the riders at the scene of the wolves' deaths? Then you can draw your own conclusions. Perhaps you may notice things we missed."

Because he was annoyed with Tree Wind, Tarkyn did not warn anyone to sit down. Consequently, woodfolk fell like ninepins as his image of the eagle took them soaring over the forest to see the wolves' approach. The group that Tarkyn had begun to think of as his home guard all knew what was coming and had managed either to sit down in time or brace themselves to stay upright.

"Tarkyn. Stop it," whispered Autumn Leaves, smothering a laugh. "This is serious."

"So is being doubted. Hang on!" said the sorcerer unrepentantly. "After the wolf attack, I'll show you the swallow's view of the hunters riding through the bush. The eagle's flight was easy, compared to this one."

The fallen woodfolk wisely decided not to try to stand up until the visions were finished. Even so, many of them looked a little pasty by the time they had seen the forest below them through the swallow's eyes as it bobbed and swooped its way through the air. The owl's view of the wolf and horsemen's arrival was more measured and they were able to recover before the images concluded.

There was a stunned silence as the woodfolk unused to Tarkyn, took in the scope of the forest guardian's connection with the woodlands.

"Of course," said Tarkyn in an off-hand manner, completely unmoved by their reaction, "I may be providing you with inaccurate or mistaken images. I don't know how you can be sure." His eyes glittered with anger.

"Now calm down, young man," said Raging Water, "No need to fly into your high boughs. I think we would all like you to be mistaken because the alternative, that someone knows about woodfolk and is trying to hunt us down, is a pretty frightening concept." He huffed out his cheeks. "However, I'm sorry to say I think your images are quite conclusive and we have a serious problem on our hands." As an afterthought he added, "It's just as well we didn't kill you. I think you're going to come in quite handy, one way and another."

This last comment finally drew a smile from the offended sorcerer. Tarkyn gave a small bow. "Happy to be of service."

"Oh my word! He's bowing again." Raging Water frowned repressively, "In that case, young Tarkyn, what else do you have to offer us as our forest guardian?"

The sorcerer thought for a moment. "Protection if you are under attack, perhaps." Tarkyn nodded at the edge of the clearing. "If a band of sorcerers or wolves came rushing in here, I could throw up a shield to protect us all, like so," A bronze dome appeared around them. "But you probably can't get out any more than they could get in." Only the conversational tone of the sorcerer's voice saved the woodfolk from wholesale panic as they found themselves trapped. "Go on. Waterstone, try to get out. It won't hurt."

Waterstone pushed hard against the translucent bronze barrier. It bulged slightly but showed no signs of giving way. Tarkyn turned to the wizard. "Is there a way of making it possible to leave the protection of the shield while keeping it strong against attack?"

Stormaway shook his head. "I don't think so....unless you can raise it a little on one side?"

The sorcerer focused on changing the shape of the shield so that it wasn't a complete hemisphere. A small gap appeared along the ground near Waterstone.

"Try that," he said to Waterstone. When the woodman looked askance at him, the sorcerer added, "Don't worry. It won't fall down on you, as long as I concentrate. But even if it does, it won't go through you." He glanced at Stormaway for confirmation. "I think the worst that could happen is that you would be pinned to the ground until I removed the shield."

The wizard nodded.

Waterstone took a deep breath and began to wriggle his way under the shield. As the woodfolk watched, the shield dropped slowly down and held Waterstone in place. His eyes widened with fear.

"It's quite safe, Waterstone," said Tarkyn, sending a wave of reassurance to everyone in general. "Tell me if it becomes too uncomfortable. I am slowly lowering that side of the shield to see what happens. At a word from you, I'll remove it."

Waterstone exerted an extra effort and after several attempts that each became more frantic than the last, pulled himself free. Even before he had rolled around and stood to face Tarkyn, white faced and angry, the shield had winked out of existence.

"Blast you, Tarkyn! That was frightening," growled the woodman.

"Sorry. You could have stopped me." Tarkyn smiled ruefully at him. "Are you all right?"

"Yes, although it was very firm pressure. I think the little ones would panic if they got caught like that."

"It's not something I would plan to happen. I just need to know where we stand if you are all trying to leave and something distracts me."

"On the other hand," said Tree Wind dryly, "we could just disappear."

"I agree." Tarkyn looked at her steadily. "Go on then. Demonstrate."

In the blink of an eye, Tree Wind was gone.

The sorcerer's mouth quirked, "Not just Tree Wind. Everyone. I want to see how safe that will make you from wolves and sorcerers." He turned around as he found himself talking to thin air. "Stars above, you people are brilliant. I wish I could do that." He turned to Stormaway. "Do you know where they are?"

Stormaway looked around carefully. "They are hiding in the trees and bushes around the clearing."

Tarkyn stood with his hands on his hips, letting his gaze travel slowly across the foliage of the trees and bushes. Gradually, his eyes tuned in and then, as he focused in on the occasional flicker of movement, he could make out the dim outline of some part of a person.

"You can come back now, if you'd like to."

Immediately he was surrounded by woodfolk as before. He frowned around the group until he spotted Autumn Leaves.

"Autumn Leaves, I distinctly remember you telling me that woodfolk don't have any magic. So what do you call that, then?"

The big woodman shrugged. "We all do it. It's nothing special."

"It certainly is special," retorted the sorcerer. "I can't do it. Neither can Stormaway, I would think."

The wizard shook his head in confirmation.

"So, how do you do it?" asked Tarkyn.

"We just think ourselves somewhere else and hidden," replied Autumn Leaves.

"And how far can you go?"

"I don't really know. Not far. It has to be somewhere in sight."

Sun Shower interrupted sharply at this point. "Do you think we can curtail this discussion until after lunch? It is getting late and the little ones are hungry. We have had the harvesters' report, and we do not need to stand around for the rest of the day answering your questions."

A flush of colour darkened Tarkyn's cheeks. "I apologize," he replied stiffly. "That was thoughtless of me. Please don't let me stop you." He swung on his heel and walked away from them down to the stream. Tarkyn reflected that he always seemed to seek the comfort of running water when he was upset.

Behind him, he could hear Raging Water saying, "That was badly done, you grumpy woman. He didn't make everyone stand there and listen to him. You could have been getting things done quietly in the background if you were so worried about it."

"I will not have that young upstart coming in here and taking over. I don't mind him being woodfolk. In fact I think he deserves it but it doesn't give him the right to monopolise our time."

Gradually, as Tarkyn listened, others joined in the argument and before long, a heated discussion was raging amongst the whole group. Leaving them to debate his behaviour, the prince slowly made his way down the bank of the stream, watching tiny fish in the shallows and waterboatmen skating across the top of the water. Soon he had left the noise of the woodfolk behind him and immersed himself in the quiet sounds of the woods.

Here, the woodlands were mostly towering old oak trees, leaves turning yellow and brown and starting to fall. The forest floor was a carpet of gold. The sorcerer focused his will for a moment and lifted himself high up into the branches of a gnarly old oak. He settled himself in the crook of two branches and closed his eyes.

After a while, Tarkyn became aware that he was being watched. Opening his eyes, he found himself face to face with a red squirrel, perched on a nearby branch. A feeling of sympathy washed gently through the air. The squirrel flicked its tail and in two quick movements, was sitting on the top of Tarkyn's raised knee. She sat there looking at him then, in an unmistakable gesture, offered him the acorn she held between her front paws.

Tarkyn smiled and accepted the gift. "Thank you, my friend."

The squirrel nodded at him expectantly and Tarkyn realised that she was waiting for him to eat the acorn. Keeping his thoughts about the flavour of acorns carefully masked, the forest guardian peeled back the hard outer skin of the acorn with his teeth and took a small bite of the acorn's pale flesh. It was every bit as bitter as he had been dreading. Using a lifetime of court training, Tarkyn managed to stop his face from screwing up in distaste and to produce a grateful smile at the same time. The unfortunate consequence of this was that the squirrel disappeared briefly to return with another acorn.

Tarkyn doggedly finished the first acorn but couldn't face eating another. Luckily he had an inspiration and pointed first to the acorn and then to his pocket. The squirrel who was a great hoarder herself, seemed to think this was an excellent plan and showed every sign of approval when Tarkyn pocketed the second acorn. He smiled with relief that the squirrel assumed was gratitude.

"So, my friend," said the prince, "Despite my best efforts, they are all still fighting over me. I think we now have four separate groups in total; those who are and are not bound by the oath, and within each of those two groups, those who resent me having any authority and those who don't." After sending out a careful request, Tarkyn began to stroke the squirrel as he talked. "Trouble is, the resentful ones see me giving orders when I'm just trying to take part in a discussion like anyone else." He sighed. "Maybe I just come across as more arrogant then I realise. Now I think about it, I certainly do a lot of the talking. Maybe I should go and find Waterstone. He'll be able to give me some perspective."

"What about me, little brother? Will I do?"

Tarkyn started, making the squirrel flicked her way quickly up a nearby branch. He looked around to see Ancient Oak peering at him from around the enormous trunk of the oak.

"Dog's teeth!" exclaimed Tarkyn. "Is this a family trait, sneaking up on people when they are having a quiet conversation with themselves?"

The woodman smiled a little uncertainly, "It must be, I suppose." He nodded at the squirrel. "Do you think you can get your little friend to come back down?"

"Sit down. I'll try."

Tarkyn looked up at the squirrel who was watching him warily from a perch about ten feet above them. He sent up an apology for frightening her, then a wave of reassurance followed by invitation. She stared at him for a few moments then flicked her way back down to him to perch herself on the knee furthest from Ancient Oak.

"Wow. That is fantastic," breathed Ancient Oak. "Do you think I could pat her?"

Tarkyn smiled. "Possibly. Let her get used to you first. I'll ask her in a minute."

The woodman frowned. "Can animals talk then?"

"Not in words. We use images and emotions instead." The forest guardian raised his eyebrows, "I've just realised. My mind linking is exactly the same as that of all the creatures but not like the woodfolk's. Stormaway thought my type of mind linking was unique in Eskuzor but it's only unique among people. It's quite common amongst everything else. Mmm, interesting, don't you think?"

Ancient Oak raised his eyebrows. "Very."

"So, big brother," said Tarkyn, taking pleasure in the fact that his older brother was in fact notably smaller than he. "Did you jump or were you pushed?"

"What do you mean?"

"I mean, did you volunteer to come and find me, or were you talked into it?"

"Oh. Well, to tell you the truth, Waterstone suggested it but I didn't mind. I figured we are going to have to get to know each other better, sooner or later."

Immediately a constrained silence fell over them as they each tried to think of something to say.

Eventually, Ancient Oak said, "Sparrow seems to have taken to you then."

Tarkyn gave a slight smile. "I've taken to her too. I'm quite surprised really. I haven't had much to do with children before."

Ancient Oak looked sideways at Tarkyn and cleared his throat. "You know, I'm not sure that I deserved that apology you gave me yesterday. In fact, I think I owe you one. I'm not surprised you snapped at me on the first day. After all, I didn't treat you well, as a stranger newly arrived among us, telling you how unwelcome you were…" He shrugged apologetically. "But I have grown up with the resentment of the oath all around me and I forgot to form my own opinion." He gave Tarkyn a warm smile. "I didn't make that mistake a second time."

Tarkyn could hear Waterstone's values reflected in his younger brother's words. He smiled in return and opened his mind to let Ancient Oak into an interchange of reassurance and query with the squirrel, before saying, "You may pat her, if you like."

When he had settled into stroking the squirrel, Ancient Oak asked, "If you don't like being left out of things, why did you leave us all to it, when you must have known we were talking about you?"

The prince's smile became underpinned with anger. "I said I don't like being left out of anything important. Frankly, people discussing my behaviour in that manner are beneath my notice and always have been. I will talk to you or Waterstone or Autumn Leaves about it, maybe a few others. But I am not going to indulge a rampant mob by taking them seriously. It matters very little what they decide I should do, because I have no intention of consulting them."

Silence greeted this pronouncement. After a few minutes, Tarkyn realised that Ancient Oak was looking white and strained.

The prince frowned and leant forward, "Are you all right?" he asked gently. "You look a bit ill."

The woodman glanced up at him. His voice was tight when he spoke. "I forgot who you truly are. And now you have reminded me. For a while there, we were just two people talking. Now, I remember that you are King Markazon's son and my liege. I apologise. I should not have been so familiar with you."

Tarkyn leaned back in a sudden movement that startled the squirrel. She flicked her tail in annoyance and in a series of swift jumps, disappeared up into the branches.

The prince sent a brief apology after her then turned to study the woodman for a few moments while he worked out what to say. "I may be King Markazon's son – and I understand completely what you are implying about my behaviour by saying that – but now, so too are you." He hesitated before continuing, his demeanour making it clear that he was sharing a confidence, not a recrimination. "And so I will tell you something that I wouldn't bother saying to the vast majority of woodfolk... I loved my father. And I lost him when I was young and nothing in my life has caused me greater regret. He may have been autocratic and volatile but he could also be gruffly kind, and he tried to be fair... But above all, he was my father... and until I came to the woodlands, I was unquestioningly proud to be his son."

After a moment, Ancient Oak replied quietly, "Do not let woodfolk resentment damage your pride in him. We have had no experience of monarchs. I was too young to be involved at the time, but I have seen the memories. King Markazon was a formidable man, used to absolute rule. From his point of view, he compromised. Perhaps if he had come to know us better, he may have compromised more. But he worked tirelessly to save the woodfolk struck down by illness." He glanced at Tarkyn. "And from what I can gather, Markazon went against all his instincts and traditions to make sure that you would be safe with us when he was gone."

"Yes, he did, didn't he... even if it was at the cost of your free will and mine." Tarkyn gave a little smile. "We are each his legacy to the other." He took a deep breath. "Ancient Oak, you may be as familiar with me as you like. You are my brother, after all. If you had heard some of the things Waterstone has said to me, you would not be so concerned. He's yelled at me. He's threatened me. He fought with me. He even told me at one stage that he didn't respect me as much as he respected woodfolk."

Still, the woodman did not reply.

Tarkyn sighed. "I may be an arrogant bastard. Autumn Leaves certainly thinks I am." He watched with amusement as the woodman's eyes widened. "In fact, I know I am, some of the time. But that doesn't mean I want, or expect to hold you at arm's length."

Ancient Oak frowned. "But you are so dismissive of all those people down there, people who are my friends and kin."

"In case you've forgotten, a week ago I offered to die for those people. I do care about them. But while they are heated up like that and arguing, most of them have forgotten that I even exist as a person. They are only thinking of me in my role and what they want from me." The prince leaned forward. "You learn over the years, when you are always at the centre of attention, that no matter what you do, there will be someone who doesn't like it. I'm not going to throw myself into an argument I can't win."

Ancient Oak looked a little as though he was thawing but said nothing further.

Tarkyn smiled ruefully at his new brother. "Feel free to pull me up any time you see me getting too arrogant or dismissive but, if you can help it, please don't withdraw from me or reject me. I'm not all bad."

At this, Ancient Oak raised his head and finally held Tarkyn's gaze. "I don't suppose anyone is all bad. And, to be fair, there isn't much that's bad about you…volatile, arrogant, excessively powerful, dismissive, thoughtless…" His mouth twitched in the beginnings of a smile.

"Oh come on. Be fair. I'm not usually thoughtless. Actually, if I am, I wouldn't notice, would I?"

Before Tarkyn had time to wander off down this particular tangent, Ancient Oak added, "…but Waterstone thinks the sun shines out of you and he does not give praise lightly."

"Does he?" Tarkyn smiled. "Well, I can tell you the feeling is mutual. If I get on with you half as well, that will be good enough…and I hope to do better than that. Waterstone and Autumn Leaves tell me regularly that I am hard work to be around. So, welcome to a challenge." Seeing Ancient Oak's frown, he added, "It's not always because of me. It's often because of who I am and how other people react…well, admittedly… and how I react."

"Like today, for instance."

The prince nodded, "Shall we go back and face the music?"

"If you're ready. Do you want a hand down?"

Tarkyn laughed. "You have missed a lot, haven't you? I was going to ask you the same question. Tell you what. I'll race you to the bottom. First to touch the ground, wins. …Go"

The sorcerer sailed out and down while Ancient Oak swung swiftly down from branch to branch and jumped the last six feet.

"Blast!" laughed Tarkyn. "You were miles quicker. It took me much less effort but I don't seem to be able to go quickly."

"You cheated." Ancient Oak was also laughing between catching his breath.

"No I didn't. I didn't say how we had to get down. I just said I'd race you."

They walked back along the stream. When they had nearly reached the clearing, Tarkyn stopped. "One more thing. This might sound silly but I give you permission to hit me."

Ancient Oak looked at him in confusion. "Why would I want to hit you?"

"Well," said Tarkyn airily, "Waterstone is always wanting to hit me and it is bad for the forest if I don't give my permission. So it's only fair that I give it to you too. Then if I drive you crazy, you have a more even playing field."

Ancient Oak shook his head in bemusement. "You're right. I have missed a lot."

Chapter 32

Following Tarkyn's exit, feelings ran high amongst the woodfolk. One strong camp argued against heeding anything Tarkyn said, wary of anyone usurping the natural authority of the woodfolk. Another more canny camp saw him as a new weapon to humour and use, as they saw fit, without allowing him into any mental discussion about their proposed tactics. When Waterstone and Autumn Leaves attempted to explain that Tarkyn would now insist on being included, they were regarded pityingly by many of the oathfree woodfolk and it was carefully explained to them that it was the welfare of the woodfolk as a whole, not Tarkyn, that was under consideration and that Tarkyn could not force them to include him if they chose not to.

"I don't know about that," growled Raging Water. "If he is a woodman, he must be included like everyone else. You can't have one rule for him and one for the rest of us."

"We can, if he can't mind talk," answered a rather unpleasant woodman from the mountains. "Or are you thinking that we should all change our way of life just to suit him? I am Driving Rain, for those who don't know me."

"We must at least keep him informed of the important issues, as they arise," rumbled Thunder Storm.

Driving Rain sneered, "You have to stand up for him, don't you? You're sworn to honour him. Well, I'm not, and he'll get no special privileges from me."

In fact, the opinions of those who had taken the oath were generally regarded as being tainted by compulsion, and so were given little credibility. And those who had stayed with Tarkyn were regarded almost as traitors by some woodfolk for having done more than the bare necessity required to fulfil their oath.

"Someone had to stay with him to uphold the oath on behalf of all who swore it," protested Autumn Leaves. "Just be glad we took the burden from the backs of the bulk of you."

"And we are proud," came Lapping Water's gentle voice, "to have been the first to realise that a new forest guardian had come among us and to have saved his life so that he can fulfil his role as our protector in the times to come."

"Bravo," said Waterstone quietly, as he headed off to seek out Tarkyn.

But as soon as he had rounded the first bend in the stream, a voice behind them said, "Not so fast, Waterstone. No doubt you're off to let your new brother know what is being said. You remember me, don't you? I'm Mudslide."

Waterstone sent Ancient Oak a brief mind message to go in his stead, and turned to face her.

Mudslide was stringy but tough, and she was not alone. Driving Rain stood solidly beside her, arms folded. He was a strongly built, muscly woodman, his nose a tribute to past fights.

"Out of all of them, Waterstone, you are the greatest disgrace to our nation." Driving Rain unfolded his arms, and closed the gap between them, balancing on the balls of his feet. "You have no excuse for the inordinate amount of time you have spent with that sorcerer. You spent days with him when he was injured. We know. And for someone who is supposed to be such a strong advocate of woodfolk ways, how can you betray your values by seeking power and privilege at the side of that interloper?"

"He is an interloper no more. He is a woodman and my brother," said Waterstone, keeping his temper on a very tight rein.

"Well done," sneered Mudslide. "You were quicker than the rest of us to realise an opportunity. Now you have a powerful sorcerer in your back pocket...and a forest guardian, as it turns out. That was a real coup. You must be loving the reflected glory."

Waterstone's eyes narrowed, "And I can now include generations of kings and queens in my family's archive. Don't forget that."

Driving Rain pushed Waterstone hard in the chest with one beefy hand, forcing him to take a step backwards. Waterstone flicked back several yards but the two woodfolk just flicked to land the same distance in front of him. But it had given Waterstone the slight respite he needed.

"Oh what? No Tarkyn to protect you?" Mudslide closed in to Waterstone's left and jabbed him in the bicep. "Where is he when you need him?"

Alarm flashed in Waterstone's eyes. "Leave him alone."

Driving Rain smiled unpleasantly, "Oh, we have no intention of risking our forests. It is you we object to. We don't like toadeaters."

He followed his words by aiming a crushing blow at Waterstone's midrift. Waterstone wrenched himself out of the way, not to his right as they had expected where Driving Rain's left fist was waiting for him but to his left, straight into the woodwoman. As Driving Rain's fist grazed past his stomach Waterstone, copying one of Tarkyn's manoeuvres, grabbed Driving Rain's fist and used the impetus of the woodman's own attack to drive him past.

Unfortunately, Driving Rain was heavier and better balanced and after a couple of recovery steps, the heavy woodman swung his whole shoulder into Waterstone just as Mudslide recovered and shoved him hard from behind. Caught between them, the air exploded from his chest and he doubled up, winded. Mudslide bent over and swung her full weight behind her shoulder to send the stricken woodman flying.

Just as Driving Rain strode over and grabbed him by his shirt front to pull him to his feet, a deep voice rumbled, "That's our friend you have there... I suggest you leave him alone."

Driving Rain hauled Waterstone upright by his shirtfront. "What? This conniving weasel? You admit friendship with him? You're all as bad as each other. You can have him back when I've finished with him."

Almost before he finished speaking, Driving Rain's eyes rolled up in his head and he sank to the ground. As Mudslide made a move towards him, Thunder Storm said calmly, "I will have no compunction about knocking you out too, if you make any further move to hurt Waterstone." She looked around to see a deadly little slingshot aimed at her head.

As Waterstone disentangled his shirt from Driving Rain's slack hand, Autumn Leaves walked over to him and put his arm around him to help him up.

"Mudslide," said Autumn Leaves over his shoulder, "I don't think much of your taste in men." He turned back to Waterstone, "Come on me old mate, let's get you away from this unwholesome company you've been keeping." He frowned as Waterstone wrapped his arm around his chest, still trying to catch his breath. "No permanent damage, I hope?"

Waterstone shook his head, and managed to get out between breaths, "No. A bit of bruising maybe. Mostly just winded."

Behind them, Driving Rain groaned and raised himself groggily on one elbow. He was shaking his head trying to clear it, just as Falling Branch rounded the bend with Raging Water hobbling behind in hot pursuit.

"What's gong on here?" demanded the old man.

"That bastard shot me," mumbled Driving Rain, pointing an accusing finger at Thunder Storm.

"Yes, and I will again if you're not careful."

"Good shooting, Thunder Storm. You knocked him out for less than a minute. That takes some finesse." Autumn Leaves transferred his attention to Waterstone, "You all right to stand on your own now?" When Waterstone nodded, he let go and addressed Raging Water, "Those two miscreants attacked Waterstone. We're not totally clear why. We just came when he called."

"They object to my friendship with Tarkyn, and think I deliberately developed it so that I can use his power." Waterstone kept his eyes trained on his shirt as he brushed dirt off it. "Of course, they're not the first to think that. Tarkyn thought exactly the same when he first knew me." He raised his head to look at Raging Water. "One of the joys of being around a power wielder."

"Stars above, Waterstone," rumbled Thunder Storm, "That was very poor thanks for all those hours and days you put in at his bedside. Fancy mistrusting you after all that time."

Waterstone gave a wry smile. "Don't think badly of him, Thunder Storm. All his life, he has been used for his influence, and cast aside when there is no more profit in associating with him. You think about it. His own brothers and two of his friends were willing to see him hanged. Why would he suddenly turn around and trust a complete stranger?"

"Why did he trust you then?" asked Thunder Storm.

"I'll tell you later," said Waterstone shortly, glancing at Autumn Leaves.

"You wheedled your way into his confidence. That's why," sneered Driving Rain.

Waterstone shrugged, "Think what you like. Whatever you say or however you threaten me, I won't leave Tarkyn's side." He didn't tell them that Tarkyn had forbidden him to leave, because he would have said the same thing anyway. He smiled. "Just as I won't leave Thunder Storm or Autumn Leaves."

"And what does your daughter think about this?" asked Mudslide casually.

"She is pleased to have Tarkyn as her uncle," replied Waterstone, his whole body tightening at the underlying threat in her question, as he wondered how to keep his daughter safe.

But Raging Water had no such qualms. He stomped up to the woodwoman and put his hands on his hips, "Mudslide, if anything ever happened to Sparrow, or to Waterstone or Ancient Oak, we would hunt you down... and Driving Rain. And we would bring the full force of woodfolk law to bear on you. You would never see your home forest again." He thrust his face up close to hers and hissed, "I will make known your words to all woodfolk gathered here. Don't you ever threaten a child again."

When Driving Rain and Mudslide had slunk off, Falling Branch turned to Waterstone, "You know, when you offered to become Tarkyn's blood brother, I thought you were brave because it would be so strange to have a sorcerer – and especially that sorcerer – in your family. But now I realise that by doing that, you have also undertaken to shoulder some of the resentment directed at Tarkyn and to endure the suspicion some people will have of your motives." He clapped Waterstone on the back. "So, I just want to say that you have my support."

"And mine," growled Raging Water.

Waterstone smiled. "Thanks. You haven't been around Tarkyn as long as we have. I walked into this with my eyes wide open. All three of us know that being around Tarkyn is hard work." His smile broadened, "But luckily, he is worth it."

CHAPTER 33

When Tarkyn and Ancient Oak returned to the firesite, lunch was underway. Consumption of food and drink had mellowed the mood a little but many people patently ignored Tarkyn or threw measuring glances in his direction.

Autumn Leaves looked up with a slight smile, "Over your huff now, are you?"

"Yes, thanks," said Tarkyn, as he sat down, refusing to be baited.

Sun Shower handed him a freshly baked flat bread rolled around dried berries, soft cheese and thin strips of some sort of meat without speaking to him.

"Thank you," he said, but without looking at her.

The woodfolk ate in silence, many obviously mind talking. Handy being able to mind talk, thought Tarkyn. It doesn't interfere with eating in the way normal talking does.

Looking around the group, Tarkyn felt that all-in-all, he had lost ground. All his careful negotiations with his home guard were in tatters. No one was including him in any conversations and in the present climate, he couldn't insist on it. He wasn't about to start a conversation and be accused of trying to dominate the group again. If people had been talking out aloud, he might have been able to chat to Autumn Leaves or Ancient Oak but not when that would be the only audible conversation. How the pendulum swang. He now felt isolated again but for different reasons.

He toyed with his food, finding he couldn't bring himself to eat the meat that might be one of the creatures he had linked with over the past few days. He picked at the his food for long enough to be polite then stood up and walked back down to the stream. This time, Autumn Leaves, Waterstone, Falling Branch, Ancient Oak and Rainstorm followed him. Ancient Oak and Rainstorm had not been a party to the attack on Waterstone but they could tell something had happened from the straight-backed defiance of the other three as they left the clearing.

By mutual unspoken consent, they found a comfortable grassy place to sit, away from prying eyes. Waterstone suppressed a grunt of pain as he sat down.

Ancient Oak directed a worried frown at him but when he received no response, spoke to Tarkyn, "You mightn't be consulting them but you are certainly allowing them to dictate your behaviour."

Everyone looked at him in surprise.

"Good heavens, Ancient Oak. That was remarkably profound," said his older brother, keeping the tone determinedly light. "Do I understand from that, that Tarkyn said he wouldn't consult with anyone? What about? About how he should act?"

Ancient Oak nodded.

"Oh well done, Tarkyn," said Waterstone scathingly. He spoke again to Ancient Oak, "So I suppose you now think he is totally autocratic, do you?"

Ancient Oak put his head on one side. "Actually, I did when he first said it. But that doesn't fit with everything you've said and the way he acts the rest of the time when he's not on his high horse." He smiled, "No, he's just a bit spiky, that's all."

The prince glared at them. "What is it about me that makes people feel free to discuss me as though I'm not here? I haven't seen you doing it to each other."

Waterstone grinned. "Sorry. It's just that you're so much more interesting to talk about than the rest of us." He gingerly changed position, only to find Rainstorm's eyes on him.

"Something's wrong, isn't it, Waterstone?" asked the young woodman. "Something has happened that you and Autumn Leaves and Falling Branch are not telling us about."

Waterstone rolled his eyes. "Save us from nosey little teenagers."

Rainstorm drew himself up, "That wasn't kind. I am only concerned for you."

"Sorry, Rainstorm. It's just that I don't want anyone feeling that they have to do something about it."

"You mean me, don't you, Waterstone?" said Tarkyn slowly. He gave a wry smile, "I would not interfere unless you agreed, you know."

Waterstone's strained face relaxed. "Not to mention that we have an agreement to share information with you that we can once more honour. Very well." He took a breath. "While you were off with Ancient Oak, two thugs accused me of currying favour with you and underlined their remarks with physical force."

"Autumn Leaves and Thunder Storm came to his rescue and Raging Water sent the thugs about their business, in no uncertain terms." Falling Branch smiled proudly, "He's a feisty old man."

Tarkyn frowned, realising that this was a sanitised version of events. "Would you have told me if Rainstorm hadn't forced the issue?"

Waterstone cleared his throat. "Yes, eventually. But I didn't want you to feel bad about the reactions our family may have to face, especially so soon after your inauguration."

Tarkyn gave a shy smile, “You asked me into your family to share with you the joys and trials of kinship, so that we can call upon each other’s strength in times of need. Remember?” He glanced at Ancient Oak. “I know people around me become subjected to those sorts of pressures. It has happened around me all my life. I promise I won’t rush in and champion your cause if you don’t want me to. I can see that defending you could well reinforce people’s suspicion that you have me at your beck and call. But, at the very least, I can be here to talk to about it. After all, I have vastly more experience of it than you do. And if you request more than that, you may have that too.”

“Thanks.” Waterstone smiled at Tarkyn and then glanced at his brother. Ancient Oak returned his smile, including Tarkyn in it. In that moment, the two woodmen and the sorcerer truly became brothers.

After a rather soppy silence, Autumn Leaves could stand it no longer and cleared his throat, “Harrumph. Anyway, I think Ancient Oak made a good point. You can’t let them cow you into silence.”

Tarkyn gave a short laugh at Autumn Leaves’ discomfort. “I have not been cowed into silence. I didn’t want to have yet another public conversation while everyone sits round, listening and judging. If other people had been talking, I would have talked too… I can’t help it if they haven’t enough courtesy not to whisper in front of one, so to speak.”

“What if they keep it up?” asked Ancient Oak.

The prince frowned. “I can’t imagine they all will. A lot of those people wouldn’t endorse a conspiracy against me. Raging Water, you people, the rest of the home guard…”

“The what?” demanded Waterstone.

Tarkyn cheeks darkened. “Oops. That’s my own private name for the woodfolk who have stood by me from the time of the accident.”

Autumn Leaves smiled. “It’s all right. I quite like it.” He looked at Ancient Oak and Rainstorm. “You two, of course, will have to earn your way into the home guard.”

Rainstorm’s eyes narrowed. “If we want to be in it.”

“And if I want you to be,” retorted the prince.

“Now you two, no fighting,” intervened Autumn Leaves who had spent a week watching them indulge in friendly bickering. “So what are we going to do about the mixed feelings of the woodfolk gathered out there?”

With a glance at Ancient Oak, Tarkyn gave a resigned sigh. “Tell me what the upshot of the discussion was.”

“Unfortunately,” put in Waterston somewhat bitterly, “those of us who have sworn the oath are not accorded much credibility… especially the home guard," he added with a quirk of his mouth. "So our influence on the overall feeling has been minimal. Added to that, the harvesters, Ancient Oak's lot, are still unreconciled to the oath, so most of them are agitating against you. With the exception of the woodfolk you have already mentioned and couple of dried up old dears you were sitting next to yesterday, the rest of them are still worried you're planning to stage some sort of a take-over."

"Well, blast the lot of them!" exclaimed the prince angrily, throwing his arms up in frustration. "They can go and sort out their own problems, for all I care. If it weren't for that bloody oath!" He scowled at them. "What's the point of becoming a woodman, if no-one is going to trust me anyway?"

"The point is that we can tell you everything you want to know about woodfolk now and you can trust us again," answered Autumn Leaves succinctly. He swept his arm around. "Anyway, all of us trust you."

Tarkyn raised his eyebrows at Rainstorm who nodded in response and said, "He's right. I trust you too. I mightn't do what you tell me but I trust you." The young woodman cleared his throat. "Trouble is, Tarkyn, you are quite forceful. The way you speak and act, well, you just assume that what you're going to say is important. Even if you listen to other people's ideas, you still lead the discussion."

For a fraught moment, Tarkyn stared at him. Everyone else held their breath. Then the prince gave a twisted smile, "I told you I was no good at being equal." He frowned around at the others. "And when were the rest of you going to get around to telling me this?"

"I didn't know you didn't know," answered Ancient Oak quickly.

Waterstone smiled at the prince. "We already told you. Remember last night when we were trying to show Rainstorm how much you negotiate and basically couldn't find a situation where you weren't running the show…even during the last week when you were unsure of your position. But now, becoming a woodman has restored your self assurance, and you're a force to be reckoned with."

Tarkyn rolled his eyes. "Fine then. So we know where we stand. I am so used to leading, that there is little hope that these egalitarian woodfolk are going to be able to stomach me as I am."

Rainstorm nodded without hesitation. "That about sums it up."

The prince gave a rueful smile. "And there is little hope that I will change because I thought I had already; and obviously I have failed dismally."

"I think you've changed," said Ancient Oak, "But maybe that's because you're now in my family."

Autumn Leaves snorted. "Of course you've changed. Only two weeks ago, we were debating whether we should all stand up when you arrive and wait to be spoken to and what else was there? …not bend over you and… I've forgotten the other ones."

"Bow. Not raise our voices to you," filled in Waterstone dryly.

For a moment, as the prince raised his eyebrows, he looked quite disdainful. "And there are many more, that I didn't even bother mentioning."

Ancient Oak and Rainstorm both watched this interchange round-eyed.

Rainstorm shook his head a little to clear it. "So. Given where you've come from, you've probably come as far as you can, for the time being."

Tarkyn nodded abstractedly in response, as he thought. Suddenly he sat up and smiled. "Aha. I know what I'll do. I'll just go back in there and read them the riot act. Then tomorrow morning, I'll go off to find Falling Rain as we originally planned. Anyone who wants to come with me can. The rest can go hang."

"What about your part of the oath?" asked Rainstorm, frowning.

"No problem at all. Ask Autumn Leaves. It's dangerous and logistically too difficult for woodfolk to congregate together for too long, isn't it? So, I have achieved what I set out to do which was to stop the threat of woodfolk killing each other over me. We're never going to attack those huntsmen by main force anyway." The prince beamed around at them all and concluded, "So, all we have to do is sort out what each group of woodfolk is doing about the threat. Then they can keep us informed so that I will know if, and how, I am needed as guardian of the forest."

"So you're going to breeze back in there, are you, and tell them all what they have to do?" asked Rainstorm in some amusement.

Tarkyn's eyes gleamed with laughter. "Yes. I think that sums it up. I'll do what I do best and lord it over them. If they hate me at the end of it, it won't matter particularly, because I'm leaving in the morning anyway."

Chapter 34

The woodfolk did not continue their silent treatment during the afternoon and evening but Tarkyn made sure that he did not speak to anyone unless there were other conversations to cover the sound of his voice. There was an undercurrent of tension, and the resentment from many woodfolk was palpable. Tree Wind could often be seen at the centre of a discontented group. She seemed to spread dissention wherever she went.

Raging Water and Falling Branch were determined to ignore the general unpleasantness and spent a lot of the afternoon talking to the forest guardian about his powers and what the dangers ahead might be. If they noticed that he spoke quietly and did not try to engage others, they said nothing about it.

The prince didn't make his move until after the evening meal. When he was ready, Tarkyn asked his home guard to stay together. Waterstone did not know why and was a little concerned at the reason for the request, but complied nevertheless.

The woodfolk were seated comfortably around the firesite as the guardian of the forest rose to his feet. A hush fell. Tarkyn towered over them and let his gaze sweep across them.

"My friends, many of you have been dreading this moment, the moment when I decide to take control." His voice resonated uncannily around the dark edges of the firelight. With some satisfaction, he watched the woodfolk freeze with shock. "It will not be for long, I promise you. Do not reach for your arrows. I will only put up a shield. If I choose to use it, with or without the oath, my power is far greater than your combined force." Looks of consternation swept his audience. "I have not tricked you or misled you. I have no intention of ruling you or making anyone else take the oath. I came here in good faith and I have had no greater joy in my life than being accepted as a member of the woodfolk."

Tarkyn put up a hand to quell the mutterings of confusion that broke out. "This morning, I tried to work with you to prepare for the coming dangers. I tried to be accommodating and diplomatic but it hasn't worked. Too many of you are unwilling to accept what I have to offer you as forest guardian. Those of you who know me, will know that I am a man of little patience. I have no intention of spending precious days and weeks winning over the doubters. So tomorrow morning, I will be leaving to continue on my trek to find Falling Rain. Anyone who cares to accompany me, may do so."

"What about your oath to protect us?" growled Raging Water.

The forest guardian began to pace slowly around the firesite. "I have not forgotten; and I will do everything I can whenever I am needed. However, I do not see the value of staying here, watching my presence sow seeds of dissension among you." He paused, "Before I go, there are some things I need to say."

The prince turned to Tree Wind and her cohort. "Firstly, you people have sworn an oath to honour, serve and protect me. Nothing I have seen today has honoured or served me. I have no doubt that somewhere the forest will be suffering for your efforts to undermine me." As he spoke, the woodfolk looking surreptitiously around the clearing, realised that leaves had fallen from the nearby trees, well in advance of the end of autumn and blotches of unhealthy fungi were marring many of their branches. He stopped before them and glared down at them. "More than that, you dishonour yourselves and all woodfolk when you betray your oath."

Watching him, Waterstone was shocked. Never before had Tarkyn used the oath as a weapon of control. If anything, in the past, he had abhorred its existence.

The prince paused, "One more thing, and this applies to everyone. If something important is being discussed, I wish to be included. I was deeply offended by being excluded from all conversations at lunchtime. In a time of crisis, you play games like that at your own peril." Without letting his gaze linger on any one group, he swept his eyes around the assembled woodfolk. "I know it is hard to include one who does not mind talk. But if the legends of the forest guardians are true, then my actions may determine your people's future. If I act in ignorance, you place your future in jeopardy."

Tarkyn continued his pacing until he stood before his own group of woodfolk Waterstone shifted a little uneasily, wondering what was coming. Tarkyn made sure he had the full attention of his audience then indicated his home guard. "I would like you all to take a careful note of these people. These are the woodfolk who, alone out of those who took the oath, have had the courage to stand by me when they did not know how I would treat them. They are the people you can thank for still having a forest guardian. And in the coming times of conflict, they are the people who will be the lynchpin of any action that the woodfolk may need to take. They will be the line of communication between all of you, and me." Tarkyn's eyes glinted in the firelight. "I would not like to hear again that their opinions were not being respected by their fellow woodfolk."

Tarkyn moved on around the fire until he was standing before the oathless woodfolk.

"Although you have not sworn the oath, if you care for your future as woodfolk and for the future of the forest, then you owe me allegiance as your guardian of the forest. I do not know what lies ahead of us but whatever happens, I would expect your support as you can expect mine. I know I already have it from many of you."

The prince began his slow circuit of the fire again. "In general, I am assuming that you will organise you own actions. However, because I am not prepared to enter into a debate that will be based more on whether I should order you around, rather than on the issues themselves, I will stipulate some basic guidelines."

He ticked them off on his fingers as he talked. "Firstly, I think you should increase the number of lookouts you have and rotate them more often so that they don't tire. Secondly, some woodfolk need to keep a constant guard on the encampment of sorcerers and make regular reports. Make sure you stay downwind of the wolves. If the encampment is too far away for mind talking, you will need to station people along the route to transmit information. Thirdly, we need a group to keep surveillance on the people travelling through the woods to find out what is happening to them and if there is any connection between the brigand attacks and the encampment. Fourthly, all woodfolk should make sure they can contact all other woodfolk. So you may need to set up other communication routes. Finally, make sure that there is a minimum number of woodfolk together at all times in case there are more wolf attacks."

The guardian of the forest spread his hands and gave a courtly bow and a smile. "Thank you for your attention. That is all I have to say. I am now relinquishing control."

Tarkyn walked back over to where he had left his wine glass sitting on a stump. Ignoring everyone, he retrieved it and refilled it from an earthen jug. Then he made his way back to his home guard and sat down among them. For a few long minutes there was a stunned silence. Tarkyn buried his face in his glass and smothered a smile.

Slowly, around the firesite, the odd conversation started up and soon the air was filled with animated chatter as the woodfolk digested what had just happened. Once there were other conversations to mask their own, the prince's home guard finally regained the power of speech.

"Stars above, Tarkyn," breathed Waterstone, "You really have been hiding your light under a bushel, haven't you? No wonder you're used to people standing up when you walk into a room. That was awe-inspiring."

"Thanks." Tarkyn finally let his grin take over. "I'm glad the silence didn't go on for too much longer. I might have started laughing."

"Your Highness, that would have ruined the effect," rumbled Thunder Storm with mock severity.

"I know," said the prince, grinning broadly. "That's why I managed to control myself."

Summer Rain frowned at him reprovingly, "Sire, I do not think your levity shows respect for these woodfolk."

"That's why I hid it, Summer Rain." He explained patiently. "And if they had shown me respect in the first place, I wouldn't have had to make that speech."

It was not long before they were joined by Rainstorm and Ancient Oak.

"I think I'll revert to my first impressions of you and then some," said Ancient Oak as he sat down. "Stars, if I hadn't spent the day with you, I'd be quaking in my boots by now."

Rainstorm was jubilant. "I can't believe you actually did it. Every last one of them shut up and listened to you from start to finish. Brilliant. Absolutely brilliant."

"Why, thank you, my friend," said Tarkyn laconically. "It's a pity I didn't make a bet with you. I never doubted for a second I could do it."

As the night wore on, more and more people plucked up the courage to come and speak to the prince. Gone were the mutterings of the afternoon. Tree Wind's oath-bound woodfolk had been effectively silenced, since no one wanted to be a party to damaging the forest or betraying the oath. All the other woodfolk realised their worst fears had already been and gone, and they were still free.

"Sometimes people just need to know where they stand," said Tarkyn, in an aside to Waterstone.

"Spoken like a true despot, my lord," replied the woodman with a grin.

Tarkyn laughed.

"Young man," came a scratchy old voice. Tarkyn turned to find Ancient Elm addressing him, "You have a very persuasive turn of phrase."

"Why thank you, Ancient Elm."

"I also wanted to thank you for showing us your journeys with the birds," the old lady continued, "although I now have a nasty bruise on my hip which I suspect was really owed to Tree Wind."

Tarkyn was instantly contrite. "I'm sorry. You're right of course. That was thoughtless of me. I didn't think of anyone getting hurt. Is Dry Berry all right?"

"I think so. She hurt her wrist a bit but she'll get over it."

The forest guardian shook his head. "No. That's not good enough. Where is she? I will have to sort this out."

"Hello young man. Looking for me?" cackled another familiar dried up old voice. "What do you have to sort out?"

"Your wrist."

Dry Berry lifted her scrawny arm and waggled her hand. She gave a slight wince but said stoically, "It's just a slight sprain. I've had a lot worse in the past. It'll heal in time."

Tarkyn looked at them both. "Would you let me heal you please? After all, you wanted to see a forest guardian at work...and I really don't want you going around telling everyone that I hurt you and then did nothing about it."

The two old women looked at each other, then back at him. "Go right ahead," said Ancient Elm.

"I'm fairly new at this. So we'll just have to see how it goes," said Tarkyn, belatedly realising he hadn't actually tried to heal anyone but himself before. "Now, close your eyes and focus on the injured part. I will send you a little of my *esse* and you must direct it to the part you want to repair."

The forest guardian placed a hand on each of their shoulders, closed his eyes and focused down inside himself to the seat of his power. He drew it up and out along his arms, through his hands and into the two bony shoulders. After a minute, Tarkyn opened his eyes and took his hands away.

"How's that?" he asked hopefully. "Any better?"

The two old woodwomen opened their eyes and experimentally rubbed the relevant parts of their anatomies. Then their faces wreathed in smiles.

"Well done, young man." Ancient Elm stood up. "I appreciate that. I have a long way to travel tomorrow and I'll be more comfortable now on the journey. It has been a pleasure to meet you and I hope we keep in touch."

Dry Berry frowned at him. "For a minute there, I thought you were going to go back on your word and meant to make us all take the oath. But I have now realised you can get exactly what you want without the oath. You're a dangerous young man but I think you're honest. I'm glad I met you...and I'm glad you are one of us now." She gave a little cackle. "To be frank, I wouldn't want you with the opposition."

Tarkyn gave a short laugh. He stood up to say goodbye and performed a small bow for them "Unless I mistake the matter, you two were gatekeepers for the decision to allow me to join the woodfolk. That being the case, I owe you a debt of gratitude and will not forget you."

As they walked away, he heard Dry Berry whisper to Ancient Elm. "See what I mean. Not much passes him by. Dangerous young man, indeed."

"Oh stop fussing, Dry Berry. You always think the worst of people…." Their last words were lost as they disappeared into the darkness beyond the firelight.

Tarkyn turned back from watching them to find Raging Water waiting to speak to him.

"Tarkyn, my boy, the legends of the forest guardians make hard acts to follow. But from what I have seen of you, you are well on your way to outstripping them all. Masterly performance this evening. Masterly."

Tarkyn put his hands on his hips and looked quizzically at the gnarly, old woodman. "Raging Water, I am not an actor. I meant every word I said."

The woodman smiled knowingly. "I know you did, my boy, even if it did strike you as amusing afterwards. But I also know you would no more kill a woodman than kill yourself. Mmm. Perhaps that's a bad example, after the other day, but you know what I mean. You didn't say 'Listen or I'll kill you.' You just pointed out that you had more firepower."

The prince grinned. "True. Anyway, I could hardly threaten to kill anyone when I've promised to protect you all, now could I?"

"Precisely. Anyway, it was clearly the best thing to do. You weren't going to be listened to properly while all the factions were fighting it out." He hesitated a moment and lowered his voice. "By the way, I saw how you healed Ancient Elm and Dry Berry. I think your older brother could do with bit of that. Nothing serious, you understand. But I think he'll be a bit stiff and sore tomorrow without it."

"Thanks. I'll see what I can do, now that I know I can do it. It's more a matter of whether he'll let me."

Raging Water nodded understandingly before giving the prince one of his hearty thumps on the back. "Well my lad, I'm sorry you're going. I would come with you but I'm getting a bit old for travelling long distances. We forestals aren't such great ones for travelling anyway. But I think Falling Branch and Rainstorm may be going with you. I'll keep in touch with you, never you fear." He leaned in towards the prince. "Try not to get too melancholy. You have a fine bunch of woodfolk there who are travelling with you. I can see why you wanted to get on well with them."

"I have you to thank for that." Tarkyn smiled and sent him a wave of gratitude. "I'm not sure why you did it but I know it was you who organised everyone to consider having me join the woodfolk."

Raging Water raised his eyebrows. "Don't you know? After all you had been willing to sacrifice; I couldn't bear to see you so resigned to being lonely. It just didn't seem fair."

Tarkyn frowned. “How did you know I felt like that? I didn’t tell you.”

The woodman just looked at him and smiled.

“Oh no.” said Tarkyn, turning a delicate pink as realisation hit. “Oh, that is so embarrassing. My blasted feelings! It’s this forest guardian thing. I can transmit feelings intentionally but sometimes they seem to transmit themselves without me even knowing it’s happening. Oh dear. Did anybody else notice?”

Raging Water laughed. “I am tempted to lie to you to save you further embarrassment but I won’t. The entire community noticed. Everyone stopped and watched you help Autumn Leaves across the stream.”

“Oh stars!” groaned Tarkyn. “That’s why everyone was suddenly so friendly.”

The woodman nodded. “You see? We’re a kindly bunch, really,” he said, grinning.

Tarkyn lifted his head and sighed. “Well, I’m glad you didn’t tell me this until after my performance, as you call it. I don’t think I could have stood up there and been so forceful, knowing I’d made such a fool of myself.”

“It’s not foolish to feel like that.”

Tarkyn looked at him derisively. “Perhaps not. But it is foolish to shout it out to everyone in sight.”

Raging Water shrugged. “What can I say? I don’t think you’re foolish. If I had, I wouldn’t have helped you to become a woodman. I think you’re strong, courageous, very clever and just a little emotionally volatile; perhaps call it passionate. Does that sound better?”

“It sounds,” said Tarkyn slowly, “like a euphemism, which is exactly what it is.” The prince straightened his shoulders. “Anyway, forget it. It can’t be undone. Thank you for your kind words and your kind deeds. I am glad there will be someone in this neck of the woods with sound common sense. I promise we’ll keep in touch.”

Part 7: The Storm

CHAPTER 35

Any plans for an early departure were thwarted by a howling gale that lashed the trees, bringing down branches and thrashing leaves off slender stems. Driving rain found its way through any chinks in the shelters, and sodden woodfolk could be seen from time to time streaking across the clearing seeking cover in more fortunate, drier shelters.

Tarkyn sat cross-legged in one corner of his shelter listening to the rain drumming on the roof. Sparrow was sitting beside him, constructing a complicated series of forest paths in the hard dirt of the floor.

He leant over her creation, frowning, "So where is the big road we crossed?"

"Down there," explained Sparrow patiently.

"Why is it there? We should be on that side of it, shouldn't we?"

The little girl rolled her eyes. "Tarkyn, you are hopeless with directions."

The prince shook his head and smiled. "I know, Sparrow. I wasn't brought up in a forest like you were. So why is the road down there?"

Sparrow frowned at him. "Because when you left us, you went straight back over the road we had all carefully crossed the day before."

"Did I? I didn't even see the road."

"Oh well done!" replied Sparrow with the awful sarcasm of the pre-adolescent. "*And* luckily you went in completely the wrong direction."

Tarkyn burst into laughter. "And now I have no idea where we were, where we are now or where we're going. So, start again. Where are we on your map?"

The little girl pointed to a spot about ten miles north west of their previous campsite.

"Right. So where were we and where are we going?" Tarkyn studied it with a frown of concentration. "Well, it could be worse. At least we've come a bit to the west."

Sparrow's eyes twinkled with laughter. "Yes, about six miles west. Marvellous! And only eight miles too far north. Daddy told me."

"Well," said Tarkyn in a thoughtful tone of voice. "When it all comes down to it, I think you should blame the owl. He's the one who chose to bring me to these particular woodfolk when I was looking for people who hadn't sworn the oath."

Sparrow frowned at him severely. "I think you're being naughty again. I think Dad would say you're trying to get out of it."

Tarkyn smiles sunnily at her. "He'd be right." Confronted by Sparrow's admonitory stare, he threw up his hands, "All right, all right. I'm sorry I've made everyone walk all that extra distance. Satisfied?"

Sparrow gave a sharp nod, her mouth tightly compressed to stop herself from laughing.

The sound of running footsteps outside was followed by someone scrambling their way through the brush screen that served as a door. A sodden woodman plunged inside, to land sprawled on the floor.

"Hello," said Sparrow. "You're sopping." She turned to the prince. "Have you got a towel anywhere?"

Tarkyn reached into a pile in the corner, extracted a towel and threw it to their visitor.

"Thanks," said the woodman as he set about drying himself off and pushing the wet hair out of his eyes.

"Stars above. Your shelter must have leaked a lot," said Sparrow sympathetically.

The woodman nodded. "It did. We only arrived here yesterday and with all that was going on, we didn't really put as much time into our shelters as we should have. Just our luck that the weather has come up so badly."

Sparrow gave a puzzled frown, "What was going on yesterday?"

"Oh, you know," replied the woodman, "That bloody prince throwing his weight around; beginning with a taster in the morning and finishing with a double whammy in the evening."

In the dim corner of the shelter, Tarkyn smiled evilly. "Yes," he said, at last attracting the woodman's attention. "I was quite proud of the double whammy."

The woodman's eyes widened in alarm. He made a dive for the door but Tarkyn's barrier reached it first.

"Not so fast, my friend," said the prince, an undercurrent of threat in his voice. "We can't have you running around in this heavy rain. You'll catch your death of cold."

Sparrow turned her gaze from the woodman to the prince and frowned at him. "Stop being so mean, Tarkyn. You're scaring him."

Tarkyn looked steadily at her for a moment. "Hmph." Then he shrugged and smiled at her. "You're right, young one. I suppose he has a right to his opinions – I'm not letting him go, though."

Sparrow smiled cheerily at the trapped woodman. "Well, that'd be silly, wouldn't it? You don't want to get wet again, do you?"

The woodman turned a stricken face towards the prince. "My lord. I apologise for my rash words. I didn't mean to offend you."

Tarkyn raised his eyebrows. "Of course you didn't. You didn't intend me to hear what you were saying. But please don't compound your transgression by offering me an empty apology."

Suddenly the prince leaned forward in the gloom to study the woodman's face. "Oh Stars above! You're Running Feet, aren't you?"

"I'm surprised you remember me," replied the woodman bitterly.

Tarkyn grimaced. "Oh, I remember you, all right. I have nightmares about levitating you and threatening to drop you. I was so angry at being unable to leave the forest and I thought you people were to blame. But that is no excuse. I should never have done it." He sighed. "You above anyone, have every right to a poor opinion of me… I apologise yet again for frightening you, then and now. I will release the shield on the door but I would ask you to stay. It's absolutely throwing it down out there."

The hunted look did not disappear from the woodman's face.

Tarkyn frowned. "I'm not ordering you to stay, only offering. If it makes you feel any better, I'll contract to stay up this end and you can stay down there." Given the restricted size of the shelter, this amounted to little more than a gesture of goodwill. He turned to Sparrow, "Do we have anything to eat?" When Sparrow nodded, he asked, "Could you get it out please and offer some to our guest – if he's staying, that is."

At Running Feet's reluctant nod, Sparrow rooted around in the corner and produced some bread and cheese with two plates. She gave one to Running Feet, saying, "It's okay, you have this plate. Tarkyn and I will share."

Running Feet looked askance at the offered plate. "I think I should be sharing with you," he said to Sparrow. "His Highness should have his own plate."

"No. Don't worry. I share all the time with my uncle," Sparrow grinned, "mainly because he never gets his own."

Running Feet was nonplussed by this answer and accepted the offered plate with reluctance.

"Oh, for goodness' sakes!" exclaimed the prince, losing patience. "It's only bread and cheese. You two have a plate each and I'll just hold mine. There. Are we all happy?"

Running Feet looked anything but happy, but wisely held his peace. When they had finished their austere meal, Tarkyn went back to studying Sparrow's map.

"If we cut the diagonal again," he said, "we can get to a place 12 miles due west of our last campsite and we will only have travelled 20 miles."

Sparrow chortled. "That's great, isn't it? Only eight extra miles."

"Ah yes, you may laugh, but that's only eight extra miles altogether" said Tarkyn, smiling. "And if we don't cut the diagonal, it will be further, I promise you."

Sparrow peered down at her reconstruction of the forest paths and became more serious. "But where are the paths taking us? That's the question. You can't just go in a straight line if it leads you through a bog or over a cliff."

Despite himself, Running Feet leaned in to have a look. "We've just come from over that way." He said, studying Sparrow's diagram. He raised his eyebrows. "You've made a pretty good job of this, young lady. Look. There's the way we came. You have to go around a small brambly patch here and there's a long exposed area of heather there. You really have to skirt around it even though it's easy walking because you are too far from cover. But basically, His Highness is right. You can cut the diagonal to get you back over the road. There's quite a good place to cross just where it bends down to the southwest before straightening out to head west again. See? There."

"Running Feet, where's the encampment?" asked Tarkyn.

The woodman glanced at the prince then drew an extra line in the dirt that extended the map out to the west. "About here," he said, "Pretty much due north of the point where you will turn to head south over the mountains."

"How far due north of our path?"

Running Feet screwed up his face while he considered it. "Twelve, maybe fourteen miles due north. Not far. You'll have to take extra care around there. They may have riding patrols that far south. They certainly will have them near the road and that will only be two or three miles north of your path."

Tarkyn whistled. "That's going to be dangerous, especially for the littlies like this one," he said, ruffling Sparrow's hair.

"I'm not little. I fought against the wolves."

Tarkyn transferred his gaze to give her his full attention, "When it comes to men as big as me on horse back, we're all going to feel little. And I don't want any heroics from you, young lady. You make sure you stay with one of us all the time. You promise? I wouldn't want to lose you."

Sparrow looked at him for a serious moment then climbed up onto his cross-legged lap and leant against him. Tarkyn put his arms around her and gave her a kiss on the top of the head. "Don't worry, little one. We'll look after you. That's why it's good to talk to people like Running Feet who can tell us what to expect."

The prince looked up to find Running Feet watching him with a strange expression on his face. Tarkyn frowned, "Is anything wrong?"

The woodman shook his head. "No. No, you're just a little unexpected, that's all."

Tarkyn smiled and gave Sparrow a little squeeze. "Oh, don't be fooled by this. I'm still the same arrogant, autocratic bastard you all love to hate. No one's bad all the time."

Finally, an answering smile dawned on the woodman's face. "I'm beginning to think you're not very bad at all."

Tarkyn gave a wry grin. "Coming from you, that is high praise indeed. You know, I never set out to be bad. In fact, to be honest, the only really bad thing I have done is what I did to you. Everything else is a matter of opinion." He looked down at the top of Sparrow's head. "And let's face it; at least I'm not as bossy as this little madam." For which statement, he received a jab in the ribs. "Ow. Just as well my ribs are healed, isn't it?"

"You are so more bossy than me," came a muffled voice. "Running Feet said so."

The prince raised his eyebrows at the woodman who looked mildly horrified at this turn of events. "Now look at the trouble you've landed me in." Tarkyn addressed the top of Sparrow's head again. "Okay. Maybe yesterday I was more bossy. But I'm not usually."

Sparrow lifted her head and Tarkyn was relieved to see she was laughing. "Oh yes you are. Daddy says so. But," she added kindly, "he says you're not as bossy as you used to be."

"Waterstone: Fount of all wisdom," explained Tarkyn. He frowned. "I really don't know what you woodfolk found to talk about before I came along. I seem to be a source of constant entertainment for all of you."

Unexpectedly, Sparrow's eyes met Running Feet's and they grinned at each other.

The prince sighed. "Well, that says it all, really. By the way Running Feet, just to put you out of your misery, we all realised I had come on too strongly yesterday morning. So I decided I might as well say everything I needed to say and then leave. Hence your double whammy." Tarkyn smiled reminiscently. "Even Waterstone was shocked by that little effort, especially by what I said to Tree Wind and your group."

He paused, then asked Running Feet, "Have you spoken much to Waterstone or to any of the others who have been with me?"

Running Feet hesitated then shook his head. "Not very much. To be honest, I didn't really want to know."

"Have any other people in the harvesters and gatherers?"

Running Feet shrugged, "Not much. Maybe Ancient Oak, but he tends to keep his own counsel. Generally, I think everyone has been trying to ignore the fact that you are here and that the oath has been invoked."

"Blast it!" exclaimed the prince. He waved a reassuring hand when he saw Running Feet flinch. "Don't worry. I'm not angry with you. But I've just realised that I have seriously overestimated how much you communicate to each other with your mind talking. I thought everything that was happening with us was being communicated to you." He took a deep breath. "No wonder there is still so much resentment among you. You're still back with your impressions of me from the first day. In fact, all you've had to work with, is me losing my temper and threatening everyone and, as I found out only two days ago, the fact that I inadvertently forced another forty hapless individuals to take that blasted oath." He looked at Running Feet. "On top of that, there are people like you and Tree Wind who would have been feeding the resentment."

Seeing the shutters go down in Running Feet's face, Tarkyn continued quickly. "Oh, I don't blame you. I don't know what Tree Wind's particular problem is, but you have every justification for undermining me." He sighed, "The question is, what are we going to do about it?" Tarkyn waved his hand impatiently. "Stop looking so worried. I'm not going to do anything to you. I want your help to reduce the resentment."

"Why should I help you?" Surprisingly, this was not said belligerently.

The prince stared at him. Finally he said, "Not for my benefit particularly, if that's what you're wondering – although I can't say I enjoy being the focal point for all that antagonism." Tarkyn frowned."I suppose there are three main reasons. Firstly, if I request your cooperation as your forest guardian, I don't want resentment to undermine the safety of woodfolk or the forest - which is what I saw happening yesterday. Secondly, I don't want the people with me to become unfairly isolated from other woodfolk because I am with them." He paused and the side of his mouth lifted into a self-deprecatory smile. "And thirdly, I really don't want you living in dread of how I might treat you all, under the terms of the oath."

Running Feet raised his eyebrows. "I'm impressed. Those are very persuasive reasons."

Tarkyn looked at him quizzically, "What did you think I'd say? That you owe it to me because of the oath?"

"Something like that. Well, you could just order me to help you."

"What? And risk the forest's welfare while you try to find ways to undermine me?" The prince shook his head. "You can't just order resentment to go away. If you could, I would have done it long ago."

"So, do none of the woodfolk with you feel at all resentful at having to serve you? I find that hard to believe."

Tarkyn put his head on one side as he considered. He gave a Sparrow a little push in the ribs and asked, "What do you think, young madam? Do people still resent me?"

Sparrow looked up and frowned, "What do you mean? Do they get mad at you? Only sometimes."

Tarkyn smiled. "That wasn't quite what I meant, but it will do." He looked up at the woodman. "Sometimes the resentment wells up. Waterstone and I came to blows over it the other day." Tarkyn ignored the shocked incomprehension on the woodman's face. "Mostly, we're all right. It's not easy, but it can be better than what I see amongst the harvesters and gatherers. And, if you ask them, I think you'll find that my little group would rather have me than not, now."

Sparrow nodded her confirmation of this.

"In fact, I think they're even quite proud of me now that we've worked out I'm a guardian of the forest."

Sparrow nodded even more vigorously. "Although he didn't look too good when he was green."

Running Feet frowned in consternation as Sparrow sent him an image of the green Tarkyn.

Tarkyn laughed at his expression. "Not a good look, was it? That was the healing force of an old oak tree. I think I might have overdone it a bit. Still, as you can see, it faded over time."

Running Feet blinked as he took all this in. He was silent for a couple of minutes, then finally said, "Very well. I am prepared to help, now that I understand why it is important. What do I need to do?"

The prince thought carefully. "Update your people on what has been happening since I arrived in the forest. Talk to the forestals and the home guard and give them a fair hearing. I promise you I haven't ordered them to say anything in particular."

Running Feet looked puzzled. "Who are the home guard?"

Tarkyn glanced at him. "Now, this is not for public consumption, but that is what I privately call the people who have stuck by me."

"Do they know this?"

"Yes. I let it slip out yesterday by mistake. They all went into deep shock but they are gradually recovering." Tarkyn laughed at the look of consternation on Running Feet's face. "No, they didn't. They don't mind. In fact, Ancient Oak and Rainstorm have aspirations of joining."

Running Feet shook his head a little as he dealt with one impression after another from the prince. He gave a slight smile and said ruefully, "Even if I do update everyone, I suspect there will always be some resentment, my lord."

Tarkyn gave a bitter laugh, "I'm sure there will be. Woodfolk such as Sun Shower know all that has happened, aren't even under oath and still resent my subtle leadership style. So it's not going to cure anything. It just might make it a little more manageable."

"So, from your point of view, what has happened since we left you?"

Tarkyn acknowledged the woodman's subtly expressed scepticism with a slight smile before sketching out events since he had regained consciousness; repairing the forest, his discussions about etiquette with Waterstone and Autumn Leaves, the run-ins with the wolves and horsemen, their efforts to disguise the wolves' fates, the discovery that he was the forest guardian, his fight with Waterstone and the subsequent healing.

When he came to more recent events, Tarkyn leaned over his niece and frowned at her. "Sparrow, block your ears and hum loudly." When he was sure she couldn't hear him, he continued, "And I gather from Ancient Oak that you have all been talking about my initial meeting with the forestals?"

"Yes, Sire. I believe they came close to killing you."

"I gave them that choice," said Tarkyn matter-of-factly. His mouth twitched in a half smile. "They thought hard about it and there were a few arrows flying around for a while there. But it was a risk I had to take. I could not allow the possibility of oathbound woodfolk having to fight other woodfolk to protect me." He shrugged. "And in the end, woodfolk honour prevented them from killing me to free you from the oath."

Running Feet considered him. "Offering your life was an enormous gesture for a people you hardly knew."

"Noblesse oblige, Running Feet," said the prince lightly, although he clearly meant it."I'm glad it remained only a gesture, though. The outcome was by no means certain, I can tell you." He looked levelly at Running Feet. "What's more, I did it in all good faith and it would be nice if it made a difference. Now, we seem to have swapped one rift for another."

At this point, the sound of humming increased significantly in volume.

"Whoops. Sorry, Sparrow," Tarkyn pulled her hands way from her ears. "I said, 'Sorry Sparrow'. You can stop now." He looked up at Running Feet with a smile. "End of discussion for the moment, I think."

By mid morning the rain had still not relented. Damp patches were beginning to show on the ceiling of Tarkyn's shelter but it had so far held. It was so dark outside that it was hard to believe it was nearly midday. Running Feet and Sparrow had explored all the possible routes on their dusty map, with Tarkyn taking an intermittent interest. Suddenly, Sparrow raised her head and looked intently at Tarkyn.

"Daddy needs to talk to you." she said. She went out of focus for a couple of minutes then reported, "Stormaway is with him. He is saying that this storm is not natural."

The prince frowned. "Oh no. I hope it's not from the oath. Ask your dad to talk straight to Running Feet, could you?" He flicked a glance at the woodman to check that this arrangement was all right and received a brief nod.

"Why not me?" asked Sparrow, much put out.

"Because it's grown up's business. They may need to use big words you won't know. Don't worry. I'll tell you everything you need to know. Okay?"

Sparrow narrowed her eyes at him but complied with his request.

Shortly afterwards, Running Feet also went out of focus. After a while, the prince said, "Stop gossiping about me and keep to the point."

Running Feet flicked back into focus. "If you can't mind talk, how did you know we were?"

Tarkyn smiled, "Stands to reason. Waterstone wanted to know what you're doing in my shelter and what you thought of being stuck with me after our last little encounter. Once he has that all sorted out, he'll know how far to trust you with relaying messages to me....Correct?"

Running Feet smiled in return. "Correct."

"So. What is Stormaway saying about this storm? Is it a backlash from someone undermining me?"

The woodman shook his head. "He doesn't think it has anything to do with the oath. He thinks someone might be trying to flood us out. The stream is rising. It's nearly up to the top of its banks already."

"Who can create a storm like this? And how on earth do they know we are here?" Tarkyn nodded at him impatiently. "Go on. Ask them."

Running Feet returned to focus very quickly this time.

"Well?"

A slight frown of annoyance appeared on Running Feet's face as he answered shortly. "Waterstone will get back to me when he has talked about it with Stormaway."

The prince took one look at the woodman's taut face and sighed. "Sorry. Please tell me if I annoy you. It's much better to sort it out than having you going off to tell everyone what a tyrant I am. I'm just worried. And when I get tense, I have a tendency to cut corners and become peremptory."

Running Feet's face relaxed. "It must be frustrating needing a translator for the mind talking."

"It is."

This conversation was curtailed as Running Feet was pressed to reply to Waterstone. After a short mind-discussion, the woodman reported back to the prince, "A wizard can drum up this sort of weather, according to Stormaway, though he would need time to create enough power."

"Hmph, when you think about Stormaway's name, it's pretty obvious really," said Tarkyn. "So, can Stormaway counter this other wizard's spell?"

"He says he may be able to but he will need more power if he is do to it quickly enough to stop flooding. He wants you to help him."

"Of course I will. But before we organise that, what about the second question? That's even more important. How do they know we're here?"

Running Feet shook his head. "Stormaway doesn't think anyone does know we're here. He thinks the storm is more general than that and that someone is possibly trying to herd us up onto higher ground…"

"….where presumably sorcerers and wolves will be waiting." The prince said nothing for a few minutes while he collected his thoughts. Then he turned to Running Feet.

"Speak to Stormaway and Waterstone. Ask for their opinions on what we should do"

After Running Feet had reported back, Tarkyn said, "I'm afraid I'm going to have to make sure a few things are put in place before I help Stormaway." He gave a wry smile. "That is a euphemism for issuing orders, in case you hadn't worked it out. I remember a captain of the guards once said to me, the more critical the situation, the more directive you must be."

"See," said a shaky little voice. "More bossy than me."

"Oh Sparrow, come here." Immediately she climbed up onto Tarkyn's lap and he wrapped his arms around her. "Don't be frightened. We will sort it out. Stormaway and I will do lots of interesting magic and make the storm go away. Now, you just snuggle up quietly while I boss everyone around. How's that?"

Sparrow just nodded and pressed herself against his chest.

Tarkyn stroked her hair and made sure she was settled before looking at Running Feet. "You're in the unlucky position of being the messenger.

Ready?" When the woodman nodded, Tarkyn said, "Right. Tell everyone I am speaking as the guardian of the forest and I need their full cooperation. Tell them what Waterstone and Stormaway have worked out about the storm."

Tarkyn waited until Running Feet indicated he had done this, and then continued, "We must make sure we have an escape route from the rising water that does not take us where they expect us. In other words, we'll need to evacuate downhill somewhere, perhaps up into trees. I don't know. I'll leave that to local knowledge to sort out. If it means we have to leave sooner, then we will."

Tarkyn waited with raised eyebrows until Running Feet nodded. "I have only just realised that you don't all keep in contact with each other using mind talk as a matter of course. So we need an inventory of all woodfolk everywhere. Do we know where everyone is? It is my fear that these hunters have captured some woodfolk somehow. It is the only explanation that fits the facts. Who is missing? Are there some people too far away to contact? We need to make sure everyone is accounted for and contactable, not just those who have come here." The prince paused again. He waved a hand. "Don't transmit this bit. How are we going? Do we have a mass rebellion yet?"

Running Feet gave a reluctant smile and shook his head. "They haven't had time to organise it yet because they can't get a word in edgeways."

"Good. I'll keep going before they do. Ready?" At the woodman's nod, he began again. "We will need to mount a rescue mission. If they have captured some woodfolk, they are probably being held at that encampment. So start talking to the people who have seen the encampment and start thinking about how a rescue can be undertaken. That's it from your friendly neighbourhood tyrant for today." Running Feet looked queringly at this, but Tarkyn smiled and nodded to send it. "I will be working with Stormaway for the next little while if anyone wants me."

The prince grinned, "Well, that should give everyone something to think about and complain about, to while away a few damp hours stuck inside."

A little voice issued from the region of Tarkyn's chest. "I think you're getting bossier."

Tarkyn laughed. "I think you're right. All my good intentions in tatters again, hey, little one?" He looked across at Running Feet. "Thank you for doing that. If you get any backlash at all from it, I want to know about it."

"Is that another order?"

The prince grimaced, “Yes, I’m afraid so. If I make it an order, you don’t have to debate whether to tell me or not. You just do it. Then no-one can blame you for informing on them.” Tarkyn regarded him quizzically. “So, I suppose I’m back in your bad books now? You may find this hard to believe but I have generally avoided giving anyone direct orders until this crisis.”

Running Feet raised his eyebrows. “It doesn’t really matter what I think, does it, my lord?”

Tarkyn frowned, “Do you say that because you think little of yourself, or little of me?”

“I’m saying it because I assume you think little of me.”

“Because of what I did to you before?” Tarkyn’s mouth twisted in a rueful smile. “I know I treated you with great disdain at our first encounter, but I didn’t know you or anyone else then…And I felt trapped and angry. Now I’ve had a chance to get to know you, I do care about your opinion. In fact, I would have sought you out to make reparation but you chose, quite understandably, to stay away from me. To tell you the truth, I am quite anxious to have your good opinion because I feel guilty about what I did to you.”

Running Feet have his head a little shake, a queer smile playing around his lips. “Then, for what it is worth, I still think you throw your weight around but you do it in support of woodfolk, not for yourself. And although I will probably still keep having nightmares about being dropped from great heights, I could not have spent these hours with you without changing my opinion of you. You are not the haughty tyrant I was anticipating. Despite my expectations, I find I like you but I’m not surprised everyone talks about you all the time. You are quite an amazing person. You take responsibility for everyone and see everything so clearly.”

Tarkyn blinked in surprise at the accolades. “I have to. I’m your forest guardian and I swore an oath to protect you. Everyone is expecting me to pull them through even while some of them hate me. But I would have to say that I don’t see everything clearly. I definitely get things wrong sometimes.”

Running Feet smiled, “I think I can attest to that. Perhaps I exaggerated slightly but you do see the overall picture very well.”

“Thank you.” Tarkyn hesitated, “Maybe when this particular crisis is over, I could help you get rid of the nightmares.” He shrugged a shoulder. “Oh, why wait? Let’s do it quickly now. It’ll only take a couple of minutes. Hang on. Am I going there or is Stormaway coming here? Could you find out please – and when?”

"They will come here because your shelter is bigger. They'll be here in about ten minutes."

Tarkyn smiled reassuringly at the woodman. "Are you willing to let me try to get rid of your nightmares? I think I can do it with my forest guardian powers."

"Have you done it before?"

"No," said Tarkyn, shaking his head, "but I have healed myself and others. Of course if you do stop having nightmares, we'll never know if it was because you met up with me and put your demons to rest or whether it was the healing. Other than that, you have nothing to lose. It doesn't hurt and it's not unpleasant."

"And you won't turn green," piped up a little voice.

Running Feet addressed Sparrow. "How do you know? Have you had it done to you?"

Sparrow nodded. "Tarkyn gave us all more energy when we had travelled through trees all day. It was quite nice, really."

"Okay. Go on then," agreed Running Feet. "What do I have to do?"

"Close your eyes. I'm going to put my hand on your shoulder. Now, think about your dream and the fear in it. As you do, I will send healing force into you. You will have to direct the force yourself to soothe the fear in the memory and gradually dissipate the nightmare. Ready?"

When the woodman nodded, the forest guardian drew forth his *esse* and sent it into Running Feet. As Tarkyn watched, he could see Running Feet's face and shoulders relaxing. When the changes stopped, Tarkyn asked, "Enough?"

Running Feet nodded and opened his eyes. He smiled and the tension in his face that no one had particularly noticed, was no longer there. "It's gone. I know it has. Thank you. Even if you were the cause, you have also been the cure. So you have made reparation, as you wanted to."

Chapter 36

Five people in a shelter made for one was proving to be logistical nightmare. Every time anyone needed to move to keep a limb from cramping up or going to sleep, the others had to re-arrange themselves to accommodate them. Sparrow was getting tired of sitting on Tarkyn's or her dad's lap but there wasn't any room for her in between.

"Don't worry, Sparrow," Waterstone was saying, "The two biggest people are leaving soon. Then we'll have plenty of room."

"Good," said a seriously discontented little girl. "Then I can show you my map and Running Feet can tell you all about it." She gave a little huff, "Well, I could have shown it to you, except you're sitting on it and it will be all smudged."

"I'm sure you'll be able to fix it up." Waterstone glanced at Running Feet who was sitting beside him while the sorcerer and the wizard planned their tactics up the other end. "It's good to see you again. We used to spend a lot of time together before… well, before Tarkyn arrived. In fact, you were always with Autumn Leaves and Thunder Storm and me. I suppose that was why you were in the frontline when his lordship lost his temper. We were just lucky he didn't pick one of us instead of you… Have you been all right?"

Running Feet turned his head to look at his old friend. "I am now but I haven't been. I couldn't sleep for weeks afterwards. As soon as I would start to drift off, I would wake with a jerk, thinking I was falling. Only recently I've been able to get to sleep but I've always woken several times a night with the same nightmare of being lifted up and then dropped."

"Oh, you poor bastard! You must have been horrified when you realised whose shelter you'd come into."

"I was." Running Feet grimaced, "What's worse, by the time I realised, I had already opened my big mouth and complained to Sparrow about His Highness throwing his weight around."

Waterstone glanced across at the prince. The woodman was pretty sure that Tarkyn would have half an ear tuned to their conversation, but he had no intention of letting that affect what he was saying to Running Feet. "Did he get angry? … Silly question. Did he get angry for long?"

Running Feet shook his head. "In fairness, he came over threatening for about thirty seconds. Then Sparrow pulled him up and he stopped. Once he discovered who I was, he couldn't have been nicer but he had already backed off before that." The woodman gave a small sigh, "I have probably done him quite a bit of damage, you know. I've twisted and derided anything good that we heard about him. And everyone was just looking for reasons to hate him. So it wasn't hard."

"And now he's forced you to send out his latest pronouncements."

Running Feet gave a small smile. "No. He didn't force me. He just assumed I'd do it." He grinned, "But he did order me to tell him if I get any kickback from it."

"Did he?" Waterstone raised his eyebrows. "In all the time I've known him, he hasn't given me a single order. Yes he did, just one. But that was just something silly between him and me," he added, making light of something that actually mattered a great deal to him.

"So he was telling the truth about that, was he? He said he was making it an order so that I didn't have to choose."

Waterstone shrugged, "You have to give it to him. That was a good reason to give an order." He paused, "By the way, just so you know, Tarkyn never deliberately lies."

Running Feet watched the prince in animated conversation as he said slowly, "So I can take it that everything he told me about his time with you people is true?"

"Yes. Of course it is. Only a fool would tell you lies that you could go straight out and disprove."

"He was courageous, wasn't he, to throw himself on the mercy of the forestals?"

Waterstone flicked a warning glance down at his daughter. "We were not very happy with him about that," he said tightly. "Tarkyn left in the middle of the night and made sure we couldn't follow him, to protect the forest. But he didn't consider how we would have felt at our failure to protect him." The woodman grunted, "Actually at that stage, he probably thought we wouldn't care. But he was wrong. We really don't want to lose him…any more than I would want to lose this little ratbag," he added, giving his daughter a squeeze and a tickle that made her twist and giggle in his lap.

Running Feet smiled but quickly became serious again. "But how can you stand having someone in charge all the time when we are all used to having an equal say in things?"

Waterstone raised his eyebrows in surprise. "Tarkyn's not in charge. Whatever gave you that idea?"

"Oh, I don't know," replied Running Feet sarcastically, "Something about his manner, the constant stream of edicts…the way he takes over all the discussions."

"He is at the heart of many discussions," conceded Waterstone. "And sometimes he does have an arrogant air about him, like last night for example. But not all the time by any means." The woodman smiled, "And the stream of edicts? We all worked them out together during the afternoon when everyone else was giving him the cold shoulder. We would have included everyone but the morning session showed us that it wasn't viable. In case you didn't notice, most of this morning's edicts, as you call them, were basically the recommendations made by Stormaway and me. Our forest guardian is the only person who can command everyone's attention at a time when we can't afford the luxury of long debates and inaction. So he's prepared to put up with being disliked to make sure we can protect ourselves."

Running Feet frowned. "He seems to have a strong tendency towards self sacrifice."

"He does when he feels it's needed." Waterstone shook his head. "It worries me sometimes. Most of it stems from the oath he swore to us, but the other morning, I'm not so sure about. From what I've been told, I'd say he was right on the edge. He didn't just give them the opportunity to... you know." He glanced down at his daughter, "I think he was almost trying to talk them into it." He looked steadily at his friend. "He was devastated by what he saw as our betrayal of him. We've sorted it out now, but he doesn't give trust easily. You have no idea how hard it was to get him to trust us after the repeated betrayals he has suffered." Waterstone's voice developed a distinct edge to it. "I would not like to see anyone develop a closeness with him and then betray his trust. They would have his home guard to answer to."

Running Feet's eyes widened. "You really do care about him, don't you?"

Waterstone shrugged, easing off the tension. "I wouldn't let just anyone into my family."

"I suppose not. I was surprised by that, I must admit, but not so much now as I was." Running Feet paused. "In answer to your unspoken question, I have no intention of undermining him any further than I already have done." The woodman glanced at his friend. "But I suppose I would say that, wouldn't I, whatever I was going to do?"

Waterstone considered him for a few seconds before replying. "No, my friend, I don't think you would. You have been honest about undermining him in the past, after all. A lot has changed since we last met but a lot remains the same and I hope you will be able to travel again with us sometime."

Running Feet surprised him by saying, "I would come with you now if I could, but the prince has asked me to help reduce the resentment among the other woodfolk. So I think I'll do that first. But perhaps I may join you further down the track."

Before Waterstone had time to reflect on the astonishing change that had been wrought in Running Feet's attitude in the course of one short morning, Tarkyn interrupted, "Right. We're off. We need a strong tree to draw strength from, so unfortunately that means getting wet."

"Are you going to be focussing as hard as you did with me?" asked Running Feet.

"Yes, probably harder." The prince raised his eyebrows, "Why do you ask?"

"Well, you can't go off without protection if you're going to lose sight of your surroundings." Running Feet grabbed his boots from next to the doorway. "Wait. I'll come with you."

Waterstone raised his eyebrows, "He's right, you know. I should have thought of that."

"What? Not the Fount of all Wisdom all the time?" quipped Running Feet, as he pulled on his shoes.

"Who said I was?" demanded the woodman.

"I did," said Tarkyn with a grin. He looked at Running Feet. "You'll need weapons. I don't have any in here. Waterstone…?"

"Wait a minute. I'll ask Autumn Leaves to come down with bows and quivers and he can go with you and get wet too. Sadly, I'll have to stay here in the dry and mind Sparrow." Waterstone promptly went out of focus.

Shortly afterwards, Autumn Leaves arrived outside. "Come on, you lot," he shouted. "I'm getting soaked out here."

When they emerged from the shelter, they found Ancient Oak had also joined them.

"Hello, little brother," he said as Tarkyn straightened up out of the shelter to tower over him. "Mind if I come along? I want to watch your magic display and I can guard your back at the same time."

Tarkyn grinned at him. "The more the merrier, although I think you're mad. I wouldn't come out in this, if I didn't have to." He pushed his already soaking hair out of his eyes. "There are some big old oaks along the stream this way. We'll use one of them. At least their branches will provide a bit of shelter." He turned to Stormaway as he walked, "Are you all right?"

The wizard nodded tetchily, "As good as I'm going to be, soaked to the skin and cold."

"I don't suppose you know any warming or dry spells, do you?" asked the sorcerer hopefully.

"Yes, I do, but we're going to need all our power to fight this storm."

"What about a shield?"

The wizard shook his head. "Come on. Just get on with it. We don't want to risk attracting the attention of whoever's creating this storm by using magic until we're ready to challenge him or her."

"All right. All right. I'm going as fast as I can without falling over in the mud."

The gentle stream of yesterday had turned into a raging torrent. In several places, the prince and his little entourage had to skirt around areas where the water had spilled over the banks of the stream.

Just as they reached the tree line, Lapping Water and Rainstorm came running through the rain to join them. Tarkyn noted their arrival with mixed feelings. He would have been glad to see either of them on their own but their joint arrival sent a twinge of jealousy through him. Resolutely stamping down on his feelings, he greeted them both warmly and returned his attention to the task at hand.

Once the group reached the shelter of the trees, there was a noticeable abatement in the force of both wind and rain.

"This one should do," said Tarkyn, patting his hand against the trunk of a tall sturdy oak. "Old, but not too old."

The sorcerer stood beside the oak and placed his right hand against the trunk. He placed his left hand on Stormaway's shoulder and waited. As the wizard closed his eyes and began to concentrate, Tarkyn looked beyond him to see a ring of faces watching intently. "I don't think I'm going to be able to focus with you people staring at us like that. Besides, I can't see how you will have any hope of protecting us with your backs to the rest of the world."

"Good point," said Autumn Leaves with a grin. "Come on. Let's back off a bit."

Once the woodfolk had redeployed themselves less obtrusively, Tarkyn closed his eyes and focused within himself to find his essence. Then he reached out through the palm of his right hand to connect with the inner strength of the great oak. When he could feel himself blending with the oak, he transferred his focus to his left hand and sent a trickle of power into Stormaway.

"Right," he said, "I'm ready. I can give you as much power as you need now. Just let me know."

Tarkyn felt Stormaway's shoulder move slightly as the wizard nodded.

Suddenly, unexpectedly, Tarkyn found his mind joined with the wizard's. He could see the storm through the wizard's eyes; sense the swirling clouds high above them and feel their source somewhere several miles beyond the stream. The sorcerer followed the wizard as he explored the extent and texture of the turbulence. It soon became clear that the clouds of the storm were slowly rotating in a clockwise direction around a distant focal point.

For the first time, Stormaway spoke. "It is easier to work with a force than against it. We will augment the clockwise rotation and add in a vertical component. That will have the added advantage of disguising our interference for longer. By the time the storm-maker realises what is happening, he or she will be unable to counteract it."

"That sounds simple enough," said Tarkyn.

"There is nothing simple about working with weather," replied Stormaway repressively. "Follow my lead."

"Am I going to use my power separately or direct it all through you?"

"Through me, to start with. Once I tune in to the movement of the storm and begin to add my force to the wind, you can break off and use your power to force the clouds upwards."

Even as he spoke, a vast green column of light thrust upwards through the boughs of the tree. As it cleared the roof of the forest, the column bent before the force of the wind just as a slender sapling would. Then the wizard directed more power into it so that instead of being pushed before the wind, the green column streamed forth, spreading out across the sky and driving the clouds before it.

There was a long delay before the effects of Stormaway's efforts translated themselves around the full circle of the storm. Tarkyn could feel the strength of the great oak pouring through him as the wizard's magic demanded more power. Then, slowly the wind increased in velocity until, after a time, it was howling through the trees.

"Now," yelled Stormaway above the roar of the storm. "Break off and drive your own power upward."

As the sorcerer removed his hand from the wizard's shoulder, his eyes flew open, glowing like lanterns in the dim light. He thrust his arm skywards and bronze light arced upward into the sky. As it hit the clouds, it spread into a glowing wall. The clouds began to build up behind it.

"Not straight up," yelled the wizard, "Angle it."

The sorcerer did not reply but the top of the bronze wall swung away from the wind. Immediately, the bank of clouds rolled up its incline.

"Higher. You have to take it higher as the cloud lifts," shouted Stormaway.

A few minutes later the wizard yelled, "I'm going to join my power to yours. We have to keep increasing the height of the wall. Keep yours steady until I take over. Then bring your hand back onto my shoulder and we'll combine forces again."

Stormaway's green magic contracted and swung back up until it was running parallel with Tarkyn's bronze wall of power.

"Ready? Now keep your eyes open, focussed on your power. Let your eyes take over from your hand."

In answer, bronze light seemed to stream from both the sorcerer's upstretched hand and his glowing amber eyes.

"Keep it steady," shouted Stormaway. "Hold your focus. Now, bring down your arm and put your hand back on my shoulder."

As soon as Tarkyn's hand touched the wizard's shoulder, the two walls of light slammed together and a wave of power rippled up from the ground to disappear into the roiling clouds above.

A short time later, Tarkyn realised he wasn't being buffeted by the wind any more. But overhead, he could still see the branches being thrashed about and he could still hear the wind's howl. As he watched, the lower of branches of the oak quietened and gradually level after level of the tree stilled. The wind still shrieked above the tree line but all around him, the forest was quiet. As the clouds rose, the rain began to ease.

"We've done it," murmured Stormaway quietly. "It will be self perpetuating from now on. The clouds are spiralling upwards.- Now, let your power go slowly. Then I'll release mine. If you can just keep your hand on my shoulder for a little longer, it might save me from collapsing with fatigue."

As Tarkyn drew in his bronze wall and redirected the flow of energy into the wizard, he rocked slightly on his feet as the force changed directions. His eyes stung and he was beginning to feel sick from the constant flow of power using him as a conduit from the oak to the wizard.

A few minutes later, the forest guardian asked in a tight voice, "Enough? I can't manage much more. I think I'm going to throw up. It feels as though I have a river running through me."

"Yes. Thank you Tarkyn. That's enough. Don't make yourself sick."

"Too late, I'm afraid." He doubled over and heaved.

"Ooh dear," remarked Autumn Leaves, appearing out of nowhere, "you've gone green again."

"I feel green."

"That was great," enthused Ancient Oak, "Absolutely unbelievable."

Tarkyn looked sideways at him from his doubled up position. "It doesn't feel great, I can tell you."

Stormaway slapped him on the back. "Don't worry, young man. The feeling will pass. You did a fine job."

The sorcerer finally straightened up, wiping his mouth on his bandage. He was a distinctive shade of pale moss green and it was hard to tell what his own pallor would be underneath it

Lapping Water looked him over thoughtfully. She spoke softly. "My lord, I don't mean to be rude, but why don't you give back some of the power to the oak? Then you might get rid of some of the green."

Tarkyn looked askance at her, thinking that being a forest guardian wasn't very good for one's image. He ran his hand through his sodden hair. "I don't know that I could stand it, just at the moment."

Stormaway gave him another gentle pat. "I think you'll find that if the power is only going out of you and not in at the same time, you won't feel that queasiness."

Tarkyn looked at each of them in turn, then resolutely placed his hand back on the oak's trunk. "All right. Tell me when my colour goes back to normal." He took a deep breath and focused on sending some of his life force back into the oak.

"Stop!" came a chorus of voices.

Tarkyn opened his eyes and grinned. "Thanks." He inspected himself. He looked healthier, although he knew his legs were still a little shaky and his stomach was right on the edge."I feel a bit better now. Probably just as well I did that. Last time I went green, I had an over-abundance of energy, as I recall, and came on rather too strongly." He laughed. "I think if I came on any stronger at the moment with the folk back there, we'd have a mass rebellion."

"They would be an ungrateful pack of bastards if they did that," responded Rainstorm hotly.

"Oh, I don't know," replied Tarkyn. "I think it is Stormaway they have to thank more than me." He turned to the wizard and said seriously, "And I thank you too, Stormaway. That was truly amazing. You have so much knowledge that I lack. And it is your skill, not mine that has saved the woodfolk from this crisis."

"I have had a few more years to accrue it, you know, young man," he responded gruffly. Nevertheless, Stormaway was clearly gratified by the prince's acknowledgement.

Looking around at the group of bedraggled but happy woodfolk, Tarkyn said, "And thank you to all of you too, for coming out in this terrible weather. I hope it was worth it."

"Best compensation I've ever had for doing lookout duty," said Ancient Oak, endorsed with great enthusiastism by those behind him.

"I think this will go a long way towards dissolving some of that resentment, Your Highness," said Running Feet.

"Perhaps," Tarkyn smiled wryly at the others. "Having just discovered that no one outside the home guard has heard much about our recent activities, I realise I still have their terrible first impressions of me to overcome."

"I thought you said you didn't care what people thought of you," said Ancient Oak.

Tarkyn glanced sideways at him. "To be honest, I may have been a bit angry when I said that. It's probably more that I can't afford to care too much."

He was distracted by sounds of shouting and cheering that grew louder as they rounded the last clump of trees. As they reached the edge of the clearing, the prince and his small entourage were greeted by the sight of all the woodfolk, young and old, completely soaked like themselves, waving and smiling at them as they walked towards them.

Tarkyn gave a puzzled frown. "What's going on?"

"How could you ask? The best sound and light show we've seen in years, possibly ever," beamed Raging Water. "We weren't going to let a little thing like torrential rain put us off."

"Tarkyn and Stormaway, on behalf of everyone, I thank you," said Sun Shower, smiling. She walked forward and patted the sorcerer on the back. "I'm sorry I called you an upstart, young Tarkyn. I could see that remark smarted. And even in the face of our antagonism, you have still fought to support us."

"And you, you old rogue," said Raging Water bracingly to Stormaway. "You might be a stubborn old bastard, but your orchestration of that attack on the storm was magnificent."

"But how did you all know what was happening?" asked Tarkyn.

Waterstone and Sparrow walked out of the trees from behind the prince. The woodman grinned at him. "Running Feet and I knew everyone would be interested in seeing some magic. So we made sure they all knew. We've been sending them images of what you and Stormaway were doing on the ground to explain what they were seeing in the sky." He smiled down at Sparrow. "And there was no way Sparrow was going to let me sit in the nice dry shelter when all this excitement was happening out here."

"We've been watching with Autumn Leaves and Running Feet," said Sparrow, with a big smile.

"Oh, have you now?" The prince looked around in a bit of a daze. He shook his wet hair and sent spray over all those stranding near him. He gave a vague grin. "Sorry about that. I don't suppose anyone has been able to light a fire in all this wet?" he asked hopefully.

"No one's tried yet but we'll have one going in no time. Then everyone can dry out," replied Falling Branch. He looked at the wizard, "Perhaps you could give us a hand with one of those spells you mentioned?"

Stormaway nodded. "I think our young forest guardian here replenished my strength quite sufficiently for that. Lead the way."

CHAPTER 37

With the assistance of the wizard's magic, a cheery, warm fire had been lit and the ground around it had been dried out. Woodfolk were all master bushcraftsmen and could have lit the fire quite easily even in the damp conditions, but they couldn't have dried out the ground. Besides which, they were all keen to see a bit more magic. As an added precaution, Stormaway placed some sort of glamour on the wood smoke so that it could not be seen against the late afternoon sky. All around the clearing, various items of clothing and bedding were hanging on every available twig or branch to dry out.

Stormaway, by nature solitary, found himself the centre of a constant ring of admirers. However, not being one to miss an opportunity, he sat back and made use of the attention so that consequently, many deals for delivery of woodland produce were struck by the end of the evening.

Tarkyn, in a similar position, was failing dismally in his attempts to keep a low profile. Given a choice, he would rather have been on the road far away from this uncertain crowd, leaving them to sort out the details of how to carry out the edicts he had made as their forest guardian. Despite the energy from the oak, he was feeling hammered by the volume of power that had run through his body. His eyes were still bloodshot and smarting and he decided that he wouldn't use them again for transmitting power unless there was no other choice.

When everyone was settled, Summer Rain approached him bearing a new bandage. "My lord, I notice you used your bandage as a hand kerchief when you were ill. So I thought you might like a new one. I've brought one for you too, Waterstone, since yours must be sodden."

Tarkyn smiled at her. "Thank you. That would probably improve the aroma around here."

"Quite possibly," she replied, betraying not a glimmer of humour.

As she unwrapped the old bandage, she leaned forward to inspect the long shallow knife wound. She frowned and ran her fingers gently along it. Tarkyn looked over her shoulder and met Lapping Water's eyes. He grimaced and grinned, knowing what was coming.

"My lord. Your arm has already healed."

Tarkyn eyebrows shot together and he looked down at his arm. That had not been what he had expected or wanted to hear.

"But," continued Summer Rain, "you have a slightly raised, bright green scar all the way along it. Very unusual. Possibly the swelling will go down over time but I'm not sure what we're dealing with here, with the green. Perhaps the oak's healing power has seeped into the tissue of your arm. Most interesting."

Lapping Water moved forward to peer over the healer's shoulder. "Very nice, Sire. Better than you would have expected, in fact," she said with a cryptic smile.

"Yes, it is rather dashing, isn't it?" remarked Tarkyn, holding his arm out to admire the scar.

Summer Rain moved on to Waterstone with her offering of bandages.

Waterstone put up his hand. "No thanks. It will dry in time. I'll just leave it."

The healer frowned. "You should not leave a wet bandage on. Your wound could fester beneath it."

"No thanks. I'll take my chances. I'll make sure I dry it out thoroughly by the fire."

As she turned to leave, her arm brushed against Waterstone's and Tarkyn saw him wince. A dawning suspicion entered the prince's mind. Twenty minutes later, Tarkyn said casually to Waterstone, "Could you come and have a quick look at something for me?"

As soon as they were away from prying eyes and ears, Tarkyn turned to him and said, "Come on. Take the bandage off."

"I would prefer not to," replied Waterstone steadily.

"Come on," urged Tarkyn, "Take it off."

Waterstone's eyes narrowed. "Is that an order?"

"Oh stop being silly. Of course it's not an order. You can be a stubborn old goat if you want to, but I know what I will see when you take it off, so you might as well."

Reluctantly, Waterstone unwound the bandage from his arm. The last layers were stuck to the wound with seeping blood and puss.

"Stars above, Waterstone, your arm is a mess." Tarkyn peered closely at the wound to check that his suspicions were right. "Rubbing dirt into a wound can cause infection, you know."

The woodman turned a dull red.

Tarkyn smiled broadly at him. "Lapping Water told me that, when she caught me doing the same thing yesterday morning."

Waterstone's tight face relaxed into a grin. "Did you do it too?"

Tarkyn nodded, his eyes crinkling with laughter. "Yes, but the oak has healed mine. Luckily, after all that effort, I still have a scar, and a green one, at that." He studied Waterstone's arm. "Come on, my friend. I think I need to give your arm some help with healing."

Seeing Waterstone frown, he added hastily, "Don't worry. I won't take the dirt out but I do think we need to get rid of some of that infection, don't you? We might need your right arm in the days to come." As Waterstone still hesitated, Tarkyn explained, "All I will do is send you some *esse*. It's up to you to direct it as you will."

The woodman nodded reluctantly and complied. When the infection had been eased, Tarkyn said, "Wait here. I'll ask Lapping Water to procure us another bandage. We must maintain your disguise, after all."

A few minutes later, Lapping Water returned with the prince.

"Put out your arm," she instructed the woodman. As she carefully wrapped the bandage around his arm, she said, smiling, "I think you should have a nice clean raised scar at the end of all this. Congratulations."

Waterstone looked anxiously at her. "You won't tell anyone, will you?"

Lapping Water raised her eyebrows. "His Highness had to put up with having his arm unwrapped in full view of everyone. Why shouldn't you?"

Waterstone looked even more anxious. "But no one knew why his arm was like that. They all think it was just the oak tree."

"Ah yes, but he didn't know it was going to look like that and he was prepared to endure the teasing."

Tarkyn directed a small frown at her. "But only because I couldn't think of a way out of it fast enough. I didn't even want Waterstone to know, let alone anyone else." He grinned at his friend. "And I have only told him now because I couldn't let him suffer the embarrassment alone."

Lapping Water let her gaze travel slowly from one to the other, as though considering the matter. Then she smiled. "Don't be silly, Waterstone. Of course I wouldn't tell anyone." She added in a sugary voice, "I think it's so sweet that you want to keep a memento. No wonder you're such good friends: You're each as sentimental as the other." She laughed at the pained expressions on their faces.

Waterstone grimaced and said acerbically, "I think just a third person knowing gives plenty of opportunity for teasing without opening it up to a wider audience."

Lapping Water shook her head, smiling. "I'm sorry. I promise I'll stop now. Shall we go and see if there's some food ready yet?"

When they returned to the gathering around the fire, discussions were in full swing about making sure they were in contact with all woodfolk and trying to work out who could be missing. A great deal of it was mind talking, but Tarkyn did not ask to be updated or included and was content to sit quietly among the animated woodfolk. Now and again, someone would try to draw him into the conversation but he kept his responses minimal.

After a while, Autumn Leaves came over and sat down next to him.

"Are you all right?" he asked quietly.

Tarkyn nodded. "A bit drained, but fine otherwise."

Autumn Leaves frowned at him, "You're not in a huff, are you?"

The prince raised his eyebrows and looked at the woodman in some surprise. "No. Why do you ask?"

Autumn Leaves shrugged, "You're so quiet, that's all."

"I am trying to be unobtrusive," explained the prince, with a wry smile. "I think I've had more than my fair share of centre stage over the last few days. I've said all I needed to say. It's up to everyone else now."

"And is everyone keeping you in the picture?"

"Not as much as we all agreed, but it's not just the home guard here. None of the others was part of the agreement we made." Tarkyn shrugged. "I can't be bothered going through all of that again. It was hard enough the first time."

"Do you want me to do something about it?" asked Autumn Leaves.

Tarkyn smiled tiredly. "No, not tonight. Let's just enjoy one evening without having to manoeuvre our way through people's antipathy. They will have forgotten their gratitude tomorrow and be ready to find new reasons for disliking me. So let's make the most of this hiatus while we can."

"You are in a huff," accused Autumn Leaves.

The prince shook his head. "No, I'm not. I just know crowd mentality.... especially a crowd laced with people who hate the oath and therefore me." He looked at Autumn Leaves. "I almost wonder if Stormaway is right to keep the oath tied to the forest's welfare."

The woodman's eyes widened in shock.

"I'm not casting aspersions on woodfolk honour, but how true to an oath can people be if their thoughts are constantly warped by resentment?" Tarkyn continued, disregarding the woodman's reaction. "Surely they would begin to rationalise small transgressions and then become more and more convinced that what they are doing is good enough. Even with the forest's welfare at stake, some people have lost sight of what is expected."

The prince became aware of woodman's shuttered face. "Oh Autumn Leaves, please don't take offence. I don't mean any of this for the home guard. But you know, I think I, or we, made a big mistake letting all the other oathbound woodfolk keep away from me. They have built me up into a big ogre in their minds." Tarkyn pulled at his dry but matted hair, trying to ease out the worst of the tangles. "And at the moment, if the oath were disarmed, I would be in more danger from them than I ever was from the oathless woodfolk."

Autumn Leaves was silent for a while as he mulled this over. Finally he said, obviously feeling uncomfortable, "I don't know what to say, really.

You might be right. If the oath has made some of these people hate you, it would only take one of them to break it and you could be in danger." He heaved a sigh. "And even though, as a people, we are honourable, you can't guarantee everyone's behaviour."

Tarkyn smiled in understanding. "You may find this hard to believe but we sorcerers also consider ourselves to be honourable - and look at the treachery that abounds in the society I have come from."

Autumn Leaves could not prevent a sceptical expression from crossing his face.

Tarkyn gave a short derisive laugh. "You see what I'm battling against. It's not just me personally. Woodfolk have a pretty low opinion of sorcerers generally." Tarkyn regarded the woodman thoughtfully. "I can see you share that opinion but you might like to consider where my own sense of honour came from."

Autumn Leaves nodded reluctantly. "I suppose you had to learn it from somewhere. And it wasn't from us because you came into the forest with it." The woodman shifted his position against the log. "Ah, but perhaps you are the exception from your society while the traitor would be the exception in ours."

Tarkyn could feel generations of royal heritage rearing up inside him in outrage at such a suggestion. His eyes glittered in the firelight. His voice was flat with suppressed anger when he said, "I think we have taken this discussion far enough. We must agree to disagree on how despicable my heritage is."

Autumn Leaves' head shot up from his contemplation of the fire. "Oh dear, I've offended you now, haven't I?"

"Would you like it if I said you were the only trustworthy woodman? That all these people around us were untrustworthy and dishonourable? I think not."

The woodman returned the prince's outraged stare steadily. "No, I would not. On the other hand, I can't point to one of them that has turned on me or cast me out in the way that some of your closest friends and family have done to you." Seeing Tarkyn's stricken face, Autumn Leaves added hurriedly, "I'm sorry. I should not have thrown that up in your face."

"It is very hard," After a fraught silence, Tarkyn said carefully, "to keep believing in myself when I have been constantly surrounded, both as a sorcerer and as a woodman, by people who would kill me as quickly as look at me, if they had the chance." He turned his eyes away to look into the fire. "It is particularly difficult to come to terms with, when I know, whether you believe it or not, that both societies are full of good, honourable people."

Moments later, Waterstone came wandering over. "Could you come and have a quick look at something for me?" he asked, echoing Tarkyn's earlier words to him.

Tarkyn frowned a little suspiciously but stood up and followed the woodman into the darkness beyond the firelight and away from the other woodfolk. Autumn Leaves walked beside him. Waterstone took them to a small clearing where the strong rays of the moon bathed the ferns and treetops in a silvery light. They could see their shadows stretching across the grass and mosses under their feet.

"Come on," said Waterstone firmly, "Find somewhere to sit. We need to talk."

The sorcerer looked from one to the other mutinously. "You relayed our conversation without telling me." Tarkyn said to Autumn Leaves.

"Come on," repeated Waterstone unequivocally, "Sit. I did what you wanted earlier, even though I didn't want to. Now you have to do something for me."

With ill grace, Tarkyn dropped himself down into a damp bed of moss. His eyes flashed in the moonlight. "I do not like having my conversations monitored by others without my knowledge, even if it is you."

Waterstone came and squatted down in front of him. "Don't get angry with us just yet. Autumn Leaves did not relay your conversation to me. He sent out an urgent request for help just a few minutes ago. So, here I am." The woodman twisted around and sat down beside Tarkyn. Autumn Leaves sat on the other side of him.

Tarkyn folded his arms and waited. He watched the woodmen's eyes to check whether they were mind talking but neither of them went out of focus. After a minute or two of silence, he said flatly, "Well?"

Waterstone gave a slight smile. "Well, nothing. I don't know why you need my help but I'm here waiting to give it when you tell me what you want."

Tarkyn frowned. "I don't need any help that I am aware of." His voice still sounded resentful.

Autumn Leaves glanced at him then addressed Waterstone. "I'm afraid my conversation with Tarkyn went badly pear-shaped. First I offended him. Then I really hurt him by which time I realised I was way out of my depth. So I asked for your help to pull us back out of deep water before we drowned."

Waterstone looked totally confused by the end of this explanation. He looked at Tarkyn. "Do you have any idea what he's talking about? Because I don't."

Tarkyn sent a smouldering glare at Autumn Leaves. “He is possibly referring to the aspersions he cast on the honour of my heritage. Alternatively he could be referring to the contrast he drew between the way people treated him and me – not to my advantage, I can assure you.”

“And still I am in the dark.” said Waterstone patiently. He turned once more to Autumn Leaves. “Exactly what did Tarkyn say that made you call for me?”

Autumn Leaves looked uncomfortable at having to repeat the prince’s conversation. “He said he found it hard to keep believing in himself when both sorcerers and woodfolk kept wanting to kill him. Something like that. Especially when he knew that both lots of people were basically good.”

“The light begins to dawn. But Tarkyn, why would you be feeling like that tonight, when everyone around you is celebrating what you and Stormaway achieved today?”

The prince gave a bitter laugh. “Because it is irrelevant. It won’t last. Tomorrow, the knives will be out once more. It has only lasted as long as it has, because I have carefully avoided saying anything at all tonight.”

Waterstone’s face tightened with concern. “Tarkyn, would you mind if Autumn Leaves replayed me your conversation with him? It might save us all a lot of questions.”

Tarkyn nodded shortly. “Go ahead.” While the woodmen were out of focus, the sorcerer stared stonily into the middle distance, arms still folded, as closed off as he could possibly be.

When Waterstone regained focus, he looked at Tarkyn speculatively, wondering how to breach the citadel. Eventually he said, “I think we should consider giving Autumn Leaves honorary membership of the harvesters and gatherers. I have rarely seen a more devious or more thorough demolition of a person’s honour, culture and worth.”

Tarkyn brought his glowering face around to stare at Waterstone. “I didn’t need Autumn Leaves to tell me all that. I know what woodfolk think about sorcerers, thanks to you. Other than that, he just crystallised what I had been thinking myself.”

“Which was…?”

“That there must be something fundamentally wrong with me, for all these people to turn against me. If enough people keep telling you the same thing, you have to start realising that what you believe is probably incorrect.”

“Hence the quips about being the friendly neighbourhood tyrant and an arrogant, autocratic bastard.”

Tarkyn frowned. “Who told you the last one?”

Waterstone gave a slight smile. "Sparrow asked me what it meant."

Tarkyn felt his cheeks go hot. "Whoops. I'd better be a bit more careful with my language around her."

"I wouldn't worry. She's around language like that all the time. As long as she knows that she is not allowed to use it until she's older, that's the best we can hope for."

After a short pause, Waterstone returned doggedly to the topic. "I don't know whether you realise this but there haven't actually been very many unkind things said to you. Admittedly, Tree Wind has been a determined opponent. Other than that, Sun Shower made a caustic remark, which she subsequently retracted. Even after your forceful speech last night, many people came up and were friendly afterwards. Most of the oathless woodfolk have been singing your praises. And you managed to befriend Running Feet, the most alienated person of all, in the space of a morning."

For a moment, Tarkyn looked convinced. Then his brow darkened and he said, "Yes but what about Andoran and Sargon, my erstwhile friends... And Kosar and Jarand? They were all willing to sacrifice me. Andoran and Sargon were absolutely ruthless about it."

"So were your brothers. They just got someone else to do it for them." said Waterstone matter-of-factly.

"So, people have set themselves against me in two completely separate societies and yet," continued Tarkyn on a note of desperate triumph following the woodman's ratification of his story, "Autumn Leaves has never experienced anything like it in his life."

"Neither have I," stated Waterstone baldly. "At least," he amended, "not until I became allied with you."

A flicker of panic flared in Tarkyn's eyes. "So there must be something about me that sets people against me."

"Of course there is," said Waterstone calmly. Autumn Leaves' eyes bugged out of his head with shock, while Tarkyn waited tensely.

Waterstone laughed and patted Tarkyn on the back. "You're a bloody prince, you fool. Neither of us has any claim to fame or to a throne or to the unwilling allegiance of a whole host of woodfolk. Of course you're going to strike problems we never have to encounter."

Tarkyn looked at him, half frowning and half smiling.

"Don't be confused between who you are and what you are," continued the woodman. "I know they are inextricable, but it is your role that has caused you the problems and drawn self interested people like Andoran and Sargon to your side and alienated Tree Wind and co, not you the person… perhaps with the notable exception of Running Feet, but even that you've sorted out now."

Finally Tarkyn broke into a full smile and shook his head. "I'm a complete embarrassment to myself, sometimes. I have just let things grow out of all proportion, haven't I?"

"Yes and no," replied Waterstone. "To be fair, you have an enormous amount to deal with – having to work out terms of engagement with every new person you meet in a much more fraught, significant way than I've ever had to..." he grinned, "except when I met you, of course."

Tarkyn's smile faded just a little. "I do get tired sometimes, you know, dealing with it all. I think that was half the trouble this evening. Not to mention that I've just done the biggest, most complex piece of magic in my entire life." He ran his hand tiredly through his hair."All those people think I want to be the centre of attention but actually it's more that they just assume that I will be. And it's tiring having everyone's eyes on you all the time, even when they're friendly eyes."

There was a companionable silence for a few minutes. Then Waterstone roused himself. "One more thing before we re-enter the hurly burly of your famous life. I don't want you making any more extravagant self-sacrificial gestures. I know you were upset and felt we had all double-crossed you, but you didn't come and talk to us about it. If you had, we would have told you about the woodfolk oath and you might have saved yourself all that angst. Instead, you dealt with it all on your own and nearly got yourself killed." The woodman smiled faintly. "I have to hand it to you. You did achieve great things that day but I think part of your success was that you felt you had nothing left to lose and so took inordinate risks."

Waterstone raised his eyebrows interrogatively and Tarkyn nodded reluctantly in reply.

The woodman continued, "Please, whatever happens, at least give us the chance to sort it out with you first and don't put yourself at unnecessary risk, for our sakes as well as yours."

Tarkyn eyed him sideways. "You sound awfully like a bossy older brother," he said, not sounding too sure that he liked it.

"Then you can have a lovely time commiserating with Ancient Oak about it," replied Waterstone, completely unmoved.

"All right. All right. Point taken." Tarkyn rose to his feet and put out his hands to haul the other two up. "Come on then. Back into harness." So saying, the prince walked with them through the quiet darkness and back into the glare of the crowded firelight.

CHAPTER 38

As soon as the prince entered the light, Ancient Oak pounced on him. "Ah, there you are. We were wondering where you'd got to."

Tarkyn threw a dry look at the other two before submerging himself in the conversation. "What did you want me for?"

"We think we've worked out who might be missing," said Falling Branch.

"There aren't many people unaccounted for. We've checked with everyone we can think of. There are only two possibilities left," continued Ancient Oak.

"Falling Rain is an obvious possibility," put in Rainstorm with a shrug. "But the other possibility is Golden Toad's family."

Tarkyn raised his eyebrows. "Golden Toad?"

"Yes," said Waterstone repressively before Tarkyn could say anything offensive. "He has a very low, stop-start sort of a voice."

"I see." Tarkyn's eyes shone with amusement.

"Anyway, as I was saying," said Rainstorm, firmly regaining the prince's attention, "Golden Toad's family contracted some sort of virus a few years ago which caused them to lose their ability to mind talk. They tend to keep to themselves down around the southern marshes."

"How very apt," said Tarkyn irrepressibly.

Rainstorm frowned briefly at the distraction but was so focused on what he was saying that he didn't catch the implication. "So we haven't been able to contact them to see if they are all right."

"So we were wondering…" Ancient Oak began but then broke off looking uncertain.

"We were wondering, Your Highness," continued Falling Branch, taking over from him. "If you might be able to use a bird or animal to look for them for us." When Tarkyn didn't reply instantaneously, he continued hurriedly. "Not if you think it would be too much of an imposition. It's just that it will take several days for some of us to travel there and that would be lost time if we could find out sooner."

Tarkyn waved a hand to silence everyone. "Of course I will help if I can. Just give me a minute to think." He paced up and down a couple of times then stopped. "How far away are these marshes and who has been there most recently?" The prince realised everyone was looking disappointed. "Give me a chance. I'm not planning to send those people back down there. I just need someone to guide my mind."

"I know the area quite well," offered Running Feet. "I'll help."

Ignoring the faint ripple of surprise that ran through Tree Wind's group, Tarkyn smiled. "Thanks. You're good at explaining terrain and have a clear eye for detail. I noticed that this morning. Do you know what they look like or what their shelter may look like? I'll need to know if I'm going to try to recruit a creature of some sort to look for them."

"If you can do that, why don't you just send in an animal to look in the encampment for woodfolk?" challenged Tree Wind, suddenly entering the discussion.

Tarkyn turned to look at her. Everyone, aware of Tree Wind's antagonism, waited with baited breath for the prince's response. "You know," he said quietly, "when I first entered the forest, I was impressed by your courage and your fighting spirit. Before I understood the structure of woodfolk society, I thought you might be their leader. You are quick-witted and intelligent. Every time you have queried my ideas, they have been sound queries, just as now."

"Of course they are," she replied caustically. "I know what I'm doing."

"Whereas I don't," supplied the prince for her.

In response, she just stood and stared at him belligerently.

He surprised her by smiling. "Of course, I don't. I've only been in the woods for a little over a month - and for a fortnight of that time, I was unconscious. You've been here all your life. Ask Sparrow. She'll tell you. I'm hopeless at directions. I couldn't even tell you where north is at the moment."

Tree Wind's expression became, if anything, more disdainful.

Tarkyn continued unabashed. "I know nothing about lighting fires, fending for myself, building shelters, recognising animal tracks, hunting, cooking. You name it, I can't do it."

A burble of quiet laughter wafted around the assembled woodfolk.

"Not only that, but I'm not particularly interested in doing a lot of those things. In fact, I am a constant drain on other people's resources." Tarkyn swept a friendly smile around his audience. "Traditionally, that's what a prince is – a constant drain on other people's resources. However," the sorcerer's voice grew serious, "I do possess skills, knowledge and power that you do not have, Tree Wind. If you will work with me instead of competing with me, I will give you free access to my skills and power. I have already done so with the woodfolk I have been with and I will do so for anyone who requests them for the welfare of woodfolk."

Tree Wind still did not reply but was now looking speculatively at him.

"And in answer to your question, I think that is a very good suggestion; to use a creature to reconnoitre the encampment." The prince did not give Tree Wind the sole right to decide. He looked around at everyone. "As you all know what you're doing and I don't; which should I do first? Look for Golden Toad down in the southern marshes or inspect the encampment, assuming I can do either? You decide and get back to me. I need a glass of wine."

A babble of voices immediately broke out behind him as Tarkyn turned away to find something to drink. Autumn Leaves thrust a glass into his hand.

"Thanks," said Tarkyn briefly, his eyes twinkling with laughter.

"You are up to tricks, young Tarkyn," observed Waterstone with an answering smile. "You are much more capable than that impression you just gave."

The prince grinned. "Of course I am, but I don't need to tell them that. Now they, and particularly Tree Wind, can feel happily superior about some things at least."

"What happened to your sanctimonious position about not giving false impressions?" asked Autumn Leaves dryly.

Tarkyn had the grace to look embarrassed. "Yes. Good point. I could say, 'But I didn't tell them any lies' but as I recall, you said that to me and I wouldn't wear it." The prince sighed, "Well, there's nothing for it. I'll have to turn back around and explain to them that I'm absolutely superior in every way."

"No," chorused the two woodmen.

"Anyway," added Waterstone, "You're not. So then you would be compounding a false impression with a string of lies."

"Well, I can console myself with the belief that they already had a false impression of me as threatening, all powerful and arrogant. So I've just replaced it with a new one in which I'm pathetic and helpless." He smiled unrepentantly at them "Perhaps the two will cancel each other out to be somewhere near the truth?"

An increase in volume behind them indicated that all was not well. When the prince turned back around, he realised that the discussion had galvanised the woodfolk into two groups, those for and those against him.

"Ooh dear," said Tarkyn under his breath to Autumn Leaves and Waterstone. "This could be going better." He surveyed the crowd. "Well, at least we are clear now on where the lines are drawn."

The prince took a deep breath and when he next spoke, his voice cut sharply through the night air, "Last night I told you that I was not prepared to countenance any debates that are based on politics, rather than on the issues themselves. Yet here we are, clearly divided over a virtual non-issue on the grounds of loyalty."

He bent down and picked up a stone. Placing his hands behind his back, he said, "Tree Wind, come over here please."

When she hesitated, he said evenly. "That was not a request."

Once she was standing before him, he explained, "The hand with the stone in it is the encampment. The other hand is the marsh. One person from each camp, please, stand behind me to make sure I don't cheat."As an embarrassed murmur greeted this request, the prince said sternly, "I'm waiting."

Once everyone was in place, Tarkyn moved the stones back and forth between his hands behind his back, then stopped. He nodded at Tree Wind. "Choose."

Tree Wind's eyes snapped. "This is ridiculous!"

"I couldn't agree more," said the prince. "Nevertheless, choose!"

Glaring furiously at the prince, she pointed at his right arm. His hand came around to the front with the stone clearly held in it.

"So be it." Tarkyn's angry gaze swept across the crowd before him. "If, at any time in the future, I become aware that the issues alone are not guiding your decision making, then I will have three courses of action open to me; I can withdraw my offer of assistance, I can make the decision myself or I can leave it to chance. None of those strikes me as being outcomes you would prefer."

The prince's eyes narrowed as he contemplated the group against him, "Once I have completed this task, I wish to speak alone to the group who chose the encampment, before any of you leaves. Either tonight or tomorrow morning, depending on how long we take. That, also, is not a request." He looked around until he spotted Running Feet, standing next to Thunder Storm. "Now if you will excuse us, Running Feet and I have work to do."

The prince turned on his heel and strode out into the darkness, with Running Feet hard on his heels. Once they were well away from the firesite, the moonlight took over and they found themselves walking through a monochromatic vista of towering trees, dark, hunched bushes and soft grasses.

Tarkyn let out a long breath. "Skies above, they're hard work." He glanced at the woodman beside him, "Thank you for your support today and this evening." He gave a fleeting smile. "Funny thing is, I actually agreed with the people who were against me. That's why I couldn't make the decision. I couldn't let down all the people who were supporting me. I would have made it if I really had to, but frankly, it doesn't matter much, one way or the other. So I was quite happy to leave it to chance."

Running Feet's eyebrows twitched together. "So all those people are going to get into trouble for making the right decision?"

"I will certainly be speaking to all those people who made the right decision for the wrong reasons," replied the prince dryly. "Whether they get into trouble, as you put it, remains to be seen."

"And the others?"

Tarkyn smiled. "You mean, those who made the wrong decision for the wrong reasons? Since they are not filtering everything I say through a haze of resentment, they will have already understood the error of their ways. At least, I hope so."

"Where are we going?" asked Running Feet.

Tarkyn shrugged, "I don't know. Somewhere outside. Anywhere really, where we won't be disturbed."

Running Feet stopped and looked around. He pointed to a shadowy space within a large stand of oaks. "That do?"

For a moment, a sense of unease rippled through Tarkyn. "Can you contact the lookouts? Check that everything is all right?"

Running Feet stared at him. "I can't hurt you, you know. I swore the oath."

Tarkyn frowned distractedly. "What? I'm not worried about that. It would be pointless for me to ask you to check with the lookouts, if I were."

The woodman conceded the point and went briefly out of focus. "All where they should be and nothing to report."

"How well would they pick up a threat that was already inside the perimeter?"

"The threat would have to get past them to get inside the perimeter in the first place," Running Feet pointed out.

Tarkyn still looked uneasy. "Twice already, I have known of dangers getting past the lookouts. The first time was a wolf that slipped through while they were watching its mate. The second was when I made it into here." He shrugged. "Maybe I just had a cold shiver, I don't know. You'll just have to be extra vigilant while I'm concentrating."

When they had settled themselves comfortably against the trunks of two trees, Tarkyn asked, "Can you recall the encampment?" Remembering Waterstone, he asked, "Will you allow me to share your memory of it? Feel free to edit it as you wish."

Running Feet interrupted, "Did Waterstone really let you have free rein with his memory?"

The prince stared at him, "Who told you that?"

"Waterstone did, of course. It had to be him, Autumn Leaves or Thunder Storm. No-one else knows."

The prince frowned, "So why did he tell you?"

Running Feet grimaced reminiscently. "I think it was just part of a fairly long-winded warning-off process that he has subjected me to for most of the day in one subtle way or another."

"I see," said Tarkyn. A slow smile dawned as he worked out the inferences. "Yes, he did give me free rein with his memory for some considerable time. Not one of my finest hours. I overused it. Autumn Leaves was very angry with me." He paused and glanced at Running Feet, "But do not fear. It was always within Waterstone's control, not mine, if you're wondering. I just took too much advantage of his good nature. – So, are we going to do this or not? You can describe the encampment in detail instead, if you would prefer."

The woodman shook his head. "No. That would be too laborious. If you can receive images, it's much better this way." He leaned forward so that his face was close to Tarkyn's. "Okay. Look into my eyes."

We are carefully upwind of the camp. We can hear wolves howling from time to time. There are scores of tall men. Some women. Many men are armed. They are wearing better clothes than the others who look like the travellers we see on the roads through the woods. There are scores of horses roped up inside the encampment. Some are wearing saddles, ready to leave. They have guards posted around the perimeter at intervals of fifty yards. All the guards are carrying weapons of some description. There are tents in the middle of the enclosure. Some men sleep in them. Many sleep under tatty pieces of canvas outside. A weedy young man walks around past the horses to check the chained wolves.

"That's the man I saw at the river with the wolf and the riders," exclaimed Tarkyn. "Sorry. Go on."

Running Feet shrugged. "There's not much more than that really. I didn't see any sign of woodfolk."

Tarkyn frowned, "If they are there, they will be inside one of those tents where we can't see them. What animal can I use?" pondered the sorcerer.

"You could start with one of the horses or even a wolf. You would think they would let the woodfolk out sometimes, if they're in there."

"The trouble is that I can't talk to them. I can only send and receive images. It needs to stay in the present tense, if you see what I mean."

Running Feet thought for a minute. "Maybe a mouse? Or a rat?"

Tarkyn laughed. "The mind boggles. But why not? I've used a swallow before and it's not much bigger than a mouse." He settled himself more comfortably against the tree. "Ready? Now I am going to have to send my mind searching for a particular little individual. So I need to know where I am going." He looked suddenly at the woodman and grinned. "You realise I haven't done this before? Autumn Leaves said you can use people's memories as maps. So can you do me a quick repeat of your trip between the encampment and here? I'll just have to reverse it."

Running Feet's eyes widened. "That's a pretty tall order. Not for me, for you. To remember a long route like that backwards when you haven't even travelled it yourself."

Tarkyn grimaced. "Yes it is, isn't it? Maybe you can take me through it once. Then, as I go back over it, give me verbal prompts to remind what should be coming next."

"I know," said the woodman enthusiastically. "I have a better idea. Why don't I just take you slowly backwards over the route in the first place? It won't be hard for me to visualise retracing our steps."

"Much better. With any luck I can be actually sending my mind out along the route in time with your image. Don't take it too fast." Tarkyn closed his eyes, then realised and opened them again. "Stars. I'll have to do this with my eyes open if I'm looking at a memory, won't I?"

Running Feet considered, "No. I don't think so. It actually might be easier if I transmit the images to you so that I can change the order of them first."

"Good. That will suit me better too," Tarkyn closed his eyes again. "Let's go."

Slowly with the help of Running Feet's images, Tarkyn let his mind move slowly out from where he sat into the forest, up over a series of wooded hills, around an open space of heather and gorse, around a huge spread of brambles, through a steep narrow valley and finally into a more open area of woodland. As his mind approached the encampment, he focused low to the ground, looking for the mind patterns of little animals. He could feel the air buzzing with chatter but he couldn't home in on any one mind. *Maybe it's too far away,* he thought. Just as he was beginning to tire, he found himself viewing the forest floor from only inches above as he scurried from bush to bush, looking for seeds and scraps. Gently, the forest guardian inserted a picture of the encampment, then the tents in the middle of it, with a sense of query.

He found his nose quivering with the smell of men, horses and wolves. He shuddered with fear but then began to scurry nervously from one bit of shelter to the next, towards the source of the smells. It took a long while to cross the open ground outside on tiny little legs, especially stopping every few seconds to sniff the air and quiver. Finally, he reached the edge of the encampment and ducked down behind someone's discarded shoe to look about. After a quick detour to sample some horse's dung, the little mouse scuttled into the nearest tent.

Tarkyn resisted a strong desire to spit out the mouse's snack.

There was no one in there but there were some tasty crumbs of mouldy bread and cheese in the corner. The mouse had another quick nibble before moving on. Suddenly he heard voices approaching. He flattened himself out and pushed his way under the back wall of the tent. A crunchy little black beetle was quickly dispatched before he squeezed himself through a small hole in the wall of the next tent. There were gigantic people in here. He scuttled into a corner to hide behind a pile of clothing. After a while, when he had gauged where everyone was, he peeped out around a piece of light brown cloth to see what was happening. Three people were sitting against the opposite wall. Two adults and a child. All three had light brown hair and green eyes. They looked frightened and dishevelled. The little mouse nipped out and snuck around into the tiny space between them and the tent wall. A long metal chain looped around the waist of each of them and disappeared under the tent wall. The mouse followed it out and found the end of the chain attached to a large metal stake that had been hammered into the ground. Then all thought of the people inside the tent vanished as the mouse saw another lovely pile of horse dung close by.

The forest guardian thanked it hurriedly and disconnected. He opened his eyes to find Running Feet staring into his face with some concern. "Are you okay? You look very pasty."

Tarkyn twisted and spat on the ground. "It is probably just that the horse dung and beetle I've just eaten don't agree with me," he answered d.

"Ooh yuk," exclaimed the woodman. "That's a bit above and beyond, isn't it?"

Tarkyn wiped his mouth. "It certainly is. But what could I do? I had to go along for the ride, when the mouse was being so brave and helpful."

"So, did you find out anything?"

The forest guardian became instantly serious. "Yes. We have a big problem. They have three woodfolk chained up inside the second tent along from the forest edge."

Running Feet went white. "Oh, no. That is our worst nightmare realised. The outside world finding out about us."

Tarkyn raised an eyebrow. "Not to mention the suffering of the imprisoned woodfolk"

The woodman waved a dismissive hand. "That goes without saying."

"So I see." Tarkyn stood up. "Come on, then. Back we go and tell the others."

Just as they emerged from the shadow of the trees, the sorcerer paused and looked back. He said nothing but shook his head as if to clear it.

"Lookouts report no unusual sightings. They will redouble their vigilance."

"Thanks Running Feet. I wasn't going to ask again but I did want to know."

"What should I do first?" mused Tarkyn. "Talk to the harvesters and gatherers or show everyone the mouse's image?"

"Are you asking me?" said Running Feet, unsure whether the prince was talking to him or to himself.

"You can give me your opinion, if you like."

"I think you should show the image first," responded the woodman. "Then they will understand the urgency of the situation."

Tarkyn smiled. "I agree. It's vital those poor people are rescued as quickly as possible. And if I don't have time to talk to the harvesters and gatherers alone tonight, I can talk to them tomorrow."

When they re-entered the firelight, a hush fell on the crowd. Running Feet, unused to being at the centre of attention, made his way quickly to sit down near Thunder Storm again. The guardian of the forest was left standing alone at the edge of the firelight.

"Rather than tell you what we have discovered, I will simply transmit the images I received from a small, very brave, helpful…mouse." There was a smattering of laughter around the firesite. Tarkyn smiled in response. "Running Feet and I chose a mouse because we needed a creature small enough to be unobtrusive that could get inside the tents at the encampment. There were some disadvantages to this choice, as you will find out." He looked around. "I will be kinder this time and make sure everyone is seated. Are Ancient Elm and Dry Berry still here? Comfortable? Good."

The forest guardian found himself a log to sit on and transmitted the images from the mouse. Although he smiled hard, Tarkyn managed to keep up the flow of images amid the cries of disgust, when the mouse indulged in its various snacks. But when the sequence was complete, he opened his eyes to a sea of white, stricken faces. The silence was deafening. After a few moments' hesitation, the prince decided to say nothing at all. Everything he needed to say, had already been said. He stood up quietly and wandered back out into the gloom.

Part 8: Danton

CHAPTER 39

Tarkyn found somewhere relatively dry to sit where he let his mind wander up among the trees until he found an owl. It was not the tawny owl that he had met before. This one was a huge eagle owl. Tarkyn sent a query about the uneasiness he had felt earlier when he had been there with Running Feet. In answer, the owl took off and winged through the surrounding trees searching for the source of the feeling. As one with the owl, Tarkyn could see the forest passing below. He flew over a herd of grazing deer, and startled rabbits back into their burrows. He watched a fox jump out of its skin as he swooped low over it. Tarkyn realised with a jolt that the eagle owl had a sense of humour. It flew tirelessly through the forest searching. Finally, a black shadow detached itself from beneath the overhang of a large beech. The eagle owl landed on a nearby branch and shook out its feathers, its eyes never leaving its quarry below. The sorcerer strained his eyes to make out what he was seeing. The black shape moved furtively into the shelter of another beech tree.

"Oh no!" breathed Tarkyn, "That's one of the elite guards from the palace." He sent a message to the owl asking just where the intruder was. When he felt reasonably sure he understood, he asked the owl to keep an eye on the guardsman and set off in search of Stormaway.

Tarkyn skirted around the edge of the firelight until he was directly behind the wizard. The woodfolk were fully occupied, discussing the images he had shown them, and planning the rescue. The prince found that he wasn't particularly interested at the moment. He knew they would speak to him about it when they needed to and right now he had more pressing matters to think about.

Tarkyn leaned forward into the firelight and whispered in Stormaway's ear. "Could I have a private word with you please?" The prince nodded briefly to the woodfolk sitting with Stormaway and retreated back into the darkness.

The wizard made his excuses and followed him away between the moonlit bushes beyond the firelight. Tarkyn waited until they were well out of earshot before he turned to Stormaway.

"We have some serious trouble on our hands," he began.

"I know we have," said Stormaway. "It will be catastrophic for the woodfolk if their presence becomes known."

Tarkyn waved an impatient hand. "No. We have other serious trouble." He waited while Stormaway dragged his mind away from the woodfolk issue. "There is an elite palace guard skulking in the woods."

Stormaway's eyes widened. "Has he seen you?" he demanded. "Has he seen any of the woodfolk?"

"No. I don't think so." Tarkyn thought about it. "Actually I don't know for sure. I felt a strange uneasiness when Running Feet and I came out into the woods. We checked with the lookouts, both before and afterwards but they had seen nothing."He ran his hand through his hair. "I don't know; maybe he was somewhere there, watching us. He is certainly out there now and the lookouts have not reported it."

Before Stormaway could ask his next question, the forest guardian answered it for him. "Eagle owl. We searched the forest until we found the source of the feeling. The owl is keeping watch over him, as we speak. He is less than half a mile away, downstream of the shelters and the other direction from where we dealt with the storm today."

Stormaway looked at Tarkyn. "We have to tell the woodfolk. They may need to disappear. Can you summon Waterstone? While you do that, I'll just get a few things ready."

Tarkyn sent a clear, strong image of himself summoning Waterstone. He hoped Waterstone didn't turn up as annoyed as Autumn Leaves had, the last time he had tried it. As it turned out, Autumn Leaves, Waterstone and Thunder Storm all arrived together at a flat run. They were panic-stricken rather than annoyed.

"After the discussion you had with Autumn Leaves about your signals, we knew this one was urgent," explained Waterstone. "What's up?"

"There's an elite palace guard in the woods out there. Elite means he's fast, strong, trained in disguise, camouflage, tracking; he's wearing black and he's very hard to spot. He made it past the lookouts without attracting their attention." Tarkyn waved a hand in the general direction of the stream. "He's hiding in the patch of beech trees downstream of the shelters. I have an eagle owl watching him and he hasn't moved for the last ten minutes."

"Has he seen anyone?"

Tarkyn shook his head, "I'm not sure. He may have seen me with Running Feet. That's when I first felt his presence. But I don't know."

Autumn Leaves looked thoughtful. "It is over a week since the last foray by the sorcerers and their wolf. Perhaps they have decided to use more stealthful means in their attempts to track us down."

"He has certainly got closer to us than the men on horseback did," Thunder Storm rumbled quietly. "If Tarkyn hadn't come out here with Running Feet, we would still be unaware of his presence."

"Or maybe he is simply hunting Tarkyn for the bounty or, if he is the king's man, for the glory of the capture." Waterstone kept his voice matter-of-fact and avoided Tarkyn's eyes as he turned to Stormaway who was now carrying a haversack. "You are the only one who can safely meet him and try to turn him away. If we all cover you, would you be willing to confront him and find out what he's up to?"

"He may kill and ask questions afterwards," interrupted Tarkyn. "They are trained to be ruthless. We will have to disarm him and tie his arms behind his back before Stormaway can talk to him safely."

"Right. We'll do that then," replied Waterstone without hesitation. "How are we going to knock him out? Slingshot or one of your power rays?"

"Slingshot. You will be able to get much closer to him undetected than either of us could. I will come with you as far as is safe and will create a link between the eagle owl and you, so you know what the guard is doing. Wait. I'll use the eagle owl's directions to show you exactly where he is. Do we need anyone else?"

"No," replied Thunder Storm. "But I think everyone must disappear. He's too close. If he comes any closer, he'll hear voices. We'll alert the lookouts, too."

Tarkyn frowned, "It seems a shame to disturb everyone when they're all deep in discussion."

Thunder Storm gave him the smile he would have given one of his children when they were being naïve, "My lord, that is what we do. It is second nature to us. They can continue the discussion mind talking."

The other two woodmen agreed and all three went out of focus briefly.

"Right, let's go."

Waterstone led the way past the shelters and followed the stream along until they reached the edge of the beech wood. He signalled for the sorcerer and the wizard to remain.

Suddenly the three woodmen were gone. The forest guardian checked with his owl. The elite guard was still pressed, motionless, into the deep shadow beneath the tree's branches. Tarkyn couldn't see any movement. Perhaps he was sleeping. Abruptly, the guard reared up then crashed to the ground.

Tarkyn turned to the wizard. "Mission accomplished, I think." He tuned back into the owl to thank him for his night's work. The owl, however, was finding the whole affair most entertaining and had no intention of leaving, so Tarkyn retained his contact. Below on the forest floor through the owl's eyes, he could see three woodmen firmly tying the guard's hands behind his back. His knives were in neat pile a few yards away. Tarkyn sent an image of knives up sleeves, in boots and up trouser legs. As a result, two more knives appeared and were added to the pile. Then the woodfolk were gone.

Tarkyn filled Stormaway in on the owl's image. "He's all yours. Do you feel able to do this?"

"I will be fine, my boy. Intrigue is the spice of my life. Let me at him." Stormaway smiled broadly and headed off into the woods.

The eagle owl turned its head and Tarkyn found himself looking directly at Thunder Storm who was sharing the tree with the owl. As the owl stared at him, Thunder Storm gave a small wave and a grin.

"Very funny," said Tarkyn to himself, with a smile. "And I used to think he was pompous."

The eagle owl was not quite so amused and returned his attention to the forest floor. Stormaway had arrived and was seating himself comfortably. He waved a hand and murmured a spell to produce a soft light, ready for the guard's return to consciousness.

Only a few minutes later, the elite guard began to come round. The woodmen had been very accurate with the strength of their slingshot. A black scarf obscured the man's face leaving only his eyes visible. Stormaway leant forward and removed the scarf to make sure the guard could breathe properly. The prince drew in a sharp breath as the man's features were revealed.

The guardsman was no older than early twenties. His blonde, wavy hair was shoulder length and his eyes, when he opened them, were a vibrant purple. He lay still for a few minutes, taking in the fact that his hands were bound. When he saw Stormaway watching, he struggled into a sitting position. He shook his head to clear it and groaned.

"Ow. That wasn't a good idea," he said. He blinked a couple of times then focused his eyes on the wizard. "Who are you? And more importantly, do you have anything to drink?"

"As it happens," replied Stormaway imperturbably, "I have water and wine. Which would you prefer?"

The young man frowned, "Water first. Then wine." He gave the ghost of a smile. "I may need some assistance in drinking them."

"I will be happy to oblige." Stormaway produced two earthenware cups from his haversack and a stoppered earthenware bottle. "Before I come any closer, may I suggest you stop thinking of your feet as weapons or we will end up in a serious argument that I will win. If you find you cannot do that, please let me know and I will tie them also."

The guard's eyes narrowed. After a moment, he said, "I think I can manage that."

The wizard carefully assisted him to take a drink then moved back out of range. "My name, sir, is Stormaway Treemaster…and yours?"

The guard's eyes had widened. "I have heard of you. I seem to remember the king speaking of you. You were his father's personal wizard, weren't you?"

"Indeed I was. I am gratified to have been mentioned," said the wizard with a touch of sarcasm, "Your name, sir? Or do you not wish to give it?"

The young man put his head on one side. "If I were on the king's official business, I would not give it to you, but I am travelling on my own affairs. And so I will tell you. My name is Danton Patronell."

"So, Danton, if you are not on the king's business, what brings you to these parts of the woods?"

"Before I answer that, I would ask what business is it of yours?" The guard shifted his weight to make himself more comfortable. "I would also ask why I awake from a thump on the head to find myself with my hands bound?" A note of contempt entered his voice. "Perhaps you are a brigand these days?"

Despite himself, Stormaway took offence. "Good heavens, man! Of course I'm not. How dare you suggest such a thing."

Danton shrugged, "One would have to say the evidence points to it from where I'm sitting."

"Young man, I have been conducting some small commercial enterprises near here. I discovered you were hiding in the woods, no matter how. I recognise an elite guard when I see one. As I would rather live to ask questions, I made sure you were unable to attack me while I find out why you are skulking in these woods." Stormaway had himself back in hand. "Some wine now?" he asked urbanely.

The young man nodded and waited for the wizard to feed it to him. The whole time, the guard studied Stormaway through narrowed eyes.

When he still did not offer any information, Stormaway asked, "Do you, by any chance, know a young man who keeps wolves?"

"Not personally, no. I have heard that there is such a man. Rumours such as this make a long night on guard duty bearable."

"I see. And do these rumours suggest who this man is or why he keeps wolves?"

The young man scowled impatiently. "I do not see the relevance of these questions."

"Humour me."

Danton eyed Stormaway belligerently for a few moments. "No. I do not know who he is and I have no idea of his intentions. Obviously, wolves would be useful for hunting or protection." Suddenly a faint smile appeared on his face. "But actually, we thought that the man must be some sort of an idiot to use wild wolves when domestic hounds would be nearly as good and a lot easier to train."

"Perhaps the wolves could pass more easily unremarked through the woodlands?"

The guardsman shrugged, patently uninterested, "Perhaps. But I can't see why that would matter."

Stormaway offered him another sip of wine but this time, as the wizard retreated to the other side of the path, the guard made a sudden lunge at him. In the space of an eye blink, the wizard's shield was up, but by then the young man had already relaxed back against the tree trunk again.

Stormaway frowned as he released his shield, "What was that all about?"

Danton gave a satisfied, unnerving smile. "I wanted to see the colour of your magic. If I had asked you, you might have lied."

"So you have established that I have green magic. Well done," said Stormaway with heavy irony. "So may we now return to the point of this discussion which is to establish why you are here?"

"It was not I who deviated from it." The guard considered Stormaway for a long time. Finally, he said, "I don't know how to say this to keep myself safe. I think you're protecting someone and if you know I'm looking for him, you may kill me to protect him."

"Why would you think I was protecting someone?" Stormaway asked quietly.

"Because of your connection to him, for one thing."

Tense silences punctuated these verbal manoeuvres as the two men fenced carefully with each other.

"I have connections with many people. Any other reason?" asked Stormaway, trying to sound puzzled.

Danton drew a deep breath, obviously aware that he was on very thin ice. "There was a storm earlier today. Nearly all day, actually. It ended this afternoon with a pyrotechnical display that would take your breath away." Danton's eyes didn't leave the wizard's face. "One stream of magic was green, the other was bronze."

"More wine?" asked Stormaway, stalling for time.

"Thank you." When he had been fed another sip, Danton continued, "Bronze is a very unusual colour for magic, isn't it? In fact, I know of only one person who has it. Don't you?"

Stormaway conceded the battle but not the war. "What do you want with His Royal Highness?"

"I would remind you that I am not on the king's business."

"So you say," said Stormaway tersely. "But neither are bounty hunters on the king's business. Not directly, anyway."

"This is where this becomes difficult."

"Oh, so it hasn't been difficult up til now?"

Danton shook his head. "Not really. Oh, it's been difficult looking for him. I've been trying to find him for weeks now. But this conversation hasn't been difficult until now. We've been fencing but I already knew the prince was here somewhere. No, the hard part will be getting you to trust me so that I can see him."

"Go on. Why should I trust you? And why do you want to see him?"

The young man wriggled uncomfortably against the tree. "I don't suppose you would consider untying me?"

"What do you think?"

Danton grimaced, "No. I wouldn't untie me if our roles were reversed. So, back to your question. Why should you trust me? You see, that is exactly what I meant about this being hard. I am his friend, but how can you know that? I want to see him again to tell him that I remain his friend if he needs me," he shrugged, "and even if he doesn't need me."

"Your cause has not been helped by Andoran and Sargon."

"Why?"

"They tried to take His Highness back for the bounty."

The young man's purple eyes widened. "No! Those bastards! I can't believe they would stoop so low."

The wizard's voice was bleak. "I can assure you they did. They tied his hands behind his back, just as I have done to you, and force-marched him through the forest, belting him across the head any time he faltered."

"How dared they?" The young man was clearly upset. "I knew nothing of this. I left Tormadell on the same day as the prince and I have been trying to find him ever since he disappeared."

Stormaway raised his eyebrows. "Indeed?"

"Yes. Indeed!" snapped Danton. "So is he all right after all that? How did he escape?"

"He has recovered but he was badly hurt during his escape from Andoran and Sargon." Stormaway shook his head. "And I'm afraid I can't tell you how he escaped. Otherwise it may be one less chance he has next time."

"Well, he's going to be very wary after that, even of me." Danton sighed. "Never mind." After a moment, he looked squarely at the wizard. "Wizard Treemaster, obviously you are in contact with him. Could you just let His Highness know that not everyone has abandoned him? Certainly I haven't, and there are other friends of his who would still be waiting for him if he could ever come back." The young man wriggled again. "I have travelled a long way and a long time to see him but perhaps that won't be possible. Still, at least I know the prince is still alive and that he has received my message. Will you promise to tell him I came to see him?"

Stormaway nodded gravely.

"One more thing. Since you are clearly protecting His Highness, what relevance do these wolves have to his safety? I would be honoured to serve him in whatever way I can."

The wizard gave him a considering stare before saying slowly, "I do not believe that they are a direct threat to him. They are merely of interest to him."

"I see," said Danton stiffly, interpreting this answer as a refusal of his offer. "In that case, there is no more to be said. While I am thankful that Prince Tarkyn has your protection, I can only hope that your strict guardianship of His Highness does not isolate him completely." When the wizard did not respond, Danton gave a small shrug. "So be it. Now to practicalities. Are you going to let me go and send me on my way? I can promise not to say where I found you. In fact, I can promise to say I didn't find you at all but after Sargon and Andoran, I suppose I might as well save my breath."

"We will not be here for long, anyway," said Stormaway. "So it is of little consequence. However, it would be better if no one knew the prince was in the forest." The wizard stood and gave a slight bow. "Now, if you'll excuse me, please?"

The guardsman's mouth twisted into a crooked smile. "I can't see that I have much choice."

The wizard lifted a wry eyebrow in response, as he headed out of the stand of beeches at a right angle to the way he had come in.

Then he skirted around until he came to stand beside Tarkyn. "Do you know him?"

"Of course I do!" exclaimed Tarkyn. "We grew up together. He's my closest friend. At least he was until I met Waterstone."

"I'm glad you added that rider," said Waterstone lightly, coming up silently behind them. "I might have had to kill him otherwise."

"You still might have to," replied Tarkyn, tension in every syllable.

Waterstone regarded his friend. "This changes things, doesn't it? So what are we going to do?"

Tarkyn shrugged. "I don't know. I couldn't hear what he said."

"Sorry." The wizard filled the prince in on the contents of the conversation.

Tarkyn shook his head. "Much as I would like to believe him, how can we trust him?" He gave a knowing smile. "Whatever his motives, there is no way he's just going to return meekly to Tormadell, if he has been searching all these weeks and now knows I'm nearby. I know him. He gave up too easily."

"What's he doing now?" asked Stormaway.

Tarkyn connected briefly with the eagle owl. "He's surreptitiously scanning the nearby trees. He knows someone will be watching him. So he's making no move to escape."

"You don't sound as though you trust him much," observed Waterstone.

Tarkyn glanced at him, "I don't know whether I trust him or not. But I certainly don't trust him to play it straight when he finds himself far from help, at the mercy of someone he doesn't know."

Waterstone smiled wryly. "I admit one does not necessarily reflect on the other. I don't think I'd be playing it straight in that situation either."

"Oh, for pity's sake!" exclaimed Tarkyn, his voice full of anguish. "What am I going to do? What are we going to do? That is my friend in there. It's one thing to talk about ulterior motives to friendships when they're all far away. It's quite another to abandon someone who, as far as I know, has stood by me and is right here in front of me."

"What do you want to do about him?" asked Waterstone gently.

Tarkyn ran a hand through his hair. "I want what I can't have. I want him to come back with us and sit around the fire and tell us all about what he's been doing." The prince began to pace back and forth. "But, obviously, that can't happen."

He stopped dead and looked Waterstone straight in the face. "I really don't think I could countenance having him killed, any more than I could have allowed Stormaway to be killed by the oathless woodfolk."

Waterstone smiled wryly. "I'm relieved to hear you say that. I would have strong doubts about our friendship if I thought you could turn around and order your friend's death only weeks after last seeing him."

Tarkyn looked much struck. "Oh. I didn't see it like that. So you understand my dilemma."

"Tarkyn, no one wants to kill him." Waterstone frowned. "I sometimes wonder what you think of us. Woodfolk don't kill everyone who comes near them. The forest would be littered with corpses if we did that. We fade away to avoid the need."

"Yes. You may fade away, but I don't. And that presents a dilemma"

Waterstone shrugged, "As long as you are forewarned, you can levitate so that you don't leave tracks. You can hide in trees or brambles nearly as well as we do. Just a minute. Let me fill in the other two."

When the woodman came back into focus, Stormaway said, "Regardless of your disappearing skills, I think His Highness is right. This man is going to dog our footsteps until he gets what he wants. He will be a constant thorn in our sides."

Suddenly, Autumn Leaves and Thunder Storm were in their midst. "The owl can see better than we can in the dark anyway," said Autumn Leaves casually.

Everyone carried on as though they had been there the whole time.

"If you spoke to this guard," asked Thunder Storm, "would he go away then?"

Tarkyn considered the matter. "I don't really know. It may depend on what I say to him and on his motives. But I do know he definitely won't go away until I do."

Autumn Leaves suddenly went out of focus for a few moments. "That was Running Feet. They wanted to know what was happening. Just a minute." He went out of focus again. When he returned, he was looking quizzical. "A group of them …"

"Which group…?" interrupted the prince.

Autumn leaves waved a hand. "Worry about that later. I don't think it's relevant at the moment."

Tarkyn experienced a rush of outrage that his question should be dismissed so lightly. He quelled it as quickly as it came but Stormaway and the three woodmen paused to stare at him.

"I beg your pardon, Your Highness," said Autumn Leaves stiffly. "I should have given your question more consideration."

Tarkyn looked uncomfortable. "No, you shouldn't. You know the issues as well as I do. I trust your judgement. It was just a matter of old habits dying hard." He gave a wry smile, "I'm sorry my feelings interrupted. Go on."

Autumn Leaves glanced quickly around the faces of the other three and received a slight nod from Waterstone. Reassured, he continued, "They were wondering whether this sorcerer might be of some use in the upcoming rescue mission at the encampment."

The other four were thunderstruck.

"He did offer to help with the wolves," said Thunder Storm slowly.

Stormaway waved an impatient hand, "Yes, but that was expressly to protect Tarkyn."

"No, it wasn't," said Tarkyn. "He meant what he said. He would be honoured to serve me in any way I asked…assuming he is true." He smiled at the sceptical looks on the woodmen's faces. "I know. Alien territory for you, but true nevertheless… But I can't see how it would work. Even if I asked him to undertake the rescue mission on his own or with me, he would still end up seeing the captured woodfolk. Where does he stand then?"

The three woodmen looked at each other then back at Tarkyn. Waterstone spoke for them, "This is uncharted territory for us. Possibly hundreds of sorcerers have now seen these woodfolk. We can't kill them all – or at least, we won't."

A little chill shot down Tarkyn's spine at the casual deadliness of the woodfolk. However, he didn't let it distract him. "But we don't even know whether we can trust him," he objected."He might have come from that encampment himself."

"We can check that out easily enough. Someone can backtrack his trail and see where he's come from," said Thunder Storm.

Tarkyn frowned. "Danton will have been careful not to leave tracks. He's an elite guard, after all."

The woodmen all looked at each other again. "And we are woodfolk. We can track anything," said Thunder Storm.

"As long as it stays on the ground," conceded Waterstone, quashing the competitive air that was developing.

"You can't track back over weeks' worth of travel, anyway," objected Stormaway. "If he has come from the encampment, and wanted to disguise his intentions, he will have approached from a different direction. You can be sure of that."

"We could use mind control on him," suggested Autumn Leaves.

The prince thought for a long minute, and then he shook his head regretfully. "No. I know it's a good idea but I can't allow you to subject Danton to losing his free will like that."

"Oh come on, Tarkyn," said Autumn Leaves in exasperation. "He's lost his free will already, sitting there with his hands tied."

The prince looked at him. "Autumn Leaves, there is a huge difference between physically containing someone and invading their mind. As far as I'm concerned, using mind control is on a par with scanning someone's memories without their permission."

When Autumn Leaves seemed unconvinced, Tarkyn continued, "Imagine if that were Waterstone sitting there, surrounded by sorcerers who considered him a threat, would you want me to order Stormaway to have unlimited, un-negotiated access to his memory?"

Autumn Leaves glared at him. "No. Of course I wouldn't. But Stormaway can be very specific about what he asks. Anyway, would you risk the safety of all of us for the sake of a small scruple?"

Tarkyn stared at him then turned and paced up and down. He tuned in to the owl for a minute to watch his erstwhile friend. In the filtered moonlight between the trees, he could just make out the guardsman sitting uncomfortably against a spreading beech tree. Danton's head was resting back against the trunk and his eyes were closed.

Finally Tarkyn turned back to Autumn Leaves and said, "No, I would not risk your safety. I would find another way to keep you safe that did not require me to violate my friend's trust in me."

"Stars above, you're annoying sometimes!" exclaimed Autumn Leaves.

Tarkyn spread his hands, "I'm sorry. I know you don't agree with me but I couldn't look Danton straight in the face if I had countenanced the use of mind control on him."

Autumn Leaves gave him a grudging smile, "No wonder your integrity galvanised the oath. Oh well. What's our next move then?"

Tarkyn shrugged, "I can go and talk to him. But what will I say?"

"Whatever it is, it will have to be true," Autumn Leaves rolled his eyes, "You wouldn't be able to lie convincingly even if we did talk you into it."

"That's what I'm worried about. The first thing he's going to ask me is who is with me."

Waterstone smiled, "You can just freeze him out as you did Stormaway."

"I can't just freeze him out when he's just spent four weeks looking for me." The prince sent an apologetic glance to the wizard. "I wouldn't have done it to Stormaway, had I known what else to do."

"Just say to him that Stormaway is with you and there are no other sorcerers or wizards nearby, as far as you know."

Tarkyn brightened. "I can say that in all good faith, although" he glanced at Autumn Leaves, "it is giving the wrong impression."

"No, it's not," said Autumn Leaves firmly. "We are not wizards or sorcerers and don't want to be, for that matter."

Tarkyn refused to be baited. "Then what?"

"Then we lead him into a trap," rumbled Thunder Storm with a note of satisfaction in his voice.

The prince started in alarm. "You what? What sort of a trap?"

Waterstone frowned and spoke severely. "Tarkyn, will you please get it out of your mind that we're planning to kill him? We don't need a trap to do that. We could have killed him any time in the past hour."

"Sorry, I'm being silly." Tarkyn drew a breath. "Okay. Let me think. You want to see if he'll betray himself, or more particularly, me?"

"Exactly." Waterstone reached up and put a hand on the young sorcerer's shoulder. "Don't worry. We are all working together on this. We are not going to knock off your friend unless…" The woodman shrugged, "…actually, I can't think of a situation where we would kill him. Even if he went berserk and started trying to kill you or any of us, we'd just knock him out and disappear."

"So what do you want me to do?"

"Spend the night with him, Sire," said Stormaway. "Here. You'd better take this." The wizard handed him a warm, light brown cloak. "I'll be coming with you. He will expect that. I have some food and drink here. But I might need a bit more to give us enough to get convincingly drunk with." Thunder Storm nodded and went out of focus. "I will pretend to drink myself into a stupor.Then when you go to sleep, we'll see what he does."

Tarkyn looked around at them all. "And will I go to sleep or just pretend?"

Waterstone shrugged. "It's up to you. There will be many of us watching all through the night. Even if he put a knife to your throat, we could knock him out with a slingshot."

"And if he put his shield up?"

"Bloody sorcerers!" exclaimed Waterstone, "So hard to deal with."

"You could say that Shturrum word," suggested Thunder Storm tentatively.

"Good idea," said Tarkyn with a smile, "if I'm awake."

"Don't worry," said Thunder Storm. "Stormaway can wake you if he gets up to anything."

"Why don't you make sure your hand is in contact with a tree so that, if the unthinkable happens, you can heal yourself before your lifeblood runs out all over the ground?" suggested Stormaway.

Waterstone handed him a piece of soft green moss. "And take this so you can translocate safely onto the ground out here if you need to escape."

Tarkyn's eyes crinkled with amusement at the end of all this. "Thank you, my friends. I think that should cover it."

Rainstorm came running up with a knapsack full of food and drink. "Good luck. Give him a chance. I hope he is who you think he is."

Tarkyn smiled at him. "Thanks." He looked at the others. "This is the woodman who persuaded me to go back and listen to what Autumn Leaves had to say, the other day. I can see he has a diplomatic streak in there somewhere. I don't suppose you have ambassadors, do you?"

Waterstone shook his head and watched with some amusement as Rainstorm flushed with pleasure at being referred to as a woodman.

"You don't happen to have a hairbrush in that pack, do you?" asked the prince unexpectedly.

Rainstorm rummaged around inside the knapsack and produced a hairbrush with a flourish.

"Thanks," said Tarkyn as he attacked the knots in his matted hair. He gradually became aware of a stunned silence and looked up. "What's wrong?"

"You're about to use yourself as bait in a trap and you're brushing your hair?" asked Autumn Leaves in bemusement.

The prince raised a quizzical eyebrow. "Appearances must be preserved as best we can. That is a court-bred man in there. He will expect a certain standard of dress and behaviour from me. I can't give him the dress, but at least I can present myself in some sort of order. Even amongst you who do not expect it, I would rarely appear as dishevelled as I am at the moment, after being in the pouring rain all afternoon."

Waterstone's lips twitched. "True." He grinned, "I have to admit, that is true."

"Mind you, if you cut your hair it wouldn't be half so hard to keep tidy," said Rainstorm thoughtfully, with a quick, conspiratorial glance at Thunder Storm.

Tarkyn eyed him. "I have no intention of cutting my hair. It took me years to grow it."

"But this fellow you're going in to talk to, his hair is only shoulder length." Thunder Storm raised his eyebrows. "So it's not obligatory to wear it long? Or is it only obligatory for princes?"

Tarkyn looked from one to the other. "No. It is not obligatory for princes or for anyone else, as far as I know. It's a matter of personal vanity, if you must know, and that's all."

"Even if it's inconvenient?" asked Rainstorm innocently.

"Even if it's inconvenient," said Tarkyn firmly. He frowned fiercely around at all of them. "I can't believe I'm allowing anyone to question my appearance like this."

Stormaway gave a smug smile. "I told you, even with the oath, one man against a nation is poor odds."

Suddenly the four woodmen and even Stormaway smiled broadly and patted him on the back.

"Go on, Your Gorgeousness," said Autumn Leaves, with a big grin, "Get in there and get at him."

Tarkyn smiled sweetly at them all. "Right. Make sure you're watching." He turned to Stormaway. "Perhaps you should release him first. Then when you are ready, you may present me."

The four woodmen vanished.

Chapter 40

Leaning back awkwardly against the beech, Danton heard the approach of quiet footsteps. He turned his head to see the old wizard returning, a soft light glowing beside him.

"This is bloody uncomfortable," he said immediately.

Stormaway merely raised his eyebrows. "Perhaps we can do something about that. If you will agree not to attack me, at least for the time being, I will agree to untie you."

The elite guard frowned. "Why the sudden change of heart?"

"I was never going to keep you bound for long. Only long enough to establish your intentions, which I think I have done." Stormaway stared at him, "Agreed?"

"Yes, agreed," said the guardsman impatiently. As soon as Stormaway had unbound his hands, he brought them around to the front and began massaging his wrists to restore the circulation. "So, may I go?"

"I think not," said Stormaway. In answer to Danton's frown, he added, "His Highness is desirous of seeing you. When you feel ready, I will present you to him."

The guardsman stood up quickly and brushed himself down as best he could. Then he stood at attention and nodded to Stormaway. "I'm ready."

At a signal from Stormaway, Tarkyn emerged from between the trees. Immediately, the guardsman fell to one knee, bowed his head and placed his arm across his chest, hand on heart. There was a protracted silence.

Finally, the prince spoke. His voice was warm but held a clear note of reserve in it. "You may rise. I am pleased to see you, Danton."

Four woodmen in the surrounding trees watched in astonishment.

The guardsman stood up slowly. "Your Highness, I am relieved to know that you are safe."

"I, too, am glad that you were not hurt in the mess I left behind." The prince waved a hand at Stormaway, "Would you be kind enough to put out some refreshments for our guest?"

Tarkyn seated himself against a beech tree and looked at the standing guardsman. "Please. Be seated."

The guardsman sat down warily, watched the prince and waited.

"I understand you have been following my trail for some weeks now," remarked Tarkyn.

"Er not exactly, Sire."

The prince raised his eyebrows. "But surely that is what you told Stormaway?"

"I could not find your trail to follow." Danton explained hastily, "I have been searching for you but not following your trail."

"And what lead you to this place?"

"Nothing really. I had heard there was some sort of gathering of people some distance to the west of here and I was on my way there to see if perhaps you were among them."

"I know of this gathering of which you speak, although I am not yet sure of its purpose. Certainly I have not yet been there myself," there was a slight hesitation, "in person." Tarkyn accepted a glass of wine from Stormaway with a nod of thanks. With a sudden change of direction, the prince asked, his voice hard, "Are you not afraid of me, if I am now known as a rogue sorcerer?"

Danton's eyes twinkled as he gave a gentle smile, "No Sire."

"And why have you come to find me?"

Danton's smile faded. For the first time, he looked distressed. "My lord, how could you ask that? I have always stood by you. In the past, I have believed myself to be your friend, although your cool reception now makes me doubt my presumption in thinking that."

The prince stared at him long and hard. "You either betray me or my brother by coming here. Which is it?"

"My lord, if you must put it like that, I betray your brother. I could not possibly countenance serving him any longer after what he did to you. Whatever happens between you and me, I will not be returning to service at the palace." The guardsman took a long draught of wine with a hand that shook noticeably. "I beg your pardon if I took too much upon myself in seeking you out."

At last Tarkyn relented, "No, my friend. You did not take too much upon yourself." Four woodmen in the trees above breathed a sigh of relief. "But nothing is at it was. Come. Let us walk for a while in the moonlight."

The prince stood up and the guardsman quickly followed suit. As they walked out from under the lacy canopy of the beeches, the moonlight threw their shadows across the clearing. The eagle owl flew out past them and into the night. Tarkyn sent him a brief message of thanks.

"Wow," exclaimed Danton, "Did you see that owl? It flew very close to us."

"Yes. It was a big one, wasn't it?" Tarkyn smiled and placed an arm briefly around his friend's shoulder. "I am glad to see you. I did not think to see any of you again." He brought his arm back down and turned to face the guardsman. "Even though I have grown up around people who are self interested and fickle, still I was shocked by Sargon and Andoran. I'm afraid I have become wary, even of old friends."

"I can understand it, Sire. I too was shocked." Danton stared around the clearing and frowned, "You know, it's strange but I keep getting the feeling I'm being watched. Who else is with you?"

Tarkyn looked away into the trees and replied carefully, "There are no wizards or sorcerers with me, other than Stormaway."

Danton shrugged. All his movements were quick and lithe. "Maybe there's another owl somewhere watching us. I saw that one which just flew past, perched in the trees above me when I was tied up, and it was certainly watching me." He grinned. "It must have decided I was too big and tough to eat."

From the back they presented as an odd pair; Tarkyn half a head taller and much broader with his long black hair falling down his back, Danton's wavy blonde hair catching the moonlight as his lighter frame bounced energetically across the clearing. They sat down on a log under the clear sky.

Danton turned to the prince and peered at him through the semi darkness. "Your Highness, I hope you don't mind me asking, but what are you wearing?"

Tarkyn laughed, thinking that tonight, his appearance was being criticised from all sides.

"What's funny, my lord?"

"Oh Danton. You are such a dandy. I'm sorry you don't approve of my new outfit." Tarkyn put up a hand. "No. Don't tell me you do. I can tell from your face and your voice that you are unimpressed."

"Well, it is a little rough hewn, if you don't mind me saying so. And the colour! So drab you can hardly be seen."

"That's quite handy, wouldn't you say, when there may be people hunting me?" He smiled, "Anyway, I didn't have much choice after my own clothes were ruined."

"Oh no, were they? What a shame." Danton became thoughtful. "And I don't suppose you brought any of your other outfits with you?"

Tarkyn eyes were alight with laughter. "No Danton, I didn't. I left in a bit of a hurry, as you may recall."

"It's going to be cold tonight. I hope you have something warm to put on. I can lend you something of mine if you like, but it won't fit very well."

"Thank you, but I do have a cloak. In the same drab colouring as the rest of these clothes."

"Ah well, as long as it keeps you warm." The blonde-headed sorcerer looked up into the clear night sky. "You know, whatever you two did to that storm blew it right away." He turned to look at the prince. "That was a lot of power I saw there. Either your wizard is unbelievably strong or you have become more powerful or both. You couldn't have done anything like that a month ago."

Tarkyn glanced sideways at him, wondering how much to tell him. "I have unearthed some talents I was unaware of, under the tutelage of Stormaway Treemaster."

The guardsman rubbed a patch of dirt he could see on the black of his pants as he continued, "And why did you send all that power up into the clouds? Why didn't you just let the storm run its natural course?"

Tarkyn began to feel he was heading into deep water. "Stormaway was teaching me how the storm worked and how to control it." The prince stood up and Danton immediately rose to his feet also. "I think we had better get something to eat and think about bedding down for the night. It will be warmer back under the trees," said Tarkyn, thinking longingly that it would be warmer still in his shelter.

"You know, Your Highness, I think you should be careful about using your magic. Your bronze magic shining high into the clouds is what alerted me to your presence here."

Tarkyn grimaced. "You may be right. I'll have to use it very circumspectly when it might be seen. Still, I would have had to risk it today anyway." As soon as he said it, the prince knew he had said more than he wanted to.

The blonde guardsman frowned, "So it wasn't just a lesson?" Danton stole a look at the prince's face and gave a short, bitter laugh. "Your Highness, just tell me if you don't want me to know something. I can read your face like a book. Perhaps I should ask you a few less questions for the time being. I don't really need to know. I'm just curious. So it can wait until you're more sure of me."

Tarkyn smiled. "I am truly sorry to be so uncertain, Danton. It is difficult to feel safe in my present circumstances." *Although it was fine before you came along,* he thought. *I'll have to repair this. If he thinks I don't trust him, we'll never trap him if we need to.* "Anyway, having come this far, I might as well tell you what I can. Stormaway thought that someone had created the storm and it looked as if it was going to lead to widespread flooding. So we decided to counteract it."

"So who would go to the trouble of creating such a storm?" asked Danton. "Whoops. I beg your pardon. There I go again. Asking questions."

The prince shook his head. "Don't worry. You can ask, although in this case I don't know the answer except to say it may have something to do with that encampment in the west."

His friend looked at him. "I thought you hadn't been to this gathering, my lord. How do you know it's an encampment?"

Tarkyn shrugged, "People have spoken about it. Stormaway is good at gathering information, you know."

They arrived back into the shelter of the trees. Stormaway had set out wine and a small feast on a mat on the ground. Warm bedding had appeared and had been set up to one side. Danton's knives were still in a neat pile a short distance away. Danton's eyes roved idly over them but he said nothing. Stormaway appeared to have imbibed a few glasses already and smoothly took over the conversation, giving Tarkyn a rest from skating on thin ice. Finally the time came to bed down. Stormaway wove his way to his heap of bedding and made a big business of lying down and getting comfortable before apparently dropping off to sleep, mid slurred sentence.

Tarkyn intended to stay awake, but after the effort of the magic and all the ensuing issues he had had to deal with, he fell asleep almost immediately. In the darkness, Danton waited motionlessly. He listened carefully to the rhythmic breathing of the sorcerer and wizard lying beside him. Then quietly, he rose in one fluid movement and slid through the dark to his pile of knives. After a furtive look around, he quickly replaced the knives into their various sheaths around his body. Four woodmen watched him intently.

Danton straightened up and scanned the trees around and above him. Then he glided silently into the gloom of the surrounding forest. Slowly he worked his way through the trees around the sleeping prince, stopping every few yards to listen and look around. When he had made a full circumference, he returned to stand motionlessly over Tarkyn, looking down at him. Beneath him, Tarkyn suddenly jerked but appeared to remain asleep. Danton shook his head, scanned the trees again and heaved a quiet sigh. He bent down, quietly extracted his blanket from next to the prince and then sat himself against a tree, wrapping the blanket around himself.

All through the long hours of the night, he kept vigil. Every so often, he would repeat his circuit of the surrounding woods and return to sit against the tree. When dawn came, the guardsman was still watching, hollow-eyed.

Stormaway rose first, looking very heavy eyed. He glanced belligerently at Danton. "Not much of a sleeper, are you?"

Danton gave a tired smile. "I'm sorry. Did I keep you awake? I tried to be as quiet as possible."

Stormaway bent a frown in him, "What were you up to?"

"Me?" asked Danton in some surprise. "I was doing what a guardsman does best. I was guarding His Royal Highness."

The wizard grunted derisively, "What? Out here, miles from anywhere, in the middle of the forest?"

Danton shrugged. "Well, after your magic display yesterday, anyone for miles around might know he was here. Besides," the guardsman frowned, "I keep having the feeling that we're being watched. I've learnt to trust my instincts. So I couldn't just go to sleep and hope for the best. I thought about putting a shield up over us all. We're sitting ducks for an ambush in these trees. But I thought it might wake His Highness."

Stormaway seemed to find this mildly amusing. "Yes, I think it might have done."

Danton threw off his blanket and stood up. He scrubbed his face with his hands, yawned and stretched himself. "Now you're awake, I might hunt around for some wood and get a fire going."

When Danton returned, Tarkyn was awake and talking in low voices with Stormaway.As he approached, the prince shot a hard, calculating look at him. Danton stopped dead, the colour draining from his face. He bowed stiffly and placed the firewood carefully on the ground. Then he bowed again and stepped backwards for several feet before turning on his heel and heading back through the forest on the pretext of finding more wood. The prince did not acknowledge him or call after him.

The blonde sorcerer wandered around, collecting wood, his mind in a daze. This was not the prince he had last seen in Tormadell. The man back there talking with Stormaway was cold and aloof. All evening, he had not unbent and relaxed. Danton began to comprehend the damage that had been wrought by the King's betrayal of his youngest brother. Although the prince had said he was glad to see him, nothing in his manner had backed up that statement. In a surge of anger and disappointment, the guardsman threw down the wood he was carrying, sat down against the nearest tree and considered his position. He had given up everything to look for the prince. And now he had found him, instead of being greeted with the welcome he had anticipated, the guardsman was faced with a cool distant prince who had lost his trust in his fellow man and in particular, in his best friend. Danton put his face in his hands and sat there, wondering what to do next.

A slight sound roused him and he whipped his head up to find the prince standing before him. He leapt to his feet and bowed.

"Your pardon, Your Highness. I did not realise you were there," blurted out the guardsman. Then he stiffened in anticipation of a rebuke as he realised he had spoken first.

He was a little surprised when Tarkyn merely said, "You may sit down again, Danton. I will sit also."

Tarkyn sat down with his arms laced loosely over his raised knees. He stared steadily at the guardsman for several seconds without speaking. Danton waited, feeling tense in a way he had never felt before with this prince. Somehow, he felt his future was on the line but he didn't know why.

Finally, Tarkyn observed noncommittally, "I see you retrieved your knives."

"Yes, my lord. I did not feel sufficiently well armed to defend you without them."

"I understand you stayed awake all night keeping watch. Thank you for your efforts on my behalf." The prince's voice was still distant. "You may need to sleep sometime today, though."

Danton looked down at his hands then looked back up at the prince. "I think I might move on, my lord. If you will permit me."

Tarkyn frowned. "What? After searching all these weeks. You stay for only one night and then leave?"

Danton looked away into the forest. "I know now you are safe." He brought his eyes resolutely back around to meet the prince's. "I find you changed, my lord, and despite your courtesy, I can tell that my advent has not been welcome. It grieves me that you no longer trust me or feel the friendship we once had. So I would prefer to move on."

"Oh blast you, Danton! You always were overly sensitive."

Tarkyn sprang to his feet in some agitation and began to pace. Danton also stood up and waited. After several turns during which the prince seemed rather distracted, he stopped dead and looked at Danton.

Suddenly, much to his surprise, the prince strode over to him, grabbed him by the shoulders and said in the warmer, friendlier voice Danton was used to, "Enough of this. Come here, my friend," and pulled him into a bear hug.

The guardsman took a moment to respond since this was now more effusive than he was used to. After a moment, though, he un-stiffened and returned the prince's embrace.

When the prince let him go, Danton's face was a picture of confusion. "Your Highness, I don't understand. Why have you been so cold towards me? And now suddenly, you're not."

"Because, Danton, I have been making a decision and I have had to conceal information from you. And you know how edgy it makes me when I can't be straightforward. And now we have decided that I don't need to do that anymore."

"We? You and Stormaway, you mean?"

Tarkyn smiled cheerfully. "No. Not just Stormaway and me."

Danton's eyebrows snapped together. "But you told me you had no-one else with you. I have never before known you to lie."

The prince raised his eyebrows. "I may have changed but I haven't changed that much. I didn't lie, although in my opinion, I came pretty close. I said there were no wizards or sorcerers with me, and there aren't."

When Danton went to speak, the prince held up his hand. "Wait, Danton. Before we go any further, we need to make a couple of things clear. Firstly, if I explain my previous behaviour to you and re-avow my faith in you, will you stay?"

Tears sprang to the guardsman's eyes, "My will is yours to command, my liege. I had thought you did not want me with you."

"I am sorry, my friend, that my welcome has been so poor. There were complicating factors, as you are about to find out." Tarkyn took a big breath. "What I am about to tell you now is in itself an avowal of my faith in you. You are about to be honoured with a trust that, until now, has only been given to Stormaway and myself. If you betray this trust, you betray your honour, yourself and me."

Danton went down on one knee before his prince. "You have my pledge, my lord. I will not fail you."

"Thank you, Danton." The prince placed his hand lightly under the guardsman's arm. "You may stand." When Danton was once more standing at attention before him. "In a moment, I would like you to meet some people. Under no circumstances whatsoever, must you use magic, knives or any kind of violence against them. Is that clear?"

Danton looked totally confused again but nodded vaguely.

Tarkyn's voice became sharper. "Is that clear?

Danton focused on the prince's face, with a puzzled frown on his face. "Not really, my lord, if there are no people with you. But I will undertake to do no violence."

"Good enough."

In the next instant, a ring of woodfolk appeared around them. Danton made a convulsive movement that he quelled at its inception. They were all dressed in the same garb as the prince and were all slightly shorter than himself. A circle of green eyes watched him. They carried no weapons that he could see but since he was wearing concealed knives himself, he didn't place much weight on appearances. He forced himself not to stare around at them all and maintained what he hoped was a courteous demeanour.

"Danton, I would like you to meet the woodfolk. I will introduce you to each of them but I'm sure we will all understand if you don't remember everyone's names at first."

A chorus of forest sounds issued forth and Danton realised that the woodfolk were commenting on what Tarkyn had said.

Danton bowed. "I am pleased to meet you. I will do my best to remember your names."

Tarkyn scanned the ring quickly and realised that there were representatives from every faction there. The prince walked formally around the circle with Danton, introducing each person with the same level of courtesy and distance. When they had finished, he swept his arm around the circle.

In a commanding voice, the prince proclaimed, "These people have agreed to allow you to abide among them. In return, you must swear a solemn oath never to reveal their presence to anyone else even, in fact especially, to the king. If you foreswear this oath, your life will be forfeit." The prince brought his eyes back to rest on his liegeman. "Kneel."

Danton went down on one knee, hand on heart.

"Do you so swear, Danton Patronell, Lord of Sachmore?"

"Yes, my liege. On pain of death, I do."

"You may rise."

With the formalities over, Tarkyn looked around and realised several of the oathless woodfolk were regarding him very strangely indeed. He left Danton in the care of Stormaway and walked over to speak to them, his eyes shining with mischief.

"What's the matter? Never seen a prince at work before, have you?"

Raging Water stared at him. "No. We have not. It was almost as interesting as your light show yesterday."

Tarkyn gave a short laugh. "That wasn't even a full ceremony just then. That was merely a small aside." He looked down at himself. "And frankly, the clothes reduced the impact." He grinned at them. "I'm much more impressive if I'm dressed in full regalia."

"Stop bragging. Let's go and get some breakfast," said Waterstone, walking up to hear the end of this. "And bring your friend with you. You don't want Stormaway bending his ear all day."

As they walked back towards the large clearing where the rest of the woodfolk awaited them, Waterstone and Danton found themselves side by side while Tarkyn was carried off by an enthusiastic Rainstorm.

Danton mused, "I was right, wasn't I? We were being watched."

Waterstone smiled grimly. "You certainly were."

"And you were making sure I didn't hurt him or try to carry him off, I presume?"

"Yes. You came bloody close to being shot a few times last night. When you retrieved your knives and stood over Tarkyn, it was touch and go."

Danton's face tightened. "And did Prince Tarkyn know you were standing by, ready to shoot me?"

Waterstone heard the tension in the young sorcerer's voice. "Yes. He knew. You have no idea how often I had to reassure him that we weren't planning to kill you." Seeing the confusion still on Danton's face, he added, "Slingshots, you know. We usually use bows and arrows but not against Tarkyn's friend."

Light dawned. "Oh, so that's how I was knocked out." Danton gave a little smile. "It's funny isn't it? I was guarding the prince against you because I could feel someone watching me. And you were guarding the prince against me."

Waterstone clapped the young sorcerer on the shoulder. "Well that's a good start. At least we have something in common."

Danton became thoughtful, "I didn't do a very good job of it, did I? You could have killed any of us at any time if you had so chosen. I should have put my shield over us."

Waterstone nodded. "Yes. You probably should, in similar circumstances. Last night however, that may have lead to some fairly unpleasant consequences. So it was good that you didn't."

"What could you have done against a shield?"

"Not much." The woodman shrugged, "But we had two accomplices who would have been inside the shield. Stormaway was not asleep at any time and we could wake Tarkyn without you being aware of it."

Danton thought back. "You woke him when I was standing over him, didn't you?" The guardsman turned bleak purple eyes towards Waterstone. "It is difficult to come to terms with such a lack of trust from someone I have felt so close to, for so long."

Waterstone smiled in sympathy. "It is difficult to come to terms with it in someone you have just recently met. I had to go to extreme lengths to get him to trust me. Tarkyn has been badly hurt. The trust will return over time." The woodman paused, "And he was not acting purely on his own behalf last night. He was protecting us; not only that, you have to remember Tarkyn wasn't a saleable commodity last time you saw him."

Danton frowned suddenly and spoke sharply. "That is no way to speak about His Highness. Furthermore, I don't think you should be referring to him simply as Tarkyn. He should be referred to as Prince Tarkyn at the very least."

"Oh ho. Up on your high horse already, your lordship." Waterstone stopped and put his hands on his hips. "Well, let me tell you something, my young buck. I call him Tarkyn because he gave me his express permission to do so and there is nothing I would ever say about Tarkyn that I wouldn't say to his face. Not only that, you will have to watch your step in the way you speak to people around here. Not everyone acknowledges the prince as their liege and even among those who do, there are serious pockets of resentment. Luckily you tried that one on me first or you might have found yourself in the middle of a nasty fight."

Danton glowered at him. "I might ask who you are, to be throwing your weight around like this."

Waterstone thought of several levelling replies he could produce but settled for, "I am no more or less than a woodman. All woodfolk are of equal rank so you are speaking to the highest rank in the forest, other than the prince."

"Or the lowest." snapped Danton.

"I can see your mathematical concepts are excellent," replied Waterstone dryly. He turned and began walking again. "Danton, I do not wish to fall out with you. I would say that you and I both spend a lot of our time standing up for our prince. I don't think he will feel very comfortable if he finds us at loggerheads."

They walked in silence for a few minutes. Then Waterstone glanced sideways at the young sorcerer. "I think I should point out that the reputation of sorcerers among woodfolk is based on the information we have had about Andoran and Sargon, Tarkyn's brothers and bandits. Tarkyn is the only sorcerer we know who has mitigated that impression."

Danton's eyes widened. He gave a low whistle. "Oh my stars! So what guarantee do I have that you people won't turn on me?"

"None." Waterstone eyes met and held the sorcerer's. "And nothing would protect you, if you tried to hurt the prince."

Danton returned his gaze steadily for several long seconds. "You are right," he said at last, turning away. "We do have a lot in common. And after that little warning, I feel rather intimidated at the thought of meeting crowds of sorcerer-hating woodfolk."

"As well you might, particularly since your arrival has delayed our response to a serious crisis."

"I beg your pardon for inconveniencing you," said Danton stiffly. Then he shot the woodman a shy smile, "But my prince's welfare is very dear to me. You have no idea what a relief it is to have found him safe. Perhaps in return for your safekeeping of him, I could assist you with your crisis. This has something to do with those wolves, doesn't it?"

Waterstone nodded, a gleam of approval in his eye. "You are no fool. I'll give you that much." He hesitated, "We would appreciate your help but you do not owe us anything. Many of us are sworn to protect the prince."

Danton snorted, "So were many sorcerers who have now turned on him. But their loyalty to the king overrides their loyalty to Prince Tarkyn."

Waterstone was on the cusp of saying that woodfolk were not so fickle when he remembered the recent conflict their loyalty to Tarkyn and woodfolk lore that they had just spent a week resolving. "It is difficult when disparate commitments come into conflict."

"Especially when stringent penalties are exacted for forsaking them."

"How true," said Waterstone warmly. "What penalty would you face for forsaking Tarkyn?"

Danton raised his eyebrows in surprise. "None, now that he is exiled, except my own conscience. It is for forsaking the king that I would face punishment."

"I see. So nothing is now compelling you to behave as you do towards Tarkyn."

"My respect and lifelong devotion to him compel it."

"Extraordinary." Waterstone fell into a reverie for a little while, before giving himself a shake and saying, "Well, having seen how you behave around the prince, I think you are going to be shocked by many things you see. I suggest you keep your reactions to yourself and talk to Tarkyn or me about it afterwards."

Just as he finished saying this, Tarkyn and Rainstorm reached the clearing ahead of them. No one stood up, although someone brought each of them a bowl of porridge and a spoon.

Tarkyn nodded his thanks and then said to everyone, "I would like to introduce Danton Patronell to you. I'll leave you to get to know each other in your own time." So saying, he sat himself down against a log to eat, next to Rainstorm.

Danton stopped dead in his tracks and stared in shock. Tarkyn looked around at him and gave a smile. "Danton, get yourself a bowl of a porridge and sit down here," he said, patting the ground beside him.

Someone thrust a bowl and spoon into the bemused sorcerer's hands as he sat down. When Waterstone joined them, he whispered, "Thank heavens you warned me. I would have ripped shreds off everyone if I'd been left to my own devices."

Rainstorm frowned at him. "What's your problem? They're just not talkative yet because they've all just woken up."

Tarkyn smiled. "I don't think that is the issue. Unless I'm much mistaken, my liegeman here expected everyone to stand up and bow."

"He's mad, prince," said Rainstorm firmly. "Why would anyone do that?"

"Prince?... You address His Highness merely as *prince*?" came a strangled query from Danton.

Waterstone was grinning hugely. "You're doing well, Danton. Just keep that outrage in check and you'll be fine. "

A few minutes later, Stormaway, Autumn Leaves and Thunder Storm came over to join them.

"So Danton," said Waterstone cheerfully, "this is the merry group who stood vigil with you and over you last night. You were lucky. At least you and Stormaway were on the ground. We four were up in the trees. You can barely move without a bough groaning; so you have to be even more careful about changing position."

"And if this blasted prince hadn't been so scrupulous...," began Autumn Leaves. He stopped as Danton choked on his porridge and went bright red. "Are you all right?" asked Autumn Leaves in some concern as he belted him helpfully on the back.

Danton nodded while Waterstone and Tarkyn grinned at each other. When Danton recovered, Autumn Leaves resumed his whinge. "So as I was saying, if this blasted prince hadn't been so scrupulous, we could have just used mind control on you and had it sorted in five minutes. As it is, all five of us, actually six of us including you, are dog tired from staying up all night."

The prince smiled at the woodman's diatribe. "I'm sorry Autumn Leaves. Thank you to all of you for doing that. At least this way I can face Danton."

Danton frowned, "Your Highness, why are you apologising? It is our duty to protect you in whatever way you see fit."

"It might be your duty," retorted Rainstorm, "But it's certainly not mine. And even if it were, I wouldn't be told how to do it."

"Yes, thank you, Rainstorm," said Tarkyn dryly. "I think we all know your views on authority."

Danton eyed Rainstorm but let the issue drop, mindful of Waterstone's warning. Instead he asked about mind control. When the whole discussion had been explained to him, he looked a little ill. "You woodfolk are scary, aren't you? I don't know how I would have felt about it. I might have liked it better than the cool welcome I received."

"You still would have received the cool welcome. But you would have been subjected to mind control as well," said Tarkyn. "And you would still have known I didn't trust you."

Danton shrugged. "I don't know why you've decided to trust me now. Just because I didn't attack the first night means nothing. If I were going to do anything, I would wait for several nights and make sure I knew what safeguards were in place, how you two would react, if anyone else was around…" He looked at the prince with his head on one side. "You didn't look as though you were ready to trust me when I came back with the wood this morning, Sire. You looked cold, and unwelcoming, and like someone I had never met before."

"It was your reaction to that expression that decided it," explained Waterstone. "We saw how upset you were. Tarkyn picked up your feelings of anger and disappointment when you threw the wood down. Those are not the reactions of a thwarted killer or kidnapper. Anger and frustration maybe; not disappointment. And then you verified it by saying you were going to leave."

"So, how did Prince Tarkyn suddenly know what you had all decided?"

The woodfolk all looked at one another. By mutual agreement, Autumn Leaves explained the prince's and their different forms of mental communication.

When Danton had digested this, he raised his eyebrows and turned to the prince. "And more importantly, why was it not your sole decision, Your Highness?"

The prince grimaced. "I think you will find very little around here is my sole decision, but least of all that one. The woodfolk have remained hidden from sorcerers and wizards for hundreds of years. It is not my place to disrupt that. Besides, just as you are, so am I pledged not to reveal their presence. So are all woodfolk. It had to be a full community decision."

"And if they had not decided in my favour?" asked Danton slowly.

"I would have argued for you, if I alone had decided that I trusted you. But I would never have revealed the presence of the woodfolk to you and I would have had to let you go on your way, even if it had cost our friendship."

Danton nodded his head briskly and surprised them all by saying, "That is as it should be. You cannot break an oath, even for a friendship."

Tarkyn could not resist throwing a small triumphant glance at Autumn Leaves.

"All right. All right," grumped Autumn Leaves. "So maybe there are two honourable sorcerers. That still leaves thousands unaccounted for."

Chapter 41

Once breakfast was over, Tarkyn looked around at his little cohort and sighed. "I suppose I had better have that discussion with the group that chose the encampment. Thunder Storm, could you please ask them to gather over on the other side of the clearing there?"

Once the woodfolk had gathered, Tarkyn stood up, ready to head over to them. Immediately, Danton also rose to his feet.

Tarkyn smiled, "No, Danton. Could you stay here for the moment, please? I need to do this alone." When the sorcerer remained standing, the prince added, "Danton, you have my permission to be seated." He looked at the others. "Perhaps you could explain about the oath to Danton while you're waiting. There is a lot he needs to know."

The blond headed sorcerer sat down but sent a glowering look around the rest of the group who had remained carelessly seated while the prince stood. As Tarkyn moved away, he heard Waterstone murmuring something quietly to the feisty young guardsman that seemed to calm him.

As the prince approached Tree Wind's group, he saw them watching him apprehensively. He noticed Running Feet and Ancient Oak sitting deep in their midst even though they had voted the other way. Tarkyn had already decided that reading the riot act would only serve to crystallise this groups' first impressions of him and would do little to further goodwill between them.

So when he reached them, he said, "Shall we all sit down so we can discuss things in comfort?" Once everyone was seated, he asked, "Why do you think I wanted to talk to you today?"

After a few moments' silence, a scowly young man, reminiscent of Rainstorm, said, "Because we supported Tree Wind's idea and you didn't like that. You want us to support your opinions. My name is North Wind."

"And what were my opinions?"

"Presumably to search out Golden Toad and his family at the southern swamp," sneered the young man.

Tarkyn looked around the group. "And what made you decide that searching for Golden Toad was my preferred option?"

North Wind shrugged, "Obvious, really. All your cronies advocated for it."

The prince frowned, "All my what?"

"You know, cronies. The people who keep company with you."

The prince's face cleared, "Ah. You must mean the people who had enough courage to endure whatever I threw at them so that you, as a people, could uphold your oath." Tarkyn took a deep breath to quell the anger he felt building up. "In actual fact, you all supported my opinion, for which I would like to thank you. Your option saved me from having to do two lots of searching."

Inevitably, Tree Wind spoke up. "So why didn't you just decide to go with the better option instead of leaving it to chance?"

"Because I do not want to decide for you. I want you to have the choice. I trust the judgement of the woodfolk. You have made decisions by consensus for hundreds of years. Last night, opinions were based on prejudice and because of that no one would shift and no decision was reached. If I had given myself the power to break the deadlock, I would have undermined the whole authority of woodfolk society."

There was stunned silence.

Eventually, when no one spoke, the prince said mildly, "None of you has given me a chance. You left me on the second day after my arrival, injured and unconscious, and haven't come near me again until two days ago. I know you resent the oath. I know you resent me. But I am not my father. He never had to live with the oath as I have done." Tarkyn ran his hand through his hair. "I am not asking you to like me or even to come near me. But I do want to make sure that your decision-making ability is not crippled by prejudice. Sometimes I will be right. Sometimes I will be wrong. Just as all of you are, from time to time. Don't use my opinion as a foil for your own. Listen to my opinion but make your own decisions based on your own knowledge. You are strong independent people. Make sure you stay that way."

Tarkyn stood up and left without another word being spoken. Tree Wind and her group watched him walk back across the clearing in silence. When eventually they spoke amongst themselves, it was clear, even from a distance that they were still stunned.

As the prince approached his own group, Danton stood up and bowed. Tarkyn wondered why he had never noticed before how intrusive court etiquette was on other people's lives. The prince acknowledged his liegeman's bow with a courtly nod then indicated that they should both sit down.

Rainstorm was round eyed. "Hi, prince. What did you do to that lot? They look pole-axed."

Ignoring Danton's pained expression, Tarkyn glanced over at them then returned his gaze to those around him. A small smile played around his lips. "I didn't get angry, if that's what you're thinking. Although I came close when one of them referred to the home guard as my cronies."

"Very restrained, Your Highness," said Thunder Storm, with a smile, "I think that remark might even have taxed my temper."

The prince raised his eyebrow in surprise. "Thunder Storm, I've never seen you even the slightest bit angry."

Thunder Storm's smiled broadened. "Perhaps I should have said, 'That remark would have taxed my temper, had I been you.'"

Danton looked on, speechless at the woodman's temerity, and waited for the inevitable set down.

Tarkyn merely waved his hand and smiled, "Much more accurate, Thunder Storm. Well, it did, but I was determined not to give them more fuel for their fire against me."

"So what did you say?" pressed Rainstorm.

Tarkyn shrugged, "Not a great deal. I said that if they allowed me to make the decisions, it would undermine woodfolk society. So basically, they should not be too influenced by my opinions one way or the other and should remain independent."

The prince then found himself surrounded by another group of thoughtful people.

After a moment, Autumn Leaves asked, "But is that what you set out to do? I thought you wanted them to listen to you as forest guardian?"

Danton frowned, "Forest what?"

Tarkyn waved a dismissive hand, "I'll tell you about it later…I do want them to listen to me. But I don't want anyone slavishly following or opposing my advice. You should know that by now." He gave a little smirk. "And I did happen to mention how they had all left me for dead when I was injured."

Waterstone smiled, "Light begins to dawn. You are a cunning bastard, sometimes, young Tarkyn."

"Thanks," Tarkyn might have said more, but he was overridden by strangled roar at his side. He turned to see Danton, hands clenched at his sides, bright red in the face, his tolerance levels overloaded, exploding with wrath.

"How dare you speak to His Highness like that?" The guardsman's voice was shaking with anger. "I have tried to allow some leeway but this is more than enough. You show him no due respect. You do not stand for him. You do not bow to him. You abuse the privilege of using his first name by being overly familiar. And now you use words to describe him that I would be ashamed to repeat."

"I was actually being complimentary," replied Waterstone mildly.

Danton turned his wrath, unabated, onto Rainstorm. "And you, how dare you just refer to his lordship as 'prince' in that disrespectful manner? And dispute his right to your protection?"

Rainstorm's eyes snapped in anger. "That's it. I'm going to have to kill him." Before anyone could stop him, the young woodman swung a fist at the guardsman but found his arm blocked. He swung wildly one fist after another in quick succession until he had connected often enough to send the guardsman sprawling.

"Rainstorm! Stop this!" ordered the prince.

But the woodman's blood was up and he took no heed. Danton scrabbled to his feet just in time to brace himself as a wiry ball of fury threw himself at him. The wind swirled leaves and dust around them as Rainstorm bore Danton over with the weight of his rush and punched him hard on the jaw.

"Enough," said the prince sharply. This time, Tarkyn did not wait for Rainstorm to respond. "*Shturrum,*" he intoned at the two men and dragged the now unresisting woodman off the guardsman. When he had created sufficient space between them, he released the spell. Rainstorm immediately turned his ire on the prince and charged at him instead. The trees around the clearing thrashed in a sudden gust of wind.

Tarkyn frowned in consternation but dealt with the immediate problem by waving a languid hand and intoning, "*Shturrum*" again, this time only at Rainstorm. He glared at the unmoving young woodman. "If you wish to be released, you will have to calm yourself first. I don't know whether you were unaware, or whether you had forgotten, but Danton guaranteed to use no violence of any kind against woodfolk. So, well done on attacking someone who couldn't fight back." The bite of sarcasm in his tone was chilling. He continued in a quiet, disdainful voice, "And I would not suggest that you continue your attack on me. You are surrounded by people who will not stand by idly and watch you do it. But before any of them has time to react, I can assure that I will send you flying to land hard against that tree behind you. Don't think you will enjoy it. It will hurt – badly. I don't impose many boundaries but there are some and you have just crossed them."

With a wave of his hand, the sorcerer released his spell. Rainstorm's face suffused with chagrin and tears sprang to his eyes. He looked around wildly at everyone, then turned on his heel and ran.

"Ooh dear," said Tarkyn quietly, "I think I may have been a little too harsh."

"My lord, how could you say so?" said Danton hotly, as he rubbed his bruising jaw. "He tried to attack you. He should be severely punished."

"He already has been," said the prince ruefully. "He is still young and his emotions are undisciplined, not unlike my own, I would have to say." Then Tarkyn turned on his liegeman and let fly. "But you, Danton, have no excuse. You presume to order these people around and to impose you own expectations on them, in direct contradiction to my own. I am very displeased. You have had the barefaced audacity to come in here and throw your weight about without even consulting me on my wishes. You are welcome to your own expectations but you have no right to impose them on anyone else."

Danton bowed stiffly. "I beg your pardon, Your Highness. I will strive to do better."

Tarkyn took a deep breath and relented, "I'm sure you will. You did well not to retaliate. Now, let me see to that jaw of yours."

"In what way, Sire?"

The prince gave a short laugh. "To heal it, Danton. One of those new skills I was mentioning." Tarkyn put his hand on the guardsman's shoulder. "Close your eyes. Now take the power I am sending you and direct it into the damaged tissue of your jaw."

Danton hesitated briefly but then did as he was asked. After a couple of minutes, he opened his eyes and gazed in amazement at the prince. "That was impressive. I've never come across anything like that before."

After a moment, Danton turned his attention to Waterstone, made him a small bow and said formally, "Waterstone, I apologise for not heeding your words. And for trying to impose my opinions on you." He ran a shaky hand across his forehead. "To tell you the truth, I feel a little out of my depth. All the rules I am used to, do not seem to apply here and suddenly, I do not know how I should behave." He looked at his prince, "The last thing I want to do is offend you, Sire. Perhaps if you could spare the time, at some point, to explain your expectations…."

"I will, Danton, but not now. You all need to get some rest. I suspect everyone's tolerance levels will improve after some sleep. Meanwhile, I need to go and repair a young woodman's opinion of himself. I believe we are all meeting at lunchtime to work out our course of action. So, Danton, I will see you in three hours' time."

Tarkyn walked off into the forest in the direction the feisty young woodman had taken. He wandered aimlessly for a while then thought about where he himself tended to go when he was upset and headed down towards the stream. The waters were still higher than they had been when he first saw them, but the stream was well within its banks and burbling calmly across the rocks. Tarkyn followed the stream around a bend and then, clearing a small overhang of bushes, came upon Rainstorm and North Wind, sitting on the bank of the stream, deep in conversation.

The prince sketched a small bow and said, "My apologies for intruding," and stepped back, preparing to leave them to it.

Rainstorm threw him a black look. “No. Please don’t feel you have to stay. I wouldn’t expect you’d want to speak to us any more, now that you have a fellow sorcerer to talk to.”

As Tarkyn paused, working out how to respond, he was startled by North Wind saying, “I don’t think his sorcerer friend is feeling much happier than you at the moment. To give him his due, the prince threw his weight around in both directions.”

Rainstorm stared angrily across the water. “I bet he didn’t call Danton a coward.”

As North Wind met Tarkyn’s eyes, the prince indicated himself and then pointed away with a query. North Wind shook his head and pointed downwards, indicating that he should stay. Tarkyn sat down quietly behind them with his back to a tree.

“I don’t think you’re a coward. Hot-headed maybe but not a coward,” said the prince quietly.

Rainstorm sent him a smouldering look over his shoulder. “Oh yeah, right. You think I would knowingly attack someone who couldn’t hit back. In my experience, that’s a coward.”

“I presume from this, that you didn’t know Danton had agreed not to use any violence?”

“That’s not the point, Your Highness. The point is, you thought I might have known and still attacked him.” Rainstorm picked up a stone and threw it with some violence into the stream.

North Wind again surprised him. “The prince said you either forgot or didn’t know when you hit Danton.”

Tarkyn raised his eyebrows, “You must have been listening closely. I didn’t think you would be able to hear from the other side of the clearing.”

North Wind gave a wry grin, “Autumn Leaves relayed the confrontation to me.”

“I might have known our peacemaker would be in this somewhere.” Tarkyn looked at Rainstorm’s stiff back and grimaced, “Rainstorm, Danton overstepped the mark and so did you. It happens to all of us some time or other. That’s when we find out where the limits really are.”

“You’re bloody lucky the prince didn’t belt the living daylights out of you, charging him like that,” put in North Wind. “I would have, in his position.”

“You couldn’t lay a finger on me, if I didn’t want you to,” sneered Rainstorm at his friend, determinedly unbending.

“I meant if I was the prince, you grumpy bastard,” he said, rolling his eyes in the prince’s direction.

Tarkyn gave an answering smile but held his peace. A long silence ensued, broken occasionally by the splash of a stones being thrown into the water. Tarkyn found himself a stick and kept himself amused by breaking it slowly into little pieces. North Wind glanced at him after a particularly loud crack as a piece of stick broke off and saw what he was doing. A slow smile dawned on his face and his eyes went out of focus. A moment later Rainstorm looked around too.

Tarkyn laughed quietly. "Would you like to see another one?" he asked, as he dropped the last of the first stick and picked up another.

"Very funny, Your Highness," scowled Rainstorm.

The prince's smile faded. "Don't call me that. I like you calling me 'prince'. Don't take what Danton said to heart. He just doesn't understand yet." Tarkyn proceeded to destroy his second stick as he talked. "And Rainstorm, I do thank you for standing guard all night long, last night. It was a long, long night for you who stayed awake. Embarrassingly, despite my best efforts, I'm afraid I slept through most of it."

Finally Rainstorm began to unbend. "I don't know how you could have, with that unknown quantity sitting so near." He threw another stone into the water. "You wouldn't be much good as a lookout," he added as a final jab.

Tarkyn shook his head ruefully. "I must have felt safe enough with you all guarding me. I told you, princes are a constant drain on the people around them. On the bright side, it's lucky I wasn't as overtired as the rest of you, or I might have waded in and returned your attack."

"I am not overtired," stated Rainstorm baldly.

Tarkyn raised his eyebrows. "Aren't you? It's probably the adrenalin then. Because the others have all gone to have a rest before the lunchtime meeting."

"Have they?" Suddenly Rainstorm yawned. "Blast! I wish you hadn't said that. Now I am tired and there's not enough time to sleep before lunchtime. If I go to sleep now, I'll feel awful when I wake up in an hour's time."

"You'll just have to hang on until this afternoon," said North Wind sympathetically.

Tarkyn frowned suddenly, "You know, North Wind, I had picked you out as a rebellious young character like our friend here but you aren't behaving like that at all anymore."

"No audience," put in Rainstorm with a cheeky grin at his friend. "I think there might be someone he is trying to impress."

North Wind jabbed him in the ribs and turned a dull red.

"I see," said Tarkyn thoughtfully. "Might I suggest that she would probably be a lot more impressed by what I've seen of you here, than what I saw of you previously. Though, to give you your due, at least you had the courage to speak to me which was more than anyone else did for a while."

"Anyway," said North Wind, with a poisonous look at his friend, "Rainstorm has it all wrong. I was baiting you because I thought you were going to rip into us." The young woodman shrugged and tinge of resentment underlined his next words. "Besides, I can't be as rebellious as Rainstorm is, because I'm under oath."

"You see? You still don't understand," said the prince in some exasperation. "I hardly ever give orders. I make requests, just as you do, and I listen when there is an objection."

"You ordered Tree Wind to come forward last night and ordered us to see you this morning," objected North Wind.

"Blast! So I did." Tarkyn ran his hand through his hair. "But if you worked with me instead of against me, I wouldn't have to."

North Wind raised his eyebrows in derision. "That's just the same as saying, 'Either you co-operate or I'll force you to.'"

"No," snapped Tarkyn, "It's the same as saying, 'Give me the same respect as you would give another woodman.'"

"But you're not just another woodman!" retaliated North Wind.

Tarkyn's eyes flickered and he went very still.

North Wind smiled faintly, "You are a woodman and you deserve to be, but you're a lot more than that. It's no good trying to pretend it's any different."

Tarkyn shook his head in confusion, "I am trying to make the oath as inconspicuous as possible."

North Wind's smile broadened. "Maybe you are, but it is there, all the same. Even aside from the oath, you are the guardian of the forest with powers way beyond ours. And however people may react, it is obvious that you are, and will be, pivotal to our survival against these hunters of woodfolk." The woodman shrugged. "So I just can't see that you're going to be respected only to the same extent as any other woodman. You're bound to be respected more, if you see what I mean."

"Perhaps. But at the moment, the same would be a good start," said Tarkyn dryly.

North Wind chuckled, "Oh, I think you've sorted that little issue out amongst my lot. I don't think you'll find them going against you without good reason in the future."

"What's so funny?" asked Tarkyn frowning.

"Your masterly argument that by giving you a fair hearing we would protect our independence."

"Don't you agree with it?"

North Wind was still smiling. "Oh yes, it's a brilliant argument. Of course, it doesn't take into account that you're better at getting your point across than most of us. But in essence, what you said is true."

Tarkyn looked at him uncertainly. "I was not trying to mislead you, you know."

The young woodman shook his head. "I didn't think you were. I think you have created a level playing field and it is now up to us to resist your arguments if we want to."

Rainstorm huffed, "At least your opinion isn't disregarded because of your age, prince, like mine is."

"I don't think that is entirely true. Sun Shower referred to me as a young upstart, as I recall. And Raging Water treats me like a young puppy most of the time. I didn't realise I was battling against that as well." Tarkyn raised his eyebrows, "So all is not as equal as it seems, after all? I wondered what authority you were rebelling against, seeing there are no ranks."

North Wind and Rainstorm met each other's eyes and nodded simultaneously.

"Oh yes. Parents and older people must be given greater respect," confirmed North Wind. "So annoying!"

Tarkyn thought back to a conversation he had had with Waterstone. "But does the respect for your opinion not depend on the experience you can bring to the discussion? In which case, isn't there a greater likelihood that an older person will have relevant experience to back their opinion?"

Rainstorm looked disgusted. "You sound just like my parents."

Tarkyn laughed. "Sorry about that. I am just trying to understand woodfolk society. In my society, rank comes before age. So courtiers deferred to me from a very young age. As far back as I can remember, even adults would bow when I entered a room."

Rainstorm eyes grew round. "What a wonderful concept. I would have loved that."

"Oh, I don't know. It's not as great as it sounds. Don't forget, both my parents and my brothers outranked me. If I threw my weight around too much, my nanny would get one of them and I would have to submit anyway and apologise for being uncivil."

Rainstorm crowed, "That would be embarrassing!"

The prince gave a wry smile. "It was. I didn't let it happen more often than I had to, I can tell you."

Tarkyn became aware that North Wind was studying him with a slight frown on his face. The prince raised his eyebrows slightly in query.

"I am beginning to realise how big the concessions are that you are making," said North Wind slowly. "That oath was designed to ensure that you would be deferred to as Danton defers to you, wasn't it?"

Tarkyn nodded shortly and transferred his gaze to look out into the waters of the stream. "Yes. It was."

"You don't have to negotiate with us at all. Far from fighting to have your opinions considered, you could just dictate your wishes, couldn't you?" pressed North Wind.

Again Tarkyn nodded. "Yes. I could."

"Not to me, he couldn't," said Rainstorm.

Now the prince did look around. He grimaced. "I'm afraid I have bad news for you on that front. Unless I am much mistaken, you are now also under the bounds of the oath." Seeing the look of horror on Rainstorm's face, Tarkyn continued quickly, "I don't know how or why, but when you threatened to attack me, there was a warning rush of wind just as there was when Tree Wind attacked me."

Rainstorm's face was white. "You bastard. You have tricked us all!"

Tarkyn lifted his hands, palms outwards. "No, Rainstorm. I promise you. I haven't. Anyway, it may not be true. It has only happened once. It may be coincidence."

Far from being mollified, Rainstorm sneered, "Let's test it then, shall we?"

So saying, Rainstorm drew his legs up under himself and launched himself at the prince. Tarkyn rolled quickly out of the way and came up into a crouch. The wind came roaring through the trees. Ignoring it, Tarkyn swivelled to face the woodman just as he threw himself towards the prince. Tarkyn raised an arm across his body and thrust outwards to deflect Rainstorm's impetus sideways, sending him sprawling on the edge of the stream. The trees around them were thrashing under the onslaught of the wind. Leaves scattered around them and whirls of dust were thrown up from the banks of the stream.

Rainstorm lifted himself onto one elbow, took in the mayhem around him and bowed his head in despair. As the air around him quietened, he rolled onto his stomach and buried his face in his arms. For several minutes, his shoulders shook silently.

Tarkyn turned a stricken face to North Wind. Once again, Tarkyn gestured at himself and pointed away to suggest he should leave. This time, North Wind shrugged uncertainly in response. The prince considered the barrier that would exist between Rainstorm and himself if he left now and decided to stay.

After a while, when Rainstorm's shoulders had stilled, Tarkyn said quietly, "Rainstorm, first and foremost, I am your friend. I promise you, I did not contrive this. It must have happened when your people said that all woodfolk were one and that you must uphold the honour of those who had sworn the oath. Either then or when I was accepted as a woodman. I don't know. I didn't design the oath and I have no power over it, just as I told you."

Silence greeted this sally.

Tarkyn continued, "I am truly sorry this has happened. I hate the destruction that is built into the oath. I can only say that I don't want anything to change between us. You and I have already worked out rules of engagement. There is no need for them to change."

"That's easy for you to say," came a muffled voice, "You haven't just lost your freedom and your autonomy and your independence." Another sob issued forth.

"Actually, I have. In the society I come from, I have." After that, Tarkyn gave up on words and sent forth waves of fellow feeling. North Wind's eyes widened and he smiled.

A few minutes later, Rainstorm sat up and vigorously rubbed the palms of his hands over his eyes. He dropped his hands and presented red eyes to his companions. He sniffed and managed a shaky smile, "So. That's the worst news I've had all week. Actually, it's the worst news I've had in all my life." He sniffed again. "No offence meant, prince."

Tarkyn gave a short, bitter laugh. "None taken. I will try to remember it's the concept and not the person you object to." Something in his tone of voice turned his sentence into a query.

Rainstorm nodded firmly. "Yes, prince. It's not you. I suppose if this had to happen, it's better that it's you than some power-mongering sorcerer."

"I would think so. I think that my brothers would be a poor substitute, for instance, if you were hoping to maintain your independence."

"So, welcome to the club, Rainstorm," said North Wind, trying to conceal a smirk and failing signally.

"It is you who are not in the club," retorted Rainstorm, making a swift recovery. "You are not a member of the home guard, as I am, regardless of the oath."

Tarkyn regarded him quizzically. "Are you? Last thing I remember, you and I were arguing about whether you wanted to join and whether I wanted you to."

Rainstorm waved a dismissive hand, "You know I did and you did." He smiled sweetly at the prince. "So, do you think we should let North Wind join?"

Realising that Rainstorm needed a way to regain an equal footing, Tarkyn raised his eyebrows and said thoughtfully, "Well, he did not stay with me when I was injured as the main force of the home guard did and he did not defy his elders by untying me, as you did." He smiled gently, "However, he did defend me against you when you were angry earlier on. Do you think that justifies membership?"

"Do I get a say in this?" demanded North Wind.

Tarkyn shrugged, his eyes smiling wickedly, "Well, there is really no point in asking you until we've decided whether you're eligible. Is there, Rainstorm?"

Rainstorm shook his head, laughing, "Absolutely no point at all."

North Wind crossed his arms and looked from one to the other. "So? Am I eligible?"

"Do you want to join? Do you realise what it entails?" asked Tarkyn. "Do you think we should let him?" he added, addressing Rainstorm.

Rainstorm nodded, smiling.

North Wind frowned suspiciously. "What does it entail?"

"You become one of my cronies, as I believe you phrased it earlier today." Tarkyn grinned. "And the other factions ignore or devalue everything you say. You may or may not consider that an attraction to the post."

Seeing North Wind looking uncertain, Rainstorm butted in, "It means you support Tarkyn. That's all. You don't have to agree with everything he says or even do what he wants. You're just basically on his side."

"It's not really anything." Tarkyn gave an embarrassed smile. "Home guard is just a collective nickname I made up for the people who have stood by me."

North Wind gave a casual nod and said, "Fine. I'll join. After this last hour I've spent with you, I wouldn't hear a word against you."

"Wouldn't you?" The prince looked startled. "You're not worried I engineered the oath on Rainstorm's people?"

The young woodman shook his head, glancing at Rainstorm. "No. I saw your reaction to Rainstorm's distress. I've learnt a lot about you in the last hour; some of it unnerving but none of it bad."

"Thanks. You turn out to be a pretty worthwhile character yourself." After a few moments, Tarkyn sighed. "Now, what are we going to do about this catastrophe with the oath? The last thing I need at the moment is another group of resentful woodfolk to win over." The prince ran his hand across his forehead. "I'm tired of being everyone's nightmare."

"Don't tell them," said North Wind baldly.

"Why shouldn't they suffer too, if I have to?" demanded Rainstorm peevishly.

North Wind frowned at him. "I thought you were in the home guard? Then grow up and stop thinking of yourself and start thinking about how to help Tarkyn - and all of us, for that matter. We need to be focused on rescuing the woodfolk from the encampment, not on dealing with a new lot of unrest."

"All right. All right.So we won't tell them. What if they jeopardise the forest by mistake?"

"I don't think they will," said Tarkyn thoughtfully. "Since I have no intention of imposing my will on them or demanding their obedience, the issue of service won't arise. They have already had their chance to attack me and haven't. They will protect me to uphold everyone else's oath and because I'm the forest guardian." He smiled, "So you see, Rainstorm, I don't think the oath will make any difference if we don't let it."

After they had considered all the angles, Tarkyn said, "So, are we all agreed? We don't tell anyone?"

The other two nodded.

Tarkyn gave a quirky smile. "And one last thing: I had better give you both permission to attack me, if you want to. You, Rainstorm, so that if your hotheadedness leads you into another fight with me, the forest won't give away that you're under oath. And you, North Wind, because if Rainstorm has permission, then it wouldn't be fair to leave you out."

Rainstorm shook his head. "You're mad, prince."

Tarkyn laughed. "I didn't say I wouldn't fight back. I might even use magic if you're too aggressive." He stood up. "I'd better get back. Oh, by the way, I might tell Waterstone. Then we'll have one person from each of the three factions here knowing. Anyway, I like to be able to discuss things with him. Agreed?"

They nodded and Tarkyn strode off through the trees leaving behind two bemused young woodmen.

Chapter 42

Danton tried to sleep but found he was too wound up. He lay on his back, with hands behind his head, studying the structure of Tarkyn's shelter. The woven and mud daubed accommodation did not compare favourably with the stone, gilded rooms of the palace. He was deeply distressed at finding the prince in a situation where he seemed to have lost all status and authority. These woodfolk seemed friendly enough but that was the trouble, really. They were overly familiar with the prince and didn't honour his exalted lineage, as they should. Danton, being of a generous turn of mind, put it down to poor education and ignorance rather than ill intent, and resolved to gently instil a more proper sense of decorum in them over time.

Danton had been shocked by what he had been told about the oath. Many things concerned him about it. Most importantly, it was clear from what Waterstone had said, that King Markazon had foreseen his elder sons' capacity for treachery and had made provision to safeguard Tarkyn. Danton pondered this, knowing that Tarkyn had not only refused to bend to the present king's ruling but had also defied his father on at least one occasion.

Danton was quite happy about the commitment the woodfolk had been forced to make to Prince Tarkyn. That was just as it should be, as far as he was concerned, and if there were consequences built into the oath, so much the better. It was unfortunate, though, that not all the woodfolk had taken it. Then there was the level of commitment demanded from Tarkyn by the oath. Danton wondered what effect Tarkyn's forced identification with the woodfolk's cause might have on the prince's birth commitment to all people of Eskuzor. He would have been even more concerned had he realised that Tarkyn had now been formally adopted into the woodfolk nation, but that was a shock yet to come.

After an hour or so of tossing and turning, Danton decided to give up on trying to sleep. He pulled aside the bramble screening and stepped outside to go for a walk instead. He nearly tripped over a little girl who was playing quietly on the path outside the door.

"Whoops, sorry," said Danton, as he stepped sideways to avoid standing on her. "Ow. That bush is prickly."

The little girl stood up swiftly and pushed back her light brown hair. "Hello. You must be Danton, Tarkyn's friend. I am Sparrow."

Danton frowned as he rubbed his scratched arm. Even children were overly familiar. However, he realised that a rebuke was not the best way to start a new relationship. So he merely said, "Hello. What are you doing playing here?" His eyes narrowed. "You're not keeping an eye on me, are you?"

Sparrow nodded quite unselfconsciously. "Dad thought you might need some help, since you're new here. So I thought I'd just play here while I waited for you to wake up." She grimaced a little. "I probably should have set up a bit further from the door. Is your arm all right?"

Danton gave a small smile, "I'll live." He abandoned his plans to go for a walk and sat down on the ground. "Do you want to show me what you were doing?"

Sparrow eyed him uncertainly for a moment, then sat down next to him and showed him a map she had drawn of the local area with all the hidden shelters drawn in. "I haven't finished it yet. I was getting it ready to show you when you got up."

Danton inspected her handiwork and raised his eyebrows. "This is a very clear map. That's the stream there, is it?" he asked, running his finger over a wavy line that ran down the middle of her diagram. When Sparrow nodded, he frowned and said slowly, "So that's the patch of beech trees we slept in last night and there's the clearing where we had breakfast."

Sparrow regarded him with some surprise. "You're quite good at reading maps, aren't you?"

Danton looked puzzled, "Why wouldn't I be?"

Sparrow shrugged and smiled, "Tarkyn is terrible at it. I thought maybe all sorcerers were."

"Are all woodfolk good at reading maps?"

"Not everyone." She smiled, "But most people are better at it than Tarkyn."

"Well, I think you'll find most sorcerers are better at reading maps than His Highness. He has never had a very good sense of direction."

"No, he's hopeless." Sparrow looked at him severely, "But you mustn't think he's bad at everything because he's not." Danton was intrigued to realise that Sparrow was now championing the prince. "Anyway," she was saying, "as he's a forest guardian, he doesn't need a good sense of direction because the animals will guide him."

Danton frowned, "I beg your pardon? What do you mean, the animals will guide him?"

Sparrow smiled sunnily at him. "Tarkyn can mind talk with forest creatures. Well, not mind talk, exactly. He uses pictures but it works the same. So he can ask an animal or bird to show him where to go or to find things for him."

A thoughtful expression came over Danton's face. "Or to keep watch over someone?" he asked slowly.

"You mean the eagle owl," said Sparrow inconsequentially. She nodded. "Tarkyn used the eagle owl to find you and then to watch you until the others came."

"I see." Danton pondered for a moment. "I suppose he hasn't had time to talk to me about the owl this morning."

The little girl put her head on one side. "Don't worry. He's not trying to trick you. Anyway, that's another thing he's hopeless at, tricking people."

Danton smiled suddenly. "You do know him well, don't you?"

Sparrow nodded, "Dad and I looked after him all the time he was sick and that's how we all became friends." She looked down at her map and started working on it again as she talked. "And now Tarkyn's my uncle, and Dad and Ancient Oak are his brothers."

Because she was concentrating on her map, Sparrow missed the look of consternation on Danton's face. As the silence lengthened, Sparrow looked up.

"And how did His Highness become part of your family?" he asked carefully.

"My Dad and he became blood brothers, so Tarkyn could become a woodman. No one has ever become a woodman ever before. That's because Tarkyn was really brave…and the oath of course."

"And who is your father?" asked Danton tightly.

"Waterstone, of course."

"I see." With years of court training coming to his aid, Danton managed to produce a small smile to cover his concern. "Same green eyes. Same light brown hair. I should have known."

Sparrow laughed. "You're silly. We're all like that."

"I know," said Danton lightly. "I was joking."

Sparrow considered the guardsman. "I like you. I'm glad you're Tarkyn's friend." She paused as she decided to confide in the sorcerer. "I felt Tarkyn's feelings when he saw his brothers riding through the forest." Tears sprang to her eyes. "They were very bad to him. People have been so mean to him and he doesn't deserve it, you know. He thought no one would be his friend any more after what happened."

Danton looked thoughtfully at her. "You know, I wasn't there, and each version I heard was more terrible than the last. But I have always been his friend and I always will be, no matter what he's done. If he lashed out and killed all those guards, he must have had a good reason."

Sparrow's eyes widened. "You think Tarkyn did that? … And you still want to be his friend?" She shook her head emphatically. "No, it wasn't like that at all." She told him Tarkyn's version and added, "But Tarkyn still thinks everything was his fault because it was his fear that made the shield go wrong."

"But I hope he can see that his brothers' action precipitated the situation and at the very least, they should share the blame," put in Waterstone, as he rounded the corner to join in the conversation.

Danton scrambled to his feet. Despite any misgivings he might have about Tarkyn being considered a member of a woodfolk family, the sorcerer was determined to behave correctly. He bowed and said, "Your Highness, I beg your pardon for not showing you due respect earlier."

Waterstone looked over his shoulder and, seeing no one there, asked, "Who are you talking to?"

"You, my lord. If I had realised…."

Waterstone cut across him, "Now settle down. What's Sparrow been telling you?"

"That you are bloodbrother to the prince," replied the sorcerer.

"True enough." Waterstone frowned at his daughter, "But I was going to let Tarkyn tell Danton that himself, Sparrow."

"Your Highness, I would never have questioned your right to tell me what to do if I had known. Why didn't you tell me then?"

The woodman frowned. "Because I was speaking to you with the authority of a woodman as I told you. I did not ask Tarkyn into my family to hang my consequence on his shirttails. I have sufficient of my own, as does every other woodman or woman." He bent down, picked up Sparrow and swung her onto his hip as he spoke. "And Danton, much as I appreciate the honour you do me in recognising my right to that title so unquestioningly, I have no wish to be referred to as 'Your Highness'."

A hint of panic flared in Danton's eyes. "Your values are so alien to me. I can't imagine anyone in Tormadell not flaunting such a connection with a prince."

Waterstone's eyes narrowed, "Now, let us be completely clear on this. I would never use any connection I had with Tarkyn, either as a friend or as a brother, to my own advantage. To do so would be to use him as a commodity and betray his trust in me." A wave of pride and gratitude broke around the three of them. Ignoring it for the moment, the woodman clapped the bemused sorcerer on the shoulder with his free hand. "Don't worry. It will be easier than you think. There are less rules in our society, not more." The woodman smiled broadly, "And just to make you feel more comfortable about it, I will undertake not to call you 'my lord' in return!"

Before Danton could react to this last sally, Waterstone called quietly, "Come on, where are you, Tarkyn? You must be here somewhere. I can feel you."

Tarkyn appeared around the bend in the track through the brambles, grinning, "I didn't mean to eavesdrop. I was just coming to find Danton and stopped when I heard what you were talking about."

Danton's looked puzzled. "How did you know he was there?"

"Didn't you feel the wave of feelings?" asked Waterstone.

Danton's face cleared, "Was that you, Sire?"A smile dawned on his face, "I can see why you feel that way. I, too, would be proud to call Waterstone my friend."

Waterstone, usually so rock solid and imperturbable, was clearly flustered by this remark. He cleared his throat and managed, "Thank you, Danton, I am honoured by your words." The woodman glanced wryly at Tarkyn. "You are a lot quicker off the mark with your offer of friendship than your liege was."

"Ah, but my liege's trust in you has paved the way for me and I do not have his experience of betrayal to overcome," said Danton gently. "To the unjaundiced eye, your integrity shows through in everything you do."

Waterstone cleared his throat again and asked the prince, "Is he always this embarrassing?"

Tarkyn gave a short laugh. "Only to people he likes. Now if you don't mind, you two, I need some time to talk to Danton before this meeting."

"Well, don't stand all over my map because I haven't finished it yet. It's to show Danton everything," said Sparrow.

Tarkyn ruffled her hair as Waterstone carried her past him. "We won't. I promise. I'll see you in a little while." He turned to Danton, "Shall we go back inside?"

When they were both seated inside the small shelter, Danton said, "I don't know why you would rather be in here than out in the forest."

"Privacy, Danton. Privacy. You can't tell whether woodfolk are anywhere near you unless they choose to let you know."

"Are there things you wish to say that they may not like to hear, Sire?" asked Danton, with a faint edge of eagerness in his voice.

Disappointingly, Tarkyn shook his head. "No, Danton, there are not. But there may be things you wish to say that they may not like to hear."

"Oh. I see. And I am free to say what I like?"

"Yes, my friend. It is much better that you talk to me about it here rather than stir up ill feeling outside." Tarkyn smiled at him, "So. What would you like to say or ask?"

Danton looked down at the ground for a while then brought his gaze up to meet the prince's, his purple eyes twinkling with mischief. "They have funny voices, don't they? It's really hard to switch from listening to one voice then tuning in on the next, isn't it?"

Tarkyn nodded, smiling, "Yes, very. You get used to it after a while but it is hard. Waterstone is often hard to hear properly when you're near a stream. Autumn Leaves' voice gets lost when a sudden gust of wind scatters leaves. Their voices blend in. I thought there was running water nearby for days when I was semi-conscious and all the time it was Waterstone talking to me."

"And it's just as well their voices are different because how are you supposed to tell them all apart?"

Tarkyn laughed. "You get used to that, too. They all look completely different from each other to me now. But they didn't at first."

Danton became more serious, "Sire, I am very confused about the proper way to act. I don't want to offend anybody but the woodfolk's behaviour towards you offends me continually. None of them show you the proper respect due to your station."

The prince regarded him thoughtfully. "And what about Waterstone, for instance? Do you think he does not respect me?"

"He doesn't use your correct title. He doesn't bow to you. He doesn't treat you with the respect due to a prince."

"Danton, that was not my question. I said, do you think Waterstone does not respect me?"

Danton thought hard. Slowly, he shook his head. "No. I couldn't say Waterstone does not respect you." A reluctant smile dawned. "In fact, I would say he respects you a great deal. In fact a great deal more than many of the courtiers who have given you all the ostensible signs of respect."

Tarkyn watched the sorcerer work his way through this new perspective. "And which do you think I would consider more valuable?"

Danton smiled, "Sire, I am not a fool. Obviously, just from the questioning if nothing else, you consider Waterstone's respect to be more valuable." He put his head on one side as he thought about it. Then he shrugged and said slowly, "And I suppose I would have to agree with you"

Tarkyn pulled a stick off the interior of the shelter and began to break pieces off the end of it. "Do you know, Danton, it has taken a long journey for all of us to get to where we are now. On my own, I have had to decide how I wanted to be treated. I could have insisted on rigid court etiquette. But can you imagine how hard it would be for Stormaway and me to train an entire nation of people in something of which they have little knowledge and consider to be mildly ludicrous?"

The blond sorcerer did not reply but looked thoughtful.

"Had I done that, they would have respected me less and resented me more. I could have forced them. In fact, the home guard would willingly have tried to learn had I insisted, but their actions would not have been marks of respect. They would have been gestures to humour me." Tarkyn sighed, "And so I chose to relinquish the etiquette in favour of developing, I'm not sure what you'd call it, perhaps terms of engagement between them and me."

Danton sounded sceptical. "And what does that amount to?"

"I respect their opinions. They respect mine. I am consulted on anything important."

Danton snorted, "I should think so."

"Ah, but when they have all worked as a mind talking unit for centuries, it is difficult for them to remember an outsider exists, let alone to include me in their debates and planning. The simplest things have required a lot of negotiation."

"And is that it?" demanded the guardsman. "Your only authority is that you are consulted?"

The prince gave a slight smile. "No. The oathbound woodfolk know that I can issue a command at any time but again, if I overuse it they will respect me less, not more."

Danton's eyes narrowed as he thought back over the morning. "Yet it seems to me that you do command a certain respect, more than your words would lead me to expect."

Tarkyn's eyes twinkled, "Well, of course, I suspect my status increased considerably when I became part of Waterstone's family." The prince rolled up his sleeve. "See my scar? It's a beauty, isn't it?"

Danton frowned at it. "Stars above, that was a huge cut. And it's gone green! That can't be right."

"That is the other reason I command respect, much more so than for being a prince. Because I am a forest guardian." Tarkyn smiled broadly, "You won't believe this but it turns out I'm a character straight out of one their woodfolk legends."

Danton's eyes grew round. "You're not serious." Then he frowned, "I can't believe you're able to trick them into thinking you're a legend. You're so bad at prevaricating."

The smile wiped off Tarkyn's face and a wave of anger hit Danton. "No. How could you think I would stoop to such a ploy? Of course I couldn't sustain a pretence like that. Anyway, I wouldn't dream of demeaning the woodfolk like that, even if I could."

The blond sorcerer looked confused. "I apologise, my lord, for upsetting you. But you can't seriously mean you're a legend…can you?" A glimmer of unease crossed Danton's face.

The prince gave a bitter laugh. "You may well wonder at my sanity. But do not fear; I am not a rogue." Tarkyn suddenly realised that Danton would only know the official version of events. "Danton, I did not attack those guards."

His liegeman managed a smile. "I know, Your Highness. Sparrow told me what happened."

"But you didn't know that, did you, when you sought me out…" When Danton gave the tiniest shake of his head, Tarkyn leant forward and laid his hand on the guardsman's knee, "Thank you, my friend, for your faith in me." He smiled as he gave Danton's knee a final bracing pat. "Having come this far, don't give up on me now. I didn't make up the legends of the forest guardian. You ask the woodfolk. Remember those special powers I told you I've developed? Apparently, they are what define a forest guardian; healing, making plants grow, communicating with animals…"

"The eagle owl," said Danton shortly.

Tarkyn nodded "And the storm yesterday? I drew the power for that from a venerable old oak tree."

Danton's eyes widened. "Did you power that whole attack on the storm?"

"Pretty much. Stormaway drew on the oak's strength through me." Tarkyn had found a green stick among the mesh of twigs that made up his shelter. He broke a piece off and proceeded to make it grow as he talked. He threw a quick glance up at his friend but returned his gaze immediately to his little project, "So you see," he said, holding up the flourishing little sapling, "Strange as it may seem, I fit their description of this mythical being."

After a short, rather strained silence, Tarkyn said quietly, "I'm still me, you know. I heard Waterstone saying to someone yesterday that a lot has changed but a lot is still the same and I guess that is how it is with you and me." He gave his friend a warm smile. "I hope, if you came to find me knowing I am exiled, that you must care for more than the court's etiquette."

"Of course I do, Sire. I care for you." After a slight hesitation, Danton's eyes twinkled, "No matter what sort of weird being you may have become."

Tarkyn laughed. "I, too, care for you and I am glad that you are here." He handed Danton the little sapling. "There. You can find somewhere to plant it and watch it grow until we leave." He grew serious. "Now Danton, there are a few things we need to sort out. Firstly, you have my permission to retaliate if any of the woodfolk attack you, but no deaths or serious injuries."

"Thank you, my lord."

"And secondly, you also may call me Tarkyn, as the others do, if you wish to. And I would like you to follow Waterstone's lead on how to treat me. Do not feel obliged to bow, nor to stand when I do, etcetera."

Danton swallowed, "I am honoured, Sire…,Tarkyn, that you should allow me such freedom."

The prince gave a little smile. "I don't think you'll find it very much different in terms of freedom. You'll still be subject to my…requests. But you can query them if you have a good reason to. I do expect respect from people including you, but not in the form of titles and points of etiquette. Just remember: the lack of protocol does not mean lack of respect. The woodfolk just have a different way of showing it."

"I will do my best to fit in."

"It would please me greatly if you could."

Danton hesitated. "Sire, you said I could speak freely?" When Tarkyn nodded, he continued, "Sire, I am concerned about your oath to the woodfolk. Where does it leave people like me?"

The prince looked at him, long and hard. Danton fidgeted, worried that he had been too bold but Tarkyn was merely thinking it through. "I don't know. I haven't thought about it, to be honest. Let me see. I have to protect the woodfolk. Their fate is my fate, their just cause is my cause." Tarkyn ran his hand through his hair. "Well, as a prince of Eskuzor, I would expect to protect anyone who needs it. So that is not necessarily in conflict. My fate is linked with all the peoples of Eskuzor and I would make anyone's just cause my own."

Danton waited, not commenting.

Tarkyn grimaced, "That, at least, is the rhetoric. In reality, I have been given the honour of being accepted into the woodfolk nation when my own people have rejected me. If legend is to be believed, I am also their forest guardian and am here to help them through difficult times ahead." Tarkyn could see that Danton was still unhappy. "You know, last night when I was worrying about your fate, Waterstone said that he couldn't see any circumstances under which they would need to kill you. He said that no matter what you did, all they had to do was knock you out and disappear. They are highly skilled hunters and could be killers, but they choose not to be. So, if necessary, I would fight against sorcerers to protect woodfolk."

Seeing Danton's consternation, he added quickly, "Saying that, I could not see why good upstanding sorcerers would use wolves to hunt down woodfolk whose main defence is to disappear."

Danton's eyes widened. "Is that what has been happening?"

"It appears so," Tarkyn leaned forward. "Danton, there will be a conference at lunchtime at which time they may ask for your assistance. You must hear their story and make your own choice. I give you the freedom to follow your own conscience. Now and in the future, I will not choose for you more than I have to."

When they emerged from the shelter, Sparrow was lying in wait to show Danton her completed map. As they walked down to the clearing, Sparrow monopolised Danton, leaving Tarkyn to walk with Waterstone.

"So, what do you think of Danton?" asked Tarkyn quietly.

Waterstine chuckled. "He's a passionate character, isn't he? I can't help smiling at the way he acts around you."

Tarkyn's eyes crinkled with laughter. "I thought you might find that amusing." But he became more serious as he glanced over his shoulder to check that Danton's attention was elsewhere before he continued, "But you know, with Danton's arrival, I feel as though the outside world has come to sit in judgement on all my decisions. I find I have to justify them all over again."

"I can imagine you would... But Tarkyn, only you can decide what your role should be, now more than ever, when you have people from two cultures around you with vastly different views. Just be clear with yourself about what you want. Otherwise, you will follow someone else's expectations instead of your own."

Something in the woodman's tone made Tarkyn frown, "You're worried about something, aren't you?"

Waterstone threw him an embarrassed glance then turned his gaze steadfastly to the path ahead. "You have no idea, Tarkyn, how glad I am that you did not force us to treat you as Danton is used to doing. For those of us who have not grown up with those traditions, it would have felt humiliating and embarrassing... Even more so, had we had to do it in front of the free woodfolk."

Tarkyn's eyes had widened in consternation. "You have never told me that before, and I wouldn't necessarily have realised it, you know." He thought back to his conversation with Danton. "In fact, I chose not to impose court etiquette because I thought you would all feel you were humouring me and would respect me less." Tarkyn smiled ruefully. "I was only thinking of my need, not yours. It never occurred to me that you might find it humiliating. Danton doesn't, as far as I know." He looked at his friend and said seriously, "Don't ever let me humiliate you. Tell me what it means to you next time. Don't assume I know."

Waterstone kept his eyes firmly on the path ahead. "I find nearly everything about the oath humiliating. The only way I can maintain my friendship with you is to try to put it out of my mind when I am with you."

Tarkyn shook his head slowly, "Ah my friend, you also have had a hard time of it, haven't you? Waiting to see how and to what extent I was going to force you all into submission."A puzzled frown appeared on Tarkyn's face. "If you hate this oath so much, why did you stay and look after me in the first place?"

"I told you at the time. I liked the way you handled yourself and you needed someone to pull you out of the morass." Waterstone shrugged and smiled, "Maybe having worked with your father and having seen the better side of him, I was more able to look past the prejudice against you than others were." He gave a short laugh. "Anyway, I refuse to let the injustice of the oath prevent me from following my principles and helping you. That's why I try to act as though it isn't there as much as I can; so that it doesn't dictate my actions one way or the other."

Tarkyn glanced at his friend, "Waterstone, I am lucky, aren't I, that you are so strong in your convictions. But you know, you can't always expect me to guess what you're feeling. I have grown up with a very different set of assumptions from you. Please tell me how you feel about decisions I make. I need your perspective to steer me through."

CHAPTER 43

When they arrived at the firesite, Tarkyn's heart sank as he realised that once again, the woodfolk had congregated in their factions around the clearing. The four of them slipped quietly in and sat amongst the home guard. Then Tarkyn had a quiet word to Waterstone who, as a result, went out of focus for a short time. On the other side of the clearing, Raging Water also went out of focus. As Danton watched, all the home guard and many of the others went out of focus as a message was passed around. Then, casually, in twos and threes, Stormaway and woodfolk stood up and change their positions so that they intermingled with the other groups.

"I thought you said you didn't control things," whispered Danton.

"I don't," said Tarkyn, all wide-eyed innocence. "At least not directly. Waterstone orchestrated that little manoeuvre."

"Hmm. I begin to see what you meant about things changing, but staying the same!"

Tarkyn and Danton were left sitting with Waterstone, Ancient Oak, Autumn Leaves, Lapping Water, Rainstorm and a slightly self-conscious North Wind. The rest of the home guard had spread themselves around. Tarkyn noticed Danton's reaction to Lapping Water with some misgiving and determined to warn him off at some more convenient time.

At this point, Raging Water stood up and said, "I believe Tarkyn, Stormaway and Danton will need to be filled in on the contents of our discussions so far. As we know from Tarkyn's reconnaissance via the mouse..."

Here Danton threw an amused look at Tarkyn, "A mouse?"

Tarkyn said sotto voce, "You should have been there when it ate the horse dung."

Danton's explosion of quickly suppressed laughter drew several glares from around the firesite.

Raging Water sent a quelling glance in their direction before giving a brief resume of their knowledge of the encampment.When he had finished, he looked around. "Any comments?"

Danton raised his hand. "Would you mind if I asked a question?"

"No. Go right ahead."

"Do you know who these sorcerers are, why they are congregated like this in the forest and why they are hunting woodfolk?"

Autumn Leaves raised laconic eyebrows, "Well, we just assumed all sorcerers were evil and were out to destroy everything that moved."

There was enough truth in this remark to create an uncomfortable pause. After a fraught moment, Danton managed to raise a smile, "I remember now. Two good sorcerers and thousands of wicked ones." He scratched his head and grimaced in what Tarkyn recognised as a deliberately disarming gesture. "It would be easier if it were that simple. But unfortunately among sorcerers, just as I've noticed among woodfolk, there are factions. Even if you rescue these woodfolk, you still need to find out what they are doing here and why they are hunting you." Looking around a ring of sceptical faces, he added, "I can assure you, this group will have a purpose and unlike your groups, someone will be running it. Even if three or four hundred sorcerers are involved in hunting you down, that still leaves the vast majority of sorcerers peaceably at home somewhere tending their crops, baking, breeding horses or whatever else they do."

Rainstorm spoke up. "Why do these sorcerer guards need weapons? Surely they can just use their power?"

Tarkyn smiled wryly. "Contrary to popular belief, most sorcerers don't have powers for fighting. Most sorcerers can just do a few useful spells like lifting objects, maybe creating shields, giving the yeast a bit of a hand in baking bread…that sort of thing. They can't evoke 'Shturrum' or stun rays or anything very useful in a fight."

"Is that right?" asked Autumn Leaves slowly, eyebrows raised. "Do you know, if you were anyone else, I would think you were trying to lull us into a false sense of security." At Tarkyn's raised eyebrow, the big woodman conceded, "But as it is, I believe you implicitly," he gave a slight smile, "although I must admit, it is a struggle."

"Can we get back to the point of this discussion?" demanded Ancient Elm in her withered old voice. "I am not concerned with who these sorcerers are. I just want our kin back safe and sound. It is my belief that we should rescue our friends first and investigate only once we have them safely back with us."

Strong murmurs of agreement around the clearing supported this suggestion.

"So, what have you decided?" asked Tarkyn.

"We haven't," replied Tree Wind.

Tarkyn frowned. "Why not? I thought you discussed it last night."

"It's the chain. We don't know how to get around the chain," said Tree Wind calmly, "We were hoping one of you magic wielders might have some ideas to help us with it."

Tarkyn looked at Danton then across the clearing at Stormaway. "Any ideas?"

Danton shook his head. Stormaway put up his hand to indicate that he was thinking and needed a moment to marshal his thoughts. Then he lifted his head and said, "I think a repeat of our hole digging exercise might do the trick." He looked around the assembled woodfolk and explained, "When the home guard had to bury the wolf carcasses, Tarkyn and I used vibrations from our magic to loosen earth in a large area. If we did that around the stake, we could just pull the stake easily out of the ground and take stake, chain and woodfolk with us as a package."

"That sounds like a good idea. Does it need two of you?" asked Tree Wind.

"Yes. You need the dissonance between two magics."

"And how long would it take and how noisy?" asked Raging Water.

Stormaway shrugged, "Not long. Two or three minutes for a small area like that. Not noisy for such a small operation. If we could get in there, it would only take a minor distraction to cover up our activities. Then the rescue could be undertaken later in the evening."

"I think I can now perform two lots of magic at once. If I practised, I could possibly do it alone," suggested Tarkyn.

"No," came a chorus of voices.

"We can't afford to risk you, if we don't have to," added Sun Shower.

Far from being gratified by their protectiveness, the prince's eyes narrowed and his mouth set in a thin mutinous line.

Before he could protest, Stormaway overrode him. "Tarkyn, you can't go into a camp full of sorcerers with a price on your head. Even if you were in disguise, your eyes would give you away…and the colour of your magic, if anyone spotted it." He paused, "It is not just your welfare at stake if anything happens to you. Anyway, your own magic will not be dissonant with itself. The two beams would synchronise."

Tarkyn's eyes glittered with anger and his mouth did not relax as he gave a short, sharp nod and dropped his gaze.

Stormaway transferred his attention and he hoped, the attention of the woodfolk, to Danton, "If you are willing, the two of us could easily disguise ourselves and infiltrate the encampment."

Suddenly, the whole gathering, as one, realised what they were asking Danton to do. There was a hushed silence.

Eventually, much to everyone's surprise, it was Rainstorm who spoke up. He cleared his throat and said self-consciously, "Danton, I'm sorry I attacked you this morning. I should have realised you just didn't understand how things work around here." He scowled around at his audience, daring anyone to comment.

Danton gave a nod of acknowledgement, "Thank you, Rainstorm. In return, I also apologise to you for forcing my views on you." He waited, clearly aware that Rainstorm had more to say.

After a moment, the young woodman continued, "Some of our ways of doing things are different. But from what I know of Tarkyn, I don't think we are so different underneath." Rainstorm shrugged, "I suppose you don't have any real reason to champion our cause, especially against your fellow sorcerers. None of us can force you to help us, if you would rather not. I suspect Tarkyn could, but wouldn't." He raised an eyebrow in the prince's direction and received a short, affirmative nod. "So it is entirely up to you. But on behalf of the woodfolk assembled here and the frightened family at the encampment, I would ask you to consider it."

Danton glanced sideways at Tarkyn before saying, "Rather than thinking of it as helping woodfolk against sorcerers, let us instead think of it as helping three victims against their persecutors and leave their origins out of it. On those terms, I believe I can support your cause."

An audible murmur of appreciation rolled around the clearing.

Stormaway's eyes lit up. "Good. That part of it is sorted then. And while we are there, we can do a bit of investigating." Seeing Ancient Elm about to object, he added, "… after we have loosened the earth around the stake."

Falling Branch shook his head. "We still have the problem of the wolves. We can't afford to be near the camp. If they pick up our scent they may be able to hunt us down, even in the trees, with the help of sorcerers and wizards."

"That leaves us a bit stuck, doesn't it?" objected Autumn Leaves. "Tarkyn can't go because he's too precious." There was a slight smile but no derision in his voice. "We can't go because we're too vulnerable. Doesn't leave any options but Stormaway and Danton and they already have a job."

Tarkyn flicked a glance at him and found the solid woodman smiling understandingly at him. He began to unbend a little.

"But if we could neutralise or eliminate the wolves, any of us could be involved in the rescue," said Rainstorm, voicing the thoughts of many.

Tarkyn shrugged, still slightly belligerent. "Anyway, unless you neutralise the wolves, they will raise the alarm when the woodfolk family leaves."

"And the problem still remains of how to get the woodfolk family out into the woods, especially if they are still wearing the chains," pointed out Raging Water.

"Can Golden Toad's family do the woodfolk disappearing act once they are out of the encampment?" asked Tarkyn, addressing his question to Autumn Leaves, the only person he was yet prepared to speak to.

A short, out of focus discussion passed between woodfolk. Autumn Leaves spoke for them. "We don't know what effect the chain will have on their ability to flick into hiding. And we also don't know whether the virus they had has affected that ability as well as the mind talking."

"So we have to assume they can't," concluded Tarkyn shortly. He shrugged, "Now I think about it, if they could do the disappearing act, they would have by now, wouldn't they?"

"Not necessarily. Not through a tent wall," replied Autumn Leaves. "We can flick around objects, but not through them."

"So, we need a distraction and a way to knock out or kill the wolves," said Waterstone, determinedly ignoring Tarkyn's ill humour and summing up the situation. "Once the wolves are out of the equation and the stake has been loosened, we should be able to sneak in during the night, knock out whoever is guarding the woodfolk, and carry Golden Toad and his family off, complete with chain and stake. Meanwhile, others of us will also need to neutralise the guards on one side of the encampment for as long as it takes to escape with them into the woods."

"That does sound like the beginnings of a workable plan," conceded Tarkyn grudgingly. Suddenly a well of humour rose to overcame his chagrin and he glanced at Autumn Leaves, knowing that what he was about to say would annoy the heavy woodman. "But I have a big problem with the fate of the wolves." He grinned as Autumn Leaves rolled his eyes. "Have wolves traditionally been enemies of woodfolk?"

"No," replied Raging Water, not quite clear why the prince was smiling. "In the past, they have steered clear of us unless, for some reason, the season is very lean and they are desperate for food."

Tarkyn became serious again. "It just seems wrong to kill them all off when someone is using them as a tool for their own ends." He shrugged, "Maybe it is being the forest guardian but I can't help thinking that they, too, are creatures of the forest…."

Ancient Elm spoke again, "It does you credit, young man, that you are concerned for the welfare of the forest creatures. However, the rescue of the woodfolk will tax us enough. If we undertake not to kill the wolves, we may be able to address their fate at another time. Will that satisfy your scruples?"

Tarkyn bowed his head in acknowledgement. "Thank you, yes. It will."

"What about that 'Shturrum' word?" asked Thunder Storm suddenly. "Does your magic work on animals?"

Stormaway considered the suggestion. "Possibly. It's better than a stun ray, which only works on one target at a time. I know Tarkyn has used Shturrum on many people at once."

A ripple of constraint washed around the firesite as various woodfolk remembered the times Tarkyn had used it on them. Several sets of eyes flashed in his direction, loaded with expressions ranging from amusement to distaste. Danton cocked a surmising eyebrow at him, but said nothing.

Aware of their responses, Tarkyn stared steadfastly at the ground with a little smile playing around his mouth. When he looked up, his eyes were brimming with laughter, "Oh well, I guess that's the disadvantage of having a forest guardian."

The constraint melted, albeit some a little reluctantly. Raging Water gave a snort of derisive laughter. "I sometimes think you're too powerful for your own good, young man."

"Scary, isn't it?" Tarkyn grinned and shrugged, his tone robbing his words of any ill intent. "Just as well I have that little spell or I'd be dead five times over by now." Before anyone had the chance to respond to this, he reverted to the original topic, "Anyway, one way or another, I'm sure Stormaway, Danton and I can devise a way to neutralise the wolves. We'll do a bit of experimenting and see what we can come up with."

"And do you want us to deal with the perimeter guards?" asked Danton.

"No thank you, young man," replied Ancient Elm firmly. "The guards cannot be allowed the chance to report back what they have seen."

Danton frowned and asked, his voice thick with suspicion, "So how are you planning to ensure that?"

Waterstone rolled his eyes, "Not another one. First Tarkyn, now you, thinking we're going to kill off everyone in sight. We'll do the same as we did to you. Slingshots. Knock them all out. We'll just have to hit them simultaneously so none of them raises the alarm at seeing their colleagues go down." He shrugged, "We couldn't use arrows even if we wanted to. Too many people would find the arrows and become alerted to our presence - which is exactly what we don't want. Slingshots just leave harmless, unidentifiable little rocks."

Danton's eyes narrowed. "You lot must be pretty good even to consider pulling off a feat like that."

"We are," responded Rainstorm promptly, smiling evilly.

Waterstone gave a short laugh. "Stop it Rainstorm!" Then he smiled wryly at Danton, "Though actually, he's right. We are."

"Good then," said Danton dryly, "As long as we all know where we stand."

Chapter 44

Within an hour, those woodfolk who were going to the encampment for the rescue or further on to look for Falling Rain were packed up and strung out through the forest. Where possible, they did not travel in single file but flowed through the forest across a broad front so that there were not many feet tramping over the same ground. The rays of the afternoon sun slanted through the yellowing leaves of old sycamors catching swirling spirals of dust in their wake. Tarkyn walked with Danton and Stormaway as they discussed plans for dealing with the wolves.

"So, do you think that you can use 'Shturrum' on animals?" asked Stormaway as he hitched his pack more comfortably on his shoulder. "And in particular on the wolves?"

Tarkyn shrugged, "It doesn't matter whether I can or can't. You won't let me go near the place."

"Well, I can't use the 'Shturrum' spell," said Danton. "Can you?" When the wizard shook his head, Danton continued, "So there's not much point in thinking about it if His Highness can't come with us into the encampment to do it."

"Perhaps I could … " began Tarkyn.

"You could not." Stormaway overrode him firmly. "The woodfolk are vowed to protect you. If they knowingly allow you to go into danger and you come to harm, the forests are forfeit. Besides which, they need your protection in return."

Tarkyn stared at him. "So. We have reached the paradox already. If I insist on going on this raid with you, the woodfolk will risk the forest if they refuse me, but they will also risk the forest if they comply because they won't be protecting me."

Stormaway nodded briskly. "Exactly. So you must not order them, or me, to take you with us into danger."

"Not to mention the trees… " said Waterstone appearing quietly beside them.

Danton frowned, "What do you mean, the trees?"

Waterstone smiled gently, "I don't think the forest will allow Tarkyn out to face such danger either. It didn't when he first arrived. None of us understood why at the time. But now it is obvious. Because he is the forest guardian, the forest is protecting its own."

"Well, blast the lot of you!" exploded Tarkyn in frustration. "Here I am trying to fulfil my vow to protect you and fight for you all and all you want to do is keep me mollycoddled and safe." He hitched his pack angrily. "What's the point in being a champion tournament fighter if I can't even put it into practice?"

"The power you drew from the tree yesterday saved us all from the storm and whatever was waiting for us on the high ground," pointed out Waterstone, walking quickly to keep up with the prince's agitated strides.

Tarkyn threw him a seething glance. "I was hardly putting myself on the line to do that. I, myself, wasn't in any danger."

"You don't have to put yourself in danger to work to protect us. You can do most things from a distance anyway," objected the woodman. He paused, "Danger is not necessarily something to be sought after.... On which point, may I have a few words in private with you?" He smiled perfunctorily at the other two. "I won't keep him long."

So saying, Waterstone turned his footsteps apart from the others, calmly assuming the disgruntled young prince would follow him. Tarkyn shot an angry parting glare at the other two and did indeed follow in the woodman's wake. By the time they were out of earshot and out of sight, Tarkyn's curiosity had gone a long way towards dampening his anger. Waterstone gave him a warm, solid smile and under its influence, Tarkyn could feel himself becoming calmer and more centred.

Eventually, he smiled back, once more on an even footing. "All right. I know. I'm being silly. I just hate feeling trapped by people's good intentions and by the forest."

Waterstone's eyes twinkled. "Not so silly. It's disappointing to miss out on the excitement, such as there may be."

"Be fair, Waterstone. It is not the excitement." Tarkyn gave a slight smile. "Well, not just the excitement."

"I do know that," replied Waterstone dryly. He hesitated, "Tarkyn, there is something I wanted to ask you." He wove his way through a thick cluster of bushes then stopped to watch Tarkyn emerge behind him. "Tarkyn, I need to ask a favour of you." He took a deep breath. "While Ancient Oak and I are undertaking this rescue attempt and afterwards if things go awry, could you, I mean would you, look after Sparrow and keep her safe?"

The colour drained from Tarkyn's face. He stared at the woodman. Seeing the prince's reaction, Waterstone's face tightened. "I'm sorry. I should not have asked you...."

Tarkyn shook his head a little and frowned fiercely. "No, Waterstone, you should ask. Of course I will look after Sparrow. I am her uncle. Remember? And I accept wholeheartedly that family members 'may call upon each other's strength in times of need.'" He waved his hand and let it fall. "I am just shocked, that's all. Your request has finally brought home to me the seriousness of what is about to happen. It's deadly serious, isn't it?" He gave a wry half smile and scratched his head. "I am offended by my own behaviour."

Waterstone gave Tarkyn a pat on the shoulder. "Don't be too hard on yourself. I know you want to play your part in protecting us."

"Yes I do, and I have to warn you, I really do not like being dictated to."

They travelled in silence for a while as they negotiated a shale-covered steep downward slope dotted with spiky bushes that provided unwelcoming handholds. When they reached the bottom of the gully, they scooped handfuls of water from a clear stream before tackling the loose footing of the next steep slope. The effort of picking their way diagonally up the treacherous shale put paid to any conversation until they reached the top of the rise.

Tarkyn stood with his hands on his hips as he caught his breath and broached the subject he had been dreading, "Waterstone, I also have something I need to say." He glanced at his friend and took a deep breath, "I am very much afraid that all woodfolk are now subject to the oath."

Waterstone looked aghast."No! They can't be."

Tarkyn smiled sadly. "I can see from your face, my friend, how much you still dread that your kin should be subject to my authority, despite all my efforts to mitigate it."

"No matter how kind or careful the subjugation, it is not freedom," responded Waterstone tartly.

Tarkyn raised his hand dispiritedly and let it fall. "Anyway, I don't want them to know."

Waterstone looked stonily at him. "What makes you suddenly think they are subject to the oath?"

"Rainstorm's attack. You had your back to the turbulence in the trees. I hope no one else noticed. He attacked me again later, just to test it and the same thing happened."

"Oh stars above, Tarkyn! How did this come about?"

Tarkyn gave the ghost of a smile, "At least you're not assuming I deliberately caused it." He shook his head, "I don't know. I think it was either when the woodfolk said they couldn't help their own people to break an oath, or when you and I joined arms in the woodfolk ceremony."

The woodman threw up his hands. "This is going to cause mayhem."

"Waterstone, you weren't listening. I said I don't want them to know."

Waterstone stopped dead, clearly thinking through all the ramifications.

"Not telling them will work on the short run to avoid more resentment provided, of course, that you don't issue any direct orders." A thought struck him. "It could just be the forest protecting its guardian."

"Maybe. I hadn't thought of that. Either way, only Rainstorm and North Wind know about it and I want it to stay that way. Unless we can be sure that it is, in fact, only the forest protecting its own, I don't want anyone else to know."

Waterstone raised his eyebrows. "Is that an order?" he asked caustically.

"Don't do this to me," said Tarkyn tiredly. "If your principles insist that you go back there and upset a whole lot of people when they need to be working together, go right ahead. I'm not going to stop you." Tarkyn turned his steps in the direction that Danton and Stormaway had taken. "And if you want to have a council of war with all woodfolk to decide how to deal with this person who has subjugated you, and stolen your freedom, just do it. I think it's time we rejoined the others."

In a woodfolk flick of movement, Waterstone was suddenly standing on the path ahead of the prince, facing him.

Tarkyn stopped and put his hands on his hips. "Now what?"

"I am sorry, my friend, for being unkind. Just as anger overwhelms you, so does resentment overwhelm me from time to time. We both know the situation was not of your making." Waterstone grimaced, "I wish I could say that I hadn't meant to upset you but that wouldn't be true. The best I can say is, that now I have upset you, I am remorseful."

The prince heaved a sigh, his face shuttered. "Life was a lot easier when it wasn't an affront to anyone if I issued an order. And life was a lot easier when I didn't know most of my liegemen. And although you may be remorseful, the damage is done. Your fundamental attitude to me is painfully clear. So, let's leave it, shall we?"

Tarkyn pushed past Waterstone and continued up the path. Moments later, Waterstone again stood before him barring his way.

The prince's eyebrows snapped together. "Now I am really getting angry. Get out of my way!"

"No!" The trees on either side of them thrashed in a sudden whirlwind. "Be angry if you like. We must resolve this."

"There is nothing to resolve!" stated Tarkyn flatly and moved forward to pass Waterstone again.

Waterstone flicked himself backwards several yards so that he was yet again standing in front of Tarkyn.

The prince's eyes glittered. "Do you know how much restraint I am using to prevent myself from throwing a spell at you?"

Waterstone gave a little bow, "Much appreciated. Although, of course, it would be cheating, wouldn't it?"

"You're using magic. Why shouldn't I?"

The woodman shook his head. "I'm not using it on you. I'm using it on me."

"That's a specious argument, if ever I heard one. You're using it to affect me."

Waterstone shrugged, "Needs must. We can't afford to be at loggerheads right now. So stop running away and listen to what I have to say."

Tarkyn crossed his arms and stared grimly at the woodman. "I'm listening."

"Tarkyn, you've always known I resented you becoming our liege lord. You saw it in my memories and I told you this morning how much I hate the oath. But that is not the most important factor in my dealings with you. Nearly always, you and I are on the same side. I'm not just supporting you because I have to…I don't have to. You have allowed us the freedom to speak our thoughts. In fact, you have insisted on it. I might wish that that freedom was not at your discretion but that is the best the situation allows." Waterstone shrugged. "I am not going to stand here extolling your virtues to convince you that you mean more to me than an imposed ruler. You must know that. I just reacted badly when the whole issue of the oath came up again. I can't undo it. I can only reiterate that I am sorry."

Tarkyn uncrossed his arms and sighed. "And I reacted badly to your resentment. Stormaway did warn me, if you remember, that I must allow for it." He started to walk along the path and this time, Waterstone turned and fell in beside him. "So, do you agree that we shouldn't tell anyone?"

Waterstone smiled, "Yes, although it would be nice to give them one in the eye."

The prince glanced at him, "I did wonder about that; whether the oath might be creating a class difference, so to speak. The free and the oathbound."

The woodman nodded shortly. "It is a bit, with, as you know, the home guard on the bottom of the heap."

"Ironic, isn't it? In sorcerer society, the home guard would be on the top of the heap." Tarkyn glanced at the woodman again before chancing his next comment, "So, it would be much better if everyone were subject to the oath, wouldn't it?"

Tarkyn watched as his friend repressed a quick frown of consternation. The woodman glanced at the prince to find him smiling in anticipation.

"Very funny," scowled Waterstone. "In actual fact, it would be easier for us and harder for them." He shrugged and after some hesitation added, "But in truth, I wouldn't wish it on them."

"No," said Tarkyn quietly, "Neither would I."

Chapter 45

When the woodman and the sorcerer rejoined Danton and Stormaway, they found them deep in conversation with Summer Rain. Stormaway looked around as they arrived and said buoyantly, "She's cracked it. Summer Rain has come up with the perfect plan for dealing with the wolves."

"Well done," said Tarkyn, falling into the natural assumption that their actions were aimed at pleasing him. After a moment, he frowned. "But I didn't know you could use magic."

"I can't," replied Summer Rain. "But magic is not the answer to all problems."

"True. So what have you come up with?"

"Poison. Stormaway can dope the wolves' food. It doesn't have to be lethal, just enough to put them to sleep for a few hours. Stormaway and I can easily concoct something."

Tarkyn beamed. "Brilliant! We were all so focused on using magic that we forgot straightforward ideas. Now all we have to do is come up with a distraction." The prince gazed around at them all. "That will be easy enough. I'll just shoot a ray of my bronze magic up into the sky from a safe distance and they will all come rushing to look for me."

Three people looked at him in consternation while Waterstone said dryly, "That would work, certainly." He continued sarcastically, "Of course, it would give your presence away and give them a signpost to the location of the rest of the woodfolk in the expedition but other than that, great idea."

"Do you think?" said Tarkyn, laughing at their reactions. "Actually, I was thinking that I could probably link up with the horses in the encampment and ask them to create a distraction. What do you think?"

"Much more sensible," replied Summer Rain repressively.

Tarkyn's eyes met Waterstone's and lit with amusement. Danton spotted this and looked quickly away, experiencing a stab of envy that he quickly repressed as being unworthy. Amidst this group of strangers, Danton suddenly felt very lonely. Gradually, he became aware of a wash of quizzical understanding seeping into him and looked up to see the prince watching him.

"I'll tell you later," mouthed Tarkyn silently.

A little ball of tension disappeared inside Danton as he smiled back and nodded.

The five of them were walking along a winding path through a grove of tall spreading beeches catching the last of the afternoon sun when Danton was finally able to speak to the prince.

"So what was that all about with you and Waterstone and Summer Rain?"

Tarkyn raised his eyebrows, "Very good, Danton. You got their names right." He smiled, "Summer Rain has no sense of humour. So Waterstone and I were just smiling about it. It can be very daunting if you crack a joke and she reacts totally seriously. I've done it often, much to my discomfort. She's a competent healer, though. She brought me through after my run-in with Andoran and Sargon."

"What happened? Stormaway said you were badly injured.

Despite himself, Tarkyn couldn't bring himself to reveal everything to his friend. "I fell out of the tree that I had escaped into. The fall dislocated my shoulder and broke several ribs. Apparently, I hit my head several times on the way down and was unconscious for nearly two weeks."

"Stars above, Sire!" Danton's eyes were round. "Those men should be horse-whipped for what they did to you."

Tarkyn smiled wryly, "Unfortunately the opposite is true. If they had succeeded in returning me, they would have been rewarded instead."

"And what is the reward, I wonder?" asked Danton in an unnervingly thoughtful voice.

Tarkyn flicked a sideways glance at him, "I don't know, but I'm sure it would be enough to set you up comfortably for the rest of your life. I would be offended, if it were any less."

Danton rubbed his hands together and grinned. "Good then. I'll just wait my chance, bung you over my shoulder and away we go. Then I can live comfortably for the rest of my life, battling it out with my conscience."

"Thank heavens for me that you do have a conscience," said Tarkyn, as lightly as he could muster.

The guardsman shrugged. "I don't actually think it would matter much if I didn't. You are strong yourself and very well protected. But even if I killed you, the woodfolk wouldn't let me take in your body for the reward. So there would be no point to it."

The prince frowned down at his friend, "Danton, you are beginning to unnerve me. Why this fixation on the reward?"

Danton glanced up into the depths of Tarkyn's amber eyes, then looked back at the path ahead. "Because you still don't trust me. I am trying to show you that you can."

"You have a funny way of going about it. You have me more worried than ever."

Danton pointed his finger at the prince, something he would never have done before. "There. You see. You are worried about me. I knew it."

Tarkyn sighed and smiled. "Stop it, Danton. You're getting all fidgety. I do trust you. I am trying to trust you as well as I know how."

"You didn't tell me how you escaped."

Light dawned. "Is that what this is all about?" Tarkyn considered him for a moment. "Why are you so anxious to know?"

Danton gave a quirky little smile. "Because Stormaway wouldn't tell me. He said it might give you one less chance next time."

"Which only holds true if you are the threat."

"Exactly. And I'm not."

"So you want me to prove my faith in you by telling you how I escaped, even though I have already proved it by showing you the woodfolk?"

"Yes." Danton took a little breath. "Please."

The prince shook his head, smiling, "Danton, you are hopeless. All right. I will tell you. But if you ever betray me, the world will not be big enough to protect you from the woodfolk."

Danton smiled sadly. "You see? And you are struggling so much to tell me. You keep avoiding it." His voice became brisker, "Look, don't worry. Let us leave things as they are. With luck, you will come to trust me again in time."

Tarkyn felt as though he was trying to clear a big hurdle but couldn't. He had gradually come to trust most woodfolk but he had had no practice with the people who had betrayed him. He shook his head to clear it. "No. I'm not being rational. You are being tarred with the same brush as my brothers and those other two and that is not fair." He took a deep breath and said quickly, "I translocated."

"Did you?" responded Danton matter-of-factly. "Well, that's impressive. And I presume that's how you escaped from the Great Hall as well? That explains why you left me no trail to follow." The guardsman beamed. "So, well done! That is a marvellous skill to have. Maybe I could learn it."

Tarkyn let out the breath that he hadn't realised he was holding and smiled, more relaxed than he had been since Danton's arrival. "Maybe you could."

Part 9: The Rescue

CHAPTER 46

On the day before the planned rescue, the sun climbed into a clear cold sky behind the dense foliage of the forest. As it rose above the tree line, the intensity of its light threw the woodland into relative shadow, making it almost impossible for any guard who might be scanning eastward for signs of life to see more than a few yards into the forest. There was no wind to carry the woodfolk's scent into the camp.

Just beyond the forest's edge, Running Feet and Tree Wind flitted along the branches from tree to tree showing the other woodfolk, particularly those who would be involved in the raid, the layout of the encampment. They had planned their reconnaissance to be early so that when they approached from the east, the glare of the morning sun would shield their presence.

Heated debates had raged, both vocal and silent, about what each person should do. The best marksmen and women would target the guards while the fastest, strongest and most level-headed were chosen to enter the encampment and carry out the actual rescue. Autumn Leaves would lead the rescue because he knew Golden Toad and thus would be most likely to keep the captive woodfolk from panicking.

Rainstorm and North Wind had been relegated to keeping guard over Tarkyn. Despite their previous eagerness to be part of the home guard, neither one was happy about his role. For perhaps the tenth time, Rainstorm pointed out that he was an excellent marksman.

Autumn Leaves nodded amiably, "I agree. You are. Which is why we need you to protect the prince."

"Thunder Storm will be there with him," protested Rainstorm.

"That is true," replied Autumn Leaves. "And he too is an excellent marksman. But he will be minding the children while Creaking Bough helps with the rescue. You can't expect him to abandon the children if they are attacked. We need more people with the prince, especially while he's concentrating."

"Truth is that you're still a little too hot headed to be in the front line, Rainstorm," said Waterstone quietly.

"Then I'll be no use to the prince if we're attacked, will I?"

Waterstone heaved a sigh. "I'll tell Tarkyn then, will I, that you aren't prepared to support him?"

Rainstorm shrugged, "Do what you like. He will understand completely. He'd rather be here himself."

"So what are you planning to do with yourself then? Because you're not staying near the encampment, no matter what," said Tree Wind firmly.

"How are we ever supposed to gain experience if we aren't allowed to take part?" demanded North Wind.

Running Feet looked from one to the other. "You gain experience in hunting parties, where our kin's lives and the whole future lives of woodfolk aren't at stake."

"But this might be our only chance," protested Rainstorm.

"I would like to think that were true," answered Waterstone gravely. "But I very much fear there will be other opportunities in the future. I don't think these people are going to stop looking for us just because they've suffered a set back – if we're successful."

Tree Wind glared at them. "The fact that you're distracting us from our task at the moment is evidence enough of your inexperience. Just be glad you have been allowed to come with us now so that you can have some idea of what we're dealing with." She turned pointedly away from them and waved her hand at the camp. "See? There are hundreds of these white canvas tents. Golden Toad could be in any of those away from the perimeter. We'll have to wait for further information from Stormaway and Danton before we make our final plans."

As they reached different vantage points, Waterstone went out of focus to share the information with Tarkyn. While they stood scanning the sea of tents before them, Waterstone suddenly jumped in fright, but quickly gave a short sigh of relief.

"What was that all about?" asked Autumn Leaves.

"That was our novice image-talker asking me where the wolves are. Tarkyn sent a truly fearsome image of a snarling wolf, followed by a query." Waterstone gave a rueful grin. "I'm sure the delay between the two was unnecessarily long and the image of the wolf unnecessarily fearsome.I think our young sorcerer is feeling bored." He swept his gaze across the tents, sending the image as he did so. "I can't see the wolves from here but I can hear them from time to time. They must be around the other side."

Suddenly Rainstorm reeled back then quickly recovered himself.

Waterstone raised his eyebrows in query.

"An image of galloping horses coming straight at me, then a query," replied Rainstorm laughing. "Well, at least that's easy enough to answer. I can see a few from here. The rest must be behind that tent." He sent the image to Tarkyn.

Tree Wind shook her head, "I think you young men all belong together, well away from here. The prince is showing no sign of possessing the sort of temperament needed for this type of undertaking."

"Oh come on, Tree Wind. We're just having a bit of fun," protested Rainstorm.

"My point exactly," she replied repressively.

Lapping Water relayed her view of this conversation minus the words to Tarkyn. The contents of the discussion were clear just watching Rainstorm and Tree Wind.

Moments later, she saw Tree Wind's eyes widen as she swayed and clutched at the tree trunk to stop from falling. A jet black raven soared up out of the trees and flapped its way slowly around the encampment. When it had finished its circuit, it glided lazily back towards the tree line. Just before it reached them, it flapped its wings to gain height then swooped down onto a branch just above them and sat calmly ruffling its feathers, watching them out of the corner of one eye.

Tree Wind was scowling furiously. "That was not funny." She received a strong sense of contrition mixed with laughter. Despite herself, she could feel herself beginning to unbend.

"That must have given you a good view," said Lapping Water innocently. "You may have to share that with us."

Tree Wind nodded reluctantly. "Yes. I know where the wolves are now. And you're right, Rainstorm; the rest of the horses are behind that tent; tethered with those we can see from here. I still don't know where Golden Toad's tent is, preoccupied as I was with staying up in the tree here."

"How come you're the lucky one to go flying with the raven?" demanded Rainstorm.

Waterstone glanced at Lapping Water before answering, "I suspect Tarkyn thought Tree Wind needed the chance to mix work with fun."

"He's an absolute menace, that prince of yours," said Tree Wind with a half smile. "I nearly fell out of the tree."

"But you didn't. And he may be my brother," added Waterstone, smiling to take the sting out of his words, "but he's your prince too."

Although she gave a small sigh, Tree Wind's smile didn't disappear. "Yes, I know." She looked around at the other woodfolk. "And to be honest," she said slowly, "I think we will be all right with him."

There was a shared moment of understanding. Although it was a small statement, it spoke volumes, as years of trepidation and apprehension were put to rest.

As the moment passed, she brought her gaze to bear on Rainstorm and North Wind and said briskly, "And so, you two, it is not a trivial task that you have been assigned. We have an oath to fulfil, and protecting the guardian of the forest ensures that we will have his help in the future against an enemy that we would struggle to deal with on our own."

After an infinitesimal hesitation, Rainstorm blustered, "I'm under no oath to protect him," he shrugged, "but I will, to help North Wind."

"Big of you," said North Wind, rolling his eyes artistically.

Watching their indifferent acting skills, Waterstone decided that a diversion was needed urgently. "So, now that we have settled that, let's return to the job in hand. How far do you think it is from the tree line to the guards?"

Lapping Water's eyes narrowed as she estimated it. "We will have to shoot about one hundred feet. That's quite a distance for the degree of accuracy we'll need. Maybe we should use blunted arrows instead of slingshots. Then we won't kill them."

"No, but we'd still have to find time to retrieve the arrows." Waterstone thought about it. "I suppose you marksmen could retrieve the arrows while the rest of us are carrying out the rescue. It does slightly increase the risk of being seen, though."

"Let's practise with slingshots and see how we go," suggested Lapping Water. "We can decide after that."

Tarkyn was squatted down playing marbles with Sparrow and the three boys when the woodfolk returned to the campsite. As soon as he saw them, Tarkyn could feel something had changed. There was a sense of released tension in the air. He cocked an enquiring eyebrow at Waterstone but only received a faint shake of the head in return. Giving a mental shrug, Tarkyn returned his attention to the marbles just as quiet little Rain on Water flicked a cracking marble into his and shot it off out of the ring.

The little boy glanced shyly up at Tarkyn and smiled, "You've lost all your marbles now." He hesitated, "You can borrow some of mine, if you like."

"No he can't," protested Sparrow hotly. "That wouldn't be fair. Tarkyn's out and that's all there is to it."

"I'm afraid she's right. But thank you for your offer." Tarkyn gave Rain on Water a friendly nudge before he stood up, "Just do me a favour and get Sparrow out next. Since I'm out, I'll leave you lot to it, for the time being."

Tarkyn walked over to join the newly returned woodfolk by the fire and accepted a bowl of porridge from Thunder Storm. As he ate, his eyes roved from one to the other trying to work out what was different. Everyone seemed friendly but more relaxed and self-assured. He noticed that there were no longer any splits between the groups and although this was what he had worked towards, he feared that, in some way, in becoming unified, they had closed ranks against him. Since Waterstone had not responded to his earlier query, he did not ask again but determined to mention it later when there was no audience.

Eventually he put his thoughts to one side and asked Tree Wind, "Did you like your trip around the camp with the raven?"

"Yes thank you, Your Highness." Tree Wind replied tartly. "Once I had saved myself from falling out of the tree. I can see I will have to become used to your levity."

Tarkyn took a quick look around to check who was listening, then rolled his eyes. "I hope you're not like Summer Rain."

Tree Wind frowned, "I beg your pardon? What's that supposed to mean?

"No sense of humour," replied Tarkyn dolefully.

Tree Wind gave a short laugh. "Stop it. Summer Rain is a very skilled healer. She is a very serious person."

"Well I hope I don't lose my sense of humour as I become more skilful at healing," replied Tarkyn with a twinkle in his eyes.

"I think you have such an overabundance of it, that a bit less wouldn't be noticed."

"You have eased my fears," said Tarkyn. "You wouldn't have noticed that I had a sense of humour if you hadn't one yourself. Now Summer Rain, you see, just thinks I make odd remarks."

"Hmm. I suspect she thinks we all make odd remarks from time to time." Tree Wind smiled, "Now, these two young men have kindly volunteered to remain here as your protectors. So has Running Feet."

"Thank you, Running Feet," said Tarkyn gravely before turning a quizzical smile on Rainstorm and North Wind. "Bad luck, you two. Drew the short straws, did you?"

Rainstorm eyed him belligerently for a moment, clearly deciding whether to admit their reluctance or whether to act hurt. In the end, he gave a crooked smile, "As it turns out, this is not actually our first choice but seeing how useful your raven proved to be, I can see the value in protecting you."

"Thanks," said Tarkyn dryly. "I'm glad you find me useful. Very heart warming."

Rainstorm almost but not quite stamped his foot. "I am trying to find a way to see protecting you as a contribution to the rescue."

Tarkyn smiled understandingly, "It's a pain isn't it? Not being allowed in the front line. I know just how you feel. If it makes you feel any better, I can assure you that I will be making a significant contribution from the back blocks here. And I will need people guarding my back whilst I concentrate." Tarkyn scraped out the last of his porridge and set aside his bowl before adding, "And to tell you the truth, it will be good to have your company. With Thunder Storm and Running Feet, we should be a cheery little crew." He paused as he thought for a moment. "That's not many woodfolk to protect four kids and me. Are you sure your skills are up to it?"

"Of course they are," retorted Rainstorm hotly.

"North Wind, you're not saying much. What do you think?"

"If you really want to know, Your Highness, I think we would be hard pressed if we really came under attack."

"I think you're absolutely right. So you will have to be super vigilant because our only hope will be to have enough warning to avoid an attack, won't it?" Tarkyn frowned at Rainstorm, "How did your concentration go the other night when you guarded me against Danton?"

Tree Wind watched in grudging admiration as Tarkyn took the boys seriously and melted their resistance like sun on snow.

Rainstorm considered carefully before replying, "It was difficult at times. We might be better to give each other breaks from time to time. We could alternate guarding with minding the kids."

"Good idea. More fun and less boring, too. Still, it won't be for all that long. Only three or four hours, I would think. So that won't be as bad as a whole night on guard, will it?"

Rainstorm grinned, "Nothing like it. The other night was the longest night of my entire life."

"And once the kids are asleep, I can share the images with whoever is not on lookout so you know what is happening at the encampment."

"Sounds a good deal to me," said Waterstone. "Come on you two. Help me set up targets for slingshot practice. Then we can see what you're really made of."

Chapter 47

Stormaway and Danton lay hidden behind a hedge of hawthorns close to the track leading to the encampment. They were both dressed in worn travellers' clothing. Danton was seriously unimpressed with the cut of his jacket but had wisely decided not to comment. Stormaway had a glamour in place that made him look old and unkempt, his features altered sufficiently to make him unrecognisable.

Every now and then a dispirited group of weary shaken travellers passed close by, flanked by armed men. The travellers did not seem to be prisoners. In fact, the armed guards were friendly, chatty and even solicitous.

"This is very strange," whispered Stormaway. "I don't understand it at all."

"Perhaps the armed guards are escorts to protect the travellers on their journey."

The wizard shook his head. "I don't think so. We are too far from the road… Why are they coming here?"

"I don't know. Maybe we'll find out more once we're inside."

"Maybe."Stormaway glanced at the sorcerer. "Are you ready? We'll fall in behind the next large group."

The sun was high in the sky by the time the next large group filed past them. Danton watched the armed men, looking for a moment when their eyes were elsewhere.

"Now!" he breathed.

They stood up and walked casually onto the road behind the group to join the stragglers. An old woman's eyes widened briefly as she suddenly found herself no longer at the rear. But life had been hard and she wasn't really interested in anything other than reaching camp and getting some food and rest. So she gave a faint shrug and kept putting one foot in front of the other.

Stormaway and Danton matched their pace and posture to those around them, hunching their shoulders and treading slowly and heavily. They didn't speak because they had nothing safe to say. Forty minutes later, they were approaching the encampment. Strangely, the guards at the entrance paid very little heed to anyone.

Danton frowned and whispered, "This lot wouldn't last long at the palace. Why do they even bother having guards if they don't even make a cursory check on people coming in?"

A chilling thought struck Stormaway. "Maybe they are more careful about people going out?"

The two men looked at each other. "There is no one going out," whispered Danton.

As they watched, they realised this wasn't strictly true. From time to time, a small group of armed soldiers would leave, heading back down the path to the main road through the forest.

The wizard and the sorcerer found themselves ushered to a place around a campfire. Helpful guards provided them with food and drink. When they were sated, soldiers showed them to a large tent where they could bed down in a corner when they were ready. Beyond that, they were left to their own devices.

"Do you know any of these people?" asked Danton.

The wizard shook his head. "Not so far. But I have a wide network. There must be someone here I know."

Danton frowned. "I think I may have seen one or two of the soldiers before, but I don't know them personally. I could have seen them anywhere."

"Let's start moving around," suggested Stormaway. "We have to find out the feeding arrangement for the wolves. We only have tonight. Tomorrow we must get it right."

"It's a short time line," said Danton, bowing slightly to an officer as they sauntered past. "I would have preferred more time but the woodfolk are anxious about their friends and I suppose the danger of discovery increases the longer we stay here."

Stormaway shrugged. "We are in no danger of discovery. We both have every right to be travelling wherever we please."

"It would help if we knew why it might be that we have come to the encampment."

The wizard looked thoughtful. "True. Let's find the stake, the woodfolk tent and the wolves first. Once we have done our planning, we can settle ourselves in around a campfire and listen to a few conversations."

They wandered around the inside of the perimeter of the encampment, trying to work out which tent housed the woodfolk. It took twenty minutes to circumnavigate. Thanks to Tarkyn's complete and utter lack of directional sense, they had no real idea where the tent was. However, they guessed that it might be on the east because they knew Running Feet's vision would have lead Tarkyn's mind from that direction.

The wolves and horses were a lot easier to find. The wolves were unhappy with their lot and several of them paced restlessly up and down the few feet of travel their chains would allow them. When Stormaway and Danton approached them, they snarled and howled, dragging at their chains in an effort to attack. Several people looked over to see what was causing the disturbance. Although the horses were roped well away on the other side of the camp, the wolves' snarling caused several horses to whinny, tossing their heads and rolling their eyes in fear.

"We'll give those wolves a wide berth then," said Danton firmly. He added quietly, "I wonder if they can smell woodfolk on us?"

"Possibly," mused the wizard. "Anyway, we don't need to get near them. We just need to find their food source."

Suddenly, they found their way blocked by a sturdy, armed guard. He was dressed in a cobbled together uniform that was a mixture from several regiments. He wore no helmet and his bald head shone in the afternoon sun. What was left of his hair was grey and shoulder length. He glared at them from under dark, bushy eyebrows and demanded, "What do you two think you're playing at, getting so close to those wolves? They're dangerous, you know. Look at that! You've disturbed the horses." He leant forward and peered closely at them, "Have I seen you before? You don't look familiar."

Danton's heart was thumping in his chest but he replied with a semblance of calm, spiced with just a dash of uncertainty, "I beg your pardon, sir, if we have upset anyone. We have only just arrived and were simply having a look around."

The guard straightened up in response to Danton's well-bred accent. "That explains it then, my lord." He gave a kindly smile, "Took your finery, did they? You must be feeling a little shaken up still. Don't worry. We're a friendly enough bunch here. You'll soon get to know us all. My name's Torgan." He looked Danton up and down, to which Danton took silent exception. Sergeant Torgan smiled disarmingly. "You seem to be in pretty good shape, sir. You might be ready to join a regiment quite soon." He glanced at Stormaway. "Your friend here could take a bit longer." He frowned, "Perhaps he has other skills we can use instead. He doesn't look like much of a fighter."

Stormaway managed to cower down and appear even more pathetic than before, "I am a tailor, sir," he whined, "Though my eyesight is not as good as it used to be. But I can still sew if someone else threads the needle."

The guard gave him a hearty, condescending pat on the back, "Good on you, old man. I'm sure there'll be plenty for you to do." He tipped his fingers to his forehead in a friendly salute, "I'd better go. I expect I'll see you around."

As soon as he was out of earshot, Danton turned to Stormaway incredulously. "Tailor? Where did that come from?"

The wizard shrugged and gave a small self-deprecating smile, "I don't know why it is, but people never think of a tailor as a threat. It's a very useful disguise."

"And can you sew?" demanded Danton.

Stormaway snorted, "Of course I can. I don't do things by halves, you know. I've been in this game for many long years."

"Well, if you've been in this game for so long, what do you make of all this?"

The wizard looked around and shook his head. "I don't know for sure but I would say they are recruiting people for something."

Danton's eyes widened, "Not for hunting woodfolk, I hope."

"I don't know. Could be. Could be for something else. We'll keep our eyes and ears open and see what we can find out."

Not surprisingly, Stormaway and Danton eventually located the imprisoned woodfolk's tent quite close to the wolves. There was no other tent with a chain issuing under the side panel attached to a metal stake in the ground. A large black crow was perched on the top of the tent pole. It flew off as they approached and settled further away in an overhanging branch.

Once they had identified the tent, they wandered around the vicinity, looking casually for guards or magical wards. Stormaway looked around surreptitiously and muttered under his breath, "Wards, Rayavalka!" and thrust three fingers outwards.

Immediately, pale splashes of green flickered in a dozen different places across the encampment. One of them flickered across the entrance to the woodfolk's tent, but there were none around the sides.

Moments later, Stormaway snapped his fingers back into his palm and the green lights flicked out.

"Mmm. Interesting, "said Stormaway. "A ward to stop people going in by mistake, or out of idle curiosity, but no real expectation of a rescue attempt."

Danton shrugged. "I can only imagine they have underestimated the woodfolk. Maybe Golden Toad and his family are playing dumb. Whoever has them trapped might think of them as wild animals if they don't speak – and wild animals wouldn't rescue their kin."

Stormaway frowned in disapproval. "Woodfolk are nothing like wild animals. Mind you, without Tarkyn's help, they wouldn't have known Golden Toad and his family were even missing, let alone where they were." Stormaway looked towards the nearest perimeter. "Okay. Let's see how many guards there are, and where."

They scanned the perimeter nearest the woodfolk's tent.

"Six that I can see," reported Danton.

"I wonder when they change the guard?"

"It's usually every four hours," replied the ex-palace guardsman. "We'll need the woodfolk to strike soon after the change so that they can be well away before the next watch discovers the unconscious guards."

A small huddle of travellers wandered past them, obviously reconnoitring their new surroundings. As Danton sauntered over to them to strike up a conversation, they bowed in response to his unconscious air of command. He frowned and threw a wry glance at Stormaway before nodding his head in acknowledgement. He offered a few desultory remarks and when they were more at ease, asked, "New here too, are you?" He nodded at the woodfolk's tent. "What do you suppose is in there with that chain going under the wall like that?"

A young girl curtsied and answered with wide-eyed nervousness, "Sir, I believe there is an injured wolf in there, sir." She curtsied again, her chestnut hair falling down over her shoulder.

Danton smiled disarmingly, "Really? I'm glad I asked. I wouldn't want to go in there by mistake and get myself mauled."

"No sir, you wouldn't," said a tall gangly youth, clearly her brother and clearly anxious to get a word in with this lordly acquaintance. "Only the wolves' keeper goes in there, we understand." He hesitated, "Will you be taking over one of the regiments, sir?"

Danton cast a quick measuring glance at the other members of their group. "I have only just arrived and do not yet know my intentions."

"My Da and uncle and me… We all plan to fight the brigands." The young man glanced earnestly at an older man standing just behind him. "Don't we, Da?"

"Yes lad, we do."

A short stocky man, presumably the uncle, joined in. "It's got to be stopped, you know. You can't have the kingdom's road rife with thugs. If the king won't attend to it, we'll have to do it ourselves."

Danton raised his eyebrows, "Do you doubt the king, sir?

For a moment, the man gobbled at him, his mouth opening and shutting soundlessly like a landed fish.

"Do not fear," said Danton with a slight smile. "I am not the king's agent. I am merely interested in the progress of popular opinion, since I have been out of touch for a few weeks."

The uncle scratched his head, "Oh well, in that case…" He leaned in a little closer. "It's not that we are disloyal to the king. It's just that he is so busy chasing his evil brother... "

Danton frowned, "Who? Prince Jarand?"

The man snorted. "No, not Prince Jarand. He is fighting to support us against the raiders. Prince Tarkyn. He's the evil bastard who destroyed half of Tormadell, and killed off all the Royal Guard and hundreds of innocent bystanders."

Danton's eyes grew round not, as they thought, at the enormity of the crimes, but at the enormity of the rumours, which had grown considerably since he last heard them.

The father nodded sagely. "Well you might boggle, my lord. No wonder the king has his hands full. The countryside is shouting for the Prince Tarkyn's blood but the king, very nobly, wants to give his brother a fair trial. Personally, I'd be happy to see the murdering bastard torn limb from limb, but the king has his standards." He shrugged. "Still, that's why we look up to the Royal Family." He sucked his breath in sympathetically and shook his head. "What a shame for them to have such a black sheep among them."

It was taking Danton considerable effort to regain the use of his vocal chords, "Harumph. Yes. Quite embarrassing for them." Feeling that he could not stomach any more of this, Danton turned to the young lady and summoned a smile for her, "And what do you intend to do while the men of your family fight brigands?"

She gave a shy smile in return, "My little sister and I will stay here in the camp and see what we can do to help. Perhaps we will see you around the campsite from time to time." Then she blushed furiously while her father scowled at her. "I beg your pardon. I did not mean to sound forward. I only meant…"

Danton glanced reassuringly at the father and broadened his smile, "I understand what you meant. I am sure we will all see each other again if we remain billeted within the encampment. After all, it is not so very big, is it?" He sketched a small bow for her. "It would be a pleasure to run into you again… all of you," he added hastily.

"Excuse me, my lord," he heard a caustic voice say behind him, "but I believe duty calls."

Danton swung around to find Stormaway's eyes boring into him. He frowned before swinging back to say ruefully, "I am afraid he is right. Until next time."

"I see you do not have the same natural difficulties with dissemblance that your liege displays."

Danton gave a short laugh. "No. Not at all, as you just saw. So it's just as well, isn't it, that Tarkyn's morals keep me in check?"

"I have no problem with a natural dissembler. I am one myself. It doesn't have to be in an unworthy cause." Stormaway regarded the sorcerer curiously, "But if I weren't here to report back to him, what then? And what of your behaviour when you were on your own, searching for him?"

Danton frowned in annoyance. "I don't dissemble with the prince," he said shortly. "I know what he wants and as far as I am able, I deliver it. Always."

As they talked, they had walked around the area surrounding the wolves looking for the source of the wolves' dinner. By mutual, unspoken agreement, they wandered further afield towards the smells of cooking food.

When the wizard did not reply, Danton continued, "And I have always tried to protect him from other dissemblers. Because he is so straightforward himself, Tarkyn struggles to understand that some people may be more devious. He knows in his head that people double-cross and manoeuvre for power and influence at the expense of personal integrity, but in his heart, he has never been able to come to grips with it."

Stormaway studied the passionate young sorcerer, "Unless I am much mistaken, you too have your own emphatic code of ethics."

Danton gave a slightly embarrassed smile, "Yes, I do. Of course I do, but not everyone at court realises that. If they did, I would have been privy to less intrigue and in a poorer position to protect my liege."

"Ah! A man after my own heart," said Stormaway as he followed his nose to large white tent. He pulled back the flap and poked his head around the corner to see several long trestle tables set up as preparation benches. Large baskets of vegetables were sitting under the tables waiting to be prepared for the night's meal. A huge cooking fire burned slowly in the middle of the tent beneath a hole in the roof; and several cooks had already begun to prepare the vegetables. As they were finished, handfuls of carrots, potatoes and chopped onions drifted through the air into large cooking pots, already simmering over the fire. Every now and then, one of the cooks directed a trickle of yellow magic into the steam and smoke to keep it on course for the hole in the roof.

At a separate table, a hefty cook was dismembering a skinned deer using a sharp hatchet. Bones and offal were thrown into a big wooden bucket against the wall of the tent. As Stormaway watched, a marrowbone missed the bucket and landed on the floor. With a slight frown of annoyance, the cook casually directed a thin stream of grey magic at the bone and lifted it off the floor into the waiting bucket before returning to his chopping.

The wizard withdrew and looked around at Danton, a satisfied smile playing around his lips. "I think I may have found the wolves' food. The meat scraps are being collected in a bucket against the back wall of the tent. Couldn't be easier, if that is the case. We'll wait around here and make sure."

"Perhaps we can loosen the stake when the wolves are eating tomorrow night."

Stormaway brushed a speck of dirt off his left shoulder. "Possibly, but the wolves are very close to that tent. It depends on whether their trainer stays with them while they eat. And whether other people come to watch them feed too. We'll watch and see what happens tonight." He then brushed down his right shoulder, by the end of which procedure he had scanned to whole area around them. "We'd better move on. We don't want to be seen loitering near the food tent. Let's stay close by but wander over and have a look at the horses. "

They sauntered around the corner of the next tent and ran slap bang into Andoran and Sargon.

CHAPTER 48

Deep in the woods, North Wind and Rainstorm eyed each other as they followed Waterstone to set up targets.

"He told you, didn't he?" asked North Wind as soon as they were out of earshot.

Waterstone nodded as he handed them chunks of yellow ochre, "Here. Mark out some targets on these trees. We'll need six or eight of them, I'd say."

Surprisingly Rainstorm didn't object, but merely asked, "How do you want them?"

Waterstone stood with his hands on his hips while he considered it, "Just draw a circle with eyes and nose. A bit above our head height. We don't need the body. We'll be aiming for their heads."

As they each began work on a separate tree, Waterstone said quietly, "I've been looking for a chance to talk to you two, for days." The woodman didn't beat round the bush. "Are you sure, Rainstorm? Couldn't it just be the forest protecting its guardian?"

Rainstorm thought carefully before answering, "I don't think so. It wasn't the trees reacting. It was the wind…and it was damaging the trees. What do you think, North Wind?"

The young woodman shook his head. "No. The trees weren't protecting Tarkyn. The wind was lashing the trees, ripping the leaves off them."

Waterstone looked at Rainstorm with concern. "And how are you? It's quite something to come to terms with, isn't it? I've had years to get used to the concept yet even now, I get upset sometimes. Still, I suppose even I have only had a few weeks to come to terms with the reality. It's hard, isn't it?"

Rainstorm nodded ruefully. "Especially when I can't talk to any of my family about it. They might drive me crazy a lot of the time but when we are sharing something as huge as this, it is hard to keep it to myself." He stood back to look at the face he had drawn. "Hmm, this one looks a bit lopsided."

"It doesn't matter. As long as it's near enough." When Waterstone had finished drawing his own target, he said, "I am impressed by the care you are showing for our people, keeping such an enormous thing secret. It takes courage to do that, Rainstorm… and strength of character." He walked over to the next large tree and began to size up where to put his next target. He glanced across at Rainstorm, "I suppose Tarkyn must have a fair idea of how you're feeling?"

Rainstorm grimaced and his eyes met North Wind's, "Ooh, I'd say he has a slight inkling. I more or less fell apart right in front of him when I found out."

North Wind gave a short laugh. "Yes, you did, didn't you? And Tarkyn was distressed about by your reaction. You could see it in his face." North Wind rubbed at one side of the face he'd just drawn and tried to extend it out further. He frowned at the messy result, "Blast! This has gone all wrong. It's fat on one side and skinny on the other!"

"Don't worry," said Rainstorm, "Mine's lopsided too."

"They'll do," said Waterstone shortly. Then he sighed, "Oh dear, Tarkyn must have had a great day that day. I followed that up by looking horrified." He smiled reminiscently, "And then, when he suggested we should keep quiet about the oath having spread, I demanded to know if he was giving me an order."

The two young woodmen stopped what they were doing and goggled at him. North Wind chortled. "Waterstone! I can't believe you'd be so, I don't know, adolescent. That's the sort of thing people expect Rainstorm and me to do. Not you."

"Thanks, North Wind," responded Waterstone dryly, "I think the oath brings out the worst in me sometimes. Come on, get on with it!" he added to cover his embarrassment.

North Wind and Rainstorm smiled knowingly at each other before moving on to start on new targets

"Anyway," continued Waterstone, ignoring their exchanged look, "I just wanted to check with you, Rainstorm, to see how you're coping.… And I was hoping it was the forest and not the oath but it doesn't look like it."

"Thanks." Rainstorm shrugged, "I'm all right. Tarkyn gave me permission to attack him in case my temper gives the game away – not that I'm planning to. I might get myself hurt if I do. Other than that, it's up to him really. As long as he doesn't suddenly start issuing orders, I don't think it's going to make too much difference."

Rainstorm stopped talking for a few minutes while he lined up the placement of the next target. When he was satisfied, he gave a little smile and continued, "Tarkyn's an impressive character, you know. You weren't there when he took on the forestals. But I couldn't believe how calm he was, faced with all those unfriendly, hostile woodfolk. If I had to follow anyone, it would be him."

Waterstone raised his eyebrows. "I'm amazed to hear you say that, especially with the oath being so raw for you."

Waterstone was taken aback. He realised that, in some ways, the young woodman accepted the prince's authority more readily than he did. Waterstone could welcome Tarkyn as a friend and a brother but he still struggled to accept him as his liege lord. *Maybe his age,* pondered Waterstone. *To me, Tarkyn is a young man barely out of adolescence. To them, he is older, a lot more powerful and more experienced in the ways of the world than they are.* "And you, North Wind? What do you think about having to follow Tarkyn?" he asked, as he sketched out a large circle on the tree on front of him.

North Wind finished adding some artistic eyebrows before he replied, "I don't like it but having met Tarkyn, it's not as bad as I had been lead to expect." He leaned backwards to see how his face was looking. "Hmm. That's a bit better…He's had such an amazing life. You know, Tarkyn's had people bowing to him since he was a little boy. Rank before age. That's what he said. What a mad concept." North Wind shook his head in wonder. "I don't know how he has managed to come in here and leave all that behind."

"He hasn't left all of it behind," said Waterstone dryly as he added in two large eyes and a rather strange sideways nose. "He still thinks rank before age."

North Wind shrugged, "Maybe, but not in the same way as he was brought up to think." He frowned reprovingly at the older woodman. "We're just bloody lucky he's not requiring us to behave like Danton. And I couldn't believe it when I realised that here he is, trying to get an equal say, when he could simply dictate to the lot of us." He paused in his creation of two almond shaped eyes to study Waterstone, "You're too close to him. You're used to him. But take a step back and you'll realise how extraordinary that is for someone who's always been used to power."

Waterstone thought back to the faint derision in his tone when he'd questioned Tarkyn's need for greater influence and for keeping a dignified distance. He realised he had basically taken it for granted that Tarkyn would have similar views to his own and that discussions around distance and expectations were curious little peccadilloes in an otherwise normal woodman. Something of this must have shown on his face because North Wind added, "I wouldn't be quibbling about the odd order here and there, if I were you."

"No, you may not," answered Waterstone grimly, "but I would. It does not sit well with me to have to obey any man. He said he would sooner die than subvert his will to anyone. That's pretty much how I feel. Maybe that's one reason I get on so well with him. Unfortunately, I must obey Tarkyn if he insists, but I don't like it and never will."

Rainstorm looked up from the eyebrows he was delicately sketching on his target. "And has Tarkyn always known you feel like this?" he asked curiously.

Waterstone gave a short laugh, "To quote you, I think he might have an inkling! We even fought over it at one stage."

"Really?" North Wind gave a low whistle.

"But I could fight him, only because he'd given me permission," added Waterstone bitterly. "And it was not a play fight by any means. I stopped it pretty quickly but even then it was too late."

Rainstorm frowned, "Too late for what?"

"Too late to stop one of us getting hurt." Waterstone glanced at each of them in turn, then dropped his eyes. "Tarkyn hadn't recovered properly from his fall and during the fight, one of his broken ribs punctured his lung. If Stormaway hadn't known what to do and Tarkyn hadn't been a forest guardian, he would have died. As it was, it was touch and go, even with all of us sharing our life force with him."

North Wind let out a low whistle. "Wow. That's scary. With that and him falling out of the oak tree, we've come close to losing the forest twice in a few weeks."

"And Tarkyn," said Waterstone with a sharp edge to his voice.

North Wind shrugged, "And Tarkyn. But, much as he's an interesting, likeable character, his loss would be our gain as long as the forest was safe."

Suddenly, Waterstone lunged forward, swinging his fist at the unsuspecting young woodman. As the punch connected solidly, North Wind was thrown over backwards. He found himself lying on the floor staring groggily at a sky that seemed to be spinning slowly through a web of overhanging branches. His jaw and shoulder hurt and he licked blood from a split lip. After what seemed like a several minutes but was actually only a moment, he lifted his head uncertainly and saw a thunderous Waterstone standing over him, ready to hit him again if he tried to rise.

North Wind wisely decided to stay where he was and dropped his head back down. "Stars above, Waterstone! I'm sorry, I'm sorry. Don't hit me again." He wiped his mouth and frowned as his hand came away streaked with blood, "I don't see why you're so upset. You just finished saying that you resent having to obey Tarkyn."

"That doesn't mean I want to lose him, you bloody snake-in-the-grass. How could you be so cold blooded about him? I thought you liked Tarkyn."

"I do. But you can't compare that with my freedom and the freedom of all woodfolk."

"But you said you wouldn't hear a word against him," protested Rainstorm.

"I haven't said anything bad about him. I told you. From the little I've seen of him, I like him. I'm just stating facts. After all, we would be a free people again if Tarkyn weren't here," said North Wind, watching Waterstone nervously.

Waterstone threw him a disgusted look then turned his wrath on Rainstorm, "And you? Do you think Tarkyn's loss would be our gain?"

Rainstorm eyed the irate woodman askance. "Are you going to hit me too, if I give you an answer you don't like?"

Waterstone clenched his fists at his sides. "No," he said through gritted teeth, "I will contain myself. I would rather know where you stand."

Rainstorm put his head on one side as he thought about it, "I like the prince and I trust him. Life was much duller around here before he came. But I don't like following orders from anyone. Saying that, he said we would stay on the same footing as before and I believe him, though I suspect there might be times when that doesn't hold true." He gave a little smile. "Besides, he's one of the few people who has any respect for what I have to say. But if Tarkyn's death could release me from this oath without the forest being damaged…." Rainstorm shrugged and glanced at Waterstone standing like a wound up spring before him. He gave a little mischievous smile, making Waterstone wait, and then admitted, "No. I wouldn't want Tarkyn hurt, even if it did release me from the oath. I guess I can cope with the oath. The 'honour' and 'protect' bits are fine. I think he actually deserves them. It's the 'serve' bit that's a struggle but I can live with it." He frowned fiercely. "I am amazed to hear myself say that, though."

Some of the tension seeped out of Waterstone.

Rainstorm glanced at the older woodman before drawing a wobbly circle then standing back to look at it. "But you hate being under this oath, don't you?" Waterstone nodded briefly. "And so does Tarkyn. What he saw in Tree Wind's memories horrified him almost as much as it had horrified us. Right from the start, he has known how much we resented the oath and him. Yet, even if he wanted to, he couldn't walk away from it."

North Wind had gingerly lifted himself up onto his elbows while he listened. "But he could have isolated himself within the forest."

"Don't worry. He's thought of that." Waterstone shrugged, "But he is vowed to protect us as we are to protect him. Anyway, that's no life for a young man to be totally isolated. This isn't just a few weeks or months we're talking about here. It's his whole life."

Rainstorm frowned, "I hadn't really thought about all that. It must have been hard for him to have had all of you hating him at the start."

"It was and it still is." Waterstone sighed, "And you and I haven't made it any easier for him with our recent reactions. And he knows he is going to have to face that in scores of other woodfolk as they realise they have come under the oath." Waterstone took a couple of paces then swung back around, hands on hips, "You know, the thing I detest most about the oath is that it muddies my friendship with Tarkyn. If I protect him or help him out of friendship, how does he know it's not just because of the oath?"

Rainstorm smiled, "Don't worry. He knows. You wouldn't be as nice about it, if it were because of the oath."

Waterstone gave a short laugh, "Huh. I hadn't thought of that. You're probably right." He took his arms down from his hips and grimaced, "But the other thing that happens is my resentment wells up and I hurt him when he's just trying to have a normal conversation with me."

"But surely he understands…" began Rainstorm.

"Yes and no," Waterstone's words unknowingly echoed Danton's; "In his head, Tarkyn understands. Stormaway warned him to make allowances for resentment. But in his heart, he takes it personally. You can see him struggling to deal with it." He looked from one to the other of them. "In the end, he's just a young man not much older than you. You might think you have the world against you at times, Rainstorm, but Tarkyn really does. At least, he did. I think he has managed to get a lot of people on side as they have come to know him. But as North Wind has so ably demonstrated, he still has a long way to go. I wouldn't be Tarkyn, for all the trees in the forest."

Rainstorm shook his head in sympathy, "No, it must be tough, fielding all that resentment… and now there's going to be more."

"I feel bad now," stammered North Wind.

"Good," replied Waterstone shortly.

"I don't mean physically. I feel bad because you think I've betrayed Tarkyn. When I said his loss would be our gain, I was thinking about the forest's safety and the woodfolk's independence. Tarkyn's existence places them both in jeopardy. It's the concept of him that I was talking about, not the man himself." He eyed Waterstone nervously, "Do you understand?"

Waterstone let out a pent up breath. "Yes, I do understand. Even Tarkyn himself gets confused about that. But do you understand that the concept and the man are inseparable? If you betray one, you betray the other. Tarkyn doesn't like it. You may not like it, but that's the way it is. To support him as a person, at the very least you have to accept him for what he is, even if you don't like it."

"If you go around saying his loss would be our gain, you'll inflame people against him again," put in Rainstorm. "We're stuck with him. He's stuck with us. You know from talking to him that he's doing his level best to make the situation as bearable as possible for everyone. We might as well just get on with it and support him."

Waterstone raised his eyebrows, "You never cease to amaze me, Rainstorm."

"Get used to it, old man. Something Tarkyn said to me made me realise that what I think is okay. I just need to figure out how to say it, so people will listen to me."

Waterstone gave a wry smile. "I'm not sure that calling me old man is going to get me on side."

Rainstorm chuckled. "You love it, really. Anyway, you're twice our ages."

"That does not make me old."

The young woodman grinned unrepentantly, "It does from where I'm sitting. Twenty is old. Thirty five is positively decrepit."

A short time later Tarkyn, sitting in the shade of an old oak, having a break from reconnoitring, watched the trio talking amongst themselves as they returned from creating the targets. He knew that Rainstorm and the oath would have been the centre of their discussion. The three woodmen parted company and North Wind headed over in his general direction. As he came nearer, Tarkyn saw his cut lip and the beginnings of bruising on his jaw.

Tarkyn called out to him, "North Wind. What have you done to yourself? Do you want me to fix your lip?"

North Wind, who was feeling guilty and that he had more or less earned his sore face replied shortly, "No thanks. I can look after myself."

"I'm sure you can." In one short phrase, Tarkyn's friendliness faded to constraint.

North Wind veered off and passed him without another word. Tarkyn watched his retreating back and wondered what the three of them had been saying. After the unexplained change in atmosphere this morning, North Wind's response to him made his stomach tighten. He grunted and, giving himself a small mental shake, returned to his view of the encampment through the crow's eyes. The first sight that met his eyes was Andoran and Sargon.

Chapter 49

Danton's face went white with shock and his mouth thinned. Stormaway became more self-effacing than ever. Andoran and Sargon's faces broke into smiles.

"Danton. Fancy seeing you here!" said Andoran cheerfully, tossing his head to flick his mop of unruly red hair falling out of his eyes. "This is great!" He frowned. "Who's your friend?" he added less enthusiastically.

Danton had recovered himself sufficiently to produce a friendly smile, "This fellow here is Threadneedle." He said, inventing freely. "He is a tailor, you know. Met him on the way to the camp here."

Andoran laughed, "A tailor, eh? With a name like Threadneedle, I never would have guessed." Andoran sketched an ironic bow, "An honour to meet you, sir. I am Andoran and this is my friend, Sargon."

Stormaway bowed to them both, "An honour, my lords." He glanced at Danton. "If you'll excuse me, sirs, I have a few things to sort out. Perhaps I will see you later."

"Perhaps," replied Sargon, his eyebrows slightly raised at the tailor's temerity.

"Well," said Andoran, watching Stormaway's retreating figure. "I don't think your friend could manage the excitement of three exalted personages all at once. Perhaps one is his limit."

Danton shook his head, smiling. "I think you may be right." He turned back to them. "So, how are you both? It is good to see you after all this time. What have you been up to?"

Sargon shrugged. "This and that. We have thrown our lot in with these people for the time being." He looked down at himself in his grey and blue jacket and dark blue trousers. "The uniforms are a bit of a deterrent but we are managing to overlook them as much as possible. Other than that, they seem a friendly team."

"So, what are you doing here?" asked Andoran.

Deciding that, as far as possible, honesty was the best policy, Danton replied, "I don't really know yet. I only arrived here this afternoon."

"So, were you amongst a group of travellers that was attacked? That's how most people get here."

"Is it?" Danton put his head on one side. "No. I just fell in with a column of people and wandered in here with them. I'm actually taking some time out to visit my grandmother down in the southwest. But I'm in no great hurry. So I thought I'd spend a day or two here."

Andoran and Sargon lead Danton to a nearby campfire. Andoran found a bottle of wine and poured measures into three glasses as they spoke. He handed Danton a glass as he sat down on a sturdy wooden chair, "That was a bad business with the prince, wasn't it?" he said, shaking his head.

"Yes, terrible," replied Danton ambiguously, unsure how to play it.

Sargon leaned forward. "You know, he must have been going off balance for a while and none of us noticed it." He waved a hand. "I mean, look at the damage he wrought at the tournament." He shook his head sadly, "And then, to attack all those guards in the palace. He killed a couple of my friends, you know. I admit I was surprised. Tarkyn never seemed to be aggressive before."

Danton frowned thoughtfully, "You did have to be careful of him when he was angry, don't you think?"

"True," agreed Andoran. He took a sip of his wine. "I blame his brothers, though."

Danton raised his eyebrows in surprise. "You do?"

"Oh yes. They should have pulled Tarkyn into line a lot earlier. You can't have a rogue sorcerer like that running free in society and endangering everyone's lives. Surely they must have realised, long before it got to that point."

"Well, to be fair to them, I didn't realise anything was wrong earlier and I probably spent more time with Tarkyn than his brothers did," said Danton. He shrugged, "Perhaps the strain of all those years of intrigue and being discounted within the family took their toll on him and he finally cracked."

Sargon leant back in his chair and said disgustedly, "Danton, you are such a soft touch. Stop feeling sorry for him. Tarkyn was a spoilt brat. He had everything any of us could wish for." He leant forward again, his wavy brown hair swinging forward. His grey eyes met Danton's and he spoke in an undertone, "More likely heredity, if you ask me. They're all a bit unstable in that family. Look at his brothers. Rampant jealousy from one and deliberate goading from the other. I ask you, is that any way to run a kingdom?"

Andoran gave a short laugh and waved his glass around, "Still, we can't complain too much. It does provide opportunities."

"Hmph. Not with Tarkyn anymore, it doesn't." said Danton shortly.

Sargon sighed, "No. Pity about that. We were well placed with him." Sargon gave Danton a measuring look, "You're not looking for him, are you?"

"Me?" asked Danton frowning. "What would be the point?"

Andoran shrugged, "The reward, for one thing. Actually that would be the only point, when you think about it. But the reward would definitely be worth it."

Danton kept his eyes on his wine. "I admit I've thought about it. He could be such an arrogant bastard, couldn't he? It would serve him right." He looked up at them and grinned, "It could be a final offering he made to us, his loyal followers, if we got the reward for bringing him in."

"That is a slight contradiction in terms, his loyal followers turning him in," objected Sargon with a smile. "But he has betrayed us by deserting us. So fair is fair." He shrugged, "Besides it would be doing a public service, ridding the world of a rogue sorcerer."

"Surely they would just imprison him, not kill him?" queried Danton.

"I think imprisonment was the sentence after the tournament," replied Andoran. "No half measures now. They want the prince's head after the deaths in the Great Hall."

Danton's eyes widened. "Oh, I see."

"That wouldn't worry you, would it?" Sargon's eyes had narrowed.

Danton gave his head a little shake and managed a smile, "No, not at all. I was just surprised, that's all. I left Tormadell soon after all this happened. So I haven't kept in touch with developments."

"So, any idea where he might be?" asked Andoran casually.

Danton ran his eyes around the encampment. "Plenty of people here. Have you asked around? Someone might have seen him." Thinking back to conversations he had had with Stormaway, he said, "I heard from some people back down the road a bit that the prince had been sighted in the northwest, maybe heading for the coast. Have you heard anything like that?"

Andoran and Sargon glanced at each other. "Yes," said Andoran. "We'd heard something like that, but that was a couple of weeks ago. He may well have left the country by now."

"Oh well," Danton put a note of disappointment into his voice, "If that's the case, we'll never catch him. Not unless he comes back, and I can't imagine that he would." He shrugged, "I'm not so desperate to get the bounty that I would travel overseas to trap him."

"That's pretty much the same conclusion that we've drawn. I just thought you might have heard something different, that's all." Andoran poured them all another wine and swept the hand holding the bottle in a wide arc, "So, here we are, in the midst of Plan B."

"And what is Plan B exactly?" asked Danton.

Sargon sipped his wine and looked at Danton. "You may be surprised at this but we are helping people who have been attacked on the road or on their farms by brigands. The king has been so busy antagonising his brother that he has forgotten to look after his subjects. A lot of people are being attacked but there are few brigands being brought to justice. The people you see around you have decided to take the law into their own hands to protect innocent travellers and farmers by fighting against the brigands."

Danton frowned sceptically, "And who is financing all this? You can't spend your life on a good cause without food in your belly and money in your pocket."

"Danton, Danton." Andoran shook his head sadly, "I'm surprised at you. So mercenary."

A little smile played around Danton's mouth. "Come on. Out with it. What's in it for you two?"

Andoran and Sargon both rocked back with laughter.

"Danton. You should have more faith in your fellow man," said Sargon, smiling. He shrugged, "Well, as it turns out, the fellow who is financing this caper is paying experienced officers, like ourselves, good money to organise and train up the rabble."

"Much better pay than the palace offers its guards. You should think about it," added Andoran.

"And who is this great philanthropist with the finance?"

Andoran and Sargon looked at each other. Andoran shrugged, "We know his name. It's Davorad, Lord of Stansbeck but we don't know him personally. He's obviously very wealthy but that's about all we know."

Sargon grinned, "From our point of view, that's all we need to know."

"You do realise, I suppose," added Andoran laconically, "that Prince Tarkyn's erstwhile entourage is not exactly flavour of the month back in Tormadell at the moment? So it suits us to be well away for the time being, while feelings calm down and events are forgotten."

Danton shook his head, "I had no idea. That seems a bit rough; to tar us all with the prince's brush. After all, we didn't put him up to any of it."

"Guilt by association," said Andoran.

"Hmm. Maybe I'll stay away a bit longer than I had planned," mused Danton thoughtfully. "I'll see. Perhaps I'll come back here and join you after I've been to see my grandmother."

"That would be great," enthused Andoran, "Just like old times. Same friends. New location. Couldn't be better."

Danton was struggling to keep his smile in place at the complete dismissal of Tarkyn as one of the friends. He put down his glass and stood up, wiping his hand across his forehead. "I'm sorry. I'm a bit tired after all this travelling. I might have a bit of a rest before dinner. If you'll excuse me? I'll catch up with you later."

CHAPTER 50

As soon as Danton was out of sight and earshot, Stormaway appeared at his side. His eyes were glittering with anger. "Neither with that family we met before nor with Andoran and Sargon, have you said a word to support your liege. So your loyalty doesn't extend as far as standing up for the prince when he's not around to hear you, then? "

"What on earth are you talking about, Stormaway? Of course it doesn't. Not if that doesn't serve his best interests."

"You could have said something to support him."

"Yes, I could have. Then I would have had those two watching my every move and making sure I was followed when I left." Danton turned his intense purple eyes on the wizard. Stormaway reeled back before the depth of implacable hatred in the sorcerer's stare. The wizard experienced a sense of relief that it wasn't directed at him. Danton spoke with cutting control. "Instead of ranting at me, you might like to consider how much effort it cost me to produce that little charade when I was nearly beside myself with rage."

Stormaway let out a breath. "I apologise, Danton. I should have realised how hard it was for you. It is very difficult for both of us to hear Tarkyn being spoken of like that. I'm afraid I misdirected my anger."

The sorcerer gave short bitter laugh. "Don't be sorry. I'm becoming used to not being trusted. It's a salutary lesson for me. You, Tarkyn, the woodfolk, everyone I am loyal to, mistrust me. And yet people I don't care about are willing to trust me almost on sight." He kicked a pebble along the ground. "It's bloody annoying."

The wizard smiled and clapped him on the shoulder. "You're such a consummate actor, my boy. I know it's harder but I'm glad you haven't turned your acting skills on us and are allowing things to take their course."

Danton looked at him through narrowed eyes. "I would have no qualms about acting a part amongst you if I could figure out what would convince you all. Unfortunately, I suspect nothing but time and experience of me will do it." He shrugged and gave a tight smile. "Oh well, on the other hand, I couldn't ask for better protection for the prince than his ring of doubters. I'd just rather be inside than outside the ring."

"You're getting there, Danton. Give it time. It will come."

Danton eyed the wizard, his gaze still cloudy with anger. "Anyway, you may yet have cause to be angry with me." His voice vibrated with passion, "No matter what the cost, no matter what the disruption to our plans, I will make those two pay before we leave here. I don't know how yet, but they will pay."

The wizard tilted his head sideways and considered the irate sorcerer, "But Danton, much as I hate to admit it, I can understand their point of view, especially if Tarkyn killed their friends. And they don't know that the fatalities were not deliberate acts of aggression by the prince."

Danton snorted in derision, "They had their chance to ask him and didn't. They kept out of his line of vision and were brutal instead. What sort of friendship evaporates without being given any chance to redeem itself?" Danton stopped walking and put his hands on his hips, "If they had killed him in righteous anger, I might have understood. But this wasn't revenge. Those friends Sargon spoke of were barely acquaintances and in case you hadn't notice, they forgot to mention to me that they had already had a run in with the prince." He shook his head. "Don't be fooled by their charm. Andoran and Sargon are only interested in the money. They couldn't lie straight in bed, either of them."

"Hmm." The wizard was thoughtful for a minute or two. "My first instinct was to try to dissuade you. But on reflection, I would have to admit that our feelings are very much in agreement on this issue. So instead, I think I had better help you concoct some form of revenge that doesn't interfere too much with our other plans."

At last Danton's face relaxed. "Oh good. This should be fun then."

Stormaway raised his eyebrows, "You weren't thinking of killing them, were you?"

Danton waved a hand casually, "Oh no, no. That would give us away. I was thinking of something much worse than that. I don't know. Something exquisitely embarrassing or humiliating, preferably painful as well."

"Ah, excellent. That sounds just the thing. I'll give it some thought."

Just then the wolves set up a din of whining and howling. Stormaway and Danton looked over to see a scrawny young man feeding them the contents of the wooden bucket. A few people were drawn to the noise but no one went too close. All eyes were on the wolves. Stormaway's eyes were on the wolf trainer.

"That man is familiar, even from the back." The wizard waited until the scrawny man straightened up and turned around. "Oh my stars! That's Journeyman Cloudmaker, my old apprentice from the days when I worked in the castle for Tarkyn's father." He frowned, "What's he doing here, I wonder?"

"He must be the sorcerer who is hunting the woodfolk. I wonder how many others know about the woodfolk?"

"He is not only a sorcerer," said Stormaway tetchily, "Think man! If he was my apprentice, he must be a wizard."

"Sorry. No offence meant, I'm sure. After all, you have also taught many sorcerers from what I've heard, Tarkyn and Markazon among them."

"None of them has been my apprentice. It's not the same thing at all." Stormaway waved a hand dismissively. "Anyway, let's concentrate on our plan for the moment." He glanced around him, "I think we could do it while they are being fed. The wolves' howls would cover the noise and no one is looking that way."

Danton frowned, "We would be in full view if anyone looked around."

"True. Well, what do you think? Risk doing it at the wolves' dinnertime or wait for Tarkyn to create a disturbance with the horses?"

"How will he know whether to create a diversion or not?"

Stormaway glanced up at the raven that had flown down out of the tree and was now sitting on top of the tent nearest to them. He leant forward and said quietly in Danton's ear, "Because, unless I'm much mistaken, Tarkyn is watching our every move."

Danton started and looked around. Then he followed the direction of the wizard's finger and saw the raven watching them. Danton's eyes narrowed and he put his head on one side as he considered the large black bird. The raven copied his head movement. Then it launched itself off the tent pole straight at Danton. As the young sorcerer ducked in alarm, the bird changed its trajectory and swooped to land neatly on Danton's shoulder.

Danton, who was not particularly enamoured of birds, especially at close quarters, steeled himself to stand slowly upright with the raven ruffling its feathers inches from his left cheek, its sharp menacing beak and beady black eye clear in the peripheral vision of his left eye.

He produced a wavering smile. "Ooh good. Up close and personal, then. Does he have to watch from this close?"

"Does Tarkyn know that you don't like birds, by any chance?" asked the wizard, smiling broadly.

Eyeing the raven, Danton said carefully, "It's not that I don't like them, so much as they make me nervous. All those feathers and beaks and claws." He frowned, "And yes, he does know."

"I thought he might," laughed Stormaway. "Come on. Let's show our raven friend the perimeter guards' lay out. Tarkyn can transmit all the information to the woodfolk."

"The raven was in the tree earlier on. I just didn't realise then, that it was being Tarkyn's eyes. So I expect he already knows." Danton winced as the raven's sharp claws dug into him. "Anyway, I can't help thinking I'm a little conspicuous with this raven perched on my shoulder."

"I couldn't agree more but until Tarkyn stops mucking around, I can't see that there is much we can do about it."

Just as the wizard finished speaking, the raven launched itself into the air, leaving several scratches in Danton's shoulder, and landed back on the nearest tent pole.

"Very funny," mouthed Danton at Tarkyn via the raven. A thought struck him and he looked at the wizard in exasperation. "Please tell me that Tarkyn is not checking up on me."

Stormaway shook his head, "You're not thinking straight. If Tarkyn were checking up on you, he would hardly let you know he was watching, would he?"

Danton smiled perfunctorily, "No. Good point. Hmm. I wonder what he made of my conversation with Sargon and Andoran. Pity he couldn't hear it. Still, just watching it would have been enough to condemn me if he didn't trust me."

"Only if I hadn't been lurking in the background. It wasn't as if you met them on the quiet."

Danton rubbed a hand across his face, "Oh well. I hope he remembers I can act. Saying that, I don't know that I could have said all those things if I'd known he was watching."

"Then it's just as well you didn't know, isn't it?" The wizard patted the sorcerer on the back. "Stop fretting, Danton. Tarkyn wouldn't be playing games with you if he were angry with you."

"True," Danton realised his hands were shaking and took a deep breath to steady himself.

"You do get yourself in a tangle sometimes, don't you? Is this what Tarkyn meant about you being overly sensitive?" When Danton nodded, Stormaway continued bracingly. "Come on. Let's plot our revenge on Sargon and Andoran so that no doubt is left in Tarkyn's mind about your loyalties."

At dusk, the raven lifted itself out of the tree and winged its way slowly against the setting sun back into the forest.

Danton and Stormaway spent the early part of the evening listening into and joining in conversations around the campfires. Danton was borne off by Andoran and Sargon to spend the evening with them, drinking and reminiscing. Stormaway was less conspicuous and therefore more fortunate, moving quietly from one conversation to the next as the mood took him.

At the end of a long night, Danton finally escaped the attentions of his enthusiastic companions, pleading a headache and resisting invitations for him to join Andoran and Sargon in their tent. He wove his way back to the tent he had been allocated and flopped down on his back beside

Stormaway in the darkness. Even in the gloom, Danton's face stood out stark and white, lined with strain.

Stormaway did not make the same mistake twice. He rolled over, took one look at the guardsman's face and whispered, "Rough evening?"

"I don't know when I've endured a harder one." He sighed. "I feel sick to my stomach with the things I've said this evening." He turned his head to look at the wizard, "And even more so with the things they have said. How much longer are we going to have to stay here?"

Stormaway extricated a hand from within his bedding and placed it on Danton's shoulder. "I'm afraid we'll have to stay for at least a day or two afterwards, especially with your known association with the prince. Otherwise, suspicion may fall on you, and consequently, on Tarkyn and alert everyone to the prince's presence in the area."

"Oh my stars!" groaned Danton. "I don't know that I can do it."

"You can, because you must," whispered Stormaway, not unkindly. "But let's see if we can incapacitate the terrible two before you have to spend too much more time with them, shall we?"

Danton's teeth flashed in the dark in a brief smile. He sighed, "I still can't retrieve all those things I've said, even if it would have been pointless to say anything else."

"Danton, look at me!" The wizard's voice, even though only a whisper, sounded harsh in the darkness. "That wasn't you who said those things. It was the person you were playing. Across the country there are hundreds of people saying things like that about Tarkyn. I've been listening to some of them tonight. Think of it as one of them. Not you. Leave it behind you, outside with the other two."

Some of the strain left the sorcerer's eyes. He smiled tiredly. "Thanks Stormaway. I'll try." So saying, he rolled over and settled down to sleep.

All through the night, a succession of large rats doggedly gnawed their way through the ropes tying the horses. By morning, only one strand of each rope was still in place. Despite the dislike some of the horses had for rats, none of them had done more than roll their eyes and stamp their feet occasionally.

In the forest, just as the first rays of sunlight hit the top of the trees, Tarkyn released his connection with the last of the rats and sank into bed.

Chapter 51

Not long afterwards, Stormaway rose and, sitting in the corner of the tent, began to work his way through a couple of ancient tomes he had brought with him in his satchel. The wolves presented no problem to him. Summer Rain and he had already devised a concoction to put them safely to sleep for the duration of the night. It was the exquisite revenge that occupied his attention.

Once Danton was up and dressed, he wandered off to procure them both some breakfast, leaving the wizard to his studics. When he returned, Stormaway glanced up and nodded his thanks as Danton handed him a cup of tea and a plate of freshly baked bread and soft cheese.

"The problem is," explained Stormaway, "that most poisonous plants either kill you quickly or only make you very uncomfortable for, at most, about three days while they go through your system." He bit into his roll and munched on a mouthful before continuing, "Now, what I'm looking for is something that will cause them grief for at least a couple of weeks. That's how long Tarkyn suffered serious pain. If I can't come up with something longer term like that, then we may just have to kill them and be done with it."

Danton eyed the wizard with something between a frown and a smile hovering on his face, as he sat down opposite him. "You have a bloodthirsty streak that I am only now beginning to appreciate." He took a sip of tea. "Of course we will have to kill them in the end. We can't allow anyone to get away with attacking a member of the Royal Family, even if the prince has been outlawed."

The wizard shrugged, "Strategically, we can't really kill them in the foreseeable future unless we can make it look accidental - and two people dying accidentally does strain people's credulity somewhat."

Danton heaved a sigh, "Yes. I'm afraid I agree with you. We will have to leave their execution until the woodfolk are safe. I think the most frustrating aspect of this scheme we're concocting is that we can't afford to let them know why they are being made to suffer."

Stormaway gave a half smile, "Not very satisfactory, I agree. But one day in the future when we are well away from here, we will let them know in retrospect, before we kill them, that they were punished."

"Hmm." Danton sipped his tea. "I can think of lots of ways of humiliating them but in every case, they would know someone had set them up or attacked them. It's much harder to find a way to make them suffer with no apparent cause."

The wizard frowned thoughtfully. "I think what I need is a combination of poisons administered in different ways. Yes, I think that might do it. Where do they get their water from?"

Danton thought about it. "They have a large wooden water barrel just outside their tent, but I don't know where the water comes from."

"And how long would that water last them, do you think, before it needs to be refilled?"

"I don't know. Maybe four or five days. Depends on their wine to water ratio, if you see what I mean."

"Hmmm." There was a protracted silence while Stormaway riffled through his books and thought through his tactics. Danton sat beside him patiently, eating his breakfast and allowing the expert free rein with his ideas. When Stormaway finally lifted his head, his eyes were glowing with satisfaction. "Right. I think I have it. Now, is there any protracted length of time that Andoran and Sargon will be away from their tent?"

Danton nodded. "Most of today. They are heading off down to the road to bring back another group of travellers. They're leaving mid morning and won't be back until close to nightfall. Thank goodness. At least I won't have to talk to them all day today."

"Excellent. We can put our long term punishment in place while they are gone and you will be able to set up their short term punishment when they return." Stormaway ticked off a list on his fingers. "We'll need to treat their bedding, their spare clothes, especially the undergarments, and a bottle of wine that they will drink tonight. I think it would be too hard to infect their food without affecting other people too. I expect everyone's meals are cooked in the same place." Stormaway frowned for a moment, "This water barrel of theirs. Does it have a tap at the bottom or do they just upend it and pour from the top?"

Danton thought back, "It's quite large. I'm sure it must have a tap. It would be refilled from the top, though."

The wizard rubbed his hands together. "Excellent. Just what we want. It is all coming together nicely. Now, you run along for a while. I need some time to prepare a few concoctions. Come back and tell me when they have gone and we'll get to work." Just as Danton was leaving the tent, the wizard called softly after him, "You know, even though I have devised several nasty experiences for them, I keep wanting to think of more. Nothing seems bad enough to repay that sort of treachery."

"No," Danton looked back over his shoulder. "Nothing is bad enough."

CHAPTER 52

Four miles away and six hours later, Tarkyn was glaring down at Waterstone. "If they can't ride, tie them to the horses. They may well be too weak to ride on their own, anyway."

"Woodfolk don't ride horses," reiterated Waterstone stubbornly.

"Well, it's about time you learnt."

"Horses leave tracks, Your Highness. We don't."

Tarkyn put his hands on his hips. "And how are you proposing to carry three woodfolk, complete with chains, all the way here then? Awkward bundle, wouldn't you say?"

"We will manage. We have four hours before the guard changes."

Tarkyn turned away and took a couple of strides to calm his temper. He swung back and demanded, "And don't you think the chains are going to make some noise and alert other people in the compound? What then? You'll be exposed to everyone's view and be unable to move quickly because of your burden."

Waterstone glared at him and said nothing.

Tarkyn threw his hands up. "And then we'll have ten imprisoned woodfolk and even more people knowing about you."

"The chains will make a lot of noise clanking up and down on a horse's back anyway."

"But at least you can be away from view inside the forest within seconds."

"Excellent," said Waterstone with withering sarcasm. "Leaving a trail a mile wide that even the dimmest sorcerer can follow straight to us."

Tarkyn eyebrows came together in a frown that had the beginnings of puzzlement amongst the anger. "Waterstone. You're being deliberately obtuse. You know better than that. We can easily extract Golden Toad and his family from the back of the horse up into the trees and let the horse keep going to leave a false trail."

Waterstone scowled disdainfully. "Any tracker would be able to see that the horse had slowed down or stopped. And its tracks would be shallower after its load was lifted."

Much to the woodman's irritation, a slow smile began to dawn on the prince's face. "And can you find no solution to this, Waterstone, my determinedly obstreperous friend?"

"Don't patronise me!" snapped Waterstone.

"If I were patronising you, I would be praising you with insufficient cause. As it is, I find nothing whatsoever to praise. You are being a stubborn, oppositional, old goat." Despite the words, the smile still hovered around Tarkyn's lips, infuriating the woodman further.

Waterstone put his hands on his hips and glowered at him. "Your suggestion is unworkable. But that is no reason to start insulting me."

Tarkyn smiled and shook his head. "Waterstone, even I can think of ways to overcome the problems you've raised. If a town dweller like me can do it, I'm sure you can. And before you accuse me of patronising you again, you should stop to consider the truth of what I'm saying." He paused and his smile broadened. "Come on. Admit it. The real problem is that you're scared of horses."

Waterstone stared at him in silence. Then as Tarkyn watched, a dull red crept over the woodman's face from the neck upwards. There was a long awkward pause.

Finally the prince said quietly "Sorry, Waterstone. I didn't mean to be flippant about something you're sensitive about. I didn't realise it would matter. There's nothing wrong with being scared of horses. Lots of people are." A thought struck him, "But if all woodfolk are scared of horses, then that really will put paid to my plan."

Waterstone dropped his eyes. He cleared his throat, "Not all woodfolk are scared of horses. There are forest ponies that we come across from time to time." He raised his eyes. "We don't use them much, though, because of the tracks. That objection was genuine."

"I know, my friend. All your objections were genuine. But that doesn't make them insurmountable."

Waterstone turned his head to look away into the trees. After a few moments, he returned his gaze to Tarkyn. "I don't know that I can do it. They are so big and unpredictable." He sighed. "When I was small, maybe three or fours years old, a hunting party came into the forest. We were watching from behind a row of trees. One of the horses broke away from the control of its rider. It lunged between the trees towards us and trampled the bush I was hiding behind. This huge animal towered high above me, its rider fighting for control. Its hoof scored the side of my shoulder as it plunged over me and off into the forest. Neither horse nor rider even noticed me but I will never forget them." He gave a crooked smile. "I've always watched hunting parties from up in the trees since then."

Tarkyn smiled, "Very wise." He hesitated, "Waterstone, you don't have to go near the horses. Others can do that. All who wish to can ride. Everyone else can escape on foot. Only Golden Toad and his family should go on horseback so that you woodfolk are in view of the encampment for as short a time as possible." The forest guardian considered his friend.

"These horses will be under my guidance. They will do whatever we think is necessary to confuse the pursuit. I will back down gladly if you truly believe this to be a bad plan. But I don't think either of us would want me to back down to pander to your fear."

"Now that would be patronising. No, I will have to deal with it somehow," said the woodman firmly. He frowned, "I wasn't deliberately misleading you with my objections just to protect myself, you know. I didn't realise my fear was driving my thoughts."

"Do you really think you need to tell me that?" The prince's amber eyes twinkled at him, "So now that we have that sorted, the question remains; is my plan workable and worth doing?"

Waterstone sat down on the ground with his back against a solid birch while he thought through his objections and possible solutions. Tarkyn sat down next to him while he waited quietly for the answer.

"Yes, on both counts," Waterstone conceded finally. "We can easily swap the woodfolk for a load of wood to keep their hoof prints at the same depth. The horses can stop under several trees so that there is no way of telling where the exchange was made. Then they can lead the pursuit far from us before they allow themselves to be caught." He looked up and grunted, "But get that self-satisfied grin off your face or I'll think of another objection."

If anything, Tarkyn's grin broadened. "I'm so pleased to discover you're not perfect. It's made my day!"

Waterstone blinked in surprise. "What? Me? You're mad. I'm always losing my temper, once so badly that I damaged the forest."

"True," smiled Tarkyn.

"And I can't manage my resentment to the point that I nearly killed you."

"That wasn't your fault. My ribs were already broken."

"Hmph. And I nearly abandoned you when I couldn't handle the pressure."

Tarkyn waved all this aside. "But you didn't. And you are so rock solid. I didn't think there would be anything that could intimidate you."

"Well, there is," said Waterstone shortly. "Anyway, have you looked at yourself lately? Nothing frightens you at all. You walked into that camp of hostile woodfolk and calmly threw yourself on their mercy."

"I don't know what made you think I wasn't frightened. Just because I didn't fall down in a quivering heap doesn't mean I wasn't scared." He shrugged. "I suppose though, to some extent you're right." Tarkyn flicked a quick glance at his friend, "My greatest fears aren't physical."

"I know," said Waterstone quietly.

Tarkyn picked up a stick and set about breaking bits off the end. "Did I mention that I saw Andoran and Sargon at the camp?" he asked casually.

Waterstone frowned. "No. You didn't happen to mention that significant piece of information and you didn't include it in your replay of your images."

"No. I also left out the fact that Danton spent some of yesterday afternoon and most of yesterday evening talking with them."

"You did, didn't you?" Waterstone turned his head to look at the prince. "You didn't consider that our safety might depend on these little snippets, I suppose?"

Tarkyn turned troubled eyes to meet his friend's gaze. "Stormaway knows. He was there in the background, at least in the afternoon. Danton knows I was watching too." He gave a slight, reminiscent smile. "I sent the raven to sit on his shoulder. He hates birds. I sent it to reassure him that I trusted him. He thought it was funny at first but shortly afterwards, I could see he seemed shaken." The prince's smile faded. "I don't know if that was because he was worried that I might be doubting him or whether it was because he was feeling guilty."

"And in the evening?"

"I didn't have time to watch closely because I was coordinating the rats eating through the horses' ropes. But I do know Danton left Sargon and Andoran's tent late in the evening. Stormaway didn't go with him at all. I hope Stormaway knows what he's doing."

"Stormaway is nobody's fool," said Waterstone reassuringly, "And to be honest, neither is Danton. If he were going to double cross us, I don't think it would be in full view of your raven or with Stormaway knowing his movements."

Tarkyn nodded. "That's what I think. That's what I hope. Unless he's doing a double bluff."

Waterstone shrugged. "If he is, the damage is already done and he will have told them of your location. We must change your location now, just in case, before we set our plans into motion."

"You realise, that if any of you are captured, Danton would know you could be held to ransom in exchange for me. He knows I would give myself up to save you."

Waterstone patted the prince on the knee. "Tarkyn, you might want to, but you couldn't. Even if those captured were threatened with execution, you couldn't agree to exchange yourself for them. You would be condemning the rest of the woodfolk to losing their livelihood, their home and their safety. They would all die, but more slowly and painfully." He smiled, "But if it's any consolation, I think Danton will have figured that out and would know that you couldn't give yourself up, whatever your wishes on the subject."

"This bloody sorcerous oath drives me crazy."

Waterstone glanced at the prince's set face. "I hope you remember our conversation about self sacrifice. I'm not sure how much you've taken it to heart. Nobody wants you to sacrifice yourself, under any circumstances. Oath or not."

Tarkyn ran his hands through his long black hair and pulled it over one shoulder. "I think we'd better get going."

The woodman put a restraining hand on the prince's arm as he went to rise. "Just a minute. You don't believe me, do you?"

Tarkyn glanced at him then looked down at his hair as he fiddled with the ends of it. "Hmm. I've been sacrificed before, for what might be considered the greater good. The next time, I'd rather do it myself than have it done to me. Anyway, this is different from last time we talked. I wouldn't be sacrificing myself because of falling out with you. It would be to save the captured woodfolk and, even more importantly, rid your society of my presence and the oath." He sighed, "I don't know that I can face a whole new barrage of resentment with the spread of the oath." Tarkyn waved a hand impatiently. "But this is a pointless discussion. I couldn't do it even if I wanted to."

Waterstone stared at him, concern written on his face. "Do you know," he said slowly, "for the first time, I begin to be glad of this sorcerous oath? Without it, you would be totally unsafe from yourself. You could talk yourself into sacrificing yourself as a way of protecting us and thereby fulfilling your side of the oath. If the forest's safety did not hinge on us protecting you, nothing would stop you, would it?"

Tarkyn looked at him long and hard, then turned his eyes away. "No. Nothing would."

"Is life so hard?"

The young sorcerer sighed. "The uncertainty is hard. Waiting for everything to fall apart is hard. Knowing that I stand in the way of everyone's contentment is hard. And in the end, knowing that my brothers, whom I have loved and lived with all my life, were willing to lock me up and throw away the key while my own mother watched, is hard. Very hard."

He flicked a glance at Waterstone, "If the people who have known me all my life can turn on me like that, how can you expect me to believe that the woodfolk, who have only known me a few weeks and have had me foisted upon them, would have any concern for my welfare beyond the oath? Why would you care if I found a way to sacrifice myself that left the forest intact?"

Waterstone's face was tight with shock. He took a deep breath, "Tarkyn, I am more sorry than you can imagine to hear you talk like that. I know your faith in your fellow man has been shaken but I did not realise the depth of your unhappiness. The questions you ask me sound rational and yet I cannot provide satisfactory rational answers to them."

"Because there are none," said Tarkyn bleakly.

"I may not be able to answer how and why but I can demonstrate that it is so," continued Waterstone, ignoring Tarkyn's interjection. "I cannot create years of friendship to justify my care for you. Anyway, it seems longevity of acquaintance by no means guarantees loyalty. I can, however, produce memories that you may scan any time at will, if you are in any doubt."

Tarkyn shook his head, "No. I would not do that to you again."

"But you must at least accept my offer as a demonstration of good faith." He waited until Tarkyn had nodded reluctantly, before continuing. "There are, of course, the things you have done and will do for woodfolk. Warning us of the wolves, rescuing us from the storm and whatever else you will do in the future as the forest guardian."

"That may be true until the danger has passed."

Suddenly Waterstone's eyes lit with anger. "Yes. But being the ungrateful people that we are, you would then expect us to turn on you, would you?"

Tarkyn glared back at him, "From my experience of the world, yes. Once my usefulness is over, if you were given the choice, then yes, I would expect to be rejected. However, since you and I will have no choice, we will both have to endure my continued tenure in the woods."

Now Waterstone was fired up, "So, I presume you do not value, as I do, your membership of my family?"

This did give Tarkyn pause. He sighed and said gently, "No, don't presume that. Being part of your family, and the acceptance into the woodfolk that goes with it, is probably the only thing that keeps me afloat when I am drowning in confusion. That, and your friendship."

Tarkyn's words took the wind right out of Waterstone's sails. He shook his head and smiled sadly, "Tarkyn, do you understand how much it signifies that I asked you to join Ancient Oak, Sparrow and me? I did not have you foisted on me by birth as Kosar and Jarand did. Nothing in the oath forced me to take you in. I chose to have you as a brother." He paused to let his words sink in. "And Tarkyn, I will never choose to let you go."

Tears sprang into Tarkyn's eyes. He turned his head away quickly and pulled away, trying to stand up. But Waterstone held him by the arm and used his other hand on Tarkyn's shoulder to drag him back around to face him.

"Come on, Tarkyn. Stay. Don't run away."

Tarkyn faced him unwillingly, his eyes bright with unshed tears, his chest heaving with restrained sobs. Waterstone wrapped his arms around the young sorcerer and held him as the dam of pent up feeling finally spilled over. Eventually Tarkyn quietened and the next time he pulled away, Waterstone let him go.

Tarkyn sat up and looked at the woodman out of red-rimmed eyes and sniffed, "Bloody Danton. I was all right until I saw him having such a great time with Andoran and Sargon. I tried to trust him. I really did. That's why I let him know I was watching." He wiped the back of his hand across his face and sniffed again. "I don't know. Maybe it will be all right. I've lost all ability to judge people, if I ever had any."

Waterstone smiled reassuringly. "Well, I've never had any trouble judging people and I think Danton is the genuine article. Saying that, I don't have much experience of sorcerers but I judged you to be all right."

"And I don't know what happened yesterday morning but when you all came back, something had changed that I didn't understand." Tarkyn glanced sideways at the woodman. "Whatever it was, brought you all closer together. I asked you, but you never told me."

"And you've been worrying about it ever since? Sorry Tarkyn, I wasn't hiding anything. I simply forgot." Waterstone looked at him, "You're tuned like a fine bowstring to the slightest change in people around you, aren't you?" When Tarkyn nodded, he continued, "Well, you needn't have worried. Quite the opposite, really. Tree Wind said she thought we'd be all right with you and suddenly everyone knew it was true. All the anxious years of waiting were laid to rest." He slapped Tarkyn on the back, "I should have told you, shouldn't I? You've achieved the near impossible, allaying everyone's fears after the way your father treated us."

Tarkyn smiled, his eyes shining with tears. He couldn't answer, so merely nodded in response.

"I guess what you picked up was that something important had happened amongst us. But although it was about you, it didn't include you."

Tarkyn took a deep breath and managed to regain control of his voice, "Food for the paranoid mind," he said shakily. He wiped his hands across his eyes and took another breath. "That, on top of Rainstorm's and your reaction to the spread of the oath and North Wind brushing me off has all been a bit much. Then Danton consorting with the enemy was the final straw."

"No wonder you were feeling so bad. You have a lot to contend with at the best of times, without all that lot adding to your woes." Waterstone grunted, "Don't worry about North Wind. He's just a bit confused at the moment. He'll come around."

Tarkyn gave him a watery smile, "I'm sorry. Some forest guardian I turn out to be, sitting here blubbing my eyes out when we're supposed to be mounting a rescue."

"Plenty of time. It's nearly sunset. They will be feeding the wolves soon but then we'll have to wait for the sorcerers to go to sleep. Let's move location and have some dinner. Then you can tell us what is happening at the encampment." Waterstone stood up and put out a hand to pull Tarkyn to his feet. "And this time, you might like to keep at least me in the picture about Danton and the other two instead of keeping your fears to yourself. Agreed?"

Tarkyn nodded. "Agreed." As he turned to walk beside Waterstone, a small private smile played around his mouth. He glanced at the woodman but said nothing.

Waterstone's eyes narrowed. "What?"

Tarkyn gave a broad grin, his red-rimmed eyes shining with laughter, "You must actually, really care about me if you could even contemplate being glad about any part of the oath."

"Of course I do, you big galoot." Waterstone raised his eyebrows. "You're not the only one prepared to make sacrifices." He stopped and put his hands on his hips. "In fact, if Stormaway tells me that he had decided to disarm the oath, I will tell him not to, at least for the time being."

Tarkyn's eyes went all watery again. He laughed through the tears. "You know, that's the nicest thing anyone has ever said to me."

Waterstone gave a snort of laughter and clapped him on the back as they turned to continue walking. "You poor old bugger. You've had a hard time of it, haven't you? I keep forgetting you're so young, too. Too much poise for your own good."

"Not at the moment."

Waterstone smiled. "No. Not at the moment. We'll take the longer path back to the others, shall we?"

CHAPTER 53

As soon as Tarkyn and Waterstone entered the clearing where the others were gathered, Rainstorm came bounding up to them, full of plans for the evening. He took one look at Tarkyn's face and frowned, "You all right?"

"Dust and not enough sleep last night," interjected Waterstone, knowing Tarkyn wouldn't be able to lie.

"I might go down the stream and freshen up a bit," suggested Tarkyn.

"Good idea." Waterstone gave him a pat on the back to send him on his way. "I'll broach the idea about the horses while you're away."

Rainstorm clung to Tarkyn's side like an eager puppy as he wandered down the path to the stream. Tarkyn glanced down sideways at him but said nothing.

"You're not all right, are you?" persisted the young woodman.

"I'm better than I was," replied Tarkyn shortly.

"So, what's the matter? Nothing I've done, I hope… other than make you feel hideous about the oath." Rainstorm looked up expectantly but, receiving only a slight smile in response, continued huffily, "Fine. Then don't tell me. None of my business anyway, I suppose."

"Rainstorm, I just finished talking to Waterstone about it. I don't want to start all over again."

"Fine. I'll leave then. You might just remember sometimes that Waterstone is not your only friend."

He turned to leave but Tarkyn put out a restraining hand. "Don't go. Come down to the stream with me."

Rainstorm eyed him belligerently for a moment, then grinned, "All right, I will and if you're very lucky I might just shut up."

Tarkyn laughed, "I think that might be a bit much to hope for."

When they reached the stream, Tarkyn dragged off his boots and waded straight in. Rainstorm watched him, horrified. "What are you doing? It's freezing in there, prince."

Tarkyn ducked his head under the water and came up gasping. "Yep. It certainly is." He shook his head and sent his long black hair flying. He grinned, "Don't tell me you're going to let me suffer alone."

"I was thinking of it, I must say."

"Come on. Don't be a wimp. Get in here," said Tarkyn before disappearing under the water again

In a split second, it ran through Rainstorm's head to wonder if this was an order. In the same instant he knew it was not. He suddenly understood what Waterstone had meant about the oath getting in the way of friendship. He put his hands on his hips and tried to work out what his natural response would be. Before Tarkyn had time to resurface, he shrugged, threw off his boots and gingerly stepped into the freezing water. This might not be what he would usually do. He wasn't sure. But it was what was needed at the moment.

Tarkyn came up close to him and blew a spout of muddy water into the air that landed neatly on Rainstorm's head and dripped in icy rivulets down his back.

"Wolves' teeth Tarkyn! Stop it! That's freezing."

"Come on. Stop standing there, shivering. Just get in. Once you're in, it gets better."

Rainstorm took a deep breath and resolutely let himself fall forward into the shallow waters. As soon as he could get his feet under him, he shot upwards, gasping. "Stars above, prince. You're mad. This is murderously cold."

Tarkyn grinned, "I know. You have a streak of true heroism in you, Rainstorm."

Even as Rainstorm's eyebrows twitched together in suspicion, Tarkyn sank under the water again. Moments later, a tug on Rainstorm's ankle dragged him under. He just had time to grab a breath before he was submerged in the icy water. When he came up spluttering, he found himself face to face with an expectant Tarkyn.

Rainstorm laughed and launched himself at Tarkyn. Tarkyn went flying over backwards and sank beneath the water. There were a few moments of quiet while Rainstorm caught his breath and waited for Tarkyn to re-emerge so that he could push him under again. The moments stretched beyond a minute and still Tarkyn didn't reappear. Suddenly Rainstorm's stomach turned over and he began to feel frantically around in the muddy water.

"Looking for something?" asked a voice behind him.

Rainstorm swung around to find Tarkyn watching him, a huge smile on his face.

"That's it. You will die," roared Rainstorm and threw himself at the prince. Tarkyn sidestepped neatly and threw Rainstorm into the water before dumping himself down into it again. They both came up spluttering and laughing and, by unspoken agreement, stopped fighting and sat side by side up to their necks in water in the deep golden light of late afternoon.

After a while, Tarkyn glanced at Rainstorm, "Do you know, there's a large owl about two trees along over there watching us. I'm not sure that she approves of our antics. She's worried about me drowning." He smiled and nodded further along the river. "There's an otter downstream there a bit. She's not happy with us because we've churned up the water. But over there behind those bushes is a sneaky little fox that has been using us as a sound screen to close in on a dim, hapless rabbit who hasn't even noticed us."

"Is that right?" Rainstorm let his senses roam through the gathering shadows of early evening but in the end shook his head. "For all my years of woodland training, I can't tell any of that." He turned his head to look at the prince. "Of course, you could be making it up."

"I could be."

Rainstorm dipped the back of his head into the water, "But of course you're not because you couldn't lie to save yourself." He lifted his dripping head back up. "You know, prince, you are very lucky to have those gifts and we're lucky to have you. Even if we can't do it ourselves, you can show us the world through the eyes of an eagle or a heron. It will be generations before anyone gets that chance again."

He let himself sink right under the water again. As he came back up he spat away the excess water and added, "Don't worry about the oath. I'm over it. I think you more or less deserve it anyway - as our forest guardian. Maybe not so much as prince, but that's a hierarchy thing, isn't it?And we don't do hierarchies."

"Thanks Rainstorm. I think you're the first person who's said that to me. Even the best of them, like Waterstone, only endures the oath at best." Tarkyn dunked the back of his head in the water and watched his long hair floating around him. "I'm not looking forward to the forestals finding out about it, I can tell you."

"Don't worry. I'll help you. If they see that I can deal with it, they'll know anybody can." In a gush of water, Rainstorm stood up and waded to the bank. He looked back over his shoulder, "Come on. We'd better get back."

They sloughed off all the excess water they could and stood there dripping, their wet clothes clinging to them.

"Ugh. That feels horrible," said Rainstorm as a gentle night breeze plastered his wet clothes against his skin, "I think we need a fire in a hurry. I'm not putting my boots back on until my feet are dry."

They trod gingerly back up the track in the dark and emerged, still dripping, into the firelight of the clearing.

"Hello, all," said Rainstorm jauntily as he headed for the fire, ignoring the raised eyebrows.

Tarkyn followed more quietly and squatted down at the fire, his hands held out in front of him to warm them. When the silence didn't dissipate, he looked around and asked, "So, what do you think about the horses then?"

Autumn Leaves appeared out of the gloom with two towels, distributed them without a word and sat down next to the prince.

"Thanks," said Tarkyn as he towelled dry his hair. "So what do you think?"

"I think the idea is good in principle. But how confident are you that you can control these horses?" asked Autumn Leaves. "As far as I know, you've only guided individual animals before."

Tarkyn concentrated on putting his socks and boots back on. "True. Even with the rats, I made the request of one who then enlisted help. And that's all I'll do this time. If I can guide the lead mare, she will guide the others."

"I see," said Autumn Leaves slowly. "Fair enough. And what about afterwards? We send them off into the distance to be recaptured or not as they choose?"

Tarkyn nodded, "Something like that. That's the other good thing about it. The encampment guards won't be able to scour the forest on horseback looking for us. And you people will be miles faster than them on foot if we need to get further away."

"You realise Golden Toad and his family will be frightened of getting up on a big horse, especially hindered by chains."

Tarkyn stared at him for a moment. "Yes. I expect they will. But frankly, that is the least of our worries…or theirs. Don't pussyfoot around their feelings. Throw them up there, tie them on and get them out of there as fast as you can. If they threaten to make too much noise, gag them. If they complain about it later, you can blame me. It's not just their welfare at stake. It is the welfare of all of us. We can't afford half measures."

"You're very forceful, all of a sudden."

"Needs must in times of war." Tarkyn gave a quick smile. "For once, we are discussing something I know about. I know how to be ruthless in combat situations, much more than you do, I suspect. I've trained in it all my life." He reiterated his instructions, then asked, "Can you do that?"

Autumn Leaves smiled, "Yes, I can do that though I mightn't have, if you hadn't mentioned it."

Tarkyn looked across at Waterstone, "And Danton?"

"We discussed Danton. Like you, we're not sure but if there is any doubt, we'll grab him. We can't afford to risk him telling the sorcerers about us."

"Maybe we should never have sent him in the first place," mused Tree Wind, "On reflection, it seems dreadfully naïve of us to have sent a sorcerer who has only known us for a couple of days back into the midst of his own kind. How could we expect his loyalty to us to override his loyalty to them?"

"We didn't," said Tarkyn. "I expected his commitment to justice and his loyalty to me to overcome his prejudices. I just hope I'm right."

CHAPTER 54

Just as the last of the sun's ray disappeared behind the trees, Danton sauntered into the food tent and asked in a loud voice, "Could I ask who cooked that marvellous meal we had last night?"

Several voices clamoured to be heard.

Danton waved a hand. "One at a time, please."

"My lord, we all had our part to play."

"Oh really? A joint effort?" The lordly blonde sorcerer raised his eyebrows. "But was there not some culinary genius behind it all, coordinating your efforts?"

A scruffy, middle-aged woman wiped her hands on her apron and drawled, "That would be me."

"Well, congratulations, ma'am, on a fine effort, especially in this makeshift kitchen." Danton kept a casual eye on the back wall of the tent, which lifted quietly from the bottom as he spoke. "And what marvel are you preparing for this evening, I wonder?"

A sprinkling of pink and white powders flowed under the flap of canvas and swirled above the bucket of meaty off cuts.

"We're having venison pie, sir." The head cook bobbed a curtsy.

"Are we indeed? Well, I look forward to it." The powders swirled gently down into the bucket and out of sight. "Still, I mustn't keep you. Good afternoon." Danton gave them all a charming smile and departed.

As he walked away, the wizard fell in beside him "Phase one completed. Now, let's see about filling Sargon and Andoran's water barrel."

Danton found a bucket and filled it at the small stream that ran through the encampment. He met Stormaway at the bounty hunters' tent. They glanced around them and when they were sure they were unobserved, the wizard instructed Danton, "Right, pour in enough to almost fill it. Leave about an inch at the top."

As soon as this had been done, Stormaway produced a small phial filled with a thick dark liquid. He poured it slowly into the barrel, being careful not to get any of it on his hands or on the outside of the barrel. He stood back and smiled in satisfaction. "Good! Phase two completed. One of our longer term surprises is now in place."

Danton raised an eyebrow.

"A nasty but mild concoction of larkspur, stinkweed and chilli suspended in oil," explained Stormaway. "The oil will float on the top of the water so, as they draw the water from the bottom, they will drink this barrelful of water free of its effects. However, as the water level drops, the tainted oil will seep into the wood of the barrel and affect the next barrel full of water. If we are really lucky and they don't work out what is happening, it may also affect the barrelful of water after that." The wizard gave a satisfied smile. "That would give them a good eight to ten days worth of very unpleasant symptoms."

"Go on then. What are the symptoms?"

"The larkspur will cause severe nausea, perhaps a little vomiting and some truly embarrassing muscle twitches. Hopefully, I have the dose right and they will escape paralysis and death. The chilli will burn their mouths and lips and the stinkweed will cause vision distortions and delirium and they will find it difficult to put a sensible sentence together. So that should add nicely to their difficulties." Stormaway gave the barrel a friendly pat and looked around briefly before slipping inside the tent. "I've only put a dash of stinkweed into the mix. We wouldn't want them so delirious that they missed the misery of the other symptoms, now would we? Of course, the severity of their reactions will depend very much on how thirsty they are. Still, I have erred on the side of caution. We don't want their suffering cut short by death, do we?"

"You're a dangerous man, aren't you?" mused Danton, raising his eyebrows.

"All men are dangerous in their own ways."

Danton followed the wizard inside Sargon and Andoran's tent. "Almost, I begin to feel sorry for them."

"Oh, we haven't even started yet," Stormaway drew out a small bag filled with dried leaves finely crushed into a light green powder. "Have you brought the gloves? You don't want to get this on your hands."

When Danton was ready, the wizard sprinkled a fine film of green dust across the bounty hunters' bedding and over their clothes. He paid particular attention to their undergarments. "Okay, Danton, rub the powder into the material until it can't be seen."

Suddenly there was the sound of footsteps in the gravel outside. They froze. The footsteps stopped for a moment then continued on past. Sorcerer's eyes met wizard's and the two breathed a sigh of relief. Danton quickly finished rubbing in the powder while Stormaway stood guard at the entrance to the tent

"Well done Danton. Phase three completed. Now, I think I'd better doctor the wine somewhere else. I don't think I can stand the tension of being in here much longer." The wizard poked his head outside and said, "Come on. Bring a bottle of wine with you and let's go back to our own tent.

Once back inside their own tent away from prying eyes, Danton produced the bottle of wine and watched with interest as Stormaway prised the cork out and added a few pinches of a dark brown powder to the wine before resealing it. He gave it a good shake, then handed it back to Danton.

"There. Phase four completed. You can take it along with you tonight when you go to visit them. Try not to drink any yourself, although it won't kill you if you can't avoid it."

Danton held the bottle up to the light and studied it. "And what will happen to me if I do?"

The wizard gave a wicked smile, "You will become disoriented and start seeing things. Not particularly pleasant even if you're expecting it although I've heard some people actually seek these experiences. However, if you don't know it's going to happen, it is frightening in the extreme. You think you are losing your mind."

"And the green powder?"

"Poison ivy and stinging nettle. I would have just left it at poison ivy. On its own, it causes severe itching and irritation, often leading to delightful infections if scratched. But sadly, not everyone is affected by it. So to make sure of their misery, I've added the nettles. Very satisfactory, don't you think?"

Danton laughed. "Very satisfactory indeed. I only hope Tarkyn watches at least some of their effects."

"So do I!" Stormaway heaved a sigh, "Right! Onto phase five. So we're going to take a chance and loosen the stake while the wolves are being fed?"

Danton nodded. "It's as good a distraction as any. Even if Tarkyn made the horses bolt, someone could still look around and see us. So let's get it over and done with."

"Are you clear on what you have to do? I won't have time to give you instructions."

"I'm clear. Let's go."

They emerged from the tent just as the wizard's ex-apprentice reached the wolves with the bucket of meat scraps. The wolves yanked on their chains and howled, teeth bared, trying to reach the meat. Danton and Stormaway walked unhurriedly and quietly behind the wolves' keeper until they stood outside the imprisoned woodfolk's tent, on either side of the metal stake. Checking that all eyes were on the wolves, they each sent a small but intense streak of magic circling the ground around the stake. Stormaway's green twanged as it touched the turquoise stream of Danton's magic. Their eyes widened in alarm but only they had heard it above the din of the wolves.

They maintained their magic streams for another long minute, on tenterhooks that someone would look around.

"Enough," said Stormaway in an urgent undertone.

The green and turquoise winked out. Danton looked around quickly, then pressed his hand against the side of the stake. It gave way easily. He righted it hurriedly and moved away. Stormaway walked off casually in another direction. Ten minutes later they reconvened inside their tent and smiled at each other with relief.

CHAPTER 55

Fireside conversations had died away and finally, the last of the sorcerers had made their way from communal fires to their respective sleeping tents. Spots of light from unquenched fires and lanterns, both inside and outside tents, were still dotted around the encampment. In a distant corner, the fretful cries of a baby signalled the presence of at least one wakeful sorcerer while the undiminished sounds of a few drink-laden voices emitted from a tent closer to hand. Half an hour later, the guards around the perimeter were replaced. Those relieved of duty did not linger and soon they too had retired.

Within the tree line, the woodfolk watched and waited for another half an hour, some stationed in the trees as close as possible to the guards' posts and the rest strung out along the ground, hidden behind trees and bushes. The baby had quieted but the nearby revellers carried on.

The raiding party could not afford to wait much longer. The moon was riding high, partly obscured by a wispy patch of cloud. Not ideal for a clandestine raid, but it would have to do. They had three and a half hours before the next changing of the guards and they wanted as much time to elapse as possible before their activities were discovered.

By mutual agreement, they swung into action. Under Lapping Water's direction, those in the trees synchronised their actions to fire simultaneously at the perimeter guards. Moments later, six sorcerers grunted and crumpled to the ground.

Immediately, light shadowy figures emerged from the tree line and sped across the open ground to the edge of the encampment. As they reached the cover of the occasional trees and bushes within the encampment's boundaries, they seemed to blend away into nothing.

Then, two sorcerers guarding the horses grunted as they were caught by waiting hands and lowered quietly to the ground. Sharp knives flashed in the moonlight and the last strands of the horses' ropes were sliced through. The horses watched calmly and trod quietly behind the fleeting shadows through the night. As they neared the sleeping wolves, some of the horses rolled their eyes but a distant presence calmed them and kept them from snorting or making any sound.

Inside the nearby tent, three woodfolk awoke to find their mouths held shut by firm hands. As their eyes struggled to become accustomed to the dark, they stared wild-eyed in to the faces of their kindred.

"Keep quiet," whispered Autumn Leaves. He waited until recognition dawned in their eyes. "Can we take our hands away?"

The three woodfolk nodded.

"We are going to slip you out under the side of the tent, chain and all. There are horses waiting outside. We are going to tie all three of you onto one horse."

Autumn Leaves could dimly see the whites of three sets of eyes in the gloom as they rolled their eyes in alarm.

"Shh. It will not be for long. And then you will be safe. Once we are safely away, we can see about removing the chains."

The imprisoned woodfolk looked frightened but nodded.

"Hold your chains still, as much as possible when we move."

Other hands lifted the canvas of the tent wall while Autumn Laves and Falling Branch helped the chained woodfolk out into the night. When they saw the wolves lying close by, they started and pulled back. The chains rattled loudly in the night.

"Shh. Don't worry. The wolves are drugged," whispered Autumn Leaves.

Woodfolk swarmed around them, lifted them up onto a placid, solid mare. Despite everyone's best efforts, the sound of the chains seemed to reverberate around the campsite. Once the wood folk were seated, ropes flew across them and were quickly tied to secure them to the horse's back. Someone passed them up the iron stake to hold.

"There are no reins," mouthed Golden Toad, panic stricken.

"Hold the horse's mane. Trust us. You will be all right. Now go!"

Autumn Leaves gave the horse a gentle pat on the rump and it walked quietly towards the perimeter of the encampment, surrounded by the other horses.

Forty yards away, in Andoran and Sargon's tent, Danton was fretfully trying to keep Andoran and Sargon's attention focused on a game of cards. An unfortunate side effect of the drug Stormaway had placed in the wine seemed to be sleeplessness. Ever since they had drunk the doctored bottle of wine, Andoran and Sargon had been jumpy and had kept looking sideways at the other two. From time to time, one of them would ask an odd question, then shake his head and looked frightened when no one else had heard or seen what he had.

Andoran sat up and listened, "Did you hear that?"

Danton, whose hearing had been finely tuned to the world outside the tent all evening, did indeed hear the quiet clop of horses' hooves. His heart leapt in his chest but he said impatiently, "Andoran, what is it this time? You keep holding us up. Play your card."

Andoran shook his head, looked uncertainly at the other two and drew his attention back to his cards.

A few moments later, Sargon's head went up. "Did you hear that?I'm sure I heard a chain being rattled."

Danton threw down his cards in disgust. "You two are hopeless to play with. How could you be hearing a chain? I haven't even seen any chains."His voice thickened with sarcasm, "Perhaps there's a ghost around here somewhere and it's rattling its chain? You would expect a castle to go with it, though. Wouldn't you?" He sighed in exasperation and picked up his cards again. "Do you think we could get on with it?"

Sargon glanced at Andoran but receiving no confirmation from him, reluctantly frowned once more at his hand. Even before he could put down another card, his head went up again. "I can hear horses too."

"Well, they are tied up nearby. Maybe they're just restless," suggested Danton, knowing he was now fighting a losing battle.

Andoran frowned, "If you can hear it too, Sargon, then it must be happening,"

"Quick. Let's see what's going on."

Because of the drugged wine, they fell over themselves several times before they reached the doorway. Once they had disentangled themselves, Andoran reeled out of the tent with Sargon and Danton in hot pursuit.

Suddenly Andoran's shout rent the night. "Hoy. Someone's stealing the horses!"

"Go!" urged Autumn Leaves. As the horses thundered out of the encampment, the woodfolk used them as cover to reach the perimeter. A few brave woodfolk threw themselves onto the backs of the passing horses but most ran out into the night and flicked back into the cover of the trees.

Unnoticed by the two bounty hunters, two dark shadows stole up from behind, hit Danton on the head and whisked him off into the night. Andoran and Sargon threw themselves clumsily but enthusiastically into the chase. As the last horse broke through the perimeter, Andoran lunged wildly and just managed to grab the tail end of Autumn Leaves' shirt. He dragged the woodman backwards and swung him around in an arc into Sargon's waiting fist. Autumn Leaves crumpled without a sound. The fleeing woodfolk, intent on their escape, did not look back.

Chapter 56

The horses cantered off through the forest, bearing their cargo of woodfolk. Once well inside the trees, they slowed to a walk and the nervous woodfolk on their backs sat up carefully and breathed a sigh of relief.

"Golden Toad, you are safe now," called Creaking Bough quietly from astride a large roan. "Just hold on for a while longer and we will take you down and get those chains off you."

The horses carried them further into the forest, but every ten minutes or so, they would stop beneath a large tree and mill around pointlessly for a few minutes before once more setting off. Eventually, they brought the woodfolk into a large clearing deep within the forest canopy. The horses came to a halt and stood quietly, facing a tall young sorcerer with glowing golden eyes and long black hair. Golden Toad and his family smothered cries of consternation.

"No. Don't be fearful. He is a friend," said Creaking Bough hastily

Waiting hands reached down to grab Golden Toad and his family and bear them off through the trees into a nearby shelter while small bundles of wood were strapped onto the horses' backs.

The guardian of the forest bowed to the horses and sent forth waves of gratitude. The leading mare bowed her head, then tossed it and snorted. The horses wheeled around behind her and galloped off into the night.

He smiled and turned back into the clearing. "Rainstorm, North Wind, where are you?" As the two woodmen swung down out of the trees to land in front of him he said, "The horses will be fine. They will circle around and eventually return to the encampment." He gave a short laugh "They could have stayed free but they like the food there and winter is coming. Where are the others?"

North Wind went out of focus for a few moments. "With Golden Toad and his family. You'll meet them when they come out. Not enough room in the shelter. Thunder Storm thought you might like to postpone telling them who you are for a while until they've settled down a bit."

Tarkyn grimaced, "I expect they don't want to see another sorcerer as long as they live. Maybe I should make myself scarce for the time being."

"No, prince," said Rainstorm firmly, "You might as well hang around. They saw you when they arrived on the horses. You probably need to reassure them that you're friendly."

Tarkyn threw Rainstorm a sardonic glance, "Like a tamed wolf, you mean?"

Rainstorm grinned. "Yes. Something like that,"

"We'll go and see how they're going." said North Wind, and the pair disappeared.

Tarkyn paced back and forth to keep himself warm while he waited for the woodfolk to recover and re-emerge. Suddenly, he gasped and reeled, an intense jab of fear piercing his mind. Almost immediately the image of a knife flashed before his eyes. *Sargon is waving the knife up close to me while Andoran leers into my face over Sargon's shoulder. As I watch, the two sorcerers direct puzzled frowns at me, arguing about something. Suddenly the knife is reversed and comes plunging towards me, hilt first.* Then the image went black.

Tarkyn staggered against a tree and leaned there for a minute catching his breath, thinking about the image he had just seen. He knew, without a doubt, that Autumn Leaves had been captured. He wondered if everyone had received that image but there did not seem to be anyone reacting around him. Maybe it's the strength of feeling that allowed me to pick it up. No one else receives feelings.

Without further thought, Tarkyn sent forth a command to Rainstorm. The young woodman appeared at his side, looking shaken.

"Sorry," said Tarkyn peremptorily. "I need your help. Now. Will you help me without knowing why? And are you willing to risk your kinsmen's ire to do as I ask?"

Rainstorm nodded without hesitation, his eyes gleaming in anticipation.

"Good. Now go back into that shelter and find a blade of grass or any piece of vegetation on those woodfolk that has come from the tent in which they were held captive. Then bring it to me without anyone knowing. Clear?"

Rainstorm frowned, "How will I know if it's from the tent or from the bushes they passed through on the horse?"

"Rainstorm, you're the woodman. You figure it out. Now go. It's urgent."

Tarkyn paced up and down, frantic with worry, while he awaited Rainstorm's return. Gradually, he calmed enough to start thinking through what he needed to do. He found a low bush, plucked a spray of berries off it and stuffed them into his pocket. Then he composed himself and sat with his palm against an oak tree. He focused on the sap of the forest and sent an image of what had happened and what he wanted to do, deep into the heart of the forest trees. Slowly a gentle breeze wafted through the woodlands and, as the branches sighed with the passing wind, the guardian of the forest knew the forest would support him.

He breathed slowly and deeply until he was calmer and then sent his mind wandering around the encampment until he found the friendly little mouse he had worked with before. He directed it to head towards the tent where the woodfolk had been kept. When he was sure it had understood and was on its way, he broke contact and set to pacing once more as he waited for Rainstorm to re-appear.

Finally, Rainstorm returned bearing a small blade of grass smeared with mud. "It's from the mud on the bottom of Golden Toads' boot. It can't be from the horse ride."

"Well done. I knew you'd figure something out." Tarkyn took the blade of grass and sat down. "Now, listen carefully. I want you to go back into the tent and give me as much uninterrupted time as you can. After twenty minutes, tell North Wind, Running Feet and Thunder Storm that you have given me this grass. They will explain the rest."

Rainstorm looked a little puzzled but he stood by his resolve to assist Tarkyn. He nodded briefly "Good luck with whatever you're doing, then."

"Thanks, Rainstorm," said Tarkyn warmly, "Now go and stall everyone for as long as you can."

As soon as Rainstorm was out of sight, Tarkyn resumed contact with the mouse. It was now in the tent that had held the woodfolk. The mouse scuttled around the edges of the tent, darting from clothing to bags to bits of rubbish. The tent was clearly unoccupied. Tarkyn broke contact, took a deep breath and focusing in the blade of grass, incanted quietly, "*Maya Mureva Araya!*"

He experienced a rushing, nauseating sensation, then a slowing down and a hesitation. For a moment, it felt as though his travel pushed at a soft barrier that gave way but then cushioned him to a gentle landing at the other end. Tarkyn opened his eyes and found himself lying on his side inside the now familiar tent. He drew a couple of steadying breaths, sat up and looked around.He spotted the mouse cowering behind a pile of clothes in the corner. Tarkyn sent out a wave of reassurance. He listened carefully. He couldn't hear any movement outside. Perhaps they have all chased off after the horses. He regained contact with the mouse and asked it to go out under the side of the tent to see what lay beyond. Tarkyn was not planning to risk his safety any more than he felt was necessary.

Once outside, the mouse snuffled about and soon picked up the scent of horse dung. Oh no! Not again, thought Tarkyn.He sent it an urgent message to keep looking around.

It's very quiet out here. Over there are a lot of nasty big animals but they are sleeping too. Wait! Someone nearby. People in that tent over there. No one else is out here. There are a few mounds of lovely dung over here though. Nice and warm.

Tarkyn pulled out quickly. He took a deep breath, carefully raised the side of the tent and slithered out beneath it. He brought his feet up under himself and waited, crouching low while he gained his bearings and located the source of the voices.

He crept to the outside of the tent and listened.

"I think he's coming around again," said a voice that Tarkyn recognised as Sargon's.

"Well, who's going to hit him this time? You or me?"

"Are you sure he's really there? I've never seen anyone like him before."

"Of course he's there, you idiot. We can both see him."

"We could talk to him…Find out who he is...what he is?"

"I don't think so. We need to sober up a bit first. He might trick us. Who knows what magic he has up his sleeve."

Tarkyn sent forth a wave of hope and friendship, with a gesture indicating silence. A fuzzy image of the two bounty hunters came back to him. They were standing over the woodman, with their backs to the door. Tarkyn didn't hesitate. In two sure strides, he entered the tent and incanted "*Shturrum*" before either of them could look around. Then he grabbed their heads and bashed them together with a resounding crunch. Sargon and Andoran fell senseless to the ground.

Tarkyn stepped over them and knelt down next to the woodman, "Oh my stars! Autumn Leaves! What have they done to you?"

Autumn Leaves' face was covered with blood and his nose was on a sickening angle. He shook his head groggily. "I don't know. Just hit me, I think. I feel sick. I think my nose is broken." He frowned vaguely. "What are you doing here? Are we back in the woods?"

"Shh. No. We're not. But we will be soon." Seeing Autumn Leaves frown deepen, Tarkyn said hastily, "Don't worry. We're leaving now."

He lifted Autumn Leaves up gently and set him down on his feet. "Can you walk?" The woodman collapsed as soon as Tarkyn slackened his grip. Tarkyn lowered him carefully back down. "No. Clearly not. Wait. I'll check outside." Tarkyn tuned back in with the mouse to find himself surrounded by a soft smelly warmth. Overcoming his distaste, Tarkyn persevered and after an initial reluctance, the little mouse good-naturedly ventured back out into the cold to look around. Nothing was moving. Tarkyn sat down with the woodman leaning against him "Okay, Autumn Leaves. Think about my hands holding you. I'm going to send some strength and healing through them into you. Just relax and accept the power."

But Autumn Leaves was too befuddled to concentrate. After a few unsuccessful attempts, Tarkyn sent his own mind out along his arms and into the woodman's body. He fed energy into the bruising around Autumn Leaves' temple and soothed the knots out of overstressed muscles. He didn't repair the nose because it needed to be set straight but he shored up the damage enough to enable Autumn Leaves to withstand the pain and to regain his senses.

Tarkyn's mind came back out of Autumn Leaves' body just as Sargon groaned and began to sit up. Without a moment's thought, Tarkyn backhanded Sargon hard across the head with the full force of his arm and shoulder, slamming him back down onto the ground. He stood up and assisted the woodman to rise

"How's that? Can you manage now?" he asked gently.

Autumn Leaves glared at him through his one open eye. "What are you doing here? You're supposed to be staying safely inside the forest."

"I would have thought that was obvious. I'm rescuing you." Tarkyn put his arm around the woodman's waist. "Let's argue about the rest later."

Tarkyn poked his head out the door of the tent and, after checking for any signs of life, supported the woodman towards the perimeter of the encampment. "Can you do your flick thing?" he asked in a whisper.

Autumn Leaves smiled faintly in the gloom. "Not yet. We need to be closer to the woods. I should be able to do it when we're about halfway to the trees. What about the guards?"

Tarkyn shook his head, "I don't know. Could be a problem. They have probably all woken up by now and I bet not all of them chased after the horses."

"Stars above Tarkyn! What are you thinking? Don't you have a plan? What if someone sees you?"

"Don't worry. I'm safe. It's just you we have to worry about." Tarkyn glanced down at the woodman and frowned, "Do you think you can run?"

Just then they heard the sound of solid footsteps and a pair of guards walked into sight along the edge of the encampment not twenty yards from them. Tarkyn and Autumn Leaves pressed into the shadow of the woodfolk's tent and held their breaths.

"It's a bloody strange thing," growled one of the guards. "It must be some clever sorcerer to be able to knock them all out at once like that."

"I don't understand why they didn't see anyone."

Tarkyn peered out from the shadow, waved a hand and intoned Shturrum softly. The two guards froze but were faced half towards Tarkyn and Autumn Leaves.

"Blast!" exclaimed Tarkyn quietly. "We can't go out there. They'll see us and be able to report back after we're gone." He looked back over his shoulder. "Come on. We'll have to skirt back around the other side of the tent."

They crept back around to the front of the tent. But as soon as they touched the canvas near the door, the magic ward lit up and set up a loud warning wail.

The sounds of running footsteps closed in from all sides. "Sorry Autumn Leaves. Nothing for it now." Tarkyn clasped the woodman close with one arm, thrust his other hand into his pocket and grasped the spray of berries. "*Maya Mureva Araya! Ka Mureva Araya!*" he intoned urgently.

Tarkyn felt himself dragged backwards at speed but his arm felt as if it was trying to lift a ton weight. He clenched hard with every fibre of his strength, his biceps screaming with the strain. He could feel himself sweating and the bile rising in his throat. He held on grimly. He felt as though he was being torn apart at his shoulder. Tarkyn reached deep inside and brought his whole being together to focus his strength on his straining arm. With a strange sensation like being dragged out of thick mud, Tarkyn and his burden suddenly came free and were catapulted onto the floor of the forest to land sprawled at the feet of Rainstorm and the other woodmen.

Tarkyn lay there gasping, too tired to move. He found himself looking up into the anxious faces of the four woodmen who were meant to be protecting him. Others were gathered in the background. He could see Rainstorm smiling in relief and a wrathful frown gathering on Thunder Storm's face. Ignoring them all, Tarkyn rolled over and looked down at the bloody woodman who lay pale and unconscious on his outstretched arm.

"Find Summer Rain. Get her here fast," he ordered. Tarkyn closed his eyes and placed his other hand on Autumn Leaves' chest. Realising he was still clutching the berries, Tarkyn threw them away and replaced his open palm on Autumn Leaves. He focused his mind through his arm into the woodman. With relief, he felt Autumn Leaves' heart beating slowly but strongly. He drew on his own diminished strength and let it flow into the injured woodman. After several agonising moments, Autumn Leaves stirred and opened his eyes. One eye was swollen nearly shut and the other was bleary and unfocused. Slowly, as Tarkyn's strength flowed into him, the woodman became aware of his surroundings and smiled rather muzzily up at the four woodmen leaning over them.

"I feel sick," Autumn Leaves pronounced slowly, "And my face hurts. But I am so glad to see you all." He let his eyes travel slowly across the branches above him before bringing his eyes around to stare up into Tarkyn's face. He gave a faint smile. "You brought us back to the forest." He frowned vaguely, "I think you'd better save some strength for yourself. That flow is feeling very wavery."

Tarkyn nodded and fell back weakly onto the ground beside him, his arm still stretched beneath the woodman.

"He needs a tree," said Thunder Storm shortly. "Come on. Help me pick them up and move them over to that big oak."

Running Feet, North Wind and Rainstorm looked puzzled, but nevertheless followed Thunder Storm's instruction without question.

"Now place Tarkyn's palm against the tree's trunk."

"Thanks," murmured Tarkyn. After a few minutes, he opened his eyes, lifted his head and twinkled up at them, "So that was interesting. I think that might be an all-time first for sorcery; translocating two people with one spell." He let his head drop down again. "Takes it out of you, though." He looked at Thunder Storm whose face seemed to oscillate between concern and anger. Tarkyn sent up a wave of reassurance that did little to reconcile the angry woodman. He closed his eyes again. "Thunder Storm. Go off and be angry somewhere else. I can't deal with it at the moment. Save it up and hit me with it later when I'm feeling stronger. I need my strength now to help Autumn Leaves." A fretful frown appeared on his face. "Where's Summer Rain?"

"She is on her way, Your Highness," replied Running Feet. "She was stationed near the edge of the woods close to the encampment in case there were any injuries. So she has some distance to cover. All those who did not ride should be returning here shortly."

The prince roused himself, opened his eyes and snapped impatiently, "Don't wait for them. Do a head count now. I don't want to find that anyone else is missing."

Running Feet raised his eyebrows at Tarkyn's tone, "Yes, my lord." He glanced at Thunder Storm and moved quickly away to concentrate on sending out the message.

Before long, the clearing began to fill with returning woodfolk. The air was full of excitement and success. But gradually, as they realised that Autumn Leaves lay injured up under the oak, the sound of voices became more subdued. Once Running Feet had returned with Summer Rain, Tarkyn extricated himself from beneath Autumn Leaves and sat up.

"I have done the best I could, Summer Rain. You will need to set his nose and check him for other injuries. Let me know if you need more healing power." He looked down at Autumn Leaves, "I'll leave you to Summer Rain for a while. Is that all right? I'll be back soon."

Tarkyn wandered down the slope to find Thunder Storm amongst the throng. Not surprisingly, he found him deep in conversation with Waterstone and Ancient Oak who had just arrived. Tarkyn squared his shoulders and walked over to join them, Rainstorm and North Wind bringing up the rear.

Taking one look at Waterstone's thunderous expression, Tarkyn waved a hand and said, "Before you get stuck into me, let me assure you I had no plans to sacrifice myself or to do anything silly. I thought it out beforehand and took precautions. The worst that could have happened was that I came back alone."

"We should have been there to protect you," said Thunder Storm shortly.

Tarkyn shrugged, "Since you are all so concerned for my safety, I could not risk you refusing my orders and jeopardising the forest. I hope you weren't too angry with Rainstorm. He did not know about my translocating, so he didn't realise what he was helping me to do." He gave a little smile, "As it turns out, I did this better on my own, anyway."

"You must not place yourself in danger like that again," spluttered Thunder Storm.

Tarkyn smiled faded and he raised a supercilious eyebrow. He spoke with cutting formality, "I beg your pardon, Thunder Storm, but I am not accustomed to taking orders. I have not been used to it and I have no intention of starting now. I now realise that Stormaway was wrong about the paradox. When I gave Waterstone permission to attack me, that permission overrode your requirement to protect me and kept the forest safe. My orders can override your vow to protect me. The paradox only exists if you refuse to obey me." He let his gaze travel around all the woodmen surrounding him."Now, I see two choices before you; either I will simply go into danger without your knowledge when I feel the need, or you guarantee to support my decisions so that I know the forest will not be placed in jeopardy."

There was a stony silence.

Tarkyn did not relent. With a glance at Waterstone, he continued, "In return, I will undertake not to place myself in danger unnecessarily. However, this has gone far enough. None of you may dictate my actions. You may express your opinions and I may refrain from dictating to you, if I so choose. But no one dictates to me."

The silence continued.

Tarkyn looked around him, "May I remind you that I have a responsibility to protect all of you, even as you must protect me?" He shrugged and his voice lost its harsh edge. "But the oath had nothing to do with this. I could not have left Autumn Leaves suffering at the hands of Andoran and Sargon while there was something I could do about it. Autumn Leaves is my friend and kinsman." The prince ran his hand through his hair. "I'm sorry if I have spoilt your celebrations. I did not intend to be quite so emphatic."

Tarkyn turned on his heel to walk away but Ancient Oak's creaking voice stopped him, "I think our celebrations would have been spoilt a lot more by losing Autumn Leaves," he said quietly. "Speaking for myself, I would like to thank you for what you did."

Tarkyn swung back around and gave a short, mirthless laugh, "Huh. Don't mention it. Anyway, I didn't do it for your gratitude.... And I didn't do it to prove a point. I did it for Autumn Leaves."

Just as he finished speaking, the three rescued woodfolk emerged from the shelter, clinging nervously to each other as they confronted this fearsome sorcerer. Tarkyn frowned to see them still chained together, unaware that his concern for them made him appear even more frightening.

"Can't we get these chains off them? They are demeaning."

"We are trying, my lord," said Falling Branch. "It will take some time, I'm afraid."

Tarkyn realised that the freed woodfolk were looking at him in alarm and softened his tone, "I beg you pardon. I did not wish to appear harsh. I will see if I can help you in a minute. Perhaps we should sit down near the fire. Then I won't be towering over you." When they were seated, Tarkyn asked, "Have you had anything to eat or drink? I know it's late but you might like something."

Golden Toad plucked up courage to reply, "I could do with a good stiff drink, if there's one around. I haven't had a wine in weeks."

Tarkyn was intrigued to hear that Golden Toad's voice was indeed deep and stop-started so that the phrases came out jerkily. Feeling trapped with this huge young man, Golden Toad glanced at the other woodfolk in supplication.

"Don't worry," said Waterstone reassuringly, "Even if he is a little autocratic, this sorcerer is not going to hurt you. He is one of us, not one of them." He glanced at Tarkyn and, despite their recent disagreement, managed a little smile, "His looks are deceiving." When they still looked unconvinced, Waterstone added, "He is my brother. Look!"

He rolled up his sleeve and showed them his scar. Tarkyn did the same.

Golden Toad looked in wonder from one to the other. "How can this be? It has never happened before."

"Long story. We'll tell you another time," said Ancient Oak as he handed them mugs of fine wine. "I can tell you this, though. Without my brother here, we would never have found you or been able to rescue you. He is a forest guardian."

"No! Are you really?" asked Golden Toad. "That's amazing!"

Tarkyn smiled disarmingly, "Yes, it is rather amazing, isn't it?"

"So, that's how you controlled the horses, isn't it?" Golden Toad turned to his wife. "Imagine that, Rushwind. A real forest guardian!"

Tarkyn was beginning to feel like a travelling freak show again. He transferred his attention to Falling Branch, "How long will it take you to break those chains?"

Falling Branch grimaced, "Quite some time. I can't get in close enough with a chisel, and a file will take ages."

Tarkyn's eyes narrowed as he thought about it, "Do you want me to try?"

Falling Branch glanced at the chained woodfolk then back at Tarkyn. "I'm not sure. Maybe."

Tarkyn caught his look and correctly interpreting it, asked Golden Toad, "How would you feel about me exerting a little magic to remove your chains? I won't go near you if you don't want me to. It's up to you."

"Will it hurt?" asked Rushwind nervously.

Tarkyn gave a slight smile, "To be perfectly honest, I don't know. If I do it, I'll try it on a loose bit of chain first and see what happens."

The rescued woodfolk looked at each other then back at Tarkyn. "Try it on the loose chain first. Then we'll decide."

"Fair enough."

The sorcerer laid out the end of the chain nearest the stake, then raised his hand and sent a thin intense beam of power into it. One of the links snapped apart with a sharp report. Everyone jumped back. Tarkyn leaned forward quickly and felt the neighbouring links. Then he flicked his fingers away shaking his hand and put them in his mouth.

"Ow. That burned!" Tarkyn mumbled around hurting fingers.

"Well, heal yourself and get on with it," said Rainstorm unsympathetically. "I've seen you do it before with the rope marks."

"All right. All right. Give me a chance. I've got blisters, you know." He took his fingers out of his mouth and shook his hand. "Ow. Just because I can fix it, doesn't mean it doesn't hurt." He took a deep breath, shut his eyes and focused his being into soothing and healing his damaged fingers. As the woodfolk watched, the redness on his fingers disappeared and the blisters melted back into the skin. He opened his eyes. "There! Feel free to be sympathetic next time." He looked around. "Right. So that's only going to work if we can shield their bodies from the heat. What could we use?"

"A thick wad of bark," suggested Waterstone.

Tarkyn nodded. "Let's try it." He smiled evilly, "Rainstorm. You can put your hand under the bark and test it this time. I will heal you if you get burnt."

Rainstorm scowled at him but realised his lack of sympathy had dumped him in it. "Fine. But you had better heal me fast if I need it."

"I will. Ready?" Once more Tarkyn aimed a thin strong ray of bronze at a link. The link cracked apart but Rainstorm didn't move. Slowly the bark began to smoulder on the outside. "Thank you Rainstorm. You've made your point. It worked. You had better move before the bark catches alight, though." Tarkyn looked at Golden Toad. "Well? Are you prepared to take the chance? You don't have to, but it will be quicker. If the worst comes to the worst and you get burnt, I can heal you."

Golden Toad looked at Rushwind who nodded, then back at Tarkyn. "Yes. Go on."

Thick wads of bark were pushed in between the chains and their waists. They lifted their arms up out of the way. "Ready?" asked Tarkyn. "I'm going to do all three of you at once. So hold still until I say."

The sorcerer took a deep breath and centred himself to steady his hand. Then he sent a short sharp pulse of bronze power into a link of each of the three chains one after another. The chains fell to the ground with a clatter and the smoking bark was whisked away by waiting hands and thrown on the fire. Everyone let out the breaths they had been holding, while the released woodfolk jumped up and cavorted about.

"Oh. It's good to be free again after all this time," chortled Rushwind. "Thank you, young man, whoever you are."

The rest of the woodfolk seemed to find this exquisitely funny. Tarkyn rolled his eyes and laughed, "It's a nice change not to be at the centre of someone's universe."

The woodfolk swung into full-scale celebrations and plied their rescued kin with wine and food. Everyone gathered around them, catching them up on births, deaths and marriages they had missed.

Eventually Golden Toad came nervously over to sit near Tarkyn. "I believe we owe you our thanks. I did not thank you properly before."

"You are most welcome. But I would have to say that I was only one among many who mounted this rescue. Do not confine your thanks to me."

"Oh, don't worry. I haven't." Golden Toad bobbed his head apologetically; "In fact I've left you until last because, well to be quite honest, I'm a little nervous of you"

"Considering the recent company you've been keeping, that is hardly surprising." Tarkyn looked gravely at him, "I don't know whether you've worked out who I am yet but I would like to say on behalf of most sorcerers that I am sorry for what you have been through. There are rogues in every society. Most sorcerers are generally kind, work hard for their living and look after their friends and families just as you do. I'm afraid you and most of the other woodfolk have developed a very jaundiced view of sorcerers. But please, at least get to know me before you judge me."

"And who are you exactly?" Golden Toad looked puzzled. "I believe you're our new forest guardian which is more than enough on its own. But I gather there is more to you than that."

Tarkyn shrugged and gave a little smile. "I am Tarkyn Tamadil, third son of King Markazon and youngest brother of King Kosar. Also known as rogue sorcerer, I'm afraid to say."

Golden Toad swallowed, "Oh dear. And holder of the Sorcerer's Oath and our long awaited liege lord."

"Yes. I'm afraid so."

Golden Toad looked into the fire as he digested this information. After a while he said, "Well, you seem pretty generous with your time and power for a liege lord. That's not what I saw at the encampment. Lords seemed much more high and mighty from what I could see of them. Not that I could see much through the cracks in the canvas."

Tarkyn laughed. "Well, I'm overlord to most of those lords. That is, I was."

Golden Toad swung his head around to look at Tarkyn. His eyes narrowed, "They're saying some pretty terrible things about you. I'm glad I met you before I knew who you were. I'd have been scared to death, otherwise."

"I thought you might have been. But not now?"

Golden Toad shrugged, "You seem all right so far. You've done nothing but try to help us as far as I understand it. Anyway, if you were as bad as they were saying, you wouldn't have become our liege lord. So a lot of it must be untrue."

Tarkyn raised his eyebrows. "You're taking this all very calmly. I thought you'd be upset when you found out who I was. I wasn't very popular with everyone else, to start with."

"No, I imagine you weren't. On the other hand, from what Ancient Oak said, I believe we owe you our freedom."

The prince grimaced, "I'm afraid that is all too true. You are among those who swore the oath, aren't you?"

Golden Toad nodded.

"Then if you remember the words, you do indeed owe me your freedom, I'm afraid. You are bound to honour, serve and protect me, as am I bound to protect and support you."

Golden Toad looked around the clearing at various woodfolk wandering around, chatting, drinking and eating, none of them paying Tarkyn much attention. He brought his gaze back to the prince. "They don't seem to be finding it too onerous. It has to be better than being chained up. No one's dragged me aside to warn me about you. So you can't be too bad."

"Don't let him get you worried about it," piped up Rainstorm from the other side of Tarkyn. "It's not as bad as you'd think it would be."

"And you'd know that because…?" asked Tarkyn, a clear note of warning in his voice.

Rainstorm shrugged sheepishly. "Just from what I've observed, you understand."

"I assumed that's what you meant," said Golden Toad, unaware of the undercurrent of the conversation. "You're one of the forestals, aren't you? Your lot didn't swear the oath, did they?"

Rainstorm cleared his throat, "No. They didn't."

Golden Toad yawned, "Does anyone go to sleep around here? It can't be long until dawn."

Tarkyn smiled, "They are just excited at having succeeded in their rescue and having you back among them. Tonight is the climax of a lot of planning, you know. Go on. You'll have to go and chat with them all before you go to bed."

As soon as he had gone, Tarkyn turned to Rainstorm. Before he could say anything, Rainstorm smiled ruefully and said, "I'm sorry. I nearly gave the game away, didn't I?"

Tarkyn waved a hand. "I'm not worried about that. You recovered quickly enough. Anyway now the rescue is over, it doesn't matter as much. It might be time to face the music soon. But not tonight."

CHAPTER 57

When the world swam back into focus, Danton found himself once more with his hands tied behind his back. His first reaction was alarm that the sorcerers had discovered his complicity in the woodfolk's activities. Then he looked around and realised that he was somewhere in the forest. Breathing a sigh of relief, he let his head drop back down. Just as he was drifting back to sleep, a feeling of intense irritation overcame him. He was tired of being mistrusted.

In the grey before dawn, the sound of birds singing in nearby trees woke him. Danton struggled into a sitting position and leant his head back against a tree. He thought about the events of the night before and knew that his actions had been misconstrued. He remembered what Tarkyn had said about the world not being big enough to hide him if he betrayed his prince. His stomach lurched in fear before anger took over. Well, he hadn't betrayed the prince and he was sick of having to prove himself.

Time passed slowly. A pale yellow sun was streaming between the sparse leaves of the trees by the time anyone bothered to approach him. Danton heard a slight rustle and turned his head to find Waterstone watching him from the edge of the clearing.

"How long have you been there?" Danton asked.

"For a few minutes."

"So. What now? Do I go on trial?" Danton's voice was scathing. "Or do you kill me out of hand as a traitor without a hearing?

Waterstone walked around and sat down cross-legged in front of the bound sorcerer. "What do you think should happen?"

Danton scowled at him, "It's too late for what I think should happen. You should have left me to get on with the job as we had agreed. Now I will be associated with your activities and will no longer be able to walk freely among the sorcerers. That severely reduces my usefulness to you and Tarkyn." He shrugged and added bitterly, "But since none of you trusts me, I am of no use to you anyway."

Waterstone considered him, his head to one side. "What could you say that might convince us? How would we know you weren't acting?" He paused, "We all watched you in action with Sargon and Andoran. Either you were acting then or you are acting now. And we saw you rush out with them right into the middle of our raid. So how can we trust what you say?"

"You can't," replied Danton flatly. "And frankly, I have no intention of putting any more effort into convincing you."

Waterstone gave a slight smile, "I can understand your irritation but it would seem, in your position, that it might be worth your while to find a way to prove your trustworthiness."

"It can't be done. I see no point in continuing an association where I am under constant examination. I supported you against my own people and this is the thanks I get. You can all go hang, for all I care."

"How do I know your display of self righteous anger isn't a ploy in itself?"

"You don't," said Danton shortly. "That's why I'm not going to even bother trying. And if you want to know, I told Stormaway that I would have absolutely no qualms about acting to you people if I could find a way to convince you of my good faith. So, you can safely assume I'll act if I think it will help me."

"Danton, have a care. You are painting yourself into a corner."

"Then kill me."

For once, Waterstone was at a loss. After a few moments he said, "For what it's worth, I told Tarkyn yesterday that I trusted you. Recent events may have strained my belief but I certainly have no intention of condemning you out of hand."

"Considering how I find myself, your faith in me doesn't impress me much," Danton retorted. He wriggled his shoulders to ease their stiffness. "And you can tell His Royal Highness that he seems to have learnt how to reward loyal service from his brothers! I thought he was better than that. But apparently not."

Waterstone's eyes glittered. He said in a voice husky with anger, "Don't you ever compare Tarkyn with his brothers!"

Danton was completely unrepentant. "Then tell him not to act like them."

"The cases are not at all the same," protested Waterstone vehemently.

"The cases are very much the same," responded Danton promptly. "They didn't trust Tarkyn. Tarkyn doesn't trust me." He glowered at Waterstone. "I'm tired of tying myself in knots only to be kicked in the teeth. I spent a month on my own, scouring the countryside to find the prince because, despite all the evidence condemning him, I stayed true to him. And when I finally found him, I was greeted with a cool reception and suspicion. Then, against my natural instincts, I threw myself into the rescue of your kin, spent long torturous hours talking to two people whom I would have preferred to kill on sight and for this, I am rewarded with imprisonment and mistrust." He tilted his head to one side. "I am loyal, and yet I am mistrusted and imprisoned. So tell me, how is that different from what happened to Tarkyn?"

Waterstone stood up and began to pace back and forth before the palace guard. Finally, he stopped and turned towards Danton, “Your behaviour with Sargon and Andoran provided us with more grounds for suspicion than Tarkyn’s performance at the tournament did for his brothers”.

Danton gave a derisory smile, “It took you a long time to think of that.”

Waterstone raised his eyebrows. “It’s true nevertheless.”

“Yes,” conceded Danton, “It is true.”

“So, can you explain what happened between you, Sargon and Andoran?”

“Yes,” replied Danton. He stared up into the sunlight streaming through the branches then looked back at the woodman. “But I won’t.”

Waterstone frowned in exasperation. “Well, can you prove your good faith in some other way?”

“Yes, I think so, but I won’t do that either.” Danton rubbed his shoulders against the tree trunk. “Have you ever sat with your hands tied behind your back? It’s bloody uncomfortable and bloody humiliating, if you really want to know. I don’t like being at the mercy of your whims and it is not something I’m prepared to put up with, every time you get the jitters about me.”

Danton took a deep breath and looked Waterstone in the eye. “So. This is the end of the road. You either trust me or you don’t. If you don’t, I suppose you’ll have to kill me because I know too much.”

Waterstone frowned, “Is self sacrifice a common trait among sorcerers?”

“Oh no. I’m not sacrificing myself. Be it on your head if you kill me. That would not be my choice. My choice is to be trusted and to live.”

The woodman’s eyes narrowed. “You’re trying to force my hand, aren’t you, without having to explain yourself?”

Danton shrugged, “You can look at it that way, if you like.”

“I don’t like having my hand forced, Danton,” came Tarkyn’s voice quietly from the side.

Danton whipped his head around to see the prince sitting motionlessly with his back against the next tree. “And how long have you been there?” he demanded. “Does none of you announce your presence like civilized folk?”

Tarkyn raised his eyebrows and asked, with an edge to his voice, “Are you implying that we, that I am not civilized?”

“I beg your pardon, my lord.” Danton stammered, his bravado evaporating, “Of course I meant no such thing.”

Tarkyn’s amber eyes bored into him. “So you think I’m as unjust as my brothers, do you? – Perhaps I am. I am, after all, tainted with the same Tamadil blood.”

This was so uncomfortably close to what Sargon had said that Danton could feel the colour seeping into his cheeks. "I didn't know you were listening to them, my lord."

"I wasn't, Danton. But I am not a fool. I know what people are saying about me."

Danton dropped his eyes. "My lord, I am sorry to have to tell you this but I spoke slightingly of you several times to Andoran and Sargon."

"I am sure you did, Danton. I would have expected no less."

Watching Danton respond without question to Tarkyn showed Waterstone, as nothing else could, the truth of Danton's allegiance.

"You had a part to play, given the unexpected presence of Andoran and Sargon," continued the prince. "I'm sure you played it to perfection."

"I did my best, my lord. It was essential not to arouse their suspicions. So I spent many long hours enduring their company and their opinions."

"And what did you say to support me against their accusations?"

Danton took a deep breath and let it out shakily. "Nothing, my lord. Nothing whatsoever."

"I see."

"I could not risk Sargon and Andoran suspecting me of associating with you, Sire."

"However," said Tarkyn icily, "No such excuse exists for what you said about me to Waterstone. So I can assume that was your true opinion of me?"

Danton brought his head up and met Tarkyn's gaze defiantly, even though fear flickered at the back of his eyes. "If you punish me when I have given you nothing but loyal service, your behaviour will be no better than your brothers'. The reason for your behaviour may be different, but the effect will be the same on the people you hurt."

Tarkyn let out a low whistle and shook his head. His face was white with anger. "Danton, you forget yourself. I think woodfolk society has affected your sense of propriety more than I expected. I can't believe you just had the temerity to say that to me."

The prince stood up and walked across to tower over Danton, "Stand up," he ordered. Tarkyn grabbed Danton and hoisted him upward as he struggled awkwardly to his feet.

"Turn around," snapped the prince. He aimed a thin, intense ray of bronze power at the bonds and disintegrated them. "Now, turn and face me."

Tarkyn stared down into Danton's purple eyes. "You are free to go."

For long moments, the pair stared in silence at each other. Danton endured the returning circulation in his wrists without moving.

"I said, Danton, you are free to go."

"I heard you, my lord," replied Danton slowly. "And I thank you for your trust. But I have no wish to leave you, Sire."

Tarkyn raised his eyebrows haughtily. "Indeed? And what should I think of someone who is prepared to serve such a corruption as myself?"

"You should think of him as a loyal friend and liegeman, who is willing to stake his life on his belief that your integrity will overcome your fear of betrayal."

"Even though I am no better than my brothers?"

"I did not say that, my lord. I said your actions against me would make it seem that way." He took a breath. "All three of you fear betrayal, but in you, it is counter-balanced by your care for people. In your brothers, it is fed by their obsession with power." Danton rubbed his stinging wrists. "My lord, for you, betrayal means personal pain. For them it is merely a counter move in a political game. You care for people. They care only for power."

Danton dropped to one knee and bowed, hand on heart. "And that is why, my lord, you are the only true hope for the future of Eskuzor and why I will serve you to the end of my days."

Tarkyn gazed down at the top of Danton's head in bemusement, shocked and moved by what his liegeman had said. He became aware that a ring of woodfolk had appeared and were watching silently. He recovered himself enough to place his hand on Danton's shoulder and say gently, "Please rise Danton. I am honoured by your loyalty and your service. I will do my best to justify your faith in me."

He waited until Danton stood face to face with him then gave a wry smile, "As to being the hope of Eskuzor, I think not. As you have just said yourself, I have no aspirations to enter into a game of power with my brothers." He picked out Ancient Oak and Waterstone and smiled, "…. any of my brothers."

"And yet, my lord," came Stormaway's voice from behind him, low and intense, reverberating around the gathering. "Your destiny is written in the stars and lives deep inside the trees of the forest. It has been clear from the day of your birth for all to see who have knowledge of such things. Your father and I always knew. That's why you had to be protected. You are not only the guardian of the forest. You are the one true hope for the future of all Eskuzor."

Afterword

As Stormaway's final words rang out, Andoran and Sargon were sitting disconsolately, four miles away, before a cheerless fire. Red wheals down their arms bore witness to the hours of itching and scratching they had endured, and their eyes were hollow from lack of sleep. From time to time they glanced uncertainly at each other, each wondering if the other had seen the strangely dressed man with eyes the colour of new leaves, face and hair the colour of walnut shells. Each of them wondered in his own isolated uncertainty whether, if he had existed at all, the strange man had had fleas.

THE SORCERER'S OATH ~ BOOK TWO

The Wizard's Curse

In the darkness of his shelter, Waterstone lay asleep, his daughter Sparrow a short distance away from him. Outside, the wind was picking up. Within minutes, the trees were thrashing under an ever-increasing gale. Suddenly, an intense wave of fear slammed into Waterstone's mind, followed almost instantaneously by a peremptory summons. Sparrow woke crying.

Waterstone had no time to comfort her. "Stay here," he said urgently, as he quickly pulled on his boots. "Whatever you do, don't leave the shelter until I call you. I'll be back as soon as I can."

Sparrow nodded bravely. "Go on. I'll be all right. Tarkyn's in trouble, isn't he?"

Waterstone answered over his shoulder as he left, "Something is wrong, badly wrong. Stay here until you hear from me."

Once outside, the woodman was buffeted by the strong winds that were now shrieking through the trees. He could hear branches breaking and the air was filled with flying leaves and twigs. Eerily, he could see the stars shining peacefully above him in a cloudless sky.

"Oh no." Waterstone murmured to himself in horror. "It's not a storm. Someone is betraying the oath. The forest is being destroyed."

Jennifer Jane Ealey was born in outback Western Australia where her father was studying kangaroos on a research station, one hundred miles from the nearest town. Her arrival into the world was watched, unexpectedly, by their pet kangaroo who had hopped into the hospital. Having survived the excitement of her birth, she moved firstly to Perth and then Melbourne where she spent most of her formative years. She took a year off from studying to ride a motorbike around Australia before working as a mathematics teacher and school psychologist in England and Australia, a bicycle courier in London and running a pub in outback New South Wales.

She now lives in Melton, a country town just outside Melbourne, working by day as a psychologist and beavering away by night as a novelist. She has written two detective novels and has just completed *The Sorcerer's Oath*, a series of four fantasy novels, of which *Bronze Magic* is the first.

Eskuzor Publishing

Made in the USA
Charleston, SC
04 July 2013